THE STONE OF VITALITY COMPLETE SET

THE STONE CYCLE COMPLETE SETS BOOK 3

THE STONE CYCLE COMPLETE SETS SERIES

The Stone of Knowing Complete Set (The Stone Cycle Complete Sets Book 1), *comprising*

- The Stone of Knowing (The Stone Cycle Book 1)
- The Cost of Knowing (The Stone Cycle Book 2)
- The Seer: A Prequel to The Stone of Knowing (The Stone Cycle)

The Stone of Authority Complete Set (The Stone Cycle Complete Sets Book 2), *comprising*

- The Stone of Authority (The Stone Cycle Book 3)
- The Struggle for Authority (The Stone Cycle Book 4)

The Stone of Vitality Complete Set (The Stone Cycle Complete Sets Book 3), *comprising*

- The Stone of Vitality (The Stone Cycle Book 5)
- The Hope of Vitality (The Stone Cycle Book 6)

THE STONE OF VITALITY COMPLETE SET

THE STONE CYCLE COMPLETE SETS
BOOK 3

ALLAN N. PACKER

LUMINANT PUBLICATIONS

The Stone of Vitality Complete Set

Comprising:

The Stone of Vitality (The Stone Cycle Book 5)
The Hope of Vitality (The Stone Cycle Book 6)

First edition (v1.0) published in 2024
by Luminant Publications

ISBN 978-1-923218-11-6

Luminant Publications
PO Box 305
Greenacres, South Australia 5086

http://www.allanpacker.com

Cover Design by Karri Klawiter
Map illustration by Brian Plush

'The Stone of Vitality' Dedication

To Adeline, Cressida, Sebastian, Reuben, Annabeth, and Genevieve.
In expectation that as you grow and develop your imaginations will thrive.
In confidence that you will think, dream, and act in a way that leaves the world better than you found it.

'The Hope of Vitality' Dedication

To Nick and Mary, fellow travelers and valued friends on the journey into eternity.

Baron Island
Savage Strait
Castel
Castel Citadel
Deadman's Pass
Steffan's Citadel
Maranelle
Duchy
of
Erestor
N
W
E
S
Arvenon
& surrounding Kingdoms

ellan
Rog
Blue Mountains
Varas
Rogand
River Dan
River Aron
Danford
Stanton
Arn River
estanor
The Plains

PART I

THE STONE OF VITALITY

THE STONE CYCLE BOOK 5

VOLUME 1—THE INEVITABILITY OF PERIL

1

A gray morning dragged painfully into a pallid afternoon, and still she didn't come. Kamash sat on the rocky promontory in growing misery, gazing out to sea. It had been more than two weeks since last he saw her.

As the sun began to set, he faced the unpalatable truth—she was gone. Her quiet intelligence would brighten his eyes no more. Her carefree exuberance had lifted his spirits for the last time. It was over.

The old man clambered slowly to his feet. As always he had brought a gift, and without a second thought he tossed it carelessly into the ocean. Then he turned his back on the endless slap-slap of the waves and trudged reluctantly across the small sandy beach, heading for his shelter.

Some of the people he'd once called friends might say he had sunk low indeed to be mourning such a loss. He didn't care. Decades had slipped by since he'd worked up the courage to sail away from his old life. He had relinquished his former friends without remorse, and they had undoubtedly forgotten him as quickly as he'd forgotten them. He had watched with no regret as the mainland dwindled in the wake of his boat. Civilization and its complexities held no appeal for him, any more than the restless human hordes that sustained it.

Choosing instead to embrace the remote exile of his island retreat, he had quickly been captivated by the wonders of a timeless world unspoiled by the vanity and folly of men.

The months turned slowly to years, and even as he celebrated his escape from the grasping avarice of his kind, he discovered that loneliness had begun to gnaw at him. Contented as he was in his own company, it was disconcerting to discover that he nevertheless needed a companion.

One morning he had noticed an injured sea lion pup, stranded in the shallows of the little beach where he liked to swim each day. Having become adept at catching fish, he offered his latest takings to the pup. Frightened and resistant at first, the young sea lion eventually accepted the gift, perhaps sensing that the alternative was starvation. Kamash's compassion was rewarded with gratitude, and in time an unlikely affection developed between the lanky land dweller and the glistening creature of the sea.

He had named her Sparkle, as much for her lightness of being as for the sunlight that bounced so readily from her body. They became firm friends throughout the seasons of her life. He swam with her when the waves and the weather permitted it, and watched her antics from the shore whenever the sea refused to respect his puny strength. She came and went as nature demanded. Sometimes she was gone for days, and on a number of memorable occasions she'd returned bringing a new pup for his inspection.

He had made a raft, and she glided effortlessly beside him as he sailed beyond the fringes of his tiny circle of land, out into the deep ocean. Once, falling unexpectedly into the water, he watched in helpless dismay as the wind quickly carried the raft beyond his reach. Sparkle had accompanied him on his long swim back to shore, nudging him encouragingly whenever he flagged and refusing to let him give in to exhaustion and despair. Somehow he made it back. Even now he marveled at his own endurance.

Kamash had always known it could not last. He made no attempt to count the advancing years, but two decades might have slipped away before he first began to notice that she was failing. One telltale sign was the increasing enthusiasm with which she accepted the fish he offered each morning.

The end when it came still haunted his nightmares. A huge shark appeared from the deep as she lay basking in the shallows, snatching her away in little more than a heartbeat.

In her youth she would have danced aside to evade the predator. That day she had barely moved. Kamash watched in unbelief as the boiling water subsided, leaving no more than a red stain to mark the passing of his only friend.

He had surged into the water in mindless defiance of the departed monster, shouting at the top of his lungs as he called down curses upon the creature and its offspring forever. When his anger eventually faded he returned to the shore, falling to his knees and crying like a baby.

Years passed before he found a way to impress another of her kind. Once more he had embraced life with energy, choosing to ignore the inconvenient reality that in time this season too must come to an end.

The absence that day of his latest companion was no surprise—having enjoyed her companionship for many years, he had long been aware that her lifespan was almost at an end.

The inevitable termination had left him bereft and alone again. What would he do now? Did he have the heart and the resolve to start over a third time?

He was no closer to an answer when night fell and he headed for his bed. Forsaken, friendless, and utterly miserable, he lay down and attempted to sleep.

KAMASH FIRST SPOTTED the sail on his daily ascent to the highest point of the island. He had occasionally observed ships in the distance before, although none bothered to approach the unpretentious pimple of land that he called home. Seeing no reason to expect a different outcome this time, he took little notice of the intruder.

He was no longer a young man, but he found the climb invigorating as always. Reaching the top, he scanned the horizon. The rocky outcrop that crowned the summit offered an uninterrupted view in every direction and provided a perfect vantage point for assessing the weather. A cloudless sky with excellent visibility awaited him; he could just make out the low smudge to the southeast that represented his nearest island neighbor.

Otherwise there was nothing visible but sea beyond the rocky cliffs that surrounded the island. Nothing apart from the sail drawing noticeably closer.

It was hard to imagine anyone wanting to explore his domain. He had deliberately settled in a location both isolated and relatively unappealing. The larger island to the southeast was well watered and boasted several beaches where a boat could safely land. And as far as he knew it had never been occupied. Kamash therefore watched on with surprise and growing unease as the ship continued to head in his direction.

The only seaward access to the island was a small beach, its white sand clearly visible below him. He maintained a simple shelter among the trees, but his main dwelling was further inland beside the only reliable spring that watered the island. Neither structure was visible from the beach, and in the current balmy weather he had no reason to maintain a fire that might draw attention with its smoke. A search party would soon discover evidence of his presence of course, but he could not imagine any possible reason why anyone would want to land a search party.

The ship drew closer, and he squatted down so his silhouette would not be visible to any sailor keeping a lookout. He was no master mariner, but he could tell there was something unfamiliar about the design of the three-masted ship. It must surely be foreign. The sailors launched a rowboat, and he watched as it found its way to his beach. Two people were put ashore—at this distance they appeared to be a slight youth and a burly man—before the boat resumed its circumnavigation of the island.

It appeared unlikely that the two trespassers would be leaving anytime soon, so avoiding them would not be an option. After so long away from his own kind, Kamash wasn't sure what to think about interacting with people again. But loneliness had nagged at him since the disappearance of his latest companion, and he could not entirely ignore the lure of human contact. Curiosity eventually got the better of him, and he made his way down to the beach.

A young woman in strange garb sat on the sand beside a thickset man who appeared to be a guard. The old man watched them curiously from behind a tree for some time before deciding to take his chances.

As soon as he stepped into the open, the young woman leaped to her feet and called out in a language he didn't recognize. Her guard drew a knife and hovered protectively in front of her.

"Greetings," said Kamash, stretching out both hands palms upward to show he was no threat. "Do you speak Rogandan?"

"Who are you?" the young woman demanded imperiously, answering in the same language. She clearly understood Rogandan, although she spoke it strangely.

"My name is Kamash," he replied. "Who are you?"

Her head went up instantly. "I am Princess Neira of the Empire of Ahr," she replied, staring down at him over her nose. "I am the treasured daughter of the emperor—may his name ever be exalted!—and the only sister of the emperor-to-be." Almost as an afterthought she flicked a finger in the direction of her protector. "This is Uman," she sniffed.

"I bid you welcome," he said with a tentative smile.

She glared at him disdainfully. "You are a commoner, little better than a dog," she told him. "Why do you not abase yourself before me?"

He raised an eyebrow. "You are not in your empire now, Princess Neira. You are in my domain." His lip curled up in a wry smile as he glanced around at the sand and the trees. "On my little island I like to think of myself as emperor."

"It isn't much of an empire," she snorted.

"It's modest," he admitted, "but it's where you've landed. I'm sure the Empire of Ahr is mighty indeed, but it must be a long way from here." He gave her a wink. "To be honest, I know almost nothing about it."

She glowered at him. "When my sailors return you will answer for your insolence!" she snapped.

He studied her for a moment. "Why have they left you here?"

"I demanded to be put ashore," Neira replied haughtily. "How can any normal person be expected to tolerate constant rocking and shaking for weeks on end? Much less the daughter of the emperor!"

"When are they coming back for you?" he asked.

"As soon as they've rowed around the whole island. I instructed them to search for a more appealing beach." She waved an arm about her disparagingly. "Even a refuse heap like this ought to have *something* pleasant to offer."

Kamash ignored the insult to his tiny empire. "Who is in charge of your ship?" he asked. "What brought you here?"

She rounded on him. "Be very careful," she warned. "I advise you not to pry into affairs beyond your station."

With no answers forthcoming from the young woman, Kamash redirected his attention to Uman. "Do you know what your captain is up to?" he asked.

Uman's face was unreadable. Perhaps he didn't understand Rogandan. Perhaps he was giving nothing away. Either way, he offered no response.

Kamash turned back to the girl with a sigh. "I'm sorry to have to tell you this, Princess, but it looks as if your sailors have abandoned you and left you to your fate."

She didn't seem at all concerned. "Nonsense!" she replied dismissively.

He shrugged. "They did indeed row around the island. Then they returned to the ship and were taken on board. I watched them sail away."

It was obvious that the girl did not believe him. But the guard had understood Kamash's words, and he appeared shaken by the news.

"Follow me for a couple of minutes, and you'll be able to draw your own conclusions," Kamash told them, pointing away from the beach.

The princess glared at him with narrowed eyes. The guard joined him without hesitation.

Ignoring the path he had worn to the summit, the old man turned instead to a nearby hill and began to climb. He emerged at the top with Uman close behind him. Neira appeared a moment later, the sour look on her face making it abundantly clear what she thought of him and his assertions.

The ship was already far enough away that the sails could barely be seen above the horizon. Had they waited much longer, the vessel's current location would have been visible only from the summit.

The immediate reaction of the princess was one of fury. She shrieked and ranted in words that Kamash could not understand. Uman did not respond, although Kamash thought he saw compassion in his eyes. When her anger failed, she threw herself to the ground and dissolved into tears.

Many years had passed since Kamash's last contact with a young woman, and he looked on helplessly. Eventually, with nothing better to suggest, he turned to the guard. "I can offer you food and fresh water," he said.

Uman nodded once, before reaching down and lifting Neira into his arms. They set off, carefully descending the path to the beach.

They had not gone far before Neira began protesting noisily in her own language. Uman put her down, and she made her way independently back to the white sand.

As soon as they reached the beach, Kamash invited them to sit. "Please, make yourselves comfortable," he said. "I will prepare some food."

The old man had departed from the mainland with a generous quantity of seeds, and after cultivating several small strips of land he had been able to establish a reliable supply of vegetables, more than enough to feed one person. He now prepared a platter of fresh produce, carving off slices of fresh fish to go with it.

By the time he returned, Neira appeared to have mastered herself, although her eyes wore a haunted look, and she seemed distracted and ill at ease.

Both of his guests came to life when the food arrived. They accepted the vegetables readily. Uman looked at the fish uncertainly before placing a piece in his mouth and chewing slowly. Deciding he liked it, he helped himself to more.

The princess had an entirely different reaction. "What is this?" she demanded, screwing up her face in disgust.

"It's fish," he said simply, "freshly caught today."

"It isn't cooked!" she protested.

"My people regard it as a delicacy served this way," he told her in surprise.

"Your people are barbarians!" she spat.

Horrified at her slur, Uman bowed a mute apology.

Kamash shrugged. "I am happy to cook some fish if you prefer it," he said mildly. "I will build a fire."

She glared at him without otherwise responding.

As he got up, Uman turned to the girl, waving his hands animatedly. The princess reacted sharply in her own language. Kamash left them to battle it out.

After completing his preparations, the old man cooked the fish absently, his mind rehearsing the unexpected events of the day. *People* had arrived. Words had been spoken to him, and he had replied. He must have said more that day than in the previous few years combined.

The new arrivals had done a lot more than just shatter the stillness. Intrigue clung to them as a web binds itself to a fly. He heaved a deep sigh. He was already missing the simple solitude he had enjoyed for so long. He wondered if he would ever get it back.

After staring bemusedly into the fire for a while, he hefted his shoulders in a shrug of resignation. He would choose to embrace his new reality. What else could he do anyway?

The first priority was to make sense of what had just happened. The princess had insisted on feeling solid earth beneath her feet again. It had been a straightforward request, but a cynical game was being played out in response. Whoever commanded the foreign ship had grasped the opportunity to dump her. She hadn't been killed outright, but she had been deposited in a place where she was unlikely to survive for long, even with the help of her protector.

The girl might be self-important and demanding, but that could hardly be a reason for abandoning her, especially if she really was a princess.

It seemed ironic that in spite of his self-appointed exile to a place of no interest to anyone, Kamash had apparently found himself caught up in a political power play of some significance. Neira was not in the emperor's direct line of succession, but she was close enough to have become a target.

When Kamash returned with the cooked fish, he saw that the food he'd served previously was gone. All of the raw fish had been eaten, presumably by Uman. Seeing Neira eyeing the latest offerings hungrily, he presented her with the cooked fish immediately.

Before she ate, she mumbled an apology. "I'm sorry." Getting out the words was an obvious struggle. He had the impression she wasn't accustomed to apologizing to anyone.

Uman glared at her pointedly, and she tried again. "I'm sorry I didn't thank you for the food." After a nudge from the guard's elbow, she grudgingly added, "And I'm sorry for calling you a barbarian."

"I've been called worse," he told her with a smile. "I accept your apology." Then he pointed to the fish. "Enough talk—the food is getting cold!"

She needed no further urging, devouring it all without ceremony.

While she was eating Kamash took the opportunity to study the guard. It seemed unlikely that Uman was related to the princess in any way, yet he behaved like a parent disciplining a loved and pampered child. He was not frightened to demand appropriate conduct from her. He had engineered her apology and prodded her until satisfied by her contrition.

The question of his identity was by no means the only mystery surrounding the guard. Uman had not uttered a word, and Kamash could only guess at the reason.

After the food had all been eaten, the old man waded into the sea and swam lazily for a while in the shallow waters adjacent to the beach. The guard soon followed him in. The princess contented herself with watching the two men from the shore.

Leaving the water first, Kamash took the opportunity to satisfy his curiosity. “Why does Uman never speak?” he asked the girl.

“He has no need to speak,” she sniffed. “It is enough for him to faithfully serve his princess.”

Not satisfied with her answer, the old man tried again. “Is he capable of speech?”

The princess frowned in annoyance at his persistence. Then she shook her head. “He has been mute for as long as I can remember,” she told him.

Kamash watched thoughtfully as Uman floated on his back, his eyes closed. If the big guard was enjoying himself, his face showed no sign of it. He was a difficult man to read.

The sun was low in the sky when the three of them gathered around the embers of his fire. The old man prepared and served a little more food, then led them to the spring. After they had slaked their thirst in its crystal clear water, he invited them to follow him to his main shelter inland.

His hut had been sturdily constructed, designed to withstand the worst of the storms that battered the island in the rainy season. It was too small for three people, but after offering his own tiny bedroom to the princess he somehow managed to find space for himself and the guard on the floor of the little living area.

Normally he had no difficulty falling asleep, but that night he tossed and turned restlessly, unsettled by the quiet sobbing of the abandoned princess. He didn’t doubt that Uman was equally troubled by Neira’s misery, but the guard respected her privacy, making no attempt to console her.

Much of the night had worn away before Kamash finally succumbed to weariness and slept.

2

The raft skipped across the surface of the water, its sail flapping in the stiff breeze. Kamash pulled hard on the makeshift mainsheet to flatten the sail. In response, the raft began to punch through the low waves, picking up speed.

"Now!" he called.

Uman put the tiller over, and the bow began to come around as the raft swung slowly across the wind. The breeze filled the sail from the opposite side, thrusting it across the boat.

"Watch out for the boom!" Kamash shouted to Neira, anxiously eyeing the swinging spar.

She dodged gracefully, clinging to the mast and laughing as spray splashed across her face. The burly guard grinned up at them both as the raft settled into its new tack.

Neira was unusually animated when they sat around the fire that evening. As always, Uman said nothing, but the light in his eye spoke almost as expressively as her words.

Kamash watched them both with considerable satisfaction. Out on the water battling with the elements had been the first time he'd witnessed either of his new friends abandoning themselves to pure delight. The hours he'd invested preparing the raft had not been wasted.

For the first few days the princess had spent the greater part of the daylight hours at the summit of the island, watching in vain for a sail to appear on the horizon. Eventually she'd been forced to accept that the ship was not coming back for her.

Her prospects must have seemed bleak indeed. Nothing had equipped her for the life she now faced. Having clearly been cosseted and indulged from her earliest years, she had acquired none of the skills needed in a primitive environment with no luxuries and few amenities.

The old man might have expected her to wallow in despondency. She had surprised him by undergoing a rapid transformation, taking only a few days to become proficient in catching, cleaning, and filleting fish. Neira even routinely dirtied her hands tending gardens and preparing and cooking food.

After a while Kamash complimented her on her helpfulness. "Your resilience impresses me," he told her. "I've never heard of a princess stooping to menial tasks."

"A princess exists to be served," she snapped. "Don't dare to imagine I'm becoming a servant."

When he didn't respond, she added fiercely, "It wasn't my choice to take up residence on this refuse heap." She swept her arm about contemptuously. "But I'm not going to mope. I'll do whatever I need to do to become stronger."

So she was dreaming of revenge. And she had realized she needed to do much better than survive if she ever hoped to achieve it.

Whatever Kamash thought of her motivation, her new competencies bore eloquent testimony to her ability to adapt.

However skilled the princess might become, an uncertain future lay ahead for her, and for them all. Kamash felt sure that Neira, at least, had little real awareness of the trouble she was in. Enlightening her wasn't something he was looking forward to, but the urgency had been growing with every passing day. That night, as they relaxed before the fire with an evening meal settling comfortably in their bellies, he decided he could wait no longer.

"We can't stay here," he told them bluntly.

They looked at him, surprise on their faces.

Neira wasn't speechless for long. "If you thought I was enjoying myself today," she said, "let me make it absolutely clear I have no desire to stay here a minute longer than I have to." When he held his peace, she asked impatiently, "What is your concern? Are we going to run out of food?"

He slowly shook his head. "It's much worse than that. I will speak frankly. Sooner or later the people responsible for leaving you here are going to return. They will be expecting to find you dead from starvation, exposure to the elements, or a combination of both. Their reason for coming back will be to satisfy themselves that your lives have indeed ended that way. They will search the island for your bodies, and they won't be happy if they find you alive. It won't go well for me either when they learn I was responsible for your survival."

Uman stared back at him, his face expressionless apart from a narrowing of his eyes. Kamash had the impression that none of this came as a complete surprise to him. Neira looked stunned.

"Unfortunately, we have no time to waste," he continued. "After they abandoned you here, it probably took them a day or two to sail to Rog, and it will take them about the same to return. I have no idea how much time they will need to finish their business in Rog, but I expect they'll only stay away long enough to be certain you have starved. We might already be out of time. If not, we will be very soon."

When the princess found her voice again, it wasn't to argue with him. She seemed remarkably willing to accept his conclusions.

"We can use the raft, can't we?" she asked. "We could just relocate to another island."

He shook his head again. "It wouldn't help. As soon as they discovered signs of permanent habitation here—and it wouldn't be possible to erase those signs entirely—they'd immediately search all of the nearby islands. It would only be a matter of time before they found us. Moving would create other problems, too. The islands near here are uninhabited, so we would be entirely on our own. We might run out of food in the months it would take to establish productive cultivated strips."

A frown creased the face of the princess as she grappled with his words.

Kamash transferred his gaze to the fire, staring absently into the dancing flames. He hadn't bothered to spell it out, but he was impacted no less than they were by the turn of events. His way of life had effectively ended the moment the sailors dumped the princess on his island.

The island had nurtured and sustained him from the day he first arrived as a refugee. It had provided him with a home as the years slipped away. But it would quickly forget him. Everything he had labored so long to build would slowly be swallowed up by the vegetation. Only his fading memories would remain.

The princess broke into his thoughts. "What can we do?" she asked, a hint of panic in her voice.

He returned a wan smile. "Our circumstances might be grim, but the situation isn't entirely hopeless. I foresaw this outcome when you first arrived, and I haven't been idle. Teaching you the rudiments of sailing was not just for your entertainment—it was an important step in my preparations. I've also been gathering supplies." He took a deep breath. "We will sail to the mainland. And we're not going to delay any longer. We leave at dawn."

Their shocked faces stared back at him.

"But how can we possibly reach the mainland?" asked Neira. "Surely it wouldn't be safe to cross the open sea in a raft. It was bad enough in a ship!"

"We won't use a raft," Kamash told her. "We don't need to. I have a boat."

THE OLD MAN sat grimly at the tiller, defying the turbulence of the sea. The wind had picked up steadily over the past few hours, and the waves tossed the little boat about unmercifully, apparently determined to unseat him. The clouds to the west were looking especially ominous, and he was unable to restrain himself from making constant furtive glances in that direction.

He had schooled his face into an unexpressive mask, unwilling to acknowledge how much the conditions were beginning to alarm him. His passengers probably wouldn't have noticed his demeanor anyway. Heads down, both of them clung wretchedly to the sides of the tiny craft. They had long since emptied their stomachs into the roiling waters.

The outlook had turned bad almost from the moment they were ready to set out from the island. For two days the weather had toyed with Kamash, presenting lowering skies that threatened storms to come. Yet the storms never eventuated. They could have left while conditions were merely difficult; instead the old man was forced to endure the frustration of wasted opportunity.

The prospect of enemies returning to trap them loomed larger with every passing day. Kamash was sure the sailors would reappear at any moment. It would be too late to leave when that happened.

In the end, caught between the certainty of the human threat and the uncertainty of the elements, he decided to hope for the best and launch the boat. He set a course for the northwestern tip of the Rogandan coastline, to the west of Rog.

He had become well acquainted with raging seas, and no less with the cold ferocity of the predators that lurked in their depths. He would be leaving all that behind him, returning to a world of ruthless tyrants and scrabbling commoners. Mercurial weather and ravenous sea creatures seemed tame compared to the perils that awaited him.

He acknowledged that the turbulent seas were at least having one positive effect—the prospect of reaching Rogand was becoming more attractive by the minute.

After promising himself he would never go back, he was now doing exactly that. He couldn't entirely comprehend his own reasons.

Risking himself to help people he barely knew presented no real mystery—he could never have retained his honor if he'd simply left his visitors to their fate. The greater puzzle was that having decided to return, he found himself readily able to do so, and only because he had long prepared against such a day.

When he originally decided to settle on the island, he no longer needed his boat. He could easily have released it to drift away with the currents, or left it to slowly fall apart on the sand. Why then, had he painstakingly sheltered it from the elements, setting aside time and effort over the years to maintain it? He told himself he was simply being prudent, retaining a way of escape in case of emergency, but his own reasoning had never satisfied him. He could only conclude that some part of him had always known that one day he would return, in spite of the risk.

That day had finally come, his hand forced by an unlikely pair of castaways. He had little idea what he would find when they reached Rogand. Embracing the easiest and perhaps also the most cowardly course, he simply decided not to think about it.

KAMASH SOMEHOW MANAGED to reef the sail as the gale began to build in strength, rigging a small storm jib instead. Then he turned the boat and allowed it to run before the storm, stern toward the waves.

It hadn't taken long for the wind to shred his jib. He'd asked far too much of his aging sails—new material would have been severely tested in these conditions.

He turned to the others and shouted, "If you have gods, now's the time to pray to them!" He had no idea if they heard him over the howling of the wind.

He threw out a sea anchor and secured the tiller. There was little else he could do now. They were at the mercy of the wind and waves.

When the sun set they were still afloat, huddling fearfully together as the sea tossed the little craft up and down. Kamash had passed far beyond the point of exhaustion, completely spent from the effort of peering ahead in the dark. He decided to rest his eyes, just for a couple of minutes...

SOMETHING DISTURBED KAMASH, dragging him out of a strange dream. Baffled and disoriented, he opened his eyes and glanced around. He was lying on the bottom of the boat with daylight shining about him. Astonishingly, the tiny craft was still afloat, rising and falling with the swell. Neira and Uman lay prostrate nearby, either asleep or unconscious. The storm seemed to have passed, and the wind had eased to little more than a stiff breeze.

A voice was calling insistently, although Kamash could make no sense of the words. Had it been the voice that awakened him?

He tried to sit up, the effort leaving him weak and faint headed. Squinting around he spotted a vessel nearby. It appeared to be a fishing boat. When the voice called again, he raised his arms in a gesture of helplessness.

For all he knew, the sailors were Varasan, or perhaps Castelan. Both kingdoms spoke the same language, but he didn't understand a word of it.

The fishing boat drew closer, and a net was thrown down to him. The men seemed friendly enough. He grabbed the net and allowed his little boat to be drawn alongside the larger vessel. A couple of the fishermen clambered down and waved him to the net, inviting him to board their boat. Then they tended to the girl and her guard. He watched them stupidly for a moment before crawling to the net and stiffly beginning to climb. Hands reached down for him, pulling him onto the deck.

They lifted Neira aboard next. Uman presented more of a challenge—it took three of them to retrieve the big man.

A fisherman offered Kamash a blanket, and he wrapped it gratefully around his shoulders. He sat on the deck as the net was retrieved. His little boat began to drift away, disappearing behind a wave only to reappear as it crested the next, all the while dwindling in size. Before long it was lost to sight entirely.

His boat might not have delivered them to Rogand, but it had at least preserved their lives. Now it was gone. The final vestige of his decades in exile had been removed. Tears threatened to well up in his eyes before he steeled himself. Now was not the time to become sentimental.

Redirecting his attention to his companions, Kamash found Uman beginning to stir. Walking cautiously across the pitching deck he approached the guard, quietly explaining to him what had happened. Neira woke as he was finishing, and the two of them hurried to her side.

"Where am I?" she asked groggily.

"We've been rescued by fishermen," he replied. "I don't speak their language—they're not from Rogand. But they have treated us kindly."

Seeing that all three of them were awake, one of their rescuers came to join them. He was the captain if his demeanor offered any clue. As soon as he spoke it was apparent that Neira understood no more than Kamash of his language.

"Rogand?" he asked, directing a finger at Kamash.

The old man nodded.

The captain rattled off a number of other words, pointing into the distance as he spoke. The only word recognizable to Kamash was 'Varacellan.'

"I think they're Varasan," the old man told his companions. "And I think they're taking us to Varacellan, their capital."

"Will there be anyone there who speaks Rogandan?" asked the princess.

"Most certainly," he replied. "Varacellan is a major trading hub, and people gather there from many places. There will be traders and diplomats from Rogand. Provided Rogand and Varas aren't at war, that is," he added. He had no idea what might have happened in the world in the decades since he left Rogand.

Neira's eyes went wide. "Why would they be at war?" she asked.

Before he could reply, a sailor arrived with food and some kind of hot drink. Kamash accepted it gratefully, nodding his thanks to the man before he left.

As soon as they were alone again, Neira faced Kamash. "I know a little of Rogand," she said. "I had a slave who taught me the language. She told me stories, too. Uman was never far away, so he heard the lessons and the stories." She stole a glance at her guard. "Most of them, anyway," she added mysteriously. "That's why he understands Rogandan." Her head went up. "He doesn't understand it as well as I do of course."

"So you were on the ship because of your Rogandan language skills?" Kamash ventured.

"Certainly not!" she snorted. "My slave taught me in secret. My father would never have let me go if he thought I would be able to communicate with the Rogandans independently." Her lip twisted up in a crooked grin. "As it was, he granted permission reluctantly. I nagged him incessantly, and even my brother decided to support me. But he only agreed because of who was in charge of the expedition." The smile faded from her face. "I expected it would be such a wonderful adventure."

Kamash gazed at her sympathetically. He wondered what the purpose of the voyage might have been. There was a great deal he didn't understand about the princess and the people who had sailed with her before abandoning her.

She recovered quickly. "Tell me about the kingdoms in this region," she demanded.

"Rogand is on the eastern side of the continent, with Lestanor below it to the south," he told her. "A mountain range that runs north-south forms the western boundary of Rogand. On the other side of the mountain range is Varas in the north, and Arvenon in the south. Castel lies to the west of Varas, and it also borders Arvenon in the south."

"What languages do these kingdoms speak?" she asked.

"We Rogandans have our own tongue, as you know," he replied. "The Arvenians, Varasans, and Castelans all speak the same language. It's generally known as Arvenian. People from Lestanor have their own tongue. And there is a Plains region to the south of Arvenon. Nomad tribes live there. They speak many different dialects."

"Which kingdom is the biggest?" asked Neira.

"Rogand is the largest, and has the most people. Arvenon is next, then Lestanor. Varas and Castel are smaller."

"And why did you think there might be a war?" she asked.

He shrugged. "Only because Rogand has fought Arvenon more than once in the past. But I know of no reason why they should be fighting now."

"You seem to know a lot about all this. Why did you leave Rogand, and how long have you been away?" she asked curiously.

"I've been away a long time. Many years," he said evasively.

To his relief, she did not pursue it further. She clearly had secrets of her own. Perhaps that was why she chose not to dig too deeply.

Before the sun set the harbor of Varacellan hove slowly into view. It was completely dark by the time they finally docked.

The captain had already shown them great consideration, and when he realized they had no money to pay for lodgings, he thoughtfully arranged for a port official to conduct them to the Rogandan embassy. The port official knew enough Rogandan to explain the captain's intentions to the old man and his friends.

Kamash was grateful beyond words. Meeting with the ambassador was precisely what he had been hoping for. Being unable to thank the captain in his own tongue, all of them, even Neira, bowed low in gratitude before waving a farewell.

As they approached the ambassador's building, Kamash tried to calm his racing heart, reminding himself he was well acquainted with dealing with royal officials. Of necessity his skills had remained dormant, but he felt sure that conventions would not have changed significantly, even over the course of his long life. Leaning closer to Neira, he whispered, "Would you allow me to do the talking, at least for now?"

She looked down her nose at him for a moment, then to his surprise she responded with a nod.

When they arrived, they were ushered inside after a short delay and greeted by a Rogandan official. "What brings you to the ambassador?" the official asked. "I heard you were rescued from a tiny boat far out at sea."

"We were," Kamash acknowledged. "We were fortunate indeed to be found by Varasan fishermen. My name is Kamash," he continued with a bow, "and this is Neira and Uman. Uman does not speak."

The official surveyed them with raised eyebrows, but didn't comment. They must surely provide a curious spectacle. The great age of Kamash would itself be an object of curiosity, and the foreign features of the others could hardly have been more apparent.

"I am sure the ambassador has more important priorities than providing comfort to shipwrecked mariners," Kamash continued. "But I am confident he will want to hear what we have to tell him."

"I don't doubt you have a story worth listening to," the official told them, "but it will need to wait until the morning. The ambassador is not available at present. In the meantime, I will arrange for food to be sent to you. After you have taken refreshments, you will be shown to our guest quarters."

The official was as good as his word. A light meal soon appeared, then they were led to a cluster of small rooms equipped with beds and other amenities. After being invited to make themselves comfortable, they were told that someone would come for them in the morning.

Entering the room assigned to him, Kamash threw himself down onto the low bed and fell immediately into a deep sleep.

3

The afternoon had almost worn away before the ambassador called for Kamash and his companions. An aide ushered them into a small reception room where the ambassador sat at a large mahogany desk, his attention fixed on a parchment spread out before him.

"The castaways, Lord Daris," the aide announced before excusing himself with a bow.

The ambassador glanced up from the parchment. He appeared anxious and distracted.

"I heard of your ordeal," he said. "A terrible business." He waved a hand vaguely. "I will arrange for you to be transported to Rog at the earliest opportunity." His eyes drifted down to the parchment again.

If Kamash was reading Lord Daris correctly, this promised to be a short interview.

"We apologize for disturbing you, My Lord. I am Rogandan and my name is Kamash," he said. "My companions understand our language, although they are not from Rogand or from any of the kingdoms in this region."

The ambassador's head jerked up. He directed a sharp glance toward the girl. "Who are your companions?" he asked.

Kamash opened his mouth to respond, but Neira got in first. She had either forgotten her agreement to let Kamash do the talking, or she'd chosen to ignore it.

"This is Uman," she said, indicating the guard. "He cannot speak. My name is Neira. We have journeyed here from the Empire of Ahr."

Neira's answer was direct, but it was more restrained than the old man might have expected. Discovering he had been holding his breath, he released it slowly, allowing the air to escape between his teeth.

Lord Daris had gone pale. He turned to Neira. "Could it be possible?" he murmured. "Are you...?"

She shot a glance at Kamash.

Apparently she hadn't entirely forgotten her promise. But the ambassador needed to know the truth, and it was her story. He nodded once.

She raised her head proudly. "I am Princess Neira, beloved daughter of our most august emperor—may his name be exalted!"

"This is...most unexpected," the ambassador stammered. He shook his head, attempting to recover himself. Pushing back his chair, he clambered to his feet and offered her a formal bow. "I am greatly honored to host you, Your Highness," he said. "I beg your forgiveness if our welcome has been somewhat lacking."

"You are pardoned," she replied condescendingly, looking down at him over her nose. "I have endured much worse in recent times," she added with a dark glance in the direction of Kamash.

The ambassador pulled a cord beside his desk, and a servant hurried in. "Bring refreshments at once for our honored guests!" he ordered.

The servant bowed and scurried away. It was apparent that they now had the ambassador's full attention.

"How did you come to be adrift on the open seas?" Lord Daris asked them.

Neira glanced at Kamash, clearly inviting him to respond on behalf of them all.

"It is a matter of some delicacy, My Lord," he said. "But the simple answer is that a few weeks ago, the princess and her guard found themselves stranded as a result of misadventure on the island where I have been living. I offered to sail them to Rog. Unfortunately for us all, my small vessel was disabled in a major storm. We somehow remained afloat until Varasan fishermen found us and brought us here."

The ambassador eyed him shrewdly. "It is obvious to me that there is a great deal more to your tale than you have revealed. Much as I respect your discretion, it is crucial that I, and other interested parties, learn the full details of everything that has happened. Once the right people are in the room, would you be willing to speak openly?"

Kamash stared back at him determinedly. "On one condition," he said.

"What is it?" asked Lord Daris.

"Both you and the king of Varas must guarantee the safety of Princess Neira and her guard."

The ambassador appeared relieved. "I can readily agree to that, and I have no doubt that King Delmar will do the same."

At that moment servants arrived bearing food and drink. After ordering that his guests be served, the ambassador directed one of his servants to find new clothing for them.

He turned to Kamash. "I am going to leave you for a while, to gather a few key people who will want to hear your news. You have my word that you will receive the guarantee you requested before anything needs to be said. I will, of course, send a full report to King Krasmir, and I have no doubt that he will underwrite my guarantee."

"Who is King Krasmir?" asked Kamash curiously.

Lord Daris gazed at him in surprise. "The king of Rogand, of course."

The old man's eyebrows went up. "I expected Agon—the son of King Ugar—would be king now."

The ambassador stared at him strangely. "How long have you been away from Rogand?"

To Kamash's relief, an aide scurried up to Lord Daris with a message, saving the old man the necessity of a reply. Upon reading the message, the ambassador regretfully informed them that he was urgently needed elsewhere. After promising he would return soon, he excused himself and hurried away with the aide.

THE SUN HAD BARELY SET when Kamash and his companions, newly clad in fine clothing, were taken to the Rogandan ambassador. On the way, Kamash sidled alongside the princess.

"Do you wish to speak for yourself?" he asked her.

"Certainly not!" she retorted. "It would not be dignified for me to talk about my abasement on your primitive island. And although I entrusted my life to your puny little boat—very unwisely as it turned out—I have no desire to glorify either the vessel or the experience by talking about it. I will withhold comment until matters of substance are raised."

The old man nodded, unable to keep a smile from his lips. Whether born and bred in empires or in kingdoms, royals were the same everywhere.

They were ushered into a lavishly appointed reception room where food and drink were being served in bountiful supply. A buzz of voices greeted them as they arrived, but all conversation ceased the moment they entered the room, and every eye turned in their direction.

The ambassador stood waiting for them along with five other people. All of them studied Kamash and his friends with considerable interest.

"Welcome!" said Lord Daris, his lips parting with the practiced smile of a diplomat. He addressed the others already in the room. "May I introduce to you Princess Neira of the Empire of Ahr, her guard, Uman, and Kamash, one of my own countrymen who has been accompanying them."

Then he turned to the new arrivals. "Allow me to introduce my other guests. We are privileged to have with us King Delmar of Varas, along with one of his senior nobles, Lord Karevis."

The Varasan king aimed a nod in their direction. Lord Karevis bowed.

"I am also pleased to introduce to you King Rupert of Castel and Lord Mardone, one of his nobles. We are fortunate that they happened to be visiting Varacellan and were able to join us."

King Rupert and Lord Mardone added their greetings.

"We are also grateful that Count Ranauld has made himself available to join us. The count is a nobleman in the court of King Steffan of Arvenon and a close confidante of the king. His presence in Varacellan is also timely."

The count bowed a welcome.

Kamash eyed them curiously. He was impressed. Four of the five kingdoms in the region were now represented. And Lord Daris had introduced the foreigners almost as if they were on friendly terms with Rogand, maybe even allies. A great deal must have changed since he was last abroad in the world.

Two kings had made themselves available at very short notice, along with highly ranked nobles representing two more. Kamash was left wondering what might have prompted such a response. He didn't doubt that princesses rarely visited Varacellan from far off empires, especially as castaways. But surely curiosity alone could not account for a gathering such as this.

His experience told him that these people had more than a casual interest in the princess. He felt sure they knew something of her already and had information Kamash wasn't aware of.

"Please," said the Rogandan ambassador, "tell us from the beginning how you came to be here. Leave nothing out. I will translate for the benefit of those who speak only Arvenian."

Kamash exchanged a glance with the princess. She nodded briefly.

Pausing for a moment to calm his racing pulse, he began. "I have been living for some years on a tiny island far from the mainland."

He waited for Lord Daris to translate before continuing.

"Several weeks ago, I watched as a boat was rowed to the little beach of my island. Two people—the princess and her guard as I later discovered—were put ashore. I watched as the sailors rowed around the island before returning to their ship and sailing away."

Muttering broke out at his words. The ambassador and his guests appeared troubled.

Kamash continued. "I made myself known to the princess and her guard and was able to satisfy their immediate need for food and shelter. After they had endured a few weeks of their unexpected isolation, I offered to sail them to Rog. My intent was to commit them into the care of the king. Soon after we left, a severe storm blew up. It prevented us from completing our journey. We might well have perished at sea had it not been for the intervention of Varasan fishermen who were kind enough to bring us here."

Heads nodded once his words were translated.

"What prompted you to risk the elements?" asked Lord Daris, frowning. "Why not simply wait for the princess's people to return for her?"

Before responding, Kamash stole a glance at the princess. She returned a tight nod, and the old man faced the ambassador once more.

"I acted out of concern for the well-being of the princess," Kamash replied. "When she first arrived she told me that she had been weary from a long sea voyage and asked to spend a short time on solid ground. The sailors were delivering her to the island in response to that request. They promised to return for her after circumnavigating the island in search for a more attractive place to land. For reasons known best to themselves, they chose not to do that."

Kamash furrowed his brows. "There can be little doubt that the sailors believed the island to be uninhabited." He paused before adding, "And also incapable of sustaining life for any length of time, given the lack of shelter and readily available food supplies."

Further muttering broke out as soon as his words were translated.

"I had food enough for the three of us," Kamash continued. "But I formed the opinion that the sailors would return at some point, expecting to find the bodies of the princess and her guard. I could only guess at their reaction on finding them alive and well. But I deemed it unsafe for any of us to remain on the island to find out."

"Who was in charge of the Ahran vessel, and what was the purpose of the voyage?" the ambassador asked.

A stubborn look came to the princess's face. "You surely cannot expect that I would disclose matters of state to foreigners," she said haughtily.

The ambassador and his guests exchanged glances.

King Delmar spoke, addressing himself to the princess.

"His Majesty King Delmar asks if you know why the sailors left you on the island," the ambassador translated.

Her reply was brief and terse. "I do not. But my father will have the heads of those responsible when he finds out."

An animated conversation broke out in Arvenian, and the ambassador turned aside for a time to participate in it.

Kamash waited patiently. Thus far he had been the only one providing information, and he would have greatly appreciated any member of his audience returning the favor. But his experience of kings and noblemen left him with low expectations.

Nor was he disappointed. The interaction that followed went on for long enough that Kamash began to wonder if the kings and their retainers had forgotten entirely that the princess and her little party were still present in the room. After a while he decided to ignore them, choosing instead to eat heartily from the tantalizing array of food and wine laid out in the reception room.

Eventually the talking came to an end.

"The hour is late," Lord Daris told Kamash and his companions. He waved at the tables still laden with food. "Please, take your fill. King Delmar is kindly arranging for you to be shown to more appropriate accommodations at the palace. We will remain here in Varacellan while a suitable vessel is being prepared. It might take a day or two, but as soon as one is available we will take ship to Rog. I will accompany you."

The ambassador addressed the princess. "I presume you would wish your guard to remain at your side, Your Highness?" he asked.

"Most certainly," she replied.

Lord Daris turned to Kamash. "All of us thank you for your efforts on behalf of the princess. You will be free to go your own way in the morning."

"He will be coming with us," the princess interjected bluntly. "I will not go to Rog or anywhere else without him."

Lord Daris raised his eyebrows, but he didn't argue. "Are you willing?" he asked the old man.

Kamash nodded slowly. He was no less surprised than the ambassador by the princess's demand, but he didn't show it. "I find myself with no pressing engagements," he said with a wry smile. "So I am willing."

"Very well," said Lord Daris. "I will see to the arrangements."

A detachment of honor guards duly arrived to escort them to their new accommodations. The palace was close enough for them to walk, and as they passed through the broad streets Kamash gazed curiously at the happy crowds that thronged them. Well before they arrived at their destination he had decided he liked Varacellan very much.

The room allocated to Kamash in the palace was noticeably different from the one he had occupied the previous night, and bore no comparison at all with his primitive dwelling on the island. The feather and down pillow beneath his head was luxurious. Nevertheless, soft though it might be, it was quickly forgotten once sleep reached out for him.

THE CITY of Varacellan glittered in the early morning light, beautiful and peaceful. Splendid as it was, King Rupert of Castel would have exchanged it in a heartbeat for the less sophisticated grandeur of his own capital city. There was no place like home when you'd slept badly and woken to a fresh day of troubles.

He had plenty on his mind. Needing to clear his head, he left the palace buildings and wandered aimlessly into the large garden within the outer walls of the castle.

Life had changed dramatically for Rupert in the years since he was crowned king. At first, deceived entirely by the former Lord Eisgold, an impressionable King Rupert had made a series of monumentally bad decisions that brought his kingdom to the brink of disaster. His blindness had also very nearly cost him his own life.

Thanks entirely to the bold initiatives of a determined band of loyalists, Lord Eisgold's duplicity had been exposed in time to save Rupert and free his kingdom. Greatly humbled by the impact of his mistakes, the unseasoned young king had chosen to embrace responsibility for his actions and learn from the experience.

Eight years had now passed since the deaths of the traitorous Lord Eisgold and Eisgold's sponsor King Agon of Rogand. During that period he had worked hard at growing into the shoes vacated by King Istel, his beloved father, struck down before his time. The nobles who rescued Rupert had unstintingly provided help and guidance, proving their value and their loyalty many times over.

Everything had been proceeding as well as Rupert could have hoped. As he slowly began to mature, he dared to imagine that better times lay ahead for him and his kingdom. As little as a month ago his world had seemed predictable and his kingdom secure. He felt sure that the troubles of the past lay behind him.

Then a ship sailed into the harbor at Rog, bearing the Grand Vizier of the Empire of Ahr. Disaster now threatened to engulf Rogand—and Arvenon, Varas, and Castel along with it. Any notion that Rupert's world was stable had been stripped away in a moment.

Dangerous as the situation was, Rupert and his fellow monarchs at least thought they understood what was happening. The arrival of Princess Neira demonstrated that none of them understood anything.

Rupert groaned aloud and shook his head. At the sound, a face he recognized appeared from behind a flowering bush.

The narrowed eyes of Princess Neira peered up at him. "King Rupert, isn't it?" she sniffed. "I don't remember the name of your kingdom."

He groaned again, inwardly this time. Why did he have to bump into the princess, of all people? And she'd spoken to him in Rogandan. He'd been working hard to master the language, but he suspected that her fluency exceeded his own.

"My kingdom is called Castel, Princess Neira," he replied.

"I see," she said, somehow managing to convey that neither he nor his little kingdom registered at all in her reckoning.

"What brings you into the garden this morning?" he asked, unable to overcome his awkwardness enough to conjure up a more sharp-witted question.

Her eyebrows drew together. "Don't women in your kingdom enjoy gardens?" she asked, a sarcastic tinge to her tone.

He winced inwardly. "Yes, they do," he acknowledged. Then, speaking mostly to himself, he added, "The real surprise is that I'm here."

"Well?" she demanded. "Why are you here?"

Was it necessary for her to be so blatant about her rudeness? Perhaps she had been hoping for solitude, but so had he.

"You're not the only one with more questions than answers," he retorted with a frown. "Nor are you the only one who'd rather be speaking your own language, and preferably to someone vaguely interested in hearing what you had to say."

She looked at him wide-eyed for a moment, then she burst out laughing.

He flushed, taken aback by her response and annoyed with himself for being so forthright.

"I'm not laughing at you," she said, struggling to suppress another chuckle. "I'm appreciating the absurdity of this situation."

Her response didn't help, and it must have shown on his face, because she added, "On Ahr-Chitani I was never allowed to spend time alone with a male. Much less one with the impertinence to treat me as an equal. My chaperones would be horrified." A new bout of giggling overtook her.

He stared back at her, unsure how to respond.

She looked at him boldly. "I must say there are aspects to the situation I'm finding very interesting." Then her brows knit together delicately. "Would you like to kiss me?"

He frowned, beginning to feel even more uncomfortable.

"Apparently not," she said, sounding a bit peeved. Then she shrugged. "I've always been told that I'm much too brazen for my own good." The trace of a grin appeared on her lips. "But this is the first time I've stooped to inviting a man to kiss me."

He couldn't prevent his eyes flicking to her lips. He felt himself blushing.

She frowned again. "Back home no one would dare of course. You're probably the first person who could actually do it without losing your head." She grinned at him.

Abruptly she glanced over his shoulder. "There's Uman! I need to leave."

And with a swish of her skirts she was gone.

Rupert shook his head. He couldn't begin to figure her out. The fate of kingdoms hung in the balance, with her positioned at the center of the maelstrom. And here she was trying to orchestrate her first kiss. What on earth was she playing at?

The stakes had never been higher for him and for his kingdom. Yet a single trivial issue occupied far too much of his attention as the morning slipped away. "Would you like to kiss me?" she had asked. The question was absurd. And his inability to banish it entirely from his mind annoyed him intensely.

4

The first glimmers of daylight slowly lightened the sky, revealing a broad beach lapped by the gentle swell of a tranquil ocean. Nestled behind the sand dunes lay a fishing village, a haven to the small boats spreading out at that moment across the bay, their sails billowing in a freshening breeze.

Suddenly a monstrous reptilian form burst from the ocean, shattering the stillness. The creature threw back its head and bellowed, the unearthly roar drowning out the cries of the fishermen. Then it bent low, opening its gigantic maw wide to enclose a fishing boat. As the mouth snapped shut, a long tail whipped out to lash another vessel, splintering timbers as though they were twigs.

Boats dodged back and forth across the bay as fishermen tried frantically to evade the monster. Their efforts were in vain. One by one the boats succumbed to its fury until nothing but wreckage remained to rise and fall with the swell.

Surging from the ocean, the beast fell upon the village, thrashing about in a frenzy until the settlement had been utterly destroyed. Then, raising its head and roaring once more, it headed inland.

. . .

Brother Ander woke with a start, struggling to separate imagination from reality. Lurching unsteadily from his bed in a tower room of the royal castle at Arnost, he shuffled to the window, sweating profusely in the cool air. He stared wide-eyed up into the brilliant display of stars, unnerved by the vividness of the dream.

As he watched, a shooting star flashed across the heavens, rapidly followed by several more. Fully alert now, the monk's brows drew together as he labored to make sense of the demonstration.

Had the dream been a premonition? Had he witnessed signs in the heavens to confirm it?

Only one conclusion made sense to him—trouble was coming. His gut tightened as he pondered the implications.

What should he do?

Once a soldier and a leader in battle, the big monk knew that the mightiest of armies were powerless to defeat some enemies. The greatest warrior could not strike down a pestilence that might be conquered by the frailest of healers. He had come to recognize that true strength was often disregarded, dismissed as weakness by those unable or unwilling to penetrate its disguise.

What should he do?

Lighting a candle, he glanced down at the scroll that lay beside it. His eye fell upon the words he had been studying before he surrendered to sleep, 'Devote yourselves to prayer, being watchful and thankful.'

A wry smile crossed his lips as he considered the seeming feebleness of prayer.

His question had been answered. Heaving a deep sigh, he gazed once more out into the night sky. Then kneeling on the rough stone floor, he directed his forebodings heavenward.

Queen Essanda had finally found time to focus on her youngest child, Princess Charlotte, to the great delight of the three-year-old. Sweet and demure, Charlotte was also unusually astute for her age.

She unfailingly showered her father with affection, but showed a clear preference for the company of her mother. Everyone said she was a miniature of the queen.

"Mother! Mother!"

Queen Essanda sighed as her sons appeared at the door. Unusually spirited, they somehow managed to commandeer a disproportionate share of her available time. Her eldest, the eight-year-old Crown Prince Aiden, hobbled into the room with an arm over the shoulder of his younger brother, Prince Leonid, recently turned six.

Little Charlotte jumped up in alarm and ran to them. "Are you hurt, Aidie? What happened?"

"I was riding, and I fell off," Aiden replied through gritted teeth. "I hurt my ankle."

"Come over here," commanded the queen. "Ava!" she called. "Could you please fetch Brother Ander? Quickly!"

"At once, Your Majesty," her maid replied, dropping her needlework and scampering for the door.

Essanda settled her injured son on a sofa and tried to make him comfortable. He appeared overwrought. After a moment's reflection, she decided she'd have been more concerned if he was pale and subdued. Children certainly had a taste for the dramatic.

The monk arrived before many minutes had passed. He walked into the room, taking in the scene at a glance. Approaching the prince, he quickly examined his ankle, moving it back and forth gently. He smiled at the queen. "It appears to be a sprain," he assured her. "Nothing seems to be broken."

He turned to the prince. "What's the problem, young Aiden?" he asked. "Have you been up to mischief again?"

"I was riding, and I fell off," Aiden repeated, not making eye contact with the monk.

"That's curious," said Brother Ander. "I wouldn't have expected that pony of yours—Prince, isn't it?—to do anything too adventurous. He seems barely able to raise a trot."

Aiden colored slightly.

The monk grinned at him. "Perhaps you fell off a horse?"

The prince didn't reply, but the look on his face was revealing.

"You didn't tell me you were riding a horse!" his mother exclaimed. "You know you're not supposed to be doing that!"

"I didn't lie!" he insisted. "You never asked me what I was riding!"

She raised an eyebrow at him.

Aiden threw up his hands. "How will I ever become a warrior if I never get to ride real horses?"

"You're much too young to be thinking about becoming a warrior," Essanda told him sternly.

"But you were only a girl when you went to battle!" Aiden protested.

"That was different," Essanda replied, "and I certainly was a lot older than eight." She frowned at him. "How did you find out about that anyway?"

Brother Ander cleared his throat guiltily. "I suspect I might have been to blame for that, Your Majesty," he admitted.

"It isn't his fault," retorted Aiden, his lips forming a pout. "Everyone in the kingdom knows about it! Everyone except us, that is."

Essanda turned to the monk with a sigh, determined to change the subject. "What does he need to do about the ankle?" she asked.

"It needs rest," Brother Ander replied. "It would help if he stays off it for a while."

"If I promise to keep away from the horses, can I ride my pony?" Aiden asked hopefully.

"Most certainly not!" his mother replied. "You heard what Brother Ander said. You need to rest your ankle."

Aiden glowered at the monk.

"You appear to be cross with me," Brother Ander observed. "Why don't you punch me? If you dare, that is," he challenged, standing before the prince with hands on his hips.

Aiden hopped up immediately. Leaning against a sofa for support, he began flailing about with both fists, grunting aloud as he strained to hit his target.

Brother Ander grinned back at him, stretching out a hand lazily and placing it on the prince's forehead. His reach was so much longer than the boy's that Aiden was unable to land a single punch.

"Argh! It isn't fair!"

Still grinning, the monk removed his hand and let the young prince pound him for a few moments. "Enough!" he cried with a laugh. "I'll need a doctor myself in a minute."

Aiden stopped punching and sat down again with a grunt of satisfaction.

The monk ruffled his hair. "Promise me you'll take better care of yourself, young prince!" he said.

Aiden grinned up at him. Then he stood once more and hobbled to the door, calling for his brother to lend him a shoulder again.

Turning to Ava, the queen jerked her head after him. The maid nodded an acknowledgment, following them out the door to keep an eye on them.

Essanda smiled indulgently after their disappearing forms. Then she turned her full attention to Brother Ander and studied him for a while. "You seem more thoughtful than usual," she said.

"You're uncommonly observant, Your Majesty," he replied. "I thought I was behaving normally."

"You were," she said. "But I've known you a long time. You have something on your mind."

"I do," he acknowledged. "I had a dream last night, a disturbing dream. And it was followed by shooting stars in the heavens."

She raised her eyebrows. "Can you tell me about it?"

He nodded. Surprisingly, he was still able to remember it clearly. He described it without further comment.

She stood silently for a while. Finally, she asked, "Did you say the sun rose over the sea?"

"Yes," he replied.

"So the setting was not Arvenon. The sun sets over our coastline —it doesn't rise over the sea."

He looked at her in surprise. "You're right! I never thought of that."

"Rogand, perhaps?" she asked.

He nodded. "Perhaps. If the dream represents anywhere known to us, it would have to be Rogand."

"So something is threatening Rogand. Do you think it's a natural disaster? A plague, or a flood?"

He shook his head slowly. "My heart says otherwise." He gazed down at her. "You understand better than most the damage caused by human greed and lust for power, Your Majesty. You and King Steffan have suffered from it yourselves."

"What can the king and I do to prepare?" she asked.

He shrugged. "I have no advice to offer, Your Majesty. I can only say I'm confident you'll find a way through, as you have in the past."

She gazed up at him silently for a moment. Then she said, "Thank you, Brother Ander. I truly don't know how we would manage without you."

He stared back at her in surprise. "I contribute so little. I do know I'm supposed to pray, and I've been doing that. For you and the king especially, because the burden of leadership weighs heaviest during difficult times. But beyond that..."

She smiled. "You do much more than you realize."

He thanked her with a bow and left.

Princess Charlotte was overdue to reclaim her mother's attention. Essanda reached out and drew her in for a hug, and the three-year-old settled in with a sigh of satisfaction.

Nevertheless, the queen was unable to entirely banish the previous conversation from her mind. Brother Ander feared that trouble was coming. She could wish it otherwise, but wishing achieved very little. Perhaps the monk was right, and they would somehow find a way through when the need arose.

She very much hoped so.

After concluding a scheduled meeting with the Castelan ambassador, Queen Essanda left the reception room to discover her husband waiting for her.

"Essanda, I need to speak with you. Urgently." The king looked worried.

She followed him into a private meeting room and closed the door behind them. "What's the problem, Steffan?" she asked.

"I've just received a dispatch," he told her grimly. "There's trouble."

She grimaced. "The dispatch is from Rog. And whatever the trouble is, it came from the sea."

His brows puckered in astonishment. "How did you know?"

"A lucky guess," she replied. "I can explain later. What's the trouble? Relations with Rogand have never been better since King Krasmir ascended the throne."

"Krasmir isn't the problem," he exclaimed. "It's much worse than that. A ship arrived from the Empire of Ahr, bearing the Grand Vizier."

"The Empire of Ahr? I've barely heard of it. It's on another continent isn't it?"

"Yes," he replied. "Going there requires a long and dangerous sea voyage. Only the boldest traders are willing to risk the journey."

"What's the problem?" she asked.

"The Grand Vizier says he was heading for Rogand on a goodwill visit. He claims they were attacked at sea as they approached Rog. The emperor's daughter was traveling with them, and she was abducted from their ship, supposedly by men from a customs ship bearing the Rogandan flag."

Essanda frowned in disbelief. "It's hard to imagine King Krasmir sanctioning such an action. What does he have to say about this?"

"He strenuously denies that any of his people were involved," Steffan told her. "He thinks it might have been pirates. It's very surprising, though, to say the least."

His brows furrowed. "The Grand Vizier says this act has brought intolerable dishonor to the empire, and the emperor will have no choice but to send soldiers to find his daughter. They will conduct a search throughout Rogand, Castel, Varas, and Arvenon! They will poke their noses into every corner of the four kingdoms looking for the princess, and they will do it with or without our cooperation."

"What? That would amount to an act of war!"

"Exactly. The Grand Vizier has promised to return with an army big enough to crush any kingdom unwilling to cooperate with them."

Essanda was horrified. "Have Varas and Castel been informed? Are Delmar and Rupert aware of this?" she asked. "And what is Krasmir planning to do?"

"I don't know what Krasmir intends to do. But he's sent urgent messages to Varacellan and Castel Citadel as well as to us." He shrugged helplessly. "That's all I know."

Essanda shook her head slowly. "What can we do?"

"I've sent for Will," Steffan told her. "We'll need him and his insights. I've also sent a messenger to Lord Burtelen, and asked him to ride to Arnost with Will."

She nodded. "It's a pity the duke isn't still with us. I always valued his wisdom."

"Yes, I'm sure it won't be the last time we'll find ourselves missing my uncle," Steffan replied. "Even if he hadn't passed away last year, though, it wouldn't have been reasonable to expect him to travel from Maranelle to Arnost."

"Are you hoping to send Will to Rog?" Essanda asked.

"The thought had crossed my mind," he acknowledged.

"He won't want to go unless Amyra is with him," she said. "I hear the two of them are inseparable. And he'll want Thomas with him too."

The king looked surprised. "Why would Will want Thomas to go with him?"

Essanda quirked her eyebrows at him. "Are you serious? Whenever anything significant is going on, he always involves Thomas."

"Well I was expecting him to take Rufe. But you're undoubtedly right. For that matter he'll probably want Jonas and Haldek and Breysen..."

"It's all very well to make light of it," she chided. "I have a feeling we'll soon be wishing there were plenty more like them."

"You're probably right," he told her seriously. "You usually are. Now tell me how you guessed the news from Krasmir."

She gazed up at him. "Earlier today Brother Ander told me about a dream he had recently," she said. "He dreamed that a monster attacked the coast. The sun was rising over the sea, so it must have been an eastern coastline. I guessed it was Rog. He got up from the dream in time to see a shower of shooting stars. After receiving a dream that was followed by a sign in the heavens, he became convinced that trouble was coming."

"How does any of that help us?" asked Steffan.

She shrugged. "I don't know. But he told me he's praying for us."

The king raised his hands in a mute appeal. "We're going to need all the help we can get," he said grimly.

5

"There's been another dispatch from Rog, Essanda."

The queen looked at Steffan hopefully. "Good news?"

He shook his head. "Nothing useful to report, I'm sorry to say."

"Is the Grand Vizier still in Rog?"

"He was still at Rog when the messenger left," Steffan replied. "The man is apparently unyielding. The Rogandans have been meeting with him every day, but the meetings have led nowhere. The Ahrans don't seem in any hurry to leave, which seems odd. There's no real reason for them to stay—other than to assess Rogandan military strength," he added darkly.

"Still, while the Grand Vizier remains in Rog the Rogandans can at least keep trying," Essanda said hopefully.

Steffan nodded. "Maybe they'll somehow find a way to get through to him. Once he leaves, it's likely that we'll see him next at the head of an invasion army."

"Any word from Castel or Varas?" she asked.

"Yes, I've heard from our ambassador to Varas. King Rupert recently arrived in Varacellan on a diplomatic visit, so he'll be able to consult directly with King Delmar. As it happens Count Ranauld is there too. He will represent our interests."

Essanda sighed. "Will and Lord Burtelen should be arriving before long. Maybe they will have suggestions."

"AIDEN! You'll never guess who I just saw riding in!"

The crown prince of Arvenon looked at his younger brother blankly. "Who?"

"It was Will!"

Aiden's eyes lit up. "I'll beat you to the courtyard, Leo!"

Both boys leaped to their feet and raced for the stairs.

The princes flew out of the royal castle at Arnost to find Will separating from the large party that had accompanied him. Having just dismounted, he was handing the reins to a stable hand.

When he saw the boys coming, he faced them with both hands on his hips. "Who might these urchins be?" he asked with a mock frown. "Young vagabonds, I don't doubt—dashing around, disturbing the peace."

He knelt with a grin, opening his arms wide to receive them. Both boys barreled into him at the same time. Knocked off balance, he tumbled backward helplessly, grasping the boys tightly to his chest. The combatants rolled about in the dirt, the boys wriggling and squirming energetically as they tried to free themselves. Loud hollering interspersed with gales of laughter issued from all three of the wrestlers.

The queen appeared on the scene, accompanied by her daughter. "Who's creating all this racket?" she demanded, peering down at the pandemonium before her. "Are those my sons attacking Lord Torbury?"

Princess Charlotte watched on wide-eyed, a giggle on her little lips.

Will staggered to his feet with both boys still hanging off him.

"I'm exhausted, Your Majesty!" he wheezed. "I've fought bandits who were less ferocious than this welcoming party."

She frowned down at her sons, an eyebrow raised admonishingly. "Let the poor man go!" she commanded.

Loud protests sounded from the boys, but they released Will as instructed.

After tousling their hair, he brushed at his clothes in an attempt to dust himself off. Then he knelt before Princess Charlotte. "Can you spare a hug for an old campaigner?" he asked.

"You're very dirty," she told him seriously. "But I think I might have one hug for you."

He reached out for her, and she leaped into his arms, squealing with delight as he swept her off her feet.

"It's an energetic end to a long journey, Will," the queen told him with a laugh. "But you're very welcome, as you can see."

King Steffan appeared. "I thought the castle was under attack!" he exclaimed. "Now I see that it's only Lord Torbury arriving."

Will bowed with a smile, Charlotte still in his arms, and the king grinned back at him.

"Your arrival is perfectly timed, My Lord," the king told him. "Please join me and Essanda." He turned to a servant. "I believe I saw Lord Burtelen riding in. Could you please ask him to join us?"

As the king led them away, Prince Aiden called to Will, "Come find us when your meeting finishes. Promise?"

"I promise!" Will called back with a laugh.

AFTER ORDERING refreshments for the weary travelers, Steffan led them to a small meeting room. They made themselves comfortable while waiting for Lord Burtelen to join them. He arrived as the food and drinks were being served.

"Thank you both for coming so promptly," the king told the new arrivals. "It's been two weeks since a disturbing dispatch arrived from Rog, and I've just received a new dispatch, this time from Varacellan. Before I share its contents, let me brief you on the situation to date."

He quickly outlined all he knew about the Ahran situation. Then he retrieved a parchment.

"This dispatch just arrived from Varas," the king told them. "The news is so bizarre it's difficult to know what to make of it. The missing princess has turned up. In Varacellan."

"Surely that's good news!" exclaimed the queen.

He shook his head grimly. "I'm afraid not. It seems she wasn't kidnapped at all. Her own people dumped her with her bodyguard on a tiny remote island and left them there to die."

The news was greeted with stunned silence.

Lord Burtelen was the first to speak. "How did she get to Varacellan?" he asked.

"Fortunately for us, the Ahrans decided to abandon them on the one remote island that was inhabited. An old hermit was living there, and he took them in and fed them. He also had a boat, and they all set out for Rogand in it. They were caught in a storm and would have died if they hadn't been rescued by some Varasan fishermen who took them to Varacellan."

"Is Delmar planning to return the princess to the Ahrans?" asked Will.

"You won't be surprised to hear there are a range of views on the wisdom of handing her over," the king replied. "There'd be no way to guarantee her safety. But they are planning to send her to Rog."

"At the very least the Grand Vizier needs to know that his lie has been exposed," said Lord Burtelen.

"It might not be possible to confront him with the truth," said the king. "He may have already left Rog by the time the news reaches King Krasmir."

"It seems that the Ahrans want a pretext for war," said Will. He shook his head grimly. "If you can't find a reason, create one. Fabricate an incident, then blame the victim. The only thing that remains is to invade."

"I fear you're right, Will," said Lord Burtelen. "Producing the princess might not stop the Ahrans. If they're determined enough, they'll find another excuse to invade."

Will nodded. "The question is why they've done this. What are their motives?"

The king spread his hands helplessly. "That's what we need to find out."

"Perhaps the princess has answers," said Will. "Do we have anyone who speaks the Ahran language?"

"I've learned that the princess speaks Rogandan, and apparently speaks it well," the king told him.

Will raised his eyebrows.

Everything went quiet until Will asked the king directly, "I'm the only person among your nobles who speaks Rogandan, Your Majesty. Were you planning to send me to Rog?"

"It did occur to me, Will," the king acknowledged.

"You've finally had a chance to settle down, Will," the queen observed. "How would you feel about leaving your family?"

"I won't deny that having a wife and children has changed my outlook on life," Will acknowledged. "But I haven't forgotten that my position of privilege comes with responsibilities—to you and to the kingdom. I'll go if you want me to."

"What will Amyra think about that?" asked Essanda.

"I'd like to discuss it with her," Will replied. "It's possible she'll want to go herself. She speaks Rogandan at least as well as I do."

"And your children?" persisted the queen.

"I'm not sure. With your permission, Your Majesties, I'll return home to properly plan for the journey. Would the delay cause a problem?"

"I trust not," the king replied. "Given you'll be starting from Erestor, it might be quickest to sail to Rog from Maranelle. That should allow you to save quite a bit of time."

Will grimaced. "I can't pretend to have positive memories of my last voyage."

"It did take you a while to find your sea legs," the king acknowledged with a chuckle. "If you're going by ship, perhaps you should take Breysen with you. He's living on your holdings now, isn't he?"

"Yes, he is. It's a good thought. I'll send a message to Newhaven to see if Thomas can come too. He traveled to Rogand with me last time."

Essanda and Steffan exchanged a glance.

"What about Elena and the children?" asked the queen.

"Thomas and Elena will need to decide that for themselves," Will replied.

He turned to the king. "I will follow through on your suggestion, Your Majesty. Traveling to Rog by sea should save a considerable amount of time."

"You'll go as my personal representative, Will," Steffan replied. "I'll prepare some letters of introduction to confirm your role. You can take them with you when you leave for home."

"Thank you, Your Majesty," Will replied with a bow.

"How many people will you take?" Steffan asked.

"Just a small party," said Will. "A large force won't be appropriate for a diplomatic mission. It could send the wrong message."

Steffan nodded his agreement. "You'll be able to consult with Ranauld when you arrive. He's currently in Varacellan, and he's planning to travel with King Delmar and King Rupert when they take the princess to Rog."

"I will look forward to meeting with him," Will said with evident satisfaction.

The king eyed Will thoughtfully. "I'm sure I don't need to remind you that you'll be going as Lord Torbury. I'll avoid any mention in your credentials about your role as commander of the Arvenian army. The less said about that the better, I imagine. It's now been several years since the war ended, and another king is on the throne. But we need to avoid any unnecessary tension with the Rogandans."

Will nodded. "Of course, Your Majesty. I have no more desire than you to resolve this or any other issue by fighting."

A NEW MORNING HAD DAWNED, and the road beckoned. After carrying out a final check of his horse's girth straps, Will swung into the saddle. With his credentials from the king stowed safely in a saddlebag, nothing remained to delay his departure.

A myriad of thoughts flooded through Will's mind as he watched his riding companions mount up. He was looking forward eagerly to seeing his wife and children again. He wouldn't be with them for long, though, and he was already suffering pangs of regret.

The truth was that wandering the world held little appeal for him now. Given the climactic events that had taken place in Rogand, those who knew Will best might have expected life to seem monotonous for him once he returned from there. Nevertheless, he'd readily found new outlets for his restless energies. Returning to his devastated holdings in Erestor with a bride, he set about the process of rebuilding, ably assisted by his new steward, Jonas. Other friends had worked tirelessly alongside him too. Rufe had taken responsibility for animal husbandry as well as security on the holdings, and Breysen, reunited at last with his family, was thriving as the community blacksmith.

Will had put down deep roots into Erestor. Having learned the hard way the value of relationship and credibility with the local nobility, he now took an active interest in the affairs of Erestor's Council of Lords. Many of the nobles had reacted coolly to him at first, but after patience and perseverance he could now count a good few of them as friends. Showing generosity at strategic moments hadn't hurt either.

The Duke of Erestor had eased him into the role, continuing to provide support until his recent death. The whole country mourned the passing of the duke, and Will missed his skillful supervision and wise counsel as much as anyone. Nevertheless, he was gratified when leadership of the council passed to Lord Burtelen, a good friend and staunch ally of Will's.

Regular visits to the capital to consult with the king and queen were still required. Once they were added to the tally, Will had more than enough to occupy his attention.

His musing was interrupted by a familiar voice. "Will, can I please have a word?"

Will turned to the newcomer with a welcoming smile. "It's good to see you, Brother Ander. Unfortunately I'm about to leave—I'm sorry I haven't spent time with you. It's been a very short visit this time."

"I understand," the monk replied. He lowered his voice. "Are you going to Rogand? Because if you are I'd like to go with you."

Unsure of how much he was at liberty to say, Will had no ready reply to offer.

Apparently understanding the reason for his silence, Brother Ander added, "I know there's trouble, but I don't know the details. Would you be willing to wait long enough for me to ask the king and queen for permission to join you?"

"Of course," Will replied without hesitation. He dismounted from his horse. "I'll let my companions know about the delay."

Less than an hour passed before Brother Ander returned. If the big man was still eager to join Will, there was little outward sign of it. At that moment he looked more sober than enthusiastic.

"The king and queen have released me and given me permission to join you," said the monk.

"Reluctantly, if I know anything about the queen," said Will with a smile. "All of them will miss you."

A horse was found for Brother Ander, and he rode out beside Will.

"The king gave me a confidential briefing," said the monk. "The situation doesn't sound encouraging."

Will shook his head. "No. Not encouraging at all."

After they had ridden on in silence for a while, Will addressed the monk again. "The queen told me about your dream. Is that why you want to join us?"

The monk shook his head. "The dream was terrifying. It didn't leave me enthusiastic about heading into the eye of the storm. The reason has more to do with my desire to visit Rogand. Brother Vangellis went there, and he learned the language. I suppose I see myself as following in his footsteps." He stole a glance at Will. "I've been learning Rogandan myself."

Will's eyebrows went up. "You'll be doubly useful then. Would you like to practice while we're riding?"

Brother Ander agreed readily.

"I'm sure you'll be happy to see some of your old friends when we reach my holdings," said Will, switching to Rogandan.

"Most definitely. I will look forward to it," the monk replied in the same language. "It's been far too long."

Will's eyebrows went up even further. "Very impressive! You clearly have a gift for languages."

Brother Ander smiled, but didn't comment.

"I'll be interested to show you the progress we've made," said Will. "And there might be some other surprises too. Involving Rufe."

The monk's eyes went wide. "A lady?" he asked incredulously.

Will nodded. "I suspect he might have met his match at last," he confided with a wink.

6

Kamash leaned over the rail, watching the water as it slid past the hull of the ship and wrestling with his thoughts.

Thus far this voyage was diverging in every imaginable way from the final ill-fated voyage of his own boat. On this ship he had been assigned a comfortable berth and given access to a seemingly endless selection of delicious food. Everything reeked of luxury and quality. None of that was surprising, of course, given the status of the passengers.

Up to that point the voyage had proven uneventful, and he'd been informed that they were already more than halfway to Rog. He was still struggling with his apprehensions about returning to the capital he had fled so many years earlier.

He was no longer ignorant about the recent history of Rogand. A little careful research and a few discreet inquiries had yielded a deluge of information. Agon had indeed ascended the throne after the death of his father, King Ugar. During his eventful reign he had managed to make enemies throughout the region, invading Arvenon and briefly annexing Varas. Frequent mention was made of his army commander, Lord Drettroth, and the name was never mentioned without a snarl.

King Agon might have alienated his neighbors, but rumor had it that he had been equally unpopular within his own kingdom. His careless disregard for the common people had resulted in widespread poverty and oppression. In the end the king had apparently been assassinated on the orders of Drettroth, his own commander, with the killer not surfacing until years after Drettroth was dead and buried.

Lord Drettroth was a person known to Kamash, although it was certainly not the same man. The nobleman he knew was fabulously wealthy, but also fat, lazy, and the most subservient of King Ugar's boot lickers. Kamash could not imagine him invading anything more threatening than a banquet hall. The man who commanded Agon's armies and ultimately brought down the king must have been the successor to the man known to Kamash, most probably his son.

There was also much talk about the Arvenian army commander, a man called Will Prentis. He seemed to have featured prominently in defeating the Rogandan invasion, and rumor said he was also present when Agon was killed.

None of this history had been provided by Rogandans. They seemed unwilling to dwell even for a moment on their former king or anything associated with him. Without exception the old man's sources were Varasan, Castelan, or Arvenian.

The current monarch of Rogand was another matter entirely. Everyone—Rogandans and foreigners alike—wanted to talk about King Krasmir. The new king had captured the popular imagination. He seemed to be a strong ruler who was tolerated by his nobles and loved by the commoners of Rogand. And he had ushered in a new era of cooperation with the neighboring kingdoms.

A single crucial question remained: what did all of this mean for Kamash? Frustratingly, he knew of only one way to find an answer—he would have to wait and see.

The arrival of Princess Neira pushed such thoughts from his mind.

She came and leaned on the rail beside him, gazing off toward the horizon. Peering at her out of the corner of his eye, Kamash wondered what she must be thinking and feeling, so far from home and targeted by enemies from her own empire. He had no desire to ask. She would speak if she had a mind to.

"You handle yourself well in front of royalty," she eventually offered.

His eyebrows rose involuntarily. She wasn't given to handing out compliments, so her praise took him by surprise.

"I wonder where you learned to do that?" she continued, narrowing her eyes to stare at him.

Kamash's heart skipped a beat. Was he so transparent? His mind in a whirl, he could think of no suitable response.

She didn't leave him suffering for long; her next comment snapped him out of his agitation entirely.

"I have decided to appoint you as my spokesperson," she announced matter-of-factly.

He turned to her with a frown. "Whatever do you mean? I can't speak on your behalf!"

"Why not?" she demanded.

"I'm not even from your empire."

Her nose went up. "What difference does that make when my own countrymen have betrayed me?"

Kamash shook his head slowly. "I can't do it, Princess. I'm willing to help you as I've done already, but I can't be your official representative."

Her mouth turned down at the corners and tears began to fill her eyes. "Here I am, far from any real civilization—alone and friendless—cut off from everything and everyone. You're the only person I've met who has shown any kind of concern for me. Now you want to abandon me too. And to the mercy of barbarians!"

She stood there sniffing pathetically, dabbing at her eyes.

Kamash could not bear it. "Please don't cry," he told her. "I'll be your spokesperson if it means that much to you."

The tears vanished in a heartbeat. "Good," she said with evident satisfaction. "You needn't worry—I'll instruct you about what you should and shouldn't say on my behalf."

Another figure emerged onto the deck. It was the young Castelan king.

"Ah, there's that other supposed royal—King Rupert, as he styles himself," she said brightly. "Goodbye, loyal spokesperson. We'll talk more later."

And with that she was gone, heading in the direction of the new arrival.

Kamash watched her retreating form in astonishment. What had just happened? Had he been played?

He sighed in resignation, shaking his head. Whether or not she'd taken advantage of him, he was a man of his word and he'd committed himself now.

Neira's arrival had upended his life. And she'd just made it more complicated than ever.

THE YOUNG KING Rupert groaned when he noticed Princess Neira approaching. Their last interaction had left him extremely uncomfortable. She was disconcerting and unpredictable, and he had no idea how to deal with her.

"*King* Rupert!" she said. The emphasis on his title seemed a trifle pointed, and the smile on her face was as oily as it was friendly. It could easily have been interpreted as mocking.

"Princess," he said tersely, with a crisp nod of his head.

She stared out over the water, the picture of innocence. "Have you been enjoying the voyage?" she asked sweetly.

He grunted noncommittally. "For the most part. And you?"

"More and more," she confirmed with a broad grin.

He remained silent, unwilling to risk even an innocuous comment.

Abruptly she turned to face him. "I suppose I should warn you," she said. She spoke casually, but her voice had taken on an ominous tone.

Rupert looked at her blankly. He couldn't even begin to imagine what might come out of her mouth next.

"My father is not likely to receive it warmly when he learns of your intentions toward me."

His brows drew together, even as his heart began to thump in his chest. "What intentions?" he asked, his voice sounding shrill even to his own ears.

"We talked about you kissing me. In the garden."

"There wasn't any conversation," he protested. "You asked me to do it! That was it!"

"Can you honestly pretend you haven't been thinking about kissing me since?" She paused, studying him intently with narrowed eyes. Then a gloating smile appeared on her lips. "There's no point in denying it! It's written all over your face."

What could he possibly say? He'd certainly thought about kissing her—he'd even obsessed about it briefly—but he'd emerged with no desire whatsoever to do it. And he certainly didn't have intentions toward her. The princess wasn't at all the kind of person he was drawn to. She was far too mercurial.

He opened his mouth to speak, but the right words didn't come readily. She seemed so volatile. How would she react if he set her down? He snapped his mouth shut again, struggling to decide what to say.

"Look, *King* Rupert. I need to be honest with you," she told him condescendingly. "You'd be quite unsuitable as my consort. It simply wouldn't work. I can't settle for a man just because he has some kind of a title. I need someone with presence, a person who can't be trifled with." She released an exaggerated sigh. "I'm sure this must hurt. But I'm being kind to you, even if it doesn't feel like it."

Patting him on the shoulder, she turned on her heel and flounced off across the deck.

Rupert blinked his eyes, trying to make sense of what had just happened. Assuming he was willing to overlook the excruciating awkwardness of the whole incident, it was actually good news, wasn't it?

He couldn't imagine her wanting to trouble him any further. As for her humiliating assessment of his manhood and her bizarre conclusions about what he wanted from her, he would simply need to ignore them.

As he stood staring down at the waves, a figure appeared beside him at the rail. It was the old man.

"King Rupert?" asked the newcomer.

"Yes," Rupert acknowledged.

"Do you speak Rogandan?"

"I do," he confirmed, nodding cautiously, "although not particularly well."

"I am Kamash. I witnessed your interaction with the princess from afar."

Rupert felt himself blushing.

"I don't know what Her Highness said to you, but I hope you will extend understanding if that should be needed. The princess has not been called upon to represent her empire before, and I'm sure you can appreciate how much there is to learn when taking on such a role." He paused, apparently choosing his words carefully. "It must be especially difficult for one who has been offered very little freedom in the past."

A guffaw burst out of Rupert before he could stop it. He looked at the old man in amusement. "You're worried about her creating an international incident, aren't you?"

The old man hesitated for a moment, then he responded with a tight nod.

"You have abundant reason to worry!" Rupert told him with another burst of laughter.

He grinned at Kamash. With no more than a few carefully chosen words, the old man had somehow managed to restore both his good humor and his sense of perspective.

He clapped Kamash on the back. "Please don't alarm yourself. I'm willing to overlook her insults and her baseless insinuations," he said, still smiling. "You can tell her I said that, too."

The young man gazed out over the sea. "The salt air is doing me good," he said. "I'm hungry. I think I'll head below decks."

Clapping Kamash on the back once more, he headed for the hatch.

Left alone to his thoughts again, Kamash grimaced as he ran a hand across his face. Things had been complicated enough already. How had he gotten into this mess?

Even if it turned out to be a disaster for him, good might still come from it. The princess might have manipulated him into a role on her behalf, but in doing so she'd shown surprising good sense. Kamash's interaction with the young Castelan king made it obvious that she needed help—help that her new spokesperson was well placed to offer. A single important question remained to be answered: would she pay any attention to his advice?

In his short time on the island with Neira, he had learned that beneath her haughty and impulsive exterior lay a good heart. She'd simply never been taken in hand. Could he succeed with her when the best teachers in her empire had clearly failed?

She had at least found herself in a unique learning environment. She had sailed into the unknown with men who were honor-bound to care for her and protect her, men who had sworn allegiance to her father the emperor. They had abandoned her to her fate. Would that crush her spirit, or would she grow from it? Humility was a necessary stepping stone on the path to true wisdom; if she chose to embrace it there was a glimmer of hope.

His stomach abruptly growled loudly. Apparently his body had no respect for his need to withdraw and contemplate. King Rupert's comment about being hungry must have triggered the reaction.

Putting his uncertainties to one side, he set off after the young king.

7

The robed and hooded priest of the dark gods stood silently, eyeing the worshipers as they approached. Stationed as he was at the busiest of the shrines under his supervision, he had little opportunity for quiet reflection.

Such holy places played an important role in the worship of the dark gods of Rogand. Common people never entered the Temple of the Dark Gods at Rog, and not even the noble born had access, except by particular invitation. All of the people instead attended one or other of the shrines dotted throughout the cities and in the countryside.

The priest assigned to each shrine came at scheduled intervals to enact rituals, to lead worshipers in chants like the Call to Fear, and to receive pledges and gifts in support of the priesthood.

The people made their petitions to the dark gods directly; the presence of a priest guaranteed that the petition would be heard by the dark gods, if not granted.

Key rites of passage took place at shrines, with priests consecrating every birth, marriage, and death. Major civic appointments and significant commercial agreements also traditionally incorporated a brief ceremony at a shrine in the presence of a priest.

This particular shrine was located in a regional town, a place of no apparent significance. Appearances could be deceptive though. A priest who kept his ears open could learn a lot, even in a backwater like this. Whatever he learned would be passed on to a senior priest who passed through the region regularly. Any information of value soon made it back to the temple at Rog.

Fewer people were attending the shrines in recent years. The prosperity and comfort associated with the reign of King Krasmir undoubtedly had a lot to do with that. People were more attentive to the dark gods when they were fearful.

Returning his focus to the worshipers, he saw that next in line was a woman he recognized—the wife of an influential nobleman. Since the time a few months previously when her only daughter had almost succumbed to a crippling illness, the noblewoman had become a frequent visitor to the shrine. The priest knew a little of her circumstances and her story—given the prominence of her husband, he made it his business to do so.

Momentous events were afoot in the kingdom, and the nobleman in question had been summoned to Rog to participate in confidential meetings convened by the king. Perhaps she knew something about the topics to be discussed, perhaps not.

Dropping the traditional gift into the locked box, the noblewoman stepped forward and bowed respectfully. Then she opened her mouth and began to make her petition to the gods.

Blotting out all other distractions, the priest leaned in, straining his ears to catch every word.

WISPS OF SMOKE rose lazily in the air, mingling with the incense that drifted up from the bowls scattered liberally throughout the chamber. This room was not the most heavily frequented in the Temple of the Dark Gods at Rog, and it was not the place from which Goultzar directed his vast network of subordinates, but he liked to spend a portion of each day there worshiping with the acolytes.

Glancing around in the hazy air, he paused to savor the atmosphere of the place. Unexpectedly recalling his reaction on first entering this temple, he shook his head in bafflement, unable to make sense of his initial revulsion.

A sharp twinge in his lower back intruded painfully on his thoughts, prompting him to push himself up from the rough stone floor to stretch uncomfortably. As Archprimus, second only to the High Priest himself, Goultzar's exalted station granted him a range of privileges. But it did not free him from the ravages of advancing age. He was no more exempt from mortality than any other priest.

An image of his leader came unbidden to his mind, and he reluctantly corrected himself: *most* priests could certainly not claim to be exempt from mortality. He still hadn't made up his mind about His Eminence. The celebrated longevity of the High Priest became ever more remarkable as the years advanced.

At risk of being caught in the grip of a thought process that was neither new nor welcome, he dismissed his musings with a frown, directing his attention instead to the observance going on around him.

Goultzar knew where he needed to focus his energy. His primary role was to direct the activities of the priests, not just here in the temple at Rog, but throughout Rogand. He had been appointed to this role—many years previously—largely in recognition of his outstanding abilities as an organizer and administrator. His overarching purpose, though, was to ensure that devotion to the dark gods never flagged. For him the significance of this purpose had grown as the years passed. It now went far beyond a mere calling; it had become the consuming passion of his life. His burning desire to express his own devotion was a key reason he participated in the daily ritual before him now.

He had only just seated himself again when a junior priest arrived, bending low to reach his ear. "His Eminence awaits you," he whispered respectfully.

The Archprimus clambered to his feet once more and made his

way to the small room where the High Priest spent each day. He knocked at the door before pushing inside.

The High Priest, seated as usual in his carved wooden chair, observed his progress with apparent disinterest, offering no greeting and failing to acknowledge Goultzar's bow of obeisance. The visitor, more than familiar with the ways of his master, was not surprised.

Goultzar sat in silence on the low stool that faced the High Priest, granting His Eminence the courtesy of speaking first.

A long silence ensued as the aged Superior observed his underling. "You are troubled," he finally offered.

Goultzar tried to mask his surprise. He shouldn't have been caught off guard by the perceptiveness of the old priest. It was true. Goultzar's thoughts had been increasingly darkened by a new concern.

"As always, nothing escapes you, Your Eminence," he said dipping his head low. He paused to collect his thoughts. "Of late it has seemed to me that zeal for the worship of the dark gods is flagging in the kingdom."

He paused to allow the High Priest to respond. No reply was forthcoming. He permitted a soft sigh to escape his lips.

"The people revere their monarch, as is appropriate." He hesitated for a moment, undecided about the wisdom of being entirely frank. "They seem almost delirious in their acclaim for King Krasmir and his reforms."

Once more he paused to allow a reply.

Knowing that the High Priest's patience far exceeded his own, Goultzar gave up waiting. "King Krasmir observes the traditions, and he does not neglect the required festivals and rituals," he said frankly. "But he shows little enthusiasm for it." Deciding at last to throw caution to the winds, he added, "Does our king respect the dark gods? Does he fear them as his predecessor did?"

The High Priest stared back at him.

Had Goultzar spoken out of turn? The priesthood had always been fiercely independent of the crown, but the Archprimus was well aware that there were limits. He clamped his mouth shut. This time he would wait for the Superior to speak, however long it took.

His mind continued to churn as he waited. Much more could have been said. Goultzar's role as Archprimus allowed him to observe the kings closely. Agon had gone out of his way to avoid the priests, and there was little doubt that the king had privately feared the dark gods. Such deference from the earthly ruler was both desirable and appropriate.

Agon's successor was different. The dark gods and their ways had no hold over Krasmir. Goultzar was certain of it, and it disturbed him deeply. The people always followed the lead of their king.

All this time His Eminence remained silent, studying the priest before him. Uncomfortable at first, Goultzar slowly began to feel affronted. Shocked by his own reaction, he turned his attention to the floor in front of him, determined not to think about anything more significant than the flagstones at his feet.

After what felt like an age, the High Priest finally spoke. "Kings are mortal."

Goultzar looked up sharply with eyes narrowed. What had prompted such a comment? Had his ancient master somehow guessed at Goultzar's questions around the High Priest's own mortality?

Both men sat in silence. Goultzar remained still for long enough that his lower back pain returned, and he began to experience pins and needles in his feet. He was soon struggling to prevent physical discomfort from dominating his consciousness.

Finally his master released him. "A man waits at the temple gate. He has requested an audience with me. You will see him."

Goultzar stood up. After sitting for so long he felt light headed, and he paused while attempting to recover himself. How could his master bear to remain motionless for so long in that chair?

At last able to trust himself to move, Goultzar bowed deeply and left the room.

Once clear of the building, he headed for the temple gates. As he walked he allowed himself to revisit his meeting with the High

Priest. His Eminence had revealed no more about his inner thoughts than he ever did. That came as no surprise. If the Archprimus was honest, he knew that he had a reputation of his own for being cryptic.

The important question was whether the Superior took his concerns seriously. The High Priest had reason to be concerned if the dark gods failed to receive the respect due to them.

The High Priest was a man who said little and moved even less. At first glance he could easily be taken to be a characterless figurehead well into his dotage. But anyone foolish enough to underestimate him soon learned that he was not a person to be trifled with. When he saw fit, the Superior acted, and acted decisively.

Arriving at the gates, the Archprimus found four hooded priests standing quietly before a man clad in strange garments. Like Goultzar, the visitor wore a hood that hid his face almost completely.

Stepping around the priests, he faced the man, studying him quietly without offering a word.

"Are you the High Priest?" the newcomer demanded impatiently.

Goultzar could not place the man's accent. He allowed the minutes to stretch out before answering. "I am not."

"I will speak to no one but the High Priest."

The Archprimus stretched a hand toward the open gates behind the newcomer. "You are free to leave."

"So who are you, then?" growled the man.

"I am the Archprimus," Goultzar replied after a dignified pause.

The visitor considered that for a moment. "The second in charge," he muttered. Then, in a louder voice, "I will speak with you. But not with these present." He swept an arm disdainfully across the little cluster of priests.

None of them moved.

The newcomer slowly pulled back his hood to reveal a hard face bearing a prominent scar below one eye. "Perhaps you are frightened, old man," he sneered, leaning forward provocatively.

Goultzar leaned forward himself until his face was inches from the stranger's. "I do not fear you," he replied with casual contempt, reaching up to pull back his own hood. He exposed enough to reveal skin etched deeply with scars and daubed with fresh blue paint.

The visitor drew back in shock at the sight. Hastily recovering, he steadied himself, schooling his features into an impassive mask.

Covering his face once more, the Archprimus nodded to his fellow priests. They slipped quietly away, leaving him alone with the visitor. "Well?" he asked.

"Does your religion provide a way to achieve immortality?"

Goultzar started momentarily. Then, narrowing his eyes, he intoned, "The gods offer life, and the gods snatch it back."

"But is there a way to bargain for extended life?"

The Archprimus frowned. "How would such a bargain be made?"

"With blood, of course," replied the stranger. "One life extended, in exchange for other lives ended before their time."

"Who has spoken to you of such an arrangement?" demanded Goultzar coldly.

"I'm not here to answer your questions," the stranger growled. "You're wasting my time. I want to speak with the High Priest."

"He is not available," the priest said flatly. Then he turned on his heel, leaving the stranger at the gate.

Goultzar had conveyed cold indifference to his visitor. Inwardly, he was struggling to contain his shock. What did the High Priest know of these matters? The stranger's questions had poked and prodded uncomfortably at his own uncertainties around the longevity of the High Priest.

Profoundly unsettled by the interview, Goultzar decided to return to the Superior immediately. Uninvited and not expected, he nevertheless pushed past the startled young priest on duty outside the High Priest's room.

The bright eyes of the old man followed him as he entered the room. If the High Priest was at all surprised by the intrusion, he gave no sign of it.

Goultzar bowed tightly before planting himself once more on the stool opposite his master. He did not wait for permission to speak. "The visitor at the temple gates came to inquire about a bargain with the dark gods. A bargain intended to deliver unending life. He wished to discuss these matters with you, and with you alone." Try as he might, he could not entirely eliminate a tone of accusation from his voice.

The High Priest responded with his habitual tranquility. "Nehrvina the Awful grants life. She reclaims it when she chooses," he said with apparent indifference.

The Archprimus frowned. He was not in the mood for riddles. "Do you know of any such bargain?" he asked bluntly.

The eyes of the Superior bored into him. No response was offered.

Goultzar sat motionless on his stool staring at the older man. He had no idea what else to do.

Finally the old man intoned, "The ways of Nehrvina are inscrutable." Then the High Priest closed his eyes, signifying that the conversation was at an end.

Confused and defeated, the Archprimus got to his feet and departed from his master's presence.

THE ARCHPRIMUS'S visitor made his way to a rough inn in the dockside district of Rog. He occasionally glanced back over his shoulder, but it didn't appear that he was being followed.

Reaching his destination, he pushed through the door and threaded his way between the revelers to a table on the far side of the public room. A stool was pushed out from beneath the table, and he sank onto it gratefully. He found a pitcher of ale waiting for him.

The face of the man opposite was hidden behind a cowl. "Did you learn anything useful, Kaifet?" The question was spoken softly.

The new arrival shook his head. "I wasn't allowed to speak with the High Priest. The fool who met with me knows nothing."

The first man grunted. "It's time to try a more direct approach."

"Easier said than done," Kaifet warned.

"You know what to do," growled his companion. "Get onto it, and don't waste any more time."

Kaifet paused for long enough to drain his ale. Then he got up and headed for the door.

NO SOONER HAD Kaifet left the inn than a rough-set man at an adjacent table pushed himself to his feet and disappeared out of the door after him. When Kaifet's cowled companion decided to leave, he was tailed as well.

None of the other patrons in the inn noticed anything unusual. For them it was just another rowdy night in a seedy establishment serving cheap ale. All they cared about was getting drunk as quickly as possible.

ONE WEEK HAD PASSED since Kaifet visited the Archprimus. It had been an unusually busy time, but the preparation was finally complete. Kaifet was ready.

A group of men stood silently beside him as he peered through the darkness toward the Temple of the Dark Gods at Rog. On that night the moon was entirely hidden behind clouds. It suited Kaifet perfectly. The element of surprise would be crucial.

"You all know what to do," he growled. "Once we're inside the temple, kill anyone who gets in your way. Not the High Priest—we need him alive."

"How many guards can we expect?" one of the men asked.

"No one has ever seen guards in or around the temple. And none of our informants are aware of priests being armed. The priests are deranged though—don't eyeball them too closely. Stay focused on what we're here to do. We go in, we grab the High Priest, and we get out. Do you understand?"

His words were met with a chorus of grunts.

He drew his sword and raised it aloft.

Twenty swords cleared their scabbards, and Kaifet crept forward, followed closely by his handpicked band.

No one was anywhere in sight when they reached the gates of the temple. Hurrying through the entrance, they headed for the main temple building where the High Priest reportedly spent his entire life.

The High Priest was a fool. He should have met with Kaifet when he had the chance, instead of hiding behind a subordinate. Secreting himself in the temple wouldn't save him.

As he approached the temple, Kaifet had the uneasy feeling that he was being watched. He brushed it off. He'd felt that way for days, without ever finding the slightest evidence to support the notion. It had to be nothing more than nerves.

Stealing around to the rear of the building, he found a door left ajar. Could it really be this straightforward? Pushing inside, he waited until all of his men had filed in after him.

It was pitch dark inside the doorway. Moving quietly forward he came to another door, also lying open. Through the door lay a chamber. Even in the dark he could tell it was large. It appeared to be empty.

Prowling across it he came to yet another large room, dimly illuminated by a small cluster of candles suspended from the ceiling. No priests were anywhere to be seen.

Three other doorways led out of the chamber—the temple building was beginning to feel like a maze. Where were the priests? And where was the High Priest hiding? His men would have no choice but to search every corner until they found him.

Choosing a door at random, he headed toward it. His men bunched tightly together behind him, their figures casting huge shadows on the walls in the candlelight. Hardened soldier as he was, he couldn't pretend it wasn't unnerving.

Seen from outside, the temple was eerie enough in the daytime. Inside it in the dark was infinitely worse. And something he didn't recognize hung in the air—a cloying odor, perhaps incense mingled with the smell of blood. He grimaced with distaste.

Reaching the door, he opened it and peered inside. Another dark space awaited. Thrusting aside his misgivings, he went through.

The smell in the air was much stronger now. It was becoming difficult to breathe. Beginning to feel disoriented, he brushed uneasily at the beads of sweat on his brow and pushed on, more lightheaded with every step.

A thud sounded behind him. Peering sluggishly back over his shoulder, he saw one of his men sprawled on the ground. Another slumped to the floor even as he watched. He blinked stupidly, dimly aware of a mounting sense of panic but unable to think straight.

Why was he here? Was there something he needed to achieve?

Such questions were beyond his grasp. Abruptly losing control of his limbs, he collapsed, his head hitting the ground hard.

FOUR AT A TIME, a steady stream of hooded priests filed from the temple. Each group hefted an unmoving form.

The procession disappeared into the night, the darkness masking the departure of the intruders as effectively as it had masked their arrival. Nothing was heard of them again.

8

Kamash stood at the rail as the ship bearing the princess and the foreign royalty glided into Rog's bustling harbor. The ship had traveled in convoy with four accompanying ships that bristled with armed soldiers, and these escorts now drew back to allow the royal vessel to dock.

Having recently visited the harbor at Varacellan, Kamash eyed the vista before him with heightened interest. The contrast could scarcely have been more marked. If the harbor of the Varasan capital exuded orderliness, the Rogandan equivalent could only be described as chaotic. The appearance of the two cities from the sea only added to the contrast. Varacellan was fair and grand with tall and stately towers. What little could be seen of Rog from the harbor was unremarkable and grimy.

The princess was probably turning away from the sight in disgust. Not so Kamash. He had gone into exile by his own choice, but the tug on his spirit could not be denied. Swallowing hard against a lump in his throat, the old man brushed a tear from his eye. He was coming home.

A great deal had changed since he last glimpsed the harbor from the seaward side. The volume of shipping had increased enormously.

A host of local vessels of every shape and size lay at anchor beside tall ships displaying the colors of other kingdoms. The proportion of ships bearing three masts had grown, and his memory told him that almost all of the vessels before him were in better repair than they used to be. Rogand had apparently prospered, and its neighbors with it.

A figure appeared beside him at the rail. It was the princess. Uman hovered nearby while maintaining a respectful distance, apparently willing to permit his mistress a private conversation with her spokesperson.

A steady breeze swept the long hair from Neira's face as she gazed toward the docks that were growing steadily closer. She shifted restlessly, unable to stand still for more than a moment. A wave of sympathy washed over Kamash. Everything familiar to the princess had been swept away, and he had little doubt that anxiety was threatening to overwhelm her.

He was not unduly alarmed. Neira was not the same girl who had stepped onto the sandy beach of his island. A new sadness cloaked her now, but she had grown stronger too. He was confident that she would win through. And she was not alone. She had Kamash to support her, as well as Uman.

"Do you feel ready to face the barbarians?" he asked, a wry smile on his lips.

She glowered at him, refusing to rise to the bait.

"They will ask questions that deserve answers," he warned her. "If you want me to help you, I need to know a lot more than you've told me so far."

Her nose went up. "Don't expect me to gossip sensitive information," she said stiffly. "You needn't think I'm stupid just because I'm young."

"I don't see you as stupid," he replied patiently. "But both of us need to understand what's going on here, and they can help."

"How could they possibly help?" she asked dismissively.

"They know a great deal more than they're telling us," he replied.

She raised her eyes heavenward, apparently unconvinced.

The old man persisted. "After we arrived in Varacellan, do you remember the reaction of the Rogandan ambassador when I told him you and Uman were not from any of the kingdoms in the region?"

She frowned. "He seemed surprised."

"He was a lot more than surprised," Kamash assured her. "He was stunned. When he realized who you were, he immediately assembled an astonishing collection of royalty. He did it in no more than a few hours."

She snorted. "There's nothing surprising about that. I'm an important person."

He shook his head impatiently. "Those royals weren't there out of politeness."

"Why were they there then?"

"That's the point! We don't know. They told us nothing. They just asked questions."

She scowled, no doubt belatedly recognizing how one sided the exchange had been. "What makes you think they can help us?"

"They could tell us what they know. That might help us understand what's going on. But we need to give them a reason to be frank with us. If we refuse to speak openly, we shouldn't expect them to do it."

The ship's sails had been reefed and its forward movement had almost ceased. Lines were thrown down to row boats, and they began towing the ship toward a dock.

The princess appeared absorbed in the scene before her. She hadn't responded to his comment. Kamash decided it was time to become bolder.

"Who was in charge of your expedition?" he asked.

Neira looked at him sharply.

"I need to know if I'm going to be able to help you," he insisted.

She glared at him for a moment, then she sighed. "The Grand Vizier of the Empire of Ahr was in charge of the mission."

"So he's the one who ordered that you be left behind?"

"Never! He would never dream of doing any such thing."

"Because he likes you?"

"Pah! He has no great love for me. But he is the most loyal and most reliable of all my father's subjects. My father would never have allowed me to come if anyone else was in command."

"Who would have ordered such an action then?"

She scowled off into the distance. "I want to know that as much as you do. I can only think it was the ship's captain. I do not know him well, and I cannot guess why he would do such a thing."

"What of the Grand Vizier? Why didn't he prevent it?"

"I have been wondering about that," she said with a frown. "I fear for his safety! The captain must surely have restrained him—or worse."

"And what was the purpose of your expedition?" asked Kamash.

She glared at him. "Enough questions!"

He shrugged. It was a start. It was nowhere near enough though.

He locked eyes with her. "If you want me to help you, then you need to trust me," he told her pointedly.

The reception that awaited the travelers was impressive by any standard. Bright banners of every imaginable color whipped in the breeze, soldiers clad in ceremonial finery lined the streets, and the royal party waited in the shelter of an arresting canvas pavilion of great size.

The king sat on an ornate throne surrounded by a small crowd of nobles. Kamash knew that King Krasmir had a wife and children, although they were nowhere in sight. The throne must have been heavy, and the old man could not help wondering how such an object had been transported to the dockside reception area.

Pushing such irrelevancies from his mind, he focused his full attention on the task at hand. Taking Princess Neira's arm, he steered her forward, noting with satisfaction that the other royal visitors stood aside to allow her through. Uman followed in their wake.

The king stood up from his throne to greet her. "You must be Princess Neira of the Empire of Ahr," he said smoothly, dipping his head respectfully. "I bid you welcome to Rogand. I trust that your voyage from Varacellan was both comfortable and uneventful."

The princess performed an unfamiliar curtsy in return. "I thank you, King Krasmir," she returned. "Our journey was brief, but pleasant. I am honored to visit your kingdom and gratified to be received so graciously."

Kamash quietly released a breath, allowing the tension to ease from his body. He had set out to prepare the princess of course, but she had proven to be an indifferent student. She must have paid some attention though, because she had remembered the king's name and observed enough royal protocol to avoid any suggestion of a veiled insult.

King Krasmir then turned his attention to his other guests, greeting King Delmar and King Rupert warmly, and welcoming others among the noble guests by name.

As the introductions proceeded, the old man allowed himself to study the Rogandan king. The monarch was a big man with bushy eyebrows and a generous beard. Loose talk had likened the king to a bear, and the comparison might have been credible had Krasmir dressed himself differently. The king's demeanor was another matter. He appeared refined and intelligent, and in no way beast-like.

There was nothing weak about the king though. Kamash sensed a toughness beneath the monarch's polished manners. Rogand had apparently done well to find itself ruled by its current sovereign.

Whatever else could be said, this king bore little resemblance to Ugar, a ruler with whom Kamash had been only too familiar.

Royal receptions were exhausting work, and Kamash had become both hungry and thirsty. While keeping a close eye on the princess, he took the opportunity to sample the generous selection of refreshments on hand.

Momentarily distracted, upon looking up he was startled to find himself staring into the face of King Krasmir.

"You are the Rogandan known as Kamash?" It was a statement more than a question.

"I am, Your Majesty," he replied, bowing deeply.

"I understand we have you to thank for the survival of the princess."

"Along with a liberal dose of good fortune," he said, managing a weak smile.

"Indeed," the king agreed. He studied Kamash closely. "I believe the princess has asked you to remain at her side."

"That is true," the old man confirmed. "She has requested me to act as her spokesperson."

"Perhaps a surprising title to confer upon a hermit," the king observed casually.

The old man bowed, but offered no other response.

"But I am told there is much more to you than meets the eye," the king concluded.

Kamash fought down the wave of panic that threatened to rise up and overwhelm him. His heart pounded painfully in his chest, and he could only hope that his agitation was not visible to the king.

The king watched him closely for a few moments before observing, "I am pleased that one of my own subjects stands beside the princess, rather than a person driven by more obscure agendas."

The old man took a deep breath, working hard to steady himself. "I will strive to further the well-being of the princess," he managed, "but my efforts will never be to the detriment of Rogand."

"I am gratified to hear it," the king replied smoothly. He studied the old man for a moment longer before adding with a shallow nod, "Please accept my personal welcome. I am sure we will see more of each other."

Kamash bowed deeply, holding the pose for longer than protocol demanded. When he rose he found that the monarch had gone.

King Krasmir was clearly a shrewd operator. He had taken the trouble to find out about Kamash, and he had skillfully reminded the old man where his loyalty lay.

Surely the king knew nothing of substance about Kamash though. How could he?

The old man stood without moving for a very long time until his heart had settled into a more normal rhythm. His interaction with the king had come as a salutary reminder. He would need to exercise unusual caution in the days to come.

SEVERAL ROBED PRIESTS were included in the delegation that greeted the foreign royalty. King Krasmir had arranged for them to be kept largely out of sight, perhaps mindful of the way their appearance affected unpracticed observers.

None of them said a word, not even to each other. They looked, they listened, and when it was over they quietly melted away.

One of them made his way immediately to the Archprimus, who led him to a private location.

"What did you learn?" Goultzar asked.

"The main arrival was a young princess. From the Empire of Ahr," the priest replied.

"The one all the fuss is about?"

The priest nodded. "I assume so."

"Who were the others?"

"The king of Varas. His name is Delmar. And the king of Castel—Rupert. There were other nobles with them, including from Arvenon."

"And what was King Krasmir's reaction?"

"He greeted them cordially. Warmly, even."

The Archprimus scowled. "Our own king, consorting with unbelievers." He spat in disgust. "Who else was with the princess?"

"A big guard. And an old man. He appeared to be Rogandan."

"Who is he?"

"I heard the king talking to him. His name is Kamash. He's the one who rescued the princess, and he's her spokesperson. He told the king he won't do anything to harm Rogand. The king seemed surprised that she picked him. Supposedly he's been a hermit."

"This hermit story sounds fanciful to me. I don't believe a word of it!" exclaimed the Archprimus. "Find out more about this Kamash.

And keep a close watch on the princess. I'll make sure the other foreigners are watched."

The priest nodded.

Goultzar frowned at him. "Was anyone aware that you were listening?"

The priest shook his head emphatically. "I know how to keep my eyes down and my ears open," he asserted.

The Archprimus placed a hand on his heart, clenching his fist before flinging open all his fingers except the little one. The priest repeated the gesture before turning and slipping away.

MUCH LATER ANOTHER of the priests present at the royal reception paid a lengthy visit to the High Priest to deliver his report. No one apart from the Superior knew of the visit, and what was said between the two men was privy to them alone.

The visit remained secret thanks to a hidden doorway in the small room set aside for the exclusive use of the High Priest. The priest used it to enter and leave the room, and during his visit he ensured that both other entrances to the room were locked from the inside.

Only a very small and select group of priests knew of the High Priest's secret doorway. The Archprimus was not one of them.

9

Amyra aimed a welcoming smile at Dahra, who had emerged looking bleary-eyed. "Good morning, Mother. Did you sleep well?" Without conscious thought she had asked her question in the language of the Aen-ur.

"Very well, thank you. For some reason I seem to need more sleep these days than I ever used to," replied Dahra in the same language. "Perhaps it's the climate," she added with a wink.

Her mother wasn't as young as she once was, and Amyra didn't begrudge her an extra hour or two of sleep. She was grateful beyond words that Dahra had chosen to leave Aen-irac and make her home on the Torbury holdings in Erestor.

Having a grandmother on hand to help with young children was invaluable, of course, especially when Will was away in Maranelle attending meetings of Erestor's Council of Lords, or in Arnost consulting with the king. But Dahra was also the last remaining link with Amyra's old life. Aen-irac seemed far away, and her life among the Aen-ur was only a memory now. Amyra had embraced a new identity, setting down roots among a different people.

"Are you happy, Amyra?" her mother asked, fixing her with a knowing look.

"You know that I am," she replied. "I get tired, of course, but I'm happy tired. I love being a mother." No further words on that topic were necessary—her own mother understood as no one else could.

"I'm quite fond of Will too," she added with a grin.

Dahra laughed at the understatement. "I always knew that the man who captured your heart would need to be special," she said. "Taming you was never going to be a job for the faint-hearted. Will seems to have risen to the challenge."

"I hope I haven't become too tame!" she protested.

"You needn't be too concerned," laughed her mother. "You've tamed the famed commander at least as much as he's tamed you."

"I'm not so sure," grumbled Amyra. "He spends a lot of time away from home."

"He only leaves because he needs to," her mother assured her. "His heart is here—with you and the children on his holding. I see it in his eyes."

Their conversation was interrupted by an insistent voice outside. "What are you about, young Jem! There'll be nothing left of the mistress's garden if you don't take those goats in hand!"

Raising an eyebrow, Amyra headed for the door. "I'll see what's going on," she called back over her shoulder with a parting wave to her mother.

She emerged in time to see a young man chasing away a flock of goats. His face was red—with exertion, embarrassment, or perhaps both.

The garden had been saved by an attractive young woman in her mid-twenties who stood glaring at the unfortunate Jem with hands on her hips. She might be slender of frame, but Amyra knew her as a force to be reckoned with.

"I appear to be in your debt, Peggy!" said Amyra with a smile.

Peggy shook her head, frowning. "Jem was swooning over a couple of girls that wandered by, instead of paying attention to his work. I hope the goats didn't do too much damage."

Amyra chuckled. "My garden is a little overgrown—I can afford to lose a plant or two, I'm sure."

Peggy gave a little bow. "I'm sorry if I'm disturbing you, My Lady," she said self-consciously. "The truth is I was hoping for your advice."

Amyra returned a smile. Looking into Peggy's plaintive eyes, it wasn't hard to guess what was on her mind. "Walk with me," she replied.

Wandering anywhere near the manor house was always distracting—there was so much going on. Constant effort was expended maintaining strips of plowed land, animal pastures and shelters, barns and dwellings, and a range of farm implements. Turning her back on the activity, Amyra led Peggy around the side of the manor house to a grassy sward beside a row of fruit trees. They lowered themselves onto a strategically placed wooden bench.

"How can I help, Peggy?" Amyra asked with a gentle smile.

"I don't understand it," the young woman replied miserably. "I thought we were getting along so well. But he doesn't seem interested in anything more than friendship."

There was no need for her to name the person behind her distress. Amyra knew she had set her sights on the formidable guardsman known as Rufe Sarjant.

As single-minded as she was kindhearted, Peggy had managed to capture a healthy share of the big soldier's attention. Nevertheless, her dream of joining him at the altar was proving unexpectedly elusive. Amyra felt sure that Rufe was drawn to Peggy too, but he seemed almost entirely lacking in confidence when it came to matters of the heart.

"You haven't done anything wrong, Peggy," Amyra assured her. "You just need to give him time."

"But how long is it going to take, My Lady?" she wailed. "I'll be in my dotage soon!"

"Peggy!" chided Amyra, barely restraining her mirth at the young woman's dire pronouncement. It was true that marrying young was the usual expectation, and it was also likely that some of the young men found Peggy intimidating. But the same might have been said of Amyra before she met Will. Sometimes you just needed to hold out for the right person. And then you had to wait until they were ready.

"Perhaps you need to try a different approach. Storming a fortress isn't the only way to capture it," she said seriously.

"Are you suggesting I should starve him into submission?" Peggy asked gloomily. "Maybe it's a good idea. I know he doesn't like my cooking."

"Whatever do you mean?" asked Amyra.

"I overheard him telling Jonas that my rock buns are well named."

"Oh Peggy!" cried Amyra, bursting into laughter in spite of herself. "If I made rock buns they wouldn't just be hard, they'd be inedible! Yet Lord Torbury seems to like me anyway. I don't think you should read too much into Rufe's comment."

Peggy didn't reply—she seemed lost in thought.

Amyra was sure Peggy truly cared about Rufe. He was a man of contradictions—both fierce and gentle at the same time—and she wondered how successful his admirer had been at understanding him in all his guises.

"What do you know about Rufe's history?" asked Amyra.

"He's been a soldier most of his life. Just like his father and his father's father before him."

"Do you understand what that was like for him?" Amyra persisted.

Peggy looked puzzled. "I'm sure it must have been frightening at times. But it's behind him now."

Could Peggy be ignorant of the specifics of Rufe's story? Even before Torbury Scarp he had become renowned as an army commander under Will Prentis. Fewer people, perhaps, were aware that he had achieved almost legendary status as a berserker in his early years on the battlefield. Amyra knew through Will that the giant guardsman had never been proud of this reputation.

Unfailingly gentle to all who knew him in normal life, Rufe had long since learned to master his impulses on the battlefield as well. But he had never entirely shaken off the shame of his early unbridled destructive impulses.

If Peggy was not yet aware of Rufe's discomfort with his past, it wasn't Amyra's place to reveal it to her.

Perhaps a different tack was needed. “Rufe is big and imposing and incredibly effective at what he does,” Amyra said. “But he’s also very good at dismissing himself. Sometimes I think he believes the credit for any success he’s achieved belongs entirely to Lord Torbury.”

“That’s nonsense!” exclaimed Penny. Remembering suddenly who she was talking to, she hastily added, “No disrespect intended, My Lady!”

Amyra smiled. “There’s no need to apologize, Peggy. I’m simply suggesting that a more delicate approach might be fruitful. Don’t expect him to always understand you. He’s spent most of his adult life interacting with men.”

The young woman was frowning thoughtfully.

Amyra rose to her feet. “Give him room for initiative, too. It might even be worth playing a little hard to get,” she suggested with a grin.

“Thank you for your kindness, My Lady,” the young woman replied, getting up and bowing gratefully.

“Off with you then, Peggy,” Amyra replied. “I hope you know you’ll be going with my best wishes!”

Returning to the manor house, Amyra found a grizzled man waiting for her.

“A good day to y’, M’ Lady,” he said respectfully, taking off his cap. “I am Hernholt, steward to Lord Beldisel.”

“I remember you, Hernholt, and I bid you welcome,” she replied. Lord Beldisel’s lands bordered the Torbury estate to the south, and Amyra had met the steward once or twice when visiting their neighbor. “What brings you here today?”

“M’ Lord has heard that y’ might be looking to buy some cattle. ’E has some very fine specimens, and ’e is willing to sell some of ’em, y’ see. Two score, if that many take y’r fancy.”

“I can ask Jonas to visit you to take a look at them,” she replied. “What’s your master’s asking price?”

An hour passed before the haggling was over. Jonas appeared not long after Hernholt had left.

"As you know, Will wants to buy a few more cattle. I've just had Hernholt here. Apparently Lord Beldisel is looking to sell some of his herd."

Jonas furrowed his brows. "There'll be a reason he wants to get rid of them," he growled. "They're probably inflicted with rinderpest."

"You're far too suspicious, Jonas!" she laughed. "Lord Beldisel might be canny, but he would never knowingly defraud us."

Her assertion was met with a noncommittal grunt. "I'll find time to inspect them tomorrow," Jonas promised. "I'll go with an open mind, but I'll also take a couple of the older retainers. Between them they know just about everything there is to be known about cattle."

THE DAY CONTINUED AS it had begun, keeping Amyra busy with a seemingly endless succession of duties almost until the time for the evening meal. Returning to the manor house, she allowed her mother to guide her to a comfortable chair. She sank into it with a weary sigh.

Before she could say a word, her daughter, Millie, burst into the room. "Mother! One of the men asked me to say that Jonas needs you!" Without waiting for a response, the girl dashed back out of the door.

Heaving a sigh, Amyra raised her hands helplessly. Pushing herself out of the chair, she set off after the disappearing form of the seven-year-old.

Her mother's voice chased her out of the manor house. "I'll keep an eye on Ethen!"

Amyra called for a horse. After mounting it, she leaned down and lifted Millie, placing the child in front of her.

"Where's Jonas?" Amyra asked, speaking in Rogandan.

"Mother!" complained Millie in Arvenian.

"You need to practice your language skills," Amyra insisted, this time using the language of Lestanor.

"Even Father doesn't speak much Lestanorian," Millie grumbled, reluctantly accepting the switch.

"No, and he regrets it!" her mother replied firmly. "Now, where is Jonas?"

"He's supposed to be at the ford," Millie replied.

Clicking her tongue, Amyra guided the horse forward. She arrived at the ford to find Jonas standing among a crowd of people beside the river. A large cart lay in the river just beyond the ford. Somehow the cart horses had been released. It must have been an extremely challenging operation, given that the cart was completely submerged.

"What happened?" called Amyra, helping Millie down from the horse.

"The cart was driven too close to the edge of the ford," Jonas replied. He shot a disgruntled look in the direction of a man who seemed unusually downcast. "It slid part of the way into the river, then the force of the water carried it the rest of the way."

Drawing him aside to continue the conversation in private, she asked, "What's in the cart?"

"A full load of produce on its way to the market," he replied. "Potatoes, carrots, turnips, cured meat, to name a few of the contents. It's not just the value of the load that upsets me," he said, "it's the time spent planting, cultivating, harvesting, and preparing it all. It's a frustrating waste. And then there's the loss of the cart."

"If the contents could be removed from the cart, would any of it be salvageable?"

"At this early stage, most of it. But there's no way to safely retrieve it."

Amyra fell silent. She glanced at the cart, then began staring intently upstream.

"Look!" a voice cried suddenly. "The water has stopped flowing!"

"There must be a blockage upriver," someone else called.

The river slowed to a trickle, gradually exposing the cart.

"Can you unload it?" Amyra asked tensely.

Jonas didn't bother to reply. He was already shouting orders. A line quickly formed, and bulging sacks and heavy barrels were passed from one person to another until they could be dumped on the river bank.

"I'll try to see what's happening," Amyra called, remounting her horse and heading for a hill that overlooked the river.

The moment she reached the top she leaped from the horse's back. She had been holding back the water with nothing but her willpower, empowered by the Stone of Authority.

Her first act with the stone, years earlier in Aen-irac, had been to hold back a river, releasing the pent up waters to end a battle before it started. Now, with water beginning to spill over the banks of the river, she diverted attention to fallen branches lying nearby. She watched as one branch after another tumbled into the river, massing until they formed an effective barrier at a point where the river narrowed.

Less effort was now required to hold back the water, and she stole a glance toward the ford. The wagon was almost empty, and Jonas had harnessed the horses to it. The horses struggled forward, dragging their lighter load out of the river and clear of the ford.

A huge volume of water had been steadily building up behind her makeshift dam, and the strain was mounting to the point where she almost couldn't bear it.

"Get out of there!" she yelled frantically. "The blockage looks like it's about to be swept away!"

Amyra watched in growing tension as people scrambled clear of the river.

Seeing that all of them had made it to safety, she released her control over the water. The dam burst with a roar, and water spewed downward, sweeping branches and other debris before it. For a brief moment the ford disappeared from view as the river overflowed its banks. Flood waters reached out to lap at the pile of salvaged produce before subsiding.

A few short minutes later, everything had returned to normal.

Amyra rode down to Jonas. "Did you retrieve all of the contents?" she asked.

"Thankfully yes. Given time it will dry out. I'm hopeful that most of it will survive a brief soaking. And the wagon is safe too," he replied. He shook his head in wonder. "That was astonishing. No one can avoid disaster entirely, but it's uncanny how often we manage to do it. I'd say that Lord Torbury is just plain lucky."

"It's her ladyship that's brought the luck," asserted one old woman, nodding her wrinkled brow wisely toward Amyra. "I've always said so."

Feeling extremely uncomfortable, Amyra turned away.

She noticed Millie looking back and forth between the river, the cart, and her mother, a puzzled frown on her face. Amyra's heart sank. Her daughter had witnessed far too many things she should never have seen. One day she might begin to put it all together.

Will would be horrified at the risk she had taken. He would tell her it was madness to use the stone in the presence of all these witnesses, and he was probably right. A brief glimpse of the wagon driver offered a different perspective though. The man looked as if he had just been rescued from a deep, dark pit, and the look on his face went a long way to convincing her that she'd done the right thing.

Perching Millie before her once more, Amyra rode back to the manor house.

Millie was rarely lost for words, but on that occasion they rode in silence. Too weary even to think straight, Amyra felt only relief.

Almost a week had passed since the incident with the wagon at the ford. For a time people could talk of nothing else, but thankfully as the days passed life settled into a more normal rhythm.

Conversation turned instead to a new topic: the smoke in the sky to the west. At first it was a subject of idle chatter, but curiosity turned to alarm as the wind shifted and the smoke increased. Dense forest bordered the Torbury holdings to the west. Timber was widely used on the farm in the construction of buildings and for a range of other purposes. All of it came from the forest.

Soon the sky to the west darkened ominously, the air becoming foul with the smell of smoke. That night people went to bed fearful of what might await them in the morning.

Biding her time until all her family were settled and asleep, Amyra stole from the manor house and crept quietly in the direction of the fire. The sky glowed red now, and the whinnying of horses could be heard from the stables. The air stung her face and lungs.

Coming to a halt just clear of the manor buildings, Amyra faced west and thrust out her arms. Almost at once she felt the change as the breeze stiffened and the wind changed direction. She was forcing the fire back onto itself.

Weariness soon forced her to lower her arms, but the gesture had never been necessary. She remained in place, directing the elements until the glow in the west had diminished and the air had cleared. Unutterably weary, she turned and trudged back to the manor house.

IN THE MORNING Amyra emerged much later than usual. Dahra was there to greet her, handing her a small bowl filled with fresh milk. After draining it gratefully, Amyra sat down, still yawning sleepily.

Dahra said nothing, calmly watching her daughter.

Before long Amyra found her mother's scrutiny unnerving. "What?" she demanded, sounding more testy than she had intended.

"The smoke has cleared," said Dahra. "People are saying that the fire has burned itself out."

"That's good to know," Amyra replied with another yawn.

Her mother continued to gaze at her. This time Amyra ignored her.

Dahra eventually broke the silence. "It's going to get you into trouble," she said quietly. When there was no reply, she added, "I should know."

"You had Drettroth chasing you," said Amyra. "This is different."

Dahra shook her head. "By the time I realized I was being chased it was already too late. If you keep using it trouble will find you."

"You're worried for no reason, Mother," Amyra said coolly.

Dahra shrugged. "Don't say I didn't warn you," she replied.

10

The sun had barely passed its zenith when Will's party reached his holdings in Erestor. Spotting Amyra outside the manor house, he jumped down from his horse and embraced her enthusiastically. Then he held her at arm's length, admiring her as she grinned back at him.

Their reunion was abruptly shattered by a shout, quickly followed by the arrival of a pair of human hurricanes. Will's seven-year-old daughter, Millie, and her younger brother, Ethen, aged five, burst from the house and leaped on their father.

A smiling Amyra observed the chaotic reunion for a while before turning her attention to Will's companions. "Thank you for bringing him back safely!" she called.

Noticing the monk, she added, "Brother Ander! It's so good to see you again."

Dismounting, the monk greeted her warmly. Having officiated at the wedding of Will and Amyra in Arnost, Brother Ander later made the effort to visit them at their home in Erestor. At their insistence, he had returned to stay with them several times in the intervening years.

Hearing Brother Ander's name, and having satisfied their immediate need to jump on their father, the children turned their attention to the monk. They were soon swarming noisily over him as well, ignoring his laughing protests at their continued assaults.

Amyra was eventually forced to intervene. "Children! That's enough! Leave Brother Ander in peace for a while."

Denied their latest source of entertainment, the children surrounded their father once more, an eager light in their eyes.

"Did you bring me a bigger bow, Father?" asked Ethen. "You promised!"

"What about the pony I asked for?" demanded Millie.

"I've only been home for five minutes," protested Will with a laugh. "Can't you enjoy my company for a while before asking for handouts?"

"A pony isn't a handout. It's an animal," Millie protested. "I was supposed to get it for my birthday!"

"And you *did* promise," insisted Ethen.

Will exchanged a glance with Amyra before rolling his eyes and shaking his head. "Oh, very well," he said. "Presents first."

Both children erupted in squeals of delight.

Will disappeared behind the horses of the party that had ridden in with him. He hadn't yet dismissed his companions, but they didn't seem in any great hurry to leave. They were clearly enjoying the spectacle too much.

When the children's noise showed no sign of abating, Amyra finally intervened. "I'd suggest you both calm down," she said firmly. "Unless you want your father to wait until tomorrow for presents."

The volume decreased at once, although the children continued to bounce up and down irrepressibly.

Will reappeared, leading a bay pony he'd collected by prior agreement from a neighboring holding. Millie ran to it excitedly and hugged its neck. The animal whickered softly, but didn't seem too upset by the attention.

Ethen observed the excitement restlessly, trying desperately to be patient.

Eventually Will seemed to notice him. "Ethen!" he said with a grin. "I almost forgot about you. Now what did I do with that bow?"

By that time Ethen was barely able to contain himself.

"Don't tease the poor boy!" chided Amyra.

"Is this what you're looking for, Will?" asked Brother Ander, holding out a bow.

"Ah, of course! Thank you, Brother Ander."

Will took the bow and handed it to his son, who held it out excitedly, his eyes shining. "It's perfect! Much bigger than my old one! Will you help me with it, Father?" he asked.

"You'd be better off asking Brother Ander for lessons," Will replied.

"Brother Ander? But he's a *monk*!" said Ethen, prompting a burst of laughter from a number of the onlookers.

"He's also a better archer than I'll ever be," Will assured his son.

Ethen looked at the big monk in surprise. "Will you teach me, Brother Ander?" he asked.

"My fighting days are long behind me," the big man replied. "But perhaps I could offer you a tip or two."

"Thanks!" enthused the boy, leaning into the bow and straining to bend it.

"Run along, children," commanded their mother. "It's my turn to have your father's attention for a while."

She turned to the other riders. "Thank you again," she said with a smile. "Please feel free to go. I'm sure you must be eager to return to your own families."

As the riders dispersed, Dahra appeared from inside the house, calling a greeting to Will and Brother Ander.

"Brother Ander will be staying with us in the manor house, Mother," Amyra told her. "Could you please make sure he's comfortable? We'll join you as soon as we've caught each other up on the news."

She took Will's arm, and they strolled off together, wandering aimlessly across the fields.

"Any dramas during my absence?" he asked.

"One of the bulls got loose," she replied. "It would have gored a child if one of the sheep dogs hadn't chased it off. And a farm laborer nearly had his house burned down. Sparks from the cooking fire set some clothing alight. Fortunately no children had been left unattended in the house at the time, because the fire was almost out of control before anyone noticed it. Some of the women were able to douse the flames with water. That sums up everything worth mentioning—at least from today," she concluded.

He grimaced, shaking his head. "I notice you made no mention of the long list of demands that were undoubtedly placed on you," he said.

"It's certainly been busy," she acknowledged breezily. She seemed eager to change the subject. "What of your time in Arnost though?"

"The news is bad, I'm sorry to say. Very bad indeed," he told her grimly. He sighed. "I've become comfortable with peace and quiet, and it's a shock to find it threatened again."

She peered up at him with a frown of concern. "Surely there isn't trouble with Rogand again?"

"There is, but not the kind of trouble anyone could possibly anticipate. It's a very long story, but I'll try to give you the abbreviated version."

Her frown turned to alarm as he outlined the facts as he knew them.

"What are the king and queen planning to do about it?" she asked.

"They want me to go to Rog," he told her.

"They want *you* to go? Surely not!" she cried. "What can they expect you to do about a situation like this?"

"I can represent the interests of Arvenon."

"Why doesn't King Steffan go? You've said that King Delmar and King Rupert are in Rog."

"Neither of the other kings have families to consider. King Steffan does."

"So do you!" she exclaimed.

Will sighed. "Let's defer this conversation for a while. I've sent a messenger to Newhaven asking Thomas to join us here. Let's discuss it when he arrives."

"I hope you're not planning to ask Thomas to go to Rog with you!"

she protested. "You can't expect him to abandon Elena and the children!"

Will ran a hand through his hair. "This isn't exactly the homecoming I was hoping for," he said.

She glared at him for a moment, then she threw up her hands. "I'm sorry, Will. I know this isn't your fault. The trouble is you're so... so responsible!"

"How can I avoid being responsible?" he asked. He waved an arm around him. "I can't take any of this for granted. I only have the holding because the king gave it to me, along with my title."

"You more than earned it!" she exclaimed. "And it wasn't exactly a gift, considering the expectations that came with it," she grumbled.

He shook his head. "Those expectations didn't come with the holding. I was carrying them long before the king made me a nobleman."

She went silent.

"You felt responsible for the Aen-ur when you were with them," he pointed out.

"I haven't forgotten," she said. "I was furious with you for knowingly putting them at risk. I thought their world would end if I didn't protect them from you."

His mouth twisted into a grimace.

"But I was wrong," she concluded. "I admit it. The Aen-ur not only survived—they finished up in a stronger position than before."

"Your concerns were not unreasonable though," he acknowledged. "It could have ended very differently."

Her brows drew together. "In any event, I left the Aen-ur behind, along with my responsibilities, and I followed you here. I've adopted a people group that isn't my own. For the second time."

A stern look had come over her face. "It's different this time though. We have a family. You think you have a heavy burden of responsibility to the king, and I understand that. You believe there's more at stake than just our family, and I understand that too. The problem is that someone has to be responsible for our family. Someone still has to bear the day-to-day burdens of caring for the children. And not just for them—for all the people here on the holding who depend on us. Whenever you're off doing your duty to the king, that responsibility falls to me."

She looked him squarely in the eye. "Now you're supposed to go to Rogand to save the world again. What if you don't return this time? One day, Will, it will get to be more than I can bear."

And with that she wheeled and left him, striding back to the manor house.

Will shook his head in misery. He understood her dilemma completely. He was not unaware of his own responsibility to his family, or to the people around him.

His farmers and workers and their families—everyone who depended on his holdings for their livelihoods—had suffered great loss because of him already. He had long since dealt with the mercenaries who had struck down his steward, Timms, and dragged away his retainers after destroying every building on the property apart from the manor house. Since that time he had done everything in his power to rebuild what had been destroyed and to ensure that the people would be well protected into the future.

But he had a special responsibility to his own family. How could he put their needs first and still fulfill his responsibilities to the king and to the kingdom? He shook his head again. He simply couldn't see how it was possible.

And the stakes had never been higher. If the king was right, not only Rogand, but Arvenon and every kingdom in the region now faced a threat of unprecedented magnitude.

That threat was the reason why Will had called for Thomas. Arvenon had been spared from disaster more than once thanks to Thomas and the remarkable talisman he bore. The Stone of Knowing might be hidden from the world, known only to a select few, but it had the potential to change the course of history.

Will stared after the retreating form of his wife. Their conversation had danced over a much bigger issue. Extraordinary as the Stone of Knowing might be, it was not the only such talisman. The Stone of Authority, once abused fearfully by the late King Agon of Rogand, now rested in Amyra's trustworthy hands. Its capabilities far exceeded anything Will had imagined possible. Amyra had used it to save the Aen-ur from certain destruction.

An uncomfortable dilemma now lay before them both. There seemed little doubt that with the Stone of Authority in her hand, Amyra was better equipped than Will to face down this latest threat. She knew it as well as he did.

It came as no surprise that Amyra was frustrated with Will and his troublesome sense of responsibility. His challenges precisely mirrored the tension she herself was facing.

WILL HAD to wait several days before Thomas appeared. When his friend arrived at the manor house, Will wasn't surprised to find Elena and their children with him. Even Haldek had made the journey, eager to see Will and Amyra once more.

Erestor might have appeared to be as peaceful and safe as it had ever been, but Anneka nonetheless insisted on sending an escort with them. In the end the party had included Rellan and Hender along with a couple of other capable young bowmen who professed a desire to see more of the world.

Millie and Ethen were enraptured when they spotted Thomas and Elena's three children, Tamara, Andy, and Delia. The two families made the effort to connect at least annually, taking it in turns to host at either Newhaven or Will's estate, so the children knew each other well. They had their share of arguments and fights, but for the most part they got along very harmoniously. The five of them soon disappeared, leaving the adults free to talk.

After gathering Thomas, Elena, and Amyra, Will invited Brother Ander, Haldek, and Rellan to join them. Of those living on his own estate, he sent for Rufe and Jonas. Then, remembering the king's suggestion, he called for Breysen as well.

As soon as everyone was assembled, he thanked them for attending and came immediately to the point. "I've returned from the capital with news," he said. "Unfortunately it isn't good news. What I am about to tell you needs to stay confidential. The last thing we want is people panicking for no good reason. But Anneka will need to know, so you're welcome to share it with her when you return, Rellan."

Thomas had gone a little pale. "I wondered why you invited me to join you after visiting Arnost," he said.

Will made no attempt to ease Thomas's mind. "Brother Ander is already aware of the situation, and I've briefed Amyra," he told them. "For the sake of the rest of you, I'll start from the beginning."

With that he launched into a detailed description of the entire sequence of events concerning Princess Neira and the Empire of Ahr. A few questions were asked as he spoke, but for the most part his audience sat listening with grim faces.

"I will be going to Rog as soon as is practicable at the request of the king," he said in conclusion, "and Brother Ander has kindly offered to accompany me. He's also surprised me by demonstrating that he's fluent in Rogandan." He grinned at the monk, who contented himself with a dip of his head in response.

"I will also accompany you, My Lord, if you'll allow me to," said Breysen.

"What about your family?" asked Will.

"Providing for my family is my main responsibility, of course," Breysen replied. "But the debt I owe you outweighs everything else. I haven't forgotten that."

Will couldn't resist shooting a glance in the direction of Amyra. Her face was unreadable.

"There is no real reason for concern though," Breysen continued. "I know from bitter experience how uncertain life can be, so for the last few years I have been laying coin aside whenever I can. My family will manage, even if something happens to me. I am pleased to say they are well connected to the community here, too."

"I accept your offer gladly, Breysen," Will told him. "Especially since the king suggested that I travel to Rog by sea to save time."

His remark was met with considerable surprise, and it took a while before the room became quiet once more.

"I traveled to Rogand with you last time, Will," said Haldek, "and I will come this time too, if you will have me. I have no desire to live in Rogand again. But lately I have been feeling that I would like to see it one last time, especially now that Agon is no longer king."

"Thank you, Haldek," Will replied. "I would be very glad to have you with us."

"I will come too," said Rufe, " although I can't speak a word of Rogandan."

"I imagine your Peggy might have something to say about that," said Will with a grin.

Rufe shook his head, a puzzled look on his face. "For some reason she hasn't been around as much lately," he muttered.

"It's about time you did some of the chasing," Jonas told him with a grin. Then he turned to Will. "You can count me in as well," he said.

"I will accept your offer, Rufe," Will replied. "I would be glad to have you too, Jonas, but I need you here. If you wanted to go off wandering again, you should never have let me see how effective you are as a steward," he added dryly. "The truth is that I'm totally dependent on you to keep the estate functioning. Everyone else depends on you as much as I do."

"It's true!" confirmed Amyra.

"As you wish, My Lord," said Jonas with a tight bow. He looked a little disappointed, but Will knew him well enough to see he wasn't too unhappy about being left in charge.

Rellan hadn't spoken yet, but Will got in first. "Don't even think about offering to come, Rellan. Both of us know what Anneka would have to say about it. We'll try to manage without you."

"I'm not sure how much I could add anyway," Rellan replied with a shrug. "But you know Anneka well enough to realize you've just made a new best friend."

Will chuckled as he pictured Anneka's reaction to hearing that Rellan wasn't going.

Important decisions still needed to be made. “I’m planning to leave for Maranelle soon after dawn the day after tomorrow,” he told them. “If you’re coming with me, you have tomorrow to complete your preparations. In the meantime, Amyra and I would like to talk with Thomas and Elena, so I’m happy to release the rest of you for the moment.”

Peggy tracked Rufe down as he was leaving the conference, her slight figure providing a stark contrast to the huge frame of the soldier. The two of them stood a short distance away, but Will was still able to make out their conversation.

“What plans are you hatching?” she asked him suspiciously.

“I’m going to need to go away for a while,” he told her. “With Will. I mean Lord Torbury.” He sounded uncharacteristically strained.

“And when were you going to tell your friends?” she demanded.

“The decision has only just been made,” he assured her.

“I can well understand his lordship turning to you for help and protection,” she told him. “He should expect nothing less from you.” Then her voice caught in her throat. “And who will provide help and protection to you?”

“I’ll be fine,” he assured her. “I’ve been in much worse situations.”

“You be careful, Rufe Sarjant! You’d better come back here in one piece!”

They moved away, and Will shook his head with a grin.

The others had left by now, and Will turned his attention to Thomas and Elena and Amyra, carefully studying them to assess their mood.

“I know I’ll need to join you,” said Thomas, “although I won’t pretend I’m excited about it.”

“If you’re going, then so am I,” Elena said doggedly.

“Why?” asked Thomas. “I can’t imagine you have even the slightest interest in going to Rogand.”

“I know it was difficult for you when you went there last time, Thomas,” she replied. “But it was a torment for me. I didn’t know what was happening. I wasn’t sure if I’d ever see you again. From now on we stay together.”

“But what about the children?” he asked.

"I'm sure my father and your parents would agree to look after them," she replied. "But if both of us are going, they're coming with us."

"I'm sorry to have to ask this of you," said Will. "But all of us understand why you're needed. And I won't deny it will be good to have the two of you with us. You seem to work effectively when you share the stone."

All eyes turned to Amyra.

"I'll be going, of course," she said stonily. "It isn't as if I have a choice."

"And the children?" asked Elena.

"They'll have to come too. Our situation's no different."

"The children will be excited to be traveling together," said Thomas, working hard at being cheerful.

Amyra grunted. She was refusing to make eye contact with Will, and he had no desire to push her. The single biggest reason she needed to go to Rog had nothing to do with him. It had everything to do with the Stone of Authority.

11

Breysen rode into Maranelle with the rest of Will's party, weary after many hours in the saddle. Lord Burtelen had kindly agreed to accommodate them until they set sail for Rog, and Breysen was looking forward to hot food and a solid night's sleep in a bed again. All of them were tired, especially the five children, but thankfully the journey from Will's holdings had passed without incident.

With their immediate destination almost in sight, Breysen reminded himself they were not on the estate now, and he was a retainer to Lord Torbury, not to Will Prentis. The challenge was that Breysen, like everyone who had fought at Torbury Scarp, thought of their commander as Will. It didn't help that some commoners had never changed their ways after Will became Lord Torbury. Some of the commander's close associates—people like Rufe, Thomas, Elena, Rellan, and Brother Ander—had known him before his elevation to the peerage, and Will clearly saw little reason for them to use his title. Even Jonas sometimes called him Will in private. And Breysen was in daily contact with Rufe and Jonas.

He sighed. He could think whatever he liked, but in public he needed to carefully watch what he said.

Lord Burtelen came to greet the small party not long after they arrived.

"Welcome! It's good to see you all," the nobleman said with a beaming smile.

"Thank you, My Lord," Will replied, returning a smile of his own.

"Have you managed to secure a ship for us?" Will asked.

"The matter is not resolved," Lord Burtelen replied with an angry frown. "We've had major problems at the docks of late—every initiative I take seems to be blocked. I gave this particular task to someone I trusted, and I was astonished to learn earlier today that nothing whatever has been done about it. I've told him to find a ship, and to do it today."

The news didn't shake Will's composure. "Let me know if I can help in any way."

Lord Burtelen waved his arms. "It won't be necessary. If it isn't resolved by tonight, I'll deal with it myself in the morning. I'll go in hard if I need to."

"The docks seem to operate by a different set of rules," Will replied. "But I'm sure you'll exercise whatever discretion is necessary," he added mildly.

"Discretion has its limits," growled Lord Burtelen. "These people behave as if they owe allegiance to no one but themselves. They've apparently forgotten who rules Arvenon, and it's about time I jogged their memory." He sighed, his shoulders slumping. "Times like these remind me how much I miss the duke. He knew how to handle the wharf rats, and they seemed to respect him."

Breysen was very surprised by the exchange. Lord Burtelen had a reputation for being even tempered as well as effective. He must be very frustrated indeed to be speaking as he was.

A squeal sounded from one of the children. Apparently noticing them for the first time, Lord Burtelen raised his own eyebrows in surprise. "Are you planning to take children with you to Rog?"

"Yes, we are," Will replied evenly. "Thomas and I will be accompanied by our wives, so our children are coming too."

The ghost of a smile lingered on Will's lips, but it seemed a little forced.

Still talking, the two noblemen wandered away, and Breysen heard no more of the conversation.

The brief interaction about the children set Breysen thinking. Will had said that the children were only there because their mothers were going to Rog. For the first time it occurred to him to wonder if Amyra and Elena wanted to go.

He thought back over the journey from the estate. Amyra had seemed unusually terse. Was it because she had come unwillingly? The blacksmith had been as surprised as Lord Burtelen when he first learned that Elena and Amyra were both taking their children. He had assumed it was because the families were eager to visit Rog, but the more he thought about it, the more unlikely that seemed.

Will and Amyra had always presented a united front to the world, but they must surely navigate tensions in their marriage as every couple did. It was easy to think of Will as floating serenely above the trivial thoughts and passions of the rest of humanity, but he was still human. In any event, whatever frustrations Will and Amyra might be harboring, he had never seen it affect the way they behaved toward their children or their retainers, and he respected them enormously for that.

A burly figure appeared at Breysen's side, and he turned toward the newcomer to find a vaguely familiar face. Abruptly it all came flooding back. The late duke had employed this man as his representative in the alien world of the docks. He looked older, and more hard bitten than ever. Most notably his left ear was now missing, leaving him with a lopsided appearance.

"Jaxin, isn't it?" Breysen asked.

The newcomer grunted an acknowledgment. "I don't remember your name."

"I'm Breysen," he returned.

"Lord Burtelen needs a ship for Lord Torbury. You can come with me."

The invitation was curt, but Breysen decided to ignore the tone.

For all he knew, taking him along might have been intended as a compliment. Weary and hungry after the long ride, he guessed that a visit to the docks would be anything but relaxing. He decided to ignore that too.

He nodded. "Let me speak to Lord Torbury first."

Having secured the nobleman's permission, he hurried off in Jaxin's wake.

The docks had once been a home of sorts to Breysen, but the sights and smells that assaulted him as he entered beside Jaxin felt foreign and unfamiliar. Was he still the same person who spent so much of his life as a sailor?

The two men made their way to the tavern they had visited years earlier in search of a suitable ship. Many eyes followed their progress. Curiously, Breysen was largely ignored, all attention being focused instead on Jaxin. The smoldering anger in the watchful eyes suggested that something had happened, because on Breysen's previous visit Jaxin had seemed entirely at ease in the docks.

Jaxin pushed past the two men guarding the tavern door. They glowered at him but said nothing. Breysen was ignored when he followed Jaxin in.

Seeing who had arrived, the bartender's eyes narrowed. He bent his head and concentrated on wiping down the bar.

Two things abruptly became clear to Breysen. First, he was surprised to discover that he did feel at home here. The men at the docks had apparently decided that he belonged, and that undoubtedly helped. Second, he was there because Jaxin was no longer sure of his own welcome. Breysen's thoughts churned as he tried to make sense of this information.

After a brief scan of the men in the tavern, Jaxin approached a grizzled sailor sitting alone at a table. Following him, Breysen recognized the man at once. It was Captain Yordin of the Nomad Lady.

Jaxin took a stool opposite the captain.

"There's a job for you, Captain Yordin. If you're interested."

The captain grunted.

Whether or not Captain Yordin had heard anything about Jaxin, he could surely read the mood of the men around him. He offered no greeting, but he didn't send Jaxin away either.

Breysen wasn't surprised. Most captains were always willing to weigh up the risks if the profit was good.

Jaxin continued in a low voice. "Lord Burtelen wants to arrange passage to Rog for a large party."

Captain Yordin's eyebrows twitched briefly, then he bent his head and concentrated on refilling his pipe.

"A trip to Rog costs extra," he mumbled.

"Why?" demanded Jaxin. "We're not at war with Rogand."

The captain grunted again. "Uncertain times," he said darkly, his eyes flicking around the room.

Jaxin shrugged. "Consider yourself hired," he told the captain, pushing himself to his feet.

"One condition," the sailor replied, holding up a hand in caution.

Jaxin paused without responding.

"If I don't get confirmation by nightfall, the deal's off."

Jaxin nodded once, then turned to leave.

Breysen followed the other man to the door of the tavern, wondering why the captain had insisted on confirmation. The answer became obvious the moment they left the tavern.

A mob was waiting for them outside. Most of the men openly carried clubs and knives, and their faces suggested they meant business.

A glance at Jaxin showed him standing stiffly alert, his face pale.

"You don't belong here," spat a voice. "Neither of you."

The mob began to push forward. Both men retreated until the wall of the tavern was at their backs. Jaxin apparently had nothing to say and no plan to save them.

"Do you want to bring Lord Burtelen's soldiers down on you?" Breysen asked them.

"You're wasting your time appealing to Burtelen," another voice growled. "He doesn't rule here."

Breysen's eyes narrowed as his memory stirred. Perhaps there was something they could do. The idea was desperate, but what other options did he have? He leaned closer to Jaxin. "Is any of this your fault?" he hissed.

"No!" Jaxin snarled back.

"Then why do they hate you so much?" Breysen persisted.

The other man scowled. "I've done nothing to deserve this."

Breysen decided to take the risk. Straightening, he faced the mob. "I appeal to the Peerless Mariner," he said, trying to keep his voice from sounding shrill.

The men confronting him looked confused for a moment. Then someone retorted, "You have no right. You don't qualify."

"We qualify," Breysen asserted, nodding his head firmly to reinforce it. "We were not challenged by the Shoal Watchers when we entered the docks. That means they acknowledged our right to be here."

The mob paused. Almost within striking distance, they had suddenly become uncertain.

"I appeal to the Peerless Mariner," Breysen repeated, more confidently this time.

For a few tense moments silence reigned. Then a voice snarled, "Suit yourself. It'll be your funeral."

Things moved quickly after that. The two men were surrounded and blindfolded before being led away roughly. Breysen had no idea where they were being taken, but he knew that if the Peerless Mariner didn't see fit to release them, they would never be seen again.

When the blindfold was eventually removed, Breysen found himself in a small dark room without windows. The last of their captors left, bolting the door behind them.

"I hope you know what you're doing with this 'appeal' to the Peerless Mariner," Jaxin said brusquely.

"I hope so too," Breysen replied stiffly. "But if it'd been left to you, our throats would be cut by now. What possessed you to come here? Were you out of your mind? It's obvious you no longer have the freedom of the docks. And why did you bring me?"

"I've done nothing to deserve this," Jaxin repeated stubbornly.

"You'll have your chance to be heard," Breysen told him, "and it better be good. Until we get to that point, leave the talking to me!"

They had been sitting in the darkness for about an hour when a small hatch opened in one of the walls. "Your appeal will be heard," a voice told them lazily. "The Peerless Mariner is busy now. You'll need to wait."

"How long?" asked Breysen.

"It's difficult to say," came the response. "Two or three days if you're lucky."

"We can wait," Breysen said calmly. "But I'm not sure about you. We didn't leave Lord Burtelen in a patient mood. If we're not back by nightfall, you can expect to see the docks swarming with his soldiers by the morning."

A snort sounded through the hole in the wall. "Lord Burtelen is no soldier. He doesn't frighten us."

"You won't be facing Lord Burtelen," Breysen replied. "The soldiers will be led by Lord Torbury."

"Never heard of him," scoffed the voice.

"He's better known as Will Prentis," said Breysen mildly.

The voice went suddenly quiet. After a pause, it resumed. "What does Will Prentis have to do with this?"

"He's the one who needs a ship. He's carrying out a mission for the king—a mission of pressing urgency. He won't take it kindly if you hinder him."

"How would you know what his intentions are?"

"I traveled with him from his holdings. We arrived earlier today."

After a further pause, the hatch in the wall snapped shut.

Before another hour had passed, the door opened to reveal an old crone. She stood in the doorway holding a candle.

"Come with me, good sirs," she croaked.

She led them to a room dominated by a long table. One wall held a number of windows, all shuttered and dark. However the table was brightly lit with many clusters of candles. She pointed them to two chairs on one side of the table, and they sat with their backs to the windows.

The door opened and seven men filed into the room. One sat at each end of the table, while the other five took seats opposite Breysen and Jaxin.

Could one of these men be the Peerless Mariner? Breysen had heard that no one had ever seen the Peerless Mariner's face, so it seemed unlikely. Was the Peerless Mariner even a person? Perhaps the title represented a group of individuals.

"Who are you?" asked the man at one end of the table.

Breysen stood and bowed. "My name is Breysen. I am a second generation sailor and onetime soldier, now in the employ of Lord Torbury, who is also known as Will Prentis."

He sat down again.

The man at the opposite end of the table responded. "Breysen—sailor, sailor's son, and retainer to the commander—is recognized."

All eyes turned to Jaxin.

He also rose, bowing grimly. "My name is Jaxin. For many years I was a retainer to the duke, and I frequented the docks on his behalf. Since his passing I have been working for Lord Burtelen." After speaking he sat down.

A long pause ensued. Eventually a third man intoned, "For the sake of the duke, whose memory we honor, Jaxin—retainer to the duke and to Lord Burtelen—is recognized."

As he finished speaking, the door opened again. Several men entered the room bearing platters of food. The platters were set on the table, with the old crone overseeing the operation.

"Eat, good masters!" she wheezed, pouring ale from a large jug into the mugs set before each person at the table.

"You have appealed to the Peerless Mariner," a different man acknowledged, addressing Breysen. "In doing so you invoked an ancient rite, one that is rarely used. Stranger though you might be, you are nevertheless qualified to make petition, as you claimed. You may state your case."

Breysen stood and bowed once more. "I made the appeal on behalf of my companion. He believes he has been wronged."

At least one of the men opposite stiffened momentarily at this statement before recovering himself.

"Will you allow him to speak?" Breysen asked.

The men around the table exchanged glances.

"Your request is unusual," another man replied. "But he may speak."

Jaxin got to his feet.

"On a recent visit to the docks I was attacked without cause," he said, "and later ejected by force. Since that time I have been unjustly mistreated and intimidated whenever my business led me anywhere near the docks. This harassment has constrained Lord Burtelen on multiple occasions. He is now frustrated to the point where armed conflict is an increasingly likely outcome. If that happens, it will serve no one well. I would argue that it has the potential to diminish the respect enjoyed by those in leadership at the docks."

"You need not concern yourself with the reputation of the Peerless Mariner," another man said tartly. "Concentrate on the matter at hand. You have made a serious accusation about your treatment at the docks. We are not familiar with this supposed incident."

"You ought to be," Jaxin replied. "The person responsible for it is sitting directly opposite me."

Breysen saw that he had fixed his attention on the man who reacted earlier.

His target scowled before blurting out, "This fool attacked my brother and offered no payment."

Jaxin glared at him. "Your brother attacked me with a club when he saw that I was alone. He told me I had no right to be on the docks. As far as I could tell his only motive was to demonstrate how tough he was. I was armed only with a knife, and his arm was injured when I defended myself. Anyone who cares to examine him will see that he received nothing worse than a superficial cut. It would be completely healed by now."

"You lie!" spat the other man. He turned to his fellows. "Evin witnessed what happened. He will confirm it."

"If you're referring to a large barrel-chested man with a bushy black beard," retorted Jaxin, "he not only witnessed it, he pinned me down while you cut off my ear! He mentioned the word 'payment' more than once as you were applying the knife. The 'payment' extracted was unreasonable, especially when compared with the hurt it was supposedly compensating for."

Dark looks had appeared on the faces of a number of the men around the table. "Other witnesses?" one asked curtly.

When Jaxin's attacker offered no response, Jaxin replied, "A scrawny man—old, with little hair, and carrying a limp—also witnessed these events. And to my eye he looked less than comfortable about the so-called justice summarily handed out to me."

Jaxin sat down.

It was apparent to Breysen that the second witness was known to others around the table. Two of the men immediately got up and left the room.

Jaxin's attacker began to sweat visibly. He had reason to. If the other witness corroborated Jaxin's account, the consequences for this man would be dire.

Breysen understood the rules as well as any sailor. No one had the right to mete out justice on the docks without the express permission of the Peerless Mariner. And if Jaxin was telling the truth, the retaliation was not just unauthorized, but excessive. Permanently disfiguring a senior retainer of the most senior civil authority figure was inflammatory, and risked an escalation that could significantly damage all parties.

While they waited, most of the men around the table turned their attention to the food. Breysen joined them without hesitation. Hungry as he was, he allowed himself the luxury of eating it slowly and properly enjoying it. Jaxin ate nothing, and neither did the man he had accused.

More than an hour elapsed before the two men returned. The others left the room, taking Jaxin's attacker with them. Even the old crone disappeared. Only Breysen and Jaxin remained at the table. Breysen helped himself to another mug of ale. Jaxin continued to sit there, a grim look on his face.

They did not have to wait long. All of the men apart from Jaxin's opponent filed back into the room and sat down again. The old crone reappeared and began pouring ale.

One of the men stood to address Jaxin. "The Peerless Mariner wishes to convey sincere regret at the inconvenience you have experienced. No one can give you back your ear, but this token should offer at least some compensation." He handed Jaxin a large bronze coin with a hole punched through the middle of it. "This coin marks you as a protected guest of the Peerless Mariner. It will grant you unfettered access to the docks, day and night, in Maranelle and in other ports. Wear it around your neck, and make sure it is visible on you at all times. None will dare to challenge you."

The speaker bowed. "The Peerless Mariner also extends cordial respects to Lord Burtelen, and expresses a desire to work together harmoniously now and into the future."

Breysen stood up and bowed respectfully. "Please convey our respects and grateful thanks to the Peerless Mariner."

Jaxin also stood. "I also extend my thanks—to the Peerless Mariner and to all of you—for giving me a fair hearing." He concluded his words with a bow.

Blindfolds were once again applied, and the two men were led from the building. When the blindfolds were removed they found themselves outside the tavern.

Jaxin headed into the tavern, and the guards held the door open for him. Breysen followed him inside. The bartender greeted them with a wink. No one else paid them the least attention. Spotting Captain Yordin still inside, Jaxin directed a nod to the sailor. Captain Yordin dipped his head in return.

They left the docks as the sun was setting.

"Now that we have a ship, we'd better hurry back to Lord Burtelen before there's trouble," Jaxin said.

He glanced at Breysen when Lord Burtelen's mansion came into sight. "What do you think will happen to the other man?" he asked.

"I don't know for certain. But it won't go well for him."

Jaxin stopped walking and turned to Breysen. "How did you know you could appeal to the Peerless Mariner?"

Breysen shrugged. "I'd heard stories from my father, and also from an old sailor who now lives on Lord Torbury's estate. Between them they've told me some curious tales." He paused. "I couldn't be certain if the old codes still hold, but it seemed likely. Nothing changes quickly on the docks."

"You have my undying gratitude," Jaxin told him soberly. "I am forever in your debt."

"Think nothing of it," Breysen replied, waving a hand.

They resumed walking. "I'm curious about the Peerless Mariner," Breysen said. "Which of them do you think it was?"

Jaxin frowned. "I have no idea," he replied. "Who do you think?"

Breysen shrugged. "I suppose we'll never know. But my money's on the old crone," he said with a wink.

12

Will clung grimly to the rail as another wave sent spray splashing across the deck. A sailor might not describe this as a storm, but the weather was beyond anything Will could cope with. None of his other family members were doing any better either.

The ship rolled drunkenly, and he leaned over the side once more, his stomach heaving painfully. It didn't matter that he had long since emptied his gut into the roiling waters—his belly refused to quit.

Breysen appeared beside him. "Not comfortable below decks, My Lord?" he asked.

"I don't think I'll ever get used to this," Will lamented. "You sailors seem to enjoy it. What's wrong with you?"

A snort of laughter escaped Breysen. "I'm sorry, My Lord, I'm not meaning to make fun of your discomfort," he said repentantly. "The truth is that I do enjoy it." The sailor-turned-blacksmith gazed at the dark clouds on the horizon. "I'm not sure I like the looks of that storm front though."

Will groaned. "Is it going to reach us?"

"We're about to round Baron Island. We'll soon be sailing east. That storm front will probably catch up with us around sunset."

"Unless I'm imagining it, the waves have been growing bigger," Will said. "Is that the storm?"

Breysen shook his head. "Last time on the Nomad Lady we sailed through Savage Strait. The captain decided against it this time. There are shoals scattered throughout the strait, which makes it too risky when the weather is rough. The alternative is to sail around Baron Island, which takes us into open sea. That's why the waves are bigger."

The look on Will's face must have revealed what he was thinking, because Breysen hastily added, "Don't worry—Captain Yordin knows his business, and this ship is well able to handle a storm on the open ocean."

Breysen's assurances offered slim comfort to Will, especially when the first in a series of huge waves came crashing over the ship.

"I'm going to check on the family," he told Breysen. After waiting for the next wave to pass, he headed for the hatch.

Both Millie and Ethen were lying in their hammocks, pale and miserable. If they noticed the arrival of their father, they gave no indication of it.

Amyra was not doing any better. "When is this storm going to stop?" she asked.

"Apparently it isn't a storm. Not yet, anyway."

She grimaced. "You mean it's going to get worse?"

He nodded. "There's a storm front coming. Breysen said it will reach us by nightfall."

She stared at him, appalled. "Why did I agree to come on this trip? And why did you let me bring our children?"

"I told you what the last sea voyage was like," he reminded her.

"I had no idea it would be this bad!" she retorted.

Will realized that further conversation was unlikely to achieve a useful outcome.

"Perhaps you should do something about the weather," he suggested. "I know you've been practicing with the stone."

"Don't start on that," she growled. "I've never attempted anything like this! And I've only ever used it in private." She glared at him. "Even if I knew what to do—which I don't!—there'd be no way to keep it quiet. Exposing the stone is the last thing we need."

She was right of course. He resolved to say nothing further about it.

Elena's face swayed into view. Her little family had taken hammocks nearby. When they first boarded the ship the five children had been inseparable. Everything had changed with the weather.

"Is there anything I can do to help?" she asked.

Amyra gazed up at her for a moment. "Not at the moment, Elena. The children are trying to rest, and I think we'll manage. Thank you for asking though."

Elena nodded, gazing at them sympathetically.

"How are your family coping?" Will asked.

"Tammi's first voyage was very challenging, but she seems to be handling it much better this time. The younger two are finding it more difficult, Andy especially. Delia's managed to get to sleep somehow."

The ship rolled drunkenly, and Elena was barely able to keep her feet.

"I'll leave you in peace," she said. "Call on me if I can help." Then with a smile and a farewell wave, she was gone.

The weather worsened as the hours dragged by. By the time the last light was fading from the sky, the ship was being tossed about unmercifully on towering waves.

Amyra and the children seemed close to breaking point. Will couldn't bear it any longer. After asking Elena to keep an eye on the children, he led Amyra onto the deck, gripping her arm while hanging on grimly to the nearest support. Spray showered them both as they gaped open-mouthed at the tempest.

"You need to do something!" he shouted, trying to make himself heard over the howling of the wind.

"I don't know what to do!" she yelled back feebly.

Breysen appeared once more. “What are you doing above deck?” he shouted. “It’s much too dangerous up here!”

He helped them to the hatch and followed them inside. Even with the hatch closed, the howling of the wind was oppressive.

“You need to stay below,” Breysen insisted. “This storm is beyond anything I could have imagined. And we haven’t seen the worst of it yet.”

“What needs to happen with the weather?” Will asked.

Breysen frowned at him, uncomprehending.

Will tried again. “What does the wind need to do?”

Breysen clearly didn’t understand, but he apparently decided to humor his lordship.

“We need a change in wind direction. The wind is blowing from the northwest.” He pointed. “It needs to blow from the southwest, more from the land.” He swung his arm around to demonstrate. “And if the wind eases, the swell will settle as well.”

“Go find Brother Ander and tell him,” Will urged. “We need him to enlist the aid of the Almighty.”

A light came into Breysen’s eyes. He nodded once before heading into the bowels of the ship.

As soon as Breysen was out of sight, Will asked Amyra, “Do you know what you need to do now?”

She stared back at him with bulging eyes. After their brief time above decks, her hair was soaked and matted from the spray, and she looked completely wild.

“I can try,” she managed, moving unsteadily toward the hatch.

“Where are you going?” asked Will in alarm. “Can’t you do it from here?”

She shook her head wearily. “I need to be able to see if what I’m doing is working.”

Reluctantly Will opened the hatch and helped Amyra outside once more. After closing the hatch, he struggled to the rail with her, barely avoiding being swept away by a huge wave that washed over the ship. Will could only hope that the captain and the sailors would be too busy to notice them.

Clinging to the rail, Amyra faced the waves, gritting her teeth in concentration. More than once she almost lost her grip as the ship rolled and pitched in the mountainous swell.

Each time Will saved her. Bending one arm around the rail, he hooked his other arm around her slender waist. Then he focused the whole of his energy on maintaining his grip.

At first Will could detect no change in the conditions. Pushed back and forth with the ship, he continued to cling on with all of his might.

The minutes passed agonizingly slowly. But a time came when gradually, impossibly, the sails began to flap as the wind changed direction. The howling of the gale appeared to diminish, and the waves no longer seemed quite so terrifying. Will watched on with awe and relief as a steady wind filled the sails and the ship settled into a new rhythm, rising and falling on a moderate swell.

A ragged cheer went up from the sailors. Will joined them, although he achieved little better than a hoarse croak.

He turned to Amyra. She appeared pale and stricken, close to collapse. With one arm still locked around her waist, he succeeded in catching her as she slumped to the deck. Hefting her into his arms, he staggered to the hatch.

Amyra slept through the night and well into the next morning. Elena and Thomas took charge of the children, allowing Will to maintain an anxious vigil by her side.

When her eyes finally fluttered open, a surge of relief flooded over him.

"You were incredible!" he breathed. "You saved us all."

She gazed back at him with weary eyes. "The children?" she finally whispered.

"They're fine," he assured her. "Below deck, playing with Thomas and Elena's children."

He brought her water and supported her head while she drank. Then he gently laid her head back onto the hammock.

Her eyes soon closed again, and he left her to sleep.

WILL STOOD ON DECK, accompanied by Thomas, Brother Ander, and a jubilant Breysen. Amyra was still resting below.

"You deserve the credit as well as Brother Ander, My Lord!" said Breysen excitedly. "It never occurred to me to ask him to help. But the wind changed and the storm subsided soon after he started praying!"

Will smiled, but said nothing. He had no desire to dent the blacksmith's enthusiasm, and he was determined not to expose Amyra's stone.

Curiously, Brother Ander seemed unmoved by the acclaim. Was it modesty? Did he question his role in the change of weather? Or was it something else?

"It was a huge relief when the storm died down," said Thomas. "I was beginning to feel anxious about my family's safety."

Will nodded. "The main thing is that the worst is behind us. And according to the captain, the ship hasn't sustained any major damage, and we're making good progress."

After a while Brother Ander and Breysen drifted off.

Thomas glanced at Will with eyebrows raised questioningly. "Was it Amyra?" he asked.

Will nodded. "I feel a bit awkward about redirecting the credit to Brother Ander."

"He doesn't seem at all affected by it," Thomas replied.

"He doesn't," agreed Will. "Is that because he doesn't believe he was responsible? Or is calming a storm of no consequence to him?"

Thomas shook his head. "I can't imagine Brother Ander sees it as unimportant," he said. "But he would see God as having done it, not him."

They stood in silence for a time.

"Where did these stones come from?" Will eventually asked.

"I have no idea," Thomas replied. "A monk who was a friend of Brother Vangellis told me he thought the Stone of Knowing might be a sky rock. And you've seen the scroll. It also suggested the stones came from the sky."

"What's their purpose?" asked Will.

Thomas raised his hands helplessly. "I don't know. But Brother Vangellis once told me he saw the Stone of Knowing as a gift."

"From God?" asked Will.

Thomas shrugged. "I suppose so."

"Wherever they came from, they're powerful," Will concluded. "Frighteningly so."

Thomas offered no response.

THE WHARVES of Rog lay before them, crowded with shipping. Delighted to have made it through an entire day without throwing up, Will stood on deck as the Nomad Lady eased her way into the harbor.

In the hours that lay behind them he had pondered Amyra's achievement with the Stone of Authority. Before long they might be facing an invasion fleet. If she could calm a storm, could she contrive to whip one up to prevent the fleet from landing?

He pictured her lying prone on her hammock, utterly spent. Her will was indomitable, but how could her body sustain another such attempt, much less an effort on an even bigger scale? He shook his head. They needed to find another way to resolve the issues.

He thrust such thoughts from his mind, aware that a pressing matter of a different kind demanded his attention. His previous visit to Rogand had been covert; this time he would be appearing openly. He had no doubt that many would see him as the architect of the catastrophic destruction visited on the armies of Rogand during Drettroth's invasion. He wasn't concerned for himself, but his family was another issue entirely. Would they be safe in Rog?

Under normal circumstances he would never have considered bringing any of them on this venture. But the Stone of Authority was too important to leave behind in Erestor, especially at such a time.

And Amyra's participation had inevitably led to the children coming as well.

He had discussed this with Amyra even before they left their holdings, and they had developed a strategy to minimize the risk as much as possible. They needed to talk with the children before they arrived, so it was no surprise when Amyra appeared on deck bringing both Millie and Ethen. Spotting him, they joined him at the rail.

"I don't want any of you to be seen with me until we're safe in the castle, or wherever King Krasmir plans to accommodate us," he told them seriously.

"Why not?" asked Ethen, puzzled.

"It might be risky for you to be associated with me," he replied. "I don't expect to be popular in some quarters here. I was the commander of the army that defeated Rogand a few years ago."

"Does Tammi have to stay away from her dad?" Millie demanded.

Will shook his head. "Thomas is fortunate to not be well known here. So there's no reason for him to stay away from his family."

"That's not fair!" cried Millie.

"Life isn't always fair, I'm afraid," Will told them.

"We can spend time with your father when we're in our own private rooms, " Amyra told the children. "We'll be playing a game while we're in Rogand too. We're going to see who's the best at listening in Rogandan while speaking in Arvenian."

"But I've been looking forward to practicing my Rogandan!" said Millie disconsolately.

"You'll have plenty of opportunities," Will assured her. "When we're together we'll speak only in Rogandan. And you'll get to do plenty of listening at other times."

"It's just a precaution," Amyra said. "People tend to speak more freely when they think you don't understand. So if any of the people we meet have plans that affect us, they might let it slip."

"Do you understand what you need to do?" Will asked the children.

They both nodded.

"You'll be well protected," he assured them. "Rufe will always be with you, and other guards too."

Noticing Rufe emerging from the hatch, Will waved him over. "I'm going to leave you now," he told his children, kissing them both on the head. Then he embraced his wife. She hugged him back, although her response felt more distant than warm.

He chose not to comment. It might have taken him a while, but he was gradually learning that timing was as important in relationships as it was in battle.

A MESSAGE HAD BEEN SENT to the palace when the ship docked, and Will remained on board, not wanting to leave the docks until his party had been formally received by the Rogandan officials.

Several hours passed before a delegation arrived from the palace. Having disembarked, Will was surprised to discover that the delegation was led by King Krasmir himself.

Horses had been provided, along with carriages for the women with children. Once they had all set out for the palace, King Krasmir pulled his horse alongside Will's.

"So you are Lord Torbury. Hosting the commander of the Arvenian army in my capital must surely rank as one of the more unexpected developments of my reign," the king told him dryly.

Will dipped his head. "I hope that my visit to Rog might prove beneficial to both kingdoms."

Krasmir contented himself with a nod. "Your countryman, Count Ranauld, has assured me that you are here only to work for the good of us all."

"That is indeed my sole purpose in coming to Rog," Will confirmed.

"For as long as that remains true, you are welcome."

"Thank you, Your Majesty."

People waved enthusiastically when they saw their king riding through the streets. He waved back serenely.

After a few minutes he turned to Will again. "I must say I never imagined myself escorting the scourge of Rogand's armies through the streets of Rog. Do you know that people here refer to you as the Lash of the Devil?"

Will kept his face impassive. "I prefer to see myself as the defender of Arvenon, Your Majesty. Your kingdom may itself face an unprovoked invasion soon, and I would expect the Rogandan people to defend themselves vigorously if that were to happen."

The king returned a wry smile. "A subtle but effective riposte. I can see that your diplomatic skills are the equal of your skills in battle." He shrugged. "Diplomacy is merely a different kind of warfare, I suppose."

Seeming to come to a decision, the king took a deep breath and released it slowly. "For my own part, I was never in favor of Drettroth's adventure, and his motives remain cloudy to me. Agon's support for the invasion was no surprise—my predecessor was committed to self-aggrandizement at any cost. You will not find me motivated by the same appetites."

Will bowed low. "I appreciate your candor, Your Majesty."

"While I am speaking candidly, it is only fair to let you know that not everyone here is equally enthusiastic about your visit, Lord Torbury. However, while I have heard many differing reports about you, all parties agree that your capabilities are unmatched. I hope they are right, because I expect we will need all the help we can get in the days to come."

Will did not respond.

"My welcome must seem ambivalent at best," the king concluded. "Nevertheless, I want you to know that I am willing to extend to you the full benefit of any doubt. Your visit enjoys my support—please do not harbor doubts about that. I look forward to working with you."

"I am grateful for your gracious response, Your Majesty," Will replied. "There is one matter that I would like to raise with you, with your permission."

King Krasmir nodded an affirmative.

"My party includes children from two families, one of which is my own. I did not expect an enthusiastic reception, so I have asked my wife and children to remain apart from me in public to minimize any risk to them. You might reasonably wonder why I brought them here at all. The reasons are personal and difficult to explain, but the intent is in no way sinister."

He faced the king squarely. "My wife and children are not responsible for any of my past actions. We have people to guard them of course, but would you be willing to extend some of your own protection over them as well?" He made no attempt to hide a tone of pleading in his voice.

King Krasmir did not hesitate. "I will see to it that your family is well protected, Lord Torbury—you have my word on that. It may be necessary at times for them to curtail their movements, but we will keep them safe. I will personally assign men I know to be trustworthy."

13

Will and Amyra sat with Count Ranauld in his apartment at the royal castle at Rog.

"It's a great relief to have you both here," Ranauld told them. "The situation is extremely delicate, and properly representing the interests of Arvenon has felt like a heavy burden. I'm beyond delighted to know that the responsibility no longer rests solely on my shoulders."

"I'm sure you've done an excellent job," Will said reassuringly. "What have you learned so far in the meetings with the princess?"

"There haven't been any meetings yet," Ranauld told him. "There is a reason," he added, apparently in response to the surprise on Will's face. "The king wanted to find out if the Ahrans had returned to the island where they abandoned the princess. The hermit, Kamash, agreed to lead a party there. Apparently he was also hoping to retrieve some personal effects he'd left there. They only returned yesterday—just a few hours before you arrived."

"What did they discover?" asked Will.

"When they reached the island they found that others had been there before them. Presumably the Ahrans returned there as expected. The ground around Kamash's dwelling had been trampled by many feet, and the dwelling itself had been ransacked."

Will pondered this information. "So the Ahrans are now aware that they dumped the princess on an inhabited island. I'm sure they would have conducted a thorough search. And since there were no bodies to be found, they also know she didn't die there as they intended."

Ranauld nodded. "The question is what conclusion they might have drawn from it," he said.

"It would have been obvious to them that someone—presumably a castaway—had been living on the island," said Will. "My guess is that they decided the princess and her guard must have put to sea with the castaway, most likely by raft."

"Only a fool would attempt those seas by raft," said Ranauld.

"Very true," agreed Will. "The Ahrans would almost certainly have concluded that the princess perished at sea."

Both men fell to musing.

Will eventually broke the silence. "What has the princess been doing in the meantime?" he asked.

"She's been seeing the sights of Rog, such as they are." Ranauld made a face. "Under heavy guard of course."

"Can you please use your channels to arrange me an audience with King Krasmir?" asked Will.

"Certainly," Ranauld replied. "I'll request a meeting as soon as the king can make himself available."

Will and Ranauld were ushered into an audience chamber in the palace. The room boasted a small throne at one end, brightly illuminated by many windows. The king had ignored the throne, sitting instead at the head of an ornate table around which a number of chairs had been placed.

"Please take a seat," King Krasmir told them as they entered the room.

They bowed. “Thank you for seeing us so promptly,” Will said, handing a letter to the king. “King Steffan asked me to present my credentials at the earliest opportunity.”

The letter from King Steffan had been written in Arvenian, but Steffan’s agents had confidently asserted that King Krasmir could both speak and read the language.

The king’s eyebrows lifted as he read it. “Your king has given you sweeping powers on his behalf, Lord Torbury. He has even authorized you to commit Arvenon to a mutual-defense treaty if you see fit. He clearly places a very high level of trust in you!”

Will bowed. “King Steffan does not want another war,” he said. “But if it is clear that Rogand is being attacked without cause by the Empire of Ahr, Arvenon will stand with Rogand.”

“I greatly appreciate King Steffan’s support,” King Krasmir told him. “And I appreciate your willingness to act on his behalf to establish a strong defense against an attack.” His face turned grim. “I regret to say that it may well come to that.”

“Standing with Rogand is also a prudent step for Arvenon,” said Will. “If Rogand falls, Arvenon and the other neighboring kingdoms are likely to be targeted next.”

The king nodded.

“There is another matter I wished to explore, Your Majesty,” Will said.

“I am listening,” the king replied.

“Count Ranauld has briefed me on recent events,” Will said. “I understand that the Ahrans sailed away from Rog before the princess arrived, and that they returned to the island where they left her. Since they did not find her there, they would have been forced to guess about what happened. I personally think it likely they concluded she left the island with the hermit, most probably by raft. That being the case, they would not have expected her to survive.”

“That is entirely possible,” acknowledged the king.

“Nevertheless, even if the news has not yet reached the Grand Vizier, at least some of the Ahrans would since have become aware that the princess is with us here in Rog,” Will continued.

King Krasmir frowned. "How can you be certain about that?" he asked.

"I can't be certain, Your Majesty. But it seems reasonable to suppose they have agents in Rog, and the princess has been openly traveling throughout the city."

The king's eyes narrowed. "Are you suggesting I should have hidden her away?" he asked.

"Not at all, Your Majesty," Will replied calmly. "I doubt that the truth about her whereabouts could have been concealed. It was probably already too late for secrecy when the Varasan fishermen found her drifting at sea and brought her into Varacellan harbor. And any serious attempt at concealment would have required her to be deprived of her liberty. From the little I've heard, she is not well equipped to thrive in such an environment."

The king did not seem entirely satisfied. "What point are you wanting to make then?"

"Your predecessor, King Agon, was able to do a great deal of damage with little more than three highly connected malcontents and a relatively modest sum of money."

"You're concerned about traitors?"

"I'm concerned about being blindsided, Your Majesty. The blows struck by the traitors were effective because we were unprepared. By the time we became aware of their intentions, it was too late to prevent their actions and impossible to undo what they'd already done."

"What are you proposing?" King Krasmir asked.

"While we are not entirely unprepared this time, we remain ignorant about the real agenda of the Ahrans. That makes us vulnerable. I would like to offer two proposals. The first is that we invest whatever resources are needed to track down the Ahran agents."

The king looked unimpressed. "Finding and eliminating their agents won't solve anything. Others will be put in place, and the replacements will be more cautious next time."

"The goal would not be to eliminate the agents, Your Majesty. I am proposing that we monitor them covertly. We need to know what they are planning."

The king considered this.

"What is your second proposal?"

"That we take strong steps to ensure that the Ahrans do not become aware of our own plans."

The king's brows drew together. "Do you doubt my commitment to security? I can assure you that our meetings will be heavily guarded. Intruders will not be allowed anywhere near the site."

Will kept his face impassive. "It is difficult to thwart a person who is sufficiently determined, especially with a lot of people actively discussing the issues and servants coming and going constantly on a range of errands. I would like to propose that the venue be changed —without notice and at the last minute—and that only those directly participating be admitted to the meeting room. No servants and no soldiers should be allowed inside. Refreshments could be served in a different location. And before we begin, participants could be admitted only if you are certain they can be relied upon. I'm sure your agents will have no difficulty identifying nobles with loose tongues. Attendees should be required to never discuss sensitive matters unless they are certain beyond doubt that no others are within earshot."

The king listened patiently until Will finished. "Suppose we implement your plan," he said, "and succeed in tightening security to the point where no word of our plans leaks out. Wouldn't the Ahran agents be forced to resort to strong measures to get information?"

"Yes, Your Majesty. I find that possibility disturbing, as I am sure you do. However we need not provoke them to acts of desperation. Some of our number can hold confidential conversations at other locations, conversations capable of being overheard by a person bold enough to risk detection. We will fill their ears with plausible-sounding plans that have no basis in reality. And the strategy should give us further opportunity to identify the Ahran agents."

"You have a shrewd mind, Lord Torbury."

THE CONFERENCE BEGAN AS SOON as the three kings and the most senior of their nobles had gathered. Will noted with satisfaction that the meeting location had been changed without notice. Indeed he was gratified to discover that so far King Krasmir had implemented every one of his suggestions.

Will had managed to include Amyra in the invitation, although they were trying not to be too obvious about their connection. He had also hoped to include Thomas along with his stone, but King Krasmir made it clear that only nobility would be allowed to participate. Since Will was unable to dream up a good enough reason to request an exception, Thomas had gone to a secure location with Elena, Haldek, Rufe, Breysen, Brother Ander, and the five children.

During King Krasmir's brief introductions to those attending the conference, Will had noted that foreigners were outnumbered at least four to one. A number among the Rogandan nobility were women, and Will found himself thinking of Lady Ona. He grimaced involuntarily.

"I expect that every one of us will make extraordinary efforts to follow through on the security measures I have outlined," King Krasmir was concluding.

The king directed an almost imperceptible nod in Will's direction, but stopped short of openly crediting him for the tightened security. Will was grateful. He enjoyed good relations with all members of the Varasan and Castelan delegations, and he felt confident they would view sympathetically any initiatives he might propose. King Krasmir's delegation was another matter. The king had introduced him as Lord Torbury, not Will Prentis, but if the sour glances directed toward him were any indication, the Rogandan nobles had no doubt about who he was. He had no desire to draw more attention to himself than was necessary.

"We are fortunate to have in our midst a man who possesses an inquiring mind," said King Krasmir. "He has used it to amass a formidable store of knowledge. I am pleased to introduce Lord Boedwyk to this gathering."

A tall thin man with bushy eyebrows got up and moved to the front of the room. He bowed as he faced the king.

"Please favor us with a summary of what is known of the Empire of Ahr," King Krasmir requested.

The king seated himself, and Lord Boedwyk turned to his audience. He began speaking rapidly in Rogandan, apparently oblivious to the fact that his words needed to be translated. Will spared a thought for the carefully selected translator sitting among the Arvenian speakers. The man already looked harried.

Was the nobleman set on delivering a none-too-subtle snub to the foreign guests? After studying him closely, Will decided that the reality was more straightforward—Lord Boedwyk's engagement with his subject was so intense it excluded every other consideration.

"Few Rogandans—and perhaps none of us present in this room—have visited the Empire of Ahr," the nobleman was saying. "To begin with, the lengthy sea voyage introduces a number of interesting challenges. I make no mention of the undoubtedly fanciful tales of sea monsters." He blinked rapidly several times and directed his attention up into the ceiling. "The Ahrans are reputedly an insular society, not naturally welcoming of outsiders. Very like some of us perhaps," he added. His mouth opened wide in a chortle, although he managed to hastily smother the sound.

Recovering himself, he continued. "The Ahrans are not unwilling to trade, but their tastes apparently differ considerably from ours. Ships have arrived in Ahr after a punishing voyage only to discover that their carefully chosen cargo was largely regarded as worthless by their potential customers. After dumping their goods at a loss, they have been left with little choice other than to reload their ship with wares that would be barely marketable in Rogand."

"Perhaps these Ahrans are simply canny traders," a nobleman suggested. "By pretending disinterest, they get the goods for next to nothing. Then in return they hand over junk, and even manage to get some coin for it."

Lord Boedwyk shook his head vigorously. "I think not, I think not," he insisted, shaking his head and blinking once more. "Cheating your suppliers has never been a workable recipe for building trade. No, no, I think it has to do with differences in taste." He frowned for a moment before smiling awkwardly and adding, "But I thank you for your contribution, My Lord. Thank you." He aimed a quick bow in the direction of the other speaker.

"I have learned about some very fascinating customs," he continued. "Ahran mating rituals are of particular interest, especially where kissing is involved." His mouth opened wide in a grin. "I could convey some captivating tales," he suggested with a throaty chuckle.

At that moment Will caught a glimpse of King Rupert. The young king seemed to be fidgeting restlessly. Will wondered what could possibly account for his reaction.

Lord Boedwyk's voice had trailed off, his eyes drifting once more to the ceiling. Will noticed others among the Rogandan nobility rolling their eyes.

"The politics and geography of the empire, Lord Boedwyk?" prompted King Krasmir patiently.

"Ah yes, of course, Your Majesty," Lord Boedwyk replied, clearing his throat with a self-conscious cough. "Please excuse my diversion. The emperor of Ahr has two children: the crown prince being the oldest, and the Princess Neira—currently our guest here in Rog—being the youngest. Neither the emperor nor the crown prince are ever referred to by name, only by their title. The chief minister of the empire is Grand Vizier Rheibas, the very man who favored us recently with a visit to Rog."

Grunts and muttering broke out at this last remark. Lord Boedwyk ignored it and pressed on.

"The climate of the empire is warmer than in Rogand," he continued, "and the population is large—much larger than Rogand by all accounts. The landmass is also large. The empire is made up of a single small continent and a large archipelago of islands, several of the islands being of considerable size."

"Does the emperor live on the continent?" another voice asked.

"An excellent question. An excellent question," the nobleman replied soberly. "The emperor does not live on the continent. His capital of Kat Ahket is located on Ahr-chitani, the largest of the islands. The main administrative center is located there as well."

"Does this emperor have a sizable army?" someone asked.

"On that topic, the reports vary widely," Lord Boedwyk said, placing his hands together in a precise movement and examining them carefully.

Will found himself warming to the Rogandan researcher. The nobleman might have unusual mannerisms, but he was clearly knowledgeable. And he seemed entirely artless, betraying no interest at all in self promotion.

"But whatever the final count might be, I think I can safely say that the number of soldiers answering to the emperor far exceeds the armies of all our kingdoms combined."

"Why does he need such a large army?" asked a nobleman.

"It seems that the emperor is frequently forced to put down rebellions against his authority. I imagine he needs a large army for that reason."

"What about his navy?" asked King Krasmir.

"All reports agree that he lays claim to a large navy," the speaker replied. "I heard of one exercise where the entire navy was gathered into the huge bay at Ahr-chitani, the large island. The ships filled the bay to overflowing." He spread his hands wide.

Another noble spoke up. "Are these ships capable of carrying soldiers?"

"They are," Lord Boedwyk replied with a vigorous nod. "Since rebellions have frequently been island-based, the sailors are very practiced at transporting soldiers and landing them from the ships."

This news was greeted with loud muttering throughout the room.

King Krasmir looked grim. "Do we have any idea why they have turned their attention toward us? What is their motivation?"

The speaker steepled his fingers.

"I cannot name their specific motivation," he said thoughtfully. "I have heard, though, that wars generally stem from one of four causes." He gazed up once more into the ceiling, and his voice took on an instructional tone. "The first and most common reason is a desire for aggrandizement on the part of the ruler. The second reason is greed —a ruler's desire to enjoy the spoils of war while expanding the borders of his own kingdom or empire."

Lord Boedwyk had become more animated as he warmed to his subject. Will listened with growing astonishment.

"The third reason is in response to internal dissension," the nobleman continued. "The ruler turns attention away from local problems by uniting the populace against a foreign enemy. The fourth is a desire for revenge or an urge to right a perceived wrong. Which of these reasons might account for the emperor's actions I cannot say, although the fourth reason is unlikely to apply in this case."

Will barely suppressed a wince. Surely only a fool or an innocent could make such statements before an audience that included three reigning kings. He shot a glance around the room. Other nobles appeared equally uncomfortable. Many were desperately trying to decide where to look.

Curiously, none of the kings seemed offended. They must have decided that these comments did not apply to them. They had probably also judged that their instructor was harmless and that challenging his assertions might only add weight to what he had said.

"Thank you, Lord Boedwyk. Your insights have been...more than usually illuminating," King Krasmir said dryly.

The eccentric nobleman got the hint. Bowing low, he returned to his seat.

"We will take a short break," King Krasmir announced. "Servants are waiting down the hall to guide you to refreshments."

The meeting broke up immediately. Most of the nobles couldn't leave the room quickly enough.

When the conference reconvened it seemed to Will that a somber mood had overtaken the participants. Many of them were talking among themselves in low voices, and King Krasmir had to speak sharply to call them to order.

King Krasmir began. "I spent time during the break with King Delmar of Varas and King Rupert of Castel," he said. "Two key questions need to be addressed as a matter of urgency. What can we do to prepare effectively for a possible Ahran invasion? What can we do diplomatically to head off any such invasion?"

Will decided it was time to actively engage. "May I ask a question, Your Majesty?" he asked.

Many of the Rogandan nobility stared at him open mouthed. He wasn't surprised—the reason wasn't difficult to guess. The infamous commander of the Arvenian armies had dared to show his face in Rog, and, instead of seizing him, their own king had allowed him to join their conference.

That was bad enough. But who could have expected to hear him speaking Rogandan as if it were his mother tongue?

"You have the floor, Lord Torbury," King Krasmir replied evenly, opening his palm in invitation.

Will stood and turned toward Lord Boedwyk. "I thank you for your informative presentation about the Empire of Ahr, My Lord. I found it very instructive, as I'm sure we all did. Were you able to discover any information about the construction of the ships in the emperor's navy? Are the vessels equipped for long voyages across open seas, or are they designed primarily for use among the islands of the archipelago?"

Lord Boedwyk rose to his feet and bowed briefly to Will. "A worthy question, Lord Torbury. And nicely expressed. Very nicely expressed indeed! Who would ever have imagined?" He shook his head. His eyes began to drift to the ceiling once more before he caught himself. "Your question is consequential, My Lord, although I am sorry to say I cannot answer it." He sat down abruptly.

Will bowed in response. "An open ocean voyage with a large fleet carries significant risk. However sizable the emperor's army might be, he will not be able to deploy it without appropriately equipped vessels and experienced captains."

"Can you look into it?" King Krasmir asked, directing his question to Lord Boedwyk.

"I will do what I can, Your Majesty," the nobleman replied.

Many of the Rogandan nobles were now speaking in low voices, shooting frequent glances at Will. From the look on their faces, his fluency in their language had not endeared him to them. They appeared more suspicious of him than ever.

He shrugged it off. He was well accustomed to being an outsider.

His question had clearly captured the attention of some though. King Delmar, sitting not far from Will, leaned over to him. "That was a key question, Lord Torbury," he whispered.

The question demanded an answer. It was hard for Will to imagine that the emperor's main fleet had been constructed for the purpose of invading a distant continent. But if the emperor was planning a foreign adventure, it was also possible that a new fleet was being built, consisting of vessels fit for the purpose.

"I am going to invite Princess Neira to join us," said King Krasmir. "She might be able to offer us some useful insights."

He nodded to Lord Boedwyk, and the nobleman rose to his feet and left the room, presumably to usher in the princess.

Will waited impatiently for her arrival. There were far too many unknowns for his liking, and the princess might hold the key to plugging at least some of the gaps. He was eager to meet her, and even more eager for an opportunity to interview her.

14

"Another ship is approaching, Captain."

Captain Gharpin nodded before turning toward the direction the sailor was pointing. A quick scan of the horizon soon revealed the ship. It gradually grew in size as it drew closer. Based on its course, it could well have been sailing from Ahrchitani. Before long it was apparent that the ship was Ahran.

The Grand Vizier appeared at the captain's side. "I understand an Ahran vessel is approaching, Captain."

"Yes, Your Eminence," Gharpin replied with a bow. As always, the chief minister didn't miss much. The captain kept his face expressionless, careful not to reveal the distaste he felt in the presence of the empire's most senior official.

"Send a signal to the ship," commanded the Grand Vizier. "I wish to enlist the aid of their captain."

Gharpin bowed again, torn between curiosity about the Grand Vizier's intentions and satisfaction at the prospect of getting the man off his ship, even temporarily.

The chief minister then disappeared below decks. He was gone for a considerable time, only reemerging as a longboat from the other ship was finally drawing alongside. Six men accompanied him, every one of them laden down with goods of various kinds. It appeared that the Grand Vizier had retrieved all of his possessions. That could only mean one thing—he intended to transfer to the other vessel. The captain was hard pressed to prevent his elation from becoming obvious.

The Grand Vizier drew Gharpin aside. "You have a new mission, Captain," he announced loftily.

Unable to guess what might be coming next, the captain stared back expressionlessly.

"You will return to the island where you left the princess. You will find she has been returned to it. You will retrieve her and make your way to the capital."

The captain bowed, although inwardly he was scoffing. He didn't trust the Grand Vizier for a moment. Nevertheless, if there was even a chance that the princess could be rescued, the mission was worth the delay in returning to Ahr-chitani.

"I must return to Kat Ahket to consult with the emperor," the Grand Vizier concluded.

The chief minister did not wait for a response from the captain. Heading for the side of the ship, he proceeded to oversee the laborious operation of lowering three of his men and all of his possessions to the boat below. The wind had been picking up steadily over the last few hours and the heavy swell made the transfer extremely challenging.

Very little could be heard above the howling of the wind and the creaking of the ship's timbers. Nevertheless the Grand Vizier persisted in shouting instructions. As the longboat tossed and turned on the waves, a number of his belongings fell out of it, quickly sinking out of sight. He turned pale with anger.

Eventually the boat, overloaded and low in the water, was rowed back to the other ship. The chief minister watched from Captain Gharpin's ship, grinding his teeth as more of his possessions were surrendered to the ocean while they were being hauled aboard.

Having offloaded its cargo, the longboat returned for the exasperated Grand Vizier and his remaining three men. The worsening conditions considerably complicated the process of transferring them to the other ship. Nevertheless they were eventually taken on board, the boat was pulled from the water, and the ship turned and set sail for the capital at Kat Ahket.

Gharpin was relieved to have finally seen the last of the scheming official. Turning to his helmsman, he ordered, "Set a course for the island where we left the princess."

The helmsman's face showed his surprise, but he made no comment.

Gharpin watched with considerable satisfaction as the boat bearing the Grand Vizier slowly diminished in size. With the chief minister finally gone, the captain took the opportunity to carefully review in his mind all that had happened since he first left Ahrchitani.

Having both the Grand Vizier and the princess on board as passengers had made the voyage challenging from the very beginning. Gharpin had no great love for the princess. She was conceited and almost unendurable. Nevertheless, she was the emperor's daughter, and the captain had openly questioned the Grand Vizier's order to leave her and her guard alone on the island. He well understood that it was folly to make an enemy of a senior official, especially one as powerful as the Grand Vizier. But, as a loyal subject of the emperor, how could he say and do nothing when her life seemed so obviously at risk?

The chief minister had informed him coldly that he had no business interfering in matters he didn't understand. Gharpin had no choice but to set sail for Rog.

When they reached the Rogandan capital, the captain caught wind that bizarre stories were being told to their hosts. Supposedly Rogandan sailors—or pirates—had kidnapped the princess. He was beginning to get a glimpse of how far the chief minister was willing to go.

After they sailed away from Rog, the Grand Vizier had commanded the captain to return to the island. Gharpin had been under no illusions when they arrived there—he fully expected to find that the princess and her guard had perished. Instead, an exhaustive search of the island revealed no trace of Princess Neira.

The Grand Vizier had casually told the captain that the princess had been collected from the island as planned. He claimed she was supposed to be returned there in time to join the return voyage to the capital of Kat Ahket. Since the timing had apparently gone astray, a ship would be sent to collect her later.

The chief minister had then retired to his cabin.

Unconvinced, the captain had quietly ordered his men to search the nearby islands. The search revealed nothing. The princess and her guard had simply vanished.

Gharpin was convinced that the Grand Vizier was spinning a series of bald-faced lies. But apart from the order to abandon the princess on the island, he had no proof of the man's duplicity.

The captain's men had found obvious signs of long-term habitation on the island. Only one explanation made any sense to Gharpin: whoever had been living there had left the island with the princess and her guard. Whether they had set out for the mainland or for another island, it seemed likely they had succumbed to the elements before reaching land at all. Without access to a suitable vessel, their chances of survival would have been very poor indeed.

Gharpin did have one immediate source of satisfaction. For the first time since departing from their home, the only people aboard his ship were his own crew. That was cause for celebration.

Six men had transferred to the other ship with the Grand Vizier. They had been handpicked, every one of them completely loyal to the chief minister. They had been as aloof and arrogant as their master. If Gharpin had dared, he would have left all of them on the island along with the Grand Vizier, instead of the princess.

Convinced that the chief minister and his lackeys had a hidden agenda, Gharpin had assigned five of his own sailors to watch them. Not one of these men was still alive. One had somehow fallen overboard during a storm, two others had succumbed to sickness—most likely poison—and the other two had mysteriously vanished at different times during the voyage. The captain suspected the last two were thrown overboard after their throats had been cut.

The loss of his men was intolerable, and Gharpin was determined to ensure they had not died for nothing. He would make sure that a full report of the princess's movements reached the emperor. The chief minister would arrive in Kat Ahket first, so he would gain first access to the emperor's ear. But the captain would not be deterred. He would make it his mission to see that the Grand Vizier's actions were exposed in full.

THE CONDITIONS WORSENED as they sailed on. Gharpin soon had no opportunity for musing.

"Captain!"

Hearing the urgent cry, Gharpin labored to the helm.

"She's sluggish!" the helmsman shouted over the wind, "Not responding properly to the tiller!"

A gigantic wave assaulted them, and the captain looked on in alarm as the ship rolled drunkenly in response. Worse, she appeared to be listing to the port side.

It made no sense. Recently built, the ship was one of the finest vessels in the emperor's deep sea fleet.

Gesturing frantically to a sailor to join him, the captain struggled to the hatch and made his way below deck. To his horror he found the lower hold awash, sea water surging about freely as the ship rolled back and forth. Numbed by the scale of the disaster, he explored as far as he dared.

The ship had been holed at the waterline in multiple locations, and water had been pouring in ever faster as the storm continued to build.

Fear was unmistakable in the eyes of the sailor beside him. Gharpin made no attempt to reassure his companion. Repairs were not an option—it was far too late for that. The only certainty was that the ship was going to sink. It was merely a matter of time.

This calamity was no accident; the damage could only have been caused by sabotage. The Grand Vizier's men must have carried out the destruction as they were preparing to leave. They had not been halfhearted. Thanks to the noise of the growing storm, there would have been no need to be furtive about their efforts.

Pushing down his fury, the captain forced his way back onto the deck, his companion behind him.

"We have to launch the boats!" Gharpin yelled to the sailor.

Wide-eyed, the man nodded once before hurrying away.

Squinting against the spray, Gharpin peered across the deck with a heavy heart. The ship carried three longboats. Between them they had nowhere near the capacity needed to accommodate the entire crew. His first instinct was to yield up his own place for the sake of one of his men. But there was no way to evade his responsibility. He needed to get word to the emperor.

Sailors were laboring to launch the boats—no simple task in the conditions. Transferring any of the crew would be an extremely hazardous operation. The sea would toss the boats about relentlessly once they were in the water.

The moment the boats had been released, Gharpin shouted the words most dreaded by every captain: "Abandon ship!"

One by one his crew obeyed, with Gharpin watching on anxiously. Satisfied that he was the last, he waited until the ship lurched in the right direction and jumped over the side.

Hitting the water hard and sinking quickly, he struggled resolutely upward to the light, resisting the remorseless tug into the icy depths below.

He broke the surface gasping for air. Bobbing about in the raging sea, his face covered with spray, he spun around trying to catch sight of a longboat. Carried up on a wave, he spotted a boat nearby and struck out for it at once. Several sailors had already climbed aboard, and they pulled him over the side.

Working frenetically, they rescued as many men as they could. Occasional glimpses of the other two boats confirmed the terrible truth—too few of Gharpin's men had made it to the precarious safety offered by the longboats.

It wasn't until an exhausted Gharpin settled back to rest that he noticed something was wrong. Spray might be splashing over them constantly, but there was far too much water sitting in the boat. A frantic search for leaks soon led him to the holes in the bottom of the boat. Someone had staved in the timbers.

He immediately ordered the men to begin bailing. Even before they started he knew it wouldn't be enough.

Salt water ran freely down his cheeks. It might have been spray, and it might have been tears. Either way, he knew they were finished.

Releasing a despairing sigh, Gharpin closed his eyes in resignation. He had been a fool. He had dared to challenge the highest official in the empire. It was always going to end badly.

THE SLEEK VESSEL beneath Bisri Ahuzza's feet slid gracefully through the swell, speeding him away from the capital of Kat Ahket. Salt water sprayed freely over the aristocrat, but it did not drive him from the rail of the ship. As special envoy to the emperor, he frequently found himself at sea, and he never tired of it.

The captain approached. "A ship has been sighted, Bisri. It appears to be Ahran."

"Send them a signal," the bisri told him. "We need to know if they have information about the Grand Vizier's whereabouts."

Only minutes passed before Ahuzza became aware that the man he sought was aboard the other ship. It took considerably longer for the Ahran aristocrat to transfer to that ship by longboat.

Climbing aboard the Grand Vizier's ship, Ahuzza was quickly ushered into the presence of the Grand Vizier of the empire.

"Bisri Ahuzza," said the chief minister, nodding a greeting.

The bisri bowed low. "Matters of a sensitive nature have arisen, Your Eminence—matters that require your urgent attention. The emperor has placed a fast warship at your disposal." He gestured in the direction of the vessel that had borne him from Kat Ahket.

The chief minister dismissed his attendants immediately. "What is the nature of this business, Bisri?" he asked curtly.

Ahuzza lowered his voice. "A rebellion has been brewing on Ahr-kasahn, Your Eminence. Reports indicate that it is about to boil over."

The Grand Vizier studied him for a moment. "What are the wishes of the emperor?" he asked.

"That you take charge of the situation and resolve the matter," the bisri replied simply.

The chief minister remained silent, his face expressionless. Then he nodded, turning away to call for the captain of his vessel.

The captain hurried to his side.

"I must leave you, Captain," said the chief minister. "My servants will remain. They can oversee the transfer of my personal effects to my palace when you arrive in Kat Ahket."

The captain bowed, and the Grand Vizier faced Bisri Ahuzza once more. "Lead the way," he said, indicating the waiting longboat.

Bisri Ahuzza stood silently in the private reception room of the governor's mansion on Ahr-kasahn. The Grand Vizier sat in state immediately to his left, waiting patiently for the arrival of a delegation. The governor of Ahr-kasahn was nowhere in sight. He had been excluded from the meeting.

Several men and women were ushered into the reception room. A tall man in late middle age strode in at their head. His face revealed tension, but he was otherwise calm. Three men and three women trailed in after him. Two of the women looked angry. All of the others looked terrified.

The Grand Vizier eyed them darkly. "I have been called away from urgent business," he told them brusquely. "Why am I here?"

The tall man bowed. "My name is Hirath, Your Eminence. Thank you for agreeing to meet with us. We are loyal subjects of the emperor, and it was never our desire to cause a disturbance. But the situation here on Ahr-kasahn has become intolerable."

When the Grand Vizier did not respond, Hirath continued.

"On Ahr-kasahn, justice is extended only to those who can afford massive bribes. Taxes have become so crushing that many have been forced into poverty. And new taxes are levied regularly—taxes that do not apply on other islands."

"Why haven't you taken these concerns to the governor?" demanded the Grand Vizier.

"Anyone who dares to raise such matters with the governor is thrown into prison, Your Eminence," Hirath replied. "The situation has become so bad that a large crowd recently gathered in the main public square to air their grievances. The governor's response was to send in soldiers."

"People were slaughtered!" one of the women moaned. "My husband and son among them!" She began to weep.

"I have been informed by the governor that the crowd was armed and aggressive," the Grand Vizier returned. "He assures me that the soldiers were merely defending themselves."

"That is not true, Your Eminence," Hirath said firmly. "Fighting did not break out until later, and only as a direct response to the massacre in the square."

"Who led the armed resistance?" demanded the Grand Vizier.

"I did, Your Eminence," Hirath acknowledged.

The chief minister studied him for a moment, then he rose to his feet. "A thorough and impartial investigation will be carried out," he announced. "Any officials who have been corrupt or negligent will pay a heavy price."

Hirath bowed. "And the governor?" he asked boldly.

"Every senior official will be investigated," declared the Grand Vizier. "That includes the governor."

Hirath bowed once more. "We thank you, Your Eminence. Your reputation gives us hope that justice will finally be done."

"Hirath will remain here," said the Grand Vizier. "The rest of you are dismissed. I can promise that your concerns will be taken seriously. But let me warn you that any new attempt to take up arms will be met with a ruthless and overwhelming response."

Hirath's companions bowed low before scurrying away.

The chief minister turned to Hirath. "You have the makings of an effective leader," he observed. "Draw closer."

Hirath bowed before stepping forward.

"You say you are aware of my reputation."

"I am," Hirath acknowledged.

"Then you know that I cannot allow you to live," the chief minister informed him quietly. "Not after you have led an armed rebellion."

Hirath had gone pale, but he did not respond.

"The only possible alternative would be to offer you a job," mused the Grand Vizier. He studied the other closely. "Something tells me a role of that nature would not suit you."

The silence from Hirath seemed to offer confirmation.

"It is as I expected," said the chief minister with a shrug.

He got to his feet. "Execute this man at dawn," he ordered.

As he prepared to leave the room, the Grand Vizier leaned in to speak quietly to the condemned man. Bisri Ahuzza was close enough to hear the comment.

"If it's any comfort to you," murmured the chief minister, "I think it likely that the governor will be executed at your side."

The Grand Vizier left the room without a backward glance.

Bisri Ahuzza hurried out behind him.

15

Bisri Ahuzza stood at the prow of the emperor's ship and watched as a tiny smudge appeared on the horizon.

A distinctive cone gradually took shape above the landmass: the crater-capped mountain that towered over the extensive island of Ahr-chitani. Fantastic tales were still told of the last time the mountain had erupted, but that was ancient history. No wisps of smoke hung over the mountain today, nor on any other day in living memory.

Beside the bisri stood the Grand Vizier of the glorious Empire of Ahr. The formidable dignitary had once been a low-ranking aristocrat known simply as Bisri Rheibas—a man with few prospects and nothing obvious to commend him. How he had ascended to the lofty rank of Grand Vizier was hotly debated.

Some pointed to his obvious abilities. On Ahr-kasahn, Bisri Ahuzza had witnessed firsthand the most recent example of the chief minister's renowned prowess. A single meeting, a swift investigation, and two summary executions had ended a rebellion that threatened to plunge one of the most populous islands in the archipelago into chaos. The Grand Vizier had almost made it look effortless.

Behind closed doors, the chief minister's opponents murmured that Bisri Rheibas could most accurately be characterized as a vicious schemer, and that his rise to prominence owed more to his effectiveness at disposing of rivals than to any honest skills. No one had ever offered proof in support of these slurs, and the Grand Vizier's supporters dismissed all such talk as malicious slander. His detractors whispered that no one with proof had ever stayed alive long enough to present it.

Bisri Ahuzza had no reason to believe the critics. Nevertheless he frequently reminded himself not to cross a man who could order executions without first obtaining the emperor's approval.

In any event, it was widely acknowledged that the emperor trusted his chief minister implicitly. That said a great deal, because Ahuzza knew that the emperor was no idiot, and he had access to more information than anyone. If Bisri Rheibas was truly devious and self-serving, he was unusually adept at keeping it hidden.

No one disputed that Rheibas was useful to the emperor. What Ahuzza had just witnessed on Ahr-kasahn amply reinforced his effectiveness.

Seeing that they were nearing their destination, Ahuzza redirected his attention to the scene before him.

As the ship approached the generous bay that led to the capital of Kat Ahket, it glided among a multitude of vessels of every size. Ships bearing two or three masts dominated the harbor, their flags and pennants snapping in the breeze, fishing boats weaved their way between the larger ships, and smaller craft ferried passengers and cargo across the bay.

Palm trees stood tall among the sturdy buildings of white stone that stretched out beyond the water's edge in every direction. Even from this distance, the towering walls of the imperial palace gleamed brightly in the afternoon sunshine.

Ahuzza stole a glance at the figure beside him. What was passing through the Grand Vizier's mind as he approached Kat Ahket? The powerful official had just returned from Rog. Bisri Ahuzza had never visited the place himself, but he had heard reports about it. The docks of Rog, with their untidy wharves and mismatched architecture, provided a squalid gateway to the Rogandan capital.

The scene here must surely offer a complete contrast. Before him lay the glorious city of Kat Ahket, the heart of the empire. It was also the main power base of Rheibas, reputed to be the most powerful Grand Vizier the empire had known.

Word of the Grand Vizier's arrival must have spread quickly, because by the time they were ready to disembark, a crowd had gathered. Most of them were just curious bystanders, but one of them carried a message bearing an imperial seal. The chief minister scanned the message briefly before securing it within his cloak.

A carriage was waiting for them, and they climbed aboard immediately. The chief minister ordered the curtains closed as the carriage rumbled through the streets of Kat Ahket. Some would assert that Rheibas disdained the dregs of the empire and studiously avoided all contact with them. It seemed equally likely to Ahuzza that he was simply weary and craved a brief moment of solitude.

Either way, Ahuzza enjoyed the view and was sorry to be shut off from the world.

Presumably the dispatch waiting for the chief minister at the docks had been a summons to the crown prince, because the carriage delivered them to the door of a gleaming residence outside the palace walls favored by the emperor's son.

It was rumored that the prince liked to conduct his business away from prying eyes at the palace. Ahuzza thought it implausible. Only a fool would imagine he could avoid the notice of the emperor. A smattering of the emperor's spies were surely numbered among the crown prince's most trusted aides.

It was, however, tempting to wonder what the emperor would think about his Grand Vizier visiting the prince before calling at the palace.

The Grand Vizier was ushered directly into a reception room. Ahuzza hung back, but the chief minister waved him forward. Perhaps it was in the interests of the Grand Vizier to have a witness to the conversation.

The crown prince was already on hand to receive his visitor.

Ignoring Ahuzza, he waved the chief minister to a seat. "Rheibas," he said. "I see you received my summons."

"Your Highness," replied the chief minister, bowing before settling himself.

The crown prince had a name of course—Ahreitas—but protocol demanded that he could only be directly addressed by his title. The emperor's son and heir apparently regarded such conventions as beneath him—he had not bothered to use the Grand Vizier's title.

Perhaps he was determined to ensure the chief minister never forgot his humble beginnings. Ahuzza had heard rumors that on one occasion when the prince was younger he had told the Grand Vizier, "I have divine blood coursing through my veins, Rheibas. What do you have in your veins? Pig's blood? Or something worse? Urine, perhaps?"

If the story was true, the crown prince must have since learned to moderate his impulses. His manner on this occasion was not openly contemptuous, but his words had nevertheless failed to show appropriate respect for the Grand Vizier. Ahuzza could only wonder what Rheibas might think about that.

The crown prince seemed to notice his father's envoy at last. He eyed Ahuzza coolly for a moment before apparently deciding that a witness held some value to him as well.

He redirected his attention to the chief minister. "I hear you have been attending to business on Ahr-kasahn. Did you follow through on my request while you were in Rog?" the crown prince asked Rheibas.

Request? Ahuzza barely refrained from snorting. The crown prince had never been given to making requests.

The chief minister dipped his head. "I did, Your Highness. One of my people has prepared a detailed assessment of the Rogandan army, as well as estimates of the armies of other kingdoms in the region. The Rogandans have a large force. The Arvenian army is smaller, although more effective by all accounts. The Varasan and Castelan armies are smaller again, but not to be entirely discounted."

"How do they compare with our armies?"

"Our armies are much larger. And more practiced at fighting, thanks to the continuing unrest on some of our islands."

The crown prince scowled.

It appeared that the Grand Vizier was delivering an indirect reminder to the arrogant young prince that his position was not entirely secure. The unrest on Ahr-kasahn, clearly known to the prince, also provided a timely reminder that the chief minister was the empire's primary safeguard against rebellion.

The Grand Vizier did not dwell on these topics. "Transporting our armies to Rogand would present the greatest challenge," he continued.

"Could their navies prevent it?"

Rheibas shrugged. "Even combined, they would not compare with our own fleet, Your Highness. Nevertheless, nothing can be taken for granted where tide and weather are concerned."

Ahreitas grunted. "These kingdoms would be weaker if driven apart," he said. "That outcome should be easy to achieve given their history."

Before the prince could speak again, the chief minister changed the subject. "Important as these issues might be, Your Highness," he said, "I am sorry to report that I bear news of much greater import."

"Has my sister gotten herself into trouble on her little adventure?" the prince asked dryly.

Rheibas bowed his head. "The news does indeed concern your sister, Your Highness. On the way to Rog our ship was intercepted by Rogandan sailors—or pirates if the Rogandan king is to be believed—and the princess was kidnapped. There was nothing our men could do to prevent it."

The crown prince snorted. "I'm not asking for whatever story you've concocted for my father," he scoffed. "I want the truth!"

The chief minister's brows bristled indignantly. "How could you imagine I would deceive you about such an important matter?" he asked stiffly.

The prince continued to glower at the official, but he subsided. "So what have you done about it?" he demanded.

"There was little we could do, either at the time or later," the Grand Vizier replied.

"How could you have allowed such a situation to arise in the first place?" demanded the prince.

"Perhaps Your Highness has forgotten who supported the princess when she pleaded with your father for permission to go," Rheibas observed coolly.

The prince glared back at him but didn't reply.

After a loaded silence, the chief minister added, "I am hopeful that our representatives in Rog will soon receive a ransom demand."

The crown prince eyed him darkly for a long moment. "Go to the palace at once!" he commanded irritably. "My father will be impatient for your report."

His Imperial Majesty the Emperor Hourahn II of Ahr sat in state in the splendor of his royal palace, surrounded by guards clad in imperial finery and waited on by an army of servants. He watched without expression as his Grand Vizier approached the throne and bowed low in homage. Bisri Ahuzza followed close behind.

Turning to his servants, the emperor flicked a finger. "Leave us," he commanded. He glanced at Ahuzza. "My envoy will remain."

All of the servants scurried away, accompanied by most of the guards. A dozen guards remained, positioned watchfully just out of earshot.

"I have been made aware of your intervention on Ahr-kasahn, Chief Minister Rheibas. Once more you have demonstrated your value to me and to the empire."

The Grand Vizier bowed humbly.

"I am, however, much more interested in the outcome of your mission to Rog," he continued, a troubled look on his face. "I am not referring to trading rights. I have heard that my daughter did not return with you. Where is she?"

A grave expression covered the face of Rheibas. "I bring terrible news, Your Imperial Majesty. The princess has been kidnapped. Our vessel was boarded before we reached Rog, by men from a ship bearing the Rogandan flag. The foreigners claimed their role was to intercept smugglers. After removing anything of value, they took the princess by force. They came with such overwhelming numbers that our sailors were unable to prevent them."

The emperor rose from his throne, pacing restlessly around it. "You did not sail alone!" he exclaimed. "Why did the other ships in your squadron not support you?"

"Our ships became separated in a storm," Rheibas told him. "We were boarded at a time when we were entirely without support."

"Have you confronted the Rogandan king?"

"I have, Your Majesty. He denies all responsibility. He asserted that the princess must have been taken by pirates."

"What has been done to recover her?"

"I made it clear to the Rogandans that they risked the fierce wrath of the emperor of Ahr if they failed to secure her. I propose that we return immediately with a fleet of our deep sea ships."

The emperor waved a hand dismissively. "You know as well as I do that any such operation would take many weeks to prepare."

"Then I implore you to send me back with as many ships as can be made available at short notice."

"For what purpose?" demanded the emperor.

"To continue to apply pressure on the Rogandans and their allies, Your Majesty. If there is a delay in our response, or if someone junior is sent to act on your behalf, it might send the wrong message."

"You will return at once," the emperor told him. "Find yourself a vessel. A small squadron of three ships will accompany you to provide protection. This will not be a show of force. Our initial negotiating position will emphasize our desire to resolve the matter peacefully. To demonstrate our intent, you will lead the negotiations, and another will command the squadron."

He glanced at Ahuzza. "The other commander can be Bisri Ahuzza."

He returned his attention to the Grand Vizier. "I have no need to explain to you the importance I place on securing my daughter's safe return, Chief Minister Rheibas. I am placing great faith in you. You have repeatedly demonstrated your formidable skills as a negotiator. When you arrive in Rog, you will inform the Rogandans that I am granting them one month to retrieve the princess. In the meantime, you do not have my permission to declare war or to make threats on my behalf. I will not enter into hostilities against a distant kingdom without clear evidence of their complicity. I expect a comprehensive report from you before the month comes to an end. Do you understand?"

Rheibas nodded, bowing deeply. "Yes, Your Imperial Majesty."

"I wish to speak with the captain of the vessel that took you to Rog," the emperor informed him. "Have him sent to me at once."

A grim look came to the face of Rheibas. "I regret to say that Captain Gharpin is not in Kat Ahket," he replied. "Knowing him to be effective and reliable, I transferred to another ship and sent him back to Rog to continue the search for the princess. I hope I did not err, Your Majesty," he concluded.

The emperor paused before responding with a tight nod to indicate his acceptance of his chief minister's action.

"You are dismissed," the emperor told them. "I will look forward to a rapid and successful outcome from your efforts."

Ahuzza left with the chief minister after both of them had bowed respectfully.

The emperor had not given the chief minister an entirely free hand—he clearly intended Ahuzza to remain independent. But the chief minister would undoubtedly find a way to achieve his purposes. He always did.

16

Kamash and the princess had been summoned to another section of King Krasmir's palace for a meeting. After being offered food and drink, they were requested to wait until someone came for them.

They had been waiting for a couple of hours when a tall and somewhat awkward looking man approached them. To Kamash's eye he had the refined air of a country nobleman, although a pair of sharp eyes peered out from beneath his rampant eyebrows.

"My name is Lord Boedwyk." The man grinned broadly as he said it, as though he had just made a joke.

Ignoring his unusual manner, Kamash returned a bow.

"Please come with me," the nobleman continued, setting off without waiting to see if anyone was following him.

Kamash accompanied him into a large meeting room, Princess Neira walking stiffly at his side with her nose in the air. At least thirty people had gathered there. Every eye turned in their direction.

King Krasmir stood to greet them. "I welcome Princess Neira and her spokesperson, Kamash, to this gathering." He addressed the princess directly. "We are looking forward to discussing recent events with you and exploring possible ways to proceed."

The king briefly introduced the others in the room. Kamash had always had an ability to remember names, and he made special note of the most important of the attendees.

A quick glance at Neira told Kamash that she was leaving it to him to respond. He bowed low. “On behalf of Princess Neira of the Empire of Ahr, I thank you for your welcome, King Krasmir, and for your hospitality at Rog.” He bowed to the rest of the room. “King Delmar, King Rupert, other honored guests.”

It was immediately obvious that this meeting was already in progress. The subtle signs told Kamash that the others present in the room had been there for some time. King Krasmir and his guests had probably already drawn conclusions based on the information available to them. It remained to see if they were willing to talk openly about that information and the positions they had reached.

“We are eager to understand the purpose of your visit to Rogand, Princess Neira,” King Krasmir began.

Kamash decided to be direct. “Before the princess addresses such questions, she has a question of her own. Having endured a great deal in recent weeks, she would be grateful to hear news of the ship that carried her to this part of the world.”

The Rogandan monarch briefly exchanged glances with his Varasan and Castelan counterparts before responding. “The ship visited Rog,” King Krasmir confirmed.

“And did they mention the princess?” Kamash asked.

“They told us that their ship had been attacked at sea and the princess abducted. They said that this act of piracy brought shame upon the empire. They promised to return with an army to search Rogand and all the nearby kingdoms for the princess, with or without our support.”

“Who told you these lies?” demanded the princess, outrage in her voice.

“The Grand Vizier,” King Krasmir replied.

The face of the princess went bright red with anger, then slowly paled with shock. She muttered under her breath in her own language.

"What are you saying?" whispered Kamash.

If she heard his question she gave no sign of it. Her face had set hard like granite.

A wave of frustration washed over the old man. How could he help her if she closed herself off to him?

"The Grand Vizier has invented an excuse to invade. Is he likely to follow through with it?" asked King Krasmir.

The princess offered no response.

The king tried again. "Do you understand the purpose of this deception by the Grand Vizier?"

Still she remained silent.

A Rogandan nobleman broke the silence. "The invasion threat is empty," he said dismissively. "Rogand is too far away. The Empire of Ahr has no ships suitable for transporting soldiers over open seas."

King Krasmir glared at the speaker.

The princess erupted.

"I have been to Varacellan as well as to Rog," she spat. "The fishing villages of Ahr-chitani outshine your pitiful little harbors. You are so proud of your ships—all of them pale beside the glory of the emperor's navy. You try to tell yourself that the emperor has no ships capable of carrying soldiers across open seas. You are an ignorant fool! The Grand Vizier has spent the past few years building just such a fleet at Kat Ahket."

The wide-eyed looks on the faces of many of the attendees told Kamash that the princess had just provided a crucial piece of missing information.

Glancing back at the princess, Kamash saw her face flush with anger as she realized that she had been goaded into saying much more than she intended. She clamped her mouth tightly shut.

The old man sighed. Each party had revealed a single piece of valuable information, but no one appeared willing to say more. He had hoped for a meeting of minds, yet the conference already seemed bogged down.

An Arvenian noblewoman, introduced by King Krasmir as Lady Torbury, addressed herself to Kamash. "Does the princess wish to return to her own country? Or would she prefer to remain in Rogand under King Krasmir's protection?"

It was an important question, one for which he had no answer. He turned to Neira. She stared back at him with tears in her eyes. "There is no one I can trust," she whispered. "No one but you, old man."

For a moment his heart melted. Then he reminded himself that the princess was capable of shameless manipulation if she thought it suited her purposes.

He tried to make sense of it all. Kamash had no doubt that the Grand Vizier's betrayal had shaken the princess to the core. In spite of her bluster in defense of the honor of the empire, she must surely be aware that she had become little more than a puppet in a bold power play. Her exalted status as daughter of the emperor had not protected her. Whatever games she might be playing at that moment with Kamash, the simple truth was that Neira was a vulnerable young woman adrift in a dangerous world.

"What *do* you want, Princess?" he whispered back.

Apparently coming to a decision, she swallowed once then turned to King Krasmir.

"It seems I must continue to intrude upon your hospitality, Your Majesty, at least for the moment," she managed.

The king's face was impassive. "If your people return, Your Highness, do you wish to be reunited with them?"

She paused for a long moment. Then she shook her head. Her face appeared stricken, and her lower lip trembled. Kamash was certain she was not faking her reaction this time.

King Krasmir nodded to Lord Boedwyk, and the nobleman led Kamash and the princess from the room.

THE PRINCESS HAD BARELY LEFT before animated conversation broke out across the chamber. Everyone seemed to be talking at once.

Will ignored it, his mind working on the problem before them. If the princess had spoken the truth, the empire had the means to invade Rogand. The reason for doing so remained obscure, although Lord Boedwyk had accurately outlined a number of possibilities. Was it the will of the emperor, or did it have more to do with intrigues fomented by the Grand Vizier? Was the crown prince in any way involved? The princess had suggested that the Grand Vizier had been building a fleet. Why?

Will wondered how the Ahran motivation could be exposed without traveling to Kat Ahket. And even if they did that, understanding the reasons might not make any difference. If the motivation was greed, what could they do about it?

Perhaps all that mattered was to vigorously prepare their defenses.

"We will meet again tomorrow," King Krasmir told the gathering. "In the meantime, do not speak of these matters to anyone. We cannot afford to allow our security to be compromised. You may consider yourselves dismissed."

As the attendees rose and left the building, Will's mind returned to the princess. She undoubtedly could have said much more than she did.

He needed to find a way to get her in front of Thomas.

King Krasmir was one of the last to leave the meeting chamber, and Will waited outside for him to emerge.

The king soon appeared, accompanied by several of his nobles.

"Your Majesty," said Will with a bow. "Could I have a word?"

King Krasmir hesitated for a moment, then he nodded. "Of course, Lord Torbury." He turned to his nobles. "Would you excuse me?"

The men bowed and moved out of earshot.

"Some of my nobles find it difficult to adjust to change," the king began. "Please pay no mind to their aloofness."

Will waved a hand unconcernedly. "I understand their hesitancy, Your Majesty," he said. "But that was not what I wanted to speak to you about. I have a request. Would it be possible for me to interview the princess? There are some questions I would like to put to her."

The king looked uncertain. After a significant pause he nodded reluctantly. “I suppose I could arrange for that.” He lowered his voice a little. “I need to avoid a situation where every noble thinks they should be afforded the same opportunity,” he said frankly. “But I would like to briefly meet with the princess myself, and I suppose I could include you in that meeting. I will need you to be discreet.”

It was immediately obvious to Will that asking permission for Thomas to join the conversation would be inappropriate.

Will was grateful to the king for his consideration. Presented with a difficult choice, the king had been willing to place his request above the need to indulge his own nobles. However Will had no pressing reason to meet with the princess if Thomas was to be excluded.

“I have no desire to place you in a delicate position, Your Majesty,” said Will with a bow. “Please ignore my request. My questions can wait until the princess next meets with the nobles.”

King Krasmir considered him for a moment before nodding his acceptance and rejoining his nobles. He was clearly relieved.

Concocting a reason to include Thomas in a meeting with the princess was clearly not going to be easy. Nevertheless, Thomas only needed a glimpse. An opportunity would surely arise before long.

THE NEXT MORNING Thomas was approached by Will. A serious look covered the commander’s scarred face.

“Amyra and I will probably be spending most of the day in meetings with the nobles, Thomas,” said Will. “Again.” His expression suggested that he expected the benefit to be questionable.

“I’ve had no success at all arranging for you to meet with the princess,” Will continued, his brows furrowed. “The princess is not always included in the meetings though. See if you can wander around where the meetings are held. The guards will prevent you from getting too close, but you might still manage to catch a glimpse of her at some point.”

The prospect of poking around where he knew he wasn’t wanted held no appeal to Thomas, but he agreed to do it. He couldn't see that he had any choice.

There was unlikely to be any real risk to him provided he kept a close eye on the people around him. If one of the guards decided he was a threat, he would become aware of it immediately—the stone would leave him in no doubt about their thoughts and intentions.

Leaving it until the meeting was well underway, Thomas set off for the meeting site. He arrived in the general area to find a large contingent of guards controlling access to the meeting rooms.

He was by no means the only curious bystander. Located as they were inside the palace grounds, for the most part people with time on their hands were probably spouses and dependents of the nobles attending the meeting. Perhaps that explained why the soldiers were making no attempt to disperse onlookers as long as they stayed well out of the way.

While waiting for something to happen, Thomas positioned himself far enough from others to avoid attention, but near enough to overhear their conversation. Having worked at his Rogandan for years with the support of Haldek, he had sufficient mastery of the language to understand what was being said around him.

"This foreign princess wanders about as if she owns the place," grumbled one woman.

"And I know for a fact that she's being helped by an old man who's Rogandan!" added another. "He's supposedly her spokesperson. What's a Rogandan doing helping a foreigner?"

"The king should have him arrested!" protested the first woman.

Abruptly all conversation ceased, a buzz going up as a few people emerged from the meeting rooms.

"It's the princess! a voice exclaimed. "And her Rogandan lackey!"

Thomas stood on tiptoes and peered forward to catch a glimpse.

In little more than a moment the figures had disappeared from sight, and the conversation around Thomas moved on to other topics.

He remained unmoving, his mouth hanging open stupidly. It had taken only a brief glimpse to leave him stunned speechless.

17

"I'm bored!" exclaimed Ethen, pushing himself away from the window. He gazed at Andy and Delia. "Let's go!" he said.

Brother Ander, the only other occupant of the room, couldn't resist a grin. If he knew anything about Ethen, he wouldn't be satisfied until he'd gotten into some kind of trouble.

At five years of age, Ethen might have been two years younger than Andy, but he was a natural leader like his father, Lord Torbury. Delia, also aged five, followed Ethen around like his shadow.

When Ethen wandered out of the room, soon trailed by both Delia and Andy, Brother Ander decided he'd better go with them. Someone needed to keep an eye on them.

Most of the Arvenian adults as well as the five children had been accommodated in an isolated wing of the royal palace at Rog. Will and Amyra were attending the conference with Count Ranauld, and Thomas and Elena had agreed to take responsibility for Millie and Ethen as well as their own three children, Tamara, Andy, and Delia. Thomas was temporarily absent on an errand for Will, but Elena had as much help as she needed from the other adults.

The building provided some space for the children to run around, but all of them were used to spending time outdoors riding horses and throwing themselves energetically into a range of other physical activities. Confining five children in a lifeless building in a foreign city for an entire day was beginning to wear down the patience of everyone.

Most of the adults had sequestered themselves in a large room that boasted several comfortable armchairs. More than once a couple of children had run into the room squealing loudly; on the most recent occasion they had been promptly sent out and told to play elsewhere.

Ethen wandered into the room currently occupied by his older sister, Millie, and Tamara, the oldest of Thomas and Elena's children. Brother Ander trailed in behind them.

At seven, Millie was three years younger than Tamara, but they seemed to enjoy each other's company. Each of them was the oldest child in their respective families, and the monk guessed that they were enjoying the break from their energetic younger siblings.

"Are you two *still* prattling away in Rogandan?" demanded Andy.

No reply was forthcoming.

"I know why you want to learn!" he told Tamara. "Mother and Father talk in Rogandan when they don't want us to understand what they're saying. You just want to listen in on their secrets!"

"And you just want to get me into trouble!" Tammi retorted. "Tattletale!"

Brother Ander stepped in before it came to blows. "Come along, Andy. You, too, Ethen," he said with a smile. "Let's leave the girls in peace. I'm sure we can find something more interesting to do."

As they were leaving, Andy mumbled "Tattletale yourself!" in the direction of Tammi.

She responded by poking out her tongue.

"Let's explore the upper story of the building," suggested the monk.

He led them onto a staircase that wound its way upward until it emptied into a narrow passage covered with worn out carpet. Choosing a direction at random, he headed down the passageway, the three children tagging along behind enthusiastically.

Coming to a closed door halfway along the passage, he tried the handle. The room was unlocked, and the three of them filed in.

The room was empty apart from two old couches positioned opposite each other. The children launched themselves energetically onto the couches, raising clouds of dust. Brother Ander headed for the passageway in search of clear air.

Ethen's voice pulled him up short. "What's *he* doing down there?"

The monk and both of the other children joined Ethen at the window, peering down to the ground below. Brother Ander realized that they were positioned almost directly above the large room where the other adults were sitting. A man, clad entirely in black, stood outside the building leaning on the wall beside one of the windows. He was clearly trying to listen in on their conversation. Royal guards had been positioned at the entrance to the building, and some were stationed at various points around the building as well. None appeared to be located anywhere nearby.

"Let's find out what he's up to!" cried Ethen, running from the room.

"Wait!" called the monk. He was too late. All three children were racing down the staircase before he could stop them.

Brother Ander reached the bottom of the staircase in time to see the last of the children disappearing outside. "Stop!" he called uselessly.

A couple of doors led outside the building. They were all locked, preventing access from outside. But the key was still sitting in the lock of at least one of the doors, and it was that door that the children had used.

Hurrying outside, he saw the children disappear around a corner of the building. A cry of alarm caused him to quicken his pace. He rounded the corner to see Ethen writhing in the grip of the man clad in black. When the huge monk swung into view, the dark figure hefted Ethen into his arms and bolted for a hedge that stood adjacent to the building.

"Go back inside and get your parents," yelled the monk to the other children.

They stood there wide-eyed, rooted to the ground. They needed to move, but he didn't have time to wait for them to do it. Sprinting for the hedge, he set off after the man who had dared to abduct the son of Lord Torbury.

Reaching the hedge, Brother Ander plunged in and forced his way through. He emerged to find two black clad men before him. He could see no sign of Ethen, until alerted by a faint cry, he caught a glimpse of him being hurried away in the grip of another man, presumably the one who had taken him.

The men waiting by the hedge both pulled knives and lunged for the monk. He swayed easily aside, avoiding their thrusts without difficulty.

Years had passed since the monk had last resorted to violence. Renouncing it was no longer a decision he questioned, nor did he doubt his ability to avoid it. Nevertheless, he had no intention of standing by while the boy was abducted. When one of the men thrust his knife again, Brother Ander grabbed his hand and squeezed, at the same time swinging his attacker around to face his companion. The second man, failing to adjust his strike quickly enough, plunged his knife deep into the side of the first attacker, who cried out in pain. The monk thrust the limp form of the injured man onto the other attacker, bringing them both to the ground with the injured man on top. The second man struggled to free himself, pinned down by the dead weight of his friend.

Ignoring the men he had forced to the ground, Brother Ander raced after the one escaping with Ethen.

The man disappeared into a stand of pines, and the monk heard the nickering of horses as he approached the trees. Catching a glimpse of his quarry ahead, he put on an extra spurt.

He emerged into a small clearing to see the man mounting a horse, still grasping hold of the struggling child. As he closed on them, a heavy blow struck him on the back of his head. He crumpled to the ground, everything around him going dark.

An anxious servant met Will as he was emerging from the conference. The man wore the livery of the king. "Could you please come with me, My Lord?" he asked.

Shooting a glance at his wife, Will found that she had also been approached by another servant.

More curious than alarmed, Will followed the servants with Amyra at his side into a small reception room in another wing of the building.

"Please wait here," they were told. "King Krasmir will join you shortly."

King Krasmir was ushered into a room to find the head of palace security waiting for him. The man appeared pale and drawn.

"There has been an incident, Your Majesty. The young son of Lord and Lady Torbury has been abducted."

"What?!" Waves of anger and distress washed over the king. "How is that possible? Our foreign guests were supposed to be well guarded at all times!"

The security chief hung his head.

"What have you learned?" demanded the king.

"The abduction was witnessed only by two of the other children. They looked out of an upstairs window and saw a man dressed in black. He appeared to be snooping outside a window of the room occupied by the Arvenian adults. The children ran outside. The man grabbed the five-year-old boy and ran off with him."

The king turned to his servants. "Round up my nobles. Immediately! I will speak with them shortly. And find the head of my agents. I will consult with him after the nobles."

The men hurried away to do his bidding.

He turned back to his security chief. "Go on," he said grimly.

"The children were followed outside by the monk who came with them from Arvenon. He told them to get their parents, then disappeared through the hedge near the building in pursuit of the abductor."

"Have you searched for the boy and the monk?"

"Yes, Your Majesty. We have found no sign of either of them, or of the abductor. The ground on the far side of the hedge was smeared with blood, and the imprints of several feet were visible. There were no bodies, and we have no way of knowing whose blood it might have been. It's possible that the monk was attacked when he reached the other side of the hedge. We also found hoof prints in the stand of trees beyond the hedge. Two or possibly three horses had been there. We have trackers trying to discover where they went."

"The chances of finding them are slim," growled the king. "Where are the other Arvenians now?"

"They have been moved to a more secure location. They are under heavy guard."

"Are Lord Torbury and his wife aware of this?"

"No, Your Majesty. They have been brought to a meeting room near here. They were told that you would meet with them soon."

A cold fury was building inside the king. "I want a full report within the hour," he barked. "I want to know how this happened and who is responsible. No effort is to be spared. Do you understand?"

The man hurried out of the room.

Another servant appeared in the doorway. "Your nobles have been assembled, Your Majesty. A few had already left, but most of them are waiting for you."

"Take me to them at once!" ordered the king.

He was led back to the room where the conference had been held. Most of the nobles were waiting for him. At the king's first glance, none of the faces revealed anything other than curiosity.

The king came immediately to the point. "The five-year-old son of Lord Torbury of Arvenon has been abducted!" he snarled.

Once more he took the opportunity to study their faces. He was not able to detect anything other than surprise and shock.

"That is indeed regrettable, Your Majesty," one of the nobles offered dryly. "It is surprising that he took the risk of bringing his children here in the first place."

"Especially given his past history," another noble added with a sage nod.

"All of you are fools!" hissed the king. "Don't you understand what this means? The boy was abducted from *my palace*. Under our very noses. Get your minds off the past and think about the future! We face the greatest threat our kingdom has ever seen. In our hour of need the king of Arvenon—the same man my predecessor tried to assassinate!—has sent us his best leader, with instructions to help us in any way he can. This incident threatens to tear our fragile alliance apart."

He stared them down. "There is no greater strategist alive than Lord Torbury. Maybe there never has been. Rogand has far more to lose than Torbury if his child is not found soon, and found unharmed!"

No one said a word.

His eyes flashed as he surveyed the nobility before him. "All of you have agents and informants. Forget whatever little schemes you have them working on. Get them onto this, and do it now!"

He glared at them coldly. "One more thing. If I should find that any of you have been involved in any way in this little conspiracy, then Malzakh have pity on you!"

Krasmir's nobles had known from the beginning that their monarch had teeth. He had chosen this moment to bare them.

They stared back at him wide-eyed.

"Get out of here!" roared the king. "Now!"

They scurried away like frightened rabbits.

WILL and Amyra stood and bowed as King Krasmir entered the room.

He faced them grimly. "There is no easy way to convey this," he said. "I am very sorry to tell you that your son Ethen has been abducted."

A cry of anguish escaped from Amyra. Will went cold inside.

Somehow Will managed to hold down his growing agitation as the king outlined what was known of the circumstances.

When the king paused, he took a slow breath to calm himself. "Who has done this?" he demanded.

"I cannot say with any certainty, Lord Torbury. My best agents are already working on it. I have also recalled the nobles who attended our conference and insisted that they use their own networks to discover whatever they can."

"Do you think any of them might be responsible?" Will managed to push the words through clenched jaws.

"It is possible," acknowledged the king. "I don't think it's likely though."

"Who else?" Will managed.

"Ahran agents perhaps?" The king shrugged. "I am hoping that our inquiries will provide some answers soon."

King Krasmir passed a hand across his face. "I can well understand how distressed and angry you must be feeling. Let me assure you that no effort will be spared to find your son."

"Thank you, Your Majesty," said Amyra with a small bow. Then her composure crumbled, and she turned away, sobbing quietly.

The king inclined his head. "I will not intrude on you further. I will assign one of my most senior aides to you. You will have direct access to me whenever you request it."

Will dimly heard him speaking to one of the royal servants. "Leave them in peace for as long as they need it. Then take them to their daughter."

With that the king was gone.

Will moved to Amyra and put a comforting arm around her shoulder.

She stood stiffly, not returning his embrace. "Why did you bring us here?" she moaned.

VOLUME 2—THE YEARNING FOR VITALITY

18

Brother Ander woke to a pounding headache. Everything was black when he opened his eyes, and he wondered if he had lost his vision. He eventually decided that it was nighttime, or that he was in a dark room.

A small shuffling noise followed by a sob sounded beside him, and it all came back in a rush.

"Ethen? Is that you?" he asked.

The only reply was another sob, louder this time.

The monk pushed himself painfully up into a sitting position. His eyes were slowly adjusting to the dark, and he guessed that he was located in a cellar or something similar. A tiny amount of light was leaking through what appeared to be the cellar door.

His first concern was for the five-year-old beside him in the dark.

"Are you injured, Ethen?" After a pause, he added gently, "I need to hear your voice. If you're shaking your head I can't see it." He waited a moment longer before repeating, "Are you hurt in any way?"

The boy's breath hitched a couple of times, but he finally managed, "No."

"How long have we been here?" Brother Ander asked. Realizing that the question was probably too hard to answer, he decided on a different approach. "Have you been given any food or water?"

"Just a bit of water."

"More than once?"

"No."

So he probably hadn't been unconscious for long.

Before he could decide what to say next, the door opened abruptly.

Ethen scurried closer, and the monk responded by wrapping an arm around him protectively.

Brother Ander squinted in the sudden light.

Two men appeared in the doorway. Both of them wore hoods, and Brother Ander could see nothing of their faces. Having apparently decided that the monk was no threat, both men clambered down the few wooden steps that led into the room, each of them flourishing a naked sword in one hand.

One of the men held up a candle, and they stood silently for a moment, peering down at the monk and the boy. Brother Ander saw that the other man was grasping a small sack. The sack was tossed onto the floor, then both men backed out of the room cautiously, pulling the door shut behind them.

Brother Ander had stolen a brief glance at Ethen while the room was still lit. The boy's face was tear-stained and grubby, but he seemed uninjured. Their prison appeared to be a wine cellar, empty apart from a couple of old barrels lying on their sides. The cellar was large and the ceiling easily high enough for a tall man to stand upright without stooping.

As darkness descended, Brother Ander scurried across the floor and retrieved the sack. Groping inside as the light vanished, he removed what felt like a lump of bread and a water skin.

"They've left us some bread and something to drink, Ethen," he said softly, settling himself beside the boy. After quietly blessing the provisions, he pulled off a lump of bread and placed it into Ethen's hand. Hearing sounds of munching, he nodded with satisfaction.

The monk unstopped the skin and tasted its contents. It was

indeed filled with water, and he passed it to the boy the moment the sound of eating ceased. Then he handed over another chunk of bread.

When Ethen had eaten his fill, he leaned in to the monk, shivering slightly. Settling the little head gently onto his own broad shoulder, Brother Ander rested back against the cold wall and closed his eyes.

Ethen's breathing gradually became calm and regular. Concluding that he had fallen asleep, Brother Ander's mind turned to other things.

The monk smiled mirthlessly. The two men who entered the room had no idea of his past reputation, that much was obvious. He could easily have taken them out, with or without their swords. But he was no longer Ander the soldier. He had learned there were different ways to bring about change.

Bowing his head, he started to pray.

The hours passed slowly. When Ethen woke, he began shivering again. He leaned in close against the big monk, apparently needing the comfort of his protective presence.

At some point the door opened long enough for another water skin to be tossed into the room.

The monk had been waiting for just such an opportunity. "You can't keep a young boy in the dark for hours on end!" he called out in Rogandan as the door was closing.

No immediate response was offered, but Brother Ander felt hopeful anyway. These men were almost certainly not planning to kill Ethen. If that had been their intention they would have done so already. Expecting a child to remain placid while confined in a small space was one thing, but keeping that space permanently dark was another matter entirely. If the men had any sense they would quickly acknowledge that.

No more than an hour passed before a scraping noise could be heard outside. Daylight appeared suddenly in one section of the room near the ceiling. It quickly became obvious that the cellar was largely below ground, with a narrow strip of window looking onto the outside world above. Some object had been removed to admit the light. The window had little depth—certainly not enough to allow even a small child to escape through it—although it was quite broad.

The window must have faced west, because through it the setting sun was visible just above the horizon. After so many hours in unnatural darkness, the sunset was achingly beautiful. The monk and the boy sat together staring out the window, transfixed by the grandeur of the passing of another day. Brother Ander could not shake off the conviction that the extravagant display had been arranged just for the benefit of the two of them.

With the sun sinking low and the light beginning to fade, Ethen turned to Brother Ander. "I miss Mother and Father and Millie. Will I see them soon?" he asked, his lower lip trembling.

"I can't say when you will get to see them again," the monk answered truthfully. "But I know that your parents will not stop searching until they find you."

"ARE YOU READY, THOMAS?"

Thomas dragged open his eyes and peered blearily up at Will. "Of course. I was just having a quick nap, but I'm awake now."

Will grunted and headed for the door.

Thomas pulled himself into a sitting position and pulled on his boots. Clambering out of his bed, he hurried after the disappearing figure of his friend.

His mind was churning with the revelations of the stone when the princess and her spokesperson emerged from the meeting. He had said nothing to Will. The drama of the abduction and the search for Ethen had pushed everything else into the background. Thomas had concluded that Will did not need another distraction at that moment.

He had known Will for a long time, and he had never seen him so driven, so grim. The hunt for Ethen had become a consuming fire. Will barely ate, he rarely slept—the only thing he wanted to do was continue the search.

From the beginning Thomas had become a necessary accomplice. He was needed because of the Stone of Knowing. Normal living soon degenerated into an endless cycle of meeting people, sorting through the confusion of their thoughts and memories, and moving on.

It hadn't taken even a day before Thomas wearied of it. His mind was soon spinning, leaving him overwhelmed.

Thomas hadn't used the stone on Will, but he sensed that his friend was struggling as never before with the desire to take possession of it. He had resisted making any request to borrow the stone, but the pressure must have been building.

Thomas hadn't waited for the issue to come to a head. He instead turned to Elena. In the end, they established a workable arrangement. Thomas went out with Will. When they returned he gave the stone to Elena. Taking Rufe along for protection, Elena went with Amyra while Thomas and Will tried to get some sleep.

Rufe knew about the stone now. Thomas wasn't sure how it had happened, but everything felt like a blur anyway. The burly guardsman hadn't seemed surprised. He gave Thomas the impression he'd long since guessed that something very unusual was going on.

Thomas pushed it from his mind. There were other things he needed to think about.

Finally catching up with his friend, he hurried along at his side.

"What can we say with any certainty?" demanded Will, his jaw set firm in stubborn determination.

"That there's no end to the intrigue in this place," Thomas replied wearily. Then he sighed. "We know that King Krasmir has a lot of spies. That's no surprise. We also know that the High Priest has spies, and the Archprimus does as well. Somehow I wasn't expecting that."

Will's brows furrowed. "And none of them know anything about the abduction."

Thomas shook his head. "Not anyone we've seen so far. It's hard to imagine that a lot of people would know about it though. If it was common knowledge they'd never keep it quiet."

"There's a missing piece to this puzzle," Will growled. "Where are the Ahran agents?"

"So far we've had no more than that single fleeting glimpse," agreed Thomas. "In that tavern. We must have managed to spook him."

"That's where we're headed," Will told him grimly. "If we can't find him in the tavern, we'll start searching the vicinity."

Thomas suppressed a sigh. It promised to be a long night.

KING KRASMIR SAT opposite the High Priest. It was the first time he had entered the Temple of the Dark Gods at Rog on his own, and he was finding everything about the place extremely distasteful. He had no choice though. There was no other way to meet with the High Priest.

The wizened figure peered back at him for a moment before dipping his head. "You are welcome in this holy place, Sire," he said.

"Thank you for seeing me, Your Eminence," the king replied.

Had Krasmir ever seen anyone so ancient? If he had, he couldn't remember it. Life seemed to somehow cling to the old man in defiance of his age.

He pulled his mind back to the reason for his visit. "I need your help," he said frankly.

One of the High Priest's eyebrows quirked upward. He offered no other response.

"There has been an abduction—the son of a visiting nobleman from Arvenon. The matter is distressing to the family. And the timing could not be worse."

A long silence followed.

"What do you wish for me to do?" the Superior finally asked, his face unexpressive.

"You have your sources of information," said the king.

The eyebrow went up again.

Krasmir shrugged. "Of late my agents have been more active than usual. As a result, very little is hidden from me." After a pause he added, "Your Archprimus also seems to have a network. His reach might not be quite as extensive as your own, but his agents are unusually energetic."

The other eyebrow went up as well.

After a long silence the king sighed. "I'm sure I have no need to make you aware of the threat posed by the Ahrans. We don't need distractions right now, and we certainly cannot afford a quarrel with Arvenon and its allies."

Had the High Priest's eyes narrowed momentarily when the king mentioned the Ahran threat? Did the priests have reasons of their own for mistrusting the foreigners?

With still no response forthcoming, Krasmir decided to be direct. "Did your people take the boy?" he asked bluntly.

The reply was immediate and unambiguous. "They did not."

"And the Archprimus?" asked the king. "What about his people?"

The High Priest's eyes narrowed, but he did not immediately reply.

Did the lack of response mean he didn't know? Or did it mean he knew but didn't want to say? Krasmir sat patiently, determined to wait for as long as it took.

"I will look into it, Sire," the High Priest finally offered.

So he didn't know.

"Thank you, Your Eminence. I will await your report with great interest."

Getting to his feet, the king offered a shallow bow before following a junior priest out of the building and back to the gates.

It wasn't until the temple grounds lay far behind him that Krasmir was able to release the tension that had gripped him during his visit to the High Priest.

Goultzar shuffled into the High Priest's familiar little room and settled himself onto the low stool opposite his master. The Superior sat silent and unmoving as always. Goultzar waited for him to speak. He didn't have long to wait.

"What do you know of the boy?" the old man asked, uncharacteristically coming straight to the point.

"What boy?" asked the Archprimus, raising his eyebrows inquiringly.

"Do not dissemble with me," growled his master.

"I have heard that a boy was abducted," Goultzar admitted. "I know nothing of it."

The Superior studied him silently through narrowed eyes for a very long time.

"You have built a network of agents that answer to you, and you alone. You have done so without my consent," the High Priest finally said. "Dismantle it. And do it immediately."

The Archprimus stared back at him open mouthed.

The old man's eyes bored into him. "You are dismissed," he said curtly.

Goultzar left the room in shock.

His mind raced, reviewing what his Superior had said and assessing the implications. Goultzar had originally built an informal network solely for practical reasons, intending only to streamline his administrative operations. Since it had no broader purpose, he had not bothered to inform the High Priest.

But over the years the network had changed as its scope gradually broadened. The changes had occurred so slowly they were almost imperceptible at first. Priests attending the shrines dotted throughout the countryside regularly fed back information. With much of it sensitive in nature, Goultzar had responded by branching off a special network. His intent had been pragmatic—he wanted to ensure that delicate information was handled appropriately and kept confidential.

Without conscious design, the network had slowly metamorphosed, developing an independent life of its own. Over time, the knowledge base grew to the point where Goultzar could have used it to manipulate people in high places if he chose to do so. Of course he never did.

By then he realized that in keeping the network secret from the

High Priest he had crossed a line. He didn't doubt that if his Superior learned of it, he would demand that Goultzar shut it down. But the network was surely essential, even if the High Priest was too set in his ways to see it. How could the Archprimus effectively promote devotion to the dark gods with no way to accurately assess the attitude of the people?

Rather than making his Superior aware of the network, he had instead become more careful and secretive than ever.

How had the High Priest become aware of his activities? Could one of his agents have betrayed him? He scowled in indignation. The agent would pay dearly if the Archprimus ever discovered who he was.

Clearly the time had come to clean house. He would dismiss his agents as instructed. Most of them. He would retain only his most trusted associates. And he would ensure that from now on they operated with extraordinary wariness.

WILL SAT with King Krasmir in a private reception room, restless and uncomfortable. He was trying his best to put a bold face on the situation.

"My wife and I were greatly heartened by the substantial reward you have offered for information about our son, Your Majesty," said Will.

"It was the least I could do under the circumstances," the king replied sympathetically.

"Have your nobles discovered anything useful?" Will asked hopefully.

"Nothing at all, I am afraid," the king told him. "I also heard from the High Priest just this morning. His contacts have led nowhere." He shook his head gloomily. "My own agents have been vigorously pursuing every possible lead as well. But I am sorry to say that in spite of our combined efforts, we have yet to learn anything definite about the whereabouts of your son."

Will worked hard at maintaining his composure. He wasn't surprised at the news, but he was still disappointed. He'd hoped irrationally that the king might have unearthed information of some kind.

The intelligence networks in Arvenon could not begin to compare with their Rogandan counterparts. The number and extent of the tendrils that crisscrossed Rogand was nothing short of astonishing. Apart from the huge web maintained by the Rogandan crown, the priests supported no fewer than two rival networks, and each of the nobles had access to extensive information sources of their own.

Thanks to Thomas and Elena and the stone, Will probably knew almost as much as King Krasmir about the various networks in the kingdom. Nevertheless, Will had no way of tapping into them. King Krasmir did, and his best efforts had yielded nothing.

"I am coming to the conclusion that the kidnapping was not carried out by any of the established groups," Will told him.

"You think the Ahrans are involved?" asked the king.

Will nodded. "How else could it have been kept so quiet?"

King Krasmir looked troubled. "If you are right—and I suspect you are—it will make our job that much more difficult. We know that Ahran agents are active in Rog, but they seem highly disciplined and probably few in number. We've been able to identify and bring in only two of them, and they've given away nothing of significance."

"All we can do is continue the search," Will concluded grimly.

"We have no intention of giving up," the king assured him. "We will continue the search until we find him."

19

Thomas and Elena sat waiting anxiously in a small room set aside for the use of the Arvenian delegation. Elena appeared calm and untroubled. It was more than Thomas could manage.

"Are you sure about the timing of this?" she asked.

"We need to take the chance while we can," he told her restlessly. "It's impossible to guess when we might get another opportunity."

After a further morning of intense activity, Will and Amyra had decided not to resume the search until the evening. Will needed time to map the sections of the city they had covered thus far. He was anxious not to inadvertently bypass areas, and he was equally determined not to cover the same ground unnecessarily.

The break left Thomas and Elena free for the first time in many days. Both of them were exhausted, and they knew they only had a few hours to themselves, but Thomas was determined to take action while he could.

The children had been left in the care of Rufe, Haldek, and Breysen. Elena in particular had felt very uncertain about both of them being absent at the same time. But the children weren't far away, and the other adults could call for Thomas and Elena if they were needed. And since the disappearance of Ethen and Brother Ander, the contingent of royal guards responsible for palace security had been strengthened significantly.

Elena was fully aware of what the stone had revealed to Thomas when he was watching for the princess and her advisor. He had not told anyone else. The frenetic search for Ethen was completely absorbing Will and Amyra, and Thomas had decided it was his responsibility to follow through on his discovery. Elena would provide all the support he might need.

The stone sat in its clasp beneath his clothing as usual, suspended on the chain around his neck. It was not in contact with his skin. It had already revealed the secrets of the person they were meeting with, and Thomas wanted this conversation to proceed as naturally as possible.

They had been waiting for about thirty minutes when a face appeared at the door. Thomas recognized him at once. It was the old man who had been acting as spokesperson for the princess.

Thomas leaped to his feet. "Thank you for agreeing to meet with us," he said eagerly. "My name is Thomas Stablehand, and this is my wife, Elena."

"My name is Kamash," the visitor returned. "I must congratulate you on your mastery of Rogandan. When I heard that you were Arvenian, I wasn't sure what to expect. And I do not speak your language."

"Neither of us speak your language well," Elena volunteered.

He turned to her. "I will say that your accent is more...pleasant to my ear than your husband's."

Thomas felt himself color slightly. Kamash apparently did not intend his comment to be taken too seriously though, because he winked at Thomas before grinning broadly at them both.

"I have been curious about your invitation," Kamash told them. "It wasn't clear from your message what had prompted it."

Thomas exchanged a glance with Elena. Then he took a deep breath.

"You seem to have been blessed with a long life, Kamash," he began tentatively.

Kamash stiffened immediately, a wary look on his face.

"We have no desire to expose your secret," Elena said gently.

The old man stared at her for a long moment. Then he slowly relaxed.

Thomas could only look on with awe. Was it Elena's words or the way she had said them?

He had wanted to communicate what they knew while reassuring their visitor about their intentions. Had it been left to him, they would have danced around the subject for some time. In Elena's gentle way she had come directly to the point, accomplishing the goal in one simple sentence.

"We heard that you left Rogand when King Ugar was on the throne," Elena told him.

"And we have heard tell of a small stone—dark gray in color and crescent shaped—that grants long life," Thomas added. "It has a name: the Stone of Vitality."

"So you put those two things together and decided that I had this stone?" he asked incredulously. "That's quite a leap."

"Perhaps it is," agreed Thomas. "But having convinced ourselves it was true, we couldn't carry on with life as if nothing remarkable had happened!"

He gazed frankly at the old man. "I cannot imagine what it's like to possess such a gift. In the wrong hands it could be terrifying. But it doesn't seem to have twisted you, Kamash."

Elena nodded. "We know that you took pity on the princess and risked your life to save her. Your compassion says a lot about you as a person."

"And it shows clearly that preserving your own life is not your overriding ambition," Thomas added.

An extended delay followed while the old man studied them both.

"I have had opportunity to observe people in many different circumstances over the years," Kamash finally told them. "I do not always read people perfectly, but I have learned to recognize ambition and greed well enough, even on brief acquaintance."

He fixed his gaze on Elena. "I see a rare goodness in you," he said. After continuing to stare at her for a few moments, he added, "The eyes do not lie." Then he turned to Thomas and studied him in turn. "You are more complicated, but I sense you are a person of integrity."

Kamash contemplated them both. "Surprising as it seems to me, I believe I can trust you."

He released a deep sigh. "I have been hiding for so long. It actually comes as something of a relief to have been discovered at last."

Neither Thomas nor Elena spoke, and after a while he continued.

"It all began many years ago. Ugar was king of Rogand, and his son Agon was a small child. I was a senior advisor to the king. It was a hazardous role. The king was both unpredictable and brutal—a dangerous combination."

The old man paused, remembering, gazing into nowhere. None of this was new to Thomas, but he sensed that Kamash needed to express it. And Thomas had been able to convey little more than a brief summary to Elena.

"We traveled south, near to the border with Lestanor. It wasn't the first such trip, and it wasn't the last. I didn't know it, but the king had somehow heard of the object you spoke about."

Kamash reached into his tunic and retrieved a small leather pouch hanging on a chain around his neck. He emptied its contents onto his hand.

Thomas and Elena both craned forward, an involuntary gasp escaping from Thomas. The Stone of Vitality lay exposed in Kamash's palm. Dull in color and trifling in size, it seemed unexceptional to the eye. Yet Thomas could still sense its power.

The old man's fist closed over the stone, and Thomas discovered that he had been holding his breath. He released the air slowly as Kamash returned the stone to its pouch and tucked it under his tunic again.

Sitting back once more, Thomas fixed his attention on Kamash's face.

"I learned later that Ugar had heard of strange reports from the border with Lestanor. Tales of men and women with remarkable lifespans. But never more than one person at a time. Rumor said that a unique talisman was responsible for their longevity. The possessor could expect to far outlast the tally of years allotted to other men and women. Ugar lusted after the talisman and was determined to acquire it. His agents haunted the region, searching out anyone who even appeared to be older than usual. As soon as they were ready to round them up, they called for Ugar to join them.

"I was included in the small company that traveled south with the king. When we arrived, every old man and woman was brought in to be examined. The soldiers were not gentle with them, and I was forced to intervene on more than one occasion. I made it my business to ensure that the captives were treated with respect. Many of the old folk were frail, and I also arranged for them to receive food and drink." He shook his head sadly.

"One night I was walking near the place where these unfortunate souls were imprisoned. One of them called softly to me. I went to him, and he gazed steadily into my eyes for a while before speaking. 'I have studied faces over many years, and I believe I can read them well. Your king is a cruel man who lusts after power,' he said bluntly. 'His ambitions will not be satisfied by attaining long life. He will only become more vicious.' He studied me again. 'You are a different kind of person.'

"He pressed something small into my hand. 'This stone will grant you good health and long life. Speak of it to no one! Your life will be short indeed if anyone else learns of it. Use its gift wisely.' Then he turned away to rejoin his companions, leaving me with the stone. He told me nothing of its origins or how he had come to be in possession of it."

"What became of him?" asked Thomas. He had seen the outline of the history clearly enough in Kamash's memory, but some details had escaped his attention.

"I don't know," Kamash replied regretfully. "I wanted to return the stone to him after the people had been questioned, but I wasn't confident I would recognize him again. I hadn't been able to see his features clearly in the dark. But it wouldn't have been possible anyway. None of the old people were ever seen again. I wasn't able to find out what became of them." He ran a hand over his face. "Knowing King Ugar as I did, it wasn't difficult to guess."

"Did the king find out that you had the stone?" asked Elena.

"No. Thankfully not. I heard that he had learned nothing useful from his captives. He eventually left the region, furious at having been thwarted. When we returned to Rog, I was fearful of being discovered. I kept the stone with me at all times. But after a while, when there was no reason to suspect my secret would be exposed, I didn't think about it as much. Until I fell off a cart and was severely injured. I recovered in an impossibly short time. No one who had witnessed the accident could stop talking about it. I knew that sooner or later the story would reach the ears of the king."

"What did you do?" asked Elena, clearly gripped by his account.

"I decided I needed to leave. Having served the king for many years, I was beyond weary—largely from the effort of trying to survive. Very few others had lasted as long. Anyone who displeased him was disposed of without a second thought. The man was unfit to rule, and his young son Agon was already showing signs of inheriting his father's sadistic nature.

"I wasted no time in making preparations. I acquired a boat and extensive supplies through the services of someone who didn't know me and never actually met me. I had become wealthy over the years, and I had many servants. I sent them away to my summer house at the coast, telling them to expect me there in the near future. I planned to set sail from that location.

"By then the only thing preventing me from leaving was fear. I knew that I would be missed, and that Ugar would not rest until I had been hunted down. I was on the brink of deciding I couldn't remain any longer when an old acquaintance from my village appeared on my doorstep. He sought me out because he had nowhere else to turn. We were acquainted because both of us lost our parents when we were young, and neither of us had other relatives to care for us. We survived

—barely—thanks to the goodwill of a couple of kind-hearted individuals in the village. They had long since passed away. This man grew up bitter and without friends, and as he aged his health failed. The other villagers wearied of him and his attitude—so much so that they eventually drove him out. So he came to me. He arrived late one night. I was alone in the house, and I took him in out of pity. He was much sicker than I realized, because I found him dead the next morning."

He smiled grimly. "I saw that I'd been granted an unusual opportunity. That night I set fire to my own house and watched from a distance as it burned to the ground. I waited long enough to be certain that a charred body had been discovered inside the ruins. From that moment, as far as anyone knew, I was dead. Then I fled to the coast. I boarded my boat secretly and left Rog behind, determined never to go back."

"Wouldn't your servants have missed you?" asked Elena.

"I'm sure they missed me," he replied, "but they didn't need me. I had made certain they were provided for. Since I had no other dependents, I made out a will in favor of those who had served me faithfully over the years."

"So that's how you came to be on your remote island," said Thomas.

Kamash nodded. "I discovered that I was well able to endure my own company," he said. "Especially with the help of a succession of animal friends. I imagine that a big risk for many hermits is getting sick or being injured, but I had no such problem. I did occasionally get sick, but I always recovered quickly. I had the stone to thank for that."

"Did you always carry it with you?" asked Elena.

"No," he replied. "I went for long periods without any direct contact with it." He shrugged. "Perhaps that will affect my longevity. I can't say with any certainty. I eventually buried it somewhere safe on the island so I wouldn't accidentally lose it."

"But you brought it to Rog with you," said Thomas.

The old man's mouth twisted up in a wry smile. "When I set out in my boat with the princess and her guard, I left it behind on the island. I'm still not sure why. I think a part of me wanted to give it up. But after we arrived in Rog I decided I'd made the wrong choice. King Krasmir wanted to send a ship to the island to see if the Ahrans had visited it on their return voyage. I volunteered to lead them there mostly because I wanted to retrieve the stone. The Ahrans had turned the place upside down, but they didn't find my hiding place," he said with satisfaction.

He gazed at Thomas and Elena thoughtfully. "This conversation is most unexpected. I certainly wasn't anticipating anything of the kind when I came here today," he said.

"Elena told you that we wouldn't share your secret without your consent," Thomas said. "You have my word on that as well."

Kamash nodded slowly. "Thank you," he said.

"And in case you're wondering, we have no desire to take the stone from you," added Thomas.

The old man's eyebrow quirked up. "You're an unusual pair," he told them.

"It's true," acknowledged Thomas. "We've been on an interesting journey ourselves."

As he exchanged a knowing glance with Elena, her lovely face lit up in a smile of affection. He beamed back a smile of his own.

Kamash grinned at them, plainly enjoying their interaction. "Perhaps I'll get to hear your story sometime," he said.

"Perhaps," Thomas returned noncommittally.

The old man's face gradually became serious. "Why did you want to meet with me today? Apart from being curious about my story, that is."

"It's true that we were curious," Thomas confirmed. "Extremely curious. And we're grateful that you trusted us enough to share your history, and especially to show us the stone. But our main reason for meeting you was because we felt constrained to let you know we were aware of your secret. It would have been inconceivable to behave as if the discovery wasn't significant."

"Are you thinking that others might guess too?" the old man asked, looking at them uncertainly.

Elena shook her head. "I don't think that's likely," she said. "As Thomas mentioned earlier, we were already aware of the existence of your stone. I can't imagine any way someone else could guess without that information."

"Where did you hear about the stone?" Kamash asked. "I've had it for decades, but in spite of that I know nothing about it apart from what the old man told me. And from my own experience of course."

"We learned of it from an old scroll in a library," Thomas replied. "The librarian thought it was nothing more than a fable."

"Is the library in Rog?" the old man asked.

Thomas shook his head. "It's a very long way from here, and not at all easy to find."

"Does anyone else know about the scroll?" Kamash asked.

"Just two other people," Thomas replied. "They're here with us in Rog, but they're rather distracted at the moment."

Kamash looked at them sharply. "Is it Lord Torbury and his wife?"

They nodded.

"Do you know anything about the abduction?" Elena asked him.

"Nothing at all," he replied without hesitation.

"What about the princess?" asked Thomas. He berated himself once more for having failed to catch a glimpse of her.

Kamash took longer to answer this time. "Not as far as I know." He looked thoughtful. "I can't imagine that she's involved. The princess isn't a bad person at heart, although in her eyes the glory of her empire takes precedence over everything. That makes her unpredictable." He shrugged. "I agreed to act as her spokesperson because I saw her as young and vulnerable. But perhaps I was mistaken. I don't know her well, and I have no real understanding of the agendas and influences that might be driving her."

The princess almost certainly knew a great deal more than she was letting on, and Thomas had a simple way to settle the issue. "Would it be possible for us to meet the princess?" he asked.

"I can try to set up a meeting," Kamash told him. "But I doubt that she will agree to it anytime soon. The questions from King Krasmir's lords, especially since the abduction, have begun to irritate her. She doesn't believe she's been shown sufficient deference as a princess of the empire."

Kamash's reply dispirited Thomas. Will had entrusted the task of investigating the princess to him, and he could only acknowledge that he had allowed himself to be distracted by Kamash and his stone. It was not the fault of the old man. No one was to blame but himself.

"I am grateful to you both for listening to me patiently," said Kamash. "If there is anything I can do for you, and especially for Lord Torbury and his wife, please let me know without delay."

"Thank you," Elena replied graciously.

"Yes, thank you," Thomas echoed. "We will contact you if we believe you can help in some way."

The old man bowed once and left the room.

After he was gone, Elena turned to Thomas. "So he knows nothing about the other stones?"

"Nothing at all," Thomas confirmed.

"I envy him," Elena said softly.

20

As the days dragged by, it became evident to the monk that he and his young charge were likely to be imprisoned in the cellar for some time. At first Brother Ander worked determinedly to discover a way to escape, but the cellar proved secure against any such attempt. Short of attacking their guards, there was no obvious way to break free of their prison.

The monk remembered the subject of his meditation on the morning he was taken. He had been studying a passage of scripture that said, *'In this world you will have trouble...'* The words had been said long ago, by a man intimately acquainted with trouble. And since becoming that man's disciple, Brother Ander had seen the truth of it demonstrated many times. It was a disturbing promise.

He sighed. He couldn't entirely shield the boy from trouble. But he would do whatever he could to guide him through it.

Having acknowledged that escape was not an option, at least for the moment, Brother Ander instead redirected his attention to occupying Ethen usefully. He knew that five-year-olds needed open air and exercise to thrive. Large as the cellar was, it must surely be claustrophobic for a child. With no possibility of altering their environment, he decided to do everything in his power to at least provide some exercise.

Finding a few old rags in the cellar, the monk fashioned them into a simple ball. Games involving throwing, catching, and kicking the ball quickly became a regular feature of every day. Ethen also became quite adept at walking one of the empty barrels around the space. At first Brother Ander steadied him with one hand, but after a while the boy could stay atop the barrel with ease as it rolled across the floor.

Occasionally their fun became sufficiently boisterous to earn them a sharp rebuke from one of their captors, but for the most part they were left to themselves.

The monk also instituted lessons on a range of subjects. Having never taught a five-year-old, he saw himself as a learner just as much as Ethen, but they soon settled into an afternoon routine of exploring a broad range of topics that included history, geography, science, theology, and medicine. Ethen had inherited his parents' facility with languages, and the two of them spoke Rogandan all morning, reverting to Arvenian for the rest of the day.

Brother Ander's life had changed so much in the previous few years. In his former life, before he met Will and Brother Vangellis, he could never have imagined being willing to spend time in this way. Yet he was content.

One afternoon as they sat together sharing the latest delivery of bread and water, Ethen asked once more about his parents.

"They'll still be looking for you, Ethen," the monk assured him. "And knowing your father as I do, I wouldn't want to be one of our captors when he finds you."

"How did you meet my father?" the boy asked.

"I knew about him before I actually met him," the monk replied. "He was commanding soldiers at Arnost, the capital of Arvenon. He was quite famous because he managed to prevent the Rogandans from destroying a large town called Danford. Later, when we were at war with the Rogandans, their army commander wanted to capture other towns, and your father set out to stop him. He took a few people with him, and I was one of them. So I traveled with him for some time."

"Tell me about it!"

Brother Ander had many stories to relate that centered around Will, and as time went by he shared them freely with Ethen. The boy listened intently, his eyes wide.

"I never knew about any of this!" he said after hearing about Will's efforts on behalf of Baron Rudungen's oppressed villagers.

The monk smiled. "Your father isn't one to sound his own praises."

The stories entertained Ethen, and they had a way of settling him too.

Difficult times were impossible to understand when you were living through them. The monk hoped these stories might show the boy that the most harrowing experiences also became the best adventures once they were behind you.

Elena crouched in the shadows beside Amyra and Rufe. They had positioned themselves behind a wagon, keeping out of sight as they watched people come and go from a tavern.

Abruptly Elena gripped Amyra's arm.

"What is it? Have you seen one of the Ahrans?" hissed Amyra.

Elena shook her head. She pointed to the woman who had just emerged from the tavern. "She's had contact with one of them."

The woman paused in the middle of the street as if undecided about which way to go.

"Do you want me to grab her?" whispered Rufe.

"There's no need," Elena replied softly. "I already know everything of value she could tell us."

She peered at the woman briefly before nodding to herself. "Wait here for a moment," she said to Rufe and Amyra. Then, ignoring their frowns, she stepped out from behind the wagon.

At first the woman looked at her warily as she approached, although she apparently soon decided that Elena presented no threat.

Elena drew close to her. "May I tell you something?" she asked quietly. "I think it will benefit you."

The woman stared at Elena suspiciously, clearly torn between irritation and contempt, but she didn't move away.

Leaning forward a little, Elena whispered in her ear.

The woman stiffened, then her eyes opened wide in surprise. Tears trickled down her cheeks, and she began to gasp, convulsively sucking in gulps of air. She abandoned any attempt to master herself, and great sobs wracked her body. No doubt realizing she would soon draw unwanted attention to herself, she scurried away without a backward glance.

Elena hurried back to the others, and they headed immediately for the palace.

"What was that about?" demanded Amyra. "If you have information from the woman, we need to get it back to Will without delay. Why were you wasting time on her?"

"She hates herself," Elena replied gently. "It's damaged her unnecessarily. I wanted her to understand that other choices are available to her."

"Her happiness isn't our responsibility," growled Amyra.

"I know you want to rescue Ethen," replied Elena, "and that's what I want too. But that woman has no knowledge of the abduction, and it only took a couple of minutes to help her."

When Amyra glared at her, Elena shrugged helplessly. "People's lives are often a mess, but sometimes a small change can tidy things up a lot. It can make a big difference to the person, and to everyone who depends on them."

Amyra showed no interest in her explanation, concentrating only on hurrying along.

How could Elena begin to explain what it was like to suddenly enter the mind of another person and become immersed in their life?

How could she hope to account for the overwhelming sense of responsibility that came over her—the pressing need to make a difference when she knew she could?

Pushing the woman's inner turmoil from her mind, she tried to refocus on what had been revealed about the Ahran agents.

AMYRA PRESSED FORWARD RELENTLESSLY, trying to overcome her feelings of anger. Elena was far too soft. Didn't she understand that every minute counted?

Their path took them down a back alley. Turning a corner, Amyra found her way completely blocked by a pile of garbage. She waved an arm irritably at the reeking mound, and the pile instantly disintegrated. Refuse flew through the air, landing on roofs and plastering itself on the sides of buildings. Ignoring the astonishment of Elena, who was immediately behind her, Amyra pressed on through the newly cleared path.

The power of the Stone of Authority had given expression to Amyra's agitation. But acting on her frustrations did little to ease them. If anything she was left feeling more unsettled than ever.

Before long her attempts to contain her distress failed miserably. Her exasperation burst out again, this time with a different target. With an open scowl, she faced Elena. "Why do you care about that woman? You don't even know her!"

"Her life matters, even if I don't know her," Elena replied calmly.

"It doesn't matter to me!" Amyra shot back indignantly. "My son has been abducted! Anyone even vaguely assisting the people who did it deserves no pity, from me or anyone else."

"I wonder if any one of us really deserves pity," Elena returned quietly.

Amyra frowned. What was that supposed to mean? Had Elena been directing her last comment at Amyra?

"Are you looking into my mind?" she demanded.

"Of course not!" Elena exclaimed. "We've told you we never use the stone on our friends, and it's true. I wouldn't violate you in that way."

A grunt was Amyra's only response. She tried to ignore the interaction, but Elena's comment still pressed in on her, whether it had been directed at her or not.

Did she deserve pity?

She had been tense and unhappy. Of course she had. Who could blame her under the circumstances? Her precious son had been snatched away.

Her thoughts swirled restlessly as she revisited her behavior and her attitude, intent on justifying herself. But a niggle of doubt would not let go. The truth was that her unhappiness had not begun with the abduction. She had been irritable and unhappy from the very moment they set out on this trip.

To begin with she was angry with Will for leaving Arvenon and going to Rog. That reaction wasn't entirely fair of course, as she well knew. Refusing the king would have been unthinkable.

It certainly was Will's fault that she was in Rog with the children though. With both parents heading to Rogand, they couldn't possibly leave the children behind.

She hadn't wanted to come; she was only there because of the Stone of Authority. Will saw her stone as an important weapon in his armory, just as he did with the Stone of Knowing. He wanted the stones available in case he needed them.

She tried to tell herself his attitude was selfish and unnecessary. But it wasn't that simple. Will didn't care about the stones for his own sake. And they were undeniably useful. Her stone had been the reason their ship made it safely through the storm. And Thomas and Elena's stone had been crucial as well; she herself had come to rely heavily on it since the abduction.

Everything had become so complicated and messy. Even so, she had a right to her anger and distress.

An image of Will's face came unbidden to her mind. He had woken that morning with a haunted look on his face. Normally so unruffled in a crisis, Will's composure had deserted him of late.

Ethen was his son too. How could he be expected to retain his equanimity?

Her husband was clearly hurting as well, and it occurred to her to wonder what she'd done to support him in his grief. She'd certainly made it very clear she blamed him.

And what about Millie? Amyra had scarcely spared their daughter a thought in the past few days.

Elena's words came to her again. *I wonder if any one of us really deserves pity.* Amyra frowned uncomfortably. Could she lay claim to deserving pity?

A groan of misery escaped her lips. Abruptly abandoning the battle to justify herself, she accepted the truth. She had been behaving badly—there was no way to pretend otherwise. She'd felt so demoralized and defeated though. What else could she do?

The royal guards admitted them to the palace grounds, and they arrived at their accommodation with Amyra still unable to find peace. She tried to push her inner conflict to one side as Will joined them and Elena passed on what she had learned.

"We saw a woman leaving the tavern," Elena was saying. "She sells bread. Two men with foreign accents approached the woman and bought a few loaves. She saw where they were staying. I can show you where it is."

"Maybe we should ask the Rogandans for support before we go in," Rufe suggested.

"No," said Will emphatically. "A big group of men moving in might alert the Ahrans. We need to take them by surprise. And King Krasmir's men answer to him, not me—I'm not willing to risk losing control of the situation. We'll take Breysen with us. The three of us can handle it. Amyra and Elena should both be resting, but we're going to need Elena. Haldek can come as well to protect her."

As they were moving out Amyra approached Will. "Be careful!" she urged him, touching him lightly on the arm.

Flinching at her touch, he turned away with a frown of bemusement. Then without an acknowledgment of any kind he hurried off, his attention entirely focused on the operation ahead of him.

Amyra stood staring after them long after they had gone. She didn't show it, but his response had shaken her. Until that moment she hadn't fully allowed herself to grasp the extent to which she had become distanced from other people.

A dull ache in her head was beginning to throb uncomfortably, and she knew she needed to lie down before the headache blinded her. Holding her head, she stumbled to her bed. An insistent thought poked and prodded at her as she lay down—she had done more than just allow herself to become distanced from others. She had been actively pushing people away. Especially Will.

WILL PULLED at the reins of the horse, and the creaking of the wagon slowly ceased as it came to a halt.

"That's it over there!" Elena said softly, pointing to a building a short distance away.

As he peered forward in the dark, Will's mouth twisted in a grim smile of satisfaction. They must surely be drawing close at last. Handing the reins to Haldek, he climbed down from the wagon, Rufe and Breysen behind him.

Haldek moved into the driver's seat and took the reins, with Elena settling herself beside him.

"Don't leave Elena's side, whatever happens," Will whispered to Haldek.

Haldek nodded without speaking.

Gesturing to his companions, Will set off casually along the street. Rufe walked a couple of steps behind him. Breysen headed away in the other direction and soon disappeared.

When they reached the building, Will waved Rufe back out of sight. Approaching the door, he banged on it three times with his fist.

Nothing happened for several minutes. Then the door opened a crack, a face peering out suspiciously.

"Good evening, friend," said Will cheerfully. "May I come in?"

"No! Go away!" The speaker could not hide a heavy accent.

As the door was about to slam in Will's face, he pulled a short beam of timber from behind his back and jammed it into the crack. Then the massive frame of Rufe appeared beside him. Throwing themselves at the door, the two men forced their way into the building.

The foreigner came at them with a sword. Dodging past him, Will moved deeper into the building. Rufe could handle the swordsman. Another man appeared out of the shadows, swinging a sword wildly in the confined space. Barely managing to avoid it, Will stepped forward and smashed his fist into his attacker's face. The man went down hard and didn't get up.

Stepping over him, Will scaled a flight of stairs. Candlelight flickered ahead of him, and he moved cautiously into a long narrow room with three beds. The room was empty. Finding no one else in the upper level, he hurried back down the stairs.

Rufe's attacker was also lying prone on the floor, and the big guardsman did not appear to be hurt.

Pausing for a moment, Will heard a commotion at the back of the building. He raced forward, Rufe close behind him, and surprised a third man trying to escape through a rear door.

Redoubling his efforts, the man finally forced the door open to find Breysen blocking his path. He barely had time to raise his sword before both men were upon him from behind. Will had picked up a large earthenware jug, and he smashed it down hard on the man's head. The man crumpled.

Rufe bent down to examine him. "He's dead," he announced evenly.

Will grunted. He hadn't intended to kill the man, but he was in no mood to be gentle.

"Drive the wagon around the back," he instructed Breysen. The blacksmith nodded, and hurried away at once.

"Bring the other two here after you've tied them up," Will told Rufe. "I'll check the rest of the building."

He didn't say it, but he hadn't abandoned hope of finding Ethen and Brother Ander locked in a basement of the building.

It wasn't until he had conducted an exhaustive search that Will finally accepted he wasn't going to find his son in this place. The exercise hadn't been a complete waste of time. He would turn the surviving agents over to King Krasmir for questioning. But only after Elena had stripped anything of value from their minds.

Barely conscious, the two men trussed up by Rufe were bundled into the wagon. After wrapping the body of the third, they loaded him in as well and set off for the palace.

Will took the reins once more, and Elena sat beside him. He had seen her examining the men closely as they were being lifted into the wagon.

"What can you tell me?" he asked quietly, trying not to sound too eager.

"If other agents are holding a man and a boy, these men are not aware of it," Elena whispered back.

"Do they know where other agents are located?" asked Will.

"They seem to have at least a vague idea," she replied. "I'm not confident I could identify the exact place, but I think I can find the general area."

"Who is their leader?" Will asked.

"They meet regularly with a man who gives them instructions. They know he isn't the main leader though. They don't know who that is, but they have their suspicions."

Will was instantly alert. "Who?"

"They think it might be the Grand Vizier."

The idea that the Grand Vizier was directing the agents personally seemed preposterous to Will, but he didn't say so. "How many agents do the Ahrans have?" he asked.

"They know of quite a few," she said. "I'm worried about what will happen if you try to take all of them on yourselves, Will," she added with a worried frown. "I think there are too many for the three of you to handle."

Will nodded. "When we came here tonight I thought these men might be the ones holding Ethen," he said, jerking a head toward their captives. "I was even hoping we might be able to free him and take him home. But now we're no closer to finding him."

"I'm sorry, Will," she said.

He shrugged helplessly. "The Ahran network is clearly bigger than we imagined. And since they haven't drawn attention to themselves, at least some of them must speak Rogandan without noticeable accents. It's time we involved King Krasmir."

21

Having once again sought out King Krasmir, Will sat with him in a small reception room.

"My own inquiries have led me to three Ahran agents, Your Majesty. Unfortunately one of them was killed when we attempted to subdue them. I have questioned the other two closely without learning anything that could lead me to my son. I will turn the men over to you whenever you are ready to take charge of them."

The king's eyebrows went up in surprise. "To achieve results like that you must have an extensive network of your own, Lord Torbury. Yet its existence has escaped my detection. I confess to being astonished."

Will smiled humorlessly. "I have no such network, Your Majesty. This connection came solely from my own very vigorous inquiries. I am sure my success is due to little more than dumb luck."

He flinched internally as he said it. Such dishonesty was uncharacteristic for him, but nothing had felt normal since his son was abducted. And he had no intention of revealing anything to King Krasmir about the Stone of Knowing.

"If we have succeeded in identifying five agents between us," said the king, "the Ahrans must have more people out there than we supposed."

"I agree, Your Majesty," said Will. "Our questioning has pointed us to the general vicinity of other Ahran agents. I am hoping you might agree to a joint operation to flush them out."

"The idea of allowing an Arvenian nobleman to participate in an operation in my own capital city is beyond unusual, Lord Torbury. But these are unusual times. I am willing to allow you to join us. On one condition."

Will raised his eyebrows. "What is that, Your Majesty?"

"That you cease your independent activities immediately." The king's face was grim. "I cannot have foreigners roaming my streets and killing people without my knowledge or consent."

Will winced. "I accept your condition of course, Your Majesty," he said, bowing low. "And I freely acknowledge that my own intensely personal interest in this matter has led me well beyond recognized diplomatic conventions and into some very murky waters. I am indebted to you for your gracious response. Please accept my sincere apologies for placing you in such a position. It will not happen again."

RESTLESS AND ON EDGE, Bolnyk waited on a low hill above a secluded beach north of Rog. As the senior agent responsible for the entire Ahran network in Rogand, he had many pressing matters competing for his attention. The arrival in Rogand of his master, the Grand Vizier, eclipsed them all.

The dim outline of a ship appeared, sailing in close to the shoreline. At almost the same moment, the first glimmers of daylight appeared in the sky, slowly transforming the dark smudges around him into a series of low hills on either side of a pale beach.

As Bolnyk waited expectantly, longboats were lowered from the ship, and dark figures clambered down into the boats. Pushing away from the ship, the sailors pulled vigorously toward the beach.

As the boats approached the shallows, Bolnyk hurried down onto the sand and called a greeting in the Ahran language.

"Get on with it!" a voice called imperiously to the sailors. Bending to their oars once more, they caught a wave that pushed the boat up onto the sand. The boat remained fast as the wave sucked back toward the sea. Two sailors leaped from the boat into the shallows, hauling the craft further onto the beach with the next wave.

Once the wave had retreated, the Grand Vizier stepped carefully out of the boat, grimacing as the sand squelched beneath him, soaking his shoes.

Bolnyk hurried forward to welcome him, bowing low. The agent led his master to a horse and helped him into the saddle. The chief minister left the beach without a backward glance.

"Update me on what has been happening since I left Rog," he commanded, pulling alongside Bolnyk's horse.

"Her Highness the Princess Neira arrived in Rog not long after you left, Your Eminence," the agent replied.

The chief minister sat rigid in the saddle, clearly stunned. Bolnyk pretended not to notice, peering resolutely forward in the dim light.

"Tell me everything you know about the princess," the chief minister growled.

The agent found himself answering many questions. They had barely finished before arriving at a large house.

"We arranged for the purchase of this farm after the previous owner recently died of natural causes," Bolnyk informed his master. "The property is situated in a sparsely settled location relatively close to Rog, and the house is well concealed in the middle of an extensive parcel of land. We have been using it as our main base. It includes a separate building that we have set aside for the exclusive use of Your Eminence."

"What of my instructions regarding the High Priest?" the chief minister asked.

"I put Kaifet, my best man, on the job. After the High Priest refused to meet with him, Kaifet went to the temple at night with a team of twenty of our best men to bring the High Priest in for questioning."

"And?" demanded the chief minister.

Bolnyk lowered his gaze. "We have heard nothing of them since."

The Grand Vizier turned away. "The priest's time will come," he pronounced. "Once we have subdued this puny kingdom we will quickly bring him to heel." He spared a glance for Bolnyk. "Leave me now. I will call for you later."

"Certainly, Your Eminence," the agent replied with a bow.

Bolnyk hurried away. The Grand Vizier would have a great deal to think about. Having served his master from the time when he was merely Bisri Rheibas, the agent knew him well enough to know how much he valued time alone and undisturbed.

LESS THAN AN HOUR passed before Bolnyk was again summoned to the side of Rheibas. A parchment, apparently a letter, lay open on a table before the chief minister. A quick glance at the fire showed singed fragments of other parchments—Bolnyk guessed that a number of drafts had been consigned to the fire on the way to the final version.

Bolnyk was aware that his master made a habit of disclosing more information to him than to anyone else, so it was no surprise when Rheibas waved a hand lazily toward the parchment, inviting the agent to read it.

Picking it up, he scrutinized it carefully.

To Her Imperial Highness the Princess Neira,

I rejoiced more than I can possibly say when I heard of your safe arrival in Rog! The news brought me comfort beyond words after the treachery of Captain Gharpin on our earlier voyage. He waited until I was confined to my cabin with illness, then he secretly arranged for his men to abandon you on the island. I was entirely unaware of his action. I wrongly believed that you were still on the ship until the moment we arrived in Rog.

For failing in my solemn duty to protect you I can only humbly apologize. I did, of course, insist that the ship return to the island as soon as possible to rescue you. I was dismayed to discover that no trace of you could be found there.

Revealing the truth to the Rogandans was out of the question. I could not have lived with the dishonor it would have brought to our beloved empire. I was left with the painful task of concocting a report that would somehow present an act of treachery in an advantageous light. I accordingly stated that you had been forcibly removed from our ship in an act of piracy, and demanded that the Rogandans find a way to return you at once. I take what comfort I can from the knowledge that I did my best to ensure that this shameful setback did not injure the empire.

Given Your Highness's unshakable loyalty, I know I can rely on you to labor mightily with me to advance the cause of your exalted father. I will look forward to working closely with you as soon as we are able to make direct contact.

I trust that this letter finds Your Highness well and in good heart, in spite of the trials you have been forced to endure.

Ever your humble servant,

Rheibas, Chief Minister of Ahr

P.S. Powerless as I was to prevent the perfidy of Captain Gharpin at the time, it gives me satisfaction to assure you that he has since been dealt with appropriately.

P.P.S. I have ordered my agent Bolnyk to retrieve and destroy this communication as soon as you have read it.

Bolnyk did not expect his master to invite comment, and Rheibas did not surprise him. The agent was well aware that this accounting of events could not be reconciled with what the chief minister had told the Rogandans, and no doubt the emperor as well. Bolnyk didn't care about the discrepancy—his loyalty was to the Grand Vizier—but it was obvious that his master was faced with a major problem.

Whether the princess would be satisfied with the chief minister's explanation remained to be seen.

"Take this letter to the princess," the chief minister commanded. "It must be delivered into her hand, and her hand alone. Do you understand?"

"Yes, Your Eminence," the agent replied.

"Make sure she returns it to you as soon as she has read it. Destroy it as soon as you leave her. You have never failed me, Bolnyk. Do not disappoint me this time."

The agent dipped his head respectfully.

The letter was at least written in the Ahran language, which offered some security from prying eyes, but he could see why Rheibas wanted it destroyed. Its very existence constituted a grave risk, and leaving it with someone as unreliable as Princess Neira would be unthinkable.

As he was about to leave, Rheibas held up a hand to forestall him. "I want a report that covers all of our agents. I'll give you two days, no longer. They know what they are supposed to be doing—I expect details on their progress."

Bolnyk bowed low. Then he headed for the door.

WILL STOOD beside the Rogandan commander as his soldiers moved silently into position in the darkness. Lord Kulferan was a man of few words, but Will had quickly seen that he was both effective and focused.

Leaning forward, Will whispered in the commander's ear. "Your men have been instructed to keep some of them alive, My Lord. For questioning." He pulled away, looking expectantly at the Rogandan. "Have I understood that correctly?"

Lord Kulferan stared back at him for a moment before nodding once.

Satisfied, Will returned his attention to the dwelling facing them. Situated not far from the bustling city of Rog, it stood alone in a field surrounded by farmland. The commander's soldiers had been quietly observing the building all day, and they had reported seeing men coming and going constantly. They expected to find at least ten men sheltering in it. Some of the men had been monitored surreptitiously, and there was no doubt that they were foreign.

Will was confident that this house was an important center for Ahran activity in the region. It could well be the place they were looking for.

Thomas hovered nearby, no doubt hanging back in an attempt to remain inconspicuous. That suited Will perfectly. The stone was the only reason Thomas was there; he needed to stay well away from any action.

The dwelling was now surrounded, with men covering every point of access. The Rogandan nobleman now raised a torch high. At the signal, four soldiers rushed to the front door supporting a small tree trunk. Swinging it back, they shattered the door in a single mighty blow before stepping aside to allow a dozen others to race into the house.

Would this be the place where Ethen was being held? Will could barely contain himself from joining the soldiers. He looked pleadingly at Lord Kulferan. After what felt like an eternity, the Rogandan nobleman turned to him and nodded. Will sprinted to the house and pushed his way inside.

A chaotic scene awaited him. Furniture lay strewn about the building, with maybe a dozen bodies sprawled on the floor. The occupants of the house had clearly put up a fight, and it had not gone well for them. Four of the fallen appeared to be Lord Kulferan's soldiers.

A staircase led upward, and Will took it two steps at a time. Reaching the top of the stairs, he emerged into a passageway that led to three rooms. Two of the rooms were empty. The door of the third had been pulled from its hinges. Inside the room a man lay unmoving on the floor. Another, seemingly uninjured, was being restrained by two of Lord Kulferan's men.

A quick glance around revealed no sign of Ethen or Brother Ander, and no place where they could have been hidden. Leaping down the stairs Will began searching for a basement.

A trapdoor lay in the floor. Soldiers must have found and opened it, and sounds of movement drifted up from below. Spotting a ladder in the opening, Will drew his sword before lowering himself into the hole and clambering down the ladder. Two soldiers with torches could be seen ahead of him, peering around cautiously.

Moving forward to join them, he was attacked from both sides. Barely avoiding the thrusting swords, he sprang deeper into the cellar before pivoting around to face his attackers. Lunging out in a series of aggressive thrusts, he forced the men back against the ladder. Both of his opponents—one stocky and the other taller—knew how to fight, and he soon had little chance to consider anything except survival.

Cries behind him suggested that the soldiers who preceded him were also under attack. Will could only hope that they would prevent anyone from attacking him from behind.

Other soldiers were now trying to push down into the cellar. The taller of Will's attackers directed his attention to the floor above, his sword flicking upward as he tried to keep them out. Driving swiftly forward, Will avoided a hasty swipe from the stocky man and took the taller one in the side. His target went down with a cry of pain. Confusion reigned as the stocky man fought Will while simultaneously struggling to prevent reinforcements descending into the cellar.

Will could not allow all of these men to die. For Thomas to be able to discover everything they knew, Will needed to keep as many of them alive as possible. Choosing his moment carefully, he leaned swiftly forward and punched the stocky man hard in the face. Stunned, the man dropped his guard. It was only for a moment, but it was enough. Punching him hard a second time, Will leaped at him and threw him roughly to the floor just as two soldiers hurried down the ladder.

"Tie him up," Will ordered. "And keep him alive for questioning!"

Leaving the new arrivals to assist their comrades in ending resistance in the cellar, Will methodically searched the cellar for hidden doors. Nothing obvious could be found in the area near the ladder. He could not examine the rest of the cellar until the fighting had ended there. More men arrived even as he was considering throwing himself into the fray, and he decided to let them do their work.

The fighting soon ended, but the cellar was now crowded with soldiers, and Will was forced to wait for an opportunity to explore the rest of it.

Eventually he got his chance. An initial examination showed nothing that looked like an entrance to a hidden room. But upon closer inspection he found a section of the cellar that had been filled with old furniture. An opening was barely visible, mostly obscured behind a large cupboard. Calling for help, he positioned himself to one side of the object and began to strain. Others quickly joined him, and the cupboard was moved aside. Behind it lay a door.

Will forced it open. With heart pounding, he grabbed a torch from one of the soldiers and groped his way inside. He found a large space filled with empty barrels—apparently nothing more than an unused extension to the cellar. Dust covered everything. It was clear that no one had visited this room in a very long time.

Struggling to master his disappointment, Will left the room and carefully examined the cellar from one end to another. Finding nothing further of interest, he clambered back up the ladder and subjected the rest of the house to a close examination. His efforts were fruitless.

The only remaining hope was for Thomas to learn something useful from the survivors. Pushing his way out of the house into the night, he saw that the Ahrans had been rounded up. They huddled together, surrounded by a large group of armed men.

Looking around impatiently, Will eventually spotted Thomas. He had positioned himself near enough to the survivors to get a good look at them without getting too close.

Will hurried over to him. "Ethen isn't here," he growled.

This information clearly was not news to Thomas. He shook his head. "No, this is not the place where Ethen and Brother Ander are being held. None of the Ahrans know anything about the abduction, either. They are only aware of their own immediate contacts. They don't even know for certain who is leading their mission."

Frustration gripped Will, causing him to cry out in exasperation. A few heads turned in their direction, but most of the soldiers ignored them.

"Do any of them know of other safe houses being used by the Ahrans?" asked Will.

"Yes," Thomas replied. "One of them knows the location of another house." He pointed to one of the Ahrans who was sitting on the ground. The man was carrying injuries from the fighting, and he looked dazed.

Will shook his head in irritation. They seemed no closer to finding his son. Already impatient to explore the next location, he would be reduced to waiting in the hope that Lord Kulferan would eventually find out through questioning what Thomas already knew.

Could he speed up the process by encouraging the commander to focus all of his attention on the one man with information worth extracting? It didn't take Will long to decide that the risks outweighed the benefits. He could think of no credible way to explain how he had acquired such knowledge. King Krasmir had already expressed surprise at the amount of information Will had unearthed with limited resources.

As far as Will was concerned, that night's operation could only be viewed as a failure. Shutting down an active cell of Ahran agents would undoubtedly be seen as a useful outcome by King Krasmir. But it made no difference to Will. His only goal was to find and release his son. Nothing else mattered to him.

Time was running short. With a serious push being made against the Ahran agents, all of them would soon be aware of it. The risk of spooking them would increase with every unsuccessful operation. Sooner or later they would decide that holding on to Ethen was too risky.

There was no telling what might happen then.

22

Weary of continually finding himself at a loose end, the young king of Castel wondered what had possessed him to come to Rog. The stakes had certainly been high when Rupert first made the decision; responding effectively to the Ahran threat was easily the most pressing issue for Castel as well as for every other kingdom in the region. But after arriving in Rog it hadn't taken long before progress stalled completely.

The initial meetings with the princess had failed to bring any real clarity about a way forward. That was no great surprise to him.

Then Lord Torbury's son had been abducted. It had only just happened, and all of Lord Torbury's friends, including Rupert, were still reeling from it.

If the Ahrans were responsible for the kidnapping as suspected, it had been an astute move on their part. All attention had been diverted away from the broader strategic threat in a determined attempt to address the immediate issue. Yet the best efforts of King Krasmir had so far yielded nothing.

Rupert felt keenly for Lord and Lady Torbury. But beyond expressing concern and support there was little he could do.

Stranded in a foreign capital with no role to play and no compelling reason even to be there, he had rarely felt so useless.

It didn't help his confidence that he'd begun so badly with the Ahran princess either. Before they left Varacellan she had done a masterful job of exposing his insecurities, standing by and witnessing his discomfort with evident relish. Supremely embarrassing as the interactions had been, he decided they revealed as much about her as they did about him. Even her spokesperson, Kamash, apparently saw her behavior as volatile and inappropriate.

The wing of the palace where the foreign contingent had been accommodated was surrounded by an extensive area of cultivated gardens. With nothing better to do, Rupert had taken to wandering both in these gardens and beyond in the extensive grounds that surrounded the palace. He had no concerns at all about his safety. Royal guards had been conspicuous even before the abduction. The palace almost seemed to be swarming with them since.

On that afternoon, Rupert had been rambling aimlessly once more in the gardens. Finding a bench beside a large hedge, he sat down and closed his eyes, soaking in the sunshine. Only a few minutes passed before his peaceful reverie was shattered by an enthusiastic yapping sound. Looking down he saw an Alaunt puppy at his feet, its eager face turned up to his. The wriggling ball of fur leaped up repeatedly, its little tail waving back and forth frantically.

Reaching down, he scooped it into his arms with a welcoming grin. The puppy was soon desperately trying to reach his face with its tongue, causing him to hold it at arms length while he laughed at its antics.

"Maxie, come back here you little truant!" called a voice.

Twisting around, Rupert saw a face framed by a hole in the hedge. A girl of perhaps eighteen or nineteen emerged from the hedge, her face flushed and her dark hair disheveled.

"I'm so sorry!" she exclaimed. "He's such a scamp!"

"It's no problem," Rupert replied. "Maxie and I have been getting acquainted." Acutely aware of his limited mastery of Rogandan, he tried to hide his awkwardness with a smile.

Apparently sensing his self-consciousness, the girl switched effortlessly to Arvenian. "You must be a member of the foreign delegation, My Lord," she offered, bowing low.

Clearly she had no idea he was a reigning monarch—how could she? He dipped his head in response, choosing not to enlighten her. Why spoil the moment by standing on ceremony?

"You speak excellent Arvenian," he said.

"Thank you, My Lord," she replied humbly. "It is a useful skill to have in a palace."

"It is indeed," he confirmed with a nod.

It hadn't escaped his notice that a high proportion of the servants assigned to the delegation spoke quite passable Arvenian. Rupert had no doubt that some of them did much more than just serve. King Krasmir's agents would be scattered among them, reporting everything they overheard.

"Foreign language skills are highly prized with palace servants in our capital city, too," he observed.

She dipped her head gravely, not managing to entirely conceal the delicate flush that tinged her cheeks.

It occurred to him to wonder if this young woman might herself be an agent. He promptly dismissed the idea. She had a delightfully artless air about her.

"What kind of service are you involved in?" he asked, glancing down at the puppy, who had nestled comfortably in his arms as he stroked it behind the ears.

"I attend to the princesses," she replied seriously. "And the crown prince."

His eyes widened in surprise. "Tell me about them," he suggested, recovering himself.

"There are three daughters and one son. Crown Prince Rimek is the oldest." She eyed him appraisingly. "You must be about his age."

He looked askance at her. "And how old might that be?"

She laughed. "I think you must be in your mid-twenties."

He brought his eyebrows back under control, granting her a modest smile. "Go on," he commanded.

She grinned at him. “Did you know that Crown Prince Rimek arrived in the world just minutes before his sister, Princess Ashloh? I think he’s been running hard ever since to stay ahead of her.” Her eyes twinkled merrily. “Then there’s the neglected middle sister, Princess Kyla. She isn’t really neglected, of course,” she assured him. “Finally there’s the youngest, Princess Teylee. She is my age.”

This latest piece of information was accompanied by another delicate blush.

Rupert found it endearing. Nevertheless he nodded wisely. “And what is your role?”

“I try to keep them out of trouble, My Lord.” A dimpled smile lit up her face.

He grinned back at her. He couldn’t help it.

“But my most important task seems to be to lend a listening ear to them,” she added seriously.

He quirked an eyebrow.

A merry laugh burst from her lips. “I don’t wonder that you doubt me. I’ve done no listening at all—I’ve been talking your ear off!”

“No you haven’t,” he insisted. Then he frowned at her. “You’ve talked about everyone except yourself. You haven’t even told me your name.”

She paused, as if uncertain about sharing such a confidence. Then she seemed to come to a decision. “My name is Tasha. And what’s your name?”

It was his turn to pause. “I’m Boyd,” he replied.

“Lord Boyd,” she corrected.

He executed a sweeping bow in response.

It never occurred to him to say he was King Rupert. And he hadn’t told her a lie. ‘Boyd’ was the affectionate nickname his sister had used throughout his childhood. He still had no idea where it came from. Having now set a course, he decided to steer by it.

“Tell me about your home and what you do there, Lord Boyd,” she said, trying vainly to bring her hair under control as she settled herself on the ground.

“Well,” he replied. “There are just two of us in my family. I have an older sister, called Sandy. She's the talented and successful one in the family."

She eyed him skeptically.

"As for my home and what I do there, I live at Castel Citadel, the capital of Castel, and I'm learning to do administration. The capital is truly striking, Tasha. The citadel is crowned by a fortress built from gray stone with tall battlements. Behind it is a towering cliff face, and below it is the city, bounded by a wall that follows a broad sweep of river. The houses are built largely of stone. It is a beautiful city. The kingdom is much smaller and less populous than Rogand, but it is prosperous and peaceful, and for the most part its citizens are contented."

The afternoon slipped away as he told her about the fishing villages by the sea, and the fruit crops famous throughout the region.

She soaked in his descriptions and smiled at his enthusiasm for his country. She also asked many intelligent questions, listening intently to his answers. He could scarcely recall a more attentive and responsive audience.

"I could keep talking for hours," he told her. "But that would hardly be fair. Tell me about your home!"

In her turn she gave her perspective on the city of Rog. Having traveled a little with the royal family, she went on to describe the attractive coastline that fringed the city and the shipping that frequented its waters. Above all, she talked about the people and what shaped them. He felt as if he was beginning to see and appreciate Rogand for the first time.

He had no idea how long they had been there. He only knew it wasn't nearly long enough.

"I've talked far too much," she said apologetically.

"But you haven't told me anything about your family!" he protested. "You've only mentioned the royals."

Before she could respond, a voice broke across their conversation. "There you are, Tasha! Whatever have you been doing all this time?"

Twisting round once more, he saw another face poking through the hole in the hedge.

"I've been chasing Maxie," Tasha cried. "He's so naughty!"

Turning to Rupert, she bobbed her head quickly. "I'm so sorry to have troubled you, My Lord. Thank you for your help with our dog!"

The puppy had found its way back to him, and she held out her arms for it. Then before he could think of a word to say, she was pushing her way back through the hedge with Maxie grasped securely in her arms.

He shook his head in bewilderment, trying to understand what had just happened. He remained in the garden, striving to convince himself he was lingering there to enjoy the sunshine.

Eventually the dark and the cold drove him inside.

THE NEXT DAY Rupert hurried out into the garden as soon as he could manage it without attracting undue attention. Making his way directly to the bench he had occupied the previous day, he was dismayed to find that the hole in the hedge had been stopped up. Until that moment he hadn't honestly acknowledged to himself how much he wanted to see Tasha again.

What was wrong with him? Having allowed himself to be flustered and humbled by the vain princess of Ahr, he was now pining for a pretty Rogandan servant girl. He knew he ought to be ashamed of himself, but it didn't stop him wishing he could spend more time with her.

With no reason to remain where he was, he headed out into the palace grounds, hoping to catch a glimpse of what lay on the other side of the tall hedge that separated the adjoining gardens. He soon discovered that a high stone wall enclosed any sections of the garden not bordered by hedges. No access to Tasha's garden would be possible from anywhere except the palace buildings. The area was private and concealed, which came as no surprise since it was apparently used exclusively by the royal family.

No passageway joined the adjacent wings of the palace. He would connect with Tasha out of doors or not at all. It was immensely frustrating to be so close to someone but with no way of seeing them, much less meeting them.

After a long period of hesitation, Rupert tentatively approached a large gate in the outer wall. Several guards appeared from nowhere, eyeing him suspiciously. He changed direction immediately, hoping he had merely seemed curious.

Over the next couple of days he tried to put Tasha out of his mind. His attempts resulted in dismal failure. He could not forget the sparkle in her eyes and her guileless laugh. His final resort was to tell himself that sudden infatuations always withered over time. What else could he do?

Ridiculous as it seemed, the week that followed Rupert's meeting with Tasha began to feel like one of the most gloomy periods he had endured for years. He hadn't felt so disconsolate since Lord Eisgold's treachery.

Then everything changed abruptly, thanks to an unexpected encounter. Walking in the outer palace grounds, Rupert heard a sound he recognized. The excited yapping of a puppy grew suddenly louder as a familiar figure bounced into view.

"Maxie! What are you doing here alone?" he asked, reaching down for the eager little Alaunt.

Moments later, several horsemen rode up. A young man about his own age dismounted and approached him.

"Does Maxie belong to you?" Rupert asked.

"He does," the other replied, reaching out for the puppy. "Thank you."

As Rupert handed over the Alaunt, a memory came to him from a brief glimpse of the royal family at the palace. "You're Crown Prince Rimek, aren't you?"

"I am," he replied.

Rupert bowed respectfully.

The crown prince gazed at Rupert with considerable curiosity. "You wouldn't be Lord Boyd by any chance, would you?"

Rupert started, his heart skipping a beat. Tasha must have spoken of him to the crown prince. Not trusting himself to speak, he nodded.

The men who had accompanied the prince were still mounted. Gazing at one of them in particular, the prince pointed at the puppy before flicking his head meaningfully to one side. Taking his meaning, the guard approached the prince and took the wriggling Alaunt. Then he guided his horse out of earshot, calling to the other guards to join him.

The prince turned back to Rupert. “You want to see her again, don’t you?”

A deep blush warmed Rupert’s face. Pushing down his embarrassment, he nodded once more.

“Are you from Castel?” the prince asked pointedly.

Rupert nodded again, more uncomfortable than ever. His unplanned deception had seemed so innocent, but it was already becoming complicated. His supposed identity would not long survive careful scrutiny.

He soon discovered that the prince had guessed the truth. “Does she know who you really are, Your Majesty?” he asked, his eyes narrowing.

Rupert swallowed. There was no way to lather this situation with honey. He shook his head. “She has no idea that I’m King Rupert, Your Highness. I know how it must seem—a king wanting to spend time with a servant girl. But I have no improper designs on her.” He shrugged helplessly. “I found myself drawn to her, and I would simply welcome the opportunity to get to know her better.”

“To what end?” asked the prince.

“I can’t pretend to have a definite goal in mind,” he replied honestly.

“You introduced yourself as Lord Boyd,” said the prince. “Did you invent the name?”

“Boyd is the nickname my sister used for me when we were growing up. As for the title, she assumed I was a nobleman, and I didn’t correct her.” He ran a shaky hand over his face. “I never set out to intentionally deceive Tasha. I just didn’t want her to feel like she had to bow and scrape around me. I never imagined the situation would become so complicated.”

The prince stared at him with an unreadable expression on his face. Then he said, “Well, Lord Boyd, this situation is undeniably complicated. Somewhat to my own surprise, I’m willing to help you. Within reason. Tasha will need a chaperone. But I will try to arrange an opportunity for you to speak with her again.”

Rupert bowed again, blushing deeply. “Thank you, Your Highness. You are most gracious.” It did not escape his notice that the prince had referred to him as Lord Boyd.

“Your Majesty,” the prince replied, dipping his head.

The prince rejoined his guards, and they rode away.

23

The chance meeting with the crown prince fully occupied Rupert's thoughts for the rest of that day. He had the clear impression that the crown prince had no immediate plans to expose him. Surprising as that seemed, it did not mean that Rupert could continue with his pretense. He owed it to Tasha to be honest with her. Assuming she was willing to meet with him again.

Being a monarch required a delicate dance. Since his disastrous miscalculations when first thrust into the kingship, he had enjoyed a relatively smooth period that spanned several years. Now his missteps seemed to be multiplying once more. Having recovered from the awkwardness with Princess Neira, he had managed to maneuver himself into a worse position. The crown prince of Rogand was directly involved this time, and he could only berate himself for his own immaturity and lack of wisdom.

He wasn't left stewing for long. Early the next morning he received an invitation to meet with Tasha that afternoon. At the appointed time Rupert was led to the location, arriving in a state of considerable agitation.

He found Tasha accompanied by a chaperone—a woman who looked like she would take nonsense from no one—and an armed guard. After briefly introducing themselves, both of the new arrivals withdrew to a respectful distance before settling down to monitor their charge.

Thankfully it took no more than a minute with Tasha to restore Rupert's equilibrium entirely.

"I hope the crown prince was not too harsh on you, Lord Boyd," she said anxiously.

"You needn't worry, Tasha. He was actually very kind."

She looked relieved. "He might seem fierce," she said with a warm smile, "but in reality he's sweet."

Her declaration felt like an arrow to Rupert's heart. There was no denying it—he'd suffered a pang of jealousy.

She was so beautiful. Her dark hair, admirably tamed on this occasion, accentuated her lovely features, and her simple blue dress emphasized her shapely figure while making her seem elegant.

He needed to speak before he became tongue tied. "I'm glad you were willing to spend more time with me," he offered, feeling himself reddening again.

She looked almost as discomposed, but she replied calmly enough. "I enjoyed being with you, and I was hoping we might meet again." She gazed at him shyly. "To be honest, I'm surprised that the prince was willing to help," she said frankly.

"I'm equally surprised," he told her. He glanced toward her protectors. "He seems to value you highly," he added, trying hard not to resent it.

Another endearing blush briefly flooded her face. "I am fortunate," she acknowledged. "More so than I deserve, I'm sure."

He frowned at her in mock anger, setting her eyes sparkling.

He opened his mouth to ask about her family before abruptly changing his mind. Their previous conversation had been veering toward such a discussion. That topic was much too hazardous, at least until he revealed who he was.

She needed to be told the truth of course, and he needed to do it soon. It didn't take long to reach a decision—he would leave it until their next meeting. A wave of relief washed over him. Delaying it would allow both of them one last opportunity to be relaxed and informal.

"How did you manage to convince the princesses and the crown prince to give you some time off?" he asked instead.

She shrugged. "It wasn't difficult. They're not as demanding as you might expect. And when the prince makes up his mind about something he can be quite determined."

Repenting of his ambivalence toward the prince, Rupert beamed at her. His smile broadened as she matched him with a radiant smile of her own.

Having sensed there was more to her than a lovely face and an attractive smile, he was not entirely taken by surprise when she asked him seriously, "What is important to you? What are you hoping to achieve with your life?"

To give himself time to think, he took a breath and released it slowly. "I have a great responsibility to those who depend on me. 'When someone has been given much, much will be required of them.' Or so I've been told."

She gazed at him thoughtfully. "I haven't heard that before. It's sobering. Where did it come from?"

"My priest says it. I think it's from our Holy Book." He gazed off into the distance. "I want to do the best I'm capable of. I know I need to be wise and compassionate in the decisions I make. I don't doubt my compassion, but I have a long way to go before I can make any claim to being wise." He rolled his eyes. "I do manage to get myself in a tangle at times. I can only comfort myself with the thought that I'm still young. I sincerely hope and expect that I will learn from my mistakes."

She didn't make light of his concerns. "Do you have wise counselors available to you?"

"I do," he acknowledged. "Some very good people have gone to considerable lengths to help me. I suppose I mostly get into trouble when no one's on hand to advise me," he added ruefully.

She gave out a merry laugh. "My father says he mostly relies on my mother to keep him out of trouble."

"It sounds like I need to get myself a wife," he replied, feeling instantly foolish for having said it.

Seeing the look on his face, she burst out laughing, a playful twinkle in her eye.

Had it been anyone other than Tasha, he would have responded with embarrassment or shame. But he felt sure she was mostly laughing at the absurdity of the situation.

Embarrassment was becoming far too much of a habit for him anyway. Casting pride to the winds, he began laughing as well, allowing himself to be caught up in the carefree attitude of the servant girl. And having relaxed, he discovered it wasn't even hard to laugh at himself.

Tasha's protectors stared at them curiously, but didn't intervene.

When they had recovered their poise, he posed a similar question to her. "What about you? What do you want to achieve with your life?"

"I want to do anything I can for the most disadvantaged and hurting," she replied firmly.

"There is no shortage of such people," he acknowledged.

She nodded. "Sometimes it happens due to natural causes. But more often injustice seems to be at the heart of it."

"Injustice or just plain cruelty," he agreed. "Like abducting Lord and Lady Torbury's son."

A fierce look came to her eye. "I would be willing to risk a lot if it meant I could return the boy to his parents," she said. "And bring whoever is responsible to justice."

He didn't doubt that she was in earnest. However much her eyes sparkled with merriment, she still radiated quiet determination.

"I hope I'll manage some adventure too," she said seriously.

He smiled at her. He could not imagine her ever leading a boring life.

Two hours passed in a moment. It was the protectors who finally ended the interaction. Rupert didn't part with Tasha before extracting a promise that she would meet with him again.

He left feeling like he was floating on air. They had covered a lot of ground, from deeply felt concerns to lighthearted banter. By the time it ended he could not remember ever feeling so relaxed with another person.

She was a servant, and a foreigner at that. Neither consideration bothered him in the slightest. He sensed they were slowly building something unique and precious.

At this early stage it remained fragile though. When they next met he would need to tell her who he was. He hoped and prayed the disclosure would not bring everything crashing down.

THE MORNING after Rupert's meeting with Tasha another invitation arrived, this time from King Krasmir. The invitation stated that His Majesty King Rupert of Castel was requested at his earliest convenience to attend King Krasmir.

A feeling of imminent doom hung over Rupert as he followed the messenger to one of the king's private reception rooms. He could only assume that his clandestine activities had been exposed. He decided grimly that he undoubtedly had the crown prince to thank for that. His mind churned as he tried to assess the implications. What protocols had he ignored? What conventions had he flouted? Was it possible that he had created an international incident?

The messenger left him alone in the room and set off to inform the king that he had arrived.

King Krasmir did not keep him waiting. He strode into the room, followed by Crown Prince Rimek and a woman who was undoubtedly the queen.

Rising hastily to his feet, Rupert offered a deep bow.

King Krasmir returned a stiff bow of his own. "This is my wife, Queen Deka," he said. "You have already met Crown Prince Rimek."

"Yes, Your Majesty." Rupert's heart sank. If the king knew he had met the crown prince, he must surely be aware of Rupert's meetings with Tasha.

"Will you understand me if I speak Rogandan?" Krasmir asked with a frown.

"Yes, Your Majesty," he replied evenly, working hard to at least project an outward appearance of calm.

"In my innocence I imagined we had more than enough to occupy our attention already," said King Krasmir sternly. "But it seems I am not to be spared a new distraction. I will come straight to the point, King Rupert. What are your intentions regarding my daughter?"

Rupert was too stunned to respond.

Krasmir frowned. "Have you or have you not been courting my daughter in the guise of a Castelan nobleman?" he demanded.

With his mouth hanging wide, Rupert glanced in the direction of the crown prince. Rimek shrugged helplessly.

Somehow mustering the composure to face his inquisitor, Rupert took a breath to steady himself. "There seems to be a misunderstanding, Your Majesty. I have met twice with one of your servants—a girl called Tasha," he replied. "It is true that I have not revealed my identity to her, but only because I did not want our interactions to be overshadowed by questions of status. I was planning to tell her everything at our next meeting."

Both the king and the queen had been studying him closely.

"He's telling the truth," Queen Deka told her husband. "Or at least he thinks he is."

"So he doesn't know," King Krasmir said to his son.

"I did tell you that, Father," Prince Rimek replied mildly.

The king grunted. Then he addressed Rupert once more. "It is my youngest daughter, Princess Teylee, that you have been meeting with. Tasha is an affectionate name used only by members of her family."

Realizing his mouth was hanging open again, Rupert hastily clamped it shut.

The king stared at him. "Now that all of us seem to be located in the same kingdom," he observed wryly, "I must repeat my question. What are your intentions regarding my daughter?"

King Krasmir's question was no less direct than before, but Rupert thought he had detected the tiniest softening in his tone.

Rupert made his best attempt at a formal bow. "King Krasmir, Queen Deka," he said, nodding to each of them in turn. "I would like to request permission to court your daughter, Princess Teylee."

The queen schooled her features into an unexpressive mask, but not before a triumphant smile made a fleeting appearance across her face.

King Krasmir appeared much less enthusiastic about the turn of events. "There are customs and protocols to be considered," he grumbled, "and there would need to be strict boundaries. Then there is the question of a dowry."

"Nonsense!" said the queen, waving a hand dismissively. "You'll frighten the poor boy away with all this palaver." She turned to Rupert with a genial smile. "You must pardon him, young man. He still thinks that Tasha is his baby. He probably also imagines that no one could ever be good enough for her." She glared at her husband.

King Krasmir glowered back at her, but he offered nothing more than a grunt in response.

"Of course we will allow you to court our Tasha," Queen Deka crooned.

With no immediate confirmation from her husband, she turned to confront him. "Well? Does this arrangement have the blessing of Your Majesty or not?"

She wasn't staring at him with hands on her hips, but from her tone she might have been.

"Very well," he finally conceded gruffly. "But I expect her to be treated properly! No more deceptions!"

"You have my word, Your Majesty," Rupert replied earnestly.

"Well, be off with you then," grumbled the king, flicking a hand toward the door.

Rupert hurried out of the room, relieved that the ordeal was over.

The crown prince followed him out. "You did well in there," he said with a grin. "Don't worry too much about Father—he isn't nearly as fierce as he seems."

"Thank you, Your Highness," Rupert replied.

"Please! Call me Rimek!" said the prince. "There's no need to stand on ceremony."

"Then you must call me Rupert," he said.

"Not Boyd?" the prince asked with a wink.

"Most definitely not Boyd!" he replied sheepishly. After a brief pause he asked, "Does Tasha—Princess Teylee I mean—know the truth about me?"

The prince smiled. "No, she doesn't. I think it's better for her to find out directly from you, and I imagine my parents will see it the same way. And a word of advice—I'd stick to Tasha if I were you."

"Thank you, Rimek."

"I'll organize an invitation for tomorrow," the prince assured him. "After that, the two of you can make your own arrangements."

Rimek clapped him on the back and headed off with a conspiratorial wink.

A servant arrived to lead the foreign visitor to his quarters. Rupert trailed behind the man with his thoughts whirling. The meeting with King Krasmir and Queen Deka had not gone as badly as he might have feared. At least he hoped he was reading that correctly.

But the whole situation had just escalated significantly. A puppy escaping through a hedge had led to an impulsive flirtation. It had seemed so harmless at the time, and it happened so quickly. Now it had assumed immense significance, for his future and also for Tasha's. He was struggling to get his head around it.

What would Tasha think about his meeting with the king and queen and crown prince? Nothing had been decided of course—no decisions could be made before she had her say. But, without her knowledge, her family had been deliberating with a foreign sovereign about her future. He didn't doubt she would have her own opinion about that.

After their last meeting, Rupert had been eager to see Tasha again. Given everything that had just happened, the prospect of facing her the next day felt unexpectedly daunting.

True to his word, Crown Prince Rimek set up another meeting in the same garden where Rupert and Tasha had met on the previous occasion. Having arrived first, the Castelan king paced up and down restlessly while he waited. He hadn't felt so anxious since his coronation.

His heart immediately began to pound the moment she appeared. Her two protectors afforded him a stiff bow before moving out of hearing range.

"Tasha, it's good to see you again," he said with a crooked smile. It was the best he could manage.

"Lord Boyd," she said with a quick nod of her head, gazing at him with an unreadable expression. She looked no less dazzling than before, but her manner seemed muted.

She'd called him Lord Boyd, which suggested she hadn't been told the truth. But she had clearly sensed that something was wrong. Perhaps her parents had been acting strangely since their meeting the previous day.

More likely the fault lay with him. He was desperately trying to behave normally, but he'd never been good at hiding his emotions.

There was no point in delaying the inevitable. His hopes and dreams were hanging by a thread, and he had no choice but to release them and hope for the best.

Taking a deep breath, he began. "There are some things I need to tell you, Tasha," he said. "I hope you will hear me out."

He could already see the light dimming from her eyes, but there was no turning back.

"My name is not Boyd, and I'm not a nobleman. Only my sister has ever called me Boyd—it was her nickname for me when we were young. My name is Rupert, and I'm the king of Castel." He paused to catch his breath. "I'm truly sorry I misled you."

She said nothing.

"I didn't intentionally set out to do it—somehow it just happened. I knew I needed to tell you the truth, but I wasn't sure how you would react. I decided to wait until we met a third time."

"Which is now," she said.

He nodded. She seemed almost relieved, and he wondered what she'd thought he might be going to say. But he wasn't finished.

"Yesterday I received a summons from King Krasmir," he continued.

A new wariness had come to her face, but she didn't speak.

"He demanded to know my intentions toward his daughter. I told him there must be some mistake. I said that I'd met with a servant girl twice, but that was all. He made it clear that Tasha and Princess Teylee are the same person. You're his daughter."

She stared at him through narrowed eyes. "And?" she asked.

"When I learned that, I requested permission from your parents to court you."

She didn't respond, so he pressed on. "Your father talked about customs and protocols and dowries. Your mother told him it was nonsense and that I was welcome to court you."

"Did it occur to you to include me in the conversation?" she asked. A dangerous tone had entered her voice.

"It did, but not until after I'd been dismissed," he admitted. "Your father took me completely by surprise! I was barely able to think straight for much of the conversation."

Her eyes were flashing now. "Do you imagine I want to be courted by someone who doesn't think to consult me when my future is being discussed?" She sent him a withering look. "You're supposed to be a king, yet apparently you don't have the nerve to stand up to my parents."

He hung his head miserably.

When he next glanced at her, her face had become expressionless again. It was almost more than he could bear.

"Goodbye, Lord Boyd," she said woodenly. "Or King Rupert, or whoever you are."

And with that she was gone.

24

Another long day was coming to an end at last for Brother Ander and Ethen. Two weeks had passed since their captivity began, and the monk had seen no sign that it was likely to end.

Something needed to change in their situation though, and change soon. Up to that point, the five-year-old had done remarkably well, but the strain was becoming increasingly evident. It had been especially difficult that afternoon to coax the five-year-old to spend time at his lessons. And in the morning he had refused uncharacteristically to speak Rogandan.

“Why hasn’t my father found me?” Ethen asked irritably. “I miss him. And I want to see my mother!”

His lower lip trembled uncontrollably, and he began to cry.

Brother Ander comforted him as best he could.

Ethen had unusual energy and intelligence, which was no surprise given his parents. The daily routine of physical and intellectual exercise established by the monk had provided an important outlet for his restlessness. Nevertheless, steering the boy through the captivity had been no easy matter. Without contact of any kind with his parents, Ethen had become increasingly tempted to dissolve into despair.

The monk resisted the threatened downward spiral with thoughtful creativity and gentle compassion, supported by fervent prayer. Having carried his own childhood hurts well into adult life, he fully understood the bitter consequences of allowing unresolved disappointment and anger to grow and fester.

'In this world you will have trouble...' The words often came to his mind now. He shook his head sadly.

His efforts to redeem the captivity slowly assumed considerable significance for Brother Ander. He even wondered if he might one day come to see this undertaking as the main purpose behind his calling as a monk.

Ethen sat down beside Brother Ander as daylight faded from the sky. Resting wearily against the monk's shoulder, the boy confided, "I'm glad you're with me, Brother Ander. I don't like the dark."

The monk gazed down at him sympathetically. "God gave us darkness as well as light," he assured the boy.

"But why?"

"Do you ever think about light during the daytime?" asked Brother Ander.

Ethen shook his head.

The monk nodded. "That's the reason darkness exists. If it weren't for the darkness, we probably wouldn't think about light at all. We learn to value light because we have to live with darkness."

The boy went quiet for some time. Then his little brow puckered into a frown. "Is that the same as liking food better when you're hungry?" Looking at his burly friend, he screwed up his nose. "I'm sick of bread, but I wish I had some now."

"That's exactly right," Brother Ander told him with a smile. "I suspect you understand these things better than a lot of grownups."

For Kamash, the familiar and comfortable patterns of his life had been upended almost from the moment he met Princess Neira. The turbulence that followed was unlike anything he had experienced before, even in his days as advisor to the unpredictable King Ugar.

Nevertheless, as he relaxed in unaccustomed luxury in the palace at Rog he found himself bored and lacking purpose. Meetings involving the princess had come to an abrupt end with the disappearance of Lord Torbury's son. The old man had no doubt that King Krasmir's attention would continue to be diverted until the matter was resolved one way or another.

Disturbingly, the rumors swirling around the palace suggested that the Ahrans were responsible for the abduction. Kamash had no way of establishing the truth. When he directly confronted the princess with the rumors, she responded evasively. He had the impression she knew no more than he did.

The princess must surely be feeling adrift herself. She had arrived in Rog as a sensation; now she was little more than a curiosity. Such a transformation must have been unusually difficult for someone who relished being the center of attention.

At first Neira had entertained herself by haunting Rog's markets, visiting them frequently, often daily. Since the abduction, King Krasmir had put a stop to that.

Kamash wasn't surprised. The Rogandans already had plenty to worry about with the Ahrans. It was asking too much to allow the princess to wander freely where her safety could not be guaranteed.

Conscious that the princess might not be coping well, Kamash decided to pay her a visit. He had been assigned a room in the same section of the palace, so he knew where to find her. And with her movements restricted, she couldn't be too far away.

The first person he encountered was Uman. The gloomy expression on the guard's face came as no surprise to Kamash. The Ahran hadn't seemed truly content since they left the island.

Kamash nodded to Uman. The guard nodded back once before turning away, ignoring him completely.

The princess spent a lot of time in a sunny room overlooking a stand of trees that lay within the grounds of the palace. Kamash headed for it, expecting to find her there. The room lay silent and empty.

Glancing out of the window, he noticed her walking swiftly away from the building in the direction of the trees. Concluding she had decided to take a walk, he headed outside to join her.

The park outside their building had become very familiar to Kamash. After so many years with the sea on his doorstep, he found it stifling to spend extended periods inside buildings. Accordingly he took every opportunity to wander outside in the open air. Guards were stationed all around the palace buildings, but they didn't interfere with their foreign guests provided they remained within the palace grounds.

Catching a glimpse of Princess Neira entering the trees, the old man set off after her. She didn't seem to have spotted him, so he needed to hurry to have any chance of catching her before she moved out of reach.

By the time he reached the trees he could see no sign of her. Guessing at the direction she had taken, he moved forward. He had been walking for only a few minutes when he heard voices ahead of him.

Without fully understanding why, he decided to remain hidden. Creeping forward cautiously, he concealed himself behind a tree, straining his ears to hear the conversation. Not a word of it made any sense to him—the conversation was clearly being conducted in the Ahran language.

Peering around the tree, he glimpsed a dark figure standing before the princess. The stranger held out something that looked like a parchment. Taking it, the princess opened it and read it slowly and carefully. The man held out a hand, and she returned the parchment. After concealing it within his clothing, the dark figure turned swiftly away and was lost to sight, leaving the princess alone.

Noticing her glancing around furtively, he pulled back quickly to avoid being seen. By the time he was willing to risk peering out again, she was gone as well. He waited for a considerable time before heading back to the building again, taking a roundabout path.

Princess Neira was emerging from her room when he reentered the building.

"Kamash!" she said vivaciously. "Where have you been? It's so long since I saw you last—have you been hiding from me?"

"I'm pleased to see you so buoyant, Princess," he replied. "Why the high spirits?"

"No reason," she assured him hastily. "I've just been for a short walk. Spending some time in the park has undoubtedly done me good." After giving him a cheery wave, she headed back to the privacy of her room.

The old man returned to his own quarters with a great deal to think about. Clearly she had been meeting with an Ahran agent, and the man appeared to have passed some kind of letter to her. Was this the first such meeting, or had it been a regular occurrence?

The change of mood in the princess raised many questions. Her contact with the agent—or perhaps the letter he had passed to her—had lifted her spirits enormously. Had the Ahrans somehow managed to heal the breach with their princess? He shook his head in bewilderment. They had abandoned her to die on the island. How could she overlook such a betrayal?

Should he inform King Krasmir of what he had seen? Uncertain and ill at ease, he decided to give himself time to think it through before deciding anything about what to do next.

THOMAS WATCHED ANXIOUSLY AS WILL PACED BACK and forth around the room. If Will's restlessness was anything to go by, he might have been dancing on hot coals.

"When I promised Krasmir not to work independently, I had no idea how it was going to turn out!" he growled. "We know exactly where to go next, but we're forced to wait while Kulferan tries to figure it out for himself."

"It isn't his fault," Thomas pointed out reasonably. "We have an unfair advantage."

"His people must be completely incompetent if they're still trying to squeeze details out of the Ahrans!" snapped Will.

"They don't know who to focus on," Thomas reminded him. "And even if they did, they can't force information out of him if he isn't willing to talk."

No further response was forthcoming, but it was nevertheless obvious that Will was not going to be placated.

Time passed in uncomfortable silence before Will seemed to reach a decision.

"We're not going to wait any longer," he said decisively.

"But we can't just ignore your promise to the king," protested Thomas.

"We won't go in with force," Will replied. "We'll head for the safe house and observe from a distance. You can watch people coming and going. All you need to do is find out if Ethen is there. If he isn't, find out the location of another Ahran safe house. We'll simply go there instead."

Thomas frowned. It all sounded very simple, but he had a feeling it was likely to prove anything but. He opened his mouth to argue but then closed it again without speaking. Will wasn't going to be convinced, no matter what he said.

How could he refuse his friend? Would he behave any differently if one of his children had been taken? Thomas sighed in resignation.

THOMAS AND WILL stood hidden behind a building, opposite the house unwittingly identified by the Ahran agent. After watching vigilantly for almost two hours, they had caught a single glimpse of just one of the inhabitants of the house. It was enough to confirm to Thomas that Ethen and Brother Ander were not being held there, and that the Ahran knew of no other safe houses. But Thomas had seen that others lived there too, and one of them might have information worth knowing.

Will was becoming impatient. "Have they somehow spotted us?" he whispered, aiming a sideways glance at his companion.

Thomas could only shrug. "It seems unlikely. We've seen no sign of anyone."

"We've waited long enough," said Will. "I'm going in there."

"You can't be serious," hissed Thomas. "On your own, with no support?"

"I'm not planning to fight them," Will replied. "I'll pretend I'm selling something."

"Selling what?" demanded Thomas, frantically trying to dream up of a way of talking Will out of such a desperate plan.

"What does it matter?" Will replied dismissively. "Just make sure you're ready to get a good look at whoever comes to the door."

With that he was gone.

Thomas watched wide-eyed as he strode across the street. Reaching the door, he hammered on it hard with an open hand before stepping back to wait for an answer.

When no one appeared, he hammered on the door again.

It wasn't difficult for Thomas to guess what was happening. The occupants undoubtedly wanted to keep a low profile. If they weren't expecting visitors, they probably wouldn't bother to answer the door at all.

With no response forthcoming, Will hammered on the door a third time. Then, apparently concluding he was wasting his time, he turned abruptly aside and headed off down the road. Thomas watched on, bemused.

Many minutes passed before Will reappeared. When he did, he bore a flaming torch in one hand, while his other hand clutched something to his chest. Stopping once more outside the door, he opened his arm to release his oddly shaped burden. A pile of sticks fell to the ground. Reaching down, Will leaned the sticks against the door, then held the torch to them.

Before long the tinder began to smoke. A flicker appeared, growing steadily brighter. Will stepped back as flames licked at the door.

Torn between astonishment and alarm, Thomas gaped open mouthed at his friend's stunt. Apparently deciding that his work had been done, Will turned away from the door and hurried back across the road.

Thomas exhaled noisily in relief as the commander rejoined him, still scarcely able to believe what he had done.

"What are you doing?" Thomas asked in alarm.

"Since they refuse to answer the door, I'm going to smoke them out," Will replied grimly. He nudged Thomas in the ribs. "Make sure you keep a close eye on that door!" he commanded.

At first the fire did indeed seem to generate little more than smoke. After a while, though, the smoke gave way to an angry red glow. And with the door now ablaze, flames were spreading upward to threaten the eaves of the building. If the occupants of the house hadn't noticed the blaze yet, then surely they would do so before long.

By the time the fire reached the thatched roof, the roar of the flames could clearly be heard in the stillness. The door crashed suddenly outward, and smoke billowed from the opening—the interior of the house must also be burning. Men stumbled into the street, coughing and gagging from the smoke.

Three men had emerged before a fourth appeared dragging a man behind him. A glance at the prone form revealed no mental activity at all. Thomas knew that the man's life had ended.

Will's purpose had been achieved though. Thomas now knew of another location they could investigate.

Other people had appeared from nearby dwellings, and shouts filled the air as people hurried to fill buckets of water to fight the fire before it could spread to other houses.

Pulling at Thomas's elbow, Will dragged him away before anyone could spot them.

As soon as they were clear of the area, Will looked at Thomas sharply. "Did you learn about any other safe houses?"

"One of the men knows of another house—that was all," Thomas replied distractedly. "What if the neighbors can't put out the fire?" he demanded, his voice wavering in his agitation. "They'll lose their houses. Maybe more people will lose their lives."

Will waved an arm dismissively. “That won’t be an issue. There’s no wind to carry embers tonight, and there’s plenty of water on hand and people to carry it.”

Thomas covered his face with his hands, his mind filled with images of people frantic to protect their homes and loved ones.

Neither of them moved. Will’s voice brought Thomas back to the present. “You’re right, Thomas. Come with me.”

Will immediately headed back toward the fire. After staring in amazement for a moment, Thomas hurried after him.

They arrived to find men and women in two ragged lines, passing buckets of water toward the fire. Up to that point it hadn’t spread, but even a casual glance showed a major conflagration threatened every house in the street.

The bucket line was not stable. Thomas saw that people were coming and going constantly, running around in a panic to retrieve belongings from neighboring houses.

Will sized up the situation in a moment. Stepping forward, his voice rang out forcefully, issuing a series of clear commands. After staring at him in bewilderment for a moment, people everywhere sprang into action. Soon the two lines had stabilized, and two new lines had quickly formed as other buckets were brought to bear. Much more water was now being thrown on the fire. The houses on each side of the blaze were being preemptively soaked as well.

Having committed himself, Will threw all of his restless energy into the task. As well as directing the operation, he joined any bucket line that faltered, shouting encouragement as he passed buckets forward.

Even with Will’s intervention, it was a near-run thing. By the time Will and his exhausted workers brought the fire under control, the original house had been entirely destroyed. The houses on either side were water damaged, but otherwise intact.

Thomas had not wasted a moment before joining one of the lines, and he labored tirelessly throughout the battle. He now collapsed in exhaustion.

Will came and slumped down beside him, utterly drained from

his exertions. His face sagging with weariness, he faced Thomas. "Thank you for bringing me to my senses, Thomas," he said. "I...I'm not proud of what I did. It wasn't intentional. I never expected to start an inferno."

Thomas placed a hand on his shoulder. "No other lives were lost. And the surrounding houses were not seriously damaged."

"But someone owned the house I destroyed." Will turned away, closing his eyes and allowing his head to sink to his chest.

Thomas could think of nothing to say.

Glancing around, he could see no sign of the Ahrans. They must have taken advantage of the chaos to slip away, taking the body of their comrade with them.

Thomas did notice that the number of people milling around had increased significantly. A body of soldiers had arrived on the scene. Too late to help fight the flames, they were working to assist the locals.

To his alarm, Thomas saw that the soldiers were led by Lord Kulferan. Worse, the nobleman had recognized Will and was striding toward them.

"Lord Torbury! What brings you here?" he asked. The question was phrased respectfully, but it was clear he would not welcome a superficial answer.

"We were in the area when the fire started, My Lord, and we decided to help," Will replied.

One of Lord Kulferan's soldiers came and whispered in his ear. The Rogandan commander frowned for a moment before addressing Will again. "I am told that you took charge of the effort to extinguish the fire." He sounded mildly surprised.

Will dipped his head. "The locals were struggling, and they seemed to need guidance. It was the least I could do."

Lord Kulferan turned his focus on the cleanup effort, directing his soldiers to help the residents and make sure that no burning embers remained to spark another fire. He nevertheless continued to hover nearby.

After a few minutes, he addressed Will once more. "Could you please join me, Lord Torbury? The king will wish to express his appreciation for your assistance. Two of my men will accompany your companion to ensure he returns safely to the palace."

"Of course, Lord Kulferan," Will replied flatly. He appeared exhausted, but Thomas knew him well enough to recognize his discomfort.

Two soldiers approached Thomas, motioning for him to join them. Waving a farewell to Will, he followed them back to his quarters.

ARRIVING AT THE PALACE, Will was ushered into a small reception room and left there alone. Feeling gloomy and disheartened, he was grateful for an opportunity to recover himself.

In the end he was forced to wait for a considerable period. It was late at night when King Krasmir finally arrived, and Will wondered if His Majesty had been called from his bed.

Getting to his feet, Will bowed low.

The king nodded in response, one of his eyebrows raised quizzically. His expression couldn't be mistaken for a smile. "I understand we have you to thank for putting out a fire earlier tonight, Lord Torbury," he said.

Will dipped his head again. "I was pleased to be able to assist, Your Majesty."

"My soldiers were told that you didn't arrive until after the fire had started. How did you become aware of it?"

"I was wandering in the area with Thomas Stablehand. The glow in the sky and the smoke made it apparent, even from a distance."

The king peered at him shrewdly. "I am also told that the people in that particular dwelling were foreigners. Do you think it possible that they were Ahran agents?"

"I did not speak to them, Your Majesty. My entire focus was on extinguishing the fire."

The king studied him silently. Then he frowned. "I will be frank with you, Lord Torbury. There has been no suggestion that you were in any way involved with whoever or whatever started the fire, and I am told that the surrounding houses were saved only thanks to a prodigious effort on your part. Nevertheless, a house that could have been harboring Ahran agents caught fire, and somehow you were on the scene. That is a strange coincidence, is it not?"

Will did not reply.

The king sighed. "This is a delicate situation, Lord Torbury. I am responsible for your protection, and I can only imagine your king's reaction if anything should happen to you. Ensuring your safety is a key priority for me. I have ordered that senior soldiers will be assigned to you, and to your countryman Rufe Sarjant. From now on both of you will be accompanied whenever you leave the palace. I trust that you will not misunderstand this precaution."

Will had nothing to say in response, and it was abundantly clear from the king's tone that the conversation was at an end. Almost as an afterthought, King Krasmir added, "And may I once more express my thanks for your help tonight."

With that, Will was dismissed. After bowing low, he turned and left the reception room.

25

Arriving at the Arvenian quarters in the palace, Thomas found himself subjected to a barrage of questions from Amyra and the others. After quickly describing all that had happened, from finding the Ahran safe house to fighting the fire, he answered their questions as best he could.

When he finished they settled in to wait for the return of Will.

The night was well advanced before Will reappeared after his meeting with the king. His face wore a grim expression.

"What happened?" asked Thomas anxiously.

"Krasmir has decided to clip my wings," Will replied with a shrug. "We should have left as soon as the fire was under control," he grumbled.

"What did the king say?" asked Amyra.

"From now on I won't be leaving the palace without one of Krasmir's men on my tail. The same with Rufe. The rest of you should still be able to do as you please."

"Does the king know what actually happened?" asked Thomas.

Will shook his head. "Thankfully not."

"Whatever were you thinking, setting fire to that house?" demanded Amyra in exasperation.

"I was doing what I could to find our son," he replied fiercely.

The others remained silent.

Amyra sighed. "The question is what the rest of us can do now that Will and Rufe are grounded," she said. "I certainly won't be giving in. I won't be attempting anything adventurous though." She raised an eyebrow in Will's direction. "Don't expect me to burn any houses to the ground."

Will winced, but didn't comment.

"Elena or Thomas can come with me if they're willing. Given what's just happened, maybe Elena is a better choice next time."

Elena and Thomas both nodded.

"Will you accompany us, Haldek?" Amyra asked.

"Of course you must count me in," Haldek replied.

Amyra's head dipped once. "Thank you all." Her face was set firm in determination. "Since Thomas has a location we can start with, we will leave early tomorrow morning—a little before dawn. We need to give ourselves the best possible chance of catching anyone leaving the house for the day."

"You should assume you'll be followed," Will warned them.

"I'll be able to tell if that's what's happening," Elena said calmly. "Provided I can catch sight of whoever is tailing us."

DAWN WAS near when Elena followed Amyra and Haldek out of the building.

"Are you sure you know where it is?" Amyra whispered to her.

"Yes," Elena assured her. "Thomas gave me the details."

"Let's be off!" called Amyra loudly, speaking in Arvenian. "I want to get to the markets early."

Dark as it was, Elena kept her eyes open. She had the stone at the ready to allow her to be certain about the intentions of anyone who appeared to be following them.

As the first light dimly brightened the sky, Haldek nudged Elena gently, jerking his head behind them and off to one side. Elena waited a few moments before casting a glance back in that direction. Two men were walking along some distance behind them. The men were talking quietly to each other, apparently taking no interest in them. But they could not hide their intentions from the stone. Elena was immediately aware that these men had been assigned the task of tailing them.

She leaned closer to Amyra. "Two of King Krasmir's men are following us."

Amyra nodded curtly. "We'll lose them in the markets. Stay close."

They arrived at the main market in Rog as the sun was clearing the horizon. Stalls were laden with produce and prospective buyers bustled about everywhere.

Elena and Haldek followed Amyra into a tent filled with carpets. They were greeted by a brightly clad woman who welcomed them with a smile and waved them to some seats, calling for tea to be served. Amyra ignored her completely, heading for the back of the tent and disappearing through a loose flap. Haldek was not far behind her. The carpet vendor watched them open mouthed. Elena shrugged helplessly before turning and following the other two out of the tent.

She found Amyra peering back the way they had come.

"Our admirers have taken the bait," said Amyra quietly. "By the time they realize we're not in the tent we'll be long gone."

With that she headed swiftly away from the tent, weaving her way through the market. Elena was hard pressed to keep up with her.

No more than thirty minutes after the sun rose, they were in position. The Ahran safe house was close by, with them located far enough away to avoid attracting attention.

They settled down to wait.

In the end they didn't need to wait long. Two men soon left the house, hurrying away without looking back. Then a third arrived, disappearing inside the house.

"Anything useful?" Amyra asked tensely.

Elena nodded. "The man who just arrived has come here from another house. And he's aware of a boy being held captive!"

Amyra gave a little cry, covering her face with her hands.

"Unfortunately he doesn't know exactly where, though," she added hastily. "It isn't at the house he came from."

A slow intake of breath greeted this news. Elena understood Amyra's reaction. This latest information might be a step in the right direction, but at that moment they were no closer to finding him.

Bolnyk had completed his report on the progress made by the agents. "There is one other matter, Your Eminence," he added tentatively.

"Well?" demanded the Grand Vizier, eyeing him suspiciously.

Berating himself for allowing even the tiniest trace of discomfort to show, Bolnyk hardened himself. "Some of our agents were foolish enough to be observed spying on the Arvenian delegation at the palace," he said. "As they escaped they were pursued by a boy and a monk. They took the opportunity to capture them both. The child is the son of the Arvenian army commander. He is being held along with the monk in an abandoned cellar in one of our safe houses in Rog."

The chief minister had gone red in the face. "What possessed the fools to allow themselves to be caught spying in the first place? And why compound their error by risking an abduction?" he hissed.

The agent didn't flinch. "I have asked them similar questions," he replied. "Nevertheless it occurred to me that the boy might provide us with useful leverage. Perhaps we can use him to drive a wedge between the Arvenians and the Rogandans." He bowed very low. "I did not raise the matter when you first arrived because there seemed to be many pressing matters that required your attention. I apologize if I have erred in these decisions."

Rheibas stared back at him, apparently assessing the possibilities.

"What do you know about the boy's father—this Arvenian army commander?" he asked.

"Very little of substance, Your Eminence," Bolnyk told him. "I will make inquiries."

"How secure are these prisoners?" Rheibas demanded.

"I believe they are very secure," Bolnyk replied. "They have been in our keeping for some days without escaping. And no one has discovered their whereabouts."

"Bring them here to me," ordered the chief minister. "I want them alive. The boy might have value as a hostage. We can use him to make sure the Arvenians do not interfere with our plans. He might also be useful to us dead, provided we make certain the Arvenian commander believes the Rogandans are responsible."

Bolnyk bowed.

"I am holding you accountable for them," Rheibas told him. "Your priority is to get them here alive. Whatever happens though, do not permit them to be rescued. As a last resort, kill them both," he added coldly.

KAMASH HAD BEEN unable to get the interaction with Thomas and Elena out of his mind. He had little concern about them exposing his talisman to unwanted attention. Something told him they would keep his secret as they had promised.

The interaction had been unsettling for a different reason. Recounting his history with the stone had highlighted the dramatic ways in which it had changed his life. The process had left him with a simple question. Would he be better off without it?

He had never sought the stone—it came as an unexpected gift. King Ugar had been the one who lusted after it, to no avail. Now Ugar and his son were dead.

Kamash had outlived them both. Did he want to outlast King Krasmir as well? Could he find the energy to adapt to a new king when Krasmir's life came to an end?

Living was a pursuit that required energy, especially when it took place around other people. And there was no escaping trouble. It came along for the ride. Trouble was inevitable, and the longer you lived, the more trouble came your way. A war with Arvenon might have passed him by on his remote island, but sooner or later another war would come—perhaps even an Ahran invasion. Would he be able to avoid that conflict too?

He faced the truth: well preserved he might be, but he was becoming weary of the ceaseless toil of daily existence.

Even on the island he had begun to tire of life. Since returning to Rog, his days had been consumed with wrestling—with Krasmir's nobles, with the princess, even with himself. The intensity of it was overwhelming. His energy for life was slowly being leached away.

The arrival of the princess brought his musing to an abrupt end. The merest glimpse of her had been more than enough to increase his weariness.

Princess Neira arrived with her nose in the air as usual. She eyed him haughtily before turning away with a disdainful toss of her head.

Kamash rolled his eyes. He had remained with her in the hope that he might be able to do her some good. Was he deluding himself?

Confronted by so many questions, he could only shake his head helplessly.

Uman belatedly arrived, positioning himself near the princess. His face, normally expressionless, suggested he wasn't entirely content.

The princess was almost strutting today, and Kamash eyed her curiously. She seemed much more buoyant than usual, and he wondered what might account for it.

"This city is unsafe for my countrymen," grumbled Neira suddenly, turning back to him with a scowl of displeasure.

"What do you mean, Princess?" Kamash asked with a puzzled frown.

"King Krasmir thinks they are wild animals, to be hunted down for sport. They are being hounded everywhere in Rog."

"How do you know that?" he asked.

"Everybody knows," she sniffed.

Her pronouncement confirmed his worst fears. "You have been in contact with Ahran agents."

Glancing at his expression, a snort of laughter escaped her. "Just look at you, Kamash! If only you could see your face!"

It was not lost on him that she had not denied his assertion. "Did your people have anything to do with the abduction of the boy?" he asked in growing alarm.

She waved an arm dismissively. "Why should I care if some grubby little brat has gotten himself into trouble? It means nothing to me."

Uman was following the interaction closely. He seemed more dispirited than ever.

Kamash faced the princess, his eyes narrowed. "It matters to me," he said. "If you're involved in the kidnapping—even if you're just aware of who has done it—you'll get no further help from me."

The princess stared at him. The irritability on her face was slowly replaced by a look of dismay. Her lower lip drooped miserably, and a tear came to her eye.

"Don't try to wheedle your way out of it, Neira," he said coldly. "I'm not interested in your manipulation. I mean what I said."

Ignoring her wide-eyed stare, he turned on his heel and strode away.

THOMAS BURST into the room in search of Will and Amyra, barely able to contain his excitement. They were exactly where he expected them to be, but the mood in the room quickly brought him back down to earth.

The children were playing energetically and noisily, to the point where he almost needed to cover his ears. Will and Amyra sat apart, haunted looks on their faces. They seemed entirely unaware of the commotion around them. Elena was shooting concerned looks at her two friends, interspersed with repeated requests to the children to tone it down. The other Arvenians had wisely fled the area.

Leaving the room, Thomas sought out Haldek. "Could you please look after the children for a while, Haldek? I need to speak with Will and Amyra and Elena."

Haldek grimaced. "These children have too much energy. They should be outdoors." Then he shrugged. "Of course. I am happy to help."

Haldek led the way back into the room. "Children!" he called. "It is time for a game with Uncle Haldek."

It took two more attempts before he managed to get their attention, but soon they were bouncing eagerly around him.

Catching Elena's eye, Thomas jerked his head significantly toward Amyra and Will and headed for the door. He led the way to a smaller room where he knew they were able to talk in peace. Elena arrived with an eager look on her face. Her companions appeared distracted and lacking energy. They looked at Thomas dully, like people who had lost hope.

"I'm beginning to think we've been approaching this the wrong way!" Thomas began breathlessly. "I just spotted Kamash—the spokesperson for Princess Neira—and the stone showed me what's on his mind. The princess has been in touch with Ahran agents—he witnessed one of them handing her a document. And he suspects she might know something about Ethen's captivity."

He seemed to have succeeded in capturing their attention. Will was frowning, and a hint of life had returned to Amyra's eyes.

"What are you suggesting?" asked Elena hopefully.

"I think we need to try to enlist Kamash's help," he replied.

"Why would we do that?" asked Will dismissively. "He's the princess's puppet."

"Perhaps not as much as it might appear," Elena replied thoughtfully. "He agreed to help her mainly out of compassion."

"I discovered that he feels very strongly about the situation with Ethen!" Thomas told them excitedly. "So much so he spoke to the princess about it. He told her he'll have nothing more to do with her if he discovers she's involved in any way in Ethen's captivity. Even if she just knows who's holding him captive!"

"That's all very well, but it sounds like he knows nothing more than we do," said Amyra. "How can he help us?"

"I haven't been able even to catch sight of the princess," Thomas replied. "Her suite is on the opposite side of the palace, and she barely seems to leave it now. If Kamash could arrange for us to meet her, we could find out everything she knows. I only need a glimpse of her, of course."

Will didn't share Thomas's enthusiasm. "Even if the princess has spoken to an agent who knows about Ethen, that doesn't suggest she's been told anything about where he's being held. She doesn't know her way around Rog, so locations would mean nothing to her. And the agents have no reason to give her details anyway."

Thomas left feeling deflated but determined not to give up.

KING STEFFAN STOOD with Queen Essanda on a battlement of their castle at Arnost, gazing distractedly into the distance. A courier accompanied by a contingent of guards had just ridden in from Rog, weary after the long journey on horseback.

"A king isn't supposed to be completely helpless. But that's the reality in this situation," said Steffan gloomily.

Essanda was holding her head. "I feel helpless, too. Will and Amyra are so far away!"

"The worst is that I feel responsible," said Steffan. "I was the one who sent him to Rog." His shoulders slumped. "Will seems to have led a charmed life, and I've taken that far too much for granted."

She shrugged helplessly. "You've never been able to protect Will when he's been off serving the interests of the kingdom. Or anyone else who's ever acted on your behalf."

Steffan threw his hands into the air. "Why did he have to take Amyra and the children? I don't understand it!"

"Would you want to be parted from your family if you were in

Will's position?" Essanda asked. "Don't forget that in our darkest time, after the attack in the barn, we had each other. I was heavily pregnant and unusually vulnerable, but when you look back on everything that happened, would you have wanted me to be somewhere else?"

"I suppose not," he admitted. "But all that aside, I can't make any sense of Thomas and Elena's decision to go, especially with their children. Apart from the risk to them, having a crowd of children running around—in Rog of all places—was almost inviting disaster!"

"I imagine Will and Amyra would have thought their children would cope better if they had friends their own age." She put a gentle hand on his shoulder. "All we can do is hope and pray that Ethen will be found alive and unharmed. At least Brother Ander is with him—we can take some comfort from that. It would be terrible if he was entirely alone."

He nodded. "I need to write to Krasmir. It's going to be delicate. I intend to convey in the strongest possible terms that I expect him to make extraordinary efforts to recover Ethen safely. But it can't come across as inflammatory." He passed a hand across his face. "I'll need you to read it before I send it."

She nodded. "Of course."

"And then I need to write to Will and Amyra. I have no idea even where to begin."

"Would you like me to draft that letter for you?" she asked.

"I would!" he told her with a sigh of relief. "However would I manage without you, Essanda?"

He put an arm around her, and she leaned in, resting her head on his shoulder.

26

For Rupert the two days that followed his calamitous interchange with Tasha were bleak beyond words. Unable to face people, he kept to himself, telling anyone who asked that he wasn't feeling well. Lord Mardone and the other Castelans who had accompanied him to Rog offered to call for a doctor, but he dismissed their concerns.

Based on the content of his conversation with King Krasmir, it seemed to Rupert that Tasha's response had been an overreaction. But even if he was right, what difference did it make?

He would have given a great deal to consult with his sister or Count Gordan, but they were far away. Elena had impressed him as both kind and unusually empathic, and he briefly considered confiding in her. But he quickly discarded the idea. She was entirely preoccupied with Lady Torbury.

Wandering alone in the garden, his melancholy was interrupted by the arrival of a servant with a visitor in tow. The visitor was Crown Prince Rimek.

The prince turned pleading eyes upon him the moment the servant had gone. "You have to see her, Rupert!" he exclaimed. "She's irritable and unhappy, and it's so unlike her! She refuses to speak to my parents."

"She won't want to see me," Rupert replied miserably. "She was very angry after I told her about the meeting with your parents. She had some harsh things to say."

Rimek nodded. "That accounts for it then," he said. "She never speaks harshly to anyone." He paused, musing. "Well, almost never. There was that time she came upon someone mistreating a horse..." He shook his head. "This is different. She's upset with herself."

"She isn't just upset with herself," Rupert assured him.

"Probably not," Rimek conceded. "Either way, you need to speak with her!"

When it became obvious that the prince wouldn't take no for an answer, Rupert reluctantly allowed himself to be dragged back to the royal wing of the palace. Leading him out into the garden, Rimek pointed him in the right direction and gave him a gentle push.

Rupert's feet carried him forward, presumably toward Tasha, although he had no idea what he was going to say to her.

Moving around a large bush, he found himself face-to-face with the princess. She looked at least as unhappy as he felt.

"What are you doing here?" she asked dispiritedly.

She had left her accusation hanging in the air when they parted. *You're supposed to be a king, yet apparently you don't have the nerve to stand up to my parents.* Those words had plagued him relentlessly since. Standing before her once more, he decided it was time he showed some spine.

"Look at you!" he exclaimed. "You're clearly every bit as miserable as I've been. Are you willing to do anything about it?"

She didn't rise to his challenge. "There's nothing I can do."

"There is something," he said. "You can hear me out."

She didn't respond.

"You owe me that much," he insisted. "I wasn't the only one who muddied the truth!"

A spark of defiance rose momentarily in her eyes, but it just as quickly died away.

Not waiting for permission, he began speaking. "I haven't been blessed with an easy life. My mother passed away when I was seven. I have a sister, Essanda, who is a wonderful person. But my father married her off to a foreign king the day after her fourteenth birthday! I was twelve years old. Once she was gone, it was just me and my father. I know he loved me, but expressing it directly wasn't something he ever learned to do.

"He was assassinated when I was seventeen. I was devastated. I became king long before I expected to, and well before I was ready for that kind of responsibility. I made some dreadful mistakes. I trusted people I shouldn't have trusted—people who were secretly working for your father's predecessor. They arranged for my food to be laced with poison, and I almost lost my life, not to mention the kingdom."

When he started she'd barely been able to look at him. Now he glimpsed compassion stirring in her eyes. She probably couldn't help herself.

"I was rescued by some wise and loyal people who risked their lives to expose the traitor and his accomplices. I gradually recovered, and the kingdom was saved. Since then I've slowly been growing into my role. I've been working hard at it, because I know how much power a king has to influence the well-being of every person in the kingdom.

"I have intelligent and capable advisors I can call upon, but it's a lonely job. Crushingly lonely at times! Plenty of young women have been lining up to ease my burden, as you might imagine. They're eager to wear the crown that sits on the head of the queen. But do any of them care about me for my own sake?" He shrugged helplessly. "I have no way of knowing."

He fixed his eyes on her face, his heart beginning to pound. "Then I met you," he said.

She was staring at him wide-eyed. He had her full attention now.

"You didn't know I was a king. You were willing to spend time with someone you thought was a nobody. You told me about yourself, and you asked me questions. And when I answered, you listened as if I was saying something worth hearing. It was intoxicating to be with someone who took me seriously, just as I was. Your eyes seemed to light up because you enjoyed being with me." He gazed at her intently. "Do you have any idea how your eyes sparkle when you're happy?" he asked.

Was that the ghost of a smile on her face?

"I haven't known you for long," he continued, "but it was quickly obvious to me that we share similar values and passions. Everything changed for me after the time we spent together. I honestly can't remember feeling so contented."

He sighed. "I knew it could all come crashing down, because I needed to tell you the truth. I wasn't sure how a carefree servant girl would cope with knowing she was being pursued by a king."

He made sure he had caught her eyes. "I didn't care that you were a servant, Tasha. I didn't care that your skin was a different color. I didn't even care that you were better at languages than me!"

That earned him a grin.

"The reason I didn't care about any of that is because I care about *you*. You might be Tasha, you might be Princess Teylee, you might be the daughter of a king who's sometimes compared to a bear."

Taken by surprise at his own brazenness, he stole a quick glance about him. "Please don't tell him I said that!" he blurted awkwardly, sparking a brief burst of laughter from her.

His face grew serious again. "Whatever people might call you and however they might think of you, to me you'll always be the unpretentious girl with the sparkling eyes who spares a thought for the most disadvantaged—a girl who was willing to treat me as someone who mattered, not as someone to be used."

She stared back at him. "That's the most wonderful thing anyone has ever said to me," she breathed.

He abandoned any attempt to calm his racing heart.

"Of course it doesn't hurt at all that you're also very beautiful. Have I told you that?"

"No, you haven't," she replied forthrightly. Her eyes were definitely twinkling now.

"In that case let me rectify the omission. You stunned me from the moment you stepped through that hedge. You have the most bewitching eyes, in case I haven't mentioned it already. And when you smile it's like sunshine bursting through the clouds." He gazed at her dreamily. "As for your figure..." His eyebrows went up, and he slowly released a deep sigh.

A beaming smile lit her face, only to be replaced by a mock frown. "You haven't mentioned my hair!"

"Your hair..." He scrutinized her thoughtfully. "It's positively lustrous," he finally pronounced. "When seen at the right moment."

A merry laugh escaped her lips. Her smile truly was a ray of sunlight on a stormy day.

He gazed at her in frank admiration. It was impossible to imagine ever getting tired of looking at her.

She met his eyes. "I'm very sorry I said such mean things to you," she told him penitently. "I've been so ashamed of myself! What I said wasn't true at all. I *am* willing to be courted by you." She flushed delightfully.

"And I don't blame you for being taken by surprise by my father. He can be fierce at times, especially on behalf of his children. But he did agree to let you court me, and that says a lot about his opinion of you."

She sighed. "I owe you an explanation for the way I behaved. Unexpectedly becoming a princess hasn't been easy for me. I've never been able to get used to the idea that I could be married off to someone just to benefit the kingdom. Maybe it would have been different if I'd been born a princess. But I wasn't. When you told me about your conversation with my father, all of my worst fears just came rushing in. My reaction wasn't fair, and I'm truly sorry for the way I treated you. I can be impulsive at times, and it gets me into trouble."

There were no words for his relief. "Thank you for being honest with me," he said earnestly. "I can't begin to tell you how wretched my life has felt since our last interaction."

"It's been just as bad for me," she confessed. "I've been desperately unhappy, and I've treated my family abominably."

Taking her delicate hands in his own, he gazed down into her twinkling eyes. "I would like to spend whatever time it takes to get to know you properly, Tasha," he said. "Can we make a new beginning?"

"I would like that very much," she replied. Then with a cheeky grin she added, "Lord Boyd."

He laughed. "You're allowed to call me Boyd—that offer applies only to you, mind—but no more of this Lord business!"

"In private I think I'll call you Boyd. When I'm happy with you, that is," she said, her lips quirking into another smile.

"That suits me fine," he said happily.

She became suddenly sober. "We need to leave," she said. "We'll get into big trouble if we spend this much time together without a chaperone."

He nodded. Her face fell for a moment when he released her hands, which didn't displease him at all. Then they headed back toward the building, maintaining a respectable distance between them.

She led the way inside.

It soon became apparent that her entire family had been watching from one of the windows.

"Well thank goodness for that!" exclaimed the queen. She eyed Tasha critically. "You finally look like your normal self again."

Tasha cocked an eyebrow at her mother. Then she turned away to introduce Rupert to her two sisters. Some time passed before her family saw fit to release him.

As Rupert approached his wing of the palace, he released a quiet whoop, barely able to contain his elation.

So much had changed since the crown prince pressed him to meet with Tasha. If he'd ever felt happier in his entire life, he had no memory of it.

King Krasmir retreated to the royal apartments that evening overcome with weariness. It had been another long day with more than its share of challenges. On his way he was intercepted by an unusually buoyant Tasha. The affectionate kiss she bestowed on his cheek went a long way toward improving his mood.

He arrived to find Queen Deka in raptures.

"It's so gratifying to see our Tasha well placed," she gushed. "She'll make a wonderful queen! Insisting that the children learn Arvenian was a canny move, even if I do say so myself."

Krasmir frowned at her. "There's a very long way to go before anything of the kind is settled."

"Nonsense," she replied decidedly. "He's every bit as smitten as she is. What he said to win her back was positively moving!" She heaved a dramatic sigh, brushing a tear from her eye.

He frowned at her. "They were supposedly talking in private! How do you know what he said?"

"I have my sources," she sniffed.

He grunted. "That explains why she begged me to give them space. I told her I had no intention of agreeing to any such request. You've just changed my mind!"

She glowered at him for a moment then threw up her arms. "Do whatever you want. Nothing will prevent me from keeping a close eye on her. I'm her mother!"

When he failed to respond, she sighed once more. "If only there was an advantageous match for Rimek. Steffan and Essanda's daughter is much too young for him."

"There's always the princess of Ahr," he replied dryly.

"Don't make light of such an important matter," she protested, frowning at him fiercely.

Then she brightened. "Our Ashloh will do very nicely for Delmar of course."

"I wouldn't count on it," he replied. "Delmar is planning to return to Varacellan imminently. I expect an announcement from him at any moment."

A look of dismay came over her face. "How do you know that?" she demanded.

"You're not the only one with sources," he grunted.

KRASMIR DIDN'T KNOW IT, but at that very moment King Delmar was indeed planning his return to Varas.

Delmar had invited King Rupert and Count Ranauld to join him.

"I'll be leaving for Varacellan as soon as my ship is ready to sail," he told them. "Two of my senior noblemen will remain to represent me."

"What has prompted your desire to return?" asked Ranauld.

"I've been receiving persistent reports about Ahrans arriving in Varacellan. Posing as merchants, of course, but many of them are undoubtedly agents of the emperor. Right now I'm needed there more than I'm needed here. If the situation in Rog changes, I will return without hesitation. It isn't a particularly long journey."

He turned to Rupert. "You're welcome to travel with me if you like. Once we arrive in Varacellan a ship can easily take you on to Castel."

"I appreciate your consideration, Your Majesty," Rupert replied. "I'm in no hurry to leave, though. I left Count Gordan in charge, and he has been sending me regular reports. He is extremely capable, and I trust him implicitly." He paused to steady himself. "My other reason for staying is that I have requested and received King Krasmir's permission to court Princess Teylee, his youngest daughter. Unless a pressing reason arises to return to Castel, I plan to remain in Rog for some time."

Delmar was taken completely by surprise by this announcement, and it was obvious that Ranauld was as well. "You have my hearty congratulations!" he said with a smile. "Krasmir is a good man, and I have only heard favorable reports about his children. I can also see many benefits in stronger ties between Rogand and its western neighbors."

Ranauld expressed similar sentiments, and Rupert thanked them both sincerely.

"This news might also help to explain your distraction of late, Rupert," Delmar told him with a smile.

A sheepish grin came to Rupert's face. "I won't deny that the process thus far has been challenging," he said. "But I am hopeful that we're on firmer footing now. Beyond that, though, it is likely that I will see more of King Krasmir in the immediate future. I would be happy to act as a conduit in passing information back and forth if it is helpful."

"I have no doubt that it would be helpful," Delmar assured him. "Ready access to King Krasmir could prove to be invaluable. I plan to meet with him one more time before I leave. Our agents have uncovered some information about the Ahrans that he needs to know."

Both of them looked at him expectantly, and Ranauld in particular leaned forward intently.

"Unfortunately it doesn't help directly in the search for Ethen," he told them. Ranauld's face fell. "There are indications that the Grand Vizier has returned to Rogand, and that he has based himself in a large farmhouse not far from Rog."

"That should give Krasmir something to work with," Ranauld said hopefully.

Delmar nodded. "Please treat this information as highly confidential. I would appreciate it if you speak of it to no one."

"Not even Lord Torbury?" asked Ranauld.

Delmar hesitated before replying. The matter was extremely delicate.

"The agents have discovered no evidence to suggest that Ethen is being held in the Grand Vizier's headquarters," he said. "For that reason it might be a mistake for Lord Torbury to redirect his attention away from Rog. The king is the one with the resources to search multiple locations at once."

Ranauld nodded reluctantly. "I see your point. I will honor your request to keep this information completely confidential, at least for the time being."

The meeting broke up almost at once, allowing Delmar to resume his preparations for departure.

Regrettably, Delmar would not be leaving with any great sense of achievement. He felt confident that his presence in Rog had strengthened the goodwill between Rogand and Varas. Beyond that, he could not identify a single return on his investment of time in Rogand.

27

Bisri Ahuzza watched as the Grand Vizier clambered up the rope ladder from the longboat accompanied by his senior agent, Bolnyk. The chief minister was clearly irritated that he could not meet the emperor's captains in a more civilized environment.

At that moment though, Rog harbor was not a place where Ahran warships could dock openly. Ahuzza had no choice but to keep his ships at sea. Whether Rheibas liked it or not, if he wanted to meet in secret with the captains in Ahuzza's squadron, the only option was for him to join them on one of the ships.

On this occasion, all three captains had joined Ahuzza, the chief minister, and Bolnyk on one of the ships.

The Grand Vizier eyed them haughtily. "As you are aware, the emperor sent me to Rog with instructions to inform the Rogandans that he was granting them one month to retrieve the princess. Events have now rendered the emperor's instructions obsolete."

The captains stirred uneasily, shooting glances at Bisri Ahuzza and at one another.

"After landing secretly, I learned through our agents that the king of Rogand has already produced the princess. Either he had her all along, or less likely, he came to an arrangement with the supposed pirates. However it came about, the Imperial Princess is now in Rog."

The news was greeted with general relief, but Rheibas did not leave them cheerful for long.

"The princess might be near at hand, but that does not mean she has attained her freedom. I have it on good authority that this King Krasmir has no intention of allowing her to return to her countrymen."

"What do you plan to do, Your Eminence?" asked Ahuzza.

"Nothing impulsive," he replied. "The situation is extremely delicate and needs to be handled with great care. I am informing you to keep you appraised of the circumstances." He turned to Ahuzza. "I must insist that you and your captains take no action of any kind without consulting with me first. I also need your assurance that my efforts will have your full support."

Bisri Ahuzza assessed the situation rapidly. Even if he had wanted to operate independently, he had no real choice. They were a long way from Kat Ahket, and while the emperor had placed him in command of the squadron, the practical reality was that the Grand Vizier outranked him. He might be independent in theory, but in practice he could not disregard instructions from the most senior official in the empire.

Embracing the only path available to him, he agreed not to act independently. He also confirmed that the chief minister had his full support.

Rheibas had maneuvered himself into position as the only person able to deal with the complexities of the situation. Ahuzza could only hope that the chief minister's legendary mastery over impossible situations would not desert him in this remote corner of the world.

AFTER RAPPING TWICE on the door before him, Bolnyk stood back to wait.

"Enter!" a voice growled.

Pushing through into a spacious study, the agent bowed to the Grand Vizier. "I understand you summoned me," he said.

Rheibas offered no immediate response, staring narrow eyed out of the window instead.

The look on the face of his master suggested he was not in a good mood. It wasn't hard to guess at the reason. The chief minister had given Bisri Ahuzza and his captains a report that accounted for the reappearance of the princess in Rog. He laid the blame at the door of the Rogandan king, accusing him of first abducting the princess then producing her when it suited him. The Rogandans and their allies would deny it of course, but that need not concern him. No true Ahran would believe the Rogandans over their own Grand Vizier.

The problem was that the princess knew what had really happened, and she could refute this story in a moment if she chose to. Bolnyk had no idea how Rheibas planned to deal with this problem.

The Grand Vizier had told the princess that Captain Gharpin had been responsible for her abandonment. Perhaps he had managed to convince her, but even if he had, this alternative account could not be reconciled with the story he had told Bisri Ahuzza and the captains.

The central difficulty was that the princess had survived, against all expectations. Bolnyk had no idea how that had happened. With her now established in Rog under the protection of the Rogandan king, his master's options were limited.

Nevertheless, Bolnyk had personally witnessed the rise of Bisri Rheibas to his current position as Grand Vizier of the Empire of Ahr. The promotion had not come as a gift. Rheibas had earned it the hard way. He would never have scaled such heights were he not a master at retrieving impossible situations.

Turning his attention to Bolnyk at last, Rheibas demanded, "The boy. The one who was abducted. Why hasn't he been brought here?"

"As you are aware, Your Eminence, King Krasmir has been pursuing our agents with unusual vigor over the past few days," Bolnyk replied. "A number of our safe houses have been overrun. I have delayed the transfer in the hope of a lull in the king's activities.

At the moment there would seem to be a significant risk of detection."

"Risk or no risk, I want it done within the next forty-eight hours," the chief minister demanded.

Bolnyk bowed.

"Is the monk still alive, and if so, why?"

"He is alive," Bolnyk confirmed. "I am told that the monk has managed to keep the boy calm and occupied. By doing so he has preserved his own life."

Rheibas grunted. "You're growing soft, Bolnyk."

The accusation was untrue, of course, but Bolnyk was well aware that the Grand Vizier was more interested in keeping his men ruthless and focused than in constraining himself with the truth.

The agent's only response was a stiff bow.

"Are you too weak to kill the boy should it come to that?" Rheibas demanded.

"Your orders are clear," Bolnyk replied coolly. "Bring them here alive. If that proves impossible, kill them both. I'll do it myself if the need arises."

The chief minister grunted.

Bolnyk knew he would never have risen to his current position if Rheibas had ever found him unable or unwilling to be ruthless. As for killing an innocent child, the chief minister knew he'd done worse than that. And he'd done it without hesitation.

"While you are here, you can give me a status report," the Grand Vizier said.

"There is one matter of immediate concern, Your Eminence," Bolnyk began. "It is possible that our location here may at some point become compromised. I have ordered one of the men to oversee the search for an alternative location."

"Why should our location be compromised?" Rheibas asked.

"Rog is seething with agents. The Rogandan king, the priests, even the Varasans have people snooping around. The father of the boy has been particularly determined. Every safe house that is compromised quickly leads to the detection of another."

The chief minister scowled. “Captured agents are spilling our secrets? I thought they were being told nothing beyond their own missions.”

“Agents are told only what they absolutely need to know. Very few have any information about other locations in use by our people.”

“How are the Rogandans learning about other locations then?”

Bolnyk shrugged. “They seem to have unusually effective interrogation techniques.”

The chief minister shook his head. “It makes no sense. A few of the weaker agents might crumble under torture, but on this scale?”

His master was right of course. It didn’t make sense.

“Do we have enough agents in place?” Rheibas asked with a frown.

“Your steady buildup over recent months has achieved what was needed, Your Eminence. I suspect our men are far more numerous than King Krasmir could imagine.”

The chief minister had certainly not been idle. As head of the spy network of the empire, he had almost unlimited resources at his disposal. The emperor might have placed the squadron of ships under the command of Bisri Ahuzza, but that was little more than a symbolic act. The Grand Vizier’s own ships were quietly coming and going from Rogand almost continuously, delivering agents, money, and anything else that could possibly be needed to further his purposes.

The Ahran web had already been well established by the time Rheibas arrived in Rog to accuse King Krasmir of piracy. It was now spreading out wider, both across Rogand and into Varacellan. Arvenon would be next.

“Our infiltration went undetected for months,” said the chief minister. “Why the sudden interest in exposing our agents? Is it the arrival of the princess?”

Bolnyk shook his head. “It is more likely related to the boy,” he replied. “We can expect pressure to be applied for as long as we continue to hold him.”

Rheibas scowled. “We’ll stay the course however many agents we lose. If the Rogandans are weeding out the careless ones, they're doing us a favor."

The agent offered no response apart from a tight bow.

"Have you investigated who is behind the raids on our safe houses?" the chief minister asked Bolnyk.

The agent's brows drew together. "I have made discreet inquiries, Your Eminence. Unlikely as it might seem, the only common factor seems to be Lord Torbury, the boy's father. My sources have revealed that bystanders frequently report sighting a man matching Torbury's description in the vicinity of raids."

Rheibas was clearly surprised. "The boy's father? How is he involved in this? And how did he conclude that his son was taken by Ahran agents? He couldn't possibly know that with any certainty. Why wouldn't he suspect the Rogandans? They were his enemies for long enough." He shook his head in puzzlement.

"I instructed you to learn more about him," the chief minister reminded Bolnyk. "What have you discovered?"

"As you already know, he is the Arvenian army commander," Bolnyk replied. "It is said he has never been defeated in battle. More than ten years ago he led the combined armies of Arvenon and Castel against a much larger Rogandan force that had invaded Arvenon and annexed Varas. His soldiers crushed the Rogandan army in a major battle at Torbury Scarp."

"This commander is beginning to interest me," said the chief minister, his lip curling in a sneer. "Holding his son might prove more valuable than I had imagined."

Bolnyk could readily guess what his master might be thinking. A man like Rheibas would find it especially satisfying to vanquish a celebrated strategist. The boy gave him a unique opportunity to demonstrate to the Arvenian commander that his run of victories had come to an end.

"He is a nobleman?" asked Rheibas.

Bolnyk nodded. "Yes, Your Eminence. He was formerly a commoner, but after his successes the Arvenian king gave him a title —Lord Torbury—in honor of his greatest victory. The Rogandan nobles despise him. Every use of his title is a constant reminder to them of their humiliation at his hands. Lord Torbury speaks Rogandan as if it were his native language, and that only deepens the insult."

"How does Krasmir view him?" asked the chief minister.

"The king is said to tolerate him. Krasmir needs an alliance with the Arvenians. He also has no strategist of his own to equal Torbury."

Rheibas nodded slowly. "Bring the boy to me alive if at all possible. If it becomes necessary to kill him though, don't hesitate. After Torbury's attacks on the agents of the empire, killing his son would be fitting retaliation."

His agent dipped his head in acknowledgment.

"There are perplexing riddles here," growled the chief minister. "What has made Torbury so certain his son was being held by Ahrans? And how has he become so effective at rooting out your agents?" He shook his head.

"Leave me now," the chief minister told his agent. "I need time to think. But before you go, I expect to be informed well ahead of time if the Rogandans are planning to move on this location. In the meantime, complete your search. As soon as you have secured a suitable base, ensure that we are ready to relocate to it at a moment's notice. If we move, we will leave this place occupied. Krasmir can raid it. Let him think he has taken out our headquarters."

Once more Bolnyk bowed.

"Another thing. You've been in contact with the princess?"

"I passed on your letter myself," Bolnyk confirmed. "And destroyed it afterward as you ordered."

Rheibas grunted. "Contact her again, and find out if she knows anything useful about Krasmir's intentions. You are dismissed."

HIDDEN IN THE DARKNESS, Goultzar conversed in low tones with two dark-clad priests. Others hovered watchfully nearby, ready to warn the Archprimus of unwanted attention.

He had dismantled his spy network as instructed. For the most part. Only the closest of his associates remained now—including the men engaged at that moment in his clandestine meeting. He could no longer meet with his supporters openly, and it was increasingly difficult to meet with them at all.

"Two of our agents have disappeared," one of the men told him.

He scowled. "Disappeared? How can they just disappear?"

"We can't say with any certainty," he was told. "They last reported in yesterday. They'd been observing Ahran agents while also dodging some of our own people."

"The High Priest's agents," Goultzar concluded darkly.

The only response was a grunt, presumably in affirmation.

"So who was responsible for their disappearance?" he growled. He didn't wait for an answer. "You've done well," he told them. "Keep me informed, and make sure you stay out of sight."

The men nodded silently. Within moments they were gone, as unobtrusively as they had come.

He glanced toward the temple building, extremely uncomfortable about his own mixed feelings upon reentering it.

Of late the atmosphere in the temple of Rog had been thicker than usual. It had nothing to do with the habitual odor that filled Goultzar's lungs and clung to his nostrils even when he ventured outside. The change in climate had everything to do with the coolness that had opened up between the High Priest and his Archprimus.

Perhaps it was more accurate to say that a coolness appeared to have opened up. The High Priest had never referred to it. He remained as taciturn as ever, and what he did say was about as cryptic as it had always been. But the subtle signs were there. He rarely called for Goultzar now, and when he did, the Archprimus felt the Superior's eyes boring into him, weighing him up and finding him wanting.

Goultzar tried to maintain his focus on worshiping the dark gods as before, but his thoughts increasingly wandered, and he was much too distracted to concentrate as he should.

He continued to direct the other priests—it was an essential part of this role—but he did so with uncharacteristic hesitancy. He had his own loyalists, but what the rest of the priests thought and whether they were choosing sides he couldn't say with any certainty. But he was conscious of feeling watched wherever he went.

Pushing aside his doubts, he headed for the door, suppressing an audible sigh as he walked inside. A familiar sense of belonging had always accompanied his return. It seemed to have deserted him, and the extent of his new ambivalence alarmed him. He made his way to his own private office, eager for solitude.

A single question nagged him incessantly: what should he do about the fault lines opening up in the temple? In his darkest moments he had even imagined putting the High Priest's famed longevity to the test. He was, after all, the designated successor to the High Priest.

The question of longevity took his mind back to the twenty fools who had invaded the sanctity of the temple. They had hoped to drag the High Priest away bodily to explore that same question—Goultzar's own agents had exposed their plans well in advance of the abortive raid, and the Archprimus had been ready for them. Having led the operation that ended with the disposal of their bodies, he had derived considerable satisfaction from the outcome. Allowing them to succeed would never have occurred to him in his wildest imaginings. Yet in recent times he had found himself daydreaming about exactly such a conclusion.

He shook his head, trying to apply himself to more immediate questions. Who was responsible for the demise of his agents? Most likely it was the Ahrans, but he could not rule out the possibility that the High Priest's men were responsible. Finding replacements was out of the question. He would be forced to make do with the dwindling resources that remained to him.

A niggling pain in the small of his back intruded on his deliberations. Perhaps the High Priest had found a way to conquer mortality, but if he had, the Archprimus wasn't privy to it.

"What progress can you report, My Lord?" King Krasmir asked his commander. "I'm not in a patient mood. We need to find Lord Torbury's son, and we need to do it soon. I've just received a strongly worded communication from King Steffan. He stopped short of holding me accountable for the outcome, but he will not be at all pleased if the matter is not resolved satisfactorily. Meanwhile, the threat of an Ahran invasion hasn't gone away, and it's getting little or no attention. The abduction has distracted us for far too long."

Lord Kulferan dipped his head in acknowledgment. "We have been pursuing information provided by King Delmar before he returned to Varas, Your Majesty. The information is promising, and I'm cautiously optimistic."

The king frowned. "How have the Varasans managed to outdo us? This is supposed to be our backyard."

The commander winced. "They clearly have an unmatched network. It's small, but it seems remarkably effective."

"The Varasans are allies—use that fact to find out as much as you can about their methods."

The nobleman dipped his head.

"What information have you learned from them?" asked the king.

"They believe that the Grand Vizier has returned to Rogand and is directing his agents from a large farmhouse somewhere near Rog."

"If that's truly what he's done, it amounts to a declaration of war," growled the king.

"I agree, Your Majesty, although we have not yet confirmed this information," Lord Kulferan reminded him. "Nevertheless we believe we have almost finished identifying likely locations that involve land transfers. We will be moving the moment the investigation is complete."

The king eyed his commander soberly. "I don't need to tell you that the death of the child is not a result I'm willing to accept. I trust you are operating accordingly."

"Of course, Your Majesty."

28

The morning after Rupert's reconciliation with Tasha, he received an invitation to meet with her. Accepting eagerly, he was escorted to a section of the palace he had never visited.

"Good morning, Rupert!" Her vivacious welcome made him feel like king of the world.

"Good morning, Tasha. I'm delighted to see you again!"

After they had exchanged pleasantries, she asked casually, "Are you interested in books?" Her face wore a simple smile, but he couldn't shake off the suspicion that her question had a right and wrong answer.

"I enjoy reading very much," he replied honestly. "So I am definitely interested in books."

"I am, too!" she told him, her face beaming with delight.

He shook his head in relief at having provided the correct answer. Apparently misinterpreting the gesture, she stared at him in alarm. "You're surprised! Is it possible you imagined I was all sparkle and no substance?"

"Of course not!" he sputtered.

"I was only teasing!" she laughed. "Nevertheless, it is a reminder of how little we know each other," she added seriously.

He nodded his agreement. There was plenty to learn about Tasha. He was confident he would never find her boring.

"There was a reason for my question," she told him. "I'd like to show you something."

An ornate door stood nearby. Pushing it open, she disappeared through it. He followed at once, trailed by her chaperones. A large chamber lay inside. Wooden shelves covered every wall, the shelves lined with books, rolled up scrolls, and piles of parchments.

Gazing about in astonishment, he admitted to himself that he had not imagined Rogand as a center of learning.

"I love this place," said Tasha, speaking in little more than a whisper.

He understood her restraint. The accumulated knowledge surrounding them was breathtaking. Approaching one of the shelves, he removed a book and opened it. After peering at it for a few moments he replaced it on the shelf.

He grimaced. "I'm afraid that I'm no better at reading Rogandan than I am at speaking it. Much worse, in fact."

Tasha chuckled. "I read Arvenian poorly," she admitted.

She led the way to another section of the library. "There are books and parchments here written in Arvenian. I've made little headway with them."

Pulling a few volumes from the shelf, he examined them carefully, finding they dealt with medicine, theology, and astronomy. Many appeared old and extremely fragile. Picking an aging scroll at random, he unrolled it with great care.

"This appears to be a history," he said.

"Can you read it to me?" Tasha asked.

Rupert nodded. "If you lose interest, let me know."

He began reading.

This chronicle is recorded by Burnett of Earlsford, scribe to King Attalnar of Arvenon.

I set out on midsummer's day with the host of the king, marching east toward the disputed lands beyond the Blue Mountains.

From ancient times the border of Arvenon has run along the eastern skirts of these mountains, giving the king a rightful claim over territory on both sides of the mountain range.

Of old these lands were sparsely inhabited, the cities of the Aen-ur lying further to the east. With the fair cities of these peaceful folk torn down by the Rogandans, the Aen-ur were pushed west, establishing themselves at last in the great fortress of Ishitar Ataye in the foothills of the Blue Mountains. Rumor had it that even this final refuge had fallen.

Following the main trading route east, we cleared the Blue Mountains and swung north. After many days and frequent skirmishes with Rogandan patrols, we came at last to the ancient fortress. Nothing but desolate ruins remained. Since the bridge had also been broken down, we turned south and followed the great river until we reached a ford.

Once most of the host had crossed, a small group of men approached from the tree line on the same side of the river.

"Who are you that trespasses in the lands of the Aen-ur?" the chief among them asked.

"I am Attalnar, King of Arvenon," the king replied. "These are my lands, and we are no trespassers."

The other man bowed. "If you are indeed the king of Arvenon, you speak truly," he replied. "I am Jae-Nairan, ruler of what little remains of the Aen-ur. It is we who are the miscreants, and I beg your pardon."

With that he waved an arm, and many archers appeared from behind rocks and trees, lowering their weapons.

King Attalnar replied courteously, "I do not begrudge you and your people refuge on our lands, King Jae-Nairan."

A man approached the Aen-ur king and whispered in his ear.

"May I suggest that your men complete their crossing quickly and

establish themselves on this side of the river?" King Jae-Nairan said. "We have experienced heavy rains in this region of late, and I have just received warning of an imminent flash flood."

King Attalnar gave the order, and the ford was cleared.

As the last of his men climbed the bank, the king was informed of the arrival of a new force from beyond the river.

A man stepped from their midst and stood at the edge of the ford. "These lands belong to Rogand," he called threateningly.

"I had not heard of it," King Attalnar replied. "These mountains have belonged to Arvenon for generations. As king of that country, I claim sovereign rights."

"Your claim is bold," sneered the other. "We shall see if you can support it." He waved an arm, and a large body of men began moving into the ford. They proceeded warily, the opposite bank being held against them.

King Attalnar was a man possessed of great learning. His subtlety was likewise rarely equaled. Raising his voice, he called out in the Rogandan tongue. "In destroying the great fortress of the Aen-ur you have awakened the wrath of an ancient sorcerer of unmatched power. He now spies out the land in the semblance of an eagle. In the guise of a bear his authority is revealed. Those who dare intrude in this region will taste his fierce anger," cried the king.

As he spoke, an eagle flew overhead, and a bear was seen eyeing the host. Although such creatures were common in these parts, many of the Rogandans hesitated.

The Rogandan commander scoffed at the words. "You will not frighten us with such tales." Calling a harsh command, he pushed forward into the ford at the head of many men.

"You have provoked the enchanter's fury," called King Attalnar. "You will face the consequences."

The words had barely left his mouth when a roaring sound was heard. Flood waters poured down the river with great force, sweeping away the Rogandan commander and every person in the ford. Even men on the far bank were overwhelmed before they could scramble to safety.

The survivors retreated in disorder, crying out in fear. The host of King Attalnar and the men of the Aen-ur watched on in awe.

When the last of their enemies were gone, King Attalnar turned to the Aen-ur ruler. "They will long hesitate before coming here again," he said.

King Jae-Nairan bowed deeply. "We are forever in your debt," he replied. "Those men were sent with the sole purpose of destroying the remnant of our people who survived the fall of Ishitar Ataye. There is little I can do to repay you, but before you return to your capital I will give you a token. It is an object of no apparent value—just a small glazed tile with a brightly colored surface—yet its worth is beyond price to us. It is a tiny reminder of the splendor of the throne room at Ishitar Ataye. There may come a time when it will be of use to you or your successors."

"I thank you," King Attalnar replied. "For my part, you are welcome to remain here, or indeed to settle elsewhere in Arvenon if that pleases you better."

"We will remain in the land that nurtured us," King Jae-Nairan told him.

The Aen-ur ruler uttered a final warning. "Be aware that your kindness to us will not endear you to the Rogandans. In turning them away from this region you have injured yourself. Their attention will turn next to Arvenon."

"Let them come," King Attalnar replied. "They will not find us unprepared."

After receiving the promised token from the Aen-ur, the king bid them farewell and led his host back the way we had come.

I, Burnett of Earlsford, myself witnessed these events.

"The scroll ends there," said Rupert.

"The scribe does not portray my forebears in a favorable light," said Tasha frankly. "Do you believe it to be a true account?"

He shrugged. “I cannot say.”

After reflecting silently for a time, she said, “I know a little of the Aen-ur. King Agon hated them and pursued them ruthlessly. In recent years my father has reached an understanding with them.”

She soon abandoned her musing. Facing him eagerly, she told him, “My parents instructed me to issue you an invitation. You must join us tonight at our evening meal!”

His heart skipped a beat, and his breathing hitched. “I…I would be honored,” he told her.

Honor it might be, but the prospect of being paraded in front of her family and their invited guests was daunting to say the least. But small and insignificant though his kingdom might be, he was a reigning monarch, and for Tasha’s sake he would do his best to behave like one.

“I will look forward to it,” he said.

“Wonderful!” she enthused.

Undoubtedly sensing his apprehension, she added, “And please don’t worry. I have no doubt that it will go very smoothly.”

WITH HIS FIRST meal with Tasha’s family underway, Rupert stole a glance at Tasha. Buoyed by her encouraging smile, he was finally able to calm his racing heart and master his breathing.

When ushered into the dining room, Rupert had been taken by surprise. Servants were bustling about in preparation for serving food and drink, but the only people seated at table were the royal family. He had fully expected to find them dining with members of the nobility, as he did in his own royal castle. Before he could decide whether it was easier or harder to be the only guest, they rose together and welcomed him warmly.

Vigorous conversation was soon underway. Rupert followed the interactions with mixed success. While it was quickly apparent that his Rogandan language skills needed work, he was able to participate remarkably well. Whenever he felt especially bemused, one of the princesses—usually Tasha—noticed his confusion and helpfully provided a translation.

The experience had been a revelation in a multitude of ways. Table manners clearly differed from Castelan customs, most of the differences being minor, but thankfully the royal family didn't stand on ceremony. Some of the food was unfamiliar, but thus far he had thoroughly enjoyed everything he had been served. Recipes for a number of the dishes would certainly be finding their way to his chefs at Castel Citadel.

The biggest surprise was the energy level, and most especially the noise. It felt like everyone was talking at once, and to his amazement King Krasmir didn't seem to mind a bit. Both the king and the queen engaged almost as energetically as their children. Crown Prince Rimek had plenty to say, but he couldn't keep pace with his vivacious twin, Princess Ashloh. The dark-eyed Princess Kyla, a beauty by any standard, was the demure member of the family. She sometimes struggled to get a word in, but it didn't seem to bother her. Tasha—*his* Tasha as a euphoric inner voice kept reminding him—was by no means the most talkative of the family, but she had no difficulty holding her own in interactions that occasionally bordered on the chaotic.

Rupert watched on wide-eyed. He'd even caught himself open mouthed on a couple of occasions when he wasn't sufficiently guarded. After getting over his initial astonishment though, he increasingly found himself enjoying the experience.

For the most part the conversation lingered around everyday topics. On one occasion, Prince Rimek had asked quietly, "Has Lord Kulferan made any further progress?"

The king's only reply was a warning glance, and the prince immediately took the hint, switching to a more mundane topic.

Rupert understood perfectly. His presence at the table was not the issue. With so many servants in ready earshot, it was safest to avoid matters of state entirely.

Queen Deka took advantage of a rare lull in the conversation to address Rupert directly.

"It is such a pleasure to have you here with us, Rupert," she said with a beaming smile.

Tasha aimed a scandalized look at her mother, but Rupert wasn't at all bothered by the queen's familiarity in using his name rather than his title. Her body language suggested she had accepted him as part of the family already, and he felt only gratitude.

"Does it remind you of meals around your own table at Castel Citadel?" she asked.

"Not even slightly, Your Majesty," he replied without hesitation.

An uncharacteristic silence settled over the table, every eye turning to Rupert. Realizing he could still play it safe by saying very little, he shot a quick glance at Tasha. The look of encouragement on her face decided him.

"I have never attended a family meal like this in my life," he confessed, "and I must say I feel the poorer for it."

The rapid flow of conversation had dried up entirely. Deciding to ignore the unwavering attentiveness on their faces, he continued.

"I come from a small family, one that only grew smaller over the years. My mother died when I was quite young. I have a few memories of her—I can still hear her laugh—but between the ages of seven and twelve my family was just me, my father and my older sister, Essanda. After my sister became the queen of Arvenon I had five more years with my father. Then he was gone too."

"For my part, I am sincerely sorry for the role Rogand played in the trouble visited upon your family," said the king soberly.

"Thank you, Your Majesty." Seeing no reason to dwell on the past, Rupert satisfied himself with a brief dip of his head in acknowledgment.

He continued. "Even before my father's passing, I never experienced family in this kind of way. If I ever have children of my own," he added, feeling his face coloring as he said it, "I want them to grow up with this, not what I had."

"You poor boy!" crooned the queen. "We will just have to adopt you for as long as you're in Rog."

"My own experience was not dissimilar to yours," the king told him. "We have my wife, and her family before her, to thank for how we are today."

Queen Deka nodded wisely. "The best way to make sure your children experience our kind of family is, of course, to marry someone who grew up with it." As she said it, she beamed a smile in the direction of Tasha.

"Mother!" protested Tasha, her face turning beet red.

"I'm merely speaking the truth," her mother insisted.

The king raised his eyebrows imploringly, causing Rimek to snort with laughter. That set Ashloh off, and before long boisterous banter reigned supreme once more.

Occasionally one of them thought to include Rupert directly in the conversation, but for the most part he was happy to listen and observe.

When the meal came to an end and they had all risen from the table, he left satisfied. And not just from eating his fill of good food. He decided his contentment was mostly due to Tasha's family making it so obvious that they accepted him.

Odd as it might be, he felt completely at home with a family he barely knew, a family who spoke another language. Only a few years previously his kingdom had been at war with Rogand. Now his fondest hope was to marry a Rogandan.

Tasha accompanied him when he left. "They like you," she told him with an elated smile. "I'm not at all surprised, but I'm still very pleased."

"You have a wonderful family," he told her. "I'm more grateful than I can say that they're so welcoming of me."

"They are very special," she agreed. "Mother can be incredibly embarrassing though," she added, raising her hands helplessly.

He laughed. "She certainly isn't afraid to speak her mind."

Tasha went silent for a moment. "There's something I need to ask you," she said, casting an uncharacteristically tentative look toward him.

"Yes?" he asked, raising his eyebrows curiously.

"My sister Kyla. I know she's much more beautiful than I am." She lowered her eyes uncomfortably.

He stared at her in surprise. After an awkward silence, he asked, "Do you think I might be wondering if I'm pursuing the wrong princess?"

She didn't respond.

"You can't have much of an opinion of me if you think I'd pursue a girl just because she's beautiful."

She winced. "I didn't mean that," she said self-consciously.

He gazed into her eyes. "Kyla is beautiful—I would never deny it. But it wasn't your looks that first drew me to you. I was captivated by you as a person! It didn't take me long to notice how beautiful you were, but on its own your appearance—or anyone else's for that matter—would not have been enough to attract me."

She was looking up at him earnestly, her eyes wide.

"When I was with your family just now, yours was the smile I wanted to see," he confessed. "Your face is in my mind as I drift off to sleep, and you are the person I'm most eager to greet when my day begins."

Lowering her gaze, she released a sigh that might have been relief. "I'm glad we've sorted that out," she said.

He wasn't entirely satisfied. "You haven't told me what you're thinking about when you go to sleep," he noted.

"No, I haven't," she agreed, a twinkle in her eye.

Not long after his first meal with Tasha's family, Rupert discovered that the princess enjoyed riding. With the help of Rimek, who had promised to assist in any way he could, suitable mounts were soon secured for them both.

When they set off on their first ride, it felt to Rupert more like a procession than a private outing. Their mounted escort consisted of six armed soldiers along with a mature woman—an accomplished rider—as a chaperone. Tedious as it was, he decided to ignore it and enjoy the opportunity to spend time with Tasha. Their escort did at least allow them some breathing space.

Their conversation ranged over many topics, from the trivial to the weighty.

"Will you miss your family when you...when you leave them?" Rupert asked.

"Undoubtedly," she told him with a smile. "Especially if some foreigner wants to whisk me away to an unfamiliar place where they eat strange food and speak a different language."

"Would you be able to cope with that?" he asked seriously.

"I expect so," she replied. "You've told me that your sister managed it, and at the age of only fourteen!"

"That's true. But she didn't have a different language or religion to consider."

"I don't expect language to present too much of a problem," she said. "Assuming we're talking about one of the western kingdoms, that is."

He responded with a chuckle.

"I hadn't given any thought to religion," she told him candidly. "My father isn't a person you would describe as devout. He does what's required, of course—that's expected of the king. My mother is more attentive to the dark gods, but it's one of many areas where I'm more like my father."

"Would you be willing to consider adopting a different religion?"

She shrugged. "I imagine it would be expected if I marry outside Rogand. The religion comes with the kingdom. But if you're asking whether I would personally embrace another religion, I couldn't answer that without knowing more about it."

"Brother Ander would be the best person for you to talk to. His Rogandan is better than mine, and I'm told he has a gift for making complicated things easy to understand. No such conversation is possible of course, since he was abducted along with young Ethen. We'll need to wait until they're both freed."

"Do you think they will be freed?" she asked, her concern apparent on her face.

"I sincerely hope so," he replied. "I don't like to think about how Lord and Lady Torbury will take it if Ethen isn't found alive and well."

A fierce look came to her face. "I wish there was something—anything—I could do!" she said passionately. "I wouldn't care about the risk."

"I feel the same way," he agreed. "Unfortunately it's completely out of our hands."

After they had been riding silently for a while, he suggested, "I'll race you to those trees!"

Without bothering to reply, she urged her horse forward, charging past him with a laugh. He took off after her, leaving the guards and the chaperone scrambling to catch up.

Rupert and Tasha's time together came to an end all too soon. When they parted their farewells were surprisingly awkward.

He recalled Princess Neira's question: *Would you like to kiss me?* The question had been as disconcerting as Neira herself, but it wasn't difficult to answer. He had no interest in Neira.

Tasha was so different.

He understood the constraints of courtship, and he would have respected the boundaries even without her chaperones hovering nearby. But it didn't make her lips any less full and inviting.

29

After a day of frustration, Elena returned to the palace with Amyra. Will met them at the door, the strain plainly visible on his face. Fortunately Thomas was waiting for them as well. Elena's face must have told him all he needed to know, because he came and put his arm around her. She leaned her head onto his shoulder and tried to will herself to relax.

"Well?" demanded Will.

Amyra threw up her hands. "Nothing! Again!"

"I'll check on the children," said Elena.

"I'll come with you!" Thomas chimed in immediately.

The two of them slipped away together.

"I don't think they can take much more of this," Thomas whispered.

Elena shook her head miserably. "You're right. Amyra is barely holding it together."

"Will she want to go out again?" Thomas asked. "If she does, I'll go with her. You need a break!"

"We have no obvious leads to follow," Elena told him. "I'm hoping she'll decide to rest. She desperately needs it."

The children were squabbling when they reached them. Haldek, Breysen, and Rufe were all trying to calm them.

Elena sighed. The general tension was clearly affecting everyone.

Rufe looked especially relieved to see them. He sidled up to Elena. "Is this what happens when people get married?" he whispered. He looked terrified.

Seeing his reaction, Elena barely prevented herself from bursting into laughter. She smiled broadly at him. "You're imagining what might happen if you marry Peggy, aren't you?" He didn't answer, but it wasn't necessary. "I don't think you need worry," she said soothingly. "Peggy strikes me as the kind of person who wouldn't be overawed by a horde of children, even if they were all big and fierce like you."

The burly soldier looked back at her, wide-eyed and shaking his head. He headed for the door with a fatalistic look on his face. His expression seemed so pitiable that she was torn between sympathy and an almost uncontrollable desire to laugh out loud. "You're good for me, Rufe," she finally managed, holding open the door with a grin that split her face from ear to ear.

Out wandering in the sunshine, Kamash noticed a familiar figure hurrying purposefully toward the trees. Diving behind a bush, he managed to disappear from sight at the very moment Princess Neira cast a furtive glance around her. Peering out cautiously from behind the bush, he was in time to see her disappear through the large hedge bordering their section of the garden.

After witnessing her earlier interaction with the Ahran agent, the old man had no doubt what the princess intended on this occasion. Not yet ready to expose her to the Rogandan soldiers, he cast about in his mind, trying to decide what to do. Abruptly remembering his time with Thomas and Elena, he recalled his offer to help Lord Torbury and his wife in any way he could.

Racing back inside, he hurried as quickly as he could to the wing where they were staying. To his relief, the person he spotted first was Elena.

"Please! Can you and your husband come with me urgently?" he cried. "I believe the princess is meeting with an Ahran agent."

"Of course," she replied at once, calling urgently for Thomas.

Thomas soon appeared, trailed by two people Kamash recognized from King Krasmir's conference. It was Lord and Lady Torbury, the parents of the abducted boy.

A burly soldier had followed them out, and Elena addressed him in Arvenian.

The big man gave a tight nod and turned back immediately, a long-suffering look on his face. Lord and Lady Torbury remained, both of them looking agitated and overwrought.

"We must hurry," urged Kamash, restraining his impatience with difficulty.

Leading them outside, he headed quickly toward the location where Princess Neira had previously met the Ahran.

King Krasmir had ordered that one of his men should accompany Will any time he left the palace. Seeing Will hurry away with the others, the soldier immediately sprinted after him.

With no horses on hand and the stables too far away to be accessible, they were forced to follow on foot. The princess reached the tree line well ahead of them. By the time they were pushing among the trees there was no sign of Neira, and Kamash began to lose hope of finding her. He also realized that he had no settled plan about what to do if they did spot her with her contact. It didn't take much imagination to guess what Lord Torbury would want to do. At the very least, he would expect the Ahran to be taken in for questioning.

As for the princess, her life would also change very abruptly if she was caught meeting an Ahran agent. Having been mostly treated with sympathy and consideration, she would likely find herself an object of mistrust and suspicion. At best her freedom of movement would be drastically restricted. She might even find herself locked away in a prison.

Kamash found the thought confronting. Was he doing the right thing?

His doubts vanished when he reminded himself that the lives of an innocent child and a monk were at stake. If the princess was even vaguely involved, she deserved the censure that would come her way.

Then, through the trees ahead, he caught a glimpse of the princess. She was talking to a man in a hooded cloak. Looking back over his shoulder, Kamash held up two fingers and pointed emphatically in the direction of the conspirators. Then he tiptoed forward furtively.

Behind him a crack sounded loudly as a fallen branch snapped underfoot. Peering ahead in alarm, Kamash saw that the intruder had heard the sound. The hooded man melted immediately into the trees. The old man set off after him, followed closely by the others. The princess stood frozen to the spot, watching pale faced as they ran past.

With no idea where the man had gone or where he had hidden his horse, they searched fruitlessly among the trees for a while before pushing into the open. They could see no sign of him.

Meeting with the princess was proving to be an immensely frustrating experience for Bolnyk. He had been charged with extracting any information of value she might have. It quickly became apparent that the mission was a waste of time. She plainly did not enjoy the confidence of King Krasmir, so she had nothing useful to tell him.

He instead found himself assaulted with words—an insistent torrent that amounted to barely coherent rambling. It gradually dawned on him that the princess, accustomed to being the center of attention, craved reassurance about her place in the world.

If she wanted coddling, she'd come to the wrong person. He simply didn't care. And even if he had the inclination to humor her, he could not afford the time.

"Take me with you!" the princess insisted. "I command you to take me to the Grand Vizier!"

"I have no horse to offer you, Your Highness," he replied.

"We will ride double," she sniffed, her nose in the air.

He shook his head curtly. "I have no such orders from my master. Even if I did, I could not simply spirit you away from King Krasmir's palace."

"*My* command overrides any order *Rheibas* might have given you," she retorted, her eyes flashing. Her disparaging emphasis on the chief minister's common name was not lost on Bolnyk.

The princess might imagine that her command was Bolnyk's most compelling obligation, but she was wrong. He had no sympathy for her whims and no interest in pandering to a fragile and sensitive young princess.

Bolnyk's situation had been beyond desperate when the Grand Vizier had plucked him from the gutter. He would have expired on the street if it had been left to the emperor. Why should he feel loyalty to a family content to sit in luxury while their people suffered around them?

Neira continued to prattle on. Princess or not, the girl was a fool—her willingness to believe the Grand Vizier's explanation in his letter demonstrated that. To have abandoned skepticism so completely she must be desperate to avoid rejection.

The chief minister placed no value on her life. Having abandoned the princess on the island, it wasn't hard to guess what he might do if she fell into his hands right now. In leaving her here Bolnyk was doing her a favor, even if she didn't have the wit to understand it.

Weary of the girl and her impossible demands, he decided it was time to escape.

The situation changed in an instant when he heard the unmistakable sounds of someone approaching. The arrival of intruders felt both alarming and fortuitous at the same time. Turning away swiftly, he fled without a backward glance, weaving his way through the trees until he came to his horse. Vaulting into the saddle, he swung the horse about and kicked it in the flanks.

Fortunately for him, his pursuers had not found him. Galloping away, he headed for the broken section of wall that allowed him access to the palace grounds.

As soon as he was free of the palace, he slowed his horse briefly. He needed to clear his head before deciding on his next move. After this incident, the city would soon be swarming with King Krasmir's men, on the lookout for him and for any unusual activity. Most alarming of all, the transfer of the boy and the monk to the Grand Vizier was due to begin at any moment. Perhaps it was already underway.

The timing of the move had seemed sensible when he scheduled it. He had decided against a nighttime operation. While the darkness offered concealment, men with nothing to hide were not given to moving loaded wagons in the dead of night. Far too many people with watchful eyes were about, and the journey could not be completed quickly, especially in darkness. The same operation could be carried out more efficiently in the daytime without attracting undue attention.

However, everything had just changed. Bolnyk's clandestine meeting with the princess had been a disaster. After the supposed sanctuary of King Krasmir's palace grounds had been breached during the abduction of the boy, Bolnyk had penetrated deep inside it once more. When the king heard about it—and that would happen all too quickly—it would surely provoke an unprecedented response.

It was difficult to imagine a worse moment to carry out the transfer. Only one option made sense—he needed to get to the safe house in time to prevent it.

Putting his head down, he urged his horse to greater speed.

Thomas peered around in frustration. The Ahran had made a clean escape.

Will appeared, his face red with agitation. "Did you get a look at him?" he asked.

Thomas grimaced. "I barely caught a glimpse of him as he was disappearing, Will," he replied, keeping his voice low. "He heard us coming! I couldn't get all the details, but he's definitely the one we've been looking for. His head is crammed with information. I don't doubt that he knows everything we've been trying to find out."

A scowl of frustration twisted Will's face.

Thomas shook his head in exasperation. There'd never been a better chance to unravel the mysteries plaguing them for so long. They'd been so close.

"Look!" said Amyra suddenly, pointing back toward the palace. Other riders had come into view. Will began calling and waving his arms frantically, causing the riders to head immediately toward the little group.

Will turned urgently to Thomas. "Do you know where to go?"

"I'm confident I can lead you in the right general direction," Thomas replied with a nod.

Both of them directed their attention to the approaching riders. King Rupert and Princess Teylee soon arrived accompanied by six soldiers and a woman.

"We need horses urgently!" said Will. "We just surprised an important Ahran agent talking to Princess Neira, and he's escaping!"

"You can use our horses," the princess replied at once, dismounting and indicating to her chaperone and her soldiers that they should do the same. King Rupert dismounted as well.

Will, Amyra, Thomas, Elena, Kamash, and the guard assigned to Will all selected horses and mounted.

"You can't go without protection," exclaimed King Rupert. "There are three more horses—three of our guards can go with you."

The soldier in charge of the princess's guard detail shook his head stubbornly. "We were assigned to protect both Princess Teylee and you, Your Majesty. Other soldiers will need to be found to accompany Lord Torbury."

"There's only one solution," said the princess calmly. "If our guards must remain with us, then King Rupert and I will go as well."

"It wouldn't be safe, Your Highness!" protested the lead soldier.

"This is Rog, not the wilds of Lestanor," she reminded him. "Lord Kulferan's soldiers will never be far away. And we're following one man, not riding into battle."

The lead soldier didn't look at all convinced.

"Our kingdom is under threat!" she added firmly. "There's a great deal at stake, and there isn't time to argue. I'm going. Do whatever you please."

With that, she remounted her horse. "Would you like to share a horse?" she asked King Rupert. "It will allow another soldier to accompany us."

The king seemed far from certain about the wisdom of joining the hunt, but she'd left him little choice. Her unyielding look seemed to decide him. Taking her offered arm, he climbed up behind her.

No doubt inspired by their example, Kamash called to Amyra. "Please!" he said, pointing to his horse's back.

Accepting his invitation, she relinquished her horse and mounted behind him.

With only three horses remaining for the princess's six guards, Elena dismounted. Thomas patted the spot behind him, but she shook her head. "I don't need to go!" she said.

The six soldiers mounted, two of them forced to ride double.

"Ask the king to send reinforcements!" the princess commanded her chaperone. "As soon as we find where the Ahran has gone, we'll send someone back with directions!"

The chaperone hurried away with Elena.

Thomas did not linger for further conversation. Turning away with Will beside him, he set off after the Ahran.

The urgency of the situation had temporarily pushed everything else from his mind, including the fact that he'd finally succeeded in getting a good look at the princess. She had nothing worthwhile to contribute to this situation, and further follow up would need to wait.

Even before leaving the palace grounds they encountered two

mounted soldiers riding patrol. The princess wasted no time in commandeering their horses.

All of her guards now had horses of their own.

Having lost his horse, one of the soldiers gave up his weapon as well. "Your sword! May I borrow it please?" asked the unarmed King Rupert. Bowing, the man unbuckled his belt and handed it over, along with the sword in its scabbard.

Even before the king had strapped on the sword, Will was urging Thomas forward. "We can't delay!" he growled. "The Ahran is long gone already!"

Locating the section of broken wall, Thomas guided his horse across it, the other riders following quickly. Loud muttering came from Princess Teylee's guards when they saw the breach. It wasn't Thomas's concern, so he thrust it from his mind and rode on.

He knew where the Ahran would be heading—even from the fleeting contact with the man's thoughts, the location had been fixed in his mind. The Ahran was heading for the place where Ethen and Brother Ander were held.

However there seemed little point in going there, because Thomas had the clear impression that the captives were imminently about to be relocated to the headquarters of the Grand Vizier. After what had just happened, the transfer would surely be accelerated. Unfortunately, he couldn't say where the Grand Vizier was based. The location was known to the Ahran, but Thomas had been unable to dig out specifics.

With no better alternative on offer, Thomas directed his horse toward the one other location accessible to him.

UPON REACHING the safe house where the boy and the monk had spent their captivity, it immediately became apparent that the house was empty. The transfer was already underway. Bolnyk gritted his teeth in annoyance. Their route to the Grand Vizier's headquarters had been decided in general terms, but he had no way of being certain exactly which roads they were planning to use.

There was, however, one segment of the journey that required them to pass through an extended section of open ground on a lightly trafficked road. Further, the road was in very poor condition, which meant that wagons were forced to travel at a slow walking pace. Because they would be exposed for a considerable period of time while passing through this area, it had received a disproportionate amount of attention during planning.

Unless his men had set out much earlier than agreed, he knew they would not yet have arrived at this location. Bolnyk accordingly hurried there, intending to join them as soon as they appeared.

He had no way of knowing it, but his own focus on this site had ensured it was the destination plucked from his mind through the agency of Thomas's stone.

BACK AT THE PALACE, a full hour had passed before King Krasmir learned about what had transpired. It alarmed him that Will was once more on the loose in pursuit of his son, even if accompanied by the soldier assigned to him by Lord Kulferan. He was even more alarmed that his daughter and King Rupert were off chasing Ahran agents, and with only six soldiers to defend them.

Calling urgently for his commander, he hastily prepared to join the search himself. Another crucial hour passed before a large and heavily armed group of soldiers set out, Lord Kulferan at their head. King Krasmir rode among them.

Heading in the general direction indicated by the princess's guards, they soon arrived at the broken section of wall. Krasmir eyed it indignantly. Such a lapse was utterly unacceptable, and he intended to have stern words with those responsible for maintaining security in the palace grounds.

Once beyond the palace grounds, they were confronted with the dilemma looming from the moment they set out—they had no idea where to go. The princess had promised to send someone back when they reached their destination, but the king refused to wait around for that to happen.

Pulling Lord Kulferan to one side, the king asked him, "Have your investigations given you any idea where the Grand Vizier might be hiding?"

"There are a number of possibilities, Your Majesty," answered the commander, as unruffled as ever. "One in particular stands out."

"Then why are we waiting, My Lord?" snapped the king. Lord Kulferan might be reliable and effective, but there were occasions when the king found his imperturbability little short of maddening.

The commander gave instructions to his men, and the column set out once more.

They were not moving quickly enough for the king. Positioning his horse alongside the nobleman, he insisted that the pace be increased. The commander calmly complied promptly with the request. Soon they were moving quickly enough even for the king.

Tracking down the Ahrans responsible for the abduction and releasing the child they held captive had always been Krasmir's most important priority. But the situation had just escalated significantly, and his gut was slowly twisting itself into knots.

What on earth had possessed Rupert and Tasha to become directly involved? If Rupert wanted to join the chase, he should have insisted that Tasha stay behind.

Krasmir shook his head. He couldn't reasonably blame everything on the young king. He knew his daughter, and he was well aware that Tasha would never have allowed Rupert to leave her behind. Nor would she have agreed to both of them abandoning the chase. The idea of pursuing the Ahran would have called out to her, whatever Rupert thought about it.

From the very beginning Krasmir had felt genuine concern for Lord and Lady Torbury following the disappearance of their son. Now, with his own daughter hunting a dangerous man with barely adequate protection, he began to catch the tiniest glimpse of what Torbury and his wife had been going through.

30

Thomas reined in his horse.

Will pulled up right beside him. "Why are we stopping?" he asked, frowning.

"This is the place," said Thomas. An open stretch of land intersected by a road lay before them, with no buildings of any kind in sight. A couple of men on horseback and several people on foot could be seen on the road, but none of them were of any interest.

Fleeting thoughts and memories had guided Thomas here—the legacy of his brief contact with the Ahran agent—but he had no idea what to expect.

Restless and on edge, Will was struggling to keep his emotions in check. "Do we need to find the nearest dwelling?"

Thomas shook his head. "I don't think so. I'm not entirely sure why this location was uppermost in his mind. I suspect he needs to pass this way. Or if not him, someone significant."

Will scowled. "I don't care about anyone except Ethen."

"I understand that," Thomas replied. "But finding the Ahran agent is the next best thing. If I can get a proper look at him, all of our other questions should be answered."

Will subsided with an effort. "You're right, Thomas. All we can do is watch and wait." He immediately began scanning the area.

The only feature in the landscape was a rise not far from their current position. Will pointed to it. "If we're going to wait, we should stay out of sight."

Thomas nodded. Both of them directed their horses over the rise and dismounted, the rest of the group not far behind them. Having positioned themselves to observe the road, Thomas and Will settled down to wait.

It seemed an ideal opportunity for Thomas to pass on what he'd learned from the princess. "I finally got a good look at the princess," he whispered to Will. "She's willing to do almost anything for the sake of her father's empire, and in that sense she's dangerous. But she isn't privy to the plans of the Grand Vizier, and she knows very little about his agents. She knows nothing that's useful to us in recovering Ethen."

Will responded with a grunt.

An hour passed without incident. Thomas could see that Will was becoming impatient, although thus far he had managed to restrain himself. Amyra had also spent time watching with them, but she was too fretful to remain in one place for long.

In the distance a wagon rolled into view. Two men sat on the driver's bench seat and two more followed slowly on horseback. The wagon had high sides, obscuring its cargo. Nevertheless, a glance at the men was all Thomas needed. In the bottom of the wagon, hidden beneath heavy covers, Ethen and Brother Ander lay bound and gagged.

As he opened his mouth to tell Will what he had discovered, several other riders come into view. To a casual observer, they had no connection with the wagon, but Thomas knew otherwise. Will, King Rupert, and five soldiers were now facing off against a dozen Ahrans.

He leaned toward Will. "It's time for one of your plans!" he said urgently, keeping his voice low.

Will tensed immediately. "Are you saying that Ethen's in that wagon?"

Thomas grabbed his arm, physically restraining him from leaping into action. "He is. But there are twelve men down there, Will! All fighters, and all well armed. Charging down there is likely to get you killed. That isn't going to rescue Ethen."

With Will straining away from him, he added tersely, "You need to know that they have orders to kill both Ethen and Brother Ander immediately rather than allowing them to be freed."

Will slowly relaxed. Peering around him, he assessed the possibilities. Behind them, the road forked, with one path continuing on and the other bending out of sight on its way to the center of Rog.

He addressed the others calmly. "We've finally found what we've been looking for," he told them.

Amyra's breath hitched, and she went suddenly pale.

"But we have a problem," Will continued. "These men have orders to kill Ethen and Brother Ander if anything goes wrong. So we need to catch them completely by surprise. And we're also outnumbered two to one."

He turned to Princess Teylee. "Could you please ride back and tell your father's men where we are?"

"If she goes, her guards go with her, My Lord," the lead soldier informed him.

"I think that answers your question, Lord Torbury," she replied tartly. "My men are needed here. And I am more than willing to do anything I can to help."

Will clearly wasn't happy about it, but there was little he could do. He turned instead to the soldier assigned to him by King Krasmir. "Someone needs to tell the king where we are. It will need to be you."

The man shook his head. "The king instructed me to stay with you, no matter what happens."

With a masterful effort, Will maintained his composure. "You are well aware of the importance placed by the king on freeing my son," he told the soldier bluntly. "Now that we've finally located him, we find ourselves unable to free him because we're outnumbered. We need Lord Kulferan here with reinforcements, and we need him now, before we lose contact with the Ahrans. If he doesn't arrive in time because you refused to notify him, the king will not thank you for sticking blindly to your orders."

Will had managed to dump a huge weight of responsibility onto the guard. Conflicted and uncomfortable, the hapless soldier could not come up with a response.

Princess Teylee resolved the matter. "You need to do this," she told him. "My men can take on the responsibility of staying with Lord Torbury."

That decided it. Mounting immediately, the soldier rode swiftly away.

Will turned to the remaining members of the party.

"I'm going to need your help," he told them. He faced Kamash. "Beginning with you," he said. "Are you willing to play a role?"

"Of course!" replied Kamash without hesitation.

"Here's what I need you to do then," Will replied.

Thomas heaved a sigh of relief. The old Will had reappeared at last.

KAMASH STRODE PURPOSEFULLY ALONG the road, careful to avoid the deep ruts that dotted his path. He soon came upon the wagon, bumping along at little better than a crawl.

"Good morning!" he called cheerfully to the driver. "It looks like slow going."

The men on the cart ignored him.

Coming to a stop, he shook his head, planting his hands on his hips. "No need to be rude," he told them. "I'm only trying to be neighborly."

The cart bumped past him without any kind of response from the driver.

"Suit yourself!" he said with a shrug. Resuming his journey, he called back over his shoulder, "Whether you're interested in hearing it or not, you're going to want to get off this road. I've heard from another traveler that a large company of the king's soldiers is heading this way, and I'm told they're riding fast. They'll be on top of you before you know it."

With that he continued his journey, not bothering to wait for a reply.

Even without looking back, he could tell that his words had caused consternation. He passed the two men riding behind the wagon. The alarm on their faces made it clear they had heard what he said. Smiling, he waved an idle hand as he passed.

Hearing hoofbeats approaching from behind, he turned his head in time to see two of the princess's soldiers approach the wagon.

"Are all of these men in your party?" one of the soldiers called roughly to the wagon driver, waving a hand to include the riders following some distance behind the wagon as well as the two immediately behind it.

The driver shook his head.

"Then you'd better pull over and let the men behind you pass," the soldier told him. "Lord Kulferan is right behind us, and he's looking for a wagon escorted by a large group of men." Then he shrugged. "I suppose it doesn't matter. He'll want to see what you've got in there anyway." He pointed into the wagon.

With that, the two soldiers rode on, one of them aiming a subtle wink at Kamash as they passed him. When they reached the second group of Ahrans, they rode beyond them without pausing.

As soon as the soldiers had gone, one of the two men riding with the wagon passed Kamash, heading rapidly back to the group trailing at a distance. Meanwhile, the driver wasted no time in pulling the wagon off the road.

The road was bumpy, but the ground beside it was much worse. The wagon slowly lurched and jolted in the direction of a stand of trees four or five furlongs away. The remaining rider followed it.

Kamash counted eight men in the second group of Ahrans. The rider from the wagon soon reached them, and after a hurried conference, all of them turned off the road, riding swiftly toward the same trees. The second group of riders soon passed the wagon. Clearly they did not want to be seen with it.

Kamash grunted in satisfaction. Lord Torbury's ruse was working perfectly.

The princess's two soldiers were under instruction to return as soon as all the Ahrans were out of the way, and he could already see them heading back. He began retracing his own steps.

As soon as a suitable gap opened up between the two groups of Ahrans, Lord Torbury, King Rupert, and the remaining soldiers would gallop over the rise and take control of the wagon.

Together they would free Lord Torbury's son and the monk, remove the horses from the wagon, and leave before the larger group of Ahrans could return.

With everything going precisely to plan, the entire situation changed abruptly. A lone rider appeared, riding hard along the path originally taken by the Ahrans. The remaining horseman beside the wagon spotted him first, calling out sharply. There could be no doubt that the newcomer had been recognized. The wagon came to an immediate stop.

It was soon apparent that the other group also knew who he was, because they were already racing back toward the wagon.

There was no longer time for Will's group of would-be rescuers to stop the wagon and free the prisoners. Once more the Ahrans had them outnumbered.

THOMAS WAS WATCHING the road as Will, King Rupert, and the soldiers prepared to ride for the wagon.

"Wait! That's Bolnyk!" Thomas exclaimed in alarm, pointing at a horseman who had recently appeared on the road. He was heading straight for the wagon.

Will hurried to his side. "Who's Bolnyk?"

"The Ahran we surprised with the princess," Thomas told him, pointing toward the new arrival and lowering his voice. "I'm finally getting a look at him. He leads the agents, and he's dangerous, Will! Don't underestimate him."

"What's he doing?"

"He's making sure his men stay together. He wants to get the prisoners to the Grand Vizier." Thomas paused before adding, "He intends to deliver them—dead or alive."

"That isn't going to happen," said Will flatly.

Thomas was squinting at Bolnyk, who had now reached the wagon. "His men have told him what Kamash and the princess's soldiers said, and he's very smart. He's guessed that it was just a ruse. He's also guessed we don't have enough people to risk fighting all of them."

"Where's Lord Kulferan?" asked Will, clenching and unclenching his fists in frustration.

"He'll be here soon," Thomas replied, hoping fervently it was true.

Will narrowed his eyes. "We can't wait—we'll attack them anyway. There mightn't be another chance."

"No! It isn't necessary to attack them now," Thomas replied urgently. "There's another option!"

"What option?" asked Will with a frown.

"I know where they're going," said Thomas. "There's a place where we can lie in wait for them. We'll have to hurry, but the wagon will slow them down."

"Lord Kulferan won't find us," Will replied.

"Not unless we send someone else," Thomas agreed.

"What makes you think this location is any good?" asked Will.

"It's the one place Bolnyk is wary about," Thomas told him.

"It'd better be worth it," Will growled.

"I sure hope so," mumbled Thomas under his breath.

They waited until the Ahrans were almost out of sight before moving. Then Thomas directed them on a roundabout ride through a forest, across a river, and over more rough ground.

By the time they arrived at their destination, Will was becoming testy. "Surely this can't be the place!" he exclaimed.

Thomas shrugged. "It's the location on Bolnyk's mind."

Will frowned as he rapidly scanned the terrain. "He might have reason to worry if an army patrol is waiting for him," he said. He pointed. "Over there."

They followed him to a rocky outcrop near a stream surrounded by trees on both banks. A rough path ran through the stream, with a steep bank on the far side.

"So they'll have to come this way?" asked Will.

Thomas nodded.

"I'd give a lot for two or three good Erestorian archers," said Will regretfully. "We'll have to make do. I need someone to watch the approaches and warn us when they're getting close."

Kamash volunteered without hesitation and soon rode away.

"Someone also needs to tell Lord Kulferan where we are," Will added, shooting a hopeful glance in Princess Teylee's direction.

She wasn't having it. "I'm not going anywhere," she told him. "You already know that my guards will leave if I go. And you need them."

Will had no choice but to accept it. "Decide among yourselves who to send. I'll be conferring with my wife and Thomas," he announced, ignoring them and heading toward the stream.

As soon as Amyra and Thomas joined him, he pointed to the path leading out of the water. "That's where we have to stop them," he said. "We need a hole so the wagon will get stuck. Or even better, so one of its wheels breaks."

With no response forthcoming, he spoke directly to Amyra. "There isn't time to dig."

She cocked an eyebrow at him. "You're the one always telling me not to use the Stone of Authority in front of other people."

"We don't have much time," he reminded her, ignoring her sally.

Turning toward the bank of the stream, she flicked a hand back and forth a few times. "That should do it," she said.

Thomas watched on in surprise. He'd barely seen the earth move, but both Amyra and Will seemed satisfied.

"I don't suppose you could arrange for the ground to open up and swallow some of the Ahrans?" Will suggested.

She snorted, not bothering to reply. She did, however, engage in quiet conversation with Will as they returned to the others.

"Who are we sending to Lord Kulferan?" Will asked.

"One of my guards," the princess replied.

Their leader looked mutinous, but eventually he pointed at one of the men. "Get back here promptly!" he ordered.

The soldier mounted and moved out at once.

Thomas shook his head. Bolnyk had boosted the Ahrans' numbers, while their own numbers had been further reduced.

"What now?" asked King Rupert.

"We keep out of sight, and we wait," replied Will.

"What will we do when they arrive?" the king persisted.

"We've examined the ground in the stream," Will replied, "and we're expecting the wagon to get stuck after it crosses. We'll attack while they're distracted trying to pull it out. That should even the odds."

He glanced at Princess Teylee. "That assumes your soldiers will be willing to help."

"The men are well aware that the king has placed a very high priority on recovering your son," she replied. "They will do their part."

"Your safety is our highest priority, Your Highness," asserted the lead guard.

"And I will be staying well away from any fighting," Princess Teylee replied.

Will nodded firmly. "That isn't open to discussion. Your father would never forgive any of us if something happened to you. Your senior guard will stay with you at all times for your protection. My wife will be at your side, and she knows how to use a weapon if the need arises. Thomas, Kamash, and King Rupert will also remain here. If anything goes wrong, none of you should hesitate—get out of here as fast as your horses will take you!"

"I will be fighting beside you," King Rupert insisted. Seeing that both Will and the lead guard were about to object, he added, "I have been training under the best fighters in my kingdom since I was a boy. You need me with you! And I'm not offering you a choice," he added grimly.

Whatever they might be thinking about it, neither Will nor the lead guard had anything further to say.

The Ahrans now had nine fighters to their seven. From the grim looks on the faces of the soldiers, they knew the odds were against them. And it wasn't just a matter of odds. It wouldn't be enough to overcome the larger force. They also needed to prevent the Ahrans from killing the captives.

Nevertheless, Thomas knew something the soldiers didn't. Amyra had access to a talisman of staggering power, and he had noticed her exchanging glances with Will. It gave him hope that there might be more to the plan than Will was letting on.

He thought it wisest not to ask.

THE HASTY RETURN of Kamash offered the first indication that the Ahrans were approaching. Thomas had an anxious moment as the old man splashed his horse across the stream, but somehow he managed to avoid the section of ground undermined by Amyra.

Pulling in behind the rocky outcrop, he told them, "They're coming. Not quickly—the wagon is slowing them down—but they'll be here before long."

31

Peering out around the outcrop, Thomas saw four horsemen ride into view, the wagon bumping along close behind them. Bolnyk and the other mounted Ahrans were bringing up the rear. All of them cast frequent glances over their shoulders. Thomas could see from the stone that they were expecting trouble, but only from behind.

As the first two riders crossed the stream, Thomas noted with surprise that the flow of water had greatly diminished. The wagon driver cracked a whip, urging his horses forward. The wagon bucked and swayed as the animals surged across the stream. No sooner had the carriage cleared the water than the ground beneath the rear wheels collapsed.

The water was barely ankle deep now. Bolnyk dismounted, shouting instructions, and the horsemen riding with him dismounted as well, approaching the wagon to examine it. A sudden noise caused them to look upstream. Before any of them could move, a wall of water smashed into the ford, sweeping the men away. Even the horses were overwhelmed, disappearing downstream. Water briefly flooded the wagon, but it was resting at a steep angle, and the water just as quickly drained away.

With a wild cry, Will rode to the ford. Recovering from their surprise, King Rupert and five soldiers raced after him.

The four mounted Ahrans barely managed to draw their weapons before they were set upon by all five of the princess's guards.

Pulling swords from beneath their seat, the two men on the wagon driver's bench jumped into the tray of the wagon and began frantically removing the covers that lay atop the load.

Will vaulted into the wagon, his sword in his hand. The wagon drivers abandoned their efforts and spun around to defend themselves. King Rupert quickly joined Will and side by side they fought the Ahrans. The space constraint made fighting unusually hazardous, but Will was in a dangerous mood.

The princess's guards brought down one of the Ahrans on horseback. When another tried to ride away, it cost him his life. The other two Ahrans now faced five attackers.

One of the princess's guards now jumped onto the wagon, attacking the Ahrans from behind. The fight in the wagon ended at the same moment the remaining Ahrans on horseback went down. Six Ahrans now sprawled lifeless on the ground.

Throwing off the remaining covers, Will finally reached his son. Pulling a knife, the nobleman cut Ethen's bonds before removing a gag from his face. Then he held the boy to him fiercely, his body trembling violently. Amyra had already left the princess, and she joined them in the wagon. Her husband pulled her into the embrace, and they stood there together, their joyous tears flowing freely.

One of the soldiers released the monk. The big man stood and stretched, his appearance disheveled and his once-white robe soiled and crumpled. Leaning toward the boy, he ruffled his hair, receiving a tearful smile in return.

All of them clambered down from the wagon, everyone talking at once, overflowing with the release of pent-up emotion and relieved distress.

As they celebrated together, a disheveled horseman emerged unnoticed from the trees. Seeing at once who it was, Thomas ran into the open, shouting a warning.

Bolnyk reached the little group at the same moment. Stepping forward protectively, Brother Ander took a vicious sword thrust to his stomach. He crumpled helplessly, his blood soiling the ground.

As Thomas looked on with horror, Bolnyk turned to Ethen, poised to strike again. Will stepped forward into his path, his sword extended. The Ahran swung downward, all of his force behind the stroke. The weapons clashed deafeningly, and Will stumbled back, desperately trying to keep his feet.

Ignoring him, Bolnyk drove his horse forward, shoving Amyra aside and knocking Ethen to the ground. The boy went down hard. The Ahran bent low, brutally plunging his sword into the boy as he lay defenseless on the ground.

Before anyone could respond, he spun his horse about and galloped away.

The princess's guards immediately took up defensive positions, but it was too late for Ethen and Brother Ander.

Through the agency of the stone, Thomas had seen the Ahran's intention. But everything had happened too quickly for him to prevent it.

Reaching their son, Amyra and Will bent over him in horror. Amyra began to wail, a piteous sound that shattered the stillness. Will had gone white with shock.

Kamash appeared at their side. Peering down at the boy, he shook his head sadly. Then he moved to Brother Ander.

Thomas brought the stone in contact with his skin, desperate for a sign that the monk's spirit still lingered. Brother Ander's life was flickering like a candle guttering in a breeze, but it hadn't yet gone out.

As he watched, Kamash bent low and placed his stone into the monk's unmoving hand. "I want you to have this," the old man whispered. Then he stood upright again, a satisfied smile on his face.

How much of what Thomas saw and heard came through his own senses, and how much through the stone, he couldn't say. But he looked on in amazement as life flowed back into the monk, filling him to the brim.

Brother Ander sat up, holding his side and wincing. Then he slowly got to his feet.

The old man leaned forward. "Don't lose that stone I gave you," he whispered. "Keep it safe and keep it hidden. It will grant you good health and long life." He nodded. "Vitality. Yes, that was the word." He studied the monk. "I think you will have more use for it than me."

Brother Ander looked baffled. Straightening his back and flexing his muscles, he peered at Kamash, at the stone in his hand, and finally down at his blood soaked robe. He shook his head in bewilderment.

Amyra's anguish reached him at last, and he shuffled to her side.

Looking down at the boy, the monk was overcome with distress. With the Stone of Knowing resting against his skin, Thomas glimpsed the toll of the ceaseless days and nights of captivity. He saw the way that Brother Ander had carefully sustained the child, laboring to shield him from the full intensity of the fear and suffering, guiding his spirit through the darkness. All of it had counted for nothing.

The soldier-turned-monk was no stranger to death. He had encountered it many times from his earliest years, eventually dealing out death himself more often than he could count. Now, as he stared at the small, limp form, indignation began to build within him. An act of casual malice had ended the boy's life, but it was not the cruelty of the deed that so provoked his affront. The monk had undergone a transformation, learning to heal, to rescue, to redeem, and in that moment, his spirit was overwhelmed with indignation at death itself.

The monk recalled the words of the man he now followed—words that had played so often in his mind. '*In this world you will have trouble...*' It came to him that the words hadn't ended there. They had continued, '*...but take courage; I have overcome the world.*'

Reaching down for the boy, he lifted him into his arms. The boy's blood stained his robe, mingling with the blood from his own wounds, but Brother Ander saw none of it. His attention was not on the grief-stricken figures huddled beside the stream, nor upon the child.

The monk began mouthing his prayers, speaking almost inaudibly, only his face revealing the intensity of his focus. Pouring out his entreaties to God, he assaulted the gates of heaven with an authority that filled Thomas with astonishment.

Thomas stood transfixed, scarcely aware of the passage of time. It was the stone that first alerted him to the faint glimmer of returning life in the child. Slowly the boy's eyes opened, and he gazed up into the face of his friend. "Brother Ander," he said softly.

Completely undone, the monk began to shudder, his entire body wracked with sobs as tears rolled heedlessly down his cheeks. The boy's parents had been looking on with mouths agape. Even before the monk had fully mastered himself, he came to them, placing their son in their arms and enfolding them in an embrace. Then all three of them lifted their voices and wailed together, tears of joy and relief flowing freely as their pain and anguish were washed away.

Ethen had lain silent in the arms of his parents throughout it all. When at last their voices grew still, he opened his mouth once more. "Mother, Father," he said. "I missed you!"

The sound of his voice set them off again.

Thomas had broken his contact with the stone as life was returning to Ethen. But he needed no assistance to feel the impact of the raw emotion emanating from his friends. He turned away, struggling to deal with his own responses.

Kamash sidled up to him, smiling and shaking his head at the same time.

Thomas took a deep breath to steady himself. "You gave him the stone," he said.

Kamash nodded. "I decided he needed it more than I did. I think I was right."

"So the stone healed him?"

"The monk? Yes, that was the stone."

"And Ethen—the boy?"

The old man frowned in puzzlement. "I can't claim to fully understand the stone, but I have always been able to sense what it is capable of. The monk was still alive when I gave it to him, and his recovery is no surprise to me. I have lived through similar experiences myself. But the boy was dead. I had no hope for him at all." He shook his head. "No, I do not think the stone can be credited with his return to life. It must surely have played a part, but your monk deserves most of the credit."

"He would say that God deserves the credit."

Kamash shrugged. "Perhaps he is right," he said. "I cannot say." With a brief nod to Thomas, he wandered away, musing thoughtfully.

Memories came to Thomas's mind of Brother Vangellis in a small hut in Arvenon, bending wearily over a stricken Ander. He recalled too the words of Ander at Hazelwood Ford after the battle of Torbury Scarp. Ander had aspired to become like Brother Vangellis. He had truly achieved his goal.

A large company of mounted soldiers appeared, and Thomas realized that Lord Kulferan's reinforcements had arrived at last. Four of the Ahrans remained unaccounted for, but it no longer mattered.

Glancing at the soldiers, he was surprised to see that King Krasmir himself had ridden with them.

"Where is the Princess Teylee?" asked the king.

"Sheltering behind that rocky outcrop, with one of her guards, Your Majesty," Thomas replied, pointing the way.

Guiding his horse around the outcrop, the king briefly disappeared. He emerged moments later, his face taut.

Spotting Will, the king rode to his side. "You have your son back!" he exclaimed. Seeing blood all over them, he asked more tentatively, "Is he injured?"

"To our astonishment, he is well, Your Majesty," Will replied with a strained smile. "Thank you for coming so quickly to our support."

"Where is my daughter, Lord Torbury?" the king asked, an edge to his voice.

Will looked at him in surprise. "I left her in safety with her senior guard, over there," he replied, pointing to the outcrop of rock.

"She is not there now," the king replied.

"Perhaps she is with King Rupert," said Amyra.

"He fought with us," added Will. "Where is he? I didn't notice him leaving."

All of them looked around, a couple of voices calling King Rupert's name loudly. There was no reply.

"Where are her guards?" asked Will.

Several men stepped forward.

Will's brows drew together. "Where is your leader—the one who stayed with the princess?"

"He was with the princess," one of them replied apprehensively. "He hasn't joined us."

Everyone fell silent.

"Is it possible they decided to follow the Ahran leader?" asked Thomas.

"Why would they do that?" asked Will, puzzled.

The king scowled. "It is just the kind of thing the princess might decide to do," he said. "Where else could they be?"

No one had an answer.

"Where did this Ahran go?" demanded the king.

"I can show you the direction, Your Majesty," Thomas replied.

"I will join you!" said Will.

"You will not!" replied the king. "Return with your son to the safety of the palace. Lord Kulferan will leave you enough men to ensure you are protected."

Lord Kulferan responded immediately, choosing a leader and telling him to retain fifty soldiers. The leader proved no less efficient than his commander, selecting the men swiftly.

Even before the process was finished, the king addressed Thomas. "Lead the way," he ordered. "One of my trackers will ride beside you."

The main body of soldiers moved swiftly away from the ford. Thomas rode at their head.

32

The moment Ethen and the monk had been freed, Rupert headed around the outcrop to satisfy himself that Tasha was safe. He arrived in time to witness a debate between Tasha and her senior guard.

"This is ridiculous!" Tasha was saying. "The fighting is over."

"We don't know if other Ahrans will arrive, Your Highness," the guard replied. "You're safest here."

Before the issue could be resolved, an Ahran reappeared, killing Ethen and Brother Ander and galloping away. They watched on helplessly, paralyzed with horror and shock.

Tasha was the first to recover. "We have to go after him!" she said.

"It's much too dangerous, Your Highness!" exclaimed her guard in alarm.

"He's right," agreed Rupert. "What could we achieve by following him?"

"We could find out where he's going! He must be heading for their headquarters." She frowned at them. "Don't you see? It won't end here. This will just be the beginning."

Rupert shook his head stubbornly. He wasn't willing to put her at risk for any reason, and certainly not on the off chance of locating the main Ahran base.

A wild look came into her eyes. "That man just murdered a child! A helpless child! And the monk as well—the one you wanted me to talk to."

Her jaw set firm. "There isn't time to argue—he's getting away."

Before they could respond, she had mounted her horse and set off after the Ahran.

Leaping onto his own horse at once, Rupert turned momentarily toward the ford. Someone needed to let the others know what was happening. But he quickly turned away. Lord Torbury and the others were distracted with grief, but more importantly Tasha was alone and unprotected. He couldn't waste a minute. Even if she knew how to defend herself, she wasn't armed. Shaking his head in frustration, he set off after her.

The guard must have come to a similar conclusion. He had set off in hot pursuit of the princess even before Rupert did.

Tasha had a head start, and her horse was fast. After riding hard for some time, Rupert realized he wasn't gaining on her at all; he was barely keeping pace with her. The guard was doing a little better, but he hadn't reached her yet.

His mind was racing—what were they going to do when they caught up with her? They couldn't forcibly restrain her.

Frustrating as this situation was, Rupert realized he shouldn't be entirely surprised. Twice in their brief acquaintance she had told him she would do anything in her power in response to the abduction. She'd said the risk didn't trouble her. And Rimek's story about her angry response to someone mistreating a horse had reinforced his impression of her concern for the vulnerable.

Tasha's huge heart for the hurting was a wonderful quality. But she had also told Rupert she was capable of being impulsive. He shook his head with unease.

Throughout the ride Rupert had not caught so much as a glimpse of the Ahran. He presumed that Tasha still had him in sight though, because she hadn't slowed. She had been right about one thing—if they wanted to follow him, there hadn't been time to argue.

The path rose before him, and for a moment he caught a complete glimpse of the chase. The Ahran had just topped a rise. Strung out behind him were Tasha, her guard, and finally Rupert.

As he watched, he saw the Ahran glance back the way he had come. He must surely have seen that he was being followed, and that his pursuers were not traveling in a group. Then he was gone. A sense of foreboding began to niggle away at Rupert.

To Rupert's relief, as the princess neared the top of the ridge, she proved she had not entirely abandoned caution. Slowing her horse to a walk, she approached the crest cautiously. He guessed that with no way of knowing what she might encounter on the other side, she recognized the danger in proceeding alone.

The instant she topped the rise, she spun her horse around and raced back the way she had come. He watched in alarm as horsemen spilled over the ridge, riding hard in pursuit.

She quickly reached the guard, and he swung his mount around to race beside her. Rupert spun his horse around in turn.

"I saw their base!" Tasha cried as she drew level with him. He swung in behind her.

A glance back over his shoulder showed seven or eight men pursuing them. They were gaining.

Rupert had already been riding hard for too long. His horse was tiring. The guard was doing no better. Both of them would soon be overtaken.

Tasha had outpaced them. When she looked back, he called, "Don't stop! Find Lord Kulferan!" To his immense relief, she urged her horse forward without hesitating.

With the Ahrans almost upon them, the guard called to Rupert, "Ride on, Your Majesty! We need to protect Her Highness. I'll try to slow them!"

But it was too late. Their pursuers had already cut them off. One of them barked a command, and three of the Ahrans set off after the princess. The remaining men rode in close, forcing Rupert and the guard to bring their horses to a halt.

The two men drew their swords, but they were heavily outnumbered.

"Throw down your weapons, or accept the consequences," said a cold voice.

Turning to the speaker, Rupert recognized the man they had been chasing. The gloating tone of the Ahran almost prompted him to do something stupid. He barely mastered himself in time.

"There's no need for violence," the man asserted.

"And yet you just murdered an innocent boy and an unarmed monk," Rupert retorted disdainfully.

The Ahran shrugged. "It was regrettable, but I had my orders. Besides, the blame lies entirely with the father. If he hadn't interfered, both the boy and the monk would still be alive."

So the Ahran blamed his murderous rampage on the grieving victims. Rupert clenched his jaw in anger.

"Throw down your swords!" the man repeated in a growl.

After a moment's hesitation, Rupert complied. The guard did the same.

They were distracted by the return of the three Ahrans who had pursued the princess. They rode in leading a dejected Tasha.

Rupert looked on in dismay.

A self-satisfied smile covered the face of the Ahran. "I bid you welcome," he said to them all, executing a clumsy bow from his saddle. He turned to the princess. "I heard your guard refer to you as 'Your Highness,'" he said, his lip curling in an ironic grin. "So you must be one of Krasmir's daughters."

He considered her thoughtfully. "Princess Kyla?" He frowned, then shook his head. "No, I'm afraid not. Much too rash. And nowhere near beautiful enough. You must be Princess Teylee."

The princess flushed with anger, but she didn't speak.

The Ahran turned to Rupert. "And 'Your Majesty,'" he said, raising his eyebrows. "I am impressed! I can only assume that I have the honor of addressing King Rupert of Castel."

Rupert chose not to respond.

"The two of you will come with me. Do not be alarmed about your fate. You are more valuable alive than dead. Don't test me though," he added in a growl. "If one of you attempts to escape, I will order the other killed. You have seen for yourselves that I will not hesitate."

As if to reinforce his message, he cast a casual look at the guard. "I have no use for him."

Rupert watched in distress as one of the Ahrans pushed forward and thrust his sword into the side of the unarmed man.

Even before the guard hit the ground, the rest of the company began to move out.

Ringed in by Ahrans with drawn blades, and anxious about the safety of Tasha, Rupert had no option but to leave the guard to his fate and ride away with them.

A bitter anger began to well up inside him. If there was a way to destroy these men and everything they stood for, he would find it.

ALMOST AS SOON AS they were captured, Rupert and Tasha had been blindfolded. Their hands were tied in front of them and secured to their saddles. The party paused after their horses had been led for only a short time. A great deal of activity was going on around them, along with frequent chatter and shouting of instructions. Rupert could not understand a word of it, but he guessed that the Ahrans were abandoning their headquarters and moving to a different location.

For the most part, the two of them were left alone. They managed to snatch a brief whispered conversation before a harsh voice demanded silence. After that they sat restless and uncomfortable atop their horses.

Eventually, after a long delay, they set out again. From the sounds around him, Rupert concluded that a large party was on the move. During the ride he tried to pay attention to their surroundings, but he quickly lost count of every rise and fall in the terrain. He did feel confident that they had crossed four streams and one river.

They rode for at least three hours before Rupert's horse was finally brought to a complete halt. He and Tasha were allowed to dismount and sit on the ground. Further hours passed before they were led into a building. After descending some stairs, their blindfolds were removed and their hands released.

Rupert found himself in a large cellar. Crude but sturdy partitions had been erected, splitting the room into three sections. A narrow space at the bottom of the stairs held a table and chairs, presumably for the use of guards. The rest of the cellar had been divided in two, with a door providing access to each and a window in the middle of the partition. A narrow skylight set high in the outer wall dimly illuminated the two sections.

Rupert was led into one of the makeshift rooms, and Tasha into the other. He found a simple bed before him, with a small table beside the bed. No other furniture adorned the space.

One of the guards placed a pitcher of water on the table along with a small loaf of bread. Then he was left alone.

Moving to the partition window, he found it had been placed at head height. Wooden strips subdivided the window, preventing either of them from climbing through the opening. The window held no glass. They would at least be able to talk together as well as see each other.

Tasha appeared on the other side of the window. Tears glistened in her eyes.

"I imagine we'll have plenty of opportunity to talk," he said brightly, speaking in Rogandan. "And there will be plenty to talk about."

Lowering his voice, he switched to Arvenian. "They're allowing us to talk for a reason. They'll listen to everything we say. But they're probably not expecting that both of us can speak Arvenian. It might take them a while to find someone who understands it. This might be our only opportunity to speak in private. We need to make the most of it."

She immediately began speaking in Arvenian. "I'm so sorry!" she said tearfully. "All of this is my fault."

"Blaming yourself won't help," he said calmly. "We'll only make it through this if we stay positive. We need to remember that everyone will be working hard to find a way to free us. They'll be more cautious after what happened with Lord Torbury's son, but they won't give up."

"Is anyone even going to know we've been captured?" Tasha asked.

"I don't think there's much doubt about that," he replied. "If they don't figure it out for themselves, the Ahrans will soon let them know."

Tears were running freely down her cheeks now. "Aren't you angry with me?" she said miserably. "I've been feeling so wretched, and you being reasonable just makes it worse."

"I'm not angry with you," he told her gently. "From all I've seen, your father is a strong ruler, and a good one. His authority hasn't been seriously challenged before. So learning to be cautious and suspicious hasn't been necessary for you. Not like it has for me. You're learning the lesson the hard way."

"Learning the hard way hasn't just affected me. My guard is dead! And I'm responsible!"

He shook his head. "You didn't murder the guard. That wasn't necessary, and the Ahran is the one who bears the responsibility for it."

He sighed deeply. "What you did was foolish, Tasha. Very foolish. But you weren't entirely wrong either. Murdering Lord Torbury's son was only going to be the beginning. And the current situation isn't entirely bad. The murder of Ethen along with our capture will cement the alliance between our kingdoms as never before. Our people will oppose the Ahrans with all their might."

"But capturing us just weakens our kingdoms," she said despairingly. "They'll bargain with our lives. And I'm afraid that my father won't be able to be strong—not when he knows my life is at stake."

He shook his head. "There's a limit to how far they can go with that. Don't forget that your father has their imperial princess in his custody. He might be able to negotiate an exchange."

Her hand was resting on the window, and he placed his own hand on it. "You're a great deal more resilient than you give yourself credit for," he told her. "We're going to make it through this, and we're going to do it together. Agreed?"

Setting her jaw, she brushed the tears from her eyes.

"Agreed?" he repeated.

"Agreed," she finally replied.

"Now, who is your favorite storyteller?" he asked, speaking once more in Rogandan.

She hesitated, but she did reply. "My grandfather—my mother's father."

"Then I want to hear his stories. Every one of them. In full," he told her.

She nodded. He had the impression that her normal self was gradually reasserting itself.

"You've told me it wasn't easy to become a princess," he added. "I want to hear what it was like to wake up one morning and find your whole world had changed."

Without waiting for her to respond, he offered another promising topic. "This is also a perfect opportunity for me to find out more about your siblings. And your mother. She seems like a determined woman!"

She cocked an eyebrow at him. "Unless you pause for a breath once in a while," she said dryly, "I'll have no hope of telling you anything."

Thomas might have pointed the way at first, but before long the tracker was doing all the work. They were moving quickly—the king made no secret of his restlessness.

Thomas's heart skipped a beat when he spotted a body sprawled on the ground ahead of them. Others saw it as well, and the whole party raced forward.

Even before he reached the prone figure, Thomas twisted the clasp to bring the stone into contact with his skin. He saw at once that it was the princess's missing guard, and that the man was barely clinging to life. He was immediately able to learn everything he needed to know about what had happened.

The king was the first to reach the guard, kneeling at his side.

The man recognized his sovereign. "I...sorry, Majesty," he gasped. The effort of talking was clearly exhausting him. "They took...her... and the king...too many."

"Why did you come here?" the king asked, speaking as gently as he could.

"The...princess. I tried...king tried...to stop her..."

The king grimaced. It was the princess who had precipitated this situation.

Getting to his feet, the king remounted. "Do what you can for him," he told Lord Kulferan.

The nobleman in turn nodded to a man who had already positioned himself beside the guard.

"Move out!" called the king, prompting the whole company to set off once more.

This time Thomas hung back. He had nothing further to offer, not until they reached the Ahrans.

The trail led to a large farmhouse not far from the crest of the ridge. This was the place Bolnyk had been heading for. Aware that the Ahran had been planning an imminent move to another location, Thomas knew that the best hope of retrieving the captives was to find them here.

The king waited while his men investigated the farm building and its barns.

One of the king's scouts soon returned. "The farmhouse has been abandoned very recently, Your Majesty," said the scout.

Thomas's heart sank. Access to Bolnyk's thoughts had not shown him where the Ahrans were heading. Having delegated the search to one of his men, the senior agent did not know specifics of the location.

The scout was pointing. "The tracks lead in that direction."

With no sign of his daughter at the farmhouse, the king was impatient to resume the search. The company was soon on the move again.

They came to a broad stream, and beyond it the tracks disappeared entirely.

"They must have ridden along the stream, Your Majesty," said the tracker. "We'll see if we can find where they left it."

The trackers were gone for some time, but they did eventually locate the trail. The company set off again, only to discover an even larger stream before them. This time the trackers searched in vain.

"There are many places where they could have left the stream without leaving tracks," one of them reported to the king. "It will take a long time to explore every possibility, and we might not succeed."

The scout's prediction proved accurate. Nevertheless, the king didn't permit them to abandon the search until darkness had almost fallen. When he finally gave Lord Kulferan permission to lead the company home, they rode away with spirits as weary as their bodies.

33

Will and Amyra stood side by side, waiting for King Krasmir and Queen Deka to receive them.

"I have my life back again," Will told Amyra seriously. He had an arm wrapped tightly around her. He'd been doing it a lot lately; fortunately she didn't seem to mind.

He didn't understand his fierce hunger for closeness with Amyra since the incident by the stream. Perhaps it was because no one else fully understood the depths they had been through.

Seeing Ethen killed before his eyes had easily been the most devastating experience of his life. As for what happened afterward with Brother Ander, he was still unable to speak about it with composure.

He knew about the Stone of Vitality now. Thomas had told him everything. As to the role it might have played in bringing Ethen back, he didn't understand it at all.

Brother Ander seemed to have no clear idea either. All he had said was, "Recovery relies on the body's natural recuperative ability. A healer simply encourages and supports that process. Sometimes an unusual outcome might be prompted by prayer, but every healing is the gift of the Creator who designed us." Gazing curiously down at the Stone of Vitality in his hand, he had added, "I imagine this little object is simply another expression of that gift."

For Will, the important thing was that Ethen had been revived. Understanding the mechanism held little interest for him.

He was, however, determined to understand how Ethen's abduction had managed to shatter his closeness with Amyra. Thankfully their relationship had been fully restored. After all they had been through together he was confident it had emerged stronger than ever.

Would their oneness have been restored if their son had died? It was an uncomfortable question.

A servant finally appeared, and the two of them were ushered into the presence of the king and queen. It was immediately obvious that Queen Deka had been crying, and the look on King Krasmir's face was painfully familiar.

The king managed to push his own problems to one side. "We rejoice with you at the safe return of your son, Lord and Lady Torbury," he said. The queen's breath hitched at his reference to 'safe return', but she managed a nod in support of his congratulations.

"Thank you, Your Majesties," Will replied.

"Some remarkable stories have been circulating about your boy and the monk," the king observed. "I hardly know what to think of them."

"Storytellers love to embellish the truth," Will replied. "Nevertheless, it seems safe to say that without Brother Ander the outcome would have been very different."

"I would like to hear more about it at some point," said the king. "For now I wanted to say that I am beginning to understand what you must have been going through, and I am sorry for the insensitivity I sometimes showed."

The king's willingness to own his behavior surprised and impressed Will. In his experience kings were rarely given to such displays.

"You were not insensitive, Your Majesty," Will replied. "You provided the practical support I needed. And I freely acknowledge that my behavior was inappropriate at times. You were well within your rights to speak and act as you did."

He could only look back with shame on some of his actions. Especially burning down the house—he still winced when he remembered the reproach in Thomas's eyes.

"It is generous of you to say so, Lord Torbury."

"It is you who was generous, Your Majesty," Will insisted. "On reflection I can see that I completely lost my sense of perspective for a while."

"How so?" asked the king.

"I allowed my own pain to blind me to almost everything else."

Arguably Amyra had been the first casualty. Having fought in a battle line, Will knew from experience the importance of facing the enemy shoulder-to-shoulder with his comrades. Yet he had failed to apply the lesson within his own marriage. It was easy to see after the event that he would have been stronger if he'd faced the challenge with Amyra. But he had let her down, withholding the support she so desperately needed.

He had since vowed to Amyra that whatever came in the future, he would face it with her. Having done her own share of agonizing, she had made him a similar promise.

"Thank you for your forthrightness," the king replied. His face was grim. "I assume you will return to Arnost now that your family is intact again."

"Yes, Your Majesty. We will travel overland."

"And the rest of your party will return with you?"

"Yes, although Brother Ander wishes to remain if you will allow him to."

"He would be welcome to continue to stay with us in the palace," the king replied. "Perhaps his services might be of use at a future time," he added vaguely.

"I will convey that to him, Your Majesty. For my part, I am planning to return to Rog as soon as my family is safe in the capital."

"Why?" asked the king in surprise.

"Because your daughter is a captive of the Ahrans. You supported me in my hour of need, and I will do no less in return."

The king raised his eyebrows. "I suppose I should refuse your offer," he said. "But I am not sure I can bring myself to do it. Your wisdom and experience will be invaluable of course. But you are also unusually well equipped to grasp the delicacy of my situation."

Will responded with a bow.

"I must somehow find a way to preserve my own sense of perspective," the king concluded with a sigh. "Perhaps you can help me with that too."

King Steffan waved the latest dispatch from Rog in his hand. "Will and Amyra are returning," he told Queen Essanda. "With both of their children!"

A cry of delight escaped Essanda's lips. "How did they manage to get Ethen back?"

"There are no details. We'll have to wait until we can hear the story from them in person."

"I am so relieved! I can only imagine how Will and Amyra must be feeling."

"Unfortunately the good news ends there," Steffan told her grimly.

"What else has happened?" she asked in alarm.

"The Ahrans have somehow captured both your brother, Rupert, and King Krasmir's youngest daughter, Princess Teylee."

Her earlier excitement vanished instantly, replaced by a look of horror.

"How could they have captured them both?" she asked in dismay.

"It seems they were pursuing an Ahran agent," he replied. "They were together because they are formally courting."

Her eyebrows went up in astonishment. She shook her head, struggling to take it all in.

He understood her confusion. He could barely make sense of it either.

"What of Castel?" she asked. "This news will be devastating for them!"

He raised his hands helplessly.

"Perhaps I should go to Castel Citadel," she said. "As a gesture of support."

"It might be a good idea," he agreed. "Provided we send a large enough escort to guarantee your safety."

"What do you mean?" she asked, frowning.

"These abductions make it clear how bold the Ahrans have become," he said. "You are aware that their agents have been infiltrating Rog and Varacellan in large numbers. I've received word from Lord Burtelen that we're beginning to see similar incursions in Erestor."

She stared back at him in surprise.

"Supposedly I am in authority over the docks at Maranelle. As you know, the reality is that the Peerless Mariner is in control. Fortunately, one of Burtelen's retainers, Jaxin, has an understanding with the Peerless Mariner's people. They monitor every ship that comes and goes, and they've been passing information freely to Burtelen through Jaxin. I've told Burtelen to be ruthless with any Ahran agents. But it would not be wise to assume that Arvenon is free of them. The same applies to Castel."

She shook her head in dismay. "So we will have further need of our army. It never ends. It will be good to have Will with us again."

Steffan shook his head. "He is planning to return to Rog as soon as his family are safe in Arnost."

"Do you know his reasons?" she asked.

"Krasmir lost his daughter almost at the moment Will got his son back. I imagine that's behind it. Krasmir did everything he could to retrieve Ethen. Perhaps Will feels obligated."

"Will is doing the right thing," Essanda asserted. "We'll just have to manage without him. It isn't only about the princess. There's

Rupert to consider as well. We need to do whatever we can toward recovering him safely."

"I agree," Steffan replied.

He sat down with a grunt, reaching for a parchment and his quill. "I sent Krasmir a strongly worded note after Ethen was abducted, letting him know that I expected his full support. It's time I thanked him for his efforts." He shook his head, still trying to grapple with the implications of this latest incident. "Given what's just happened, I will also express our deepest concern and offer our full support in his efforts to recover his daughter and Rupert."

As far as Bolnyk was concerned, the location chosen by the priest for the meeting would have seemed desolate in the daytime. On a dark night it was positively eerie. He waited restlessly, the chief minister at his side.

"Where is he?" demanded the Grand Vizier. "He should have arrived by now."

"I am told that priests do not reckon time in the same way as normal people," Bolnyk replied evenly.

At that moment a dark cloaked figure appeared abruptly before them, barely distinguishable from the darkness. His sudden arrival, without warning from the guards, almost startled Bolnyk out of his wits.

A voice came from within the priest's cowl. "I bring you greetings," he said coldly.

"I greet you in return," said Rheibas. "I trust all is well with you and your...your people."

"How can anything be well when a monk has established himself in the royal palace?" growled the voice. "The pretender styles himself as a healer."

The Grand Vizier offered no response.

"Do you intend to honor your agreement?" asked the priest.

"I do," Rheibas asserted.

"What guarantees do you offer?" the priest persisted.

"The same guarantees you offer me," replied the chief minister coldly. "None at all."

The priest fell silent.

"I will do my part," Rheibas told him. "I suggest you focus on doing yours."

Then suddenly the dark figure was gone. Bolnyk peered into the darkness in confusion. It almost seemed that he had vanished.

"It is time we were gone," the chief minister told Bolnyk.

Mounting up, they rode away, their guards trailing behind them.

Bolnyk cast a last glance back over his shoulders. The priests could only be described as unnerving. He would be wise to keep a very wary eye on them.

RUPERT WOKE from a deep sleep to find rough hands shaking him. Three men were standing beside his bed.

"Get up!" one of them ordered curtly.

As soon as he complied, his hands were tied in front of him. Shoved toward the door, he headed up the stairs. Tasha was ahead of him, her hands tied as well. Once they reached the top of the stairs they were led out of the building into the darkness.

After being taken to waiting horses, they were instructed to mount. Once more their hands were secured to their saddles. Tasha was silent, but she seemed reasonably calm, and he gradually allowed himself to relax.

Looking around curiously, he saw that they had been imprisoned in a large farm building that stood alone in a broad open space. Their stay had been surprisingly brief.

Intense activity was going on all around them. It didn't appear to Rupert that the building was being abandoned entirely, but a number of the occupants were clearly preparing to leave.

Eventually a group perhaps twenty strong rode away into the night, the two prisoners positioned in the middle of the column.

They had been riding for little more than an hour when Rupert began to smell sea air. Before long he could hear the crashing of waves onto a beach.

Clearing the clouds, the moon granted him a glimpse of two longboats drawn up onto the sand. A ship was anchored further out to sea. The implications were alarming, and his unease grew as the column made its way onto the beach.

Rupert and Tasha were ordered down from their horses and led to one of the longboats. When they tried to get Rupert into the boat he began to struggle until a voice growled, “If you value the life of your friend, you’d better cooperate.” All the fight went out of him.

Others clambered aboard, and the longboats put out to sea. When they reached the ship they were expected to climb a rope net hanging over the side of the boat. The task would have been difficult even without his hands being tied, but there was little risk of him falling. One man climbed on each side of him, grabbing him if ever he lost his grip. They were probably willing to manhandle him all the way to the deck if necessary. Tasha was similarly shadowed.

The minute they reached the deck, men with lanterns hurried them to the hatchway, leading them down into the bowels of the ship. Finally they reached a modestly sized storage room. Once inside, their hands were freed. In the lantern light Rupert saw that the space boasted two hammocks and little else.

After setting down a single lantern with a candle, the Ahrans filed out, shutting and bolting the door behind them. The sound of footsteps slowly faded as the men departed, leaving their prisoners alone in the confined space.

When quiet sobbing filled the room, Rupert made his way to Tasha. She had slumped to the floor.

Sitting down beside her, he drew her close, guiding her head onto his shoulder. “At least they left us together,” he whispered.

They sat uncomfortably on the hard wooden floor, lurching back and forward with the motion of the ship and clinging miserably to each other.

After a few minutes her sobbing stopped. Her breathing slowed, and she sat up straight.

"Where do you think they're taking us?" she asked. Her voice was quavering, but she seemed calm again.

"I don't know," he replied. "Beyond the reach of anyone who might want to rescue us, I imagine."

"No one will have any idea where to find us," she said dejectedly.

"No," he agreed. "If we're going to escape, it will be up to us."

They fell silent.

After musing darkly for longer than was healthy, Rupert frowned.

"We'll make it through this, and we'll do it together," he said defiantly. "Agreed?"

"Agreed," she replied, her voice clear and unwavering.

34

An endless succession of waves rose and fell, moving with the tide and a gentle breeze. Pitching about on the swell was a cluster of driftwood, the upturned remnants of a longboat. Two men lay sprawled across the wreckage, lost in the vastness of the open ocean.

How long they had been adrift in the water, Gharpin couldn't say. Nor could he clearly recall the reason why he was so determined to stay alive. All he knew was he needed to cling desperately to life for as long as possible. It surely couldn't be too much longer.

He wondered when last he had eaten, or drunk fresh water. Vague recollections of a rain squall came to mind, of lying face up with his mouth wide to capture the life-giving drops.

A smudge on the horizon had steadily been growing in size, and it dawned on him that they were drifting close to an island. Slowly, painfully, he began to move his dangling legs, hoping his feeble efforts might direct the makeshift craft in the right direction. He continued kicking until, spent by the effort, he lost consciousness entirely.

He woke to find himself floating near a sandy beach, tantalizingly close to the shore. With each wave the tide drew the wreckage in toward the sand before sucking it back out again. A bigger than usual breaker rolled in, and Gharpin called upon a final reserve of strength as dry land beckoned. Clutching hold of his prostrate companion and waiting until the wave reached its furthest extent, he tumbled off the wreckage and dug into the sand. The wave sucked and pulled at him as it retreated, but somehow he clung on.

When it had gone, he crawled forward a full body length before slumping in exhaustion. He knew he had no strength to haul his companion further up the beach. He could only allow the tide to do whatever it pleased.

Several hours must have passed before his eyes opened once more. He was lying above the waterline, the waves lapping gently below him. His companion had not moved.

Dragging himself the short distance to the other sailor, he saw that life had departed from him. After coming so far, his shipmate had stumbled as safety beckoned at last.

If Gharpin could have managed it, he would have scooped out a shallow grave in the sand. But any such gesture was beyond his capacity. Spotting a stream trickling down onto the beach, he crawled to it instead, struggling as far upstream as he could manage. The water tasted surprisingly fresh, and he took his fill before lying down beside the stream. He drifted off to its merry tinkling.

It was late morning when he awoke. After once more slaking his thirst, he managed to struggle to his feet. No sign of his companion's body remained on the beach. The sea had apparently claimed him.

It was just Gharpin now. He didn't doubt that he alone had cheated the elements—the sole survivor of his entire crew.

This latest reminder of the treachery of Rheibas infused him with fresh determination. He would do more than just cling to life in this place—he would thrive. The island appeared to have a ready supply of fresh water, so his highest priority would be to find food and shelter. Since he knew how to catch fish using available materials, seafood would provide the foundation of his diet.

Somehow he found the strength to climb a low hill. No other land was visible nearby. Perhaps if he climbed to the highest point of the island, he might glimpse another tiny splotch on the horizon.

Glancing about in every direction, he saw that the island on which he stood was extensive. That encouraged him. Nesting birds might make their home here. If they did, their eggs would supply a welcome addition to his menu.

The island also boasted an accessible beach—the one he had washed up on. That encouraged him too. If fishermen ever came there to replenish their water supply, they might provide him with an opportunity to escape.

On his way back to the beach he stumbled upon a hut. Could it be possible? Had he washed ashore on an inhabited island? Heart pounding painfully, he approached the structure, calling out a greeting before pushing inside. Quickly realizing that the hut lay abandoned, he slumped to the floor, struggling to overcome a crippling sense of desolation. He remained there until sleep claimed him once more.

A new day had dawned when he discovered the cultivated strips of land. Left untended, they were overgrown and marginal, but he was confident that at least some of the crops could be coaxed back to life. His prospects were surely improving.

It wasn't until he found the strength to climb the highest point of the island that a growing suspicion was confirmed. Unlikely as it seemed, he had arrived at his intended destination. Drifting in the boundless expanse of the ocean, a helpless subject to the wind and tides, he had somehow reached the island where the princess had been abandoned.

The Grand Vizier had been lying, of course—there was no sign of her, just as Gharpin expected.

He was alone, but he was alive. He would endure, and he would never stop searching for a way to exact revenge on the slithering creature who had destroyed his ship, doomed his crew, and condemned him to this forsaken bolthole.

EPILOGUE

Kamash sat at the tiller, relishing the salt air that filled his lungs. The wind might be whipping his hair about wildly, but for the most part the elements seemed intent only on reinforcing his smile.

He watched with delight as his little craft rode the swell and capered in the wind. It was a beautiful vessel. It wouldn't be easy to abandon it when the moment came.

He had Lord Torbury to thank for the boat. The grateful nobleman would probably have given him almost anything he wanted. After laying bare Kamash's longing to renew his solitary life, Lord Torbury had enlisted the aid of his friend Breysen to locate an ideal little craft. In spite of the nobleman's eagerness, Kamash had wrestled with himself long and hard before accepting it. He had admitted freely that he disliked being obligated to anyone. Lord Torbury had pointed out that he was heavily in Kamash's debt. By refusing the gift, he would be dooming Lord Torbury forever to just such an obligation.

In the end Kamash had yielded and taken possession of the boat. Now, with Rogand disappearing in his wake, he was willing to admit that any other decision would have been foolish pride.

King Krasmir himself had sought out Kamash before he left. "When you arrived in Rog, you promised never to do anything to the detriment of Rogand. You have kept that promise, and I thank you for it."

Kamash had offered a bow in return.

"I understand you were responsible for exposing the meeting between Princess Neira and the Ahran agent that led to the recovery of Lord Torbury's son. I thank you for that too." He paused before adding, "That meeting also led to the series of events that ended in the capture of my daughter. But I am not so unreasonable as to lay the blame for that at your feet."

The old man winced. "I sincerely hope that your daughter will be returned to you very soon." He could find nothing else to say.

The king had changed the subject. "I understand that you no longer wish to act as Princess Neira's spokesperson," he continued.

"That is correct, Your Majesty. I told her that if I discovered she had any awareness of the abduction, I would no longer act on her behalf. I cannot represent a person who places the glory of their empire above every other consideration."

King Krasmir nodded in satisfaction. "Lord Torbury has informed me that you are leaving the mainland. I wish you safe travels."

"Thank you, Your Majesty," he had said with a final bow.

They parted without further comment.

He had sought out Princess Neira before he left. She no longer had her freedom. Heavily guarded, every moment of her life was closely monitored. Their time together had been strained, which was hardly surprising since he had been the one who exposed her meeting with the Ahran agent. But he had meant it when he wished her well.

It was a great relief to him that she was no longer his problem. Uman at least remained with her, although he seemed more despondent than ever.

Perhaps the advance and retreat of Kamash's relationship with the princess best symbolized his reengagement with humankind in general. At first, after so many years alone, a part of him had welcomed human contact. He had quickly wearied of it. He wouldn't miss the political machinations, nor the frustrations that came from dealing with difficult and capricious people.

The absence of a few individuals might cause him regret. He was glad to have met Thomas and Elena, the Arvenian couple who uncovered his secret. The three of them shared a very pleasant evening over dinner before he took possession of the boat. For the most part, though, he felt only eager anticipation at the prospect of being alone once again.

Loneliness would not greatly trouble him, but the absence of the stone would prove more consequential.

He thought about the times it had healed his hurts and even saved his life. On one occasion, while wading in shallow water, he had come upon a strikingly colored sea snake. When he approached too closely, the creature had bitten him. By the time he reached the stone he was panting for breath and barely capable of crawling. Upon clutching it, the venom quickly lost its potency.

He winced as he remembered the time he broke his leg. The injury itself was not life threatening, but he could not have lived long if he'd remained disabled. Once more he had dragged himself to the hiding place of the stone. The effort cost him dearly—he had barely managed to grasp the object in his hand before swooning. When he regained consciousness, his leg was completely healed.

The other impact would be on his life span. Nevertheless, he had no regrets about letting the stone go. When he was young he could never have imagined tiring of life, but of late he had felt increasingly worn down. Everything had its season, and the time had come to pass the talisman to another.

There would be a time to die too. He would face that when it came.

For now it was enough that he was going home.

He was returning to his island. Its location was no longer his secret alone, and he had no way to be certain that others would leave him in peace. But he intended to abandon his previous dwelling and establish a new one in a hidden location. He knew just the place. He would keep it well stocked with water and fresh provisions. Anyone who cared to could land and search the island. They might find his cultivated strips, but as long as he spotted them in time, they would never find him.

None of that would matter until he arrived at his destination. In the meantime, with sturdy timbers beneath his feet and the wind whistling about his sails, he was more than content.

The End

The saga continues and concludes in
The Hope of Vitality

PART II

THE HOPE OF VITALITY

THE STONE CYCLE BOOK 6

VOLUME 1—A HARVEST OF CONFUSION

1

The sun had disappeared below the horizon, and its afterglow was slowly fading from the sky. Kamash sat spellbound beside the tiller, gazing upward as the lesser lights emerged, unveiling their grandeur in a dazzling display that stretched from horizon to horizon. The moon was yet to rise, and not even a wisp of cloud intruded upon the brilliance of the tiny stars that winked down at him.

The boat rolled ceaselessly beneath him, plowing swiftly through a low swell kicked up by a steady breeze. A dorsal fin abruptly broke the surface, and dolphins sported exuberantly about the little craft. They were no sooner gone than a new delight presented itself. Glancing back over the stern, he found a glow of phosphorescence trailing in the wake of the boat.

Had the ocean and the heavens collaborated in a salute to the old man's return?

Facing forward once more, he noticed a dark mass on the horizon —a telltale sign that his destination was almost within reach. Kamash's heartbeat quickened in anticipation. He had never been so ready to say goodbye to the complexities of civilization and the incessant demands of other people.

A part of him wondered if he would miss contact with his kind, but he thrust such thoughts aside. Long years of isolation had shown him he could manage very nicely on his own.

A full moon obligingly appeared as he drew near at last to the familiar little beach. As the hull scraped across the sand, he was confronted again with a question that had plagued him for weeks. Should he release the boat, allowing it to drift away the moment he landed?

The little craft was a thing of beauty. It had served him faithfully in the brief time since he took possession of it, returning him speedily and without incident to his island. Even the idea of abandoning it felt somehow disloyal.

It was a crucial decision—one with the potential to define his future. While he could not imagine another foreign princess appearing suddenly to confound him, the day might come when he himself needed help of some kind. And in spite of his eagerness to escape Rog and its relentless bustle, an entirely different thought had been nagging away at him. Would a time ever come when he craved human contact once more?

A reckless streak in him wanted to simply set the boat free and ignore the consequences. The cautious side to his nature firmly resisted any such notion.

In the end he settled on a compromise—he would defer the decision until the morning.

Leaping onto the sand, he pulled the boat clear of the waves. After sitting for so long, activity felt invigorating, and he found himself eager for more. His restless feet took him to the location where he had previously stored his boat. He'd moved his former craft using thin tree trunks as rollers, and they were still where he'd left them. Carrying the makeshift rollers to the beach, he laid them out and upended the little vessel onto them. He had brought a range of supplies from Rog, and after placing them on top of the hull he carefully pushed the load across the beach and into the trees. Having maneuvered the boat into its resting place, he relocated his supplies beneath it with the intention of retrieving them in the morning.

After first arriving on the island so many years earlier, he had woven a large mat, throwing it over the boat to protect it from the elements. He had replaced the mat more than once over the years, but the most recent version still appeared usable. Tossing it across the hull, he piled some fallen branches on top for good measure.

He had told himself he would defer any decision about keeping the boat, and securing it in this way was hardly consistent with that plan. But he didn't care.

After a long voyage followed by tiring exertion, he was more than ready to lie down. The prospect of exploring his old dwelling in the dark held little appeal, and the weather was mild. Exploration could wait until the morning. Heading back to the beach, the old man made himself comfortable in the sand. He was soon asleep.

DAYLIGHT WAS SHINING BRIGHTLY when Kamash awoke. He opened his eyes to the sight of a stranger staring down at him. Startled and alarmed, he leaped to his feet and took a hasty step backward.

The observer, bearded and unkempt, didn't move. Ragged clothes hung from him, and long hair dangled untidily about his face. He appeared quite wild.

"Who are you?" asked Kamash nervously.

For a moment the man said nothing, then an animated flow of words burst from him. Kamash could not understand a word of it. It didn't sound like Arvenian.

"Ahr?" he asked.

The man nodded vigorously, responding with a simple question of his own. "Rogand?"

Kamash nodded in his turn.

The Ahran began speaking again, slowly and loudly, as if to a child. He pointed first toward the sea, then back to the island. His efforts were fruitless—Kamash could only shrug in response.

Deciding they needed to start somewhere simpler, the old man pointed to his chest. "Kamash," he said.

"Kumm-ash," the stranger repeated. A finger jabbed at his own chest. "Ghar-pin."

"Gharpin," Kamash repeated, before adding pointedly, "Welcome to *my* island."

A frown of puzzlement came to the Ahran's face as he scanned the little beach. He swept a hand toward the sea before pointing at Kamash. When the old man offered no response, Gharpin's hand bobbed up and down rhythmically, as if riding waves, before plunging precipitately. Then he turned expectantly to Kamash, his eyebrows raised.

Gharpin was plainly wanting to understand how the new arrival had reached the island. Almost certainly a castaway himself, he appeared to be asking if Kamash's ship had sunk. Such an outcome must seem incomprehensible in view of the mild weather, but what else could the Ahran conclude with no ship visible anywhere?

Language barriers had their frustrations, but at that moment Kamash was glad he had no way of explaining his situation to the stranger. Witnessing the intensity of the Ahran, it didn't take much to guess what Gharpin might do if he knew a seaworthy vessel was present on the island. And his brief exposure to Ahrans had given the old man more than enough reason to exercise caution.

In concealing his boat the previous night, Kamash had acted on little more than a whim. That action suddenly took on a new significance.

For the moment it might be safer if Gharpin remained ignorant about the boat. That revelation could wait until Kamash better understood who the Ahran was and what his intentions might be.

GHARPIN WASTED no time in taking Kamash on a tour of the island and its facilities. The Ahran's efforts in rejuvenating the cultivated strips were impressive, and his careful labor had already seen reward. The bones around the cooking fire also suggested he had used available materials to good effect in catching fish.

The remodeling of Kamash's dwelling was another matter

entirely. The old man was shocked to discover that large sections of two walls had simply vanished. Apparently oblivious to Kamash's reaction, the Ahran chattered away proudly as he pointed to his supposed improvements.

Kamash could only shake his head in dismay. He tried to remind himself that Gharpin could not guess he had caused offense—he had no way of knowing he was talking to the original architect.

Over time the rationale for the Ahran's changes became apparent. The dwelling was now considerably more light and airy than before, and much better ventilated. That might be well and good, but Gharpin had never needed to weather the storms that buffeted the island during the rainy season.

The building would need to be repaired before bad weather set in. Assuming they remained on the island.

LEARNING to respect his new companion didn't take Kamash long.

It wasn't difficult to warm to Gharpin. Hardworking and capable, the Ahran was also generous and considerate. He freely shared everything he had, and he graciously yielded to Kamash the single bedroom in the dwelling. Perhaps he had concluded that the older man needed its limited comfort more than he did.

Thus far Kamash had reached no understanding of why Gharpin was so driven. For driven he certainly was. Although the castaway was making the best of his situation, he seemed impatient—at times desperate—to escape from the island.

The life of a hermit did not appeal to everyone, of course, but that didn't seem to be the issue. Although Kamash's interactions with Gharpin were almost entirely limited to hand gestures, he nevertheless sensed a passion burning just below the surface of the man. There was something he wanted to do, and he wanted to do it badly.

Not long after Kamash had arrived on the island, Gharpin had beckoned him over. Using a stick to draw in the dirt, he scratched out a rough depiction of a raft. Staring intently at the new arrival, he had waited for a reaction.

Kamash responded by using one hand to represent the waves, rising and falling rhythmically. He then used his other hand to represent the raft, riding the waves. The wave hand began to rise and fall more vigorously, causing the raft hand to buck and sway wildly. Then the wave hand smashed repeatedly into the raft hand, eventually causing it to sink below the waves.

Gharpin understood the meaning well enough, and he walked away with a long face.

The following day Kamash noticed Gharpin carefully examining the trees on the island. It came as no surprise when the Ahran showed him a sketch of a boat in the dirt.

The design might have been simple, but it was nevertheless a commendable effort. Unfortunately it was also worthless. Without suitable tools they had no way even to begin such an undertaking.

Escaping the island was clearly an obsession for the Ahran. With a perfectly seaworthy vessel readily to hand, the old man began to feel increasingly guilty about concealing it from his companion.

However, with no way of knowing what Gharpin was planning, Kamash concluded the only safe course was to remain silent.

"SAND," said Kamash, lifting a fistful of tiny white grains and allowing them to flow between his fingers back onto the beach.

"Cahn," responded Gharpin.

The old man pointed to the water. "Sea," he said.

"Ahr," the other replied.

"Ahr?" asked Kamash in surprise.

"Ahr," Gharpin repeated firmly.

So the Empire of Ahr was named for the sea. Interesting, but perhaps not surprising since it encompassed a cluster of islands.

Then it occurred to the old man that he might not have been sufficiently specific. Was it possible that Gharpin understood him to mean "water" when he pointed to the sea? Might "The Empire of Water" also be a possibility?

Shaking his head at his own slow-wittedness, he headed along the beach toward the stream, beckoning to the Ahran to join him. When they reached it, Kamash pointed to the flow and said "stream." Then he splashed into it and bent low. Filling his cupped hands, he stood up and said "water," as the liquid spilled through his fingers. Finally he strode across the sand and repeated the exercise in the shallows of the sea.

Gharpin appeared to understand. Scooping water into his own hand, he said, "phlu." Then he added, "nath-ahr," indicating the stream.

Kamash nodded with satisfaction. So "ahr" did mean "sea." And the Ahran word for stream appeared to be a derivative of it.

In spite of this small success, language acquisition was not coming easily to Kamash. His advanced age was undoubtedly hampering his endeavors, but he was willing to acknowledge that his limited improvement had more to do with a lack of ability. After a couple of weeks of growing frustration, Kamash decided to give up the struggle and abandon his attempts entirely.

Learning Ahran hardly seemed necessary anyway, considering Gharpin's steady progress in learning Rogandan. Redirecting his energies toward helping the other man offered Kamash a more useful focus.

The two men spent several hours each day cultivating, catching, and preparing food. The bulk of the remaining time was occupied working on Gharpin's Rogandan. Highly motivated to learn and surprisingly proficient, the Ahran worked hard on vocabulary and pronunciation while wrestling with the rudiments of grammar. Fortunately for both of them, Kamash proved to be a better teacher than a student, and he derived almost as much satisfaction as Gharpin from the Ahran's achievements.

From the beginning the two men had made extensive and effective use of sign language. Engaging in simple interactions in Rogandan expanded their communication enormously.

As the days turned into weeks, the outline of Gharpin's story slowly took shape. By the time a month had passed, Kamash knew that Gharpin had commanded a ship, that he and his crew had been the victims of sabotage, and that someone of high rank had been responsible. Details were far from clear, but Gharpin may even have been suggesting that the perpetrator was the most senior official of the Empire of Ahr, the Grand Vizier.

As they interacted, a number of tantalizing hints also suggested that Gharpin might have been involved directly with Princess Neira. On occasion Kamash thought he recognized her name, but when he repeated it Gharpin looked at him blankly. Perhaps the problem lay with his pronunciation, or perhaps the Ahran had simply been using a word that sounded similar. Either way, language was proving an insurmountable barrier, to the frustration of both men.

Even without knowing the full details of his story, Kamash had now seen enough of Gharpin to feel confident the Ahran did not represent a threat to Rogand. Accordingly, he decided the time had finally come to show him the boat.

Fearing that his companion would want to sail away the moment he saw it, Kamash waited until the sun had almost set before leading him to its hiding place. Throwing aside the branches and pulling off the protective mat, he revealed the little craft.

Gharpin's eyes went wide. "You have boat!" he said. Then he turned to Kamash. "*We* have boat?" he asked.

Kamash nodded.

The Ahran gazed thoughtfully at the little vessel for several minutes. "Now, I think," he finally said, before adding, "Tomorrow, we talk?"

Kamash nodded again, and they turned their backs on the boat, setting off for their shelter.

That night the old man's thoughts churned restlessly as he waited in vain for sleep to take him. He had been more than a little relieved at his companion's restraint—Gharpin had not even attempted to closely examine the boat. For all his drivenness, the Ahran was apparently less impulsive than Kamash might have expected. Nevertheless, Kamash didn't doubt that the shipwrecked captain would want to leave, and soon.

A difficult choice lay ahead.

Gharpin was an accomplished sailor who needed no help from an old man. The simplest option would be to give him the boat and remain on the island when he left. The loss of the craft was of no real concern to Kamash—he had never made a final decision about keeping it anyway.

While it might be the simplest solution, somehow it didn't sit right. If he understood correctly, Gharpin had lost his ship along with his entire crew as a result of deliberate sabotage ordered by an Ahran official. The most likely reason was that the official wanted to silence him. What secrets was Gharpin hiding? And what would happen when he suddenly reappeared after mysteriously escaping a watery grave?

And where would he go? Sturdy as the little boat might be, Gharpin would never be able to sail as far as the empire. If he tried, then sooner or later he would encounter an Ahran ship. Any such encounter could prove fatal if a powerful official wanted him dead.

His future would be equally uncertain if he sailed to Rogand. He couldn't pass himself off as Rogandan, and Ahrans were not exactly held in high honor in Rog at that time.

Kamash sighed. He would never be able to live with himself if he abandoned Gharpin to his fate. That left only one practical alternative—he would need to accompany his new companion to Rog and advocate on his behalf to King Krasmir.

In his innocence the old man had imagined he'd escaped human turmoil and intrigue forever. With a heavy heart he faced the reality that he was about to be thrust back into human society once more. And right into the center of the maelstrom.

2

King Rupert of Castel stirred, waking from a nightmare that lingered at the edge of his awareness. Where was he?

His world lurched suddenly, accompanied by the loud creaking of timbers and the swaying of a hammock beneath him. Everything abruptly came flooding back.

Was Tasha still at his side?

Propping himself up on one elbow, he peered into the darkness, trying to make out the other hammock in the storage room where they had been imprisoned. He could see nothing. The single candle left by their captors had gone out, and no light penetrated this deep into the bowels of the ship.

Rupert lay back quietly again, confident he could not have slept through Tasha being removed from the room. She was most likely asleep. If so, he saw no reason to disturb her.

With nothing else to distract him, a torrent of thoughts raced through his mind. He knew King Krasmir would be searching for them; the Rogandan monarch would never rest until he had freed his daughter. The Ahrans had made that task much more difficult by removing the captives from Rogand though. He wondered if they were being taken to the capital of the empire, Kat Ahket.

The disruption would by no means be limited to Rogand. Castel would be forced to continue without its king. In his absence, Count Gordan had been acting as regent, and Rupert had every confidence in him. But what would Gordan do if the Ahrans decided to bargain with Rupert's life? And how would King Krasmir react if he was forced to choose between his daughter and the interests of his kingdom?

What would become of them all? As for Tasha and him, they had fallen into a deep, deep hole, and Rupert wondered if they would ever make it out again.

Unwilling to dwell on the worst possible outcome, he reminded himself that Princess Neira was under heavy guard in Rog. Perhaps an exchange could be arranged.

"Are you awake?" a soft voice asked.

"Yes, I am," he replied eagerly. "Did you manage to get any sleep?"

"Not much. Not as much as you."

He frowned in the dark. "How do you know how much sleep I got?"

Her reply was blunt. "You snore."

A deep flush warmed his face. For reasons he couldn't understand, this simple pronouncement did almost as much to deflate him as everything that had happened so far.

"Not loudly," she added belatedly. "Just enough that I knew you were asleep."

With his perspective restored, he confronted his own sensitivity. How did princesses manage to be so effective at discomposing him? Did it come naturally to them, or did they learn it as part of their training? He ran a hand across his face, grateful that the darkness concealed his embarrassment.

For a time there were no sounds apart from the noises of the ship.

A quavering voice eventually broke the silence. "Do you hate me, Rupert?"

Taken by surprise, he responded as cheerfully as he could manage. "How could I hate a person who's joining me on the adventure of a lifetime?"

Her choked off response might have been an ironic snort. More likely it was a sob.

When she said nothing further, he added, "We're not going to let them beat us, Tasha!"

A full minute must have passed before she responded. "No. We're not." Her words were accompanied by a loud sniff, but her voice was steadier.

WITHOUT DAYLIGHT it was difficult for Rupert to judge the passage of time. Their isolation was interrupted only when their captors brought food and water, occasionally leaving behind a flickering candle to chase away the darkness for a while.

It might have been two or three days before they were eventually led from their prison and rowed to what appeared to be a small island bustling with activity. Uncomfortable after so long in the dark, they climbed out of the longboat onto the beach, covering their eyes against the dazzling light. Having delivered the prisoners, their captors returned immediately to their ship, leaving them to the dubious mercies of the men already on the island.

Glancing around uncertainly, Rupert saw a large group of men hard at work erecting several structures, directed with unruffled efficiency by a wiry man with a thick beard. Building materials lay scattered about an open space beyond the beach. After a brief glance toward the newly arrived prisoners, the workers and their overseer ignored them entirely.

Glancing out to sea, Rupert saw a second ship lying at anchor off the beach, presumably the vessel that had transported the men and materials already on the island.

Released into an open space at last, he began pacing back and forth restlessly.

It took a supreme effort to calm himself for long enough to check on Tasha. "Are you well?"

She responded with a halfhearted nod. Emotionally exhausted by the ordeal, she seemed wooden and detached.

. . .

By the time the sun set, workmen had erected several simple huts.

The bearded overseer strode purposefully toward them. "My name is Dessue," he said in passable Rogandan. "I am in authority on this island. Please follow me."

Two huts had been built apart from the others, and he led them to the nearest. "This will be your hut," he told Rupert. Turning to Tasha, he pointed. "Your hut is behind it."

"Thank you," said Rupert tightly.

Speaking courteously to any of their captors cost him an effort, but he remembered his father saying that a king should behave like one, whatever the circumstances.

Dessue assessed him. "You have spent a long time in the dark." His tone was gruff, but not unkind. "Hot food will be brought to you as soon as my men have prepared it." He nodded once, then he left them.

Rupert and Tasha sat together outside Rupert's hut. More comfortable in the dim light of dusk, they gazed out at the waves breaking endlessly onto the rocks.

Some life had returned to Tasha. "Our situation seems to have improved," she observed.

Rupert nodded once. "Let's hope it stays that way."

Food was brought to them as Dessue had promised. Simple as it was, the meal seemed sumptuous after the provisions tossed indifferently into their prison room on the ship.

The events of the previous few days had taken their toll. Rupert felt weary beyond words. Tasha was clearly in no better state. "I need to sleep," he told her. "I won't be far away. Call if you need me."

She returned a sleepy nod, and they retired to their huts.

Rupert's sleeping quarters might have been basic, but at least the low bed was not swaying. The guards did not disturb him, and he slept soundly for the first time since his captivity. In the morning he discovered that Tasha's experience had been similar.

After another meal was delivered, Dessue paid them a second

visit. “I trust that your huts are adequate.” After a nod from Rupert, he told them, “I have been given responsibility for keeping you safe and in good health. You may wander the island freely. Two guards will accompany you at all times, but that is purely for your own safety.” He addressed Tasha in particular. “My superiors have made it clear that you are not to be interfered with in any way, and I have made sure the men are aware of that.”

Rupert managed another muted thank you. But whether he showed it or not, he was greatly relieved by Dessue’s assurance to Tasha.

“You will not be treated badly if you behave well,” Dessue promised curtly.

The moment he had gone, Tasha stood up and stretched. “Shall we see if he was serious about letting us explore the island?” She sounded remarkably buoyant.

Rupert did not hesitate. “Certainly! I need exercise!”

Leaving the beach and the huts, they headed into the trees.

“We’re being followed,” he whispered, jerking his head behind him.

She peered back over her shoulder at two guards who had set off after them. “Should we try to lose them?”

He shook his head. “Let’s not push the boundaries. We don’t want Dessue deciding he’s been too lenient.”

The guards followed at a distance, but it soon became apparent they had no intention of intruding. After a while Rupert was almost able to ignore them.

They hadn’t walked far when a steep hill rose before them, its tree lined slopes obscuring the summit.

Tasha gazed up at it. “I wonder if that might give us a view across the whole island.”

After a glance back at their guards, he shrugged. “Let’s find out.” He had no idea if the hill was off limits. If it was, it would soon become obvious.

The guards made no attempt to stop them, and they reached the top puffing from their exertions. Peering back down the slope, Rupert saw the two men leaning against trees some distance below them. They had avoided the steepest part of the climb while choosing a location that would allow them to see whenever he and Tasha left the hill. Eavesdropping did not appear to be on their agenda.

Putting the Ahrans from his mind, he allowed himself to appreciate the view. Blue ocean could be seen in every direction. Three smaller islands lay not far away. Apart from visible greenery—presumably trees—none of the three appeared to be any more than featureless lumps of rock. Tiny smudges on the horizon hinted at other islands further away. As far as Rupert could tell, no landmass of any size lay within reach.

Their own island was modestly sized and covered with vegetation. Birdlife was plentiful, and the barking of sea lions carried faintly to their current position. He guessed that a range of marine birds and animals used the island as a breeding ground.

Apart from the beach where they had landed, only one other strip of sand was visible. It was small and inaccessible from the surrounding cliffs. The rest of the coastline appeared rocky and forbidding, at least to humans.

"Where are we?" asked Tasha.

Rupert shook his head. "I have no idea. We might be halfway to Ahr-chitani for all I know."

The princess peered off into the distance. "If we hadn't been sailing for so long before we arrived, we might be near the Rogandan coastline. There are plenty of islands to the north of Rogand."

"There are islands off the coast of Castel and Varas as well," he replied. "It would take longer to sail there, so I suppose one of them might be a possibility."

She peered around at the island, screwing up her face. "It certainly isn't appealing, wherever it's located. Unless you happen to be a sea lion, I suppose."

He snorted. "No. I imagine the Ahrans wanted somewhere that wouldn't attract attention. If so, they chose well."

. . .

For better or for worse this place was now home. As the days slowly passed, they did their best to adjust. Dessue occasionally visited them. The visits were brief, and Rupert saw no point to them, but the Ahran was at least making an effort to be accessible. Although neither he nor his guards showed them any particular deference, they served an adequate meal twice each day while apparently expecting nothing in return.

The first sign of change was the arrival of an Ahran ship. Having spotted it in the distance from their hilltop lookout, they made their way to the beach, curious to see what was happening. Keeping out of sight among the trees, they watched as supplies were unloaded and the boat returned to the ship carrying several passengers.

"Is that Dessue in the longboat?" asked Rupert in surprise.

"It appears to be. Perhaps he's meeting with the ship's captain."

As they watched, half a dozen men they didn't recognize were rowed to the island. The men had all the appearance of new arrivals intent on settling in. The impression was confirmed a couple of hours later when the ship raised anchor and departed. It left with Dessue still on board.

Rupert couldn't shake off a sense of foreboding, but he decided to put a positive face on it. "It looks like we're going to have a change of administration," he said, speaking as cheerfully as he could manage.

"So it appears." Tasha sounded less than enthusiastic.

Dessue's replacement wasted no time in making his presence felt. Within the hour he approached their huts, surrounded by guards. Assessing the captives through narrowed eyes, he spoke to them in Rogandan. "I am told that my predecessor treated you as guests. You are not guests—you are prisoners."

He eyed them coldly. "Your food will be provided, in keeping with the emperor's benevolence to prisoners throughout his empire. However, I will not tolerate laziness. You can no longer expect my men to do menial tasks on your behalf. Do them yourselves. The work of preparing your meals will, of course, fall to you."

With that he turned on his heel, leaving them gaping open-mouthed.

Tasha made no attempt to hide her contempt. "He didn't even bother to tell us his name!"

Rupert gazed uneasily at the retreating form of the Ahran. "I wonder if he's planning to restrict our freedom of movement."

It didn't take long to find out. To Rupert's surprise, nothing was done to hinder them when they next set off on a walk. Two men followed them as before. The guards had now become blatant in their efforts to listen in on Rupert and Tasha's conversations, but apart from that no obvious differences emerged.

For the next few days, life continued much as it had under Dessue. Everything changed when they went for a long walk.

Having climbed the tallest hill on the island, they stood gazing at the horizon.

"I'll race you to the bottom!" said Tasha with a grin, bouncing off toward the trees below without waiting for an answer.

Rupert hesitated for a moment. Then, throwing caution to the winds, he set off after her.

Careering down a steep slope dodging trees was more than enough to occupy his full attention. But he was drawing close.

Hearing him coming, Tasha put on an extra burst of speed. As she drew away from him, her laugh turned into a cry of alarm as she lost her footing and tumbled down the slope.

Rupert watched in horror as she rolled helplessly downward, her head barely missing more than one tree. Tumbling into a ditch, she came at last to a jarring halt.

Frantic and agitated, Rupert hurried to her side.

She stared up at him, pale and wincing with pain. "My ankle! I think I might have broken it."

Rupert called to the guards. "Come and help me!"

To his astonishment, they ignored him completely. They must surely have witnessed the whole episode. Yet they appeared unmoved by Tasha's plight.

"Your master will hear of this!" Rupert growled.

Their response was a harsh laugh.

Helping Tasha upright, he placed her arm around his shoulder.

She took a tentative step forward, Rupert bearing her weight as best he could.

"Can you manage?" he asked.

She nodded tightly, and they set off for her hut.

Every hop jarred her injured ankle, and more than once she cried out in pain. The indifference of the guards and their refusal to help incensed Rupert. He gritted his teeth and tried to limit his focus on where to place his next step. Nevertheless, his fury grew as the minutes dragged painfully by.

By the time they reached her hut, Tasha was barely able to cope with the pain and the shock. After making her as comfortable as he could, Rupert hurried off to find the Ahran leader.

The man was not alone when Rupert found him. Wisdom dictated that any interaction should take place in private, especially since most of the guards understood at least some Rogandan.

Rupert was too angry to care. "The princess has seriously injured her foot! She needs urgent medical attention! Your guards have done nothing whatever to help!"

The two guards had arrived at the same time, and the leader immediately addressed them in their own language. After a rapid interaction, he turned to Rupert indifferently. "The prisoner has injured herself as a result of her own foolishness. I do not regard that as an emergency—for me or for my men."

Rupert's tone became icy. "Your predecessor told us he had been given responsibility for keeping us safe and in good health," he snarled. "If the princess is crippled or worse because of your neglect, you'd better kill me! Because if you don't, when I eventually meet your master I'll make sure he fully understands your attitude toward your responsibilities." He fixed the leader with a furious glare. "And if you do kill me, you'd better have a good explanation for killing one hostage and crippling the other."

Rupert spun on his heel and left without waiting for a response.

No Ahrans appeared, and Rupert spent an anxious night trying to care for Tasha.

Not long after the sun rose, a small group of Ahrans arrived. The leader was among them, and he glowered at them both. Rupert ignored him.

One of the Ahrans approached Tasha. "May I examine your ankle?" he asked calmly in Rogandan.

When she responded with a tight nod, he worked the ankle carefully from side to side. Then he probed it thoroughly. Rupert could see he wasn't trying to be rough, nevertheless the princess winced with pain as he worked.

The healer finally completed his work. "Your ankle is badly sprained, but not broken," he told Tasha. "You need to avoid putting weight on it until the swelling goes down."

The leader spoke sharply to the healer in their own language. The exchange was brief and terse. When it was over, the leader turned to Rupert with a sneer.

"Since you have demonstrated that you cannot take proper care of yourselves, I must treat you like children. My men will be instructed to prevent you from climbing hills or trees. They will also make sure you never go out of your depth into the sea. If you do not comply, your movements will be severely restricted."

He left without offering them an opportunity to reply, striding swiftly away. His guards followed close behind him.

"How did you convince them to examine my ankle?" asked Tasha.

Intent on avoiding details, Rupert responded with a noncommittal grunt. He managed to present a calm face, but inwardly he was on edge.

He felt sure he had made an enemy of the leader. And sooner or later the Ahran would find a way to hit back at him.

3

A week after Tasha's accident, Rupert sat beside her as they prepared their evening meal over a crackling fire.

Tasha aimed a wry smile at him. "The Ahrans seem to have lost interest in us entirely."

"I'm very happy to be ignored by our enemies," he said grimly. "Especially since we're essentially helpless."

She tossed the hair from her face. A couple of stray locks remained, and he had to restrain himself from reaching out tenderly and tucking them behind her ear. The impulse was a welcome distraction from the simmering anger that constantly threatened to overwhelm him of late.

"I don't really mind being ignored," she continued. "It is an adjustment though. When I became a princess I was instantly surrounded by fuss. It was so irritating! I used to long to be free of it. Now that the fuss has gone, it feels strange."

Rupert grunted. Having been surrounded by fuss from the moment of his birth, he understood perfectly.

"I'm happy to do routine tasks though," she said with a smile.

He shrugged. "It isn't as if we have anything more meaningful to do."

She ignored his bleak mood. "I've never needed to cook for myself before. Some of our early attempts were forgettable, but I think we're becoming quite good at it." A dimpled smile lit up her face as she sniffed the food before them.

He fixed his full attention on her, gazing at her in frank admiration. "I don't know how you do it, Tasha. Cheerfulness seems to bubble out of you." He shook his head. "I'm struggling to find anything positive to focus on. I don't think I could do this without you."

Once Tasha had fully recovered from her injury, the two of them resumed their daily walks. Although they were no longer able to scan the horizon from the highest point on the island, they were otherwise still permitted to wander freely. They soon established a routine that incorporated at least one extensive walk around the island each day.

The benefit to Rupert went beyond exercise. He discovered he needed a change of scenery to help lift the grim mood that typically settled on him when he woke each morning. He hadn't been accustomed to thinking of himself as moody, at least not in the years that followed the dark period of Lord Eisgold's betrayal. The captivity, especially under Dessue's replacement, had changed that along with so much else besides.

Rupert and Tasha set off on their daily walk with two guards trailing them as always. To all appearances the guards followed without enthusiasm.

The small party took a route that led them past a pool fed by a reliable spring. The crystal clear water of the pool had called out to them from the moment they first discovered it. On that initial occasion, finding that their guards had no objection, they had jumped in and enjoyed a brief swim. The water was bracingly cold at first, but they soon adjusted. A swim became an important part of their routine whenever the weather permitted it.

Shallow at the edges, in its deepest section the water reached to Tasha's chin. The pool was wide enough to allow plenty of room to swim or splash about as their fancy took them.

Having arrived at the pool on their latest walk, Rupert stood beside it mustering the courage to brave the cold and plunge into the water. Stepping up behind him, Tasha pushed him squarely in the back, pitching him bodily into the water. He emerged shivering, a howl of protest on his lips. Tasha looked on unrepentantly, giggling with glee.

Slapping the surface of the pond with the palm of his hand, Rupert directed a stream of water at Tasha. His aim was perfect, and she squealed as cold liquid doused her. Taking advantage of her distraction, he surged from the pool and dragged her in. Both of them were now completely soaked, and after a brief wrestle they fell apart, laughing helplessly.

Dripping from head to toe, Rupert stood in the pool with hands on his hips, shaking his head in mock outrage at Tasha's surprise attack.

At the same time, he couldn't help but be grateful to her. Once more her buoyancy and cheerfulness had lifted his mood, granting him a moment's respite from the harsh realities of their situation. How could he have endured these weeks without her?

"While I'm here, I might as well take the opportunity to bathe," Tasha said in Rogandan, glancing pointedly at the guards as she said it.

The guards had been ignoring them, apparently finding their behavior foolish and beneath their attention. Now they shrugged and turned away, retracing their steps back through the trees.

The guards had previously respected Tasha's need for privacy when she bathed, and that occasion proved to be no exception. Rupert was grateful for their consideration, much as it surprised him.

Curiously, while the guards accommodated the princess's need for privacy, they still showed concern for her safety. The first time she had set out for the pool to bathe, the guards made no move to follow her. They had, however, insisted that Rupert accompany her. When he refused, they had made it clear they were not offering him a choice.

The situation raised challenges of its own for Rupert. Tasha was a beautiful young woman he cared deeply about, and it wasn't easy to remain detached as she undressed to wash herself and her clothing. He kept his back to her and tried to fix his mind on other things.

When she finished, he took his turn to bathe. She had always shown him the same courtesy, and without any apparent struggle. If he was honest, he found the discrepancy unsettling.

Pushing such thoughts from his mind, he focused on washing himself.

A deep sigh of contentment from Tasha interrupted his thoughts.

"I needed that!" she said. "In the palace there was always someone to prepare my bath and whisk away my dirty clothes. I took it far too much for granted! Now that it's gone, I can't pretend I don't miss it. I'm not myself in filthy clothes. Cleaning them properly is impossible here, but some attempt is better than nothing. And I can't tell you how good it is just to rinse my hair—I try to pretend it's been properly washed. Now I feel ready to face the world again."

He chuckled. "I'm ready to face the world too," he told her.

Stepping from the pool he made his way to her side. Seeing her smiling up at him, he reached for her hand. She placed it in his without hesitation.

He glanced around. "This wasn't exactly what I had in mind when I set out to court you."

"Our island exile hasn't exactly been romantic," she acknowledged. "But we're in an impossible situation. Thank you for helping me through it."

He returned a wan smile. "You've helped me much more than I've ever helped you. I couldn't have survived without your cheerfulness."

They stood in silence for a time, staring off into the distance.

"What are we going to do, Rupert?" she eventually asked.

He shook his head grimly. "I don't know. But as soon as an opportunity comes I'm going to seize it, however slim the chances."

RUPERT PAUSED to stretch his back, wincing at the protest from muscles he hadn't known he possessed. A steady breeze nagged at the untidy locks draped across his brow, and he wiped irritably at the sweat that dripped incessantly down his face.

A group of Ahran guards lounged idly no more than a stone's throw or two away, watching the captives with bored expressions. Rupert aimed an angry glance in their direction.

"Ignore them, Rupe," urged Tasha quietly. "They're not worth it."

For her sake he wiped the scowl from his face, shifting his attention to their shelter. Before bending to the task once more, he briefly glanced up at the sky. If he knew anything about cloud formations, wild weather would be upon them before long. They needed to work faster if they had any hope of completing the repairs to Tasha's shelter by nightfall. Perhaps sensing his unease, his companion quickly resumed her own labors.

From the moment their captors had ceased helping with practical tasks, the Rogandan princess had insisted on working alongside him whenever they needed to exert themselves. She asserted that she had become physically stronger as a result and more capable than ever before, and it was undeniably true. But the calluses on her hands confronted him with a persistent reminder of the disrespect shown her by their enemies.

To be fair, their small huts had been erected by the Ahrans. But that felt like an age ago. As time passed, more and more dwellings had been damaged by storms. The worst storm so far had descended on them the previous day, and by morning few buildings remained habitable. The guards quickly repaired their own huts, but they made it clear they had no intention of working on the huts of their captives.

Thankfully Rupert's hut had remained largely unscathed. The same could not be said for Tasha's dwelling. Perhaps her structure had been unlucky; perhaps less care had gone into its construction. Either way, they were left with no choice but to attempt a repair job themselves.

When Rupert asked for tools, the guards handed them over willingly enough. Their only requirement had been that the tools must be returned before nightfall.

He had the impression the guards didn't believe them capable of making effective use of the implements. They weren't far from the mark—with or without tools the task was almost beyond them. Rupert and Tasha had watched their huts being built, but neither of them had any personal experience of building, and they found repair work much more challenging than they had anticipated. Nevertheless, they persevered with dogged determination.

Rupert perspired profusely as he worked. He had long since stripped off his shirt in an attempt to cool off, although it made little difference. There was a time when he would have felt embarrassed to be so exposed before Tasha, but the trappings of refined society had rapidly been peeled away in the weeks of isolation. The changed reality demanded a different set of practical priorities.

"What if we don't finish in time?" Tasha asked, a trace of anxiety in her tone.

"Then you can have my hut," he replied evenly.

"But what will you do?" she asked.

"I'll sleep in the open."

She shook her head. "That won't work. If there's no other option we'll share a hut. We can find a way to make it work."

"I'm not going to even consider the possibility of failure," he said grimly.

Glancing once more at the sky, he bent his back and began again with renewed energy.

THE STORM HAD PASSED. Tasha's hut had taken a battering, but their makeshift repairs had done the job, and it had survived intact. With the sun shining once more, Rupert and Tasha took the opportunity to bathe at the pool. They welcomed the chance to forget about buildings and manual labor, and especially to leave behind their guards.

After visiting the pool they returned to the beach and gazed out to sea. Open ocean stretched off into the distance, not even the tiniest speck of land intruding upon the blue expanse. The emptiness only served to emphasize their isolation.

Then a ship sailed slowly into view around the island, anchoring off the beach. A boat was lowered into the water, and sailors rowed it toward the beach.

Were their guards being relieved again? It was an uncomfortable thought after what happened last time.

The Ahran leader met the new arrivals and conferred with them for many minutes. Then a group of guards headed purposefully toward the huts.

"What are they going to do?" asked Tasha uneasily.

Rupert stood up resolutely. "I have no idea. But I intend to find out."

Even before they reached the Ahrans it became clear that they were demolishing Tasha's hut.

Hurrying to the site, Rupert confronted them indignantly. "What is the meaning of this? We worked ourselves to the bone repairing that!"

An unfamiliar guard stepped in front of him. "Two huts are unnecessary," he growled, speaking in Rogandan. "One is more than sufficient for you both."

"Surely you're not suggesting we move in together!" Rupert retorted, shaking with anger.

Tasha placed a hand on his arm, but he refused to be placated. "This is unacceptable!" he shouted.

The new guard glowered at him. "You think yourself so high and mighty," he sneered. Switching effortlessly to Arvenian, he taunted, "Where is your kingdom now, pitiful little monarch? You deserve no more honor than a flea!"

A cold fury rose up in Rupert. The guard didn't wait for him to do something foolish. A fist smashed into his gut, causing him to double over in pain. A heavy blow to the head sent him crashing to the ground. The guard began kicking him viciously, and he curled into a ball, trying to protect his head with his arms.

The last thing he remembered before losing consciousness was an enraged Tasha leaping at the guard, screaming at the top of her lungs.

RUPERT GROANED. His head throbbed unmercifully, and waves of pain flooded his body.

When he opened his eyes, Tasha's face swam into view. Her look of concern was marred by an angry welt over one eye.

"What did they do to you?" he managed weakly.

"Not much. That brute of a guard slapped me hard enough, but I wasn't badly injured." She snorted. "He went away with some injuries of his own. He pretended not to feel it, but those scratches won't heal for a while." Her lip curled in grim satisfaction.

A damp cloth appeared in her hand, and she dabbed gently at his forehead. It stung, and he winced involuntarily.

"I'm sorry," she said.

He waved aside her apology, closing his eyes again in an attempt to settle himself.

"Where are we?"

"In your hut," she told him.

Speaking was difficult. He closed his eyes to rest some more.

After a while he rallied enough to ask, "Why?" His head was too fuzzy for him to better express his confusion about the new dramatic downturn in their circumstances.

"I've been asking myself the same question," she said with a sigh. "The new guards apparently came with new orders. We'll find out before long what that means in practice. I suspect we'll end up with a lot less freedom. The guard who beat you speaks Arvenian, too, so we won't be able to talk so freely anymore."

Everything had changed so abruptly. Their previous situation seemed almost pleasant by comparison.

His mind was spinning. "They destroyed your hut," he managed.

Tasha didn't respond immediately.

"Perhaps they're trying to force us together," she finally offered.

"I don't understand," he said with a frown, wincing when it set his head throbbing even more.

"We'll need to share a hut from now on."

He stared up into her face, uncomprehending.

She shrugged. "I don't know anything for certain, Rupe. I can't pretend to understand them."

Still unable to think straight, he waited patiently for her to say more.

After a pause she asked him, "Have you ever wondered about their behavior when I bathe?"

"They stay away," he replied, remembering not to frown again. "That's worth something." They were doing it out of respect for her privacy. Weren't they?

"They insist that you accompany me," she said. "Why?"

It seemed obvious. Even though they'd been ordered not to interfere with her, it made no sense to let her wander the island alone. "They wanted me to keep you safe. Why else?"

She went silent again.

He worked hard at marshaling his thoughts. "Are you suggesting the guards wanted us to sleep together?"

She gazed down at him. "Why else did they leave us alone at the pool?"

The idea made a weird kind of sense. He'd respected the boundaries, difficult as it had been. They probably hadn't expected that.

Thoughts began to come in a rush. From the beginning the guards had stayed well clear of them at night. Then it occurred to him that more than once he'd noticed the guards sniggering as the two of them headed toward the stream.

Even after Rupert had provoked Dessue's replacement, the Ahran had never forced them apart. It would have been an effective way of hitting back at Rupert, and the leader must surely have realized that.

Their captors' next step had been refusing to repair the damaged hut. With a storm closing in, Tasha herself had voiced the possibility of sharing the other one. Somehow they had managed to repair the hut themselves.

Perhaps the new guards arrived with orders to speed up the process. Since the two captives weren't taking the hint, the Ahrans had abandoned subtlety. The first step was to demolish Tasha's hut. Assaulting Rupert completed the picture.

It all added up. Separate sleeping quarters were no longer an option. Even if both huts had still been intact, Tasha needed to care for Rupert. They had literally forced him into her loving arms.

A number of things had previously seemed bewildering, but everything was slowly becoming as clear as a mountain stream.

How could he have been so blind?

From the beginning he'd believed the Ahrans were holding them for political leverage. The captivity offered an ideal opportunity to manipulate the kingdoms of Castel and Rogand. Now Rupert wondered if he understood them at all.

What could they possibly achieve by driving Tasha into his bed? Were they trying to weaken his standing in the eyes of the Rogandans? Or was there a different agenda?

Thoughts and possibilities rattled around in his head until he felt dizzy.

Try as he might, he could make no sense of it.

4

Bisri Ahuzza stepped forward into the throne room of His Imperial Majesty the Emperor Hourahn II of Ahr. He had positioned himself to one side of the Grand Vizier and a couple of paces behind him. As soon as they approached the throne, both men came to a halt and stooped low.

Ahuzza had always found the throne room intimidating. He couldn't help but be struck once more by the casual arrogance of its splendor, and the menace of the endless ranks of armed guards clad in imperial attire. He wondered if Rheibas ever experienced a similar reaction.

The emperor did not look pleased to see his most senior official. If the chief minister was aware of the emperor's mood, he gave no indication. As ever, The Grand Vizier presented a calm and unruffled demeanor.

The emperor fixed Rheibas in a glare. "I have been informed that my daughter is currently in Rog. What have you done to ensure her safe return to Kat Ahket?" he demanded.

"I regret to say that the Rogandan king has imprisoned her, Your Imperial Majesty. After the duplicity shown by the Rogandans in her original disappearance, it is difficult to predict what they will do next.

It is safe to say that restoring her to Your Majesty is not currently high on their agenda."

"And what of the disappearance of the king of Castel and the Rogandan princess?"

"I hardly know, Your Majesty," the Grand Vizier replied with a puzzled frown. "But it seems to be a vulgar business."

The emperor frowned. "The Rogandans claim that they were abducted by Ahrans!"

Ahuzza tried to mask his surprise. He was not aware of their disappearance, much less any claim that Ahrans were involved.

He could only admire the effectiveness of the emperor's intelligence gathering. The chief minister was head of the empire's spy network, but the emperor clearly had independent sources of his own.

Rheibas did not falter. "Any such claim is a monstrous falsehood, Your Majesty," he said firmly. "The Castelan king was apparently courting the princess. It has been suggested that he absconded with her, perhaps out of fear that his suit was about to be refused by her father. I imagine the two of them will be discovered sooner or later in some remote bolt hole. It would not shock me if the Rogandan princess is found to be expecting a child."

The chief minister dipped his head sadly. "The shame of such behavior must be difficult for the Rogandans to bear. But blaming the empire is dangerous folly. Perhaps it is an attempt to divert attention away from their own actions in making a hostage of Her Imperial Highness Princess Neira."

The emperor did not seem happy, but the chief minister was unfazed.

"If you would assign to me four or five thousand soldiers and the necessary ships to transport them, Your Majesty, I believe I could quickly resolve the current impasse."

The emperor's eyes narrowed. "I will approve no such thing!" he protested. "Do not expect me to support a military adventure in Rogand, Chief Minister. Not without much stronger cause. Get back there promptly, and find a way to resolve the matter without squandering the lives of my soldiers or plundering my treasury."

Rheibas bowed. "My diplomatic efforts will be redoubled, Your Majesty."

"You are dismissed," growled the emperor.

As the chief minister backed away, the emperor added, "Remain here, Ahuzza!"

Bisri Ahuzza stayed where he was, bowing respectfully.

As soon as the Grand Vizier had gone, the emperor turned to his envoy. "What do you make of this business involving the Castelan king and the princess, Ahuzza?" he asked.

The bisri shook his head. "It is the first I've heard of it, Your Imperial Majesty. My ships were not able to dock at Rog, so we remained at sea the whole time. We had contact with Ahran trading vessels, but the news I received through them might have been little more than hearsay. Do you believe your sources are reliable?"

The emperor waved a hand indifferently. "In this particular case the information is third or fourth hand—I wouldn't have let Rheibas off so lightly if I had real reason for concern. Nevertheless, this situation has provided me with an opportunity to remind him that I have sources of my own. I lean heavily on him, but I will never allow myself to become entirely dependent on one official, however effective."

Ahuzza nodded. "I understand, Your Majesty. You instructed me to operate independently when you gave me three ships and sent me to the region, but in practice the chief minister was my only source of reliable intelligence."

The emperor grunted. "That situation has to change!"

He directed a troubled glance at Ahuzza. "What have you learned of my daughter?"

"I am aware that she was taken by pirates—or perhaps by the Rogandans—and is now being held in Rog by the king. Beyond that I know very little, Your Majesty. According to the reports I received she is quite well. I doubt that the Rogandans would risk mistreating her.

As to what it would take to retrieve her, I cannot speak with any authority."

The emperor scowled. "There is far too much I don't understand about what is going on in Rogand," he said. "And I find some of the priorities of my chief minister perplexing." He shook his head. "Rheibas is a master at resolving political crises with little fuss and minimal loss of life. Why hasn't he been able to secure the release of my daughter? Why his fixation with a military solution? And on the other side of the world! There are subtleties here I don't understand."

The bisri decided it was wisest to say nothing.

The emperor continued, "When Rheibas sails for Rogand, you will return as well with the ships you commanded last time. As before you will operate independently from the chief minister. But this time you are to establish your own contacts with the Rogandans."

His face set hard. "I want my daughter back! And I want her back without a war! I cannot be expected to make sound decisions without reliable information, and I am no longer willing to limit myself to one person's perspective on such a delicate situation. Too much is at stake! Make no representations on my behalf, but ferret out everything that is happening. Do it discreetly. When you learn anything of relevance, I want to know about it immediately."

Bisri Ahuzza bowed.

"You are dismissed," the emperor ordered.

THE GRAND VIZIER'S summons to the royal palace had not extended to Bolnyk. Accordingly, Rheibas's senior agent made his way to the Grand Vizier's palace to await his master's return. As soon as the audience with the emperor came to an end, Bolnyk expected the chief minister would want to meet with him.

He was not disappointed. Rheibas appeared sooner than the agent expected.

The chief minister pointed the way to his private conference room, and Bolnyk followed him in.

Calling for a servant, Rheibas ordered refreshments before adding, "Make sure I am not disturbed! Under any circumstances."

The servant left, closing the door behind him.

"We have work to do, Bolnyk," the chief minister said grimly. "As I expected, the emperor is not inclined to give me a free hand in Rogand. We will need to use other means to achieve our goals."

Dipping his head in silent acknowledgment, Bolnyk aimed an inquiring look at the chief minister.

"Applying military pressure is not an option in the short term," Rheibas told him, a sour look on his face. "Nevertheless, we have the resources we need. It is a simple matter of applying appropriate leverage in the right place at the right time."

"I await your command, Your Eminence," Bolnyk assured him.

Pulling out a map labeled "Arvenon and Surrounding Kingdoms," Rheibas bent low over it. "This is what I need you to do."

With the conference at an end, Rheibas met his senior agent's eyes. "Do you understand?"

"I do, Your Eminence," Bolnyk replied, pushing himself to his feet and offering a tight bow.

Attentive as always, he waited patiently for the chief minister to dismiss him. He intended to allow himself a few minutes to relax in his own modest quarters in the palace. Any respite would have to be brief. There were things he needed to do.

The chief minister had other ideas. "Come with me," he barked.

Following Rheibas through a seemingly endless succession of echoing corridors, Bolnyk eventually found himself before a metal door in an unused wing of the palace.

Two guards stood outside. At the approach of the Grand Vizier, they snapped to attention.

"Open it," growled Rheibas. "Then leave us."

One of the guards unlocked the door. Tugging hard, he pulled it open. Given its thickness and weight, it must have been soundproof.

A dimly lit room lay within. Bolnyk caught a glimpse of a miserable and bedraggled man, his face vaguely familiar, sitting on a low bed. Bolnyk decided he had spotted him on at least one other occasion, although he knew nothing of the man's history.

Rheibas flicked a hand, and the guards withdrew, positioning themselves out of earshot. Rheibas ordered Bolnyk, "Wait here." Entering the room, he leaned heavily on the door to push it closed. In spite of his efforts, it remained slightly ajar.

A brief conversation ensued between the two men. Bolnyk caught no more than snatches of it.

Rheibas's growl reached him faintly. "You...accompany me... Rogand...convince me or...sharks."

"But...but I...I showed you...the..." the man sputtered loudly.

"Silence!" shouted Rheibas, cutting him short.

Bolnyk heard no more than muffled voices until Rheibas emerged.

Waving over the guards, the chief minister waited until they had secured the door, then he headed off, Bolnyk beside him.

As they walked, Rheibas issued a rapid series of instructions. "I am making you responsible for this imbecile. Bring him to my ship just before we leave for Rogand. Place him aboard in a secure location where no one can talk to him. The man is deranged, but in Rogand I might be able to find a use for his ravings, given the right audience. I expect him to arrive safely and in good health, but beyond ensuring that, do not speak to him or waste a minute of your time with him. Do you understand?"

When Bolnyk responded with a nod, the chief minister turned on his heel and walked briskly away.

The senior agent watched his master turn a corner and disappear. Then he gazed thoughtfully back the way they had come.

What possible interest could Rheibas have in the bedraggled creature hidden away in the room? What had the two men been talking about? And what audience could possibly benefit from the ravings of a madman? Was Rheibas looking for ways to confuse his enemies?

Bolnyk set off for his rooms absorbed in his thoughts. He knew better than anyone how dangerous it was to pry into his master's business, and he had no intention of crossing that particular line.

Nevertheless, the situation was intriguing. A lunatic held no interest for him, but he couldn't pretend his curiosity wasn't roused, if only because the chief minister usually confided in Bolnyk, yet the senior agent knew nothing of this prisoner.

RAGING seas made the voyage unusually hazardous for Bolnyk and the other passengers on the ship that bore the Grand Vizier toward Rog. Tossed about unmercifully, the senior agent had ample opportunity to ponder darkly the strange fascination that drew his master so far from home once more. Rheibas had invested considerable resource into establishing a presence in the region, to say nothing of the elaborate scheme involving the princess. Yet his senior agent had no idea what he was striving to achieve.

After a series of unusually mountainous waves had slammed into the ship, Bolnyk remembered the prisoner. He had seen him safely aboard, but Rheibas had also given him responsibility for delivering the prisoner to Rogand safely and in good health. Accordingly after collecting a loaf of bread, a lump of cheese, and a skin of wine, he lurched his way below decks to the section of the hold where the man was located.

Unbarring the door of the prisoner's room, he pulled it open and stepped inside, holding high a candle. The flickering light revealed the prisoner standing in a dark corner, swaying unsteadily with the rolling of the ship. The chains clanking around the man's ankles confirmed there was no risk of him escaping.

He threw the food onto the floor near the prisoner.

The man was eyeing him curiously. "You're the Grand Vizier's lapdog," he observed, speaking in Rogandan.

"You have no idea who you're talking to," Bolnyk growled, firmly gripping a nearby beam of wood in an attempt to stay in one place.

"Probably not," the man acknowledged. "But I do know that the Grand Vizier trusts you implicitly."

"How do you conclude that?"

The man might have been shrugging, but it was impossible to be certain with the pitching of the ship. "He allowed you to see me, and he hasn't executed you yet."

The senior agent scowled. It was infuriating to think that a miserable lunatic might be privy to information the chief minister had kept from him.

He wondered again who the man was and what the chief minister wanted him for. He hadn't forgotten either that Rheibas ordered him not to speak to the man at all.

Strangest of all, if the man was insane, he certainly hid it well.

Curiosity kept him lingering.

The man seemed to sense it. "He hasn't told you, has he?"

With no response from the senior agent, a mocking grin came to the man's face. "Of course not," he smirked. "He would never share the knowledge with *you*."

Anger welled up inside Bolnyk. Who was this cur to flaunt his secrets? He stepped closer, raising a hand to wipe the smirk off the ugly face.

The man shrank away, wincing fearfully. "I'll tell him!" he shrieked.

Bolnyk stopped short before landing a blow. Turning his back on the prisoner, he staggered away, reeling with the motion of the ship.

Galling as it might be, the man was right. Bolnyk had been ordered not to communicate with the prisoner. He would have some explaining to do if he left the man with an injury.

The interaction had left him with more questions than ever. Still simmering, he headed away, acknowledging to himself that his anger was directed as much toward Rheibas as it was toward the prisoner.

5

Will Prentis sat with King Steffan and Queen Essanda of Arvenon in the king's private audience chamber in the castle at Arnost.

"Can you describe the mood in Rog?" the king asked Will.

Will's face grew grim. "Even before we left, King Krasmir was upending the city in his search for the princess and King Rupert," he replied. "He found no sign of them."

"Has he tracked down more of the Ahran agents?"

"He has. He somehow came into possession of a document listing the safe houses of Ahran agents throughout Rog and the surrounding countryside. He asked Lord Kulferan to surreptitiously observe a few of the sites to verify the document's accuracy. When it checked out, Lord Kulferan carefully planned a series of raids before dawn one morning. The locations were raided simultaneously to prevent agents from warning their comrades. They netted a couple of hundred Ahran agents."

The king looked shocked. "So many!"

Will nodded. "Lord Kulferan's investigations revealed that some of the agents had been there for almost two years."

"This has been long planned," King Steffan observed grimly.

"Why would the Ahrans take the risk of writing down the locations of their safe houses? Much less leave such a document lying around? It makes no sense."

Will shrugged. "It probably wasn't the Ahrans. The document was written in Rogandan, and it seems more likely that it was put together by someone else. The priests of the dark gods have their own sources of information, and the Varasans have a very effective network too."

Will didn't say so, but he himself was the author of the document. He had prepared it not long before he left Rog with his family. The information had come entirely from Thomas through the agency of the Stone of Knowing. Bolnyk, the man in charge of the Ahran agents, had unwittingly revealed the locations when Thomas finally got a good look at him. Not being literate in any language, Thomas had called upon Will to write it all down. Will had left the document where he knew King Krasmir's people would find it.

"Did they learn anything at all about the likely whereabouts of King Rupert and Princess Teylee?" asked Queen Essanda.

"Unfortunately not," Will replied, shaking his head. "They were able to identify what appeared to be the headquarters of the Ahrans, but the leader of the agents wasn't there when they raided it. There were signs that the king and the princess had been held there, at least briefly. At the time we left Rog, Lord Kulferan's men were still interrogating the Ahrans. I suspect they will discover that King Rupert and Princess Teylee were taken away by ship."

This last piece of information was much more than a suspicion. Having seen the Ahran prisoners himself not long before leaving Rog, Thomas knew that several of them had witnessed the two captives boarding an Ahran vessel.

Will had decided it was wisest to let Lord Kulferan extract this information for himself. If the Rogandan commander failed to arrive at the truth, Will could always arrange for the information to be passed on indirectly, as he had done with the locations of the Ahran safe houses.

"Are you still planning to return to Rog?" asked King Steffan.

"Yes," Will told him. "I made a promise to King Krasmir, and I intend to keep it."

"How does Amyra feel about that?" asked Queen Essanda.

"She isn't excited about me leaving, of course, but she understands. She will remain here in Arnost with the children this time." He shook his head with a sigh. "Both of us have great sympathy for King Krasmir and Queen Deka. We have some idea of what they must be feeling."

For a moment the queen's own grief showed plainly on her face. "I am every bit as eager as the Rogandans to see the captives returned safely," she said quietly. Her eyes had become moist. "I am anxious for my brother! And for his kingdom!"

The king quickly moved the conversation in a different direction. "Will anyone else be returning with you, Will?" he asked.

"Just Thomas," Will replied.

The king raised an eyebrow, but he offered no comment on Will's choice of companion.

"You're not taking Rufe?" asked the queen.

Will shook his head. "It wouldn't be fair to him. He would be the only one who can't speak any Rogandan. And if it ever should come to fighting the Ahrans, you'll need him here."

The queen seemed satisfied.

"Reluctant as we are to let you go, Will," said the king gravely, "all of us want to do whatever we can to support King Krasmir and Queen Deka in their efforts to retrieve King Rupert and Princess Teylee."

WILL STOOD HOLDING Amyra at arm's length, drinking in the sight of her. He wanted to remember her just as she was while he was gone.

After a few moments he turned away with a sigh, gazing out of one of the tall windows that illuminated their rooms in the royal castle.

"Are you sure you want us to stay here in Arnost?" Amyra asked. "I expect we would be safe back home in Erestor."

He shook his head. "I'd prefer to wait until our whole party can return together, with an armed escort," he said. "These are uncertain times, and it would be risky to make assumptions about how safe it might be to travel."

She shrugged. "Since Thomas is going with you, I am sure Elena will stay in Arnost with their children as well."

"You'll be able to enjoy a bit of relaxed time with her," Will suggested.

Amyra winced. "I have some distance to travel before we can truly relax together. I'm not proud of the way I behaved at times when we were in Rog. I'll be grateful for an opportunity to make it up to her."

"I don't think you need to be too concerned," Will told her. "Elena is a remarkably gracious person."

"She is," Amyra agreed. "Although that doesn't absolve me."

After a few moments' silence, Amyra casually added, "I will, of course, be sending the Stone of Authority with you."

Will didn't try to hide his shock. "But it's yours!" he exclaimed. He shook his head stubbornly. "I've never wanted responsibility for any of the stones. You know the reasons."

"I understand perfectly, Will," she replied. Stepping closer and slipping an arm around his waist, she rested her head on his shoulder. "The fact that you *don't* want the stone is a good reason why it will be safe in your hands."

He received her embrace, but he remained unconvinced.

"The stone is the reason I needed to go to Rog with you last time," she reminded him. "Having access to it will be just as important when you return."

When he still didn't respond, she became animated. "We don't know what will happen! The stone might play a crucial role."

"I have no experience whatsoever in using it!" he protested.

"Then practice!" she exclaimed. "We'll make time before you go."

Clearly recognizing he wasn't convinced, she added insistently, "It's perfectly sensible, Will. Thomas and Elena have been sharing their stone for years now, and nothing but good has come from it."

He grunted.

Having long since concluded that possession of a stone would be especially perilous for someone in his position, he couldn't simply ignore his misgivings. The more so with that particular stone. Who could guess where it might lead?

THOMAS STOOD with Will at the rail of the Nomad Lady, gazing out over gently rolling seas. A steady breeze had been driving the ship forward at a rapid clip, and the favorable weather showed no sign of changing.

It felt like an age had passed since Thomas had parted with Elena at Arnost.

"Try to be careful, Thomas," she had said, a nervous frown creasing her lovely face.

He had contented himself with a reassuring smile in response. He knew better than to make promises about the future.

Neither his children nor Will's children seemed too troubled by the departure of their fathers. They had the run of the castle. Crown Prince Aiden, Prince Leonid, and even little Princess Charlotte had quickly been drawn into their games. Not surprisingly, it didn't take long before squabbles broke out. Amyra and Elena would have their hands full.

In spite of his ambivalence about sea voyages, Will had decided the most straightforward journey to Rog was by sea. After riding west to Maranelle, they had once again found Captain Yordin available and willing to transport them. The Nomad Lady had begun to feel like an old and trusted friend.

As if alerted by Thomas's thoughts, the captain joined them at the rail.

"We're making excellent time, M'Lord," he told Will. "Baron Island is behind us, and we should clear Savage Strait before long."

"That's encouraging news, Captain," replied Will. "As you know, I'm eager to arrive in Rogand as soon as possible."

Captain Yordin glanced briefly at the seas and up at the sky before nodding in satisfaction. "I see no reason to put in at Varacellan, M'Lord. If these winds continue, we can sail directly to Rog."

Will dipped his head in acknowledgment.

A puzzled look came to the grizzled face of the old sailor as he gazed up at the sky. "The wind seems to have settled down nicely. It was beyond understanding earlier." Peering over the rail, he added, "And I've never seen so many dolphins."

After shaking his head in bafflement, the captain offered a respectful nod and headed away in the direction of the wheel.

Thomas grinned at Will. "Was that you playing with the wind earlier?" he asked.

A pained look came to Will's face. "Yes, it was," he admitted. He frowned in frustration. "I can't get the hang of it at all! Controlling the elements is Amyra's thing."

"And the dolphins?" asked Thomas.

Will's mouth twisted in an impish grin. "That's me."

He flicked a finger, and two dolphins burst from the water, chittering loudly.

Thomas gaped open-mouthed.

Will returned a wink. "I seem to be having a bit more success with living creatures."

"And people?" asked Thomas after a pause.

"Never!" growled Will fiercely. "I will *never* forget what it's like to be compelled against your will."

His face became calm again. "After insisting for years that I had no desire for a stone, you must be wondering what I'm about, Thomas."

Thomas raised an eyebrow.

The commander sighed. "I told Amyra I didn't want it. *And* that it wasn't safe for me. She refused to listen." A wry smile creased his face. "Some of the blame falls on you, Thomas! You and Elena gave Amyra the idea. You're so effective at sharing the Stone of Knowing." He gazed at the dolphins sporting around the bow wave. "This arrangement isn't permanent though. After this is over, she'll be getting it back. For good."

. . .

The winds had continued to be favorable. Varacellan lay behind them; they had entered Rogandan waters.

Thomas's conversation with Will was interrupted by a cry from the lookout. "Ships on the horizon! Three-masters!"

"How many?" shouted the captain.

"Three o' them, Cap'n!" the lookout replied.

Will made his way to Captain Yordin, Thomas trailing behind him.

"We need to be wary," the captain told them soberly. "Sightings of Ahran vessels in these waters are on the rise. Some of them are warships."

"What do you propose to do?" asked Will.

"Outrun 'em if we can," the captain replied determinedly.

Sailors began dashing about as the captain shouted orders. Sails were unfurled until every available piece of canvas was catching the wind.

"They've spotted us, Cap'n," shouted the lookout.

The masts were now visible to everyone on board. It soon became apparent that the ships were heading directly toward the Lady.

"Can you do anything to help?" Thomas quietly asked Will.

He shook his head. "I'd likely slow us down," he said grimly. "If Amyra was here it would be a different matter."

Tension grew as the three-masters drew ever closer.

"They're Ahran ships—no doubt about that," grumbled the captain.

Eventually, the tall ships began to overhaul them. Captain Yordin had long since passed out weapons to his crew, but it was going to be a one-sided battle if it did come to fighting. The decks of their pursuers were lined with soldiers.

As one of the foreign vessels drew alongside the Lady, shouts of command rang out, and the Ahran soldiers withdrew, lining up to take their turn descending into the hatch. After a few minutes the deck was almost empty.

"Let's find out what they want, Captain," said Will. "I'll talk to them. It appears that they're not looking for a fight."

The captain frowned in response, but he didn't argue. Ordering a couple of men to prepare to launch a longboat, he shouted orders for the other sailors to reef the sails.

As the Ahran sailors slowed their own ships, a man appeared on the deck of the nearest vessel. If his dress and bearing offered any indication, he was a nobleman. Twisting the clasp beneath his tunic, Thomas brought the Stone of Knowing into contact with his skin.

Will appeared at his side. "What can you tell me about our friend over there?" he asked quietly.

"He has access to the emperor," Thomas replied, "and he shows no sign of aggressive intentions."

The captain joined them before Thomas could say more. "The longboat is ready to launch."

Will nodded. "I'll take Thomas with me. We'll go unarmed. No need for guards—we don't want to send the wrong message."

Captain Yordin looked doubtful, but he nodded curtly.

A rope ladder was lowered when they reached the other vessel, and they climbed aboard. The Ahran nobleman stood ready to receive them.

Another man stood at the nobleman's side. It quickly became clear that he was there as an interpreter. He nodded a greeting. "Do you speak Rogandan?" he asked politely.

"We do," Will replied.

"Are you the captain?" he asked Will, pointing to the Nomad Lady.

"I am not. My name is Lord Torbury. I am an Arvenian nobleman. This is my friend, Thomas Stablehand."

The interpreter bowed before speaking rapidly to the Ahran nobleman. After they had conversed briefly, he bowed again.

"My name is Ronizah," he said. He indicated the nobleman. "This is Bisri Ahuzza."

At the mention of his name, Bisri Ahuzza performed a tight bow of his own.

"Could you please accompany us to the bisri's cabin? He would welcome the opportunity to speak with you."

Will shot a brief glance in his direction, and Thomas returned an untroubled expression. Will knew him well enough to take his meaning.

"Certainly," agreed Will, returning his attention to Ronizah. Sending a cheerful wave to the men lining the decks of the Nomad Lady, he set off after the two Ahrans, Thomas at his side.

6

Of the Arvenians, only Brother Ander remained in the Rogandan capital. Kamash had sailed away to his island, leaving the Stone of Vitality in the monk's care. Will and Amyra and Thomas and Elena and their families had gone as well, no doubt impatient to consign their Rogandan misadventures to the past. Count Ranauld had long since departed with the rest of the delegation.

As the days passed, Brother Ander could have found ample opportunity to regret his decision to stay, had he been willing to entertain such thoughts. But he felt sure there was a reason why he needed to be there. It just remained to discover what it was.

The palace grounds held mixed memories for him, but he frequented them anyway, appreciating the opportunity to stretch his legs in the fresh air. Two armed guards trailed behind him everywhere he went—a visible legacy of the Rogandan king's unwillingness to allow further mishaps to befall guests staying at his palace.

His friendly attempts to engage the guards proved futile. One of them, known as Kyleth, rarely said a word to him, although he had plenty to say to his companion. The other, Ghonik, scarcely spoke at all. In time the monk learned to ignore them.

A couple of weeks after the other Arvenians had left, Brother Ander received a message through Kyleth. Given the soldier's obvious reluctance to speak to him, the monk wondered why Kyleth passed it on at all. Perhaps whoever sent the message had called in a favor.

The message requested a meeting at his earliest opportunity. He saw no reason to refuse. He had time aplenty on his hands, and King Krasmir had placed no restrictions on his movements. Accordingly he invited Kyleth to arrange a meeting.

Whoever sent the message must have felt a pressing need for urgency, because the monk found himself being led to a secluded setting in the palace grounds that same afternoon.

The location surprised him, given that access to the palace and its grounds was heavily restricted. Quite apart from the location, Brother Ander couldn't account for anyone wanting to meet with him at all. As far as he knew, few Rogandans were even aware of his existence. He therefore approached the interaction with considerable curiosity.

Kyleth and Ghonik seemed more reserved than usual as they led him to the meeting place. While not exactly furtive, they didn't appear relaxed. He felt no undue concern about his safety, but the clandestine nature of the interaction thoroughly roused his interest.

It soon became apparent that their destination was a heavily wooded section of the palace grounds. As they approached, he caught sight of a cloaked figure standing restlessly among the trees. The petitioner proved to be a soldier in late middle-age. Once Brother Ander came into view, the man made a visible effort to calm himself.

Kyleth was inquisitive to the point of being nosy, and even Ghonik hovered close at hand. The gray-headed inquirer glared at them until they moved out of earshot, Kyleth mumbling audibly under his voice.

The moment they were gone, the man turned to the monk. "My wife is very ill," he said, not even pausing to introduce himself. "I would be grateful if you would come and heal her."

Brother Ander's eyebrows went up in surprise. "Why call on me?"

"My nephew is a soldier. He was with you at the ford," the man replied. "When you healed the boy."

When the monk didn't respond immediately, the man became restless again. "The boy was dead—my nephew had no doubt!"

"I will visit your wife," Brother Ander said reassuringly. "I don't know if I can help, but I am willing to pray for her. If she is healed it will be God you need to thank, not me."

"Will you come now? She doesn't have much time."

"If you wish."

The man nodded in relief. "My name is Tarvek. My wife is called Vehmina. Please come with me."

He set off rapidly, checking frequently to assure himself that the monk was following. Kyleth and Ghonik trailed along behind.

Tarvek led them rapidly out of the palace grounds and onto a thoroughfare that led toward the heart of Rog. He moved so quickly that Brother Ander was almost forced to run to keep up with him.

They turned off the main road and wound through a number of side streets, eventually reaching a modestly sized house. Pushing through the front door, Tarvek held it wide for the monk. He ignored the guards entirely. They made their own way in.

Brother Ander followed Tarvek upstairs into a dimly lit room, the guards close behind them. A woman lay on a low bed, unmoving and deathly pale. He examined her closely, touching her forehead, examining her eyes, and listening to her breathing. His extensive experience as a healer told him she was close to death.

He knew there was little he could do, but while weighing up his limited options, he decided to offer a prayer of blessing. The Stone of Vitality lay in a pocket of his robe, and he fingered it absently with one hand as he prepared to pray. Placing the other hand on Vehmina's head, he mouthed a blessing followed by an entreaty.

The change in the patient's condition was as swift as it was astonishing. Opening her eyes, she looked up at him and smiled.

"I'm thirsty," she announced.

Tarvek bustled about the room in agitation, alternately hugging his wife and plying her with water and wine. He tried repeatedly to press payment into Brother Ander's hands, and it was only with great effort that the monk prevented him.

The situation quickly began to feel uncomfortable to Brother Ander. Anxious to leave, he murmured a farewell and made his way downstairs, pushing through the door of the house. He emerged into the street to discover a small crowd outside the house.

Kyleth and Ghonik had followed him out of the door. Stepping past him, they shoved the inquisitive onlookers aside before bustling him back toward the palace.

Tarvek was not the only one surprised by the sudden recovery of Vehmina. The monk was equally taken aback by what had happened.

Almost from the time he became a monk he had been a healer, calling upon herbs, his ever-expanding medical knowledge, and his growing confidence in prayer to treat the sick. Ethen's miraculous recovery had been something entirely different. While never fully comprehending it, he concluded at the time that the Stone of Vitality had somehow boosted the potency of his prayers.

To all appearances, something similar had just happened again. The Stone of Vitality alone couldn't account for it. He'd been touching it when he first placed his hand on Vehmina, but the healing hadn't come until he prayed.

Brother Ander's own limitations as a healer had long been a source of frustration to him. Was it possible that his prayers, when supported by the stone, granted him access to a much more effective way of bringing relief to the sick and injured? He eagerly looked forward to further opportunities to find out.

BIG NEWS TRAVELED FAST throughout a city, but even Brother Ander was surprised by how quickly word of the woman's healing spread. He rose the following morning to find himself besieged by requests for help.

The evident misery that lay behind the appeals stirred his compassion. Accordingly, he headed for the palace gates not long after the sun had risen.

Kyleth and Ghonik accompanied him as always, although they did not hide their reluctance. The remarkable recovery of Vehmina the previous day had left them no less wide-eyed than Tarvek. Yet both of them now seemed cautious and uncertain. Up to that point, their role as his guards had been relaxed and undemanding. Were they sensing that everything might be about to change?

Stepping through the gates, Brother Ander was greeted by a small crowd. Hope and despair warred within many petitioners, the tension evident on their faces.

Two people began to argue loudly about who had the right to be seen first. A scuffle broke out, forcing the two guards to intervene. Quickly eyeballing those who had taken no part in the fight, Ghonik selected a woman holding a child who was clearly in pain.

Dispensing with his usual examination, Brother Ander immediately prayed for the child while grasping the Stone of Vitality. The gathered petitioners went quiet as they witnessed an immediate and remarkable transformation in the child's condition. Immediately a crowd of people pushed forward demanding attention. Chaos threatened.

Filled with confidence after witnessing the effectiveness of prayer supported by the stone, Brother Ander held up his arms for quiet. As soon as the noise abated, he addressed the crowd. "Please be patient!" he called. "I will try to see you all."

Having responded to the first couple of petitioners, he saw that a line had formed. It grew in length even as he watched, snaking back and forth as new people joined it. Taking a deep breath and exhaling slowly, he called forward the next person.

Weeping sores, broken limbs, blind eyes—almost every imaginable disorder confronted him. He refused to be daunted. Some conditions he recognized, some he did not, but every one of them yielded to his earnest entreaties augmented by the power of the stone.

The sensational recoveries might have appeared effortless, but for reasons he did not understand, they came at a cost. He barely noticed any impact from the first two or three healings, but after that he soon became profoundly weary. What he appeared to be achieving with little effort quickly drained him to the point of exhaustion. After every new healing he was forced to rest, and for longer each time.

The passing hours became a blur. People came and went until he was barely able to focus.

Eventually an authoritative voice rang out, calling an end to it. Looking up wearily Brother Ander found Tarvek and Vehmina facing the crowd.

"The monk needs to stop!" Tarvek called. "He is close to collapse! We will ask him to come tomorrow to Ugar's Repose. It is a well known landmark—the low hill to the southwest of the city. For now he needs to rest!"

Grumbling broke out at the suggested delay, but his condition must have been obvious to everyone, and the people accepted Tarvek's words. To Brother Ander's relief, the crowd slowly dispersed.

After agreeing to Tarvek's proposal and thanking him sincerely, the monk dragged himself back to the palace. Kyleth and Ghonik followed silently. He barely noticed them.

Reaching his rooms, he gulped down some water before collapsing onto his bed.

Brother Ander woke before dawn to a dull pain throbbing in his head. He had barely eaten the previous day, and his stomach rumbled uncomfortably.

As usual, food had been delivered to his rooms, and he worked away at it steadily. Water had been provided as well, and after drinking freely his head began to clear.

Intending to set off for the palace gates, he left his rooms to find his guards waiting for him.

"You need to remain in the palace," Kyleth said bluntly.

The monk's eyebrows furrowed. "Why?" he asked, baffled at the thinly veiled hostility in the guard's tone.

Kyleth said nothing.

"It is safer here," Ghonik offered. His manner conveyed caution rather than antagonism.

"Thank you for your concern," said Brother Ander. "But unless the king insists I remain here, I will go. I made a promise to Tarvek and to the people."

With that, he set out determinedly for the gates. The guards followed close behind, Kyleth glowering at him and Ghonik looking concerned.

Tarvek was waiting for him. He seemed ill at ease.

"Is anything wrong?" asked the monk.

Tarvek lowered his voice. "We can expect trouble. Some of the priests have been stirring up the people. I have just come from Ugar's Repose. People began gathering there early this morning, but not everyone is sympathetic, and some of the sick have already been driven away."

Brother Ander wasn't entirely surprised. Bringing relief to suffering people wasn't likely to win over the priests of the dark gods if they perceived him as muscling in on their territory.

It made no difference. He had the means to help the afflicted, and he had no intention of ignoring them.

Tarvek led the way to Ugar's Repose, the guards following close behind. Ghonik wore a look of concern; Kyleth was scowling.

If Brother Ander had expected a sea of eager faces when he arrived, he would have been disappointed by the sullen glares that greeted him instead. A few in the crowd wore hopeful expressions, but the restless throng before him bore all the indicators of a mob. No priests stood nearby, although he spotted a couple of men wearing their distinctive black garb at the rear.

"You're not wanted here," a rough voice called.

"Go back to where you came from, foreign scum!" shouted another.

The hecklers were interrupted by an energetic woman who pushed her way to the front. She looked frail, but she was determined. "Let me through," she demanded.

Several of the bystanders jeered at her. "Go home, old woman," scoffed one.

"I ain't goin' nowhere!" she informed them tartly. "I waited in line for hours yesterday, and now it's my turn!"

With that, she approached Brother Ander boldly.

The monk greeted her with a gentle smile. Placing a hand on her head, he prayed for her.

"It's gone!" she shouted, a look of astonishment beaming from her face. "The pain is gone! Thank you! Thank you!" She bent low to him before capering about joyfully.

The reaction of the woman seemed to further rile the crowd.

"Think you're in charge around here, do you?" a voice snarled.

"Who are you to interfere with the will of Malzakh?"

"Keep your pretend god to yourself! We follow the dark gods of Rogand!"

Shouts of agreement followed this last statement. Clubs appeared, and men stepped forward menacingly.

"It's time to go, Brother Ander!" Tarvek called urgently, backing away in alarm.

The monk glanced instinctively at his guards. Ghonik began moving forward to defend him, but the crowd shoved him aside. Kyleth hung back out of harm's way.

Brother Ander didn't blame either of his guards. Two of them could not protect him against a mob.

He held his ground, facing the men who threatened him. "I bear you no ill will," he told them.

His calm demeanor seemed to enrage them further. Rushing forward, they began punching and shoving him. Pushed back and forth, he lost his footing and went down. Men surrounded him, kicking and beating him unmercifully. Curled up defenseless on the ground, he tried to protect his head with his arms.

Pain overwhelmed his senses. The frenzy continued unabated until a voice dimly reached him through the agony, "Soldiers are coming!"

The blows ceased, but his suffering continued.

Darkness rose up to claim him. With his consciousness slipping away, his limbs slumped nervelessly. Sliding deeper into his robe, a hand came to rest upon the Stone of Vitality.

7

From the moment they arrived at Ugar's Repose, Ghonik could see there would be trouble. He had more than enough experience to recognize the signs.

This was not the crowd that had pressed in eagerly to the monk the day before, frantic in their enthusiasm to be released from their suffering. Today a sea of grim faces awaited the new arrivals, and the guard's unease grew the moment he spotted the dark-clad priests at the back of the mob.

It hadn't been difficult to predict what was coming. His own cousin was a priest of the dark gods, and Ghonik could readily imagine what he would have to say about foreign monks being permitted to roam the streets of Rog, stirring up the masses. Sooner or later the Arvenian would get what was coming to him, and loyal followers of the dark gods would surely applaud when it happened.

Kyleth had already made it obvious his sympathies lay with the priests. Given the way he despised foreigners, it was hardly surprising. When first assigned to the monk, he had accepted the duty with an oily smile. Around Ghonik, he made no attempt to hide his true feelings.

Yet this man was no ordinary foreigner. Who else healed the sick with a touch? Ghonik had always bowed without question to the dark gods. But he had never heard of their priests giving sight to a blind woman or mending a crippled leg.

He himself knew a soldier who witnessed the murder of the Arvenian commander's son. The soldier insisted that the boy had been dead, and that he returned to life after the monk lifted him into his arms and prayed.

The story hadn't convinced Ghonik. Not until he had seen the monk in action himself.

He doubted no longer. And he had never felt so conflicted.

Whatever his own uncertainties, his duty was to keep the foreigner out of harm's way. From the moment they arrived at Ugar's Repose, it was obvious to Ghonik that he should have done more to keep his charge from coming there. Passions had been roused, and the healing of the woman only inflamed the fury.

When the mob began to move in, Ghonik had stepped forward to do his duty. The crowd had muscled him aside. Tarvek would have tried to do something if Kyleth hadn't forcibly restrained him for his own safety. Kyleth himself made no attempt to intervene.

It took only moments before protecting the monk became impossible. There were simply too many assailants.

In the end Ghonik could only look on helplessly while the monk was brutally attacked.

The approach of a patrol of Lord Kulferan's soldiers brought an end to the assault, but it was too late for the victim. No one could survive such a savage beating.

Looking toward Kyleth, Ghonik caught his eye. The other guard shrugged apathetically, his manner conveying complete disinterest in the fate of their charge. Ghonik turned away with a scowl. His partner had the sensibility of a weasel.

Peering down at the victim once more, Ghonik wondered gloomily what they should do with the body. He couldn't begin to imagine what they were going to say to the king.

Then, impossibly, the monk stirred. His eyes blinked, and he drew in a shuddering breath. Then he sat up.

Ghonik stood open-mouthed with amazement. Kyleth had gone pale.

Apparently unaware of their reaction, Brother Ander stretched his limbs awkwardly before clambering to his feet.

Wincing, he smiled wryly. "I apparently didn't receive a warm welcome," he offered.

The magnitude of the understatement left Ghonik speechless.

Tarvek hurried to the monk. "Brother Ander, how is it possible? Your injuries!"

"I imagine it looked worse than it was," the big man returned. "I don't seem to have suffered any real harm."

The captain of the army patrol rode up, bringing their interaction to an end.

"What was the cause of the disturbance?" he demanded. "Is there a problem here?"

"No problem at all," said Kyleth brightly. "Just a minor misunderstanding. We were able to resolve the matter, so there's no cause for concern."

The captain looked less than convinced, but with no obvious need for his intervention, he soon wheeled his horse about. Signaling to his men, he led them away at a trot.

Kyleth sidled up to the monk. "Brother Ander," he said, "Congratulations on your magnificent recovery! I never doubted the outcome for a moment." He lowered his voice. "I think I might know someone who is very unwell and could benefit from your services, if you're willing."

"Of course. I'm happy to do whatever I can to help people," the monk replied. He seemed a little unsteady. "Perhaps tomorrow," he added tentatively.

Kyleth nodded with satisfaction. "Excellent! I'll set something up for tomorrow afternoon."

"We must return Brother Ander to the palace!" said Tarvek. Taking the big man in hand, he gently began steering him toward the city.

Kyleth fell in beside Ghonik. Leaning forward conspiratorially, he spoke in an undertone. "This could work out very well for us," he said. "I know a person with more coin than he knows how to spend. He has major health problems, and he'll pay handsomely for a bit of personal attention from our good friend here." He jerked his head toward the monk. He rubbed his hands. "Once he's sorted out, there'll be plenty of others."

Ghonik scowled at him. "What about the dark gods?"

"My loyalty hasn't changed," growled Kyleth. "But the priests will need to lie low for a while after what just happened. In the meantime, business is business!"

Ghonik made no attempt to hide his utter contempt for Kyleth and his proposal.

Kyleth rolled his eyes at his partner's reaction. "Suit yourself," he said with a shrug. Turning his back on Ghonik, he hurried forward to catch up with Tarvek and Brother Ander.

KYLETH WASTED no time before setting up a meeting with the sick acquaintance he had mentioned. The following afternoon was not far advanced before Brother Ander once more found himself leaving the palace with his guards.

This time they traveled in a covered wagon.

"You had an energetic day yesterday, Brother Ander," Kyleth explained. "It's only right that we spare your legs."

The monk suspected the mode of transport had more to do with keeping him out of sight than preserving his energy. Having already had more than enough excitement, he saw no reason to complain.

The wagon rumbled through the streets of Rog, carefully bypassing the seedier side of the city. Glancing out of the back, he noticed the dwellings becoming bigger and more pretentious. Eventually they came to a brief halt before being admitted through ornate gates into an expansive courtyard surrounded by high walls.

Climbing out of the wagon, he looked around. The mansion

before him surely belonged either to a member of the nobility or to a merchant of considerable means.

Hurrying to the entrance porch of the mansion, Kyleth announced himself to the pair of servants standing outside the large double doors.

Brother Ander turned to Ghonik. “Your partner seems to have overcome his reservations about this assignment,” he observed.

Ghonik did not respond, rolling his eyes briefly before turning away.

The monk turned his attention once more to Kyleth, eyeing the guard thoughtfully for a long moment. It wasn’t possible to hear what was being said, but to all appearances the guard was engaged in an animated negotiation with a senior servant of the household.

Kyleth’s real agenda abruptly became clear. The monk wondered how he could have become so blind. A wry smile twisted his lips as he recalled that he had once been as cynical as the best of them.

They were soon ushered inside and led to a large room that overlooked an extensive garden. An elderly man lay sprawled awkwardly on an elaborately decorated recliner, flanked by a woman who appeared to be his wife. Their host greeted them distractedly, making no effort to get up.

A servant stood at the man’s side, and he offered the visitors a tight bow.

“I welcome you on behalf of Roethen, the master of this house,” he said.

Kyleth bowed in his turn. “Knowing as I do the difficult circumstances endured by your esteemed master,” he replied, addressing the servant, “I have taken the trouble to bring here a healer of some renown. His name is Brother Ander.” He indicated the monk before turning to the master and bowing again.

Roethen turned dull eyes upon the supposed healer. If the man harbored any hope of a cure, it was not apparent.

Throughout his years as a healer in Arvenon, the monk had occasionally found himself in similar situations. Knowing that payment would typically be withheld until some kind of treatment had been provided, he guessed that opportunity still remained to establish boundaries.

"I am very willing to pray for Master Roethen," he said, "although I need to make it clear that my services are not for sale."

The servant looked bemused at this statement, so he added, "I will not accept a fee. Not under any circumstances."

The astonishment on Kyleth's face was quickly replaced by a look of fury. Nevertheless, he said nothing.

The monk ignored him, approaching Roethen instead. "What are your symptoms?" he asked quietly.

"Chest pain. Shortness of breath. Extreme fatigue," the master wheezed.

"May I place my hand on your shoulder?" Brother Ander asked.

The servant looked doubtful, but Roethen nodded. Resting one hand on the sufferer while grasping the Stone of Vitality with the other, the monk spoke a brief prayer.

Roethen's eyes went wide in surprise. He sucked in a deep breath, then rose from the chair. "The pain has gone!" he exclaimed.

Ignoring the shocked faces around him, he began pacing jubilantly about the room. "Double the requested fee, and pay it immediately!" he commanded his senior servant.

Brother Ander shook his head stubbornly. "I found you in great need and with little hope for improvement. The same could be said of many others whose suffering has more to do with reduced circumstances than ill health. If you wish to express gratitude, use the fee to ease the burden of the disadvantaged."

"Gladly, if that is your desire," Roethen replied expansively. "See that it is done," he ordered his servant. "But first—refreshments for my honored guests!"

It didn't take long before the monk discovered that others among the master's family and servants also nursed significant ailments. He insisted on ministering to everyone who needed his help before returning to the palace. The result was that Roethen's household was buzzing by the time they left.

Roethen might have been delighted with the outcome of the visit, but not everyone shared his enthusiasm. Kyleth made no secret of his animosity toward Brother Ander, and the atmosphere in the covered wagon was thick with tension as it rumbled through the streets of Rog on its way back to the palace.

The guard's conflict of interest made it obvious to the monk that the time had come for change. It wasn't just that the current guard assignments were no longer workable. Brother Ander wanted to leave the city—to go where he could work among the poor and disadvantaged without attracting so much attention. He especially needed to avoid drawing a crowd.

Accordingly, Brother Ander decided he would apply for an audience with the king as soon as he rose the next morning.

KING KRASMIR RETIRED after a long and demanding day to find his wife waiting for him. It didn't come as a surprise.

"You were uncharacteristically silent during dinner this evening," he told her.

"I was recalling the time Rupert first joined us for a meal," Queen Deka replied. "He seemed to fit in so well! Everything went wrong so quickly after that." She brushed tears from her eyes. "I miss my Tasha so much. What has become of them both?"

Putting an arm around her, he held her close.

"No one has any idea. No one except the Grand Vizier." His face twisted into a scowl. "The day will come when I get my hands on that serpent!"

She gradually managed to calm herself. "What about this monk? I have been hearing such stories about him! Supposedly the Torbury boy—Ethen—was dead! The monk brought him back to life. One of my maids knows a soldier who witnessed it."

"I've heard the stories too," he acknowledged. "Brother Ander apparently has a remarkable gift for healing. He's been out and about in Rog putting it to use, and it's made him enemies. Some of the priests have apparently decided he's an abomination."

"Ha! It's a simple case of jealousy. I've never heard of the priests healing anyone!"

"Be careful what you say, my dear. The priesthood is an important institution in Rogand. Whatever the motivation of the priests, I can't simply wish them away. And neither can he. The priests stirred up a mob, and he was almost killed."

She stared at him in alarm. "You can't let that happen! This Brother Ander was on hand when he was needed last time. I want to know he'll be there when *we* need him!"

"I can't insist that he wait around in Rog on the off chance he's needed one day."

She opened her mouth to speak, but he got in first. "I will arrange for him to be properly protected. And I'll make sure he can get here quickly if we ever do need him."

"THANK you for being willing to speak with me, Your Majesty," said Brother Ander with a deep bow.

King Krasmir waved him to a seat.

"I hear you have become famous," the king observed evenly.

The monk winced. "That was never my intention," he replied. "I apologize for any disturbance I might have provoked."

The king brushed aside his apology with a wave of his hand. "I do not hold you responsible for what happened at Ugar's Repose." He sighed. "My men have tried without success to identify your attackers. I am just glad you avoided serious injury."

"You are well informed, Your Majesty," observed the monk, dipping his head respectfully.

"The abduction of Lord Torbury's son changed everything," replied the king soberly. "It became clear to me that the safety of foreign guests in Rog cannot be ensured without active effort. That is the reason I assigned guards to accompany you. Regrettably, I understand they have been of little value."

"I do not wish to criticize them," the monk assured him. "Two men could not be expected to hold back an angry crowd."

"Even if they wanted to," the king finished dryly.

When the monk said nothing, the king changed direction. "I'm sure you have a reason for wanting to speak with me."

Brother Ander nodded. "I do, Your Majesty. If you will grant your permission, I will leave Rog for less populous areas. Helping people is an important priority for me, but I would like to do it without attracting notoriety. That might be easier if I go where I am unknown and avoid staying in one place for too long."

"You will be a loss if you leave Rog," the king told him. He hesitated for a moment before continuing. "We intend to find our daughter, Brother Ander. But we can only guess at her condition when we do." His brows furrowed. "I will be frank with you. You have developed...a reputation. My wife takes considerable comfort from knowing you are near at hand." He peered at Brother Ander. "As do I," he acknowledged openly.

"I will come the moment Your Majesties call," the monk assured him.

The king returned a brief nod. "There is no certainty we will ever need your services, of course. It would be nothing more than self-indulgence to keep you here just in case, especially when many others could benefit from your gifts. I will gladly grant you permission to go."

Brother Ander bowed gratefully.

"There is still the matter of protecting you," the king said bluntly. "I will arrange for different guards to be assigned to you."

"Perhaps you could offer my current guards a choice. I suspect that one of them at least would be glad to be released. I cannot be certain about the other one."

The king grunted. "From everything I've been told, you are more generous than they deserve. Nevertheless, I will consider your suggestion."

A crisp nod from the king indicated that the interview was at an end. Brother Ander left after bowing deeply.

8

When Brother Ander emerged from his rooms the next morning, he found Ghonik waiting for him as usual. There was no sign of Kyleth.

A burly guard stood beside Ghonik, and the new arrival greeted the monk with a shallow bow. "I am your new guard," he said. "My name is Dannhur. Ghonik and I will be accompanying you wherever you choose to go."

"I am pleased to meet you," the monk replied with a smile. "I am Brother Ander."

At first appraisal, Dannhur appeared relaxed and confident. The new guard was in turn calmly appraising him, and Brother Ander couldn't help wondering what he was thinking. The monk stood slightly taller, but size didn't count for everything. Years of experience told him that Dannhur was not a fighter to be underestimated.

In contrast to his partner, Ghonik seemed uncomfortable. "We will protect you with our lives," he said. "The king personally made it clear what he expects of us."

"I am grateful to you both," the monk replied. "But I have no desire to see anyone put in harm's way on my account!"

"We volunteered for this assignment," Dannhur informed him.

"Why?" Brother Ander asked candidly.

"I have a sister," Dannhur replied. "Her son is the joy of her life, and he was dying. She tried everything, and no one could help him. Not until you appeared. You healed him."

When Brother Ander glanced at Ghonik, the guard shrugged. "I've made some bad choices in the past, and I didn't need this assignment to be my latest failure. I wanted a second chance. Besides, I owe it to you."

"You owe me nothing," Brother Ander assured him with a shake of his head. He faced them both. "Please do not burden yourselves unnecessarily. My times are in God's hands."

Neither of the guards responded. Perhaps they saw his views as strange. If so, it didn't trouble him, and he saw no need to try to convince them otherwise.

It was time to consider the future. "I am planning to leave Rog," he announced.

Dannhur nodded. "We were told to expect that. When do you plan to set out?"

"Right now. The weather seems perfect for wandering in the countryside." Glancing up into a blue sky interspersed with fluffy clouds, the monk could only smile with anticipation.

"We won't need to wander on foot," Dannhur informed him. "The king has arranged horses for us."

Seeing the monk's eyebrows raised quizzically, the guard added, "I believe he is hoping to be able to call us back to Rog quickly if the need arises."

The news came as no surprise to Brother Ander. "A mount could certainly prove useful at times," he acknowledged. "When there's no urgency, though, I'll be doing as much walking as the horse."

After a brief discussion the men decided to head west, away from the coast. Dannhur suggested they travel on horseback until well clear of Rog. He also suggested that Brother Ander conceal his features under a hood. Having no desire to revisit the recent turmoil, the monk readily agreed to the suggestions.

They were on their way before another hour had passed. Long before sunset, all traces of the city had disappeared behind them. With the guards now willing to slow the pace, Brother Ander dismounted and removed his hood. Then replacing the reins with a halter, he led his horse forward on foot, reveling in the late afternoon sunshine.

When darkness fell, the men gathered sticks and built a fire. After sharing a simple meal, they settled down for the night.

It had been far too long since Brother Ander last lay beneath a blanket gazing up at the stars. Luxurious beds in royal palaces might be well and good, but a setting of this kind seemed fitting for a man of his calling. Breathing out a sigh of satisfaction, he allowed his eyes to droop closed.

BROTHER ANDER'S small party had been walking through scrubland for most of the afternoon when Ghonik spotted a scrawny sheep. Glancing sharply around, he spotted two more. Instantly alert, he called a warning to Dannhur.

"We need to get away from here urgently!" he exclaimed, keeping his voice low and pointing to the sheep.

Dannhur understood at once. "Warn the monk!" he said.

Brother Ander had been striding ahead of the others. Ghonik looked up to see him disappearing over a small rise.

Ghonik hurried after him. Topping the ridge he saw that he was already too late.

Half a dozen shepherds were sitting around a small fire. Seeing the monk, they leaped to their feet.

Instead of fleeing while he could, he called a greeting and headed down to them.

What was he thinking? Brother Ander was probably unaware of their reputation of course, being a foreigner. Ghonik knew only too well. Even soldiers avoided shepherds unless they enjoyed overwhelming superiority in numbers.

From their earliest years, shepherds learned to be handy with a knife and deadly with a slingshot. It was therefore no surprise to see the men before them armed with long, wicked looking knives. Several had slingshots in their belts.

"Welcome!" called a rough voice.

Quickly surrounding the monk, the shepherds slapped him on the back, guffawing loudly. Their good cheer seemed forced to Ghonik.

Dannhur had joined him on the ridge. "They're well armed," the big soldier said grimly, "and there are a few too many of them for my liking. Stay close. We'll fight back to back if we need to. I'm not going to sell my life cheaply!"

With that, both guards headed down to join the gathering around the fire. Several of the shepherds moved to let them through, a couple of them eyeing the horses a little too obviously.

A wizened shepherd with gray hair and a game leg—clearly the leader of the group—was addressing the monk. "I am Yetvar, and I bid you welcome." He eyed the visitor closely. "You're a foreigner," he said bluntly. "What brings you to these parts?" The shepherd's tone suggested his genial demeanor could disappear in an instant if it suited him.

"I'm a healer," the monk said simply. "My name is Brother Ander. I'm wandering the countryside doing whatever I can to help people in the name of God."

"A healer, eh?" The man gave him a calculating look. "That might come in handy. And what about these two?" He jerked his head in the direction of the two guards. "Are they healers as well?"

A burst of mocking laughter from the shepherd's companions accompanied his question.

"This healer is under the personal protection of the king," growled Dannhur.

"Ooo. We'd better be careful then, boys," said one of the shepherds. His wide-eyed expression was greeted with a new round of laughter.

The leader bared his teeth in a crooked grin. "They're just having a bit of fun," he said gruffly. "Pay no mind to it. Me old mamma now, she could use a healer. She's back at our little village. The place might be humble, but it's what we call home. You'll all join us there. No arguments, mind—I won't take no for an answer!"

"We will gladly accept your invitation," said Brother Ander. "And I will do whatever I can for your mother."

Yetvar ordered two of the shepherds to remain with the sheep. Then he set off, hobbling determinedly toward the village with the monk and the two soldiers following close behind. The remaining shepherds trailed behind them, murmuring under their breath.

Both soldiers sidled up to Brother Ander. Dannhur leaned forward. "What do you think you're doing?" he whispered incredulously. "There won't be any mother at the village! All he wants is our horses. Shepherds lie from the moment they first open their mouths!"

Ghonik nodded emphatically.

"They'll put knives in our backs, and at their village they'll do it with the least risk to themselves," Dannhur hissed. "We're stepping into our own graves!"

"I'm sure we have no need for concern," the monk replied mildly. "It will all work out. God will protect us."

"That's well and good for you," growled Dannhur, "but our gods are not so considerate. I can already imagine Malzakh licking his lips."

At that moment the village came into sight, cutting short their conversation.

Children and a few old people appeared, along with more shepherds, all of them rough and unsmiling. Both of the soldiers eased closer to the monk. Dannhur looked every bit as uneasy as Ghonik felt.

Yetvar disappeared into a low hut, reappearing beside a stooped and wrinkled woman. It soon became obvious that she was Yetvar's mother, but it offered little comfort to them.

She began a tirade the moment she emerged.

"You're a cursed fool, Yetvar!" she spat. "I knew it from the moment you were born. Why bring soldiers here? It would have been tidier to slit their throats where you found them!"

Ghonik tensed further. His hand was itching to draw his sword, but he knew it would be seen as a provocation.

"The monk claims he's a healer," the shepherd snarled. "If he can't fix you, I'll carve him into little pieces myself."

"No one can fix me," she spat. "Certainly not this idiot. He must be soft in the head if he agreed to come here!"

The monk stepped forward. "I'm Brother Ander," he said with a smile. "I'm pleased to meet you."

"I'm pleased to meet you," she repeated in a mocking voice. Hobbling closer, she slapped him in the face, following it swiftly with a kick to his shins.

When she swung her arm to hit him again, he grabbed her wrist and held it firmly.

"You dare lay a finger on me?" she shouted in fury.

As Brother Ander muttered a hasty prayer, several shepherds moved in, knives in their hands. Ghonik and Dannhur drew their swords and prepared to fight for their lives.

"Wait!" the woman yelled. She turned to the monk. "What did you just do to me?" she asked, her voice catching in her throat.

"I did nothing," he told her forthrightly. "It was God who healed you."

She stretched her neck, twisting and turning energetically while bending her back. "The pain—it's gone! Completely!" she said in wonder.

The villagers looked on in bemusement, some with knives still raised.

Brother Ander turned to Yetvar. "What causes your limp?"

After a moment's uncertainty, the leader replied. "Gout. It's troubled me for years."

Tentatively stretching a hand toward Yetvar's shoulder, the monk asked, "May I?"

The shepherd eyed him suspiciously for a long moment before nodding.

As Brother Ander prayed, a look of astonishment came to Yetvar's face. "Put away your knives!" he ordered. "All of you! And bring out anyone who's sick."

The monk immediately became very busy. By the time the sun set, he had exhausted himself praying for each of those seeking relief.

The mood in the village had changed dramatically from the moment the old woman was healed. Even the two soldiers had become welcome guests, and it was a merry party that gathered around a huge communal fire to share a meal that night. After belated introductions by Yetvar, the shepherds brought out the best they had to share with their visitors. The preparations were overseen by his mother.

Ghonik watched, fascinated, as the old woman bustled cheerfully about. Her high spirits were clearly having an effect on others in the community.

Finding himself beside the monk, he nodded toward Yetvar's mother. "Is she the same person?" he asked dryly.

Brother Ander smiled, speaking a word that Ghonik did not recognize. Seeing the guard's blank expression, he said, "It's an Arvenian word. It means 'Vitality.' She's come alive again."

After a pause, he added, "She'd lost hope."

"Because of her ailments?" asked Ghonik.

"It's hard to say." The monk waved an arm around the settlement. "These people live hard lives. If she told us her story, I suspect we'd hear of disappointments and suffering beyond anything we could imagine."

Ghonik was struggling to make sense of it all. "And getting well has given her hope?"

Brother Ander shrugged. "I don't exactly understand how it works. Vitality and hope go together, although I can't say which follows the other. I do know that losing hope sometimes cripples more than just the spirit. It's difficult to be truly alive without hope of some kind."

The arrival of Yetvar cut short their conversation. "Stay with us," the shepherd urged. "For as long as you like!"

"Thank you," Brother Ander replied, "but we must leave in the morning. Others need our help."

"I won't let you go without a gift," Yetvar insisted.

Returning to his hut, he retrieved a woolen belt, made from thick strands of rough woven yarn. Metal clasps bearing a distinctive ram's horn pattern adorned the belt.

He presented it to Brother Ander. "Wear this prominently," he said. "No shepherd anywhere in these parts will give you trouble."

The monk thanked him, promising to wear the belt proudly in memory of the friendship of Yetvar and his fellow villagers.

GHONIK LAY down to sleep that night without fearing for his life or even for his horse.

The day had ended spectacularly, in spite of the earlier lurch from peaceful to ugly. After everything he had witnessed thus far, he had reason to expect the following day would end well too, whatever challenges it might bring.

He was under no illusions. Sooner or later the priests would catch up with them. Unless, of course, some nameless group of bandits killed them for their horses first.

He wasn't going to worry about the future though. For the first time in years he had no regrets about the choices he'd made.

9

Entering a small but well appointed cabin toward the stern of the ship, Thomas and Will accepted seats around an ornate wooden table, Bisri Ahuzza and Ronizah settling themselves in chairs facing their guests.

While drinks were being served, Thomas took the opportunity to study Bisri Ahuzza closely. As always, the stone revealed a treasure trove of information. He was able to witness the bisri's audiences with the emperor and his meetings with the Grand Vizier. Unfortunately, remembered conversations were of no value to him since he did not understand the Ahran language.

The process was far from straightforward, but Thomas was able to deduce a considerable amount of information from the interactions. To begin with, Thomas had enough experience with the stone to spot the difference between memories and imaginings. He soon saw that the bisri was no different from Arvenians or Rogandans. While Ahuzza conversed with someone, his imagination was hard at work. When he was speaking with the emperor, his mind pictures provided clues to the topics discussed. Importantly, nothing the bisri had imagined during conversations with the emperor offered any hint of armed conflict.

At one point Will glanced in his direction. Thomas made sure he maintained a calm and relaxed expression on his face.

The interaction began with a question from the bisri through the interpreter.

"Do you have any official status on behalf of your king, Lord Torbury?"

"I do," Will replied. "I am traveling to Rog as the representative of King Steffan."

The bisri's expressionless face revealed no sign of the surge of excitement he felt at this news. Thomas saw that Will's response had prompted the memory of one particular interaction with the emperor. At the time, the bisri had been picturing himself engaging gravely with a faceless foreign monarch.

"Are you on good terms with the Rogandan monarch—King Krasmir?" Ronizah asked on the bisri's behalf.

Will's eyes narrowed. "If you are looking for ways of driving a wedge between our kingdoms, Bisri Ahuzza, you are wasting your time," he replied curtly.

Hearing the translation, the bisri responded with energy.

"You misunderstand me! I was merely hoping that you might be able to help me gain access to King Krasmir."

"For what purpose?" demanded Will.

"To allow me to accurately convey to the emperor the views held by the rulers of this region."

"And what does the emperor propose to do with this information?" Will asked coolly.

The bisri appeared taken aback at Will's tone. "His Imperial Majesty wishes to be made aware of possible steps the Empire of Ahr could take to help resolve any...misunderstandings between our peoples."

"If your emperor truly wishes to resolve misunderstandings, he can begin by releasing King Rupert of Castel and Princess Teylee of Rogand—unharmed!"

"The Empire of Ahr had nothing to do with their disappearance," the bisri insisted.

"You speak out of ignorance, Bisri," Will replied grimly. "Either that or you are a blatant liar. Both Thomas and I are personally aware of the circumstances of their disappearance."

At a brief glance from Will in his direction, Thomas confirmed the statement with an emphatic nod.

"Their abduction was by no means the first such provocation. Ahran agents abducted my own son!" Will's voice had taken on a dangerous tone. "I was able to rescue him, but only after a protracted and debilitating search. The man who had taken my son responded to the rescue by attempting to murder him. King Rupert and Princess Teylee were present, and in the confusion they pursued him with one of their guards. They were surprised and captured by a group of your agents—led by this same man."

Thomas decided it was time for him to speak. "These agents killed the guard who accompanied the king and the princess," he said calmly. "I was present when King Krasmir found him. The guard was near death, but he lived long enough to confirm what Lord Torbury has told you."

Thomas saw that the bisri was not convinced by Will's claims. "And who is this supposed abductor?" he asked dismissively.

"His name is Bolnyk," Will replied. "He is one of your Grand Vizier's senior agents."

Will's response took the Ahran by surprise. The bisri knew of Bolnyk.

"If I ever encounter Bolnyk again," Will concluded stonily, "I will kill him myself."

Bisri Ahuzza's face hardened at Will's threat. "Since you wish to speak of abduction," he growled, "there is the matter of Her Imperial Highness Princess Neira."

"I have met with the princess personally," Will informed him. "She made no mention of abduction. She spoke of being left on an uninhabited island with her guard. If you doubt me, speak to the captain of the ship that carried Princess Neira and your Grand Vizier to this region. I believe his name is Captain Gharpin."

With no response from Ahuzza, Will continued. "She was abandoned by your Grand Vizier and left there to die. Fortunately for her, the island was inhabited. A hermit was living there, and he rescued her and her guard. They eventually made their way to Rog."

Pushing back his chair noisily, Ahuzza rose to his feet. "In sailing to this region, it was my sincere hope and belief that the empire could reach an understanding with your kingdoms. But it seems that these...fantasies of yours will be expected to form the basis of any conversation. I am beginning to see that I was deluding myself."

The bisri offered them a tight bow. "Ronizah will arrange for you to be returned to your ship."

Will got to his feet. "I was fortunate enough to recover my son, but the same cannot be said for King Krasmir. His Majesty personally heard the testimony of Princess Teylee's guard before the man died. If you or others from your empire desire a fruitful engagement with him, do not expect a warm welcome if you persist in describing the abduction and continuing captivity of his daughter as a fantasy." He left after a tight bow of his own.

As soon as the Nomad Lady's longboat had left Bisri Ahuzza's ship, the Ahrans hoisted sail and departed.

Thomas and Will climbed aboard the Lady to find Captain Yordin waiting for them.

"No idea what you said, M'Lord," Captain Yordin told Will as he watched the ships dwindling into the distance, "but looks like you scared 'em off." The old sailor peeled back his lips in a grin of satisfaction.

The commander's only response was a grunt.

Before long Will found an opportunity to draw Thomas aside for a private conversation.

"My diplomacy skills are getting worse, not better," he growled.

"You shouldn't blame yourself, Will," Thomas countered. "It's deeply personal to you. And to King Krasmir. Bisri Ahuzza doesn't have the same stake in the outcome."

Will wasn't willing to let himself off so easily. "I can't afford to let it be personal. We'll never beat them if emotion gets in the way."

"If it's any help, Bisri Ahuzza wasn't as totally dismissive as he might have seemed. You at least sowed seeds of doubt in his mind."

"What are the emperor's expectations?" asked Will.

"I can't say with any confidence. But I get the impression the emperor sent Bisri Ahuzza to Rogand so he doesn't have to rely solely on his Grand Vizier."

Will frowned in annoyance. "If that's true, I should have worked harder at building some kind of rapport with Ahuzza."

"He needed to hear the truth sooner or later," Thomas said. "And he had to know what to expect if he meets with King Krasmir. It wouldn't end well if he takes the same approach he used with you."

Will's brows drew together. "If the emperor wants diplomatic contact, it better not happen through his Grand Vizier. Not that he would ever be stupid enough to show his face in front of Krasmir. No, this Bisri Ahuzza will need to take the lead if anything's to be resolved. Next time I meet with him—if there is a next time—I'm going to be more measured."

"WHICH DIRECTION, BISRI?" asked the captain.

"Continue on a course for Rog," Bisri Ahuzza replied. "Find an anchorage where we can remain concealed."

After bowing low, the captain shouted an order to his helmsman.

Ahuzza gazed distractedly at the captain as he went about his work. He suspected that if the man had dared, he would have asked about the meeting with the Arvenians. Ahuzza wasn't sure himself how he would characterize it.

"Join me, Ronizah," he commanded, heading for his cabin.

The interpreter hurried after him.

As soon as they were seated, Ahuzza faced the other man. "Well, what did you make of them, Ronizah?"

"The Arvenian lord was all bluster!" The interpreter raised his hands in disgust.

"And the one called Thomas?"

Ronizah shrugged. "He gave almost nothing away."

"He was difficult to read," agreed Ahuzza.

"I thought you handled it well, Bisri!" the interpreter gushed.

"I'm not so convinced."

"You were clear and uncompromising! You called their stories what they were—fantasies."

Ahuzza frowned. "If I'm any judge of character, that Lord Torbury believed what he was saying."

"He might believe it, but that doesn't make it true, Bisri," insisted Ronizah.

The bisri remained silent, wrestling with his thoughts. He had now been directly exposed to the accusation that the Rogandan princess and Castelan king had been abducted by Ahrans, with the blame laid at the feet of Rheibas's senior agent. Yet Rheibas himself—before the emperor and in Ahuzza's hearing—had denied any such involvement.

"The Arvenian accused the chief minister of attempting to murder Her Imperial Highness Princess Neira!" Ronizah protested.

"Yes," mused Ahuzza. "He did."

An anxious look twisted Ronizah's features. "Please, Bisri! Do be careful!" he urged. "No one wants the chief minister as an enemy!"

Ahuzza's eyes narrowed. "I have no intention of making the chief minister an enemy," he said sharply. "Nor do I believe the monstrous claim involving Princess Neira."

The account had indeed been more than the bisri could stomach. The Arvenian nobleman had the audacity to assert that the chief minister tried to kill the emperor's daughter. Any such claim was not merely outrageous, it was a grave insult—not just to the chief minister, but to the empire he so energetically represented.

After eyeing the interpreter for a few moments, he said evenly, "Thank you for your insights, Ronizah. You are dismissed."

Rising and bowing low once more, Ronizah left the cabin.

Ahuzza watched his retreating back testily. Not for the first time, he wondered where Ronizah's loyalty lay. Pushing himself up from his chair, he paced restlessly about the small cabin.

When the emperor had set him the task of making independent contact with the Rogandans, he imagined that his biggest challenge would be to find an interpreter fluent in Rogandan. He had stumbled upon Ronizah the very next day. Ahuzza knew nothing of the man before they met, but a quick investigation confirmed that Ronizah's credentials were impressive.

Even at the time their chance meeting had seemed uncanny. Now Ahuzza wondered if chance played any part in it.

It wouldn't surprise him to discover that the man answered to Rheibas. The interpreter's caution about making an enemy of the chief minister sounded like the kind of thing Rheibas might say. It might almost have been a veiled threat.

The emperor had tasked Ahuzza with keeping an eye on Rheibas. Had Rheibas in turn tasked Ronizah with keeping an eye on him? There was an undeniable symmetry to it.

He frowned. Unsettling as these questions might be, there was more at stake here than Ronizah's loyalty. What was the truth about the shocking series of claims made by the Arvenian nobleman?

He was certain that Torbury believed what he was saying. But could Ahran agents really have been involved in the kidnapping of Torbury's son? And could they have abducted the Castelan king and the Rogandan princess as well?

Ahuzza could readily see the political potential from such actions —assuming the goal was to destabilize the local kingdoms. But why would Rheibas engage in activities of this kind? What was he hoping to achieve by it?

As for leaving Princess Neira to die on a remote island, it seemed too far fetched even to consider. Yet Lord Torbury had insisted he heard it from the mouth of the princess herself.

It was quickly becoming clear to Bisri Ahuzza that the emperor had done him no favors in assigning him this task. Political maneuvering had never appealed to him. He was much too straightforward for his own good. As for provoking the chief minister's wrath—the prospect was unnerving.

Nevertheless the emperor himself had charged him with making discreet contact with the Rogandans. He was not expected to make representations on the emperor's behalf, and it was not his responsibility to fix anything. But he had been told to actively monitor the situation.

He knew that Rheibas was unlikely to welcome his involvement, however hard he tried to avoid entanglement in whatever games were being played here. But like it or not, the emperor had given him a job, and he intended to do it.

10

At a nod from King Delmar a man was admitted to the small reception room in the royal castle at Varacellan. After bowing low, the new arrival stood silently before the king.

The king directed his gaze toward the other servants in the room. "Leave us," he commanded.

They quickly departed, closing the door behind them.

"What do you have to report, Maran?" Delmar asked his senior agent.

"Most of the Ahran agents have been dealt with, Your Majesty, including recent arrivals. We allowed a few to slip through as you ordered. They are now being watched closely."

"Have you learned anything useful?"

"Unfortunately our efforts have been hampered by language. Few of our agents are fluent in the Ahran tongue. However the agent I mentioned to you is now ready for assignment, and our plans are well advanced."

"I wish to meet with this agent."

"Of course, Your Majesty. It would be prudent to set up a meeting well away from prying eyes."

"Make it happen."

. . .

THE NIGHT WAS WELL advanced when the king was led toward a dark alley not far from the royal castle. Clad in a hooded cloak, he could have been just another wealthy merchant protecting himself from the evening chill.

A dozen guards led by Lord Karevis spread out protectively around the king as they went. All of them had been personally selected by Karevis, and by his orders they were cloaked and hooded like the king. The Varasan army commander was leaving nothing to chance.

Reaching the narrow alley, the group stretched out along it until they came to a broad common located almost directly below the castle. Delmar was familiar with the site. At most times during daylight hours it was frequented by townsfolk who strolled among the many trees that dotted the expanse or relaxed on the lush green turf.

After dark the setting could only be described as eerie. Bathed with thin light from a pale moon and devoid of any sign of life, the park was the perfect location for a clandestine meeting. The guards seemed on edge, and Delmar understood completely.

A man stepped out of the shadows behind the trunk of a large poplar, bowing to the king and whispering a previously agreed watchword. The king managed to recognize the voice of the agent who had met with him earlier.

Pointing to a small cluster of trees nearby, the agent murmured, "Over there, Your Majesty."

With a tight nod the king followed the agent into the trees, several guards shadowing them watchfully. Guards positioned themselves just inside the tree line. The agent stepped deeper into the trees, the king at his side.

A new figure appeared suddenly in front of them. Startled, Delmar reached for the hilt of his sword. Then the agent quietly greeted the newcomer, and the king willed himself to relax.

Delmar had not anticipated someone slight in build, and he

stared at the new agent curiously, trying without success in the dim light to get a glimpse of the hooded face.

"Your Majesty, I am honored."

The soft voice caught him entirely by surprise. He hadn't been expecting to meet a woman.

"Who am I speaking to?" he asked.

The woman chuckled—a melodious sound that seemed out of character for an agent. "Who would you like to be speaking to?"

Unsure how to respond, he said nothing.

"I mean no disrespect, Your Majesty," she offered. "I use different names, depending on the circumstances."

Her speech suggested she was noble by birth, but he couldn't place her accent. It must have been either Castelan or Arvenian.

Abruptly, her posture changed. "I be just a wee farmer's lass, ya see." She changed again. "Fresh mussels, Y'Worship? Octopus? Whateva y'r 'ungry for, I got it!" Her wheedling voice was coarse and guttural.

He gaped in astonishment at the transformation.

Without missing a beat she spoke a sentence in what he knew to be fluent Rogandan, before switching effortlessly to a language he didn't recognize at all.

"Were you just speaking Ahran?" he asked.

"I was, Your Majesty," she replied calmly, once again in the tones of a woman of noble birth. Her accent now clearly placed her as a native of Varas.

"I suddenly understand why you hesitated to supply a name!" he told her.

She laughed lightly, a cheerful sound in that dark place. "You may call me Maive."

"Very well, Maive." He hesitated. "Why are you doing this? Why become an agent?"

"My story would make a long and sorry tale, Your Majesty. It is enough to say that I have reason to do anything in my power to thwart the purposes of the man who clearly has designs on Varas and the kingdoms around it."

Unable in the darkness to catch the tiniest glimpse of Maive's face behind her hood, Delmar had no way of reading her. But he trusted Maran implicitly. She appeared capable of presenting herself as whoever she wanted to be, but his senior agent was not easily taken in. Before recommending her, he would have thoroughly investigated her character, her history, and her motivations. He would never have allowed her to meet with the king if any doubt remained about her reliability.

"Thank you, Maive. We are profoundly grateful that you have made your skills available in support of the well-being of Varas. Please be careful! Take no unnecessary risks. It will serve no one but our enemies if you come to any harm."

"I am grateful for your consideration, Your Majesty." She bowed. "Until next time."

Then she was gone.

She hadn't waited to be dismissed, but he was not offended. How could an agent thrive when constricted by convention?

As he headed back to the palace, it occurred to him that he applied a different standard to Maran and his other agents. Maive was different though.

He acknowledged wryly that she managed to be both mysterious and beguiling at the same time.

DELMAR STOOD with Maran on a castle balcony overlooking the city of Varacellan. To all appearances, nothing had changed. People were going about their business as always. Yet Delmar sensed that his kingdom was poised on the brink of a precipice.

However vigorously his agents rooted out Ahran infiltrators, others arrived to replace them. Most insidious of all, they came with gold—a seemingly unending supply of it. His own coffers had received a welcome boost from the small hoards seized already by his agents.

Gold shone with a sparkle all of its own, and there was no way of knowing how many of his subjects had been seduced by its glitter, agreeing to turn against their own people for the right price.

Seeking a more cheerful topic for rumination, Delmar's thoughts drifted in a different direction. The new agent had thoroughly roused his curiosity. The fact that he had never seen her face must surely be contributing to her mystique. He sometimes wondered if a single glance at her in the daylight might be enough to extinguish his fascination entirely.

He released a quiet sigh, at a loss to account for his own foolishness. Nevertheless, curiosity could not be denied. "How has your new agent been acquitting herself?" He hoped he didn't sound too interested.

"Her involvement has been invaluable, Your Majesty. We are preparing to take down what we believe to be the Ahran headquarters. Thanks to her we have considerable insight into their activities."

"What have they been doing?"

"They have been working hard at recruiting informants—and turning them into collaborators whenever they can. We have identified a number of people they have compromised. We'll be moving on them soon."

Delmar had the feeling something else was on Maran's mind. "Is there more?" he prodded.

The agent's brows drew together in frustration. "They seem to have an overriding goal, but we haven't been able to find out what it is. None of them speak of it directly."

"Keep me informed if you learn any more."

Maran bowed. "I will notify you the moment we uncover anything of significance."

THE HOUR before sunset saw King Delmar threading his way through the streets of Varacellan. A modest contingent of guards accompanied him, Lord Karevis among them.

Market day was drawing to a close; the sale of most wares had ended, and people were flocking around the ever-popular food stalls.

The king welcomed opportunities to mingle with his subjects, and people had learned to expect a brief visit from him at that time of the week. He had long since concluded there was no better time or place to quickly assess the mood of the populace.

"Your Majesty! Will you try one of my special fish cakes? Everyone agrees it's food worthy of a king!"

Delmar smiled, enjoying the vendor's enthusiasm. "Thank you, but I've eaten already. Perhaps next time."

"Over here, Your Majesty! I have a bracelet guaranteed to win the heart of any fair maiden."

The king smiled and waved, moving on without further acknowledgment. The vendor had touched on a delicate topic. Delmar would not produce an heir until he found himself a queen. It hadn't escaped him that the issue was a topic of animated conversation among his subjects.

As the light began to fail a sudden commotion shattered his musings. A runaway horse, with cart attached, was careering out of control, knocking over stalls and scattering vendors and customers in every direction. Delmar stood directly in its path.

Seeing the folly of any attempt at heroics, he threw himself aside with a shouted order to his men. "Stop that horse!"

Several guards grabbed at the traces as the horse passed, but all were thrown to the ground. None succeeded even in slowing the animal.

Sudden cries of alarm rang out from his scattered guards. Struggling to his feet he saw men with drawn swords setting upon his guards. None of those felled by the horse proved able to defend themselves. The rest were soon fighting for their lives.

He gaped in disbelief, unable to credit such a brazen attack in his own capital. Then five of the attackers broke away from the fight, heading straight for him.

Karevis, sword in hand, leaped into their path, furiously engaging two of them at once. The others ignored him, their full attention on Delmar.

"Run!" shouted Karevis.

With the attackers almost upon him, Delmar took the commander's advice and sprinted away. He'd been trained to fight from his boyhood, and he had no reason to doubt his capabilities. But he also possessed a cool head. Taking on three men with unknown fighting skills was risky at best.

Speedy and fit, he decided that running was a good strategy. Varacellan was routinely patrolled by his own soldiers. Provided he lived long enough he would stumble upon them eventually.

Turning the first corner that presented itself, he raced away from the market. The street bent away before intersecting with another broader street that led toward another heavily trafficked part of the city. Delmar didn't hesitate, dashing around the corner and flying down the middle of the broad avenue. A glance behind showed him gaining ground on his pursuers, but they were not giving up.

Townsfolk gaped open-mouthed as he sped past alone. Turning a corner, then another, he burst out onto a busy street. Frustratingly, no soldiers were anywhere to be seen.

As he glanced around, he realized that he would soon be recognized. Someone was sure to give him away by drawing attention to him with no awareness of the consequences. Accordingly he moved quickly to the side of a building that protruded into the street, hiding himself in the deepening shadows on the far side. Panting from his exertion, he peered out cautiously from his hiding place, waiting for the Ahrans to appear.

He had barely recovered his breath when a figure appeared before him, hemming him in. Reaching for his knife, he was startled by an urgent command.

"Take off your cloak! Quickly!"

The speaker was a woman. Although he couldn't place her, he removed his cloak, acting on instinct.

She grabbed it from him, tossing it aside into a pile of trash. Then she whisked off her own cloak—a thin garment colored a bold blue—and threw it across his shoulders. As Delmar's pursuers rounded the corner, she pulled him into an intimate embrace.

Choosing the same direction as Delmar, his pursuers headed toward the king. The men had sheathed their swords and hidden them below their cloaks, but all of them had their hands on the hilts. As they drew closer, he bent low, burying his face in her neck.

One of the passing Ahrans aimed a probing glance at them both, and she rounded on him, snarling. "Find a woman of your own!" Then, taking Delmar's head in her hands, she drew him close and kissed him on the lips.

Too startled to know how else to respond, he kissed her back.

His rescuer paid no attention to the Ahrans as they hurried past in search of their quarry. Even when they were surely long gone, she did not pull away. Nor did he.

Later, he was never sure precisely when it dawned on him who she was. Nor could he identify the exact moment when a clever diversion became a tender kiss. He only knew that something had shifted inside him.

He drew back at last, impatient to gaze upon the face of Maive.

She stared back at him uncertainly, her cheeks faintly flushed.

After a charged silence, she seemed to recover her poise. "Why were you alone, Your Majesty? And with Ahrans at your heels!"

"I hardly understand how it happened myself," he replied. He gazed at her in wonder. "How did you find me?"

"I noticed you when you hid. Then I saw the Ahrans. We've been watching them, so I knew who they were. When I realized they were searching for you, I decided to improvise."

"To great effect! Thank you for rescuing me!"

She looked up at him uncertainly. "Please pardon my forwardness. I'm sure you don't need me to say that the kiss meant nothing."

He tried to ignore the sinking feeling in his gut. "Of course! It's all in the line of duty. No doubt you often find yourself doing such things."

"Far from it, Your Majesty." Her tone was unexpectedly sharp. "There are lines I refuse to cross, even in the service of your kingdom."

"I didn't mean to suggest..." he stammered awkwardly. He took a breath. "What I meant was..."

Struggling to find the right words, he spotted Karevis, searching anxiously. The commander was trailed by one of the guards, other soldiers close behind them.

With a groan of frustration, he stepped into the open, reluctantly accepting that this conversation would need to wait.

Karevis spotted him at once. "Your Majesty!"

The relief on the commander's face was unmistakable. "I barely recognized you! What happened to the Ahrans?"

"They got away. I didn't need to defend myself though, thanks to my rescuer." He turned back to Maive with a grateful smile.

She was gone.

By the time he returned his attention to Karevis, the commander had retrieved his discarded cloak. "That's an impressive disguise," he said admiringly, pointing to Maive's blue substitute.

Delmar could find nothing to say.

It belatedly occurred to him that Maive might not have been the only one who recognized him. Had other townspeople seen him kissing her? He decided he didn't care.

Failing to notice his discomposure, Karevis surrounded him with soldiers and bustled him back toward the palace. The king went meekly, trying desperately to set his thoughts and emotions in order.

KING DELMAR SAT in a small palace reception room with Maran and Karevis.

"How could such an attack happen?" he asked. "Right here, in the heart of my capital!"

Maran hung his head. "We were ready to move on the Ahrans.

Clearly we waited too long. And they had considerably more men here than we realized."

"Were they responsible for the runaway horse?" asked the king. "Or were they simply taking advantage of it?"

The senior agent exchanged a glance with Karevis. "We can't be certain, but we think it was carefully planned."

The king raised an eyebrow inquiringly.

"You would have noticed they wasted no time in setting off after you," Karevis observed.

"We suspect that you were always the target," confirmed Maran. "You arrived as the markets were closing—as you almost always do—so they put their plan into action."

"Were they hoping to capture me? Or kill me?"

"We don't know."

The king met his commander's eyes. "What happened with the two men you were fighting?"

"I brought one of them down," Karevis replied. "One of your guards helped me deal with the other one."

"So the guards fought off the other Ahrans who attacked us?"

"Eventually. Three of the Ahrans left to chase you. That evened the odds. Even so, only one guard was still capable of fighting when it was over. It didn't matter. By then the place was swarming with soldiers alerted by the disturbance. I took a few of them and the remaining guard and we went looking for you. It was a while before we found you."

"Fortunately Maive reached you first," Maran observed.

"Yes, it was thanks to her that I escaped. How did she come to be there?"

"It was pure luck that she was there at all. And that she spotted you when she did," Maran replied.

Delmar couldn't help himself. "Where is she now?"

"She's left the kingdom."

"Why?" He couldn't hide his shock.

"It's possible that one of the missing Ahrans might put the pieces together. We couldn't take that chance—she's too valuable. We needed to get her away from Varacellan. She learned of a high risk mission outside the kingdom and had no hesitation in volunteering for it." Maran sighed. "I won't deny that she'll be a big loss."

Delmar opened his mouth to berate Maran for sending her away without consulting him first. He barely checked himself in time. He reminded himself that Maran didn't need his permission, and he was only seeking the best outcome both for Maive and for the kingdom.

All the same, it was frustrating. None of this would have happened if she hadn't needed to rescue him. It belatedly occurred to him that there might be more to her departure. Was it possible she was fleeing from him? He wasn't willing even to consider such a possibility.

He wanted to ask for details about her mission, but he knew it wasn't appropriate. Nevertheless, he wasn't going to give up. He would find a way to reach her.

THE DAYS PASSED, and Delmar could not get Maive out of his mind.

He knew almost nothing of substance about her. He didn't even know her real name.

At least he'd finally seen her face. She was no classic beauty, although there was something beguiling about her eyes as she gazed up at him. He longed to see her again, to properly appreciate and remember her. It occurred to him that he'd never seen her smile, never shared a lighthearted moment with her.

The more he dwelt on it, the more his sense of loss grew, until it came to feel like a crushing weight.

He winced whenever he thought of his ill-considered words to her. He hadn't intended to hurt her—he'd been thrown off balance by her assertion that their kiss meant nothing.

It was possible she had been telling the truth, but his heart told him otherwise.

He remembered how it felt as he nestled into her neck. His heart had raced as she drew his face closer. He sensed again her warm breath on his cheeks and the sensation of her lips exploring his own.

Everything had changed in that instant. Until then he had failed utterly to anticipate the raw power that lurked behind a simple kiss.

Now she was gone, far away, beyond his reach.

Would he ever see her again?

11

Steffan arrived in the queen's private chambers to find her overseeing the final preparations for her visit to Castel. Seeing the king arrive, the servants bowed and hurried from the room.

A troubled frown furrowed his brow. "This trip makes me nervous, Essanda!"

She smiled up at him. "Rufe will be riding with me, along with five hundred of your best soldiers." Seeing his reaction, she added, "We're not at war, and there isn't the faintest hint of internal dissent. The only possible threat is from the Ahrans, and I don't see what they could do. We'll be nowhere near the ocean at any point in the journey. How could they even get to me?"

Steffan grunted noncommittally.

Stretching up on tiptoes, she kissed him lightly on the lips before fixing him with a knowing grin. He could guess what she was thinking. She knew him well enough to know that it made no difference how many soldiers Rufe took—he wouldn't be satisfied until she was safe in the royal castle at Arnost again.

"Gordy will take good care of me," she said soothingly.

"Count Gordan is effective," Steffan conceded, before adding darkly, "Most of the time."

"You surely can't be referring to the morning I slipped away from him during the Battle of Torbury Scarp!" she protested. "That was years ago! And it was hardly his fault."

Steffan grunted again. "If it's any comfort to you, I agree he was a sensible choice as regent in the absence of your brother."

She raised an eyebrow ironically. "I'm greatly comforted."

He conceded a reluctant grin.

Her face became serious. "You said you had a dispatch from him this morning."

He nodded. "He's arranging for a detachment of his soldiers to meet you at Deadman's Pass. They'll accompany you to Castel Citadel."

"Wonderful! Then you have nothing to worry about," she said, leaning in to him.

He responded by pulling her into an embrace, wrapping his arms tightly about her.

After a few moments he released her with a sigh. "It won't be the same—for me or for the children—until you're back home again."

"I'll miss you all terribly!" she assured him. Then she added soberly, "This is an important opportunity to demonstrate our support for Castel. The kingdom has faced a great deal of upheaval in recent years. I can only imagine what the people must be feeling now they're facing even more uncertainty."

He nodded. "You're right of course. It's the only reason I'm willing to let you go." He glanced around at the chaos. "I'll leave you to your packing. There are things I need to attend to."

He left her with a smile, but inwardly he did not feel happy. A vague sense of unease had settled on him. He tried to tell himself it was mere foolishness, that there was no real reason to be concerned about her safety. Yet bitter experience had taught him just how unpredictable life could be.

With the border of Castel almost within reach, Rufe rode back down the column, checking on the men.

"We'll be crossing the border soon, men!" he called as he passed. "Never forget you are representing King Steffan and the Kingdom of Arvenon!"

Rufe had no doubt the soldiers would acquit themselves well, not least because he had selected their leaders himself.

When he reached the middle of the column, he came upon Queen Essanda.

"Why are we slowing down, Rufe?" she called inquisitively.

Her curiosity was understandable. For her own safety she had been placed far from any possible action. That also left her with little chance of seeing anything interesting.

"Deadman's Pass lies not far ahead, Your Majesty," he told her. "Our scouts are riding forward to make contact with the Castelan border guards."

"My thanks, Rufe, to you and your men for guiding me here safely. It's been far too long since I visited Castel." She concluded her words with a merry wave.

Rufe waved back, a grin on his face. In spite of long hours in the saddle and often primitive conditions when they camped at night, the cheerfulness and gratitude of the queen never wavered. When combined with her good-natured approachability, it came as no surprise that she was wildly popular among the men.

Having delivered his message to all of the men, Rufe turned his horse and rode forward at a canter until he reached the head of the column.

By the time he arrived, the column had come to a halt. Three of his captains were conferring to one side, and he rode over to them.

"What's the hold up?"

"The border post is deserted," one of them replied. "There's no sign of Castelan guards."

Rufe frowned. The Castelans had maintained a border post at the Arvenian end of Deadman's Pass for longer than anyone could remember. He knew that no Arvenian guards were stationed at the border, and he was aware of the reason. To begin with, King Steffan had inherited an almost uninterrupted history of peaceful relations between Arvenon and Castel. Having then married a native of Castel, the king was more than content to leave the pass in the hands of his allies.

"Did any of the scouts venture into the pass?" asked Rufe.

"No. They were reluctant to cross the border without approval from the Castelans."

Rufe nodded. "They did the right thing." He addressed two of the captains. "Choose fifty men and tell them to report to me. Make sure they're all capable archers. The rest should remain on high alert until we understand what's going on. Escort the queen to a position that's safe and defensible."

They nodded grimly, riding off immediately to carry out his orders.

He turned to the remaining captain. "You're with me, Hennis." He indicated the fifty men assembling nearby. "As soon as our preparations are in place, we'll head into the pass."

Almost half an hour had elapsed before the other captains reported back.

"I'm leaving you in charge of the column," Rufe told them. "Your priority is the queen. If anything happens, get her somewhere safe without delay."

They nodded. "What about you, Rufe?" one of them asked.

"Forget about me," he replied. "I'll have plenty of support."

He signaled to the men, and they moved out together, heading for the pass.

They came upon the border post almost immediately. It was indeed deserted. Dismounting, Rufe carefully examined the sturdy little building and its surrounds.

"There are food scraps here that are still fresh," he called to Hennis. "And the coals at the bottom of the fire pit outside the building are still warm. The post was occupied until quite recently."

Remounting, Rufe rode cautiously into the pass, trying to guess where enemies might have positioned themselves. Hennis rode beside him, tense and alert.

Rugged slopes stretched out before him as far as the eye could see. Rufe knew that the pass offered the only way of penetrating the mountain range that comprised almost the entire southern border of Castel.

From a military perspective, he could only admire the terrain. The mountain range with its solitary pass provided a formidable boundary between the kingdoms.

Readily defensible at many points, Deadman's Pass was aptly named. During the war with Rogand, the pass had been seized and held by a determined band of Rogandans. King Steffan's soldiers had eventually forced their way through, but they had paid a high price in human lives.

They had not ridden far before Hennis called softly, "Over there."

Following his pointing finger, Rufe saw two bodies. With no one else anywhere in view, Rufe dismounted again and examined them. "They haven't been dead for long," he said.

Once more they moved forward, more alert than ever. Rounding a bend in the pass they were challenged by a somewhat unsteady voice. "Are you Arvenians?"

"We are," Rufe confirmed. "Show yourself!"

Three men stepped into the open, raising a ragged cheer.

Signaling to Hennis to join him, Rufe dismounted and drew them aside. "Are you Castelan border guards?" he asked.

"We are."

"What happened here?"

"We were attacked. From Castel—from behind. Not long after dawn. We were taken completely by surprise."

A second man chipped in, "They killed our leader and another guard. We scattered and hid. For a while they tried to find us, but they soon gave up and left."

"Which way did they go?"

"Back down the pass toward Castel."

"How many of them?"

"Maybe six or seven. There wasn't any way to be certain."

Rufe scowled. "Do you know who they were?"

"No. But they were openly speaking another language."

Rufe exchanged a glance with Hennis. His captains had been briefed before they left Arnost; Hennis would be well able to guess the identity of the attackers.

"Count Gordan was planning to send an escort to meet Queen Essanda," Rufe told them. "Have you seen any sign of it?"

"No, but we've been expecting them. They can't get here soon enough!"

"Go and bury your friends," Rufe told them. "A couple of my men will help you. The rest of us will move forward to see if we can find any sign of your attackers."

The Castelans hurried away, relief evident on their faces. Rufe shook his head. Clearly they had not been well briefed on present realities.

The sound of their horses' hooves echoed from the hard rock as they rode forward. The pass was otherwise as silent as the grave. Rufe fully expected to find the way blocked and held against them, but they saw no sign of another living being until they reached the Castelan end of the pass.

They halted their horses and gazed out across the rolling green fields of Castel.

"Look, Rufe," called one of the men.

A body of men was riding toward the pass.

"It's probably Count Gordan's soldiers," Rufe suggested to Hennis. "But we can't afford to take any chances. Form up the men into defensive positions."

Something didn't seem right to Rufe. The incoming riders seemed too few in number to be Count Gordan's escort. Nevertheless he waited calmly until they came within hailing distance.

A rider separated himself from the column and called out, "Who are you?"

"We are Arvenians," he called back.

"Escorting Queen Essanda?"

"Yes."

"Excellent! I will join you." The speaker urged his horse forward, not bothering to wait for his men to catch up.

Rufe shook his head, unable to comprehend the heedless behavior of the Castelans he had met so far.

The new arrival rode up with a flourish. "Well met! I am Lord Thorsel. Count Gordan sent me to escort the queen to Castel Citadel."

"I am Rufe Sarjant."

Lord Thorsel's eyebrows went up, and he briefly dipped his head. "I am honored to meet you. King Steffan clearly places a high value on the safety of his wife!"

"How many men do you lead, My Lord?"

"One hundred. I thought it to be excessive, and told Count Gordan as much. He wanted to make it clear that the queen's safety is paramount. How many men have you brought with you?"

"Five hundred of King Steffan's best soldiers," Rufe replied evenly.

The Castelan was too surprised to respond.

Rufe saw no reason to indulge the nobleman. "You will need to reestablish your border post. The guards were attacked earlier today —from the Castelan side of the pass. Two of the five men were killed, including their leader."

Lord Thorsel was not unduly dismayed. "I am sorry to hear of their losses. Most likely it was robbers. I will order some of my scouts to look around for any sign of them." Seeing the look on Rufe's face, he added tersely, "Do you have a different explanation for the attack?"

"I have no proof, but I suspect that Ahran agents might have been responsible."

"Surely that's absurd! Why would you think that?"

"The guards reported that their attackers spoke a foreign language."

"They must have been Rogandans, then. If the guards were not imagining things. Why would Rogandans attack the pass? We're finally at peace with them."

"Have Ahrans been infiltrating Castel?" asked Rufe.

"There have been a few reports. But nothing worthy of undue alarm. Why?"

"Large numbers of them have entered Varas and Arvenon. Even more so Rogand."

"All of those kingdoms have major ports. Castel does not. That's undoubtedly the reason for the difference."

Rufe shook his head. "Ahran vessels foolish enough to dock in Rog are impounded and searched from stem to stern. Ahran agents are being put ashore on remote beaches."

"We have no evidence of any such activities in Castel. Perhaps our kingdom holds less appeal to them."

It was obvious that Lord Thorsel had no intention of taking the Ahran threat seriously, and Rufe saw no point in pursuing the issue further. He was confident Count Gordan would see it very differently.

"So you will entrust Queen Essanda to our care from here?" Thorsel asked.

Rufe was unyielding. "King Steffan made it clear we were to escort her to Castel Citadel, and remain there until she is ready to return."

Lord Thorsel's eyebrows had gone up again. "It's all a little irregular." He paused for a moment. "Arvenon is an ally, of course. I am sure Count Gordan will be willing to make your men welcome." Then he snorted. "As long as they behave themselves."

Rufe ignored the nobleman's ramblings. Queen Essanda would go to Castel Citadel accompanied by King Steffan's full escort, or she wouldn't be going at all.

The Castelan did at least follow through on his offer to have the area scouted. He also instructed his captains to meet with the surviving border guards. Having dealt with the practicalities, he asked to be presented to the queen.

Hennis's men escorted Lord Thorsel through the pass, Rufe at their head. When they reached the queen, Rufe introduced the Castelan nobleman.

"Your Majesty!" exclaimed Lord Thorsel, bowing low. "I bring the greetings of the regent, Count Gordan, and the entire Castelan court.

It is a great honor to welcome you back to the land of your birth. All of us are in shock after the appalling abduction of your brother, His Majesty King Rupert, and we are grateful for your consideration in our hour of distress."

"His Majesty King Steffan extends his greetings, as do I. He asked me to assure you that Arvenon will do anything it can to support Castel at this time. Securing the return of my brother to his throne is a high priority for our kingdom too."

Rufe excused himself and departed, more than willing to leave diplomacy to those better suited to it.

He headed first to Hennis. "Have the Castelan scouts discovered anything?"

Hennis shook his head. "No. But their captains are at least taking the attack on the border post more seriously than the nobleman."

"Are they blaming robbers?"

"Not at all. They questioned the survivors closely, and they've drawn the same conclusion as us."

Rufe nodded in satisfaction. "Brief some reliable messengers, and send them to King Steffan. He needs to know everything that happened here today."

THE REMAINDER of the journey to Castel Citadel proceeded without incident, and Rufe experienced considerable relief delivering the queen safely to Count Gordan. He had asked her to request a meeting with the Count, and she arranged it as a matter of urgency. Before the day of their arrival had ended, the regent led Rufe and Queen Essanda to a private reception room in the castle.

"I have been briefed on the events at Deadman's Pass," the count began. "I fully concur with your views, Rufe. I can only conclude that the Ahrans have a larger presence in Castel than any of us had realized. This is not the first occasion when events have gotten away from me. I intend to respond much more vigorously this time."

Rufe nodded in satisfaction. "I never doubted you would take the threat seriously, My Lord Regent."

Gordan's brows had drawn together. "One thing I cannot make sense of. Why attack the border post?"

"I have also given that a great deal of thought," Rufe replied. "Undoubtedly Will would grasp the purpose behind it in an instant, but he isn't here. Is it possible that the Ahrans planned to pose as border guards, and attack the queen as she passed?"

"It seems unlikely to me, Rufe," Queen Essanda replied. "What would they gain by it? They would only strengthen the resolve of the allied kingdoms in opposing them."

"Could they have been sending a message?" asked the count. "Issuing notice that no kingdom is beyond their reach?"

None of them were any wiser when they left the meeting. But the count had promised to spare no effort in hunting down Ahran infiltrators. He intended to begin the operation at dawn on the following day.

THAT NIGHT RUFE retired to his assigned room in the royal castle weary to the point of exhaustion. He had barely fallen asleep when he was roused by a servant. "The regent needs to meet with you urgently!"

Hurriedly throwing on his clothes, he followed the servant to a different section of the castle. Count Gordan and several senior nobles were seated around a large wooden table. He appeared to be the last arrival.

As soon as Rufe had been settled in his place, the count rose shakily to his feet, his face ashen.

"I have the most appalling news to report," he told the gathering. "I regret to say that Queen Essanda has been abducted!"

Chairs crashed to the floor as people leaped to their feet. Cries of dismay echoed around the chamber. Rufe sat with jaw agape, paralyzed with horror.

"Who has done this?" a voice cried.

The count ran a shaky hand across his brow. "It appears to be the work of Ahran agents. Our Arvenian friends warned me. I have been planning an operation to hunt them down—it was to begin tomorrow." His head sagged. "I have left it too late."

"What is known of the circumstances, and what is being done to retrieve the queen?"

Rufe eyed the speaker dully, grateful that at least someone appeared to have kept their head.

The regent recovered himself. "Her Majesty went for a walk in a secure private garden, accompanied by two guards," he replied. "Someone—presumably acting on behalf of the Ahrans—left a side gate unlocked. A small group of armed men somehow penetrated palace security. They overpowered the guards and took the queen. The guards were seriously injured, but they will survive. One of them reported that the abductors were speaking a language he didn't recognize."

Count Gordan clenched his fists. "None of this could have happened without active participation from our own people, undoubtedly compromised by Ahran gold. When we find those responsible—and we will find them!—they will be shown no mercy!"

He glanced around the table. "The city is being searched right now, and every access road will be strongly guarded. Soldiers are already spreading out across the countryside. All of us must use whatever means we have at our disposal to track down the perpetrators." He directed his attention to Rufe. "Under the circumstances, I doubly appreciate the strong force you have brought to Castel, Rufe. I would be grateful if you and your men would secure Deadman's Pass. It seems unlikely that the Ahrans would take the queen into Arvenon, but desperate men sometimes do surprising things."

Rufe pushed himself to his feet and bowed an acknowledgment. With a meaningful task assigned to him, his sense of purpose was returning. He would rouse his men and leave for the border the moment the gathering was dismissed.

Even a glance at Count Gordan made it obvious that the blow had hit the regent hard. Rufe knew that the count's affection for the queen dated from her childhood, and that he had been appointed her protector after her arranged marriage to King Steffan at barely fourteen years of age.

Rufe was no less devastated. Over the years he had watched in growing awe as she grew and matured, applying her energy and wisdom for the benefit of the kingdom she had so freely embraced. After assassins attacked both her and the king, he had witnessed her courage in the most harrowing of circumstances. Heavily pregnant, and with a gravely wounded husband at her side, she had endured with grace the seemingly endless retreat to the safety of Newhaven.

But Rufe had weightier reasons for his distress. He knew this would only be the beginning. Alone of those in the room, he had already endured the nightmare about to unfold. He had lived through the aftermath of Ethen's abduction, looking on helplessly as a frustrated and previously unshakable Will Prentis slowly fell apart.

The rejoicing at Ethen's eventual escape had quickly been muted by an even more devastating blow—the abduction of the ruling Castelan king and the Rogandan princess he was courting.

Now it was happening again. This latest masterstroke assaulted the very heart of Arvenon.

A single question haunted Rufe. What could he possibly say to King Steffan?

12

Will stood on the gangplank of the Nomad Lady, grateful to have reached Rog safely and eager to disembark. "Thank you, Captain Yordin. It has been a pleasure to sail with you, as always."

The captain bowed. "The pleasure is mine, Lord Torbury. You will always find a welcome on the Lady."

"Do you know who the king is sending to meet us?" asked Thomas as they stepped onto the dock.

Will shook his head. "The message didn't say."

While they were waiting, he walked toward the stern of the Lady, not pausing until the ship lay behind him. Gazing across the water, his attention was caught by a fishing boat returning home. The fishermen did not look happy. As they drew nearer, he heard them grumbling about their catch. At that moment, a large fish leaped from the water into the boat, followed immediately by another. The fishermen watched in astonishment as fish after fish launched themselves from the water and into their boat, flopping about at their feet.

Belatedly noticing what was happening, Thomas glanced at Will with an eyebrow arched.

"What?" asked Will innocently. "I'm sure you took the chance to practice in the early days."

Thomas rolled his eyes.

A group of soldiers in King Krasmir's livery found them before they could say more. The captain led Will and Thomas on foot through the docks to a place where horses were being held in readiness. As soon as they mounted, the soldiers took them through the streets of Rog to the royal palace. The captain ushered them into a reception room.

The king had already arrived. Nodding his thanks to the captain, he rose to greet them. "I am glad to welcome you once more to Rog, Lord Torbury. These are challenging times, and your wisdom will be greatly valued. You are welcome too, Thomas Stablehand."

Both men bowed. "We will willingly do whatever we can to help, Your Majesty," Will replied.

The king indicated the captain. "Your escort will show you to your rooms, Thomas. Please make yourself comfortable."

Thomas bowed again and left the room. The king waved Will to a seat.

It troubled Will to witness the state of his host. The face before him was drawn and haggard, as if the king had aged prematurely.

"Your arrival is timely, Lord Torbury. I have just received a request to meet with the Grand Vizier himself." The king scowled. "The man has a nerve coming here openly! I intend to meet with him though. I want to look my enemy in the eye."

Will nodded. "We had an encounter with three Ahran ships during our voyage, Your Majesty. We met with another Ahran, a man named Bisri Ahuzza. He claims to have been tasked with meeting you, with a view to conveying your views to the emperor."

The king snorted disdainfully. "His agents have abducted my daughter! What does he expect my views to be?"

"The bisri was dismissive when I told him the facts. If I am any judge of character though, this Bisri is not posturing. It may well be that neither he nor the emperor is aware of the truth."

"Then the emperor is a fool."

"Perhaps. It may also be that his Grand Vizier is deceiving him. He appears to have sent another envoy to form an independent assessment. That might suggest he has questions about the reports he's received from the Grand Vizier."

"What are you proposing?" growled the king.

"That we look for an opportunity to engage with the bisri. If the Grand Vizier is furthering an agenda of his own, it might be possible to drive a wedge between him and the emperor."

The king grunted again. He might not be entirely convinced, but he hadn't brushed aside Will's views either.

"Who will be meeting with the Grand Vizier?" asked Will.

"Apart from me? You, if you're willing!"

"Certainly, Your Majesty. I'm just as eager to see him face-to-face."

"The head of my security network will be there of course. Lady Tulinay—you would have met her briefly."

Will nodded. He did remember meeting her. He had also read the reports. Head of the security network meant she was tasked with oversight of the king's foreign and domestic agents. The Rogandan spy network was vast and sprawling, with a long-standing reputation of inefficiency. Tough as steel and a ferocious organizer, Lady Tulinay had made an immediate difference after her appointment.

"I'm also planning to include Lord Kulferan, Lord Boedwyk, and an interpreter. That will be more than enough participants."

Will's eyebrows went up involuntarily at the mention of the eccentric nobleman, but he chose not to comment.

The king had clearly settled on his attendee list already, and it came as no surprise that Thomas was not invited. Why would he include an Arvenian commoner? It made no difference though. There were other ways to expose the Grand Vizier to the Stone of Knowing. Will would ensure that Thomas was positioned where he could see the Ahran official as he entered the palace.

At a call from the king, an aide joined them in the room.

"You've had a long voyage, Lord Torbury," said King Krasmir. "I imagine you'll appreciate an opportunity to relax. The meeting with the Grand Vizier will take place mid-morning tomorrow. I'll send someone to collect you in good time."

Rising from his seat, Will bent at the waist. Then he followed the aide from the room.

He headed to his quarters with his mind already hard at work, churning through the best approaches to take in the coming meeting.

Bisri Ahuzza climbed up a rope net toward the deck of a Rogandan warship, close behind the Grand Vizier and his translator. Ronizah clambered up after them.

The significance of the location was not lost on Ahuzza. Could there have been a more obvious way to say they were not welcome on Rogandan soil? He wondered what had prompted such hostility from their hosts. Could it truly be nothing more than a pretense, a cynical mixture of false accusations?

Not for the first time, he recalled the wild claims made by the Arvenian nobleman while visiting his ship. The problem was that Ahuzza had encountered many habitual liars, both at court and among the masses. The Arvenian showed none of the obvious signs.

Whatever the truth might be, he anticipated a frosty reception. A reception of any kind would be far more than Rheibas deserved if half of the nobleman's assertions were true.

The Arvenian had named Bolnyk. How did he know his name? What had Bolnyk been doing in Rogand? Ahuzza knew the agent to be ruthless. He had also long believed he was loyal to no one but Rheibas.

They emerged on deck to find five men and a woman waiting for them. Guards stood to attention on every side.

Ahuzza immediately recognized one of the men as the Arvenian who came aboard his ship. He had introduced himself as Lord Torbury. The man clearly recognized Ahuzza too, because he offered him a faint nod.

Clearly Torbury was on intimate terms with the Rogandan king. That much at least of his story was true.

King Krasmir's gaze passed briefly over Ahuzza before settling on the Grand Vizier. His glare offered no hint of welcome.

The woman addressed the Ahrans. "You have requested an audience with His Majesty King Krasmir," she announced coolly.

Ronizah deferred to his colleague, allowing him to translate her words on behalf of all the visitors.

The Grand Vizier glanced about him. "The Empire of Ahr is accustomed to receiving foreign emissaries with more respect," he said bluntly.

The king waited patiently for his own translator to relay the words. "The Kingdom of Rogand is accustomed to dealing with murderers and abductors as they deserve," he replied coldly. "Count yourself fortunate. You are only being received at all out of respect for your absent emperor."

"I am here for one reason only," the Grand Vizier stated. "I wish to secure the release of Her Imperial Highness Princess Neira."

"Then you are wasting your time," the king informed him. "The only topic I am willing to discuss is the safe return of Princess Teylee of Rogand and King Rupert of Castel."

"Why should I be blamed if two young lovers have absconded from under your noses?" sniffed Rheibas.

Fury twisted the features of the king.

Rheibas forestalled him. "I have information that the Arvenian queen—the sister of the missing king—knows where they are and is secretly planning to visit them. I have also more recently learned that some of my sailors stumbled by chance upon their hideaway," he said evenly.

Ahuzza saw anger and confusion on the faces before him. He studied King Krasmir in particular. If he could read people at all, the king was no more an actor than his Arvenian friend.

"If you have nothing to hide, then tell us the location of this supposed hideaway," said Lady Tulinay.

"Gladly," Rheibas replied. "As soon as you release to me Princess Neira."

"Are you hoping for an opportunity to finish her off properly this time?" asked Lord Torbury coolly.

"Ah. Lord Torbury, I presume. I've been hoping to meet you."

The Arvenian's face set hard. "And I've been interested to set eyes upon the man responsible for the abduction of my son. Did you order it yourself? Or did you simply take advantage of the grubby activities of your agents?"

Rheibas sneered at him. "Your ignorant insinuations do nothing to flatter you."

"I know more than you could possibly imagine," Lord Torbury replied, his lip curling in disdain. "Your senior agent, Bolnyk, abducted Princess Teylee and Prince Rupert. He did it immediately after he tried to murder my son."

The chief minister was a master at giving nothing away. Nevertheless, Ahuzza saw his eyebrows quirk momentarily. Was he surprised that Torbury knew Bolnyk's name and his role? Or was there something Rheibas hadn't already heard about Torbury's son?

The conversation was becoming uncomfortable for Ahuzza, and with a start he realized why. The polished manner of the chief minister, so familiar to the bisri, had never felt so false. The raw anger radiating from the Rogandan king and his Arvenian ally could not have been contrived. It was real. The contrast was marked, and it disturbed him.

Noticing Ronizah shooting occasional glances in his direction, he resolved to keep an impassive mask on his face.

He berated himself again for his naivety in hiring the man. It was too late to find an interpreter who owed nothing to the chief minister. With no alternative at hand, he was stuck with Ronizah.

Lord Torbury startled him out of his musing. "I am glad to see you again, Bisri Ahuzza."

Acutely aware that he'd said nothing to Rheibas about his meeting with Torbury, Ahuzza dipped his head to hide his momentary confusion. His reaction was unnecessary of course. The chief minister had undoubtedly received a full report from Ronizah.

And what reason did he have to be discomposed? The emperor himself had charged him with making independent contact with these people.

"I am glad to see you too, Lord Torbury," he returned.

"At our last meeting you questioned my description of Princess Neira's abandonment. I referred you to the man who captained the princess's ship. He spent time in Rog after the ship arrived, and his account was very enlightening. His name is Captain Gharpin. Have you spoken with him?"

The Grand Vizier interjected. "The captain you refer to has nothing of substance to offer on this matter," he said dismissively. "Sadly he was lost at sea."

Lord Torbury stared at him calmly. "Are you completely certain about that?"

The chief minister's eyes narrowed. He offered no response, but Ahuzza sensed what might have been unease. Did the Arvenian know something Rheibas didn't? Or was he bluffing?

The woman spoke quietly with the king before addressing herself to the chief minister. "King Krasmir has requested that I bring this meeting to an end. Do not expect to be received again, Chief Minister, unless you first return Princess Teylee and King Rupert safely to us." She concluded her words with a crisp bow.

Rheibas said nothing, but the bisri saw that he had gone white with anger.

She turned to Ahuzza and bowed again. "As the emperor's envoy, we would be glad to engage with you again on a mutually convenient occasion."

Returning a tight bow of his own, Ahuzza headed for the rope net, preparing to lower himself over the side. One of the Rogandan servants approached him to offer assistance. As the man helped him over the side, he surreptitiously slipped a small note into his hand.

Curious as he was about the content of the note, a single thought occupied his mind as he descended to the boat waiting below. A difficult conversation with the chief minister lay ahead. He wasn't looking forward to it.

WILL WATCHED SILENTLY with the others as the Ahrans were rowed away to their own ship. If only Thomas had been present. The king's decision to hold the meeting on a ship—not communicated to Will until they were leaving for the docks—had denied Thomas any opportunity to catch a glimpse of the Grand Vizier, even from afar.

When they were gone King Krasmir threw his hands into the air. "That wretch as good as admitted his people were holding Tasha and Rupert. How can we find out where they are?" Tension strained his face.

"I will send out ships to check islands in the region," Lord Kulferan said.

"Can I make a suggestion, My Lord?" Will asked the commander. "Order them to search out Ahran vessels and shadow them secretly. If we're fortunate, the Ahrans might lead us to wherever they're being held."

"Do it!" the king ordered Lord Kulferan.

The nobleman bowed an acknowledgment.

The king frowned. "What do you make of this claim about Queen Essanda?"

"It's absurd," replied Lady Tulinay.

"I found it alarming, Your Majesty," said Will soberly. "He might be planning to abduct her as well. I expect her to make a goodwill visit to Castel to offer them support. She would be especially vulnerable while traveling. I need to warn King Steffan. If I prepare a dispatch, would you be willing to send it to Arnost as a matter of priority, Your Majesty?"

The king nodded distractedly. "Of course."

Will bowed.

"The emperor must have questions about what's going on, or he wouldn't have sent an independent envoy," exclaimed the king. "What use can we make of this Bisri Ahuzza?"

Lady Tulinay did not hesitate. "I believe we need to build rapport with him, Your Majesty. It might weaken the Grand Vizier if we limit our communication to the bisri."

"It might also get Ahuzza killed," Will said grimly.

She frowned. "He's the emperor's envoy. Surely it wouldn't be easy to simply get rid of him."

"The Grand Vizier doesn't seem over-particular about who he eliminates," Will reminded her. "He was willing to kill the emperor's daughter. And apparently for no other reason than to create an incident he could use against us. The man has no scruples."

Will's brows drew together. "We must not underestimate him. He's accustomed to manipulating the truth to suit his own agenda, and he's extremely good at it. He had Ahuzza completely convinced when we first met. If the bisri is starting to have doubts, the Grand Vizier will see him as a liability."

"Then we've already put him in danger," said Lady Tulinay. "I was studying him carefully, and I had the clear impression he's becoming conflicted."

Will nodded. "I believe you're right. A change of heart will only work in our favor if Ahuzza manages to stay alive."

"There's little the emperor can do to save him," added Lady Tulinay. "He's too far away."

King Krasmir was frowning. "What *is* the emperor's attitude to all this? Surely he would be furious if he knew the games his chief minister has been playing!"

Will shrugged. "Without direct access to him, we can only guess, Your Majesty."

Lord Boedwyk gazed absently up at the mast, his brows drawn together thoughtfully. "Consulting directly with His Imperial Majesty could be...enlightening." He sighed deeply. "If only the voyage to Kat Ahket was not so long. Perhaps distance is emerging as our greatest enemy."

Lady Tulinay looked sharply at Boedwyk for a moment before apparently deciding to ignore him entirely. "Bisri Ahuzza is the emperor's eyes and ears," she said, "so it's in our interests to have him report back. Since getting rid of him is likely to become a high priority for the Grand Vizier, preserving his life must be a high priority for us."

"We can try to warn him," said Lord Kulferan.

King Krasmir nodded. "Do it," he said. He turned to Will. "What were you saying about the Ahran captain, Lord Torbury? The one who brought the princess here. Is he still alive?"

Will shrugged. "We all know that the Grand Vizier is lying about what happened to Princess Neira. I decided to see how he would react if he thought we had solid evidence against him. I knew the princess mentioned Captain Gharpin by name. However, I need to make it clear there was no truth to anything I said, Your Majesty. As far as I know, while he was at Rog the captain never spoke about what happened with Princess Neira. And I have no grounds for believing he didn't perish at sea. I was baiting the Grand Vizier. I wanted to see how he would react when he wasn't the one controlling the information flow."

"He didn't like it," said Lady Tulinay decidedly.

"Maybe not," growled the king. "But how does that help us?"

"People make mistakes when they think they're losing control," said Will. He shook his head. "But we've done nothing to hurt him yet. He's as dangerous as ever."

"And we still don't know his agenda," said Lady Tulinay. "Even though I have my best agents working on it."

"To find a way forward we need the emperor involved," said Will. "Bisri Ahuzza is the key."

"Our priority is simple—to free Princess Teylee and King Rupert!" insisted the king. "Never lose sight of that!"

They made their way back to Rog without further comment.

Will returned more determined than ever. Having looked his enemy in the eye, he wanted only one thing: to see him brought down.

Bisri Ahuzza crouched wordlessly in the prow of the longboat as they glided away from the Rogandan vessel. The Grand Vizier sat facing him. The interpreters had found places of their own further back in the boat.

"So I have seen my celebrated adversary at last!" crowed Rheibas. He appeared to be in unusually high spirits. "I trust I appeared suitably shaken by Torbury's ridiculous assertions."

Too discomfited to speak, Ahuzza stared back at him.

"Already he will be composing a dispatch to his king. To no avail." He curled his lip. "The man is vastly overrated. It is beyond time for him to be humbled."

The boat pulled alongside the Grand Vizier's ship.

Rheibas prepared to climb aboard with his interpreter. "Return the bisri to his ship!" he ordered the sailors.

Then, bending low to Ahuzza's ear, he mouthed, "Be careful, Bisri. Be very, very careful."

13

Kahrlin shoved his captive forward roughly. In response the queen gave out a muffled cry, but she was wasting her time. The Ahran had tied her gag himself. No one would hear, however hard she tried to yell.

He smiled in grim satisfaction. Thus far the Castelan fools who accepted his money had done what he paid them to do.

Pulling the cloaked and hooded captive to an abrupt halt in the shadows of a building, he nodded to Akohlsa, the agent assisting in that night's extraction.

His confederate disappeared around the corner. The minutes dragged, and Kahrlin grew increasingly impatient. Before he could decide to do anything rash, Akohlsa reappeared leading a horse with a wagon. Empty barrels lay in the wagon beneath a thick waterproof covering. Akohlsa had already pulled back the covering, revealing a narrow space between the barrels.

The queen's arms had been tied in front of her. The two men now bound her legs and dumped her unceremoniously in the wagon, throwing the covering over the barrels and the prisoner.

Both men climbed onto the driver's bench, Kahrlin taking the reins. Clicking his tongue, he guided the horse toward the city gates.

It was imperative that they escaped the city before the regent's men locked it down.

One final hurdle remained. The guards at the gates had been bribed handsomely to keep the gates open and to ask no questions. There were never any guarantees though. Shifts could be changed, and the new guards at the gate might cause problems. There was little he could do about that. The guards he bribed would not receive the bulk of their payment until after the wagon was safely through the gates. That gave them an incentive to be on duty as expected.

The wagon rolled slowly away from the palace. Thus far there had been no hitch of any kind in Kahrlin's carefully laid plans. Faint cries sounded behind them as they approached the gates. The queen's fallen guards must have been discovered. The alarm had been raised. Time was now pressing.

Kahrlin's heart began to race. The temptation to goad the horses into a gallop grew as every minute passed. He resisted the urge, and they clip-clopped forward steadily as before.

To his relief, the gates lay wide open. If the guards had heard the distant cries, they were choosing to ignore them. Chatting casually to each other, they waved the wagon through.

Increasing the pace to a trot, Kahrlin crossed the bridge and swung the horses north. The hunt must surely be up now, but a safe house beckoned just clear of the city. He gave the horses their heads, and the wagon raced on into the night.

For the first time he allowed himself to enjoy a measure of satisfaction. He had every reason to be satisfied—this operation would be his crowning achievement. The groundwork had been laid slowly and patiently, the preparations meticulous at every stage. Arrangements were firmly in place well before the Arvenian queen arrived.

The single biggest challenge had been finding a way to lure the queen from the safety of her apartments into the open. Countless plans had been explored and discarded. In the end, Kahrlin had reluctantly concluded she would need to be extracted while she was sleeping. It was the highest risk solution, but he could see no alternative. Then, as the two of them lay hidden in readiness, she had decided to go for a walk—in the open, and with only two guards. He wanted to laugh out loud.

The horses were tiring when he finally guided them off the main road and down a narrow lane. Reaching the end of the lane, he steered the wagon toward a large barn beside a lonely farmhouse.

They had done it. The Arvenian queen had been plucked from the castle under the noses of her hosts.

The Castelan regent clearly had no idea what was taking place in his capital that night. The fool had no idea how thoroughly Kahrlin's agents had sidestepped his every attempt at security.

A wry smile came to his lips. He could only imagine the panic of the people he had bribed when they learned they had assisted in the abduction of their own former princess. He had spun them a yarn about pilfering barrels of wine from the over-stocked royal cellars. The fools had accepted the tale only too readily when they caught a glimpse of bags bulging with coins.

Their heads would roll once the regent's men ferreted them out. That suited Kahrlin perfectly. He had no interest in leaving behind loose ends.

After two weeks hiding out in a barn not far from the city, Kahrlin was more than ready to risk the next stage of the journey out of Castel. The queen had not proven especially difficult to manage, but he had already wearied of this assignment. He would never be able to relax until he had handed responsibility for her to someone else.

The mission held promise of becoming a huge success. If they were able to complete it as planned, he had every expectation of further promotion. At the very least he would be lavishly rewarded for his efforts. None of that would happen unless they made it to the coast undetected.

Assuming they reached the coast, a longboat would pull in to a remote beach and row the captive to an Ahran ship lying offshore.

Kahrlin and his small team would join them, remaining with the ship until they were handed their next assignment.

Getting to the coast undetected was easier to imagine than to achieve. The first problem was that the roads were swarming with soldiers. Ahran agents posing as merchants reported that access to the coast was regulated with unusual energy. Worse, people in every town and village in the kingdom had been asked to report abnormal activity or suspicious strangers. Under these circumstances it would be a remarkable achievement to make it halfway to the sea.

None of this came as a surprise to Kahrlin. From the beginning he had assumed a vigorous manhunt would be mounted. In response he and his confederates had come up with a simple, if unusual, plan.

The first step had been the preparation of a suitable mode of transport. A wagon with tall sides had been acquired and a false bottom installed, deep enough to accommodate a person lying prone. The ceiling and the base of the receptacle had been lined with thick wool, and pairs of metal brackets placed at one end. The false bottom had been cleverly designed to allow a section of it to be removed for easy access to the hidden space.

The intent was to place the queen inside the false bottom, lying on a layer of wool and with another woolen layer above her. Her ankles would be fastened to the metal brackets and her wrists tied. There would be enough space to wriggle around and turn her head, although movement of her body would be severely constrained. Sections of the wagon floor not covered by wool had sufficient gaps to permit adequate circulation of air.

One of Kahrlin's men tested the prison to ensure that the sound of any movement would be muffled effectively by the wool. He emerged unnerved after a few minutes in the confined space. Kahrlin sneered at his reaction, mocking him as nothing more than a baby.

Later that day the queen was forced to drink wine laced with crushed opium seeds. Dazed and disoriented, she was laid in her new quarters and secured in position. As soon as the false bottom was put in place, the wagon swung in behind a somber procession.

Leading the procession was an open wagon carrying nothing but a coffin. Immediately behind it was a carriage full of mourners. Their baggage had been collected earlier and placed on the false bottom of the wagon hiding the queen.

The genius of this solution to the Ahrans' dilemma was its simplicity. Several agents had searched the capital and the surrounding countryside until they identified a family with roots in a seaside village who had suffered a recent bereavement. The deceased was the patriarch of a small but tight-knit family, and his widow was surprised and touched to learn that an unknown benefactor had offered to pay all expenses associated with transporting the deceased to his home village and burying him there.

No reason existed for the procession to be secretive in any way. The corpse truly was that of a loved husband and father, and the mourners close relations who were genuinely grieved. None of them had any notion that the procession included several Ahran agents, nor that an abducted queen lay hidden beneath their baggage.

The procession inevitably attracted considerable attention. At the first town soldiers brought it to a halt, insisting on opening the coffin to check the corpse. They also briefly checked the baggage wagon without finding anything untoward.

At first distressed, the mourners were persuaded to be understanding. When the same thing happened at the next town, the widow became agitated. Emotions boiled over at the third enforced stop.

Quickly realizing that the situation was unsupportable, town officials arranged for soldiers to escort the mourners to their final destination. After that, neither the mourners nor their cargo were hindered in any way.

The journey took several days to complete, but thankfully the largesse of the benefactor extended to comfortable lodgings along the way.

Kahrlin's agents, all hand selected, looked like Castelans and spoke their language without noticeable accents. Posing as hired labor, they unloaded the baggage from the wagon at each overnight stop, reloading it the next morning.

Once it was fully dark, the queen was released and allowed to eat, drink, and stretch her legs. After long days spent in a confined space, the strain on the captive was extreme. More than once they removed the cover to find her unconscious. Whenever they returned her to her prison she resisted fiercely until they administered the drugged wine.

Kahrlin didn't care. In his eyes she was worth little more than another item of baggage. As long as he could deliver her alive and in one piece, he would be more than happy.

The last overnight stop was in a town not far from the coast. Local laborers were hired to take the place of the Ahran agents, both for the final leg of the journey to the coastal village and for the entire return trip to the homes of the mourners near the capital.

Kahrlin himself made sure the new laborers understood what was expected of them. While he was thus engaged, the queen was transferred to another wagon that other agents had prepared for their arrival. On this occasion she was bound and gagged but not otherwise confined.

Once the whole town was soundly asleep, the wagon rolled into the countryside, passing slowly in the dim moonlight over rough trails and rolling hillsides until it eventually came to a halt at the edge of a small beach.

Lifted from the wagon, the queen was carried bodily to a waiting longboat and dumped without ceremony into the bottom of it. Lying trussed at the feet of Kahrlin and his team, she was rowed to a waiting Ahran vessel.

A rope net was lowered from the deck, and the queen was placed within it. As soon as it was hauled aboard, the remaining passengers clambered up rope ladders onto the deck. The ship then raised anchor and departed.

Kahrlin finally allowed himself to relax. His efforts would be sure to attract the attention of the chief minister. And why not? His plan had been bold and imaginative, and he had executed it with his usual finesse. Unlike some of his fellow agents. His lips twisted into a smirk.

Bolnyk might be the chief minister's senior agent, but he could never be accused of finesse, much less of imagination. His recent successes looked impressive on the surface: capturing the Arvenian commander's boy, the Castelan king, and the Rogandan princess. But he deserved no credit for taking the boy. He only became aware of the abduction after it was done. Bolnyk's contribution had been to botch the boy's transfer. He had been forced to kill the child, ending any value he might have had as a hostage. As for capturing the king and the princess, that had been dumb luck and nothing more.

Bolnyk might be loyal, but he was also dull and uninspired. Sooner or later the chief minister would weary of him. When he did, Kahrlin intended to be seen as the obvious replacement.

As the shoreline slowly faded from view in the dim light, one of the sailors approached Kahrlin. "The captain invites you to join him."

Kahrlin followed the sailor to the captain's cabin and went inside.

"Welcome!" The captain greeted him enthusiastically, his face alight with satisfaction. "A job well done, Kahrlin! Well done indeed!" He handed the agent a goblet of wine. "A toast! In celebration of the perfect outcome to an extremely challenging mission!"

The two men sat together well into the night, laughing and drinking with increasing abandon.

THE FOLLOWING MORNING, a somewhat unsteady Kahrlin joined the captain at the mast. The queen, finally released from her bindings, stood nearby, silently staring out to sea. She made for a pitiful sight. With her cloak held close about her, and her face obscured almost completely by her hood, she seemed intent on hiding from the world.

The captain nodded in her direction. "From what you've told me, your queen showed considerable fortitude, considering everything she's been through in the last few weeks."

Kahrlin raised an eyebrow. "She can hear what you're saying."

The captain shrugged. "Hearing is one thing; understanding is another. I've been reliably informed she doesn't speak a word of our language."

"I was told the same thing, and I can confirm it. It became

intensely frustrating in the weeks she was with us. She doesn't even understand Rogandan. We had to lower ourselves to speaking Arvenian if we wanted a response." He spat onto the deck.

"Mentioning her fortitude was not intended as a compliment," the captain told him. "I just couldn't help wondering how our own Princess Neira might have handled similar conditions."

Kahrlin snorted before he could prevent himself. "I can well imagine!" He gazed at the forlorn figure. "What have you been ordered to do with her?"

"I've been instructed to drop her off at a remote island. I wouldn't be surprised if the chief minister himself decides to entertain her sooner or later."

Kahrlin grunted. "In that case, she'd better enjoy the voyage. If her last few weeks have been difficult, it's going to get a lot worse."

WITH SOME MEASURE of freedom restored at last, the captive made her way onto the deck, avoiding the stares of the sailors. Some faces wore sneers, and a couple showed pity, but what did it matter? These sailors could do nothing to help her, even if they wanted to.

Swaying with the pitching of the deck, she headed for the rail. Grasping hold of it to steady herself, she stared off into the horizon.

The last few weeks had been a waking nightmare, coming to a head in the extreme conditions of her confinement in the wagon. The experience had been terrifying. She had heard tell of people with a crippling fear of confined spaces; she understood completely now.

It wasn't just the terror of being trapped. Her arms and legs had ached continuously from the forced inaction. Although her nose had never been deliberately blocked, at times she feared the gag would suffocate her. Constantly hungry, with only opium-laced wine to drink, and with her bladder full to bursting, even the release of crying out was denied her. Frequent lapses into unconsciousness had been the only reason she was able to endure the ordeal.

Whenever they were not traveling and she was released for a time, the only faces she saw were harsh and unyielding.

She had known times of suffering in the past, but this experience highlighted how fortunate her life had been. With the future dark and uncertain, she chose to revisit the past, savoring the many things she had to be grateful for.

It would have been easy to grieve what might have been, but she refused steadfastly to lose herself in daydreams. Fantasies could not prepare her for what lay ahead.

Only one thing mattered now. The chief minister would come to her.

She knew what she needed to do, and she was ready for it. Having so far played her role to perfection, she only needed to stay the course until she reached the end.

Maive leaned forward on the rail, dreaming of revenge.

14

Rufe sat in his tent, head buried in his hands, still unable to come to terms with what had happened at Castel Citadel.

Following the regent's shocking revelation, Rufe had led his men back to the border to seal up Deadman's Pass as he had agreed. It took no more than a moment to decide he would base his force on the Arvenian side. Castel held bitter associations for him now.

Before setting up camp, he had assigned guards to keep a watch over the pass from the Castelan end. A strong contingent of his men now stood on alert at the Arvenian end of the pass, near the Castelan border post.

Rufe's men had arrived to find the post abandoned. No doubt the Castelans would reestablish it at some point. In the meantime the regent had more pressing matters to deal with. He also knew the pass would be well guarded by Rufe and his men.

Late on the first day after they had arrived, one of his scouts sought him out. "A small group of riders is approaching from Castel, Rufe."

His heart leaped. Was it possible that the Ahrans truly were trying to escape into Arvenon with their captive?

Rufe called for Hennis. "Allow the riders to enter the pass. Then block their escape from both ends. Avoid fighting at all costs."

Hennis nodded and hurried away.

Much as Rufe longed for a chance to free the queen, he knew he needed to temper his enthusiasm. The reality was likely to be much less encouraging. The unknown riders would probably turn out to be nothing more than a new set of border guards.

Rufe moved to the mouth of the pass and sat on his horse waiting for word.

Almost half an hour had passed before Hennis reappeared. Approaching Rufe, he drew him aside. "Only one of them rode into the pass. He knew we were here, and he wants to speak with you."

"Who is he?"

Hennis raised his hands helplessly. "I have no idea. He won't talk to anyone except you."

"You're with me," Rufe told Hennis, heading his horse into the pass.

They had ridden all the way to the Castelan end before he caught sight of the rider, surrounded by Rufe's men.

"We've checked him, and he isn't armed," Hennis said quietly as they approached.

"What do you want?" Rufe asked.

"May I speak with you in private?" the stranger returned.

After a moment's hesitation, Rufe returned a tight nod. "We'll do it right here," he said, signaling his men to back off. The men moved out of earshot, remaining close enough to provide support if it should be needed.

The stranger wasted no time. "I have someone with me who would like to speak with you. The matter is highly confidential."

Rufe was not impressed. "I have no idea who you are or what your purpose is. You surely can't expect me to go anywhere alone with you."

"Would it be acceptable to you if the meeting takes place close to the mouth of the pass? My men will keep their distance if yours do the same."

Far too many things could go wrong with this arrangement. However, Rufe couldn't see how anyone apart from himself would be at risk. He nodded curtly. "The meeting can take place over there," he said, pointing.

The other man nodded his agreement.

"And I want all of you dismounted," Rufe said firmly.

After a brief nod, the other man rejoined his companions.

Calling Hennis to his side, Rufe issued instructions. "I've agreed to meet one of them over there. Be prepared to move quickly if there's any sign of treachery. If I raise my right arm, send me support, and round the others up. Don't let any of them get away." He gestured toward the group of riders.

Hennis nodded once before returning to the men to issue orders of his own.

Rufe moved to the agreed position and waited. A cloaked and hooded figure emerged from the group of dismounted riders and walked toward him. A strange sensation washed over him as the person approached.

He was greeted by a soft voice. "Please don't react in any way, Rufe. It's extremely important." The voice rendered him speechless. She continued, entirely unnecessarily, "It's me. Queen Essanda!"

"Your Majesty!" he finally stammered. Keeping his voice low required incredible restraint. All he wanted to do was shout in exhilaration at the top of his lungs.

"How is this possible?" he breathed, shaking his head in wonder.

"It's a long story. Don't worry, I'm planning to tell you everything. Do you have anyone with you who knows the way to Newhaven? It needs to be someone discreet and reliable."

He nodded. "Hennis, one of my captains, was with us in Newhaven. I trust him implicitly."

"Please get him. I'll ask Galvas, my new protector, to join us."

The small group assembled, and Rufe moved them to a location nearby that boasted a couple of fallen logs. They sat down, trying to make themselves comfortable.

"This is Galvas," the queen began. "He's a Varasan agent, and also the main reason I'm not currently in the hands of the Ahrans. It might be simplest if you provide some background, Galvas."

The Varasan nodded. "I need to make it clear that everything you will hear today is highly confidential. Do you understand?"

Rufe and Hennis both nodded. "Yes," they replied in unison.

"You may be aware that Ahran agents have become bolder and more determined in recent times. You probably don't know that King Delmar recently escaped an attempt to either kill or capture him—we can't be sure which. The Ahrans struck in Varacellan, in the open, while he was surrounded by guards. They very nearly succeeded. They were thwarted only thanks to quick thinking on the part of one of our agents."

He sighed. "King Steffan and King Krasmir both understand the full extent of the threat, and they are responding vigorously to Ahran infiltration in their own kingdoms. We tried to convey the danger to a number of the regent's people, but none of them were willing to be convinced that Castel is a target.

"As a result, we increased our presence in Castel with a view to limiting the damage the Ahrans could do. Some time ago, after the planned visit of Queen Essanda became public knowledge, we learned that the Ahrans intended to take advantage of the opportunity to move against her. We therefore stepped up our efforts to monitor their activities."

"Do you know why they attacked the border post here at Deadman's Pass just before we arrived with the queen?" asked Rufe.

"I can't be certain," Galvas replied, "but I can venture a guess. I suspect it was an attempt at misdirection."

Rufe frowned. "Misdirection?"

"They wanted you, and the Castelans, to believe that the queen was vulnerable in the countryside, outside the thick walls of a castle. They wanted you all to relax when she reached the safety of the capital, because that was always where they intended to strike."

Rufe nodded slowly. "So the attack on the border post was merely a diversion."

"Yes. The truth was that they couldn't hope to assemble a force large enough to seriously challenge her escort, so she was never in serious danger out here."

It all made sense. And the ruse had achieved exactly what the Ahrans intended.

"We learned that their agents were splashing money around. One of our people was able to connect with them. They paid him handsomely to supply a load of empty wine barrels. While he was with them he heard them speaking in their own language. He asked innocently if they were Rogandan, and they told him they were not, but that they had learned the language while trading with Rog. They said they used it when they didn't want others listening to their conversation. He got the point and said nothing further. Fortunately for us, he knows a little of the Ahran language. They continued to converse, and he was able to overhear a great deal of it. When we put the pieces together later, we were able to guess at both their intention and the approximate timing."

Queen Essanda took up the story. "I had barely arrived and settled in my apartments when a servant came to my room. She's a loyal Castelan who also works for the Varasans. She told me the Ahrans were planning to abduct me that night. I found it very difficult to believe at first. She brought in another woman who was about my height and with hair roughly the same color and length."

"The same woman responsible for rescuing King Delmar," interjected Galvas.

"This other woman wanted to dress up in my clothes and head out into the gardens adjoining my room. She said her goal was simply to lure the Ahrans into the open. I asked if Count Gordan was aware of this plot, and both of them insisted that no one could know. They were very persuasive, and my instincts told me I could trust them. I couldn't see what I had to lose, so I agreed to their plan."

She nodded to Galvas, and he continued. "Our guesses about the timing proved to be correct. We didn't expect them to be right there and ready to act immediately though. And our agent wasn't supposed to let them take her. We still don't know what went wrong, although we're starting to wonder if she had an agenda of her own. I understand she has reason to hate the Ahran Grand Vizier. It's possible she decided that posing as Queen Essanda would allow her access to him."

"I saw it from my rooms," the queen continued, "and it was terrifying. It happened so quickly. The two guards were overwhelmed and the agent was whisked away before I could fully understand what was going on. Galvas arrived immediately afterward." She turned to him. "I have no idea how you gained access to the castle, much less to my apartments."

"That isn't important," he told her. "What did matter was getting you to safety."

"Which also meant concealing the truth from the regent," she added.

"Why?" asked Rufe. "The poor man was completely devastated."

"He could never have been completely credible if he knew it wasn't true," said Galvas. "He was told what really happened the next day. He agreed to keep it secret, not just for the continuing safety of the queen, but especially for the safety of our agent."

Rufe nodded slowly. "If they found out the truth, they would kill your agent in a heartbeat and try again for the queen. What about the manhunt though?"

"The manhunt is real. Whatever our agent's reason for letting them take her, we desperately want to find and retrieve her." Galvas shook his head. "As you have heard, she looks remarkably similar to Queen Essanda. In her royal garments, anyone who hadn't already met the queen would almost certainly be taken in. There is one small but important discrepancy, though. Her eyes are not the same color as the queen's. If she meets an Ahran who is unusually well informed, it would be disastrous! We need to find a way to release her as soon as possible."

Rufe's head was spinning. There was little he could do about the agent's situation, but the queen was another matter. "What are your plans from here, Your Majesty? You asked about Newhaven."

"I think that's the safest place for me, at least for a while. Until the agent is freed—and until the Ahrans can be properly dealt with—it's important that no one knows I'm alive and free. I suspect that Anneka and Rellan might be willing to isolate Newhaven again, at least for a while."

"And what about King Steffan?"

Galvas responded. "It's painful, but he needs to be told the official story like everyone else. He won't need to pretend when he reacts to it. But we won't delay too long before telling him the truth."

"Even after he finds out I'm safe, he'll be furious at the Ahrans for trying to abduct me," said the queen. "He'll hunt them down with no less energy than if they'd succeeded. And at least he'll know I'm safe in the meantime."

"How can we get you to Newhaven?" asked Rufe. "Our soldiers will need to be kept in the dark as well."

"If you're agreeable," said the queen, addressing herself to both Rufe and Hennis, "Hennis can ride to Newhaven, with a couple of soldiers for his protection. The soldiers don't need to be told why they're going there. When you arrive, Hennis, you can ask Rellan to meet me in the same place he met us last time. I'm confident I can locate it again. Galvas and his men will deliver me there."

"You'll undoubtedly be concerned about the queen's safety with a small escort, Rufe," Galvas acknowledged. "But remember that no one believes that she is at large, so there's no reason for anyone to be looking for her."

"I can see the sense of the proposal," Rufe told him. "I also think it's wise to limit the number of people who know her exact location. So I appreciate your willingness to hand her over to Rellan before she reaches her destination."

Galvas bowed. "It seems we have an agreement. I hope Hennis can leave as soon as possible. We will follow immediately, but I expect we will travel more slowly. I would suggest that Hennis should be present at the handover to Rellan. He can then return here to report back to you, Rufe."

"I will choose a couple of men and leave at once," Hennis told them. "You can be assured of my complete silence on all these matters."

"All of our kingdoms are in your debt, Galvas," Rufe told him. "That applies to every one of King Delmar's agents, and not least the woman who willingly took the place of the queen."

RUFE WAITED IMPATIENTLY for the return of Hennis. Most especially he wanted confirmation that the queen had been safely delivered to Rellan.

The day after the queen had ridden through the pass, one of the regent's dispatch riders arrived, heading for Arnost. Unusually, he was accompanied by five armed guards. The following day a second dispatch rider passed through, heading for the same destination. He was similarly protected.

It wasn't difficult to guess what King Steffan would read in the two dispatches. He would be aghast when he read the first. The second would leave him both relieved and angry. Rufe was glad he wouldn't be there to witness it.

By the time Hennis finally returned, Rufe was becoming agitated.

"Did it go smoothly?" he demanded.

"Very smoothly," Hennis told him. "Anneka and Rellan were very willing to host the queen. They will cut off all contact with the outside world until we send word that it's safe for the queen to reemerge."

Rufe released a sigh. He could finally relax. "What happened with the Varasans? They didn't return this way."

"We rode with them for a short time," Hennis replied. "They asked us to guide them to Steffan's Citadel. They crossed into Erestor, heading for Maranelle. I believe they were planning to board a ship there. Perhaps they're planning to return to Varacellan. They didn't say."

"Wherever they're going, I hope they arrive safely," said Rufe. "We owe them an enormous debt."

15

The candle flickered and guttered, but Goultzar was not troubled by its tenuous glimmer. The Temple of the Dark Gods at Rog had always been a drafty place. Stepping forward unhurriedly, he reached a small door at the rear of the temple. After pausing long enough to snuff out the candle, he passed silently through into the cold night air beyond.

Moving confidently in spite of the darkness, he made his way to the outer wall of the temple compound. Peering back in the direction he had come, his eyes were drawn upward into the night sky, captured by the brilliance of the stars. He noted the empty section of sky where the temple buildings blotted out the twinkling lights. At first glance it almost appeared that the temple had reached hungrily into the heavens and consumed every star within its reach.

The mental image seemed symbolic. It brought to mind his Superior, the seemingly ageless High Priest, greedily snatching at years that did not belong to him.

Hearing a movement off to one side, he stiffened. Other movements followed, and softly murmured greetings reached his ears as several dark-clad forms loomed beside him. Even in the darkness he had no difficulty recognizing his agents. They were a diminished gathering—the lingering remnant of a once vigorous multitude.

"Worship of the dark gods is flagging in Rogand, and no one makes any attempt to arrest the slide," the Archprimus told them. "We have pledged ourselves to resist the decay with all our might. A new opportunity will soon arrive. Remain alert, and be ready to respond to my call at short notice."

Following a time-honored practice, Goultzar placed a clenched fist over his heart before flinging open all his fingers except the little one. After repeating the gesture, the others turned away and melted into the night.

Goultzar marched through the temple, ignoring the buzz that spread among the robed priests. He knew his appearance at that particular moment would distract them from their worship, but he didn't care.

An angry scowl came to his face as he saw the openly baleful expressions on many faces. Once his authority in this place had been unquestioned. He glared back at them. They could despise him all they liked—he had never been driven by a need for approval.

Some priests remained sympathetic, reduced though they might be in number. They kept their heads down and their opinions to themselves, and he encouraged them to do so. The tide had turned against him, and he saw no benefit in allowing his supporters to draw attention to themselves.

He found the priest he sought in an antechamber off the main worship area. "Ah, Zattu. Here you are."

From the way Zattu was backing away, Goultzar might have had the plague.

"I understand you were responsible for reassigning Atmek," the Archprimus offered mildly.

A wary look had come to Zattu's face. He nodded.

"You sent him to a small village near the border with Lestanor. Why that particular choice?"

Zattu's eyes narrowed. "I understand the worship of the dark gods has flagged in the region. I believed his talents would be appreciated there."

"And you did not consult with me before arranging the transfer?"

"I know you are a busy man, Archprimus."

"I see. I appreciate your thoughtfulness in sparing me such trivial details."

"I trust that I did not err."

"Not at all. I am grateful to you for alerting me to the need in that particular part of the kingdom. So much so that I have decided to transfer you there."

A shocked look covered Zattu's face.

"Atmek is needed for a special project, so I have recalled him. He is on his way back to Rog. But the credit must go to you for highlighting the need for a priest with organizational talents in the region. It seems appropriate that you take his place. You will leave immediately."

Zattu's eyes had gone wide.

"A cart is waiting outside for you now."

A sea of faces watched intently as Goultzar shepherded the horrified priest across the temple and outside into the open air. A cart stood ready as the Archprimus had promised. Goultzar stood with arms folded while Zattu climbed aboard. Then he nodded, and the cart rolled through the gates of the temple compound and joined the main road.

He reentered the temple, more than satisfied with his efforts.

Zattu had spoken the truth when he described Goultzar as a busy man. Overseeing the activities of priests throughout the kingdom was a monumental undertaking, and the Archprimus had long drawn upon assistance from a number of other priests, Zattu among them. However, the assignment of priests to vacant positions was a task he had rarely chosen to delegate.

More particularly, Atmek was one of Goultzar's most important supporters, and certainly not a man ever to be banished to the outer fringes of the kingdom. It seemed unlikely that the High Priest was directly involved. If he had been, such interference would have been unprecedented. Nevertheless, Goultzar had no doubt that Zattu had acted in what he believed were the High Priest's best interests.

In any event, justice had now been done, and Zattu's punishment fitted the crime perfectly.

A couple more days passed before Atmek reappeared. He sought out Goultzar the moment he arrived.

"My thanks to you for recalling me, Archprimus. I was beginning to think my life was over in that forsaken backwater."

"I am glad to have you back, Atmek. You are needed here more than ever. I am sure Zattu will do a fine job in your place."

Atmek's lips twisted into an ironic smile when he heard who was replacing him.

"Zattu has done me a favor," Goultzar conceded. "He has shown me the strategic potential of assignments. I acknowledge that I have failed to use them effectively in the past; however, I am already hard at work correcting that error."

"Is there any way I can be of assistance?" asked Atmek.

"Certainly. Draw up a list of names for me. Focus on priests who could most benefit from such an assignment."

THE TEMPLE soon witnessed a steady stream of departures as priests set out for uncelebrated destinations throughout the kingdom. The affected priests had not been selected randomly.

Even before a week had passed, a dramatic change had taken place in the tone within the temple. For the first time in many months, Goultzar's progress through the temple was not marked by hostile stares. The experience of receiving the respect due to his office had ceased to be a faded memory. His detractors had now become the priests anxious to remain out of sight.

Over the years his mission to foster devotion for his gods had become much more than an obligation—it had become a fervent obsession. All of that had been pushed aside by the tensions that simmered within the temple. Now he again worshiped freely with the acolytes, breathing in air heavy with incense and the sickly sweet smell of blood. Once more he invested energy in promoting devotion to the dark gods. In doing so, he was beginning to rediscover his earlier passion for his calling.

Then he received a summons to attend his Superior. He responded without enthusiasm. A considerable period of time had elapsed since he last visited the High Priest, and he had been more than content with the estrangement.

He arrived to find very little had changed in the High Priest's little chamber. The leathery skin of His Eminence appeared more stretched than ever, if such a thing was possible, but he still fixed Goultzar with the same unwavering stare.

Try as he might, Goultzar could not entirely ignore the protests of his aching body as the minutes dragged by. The stool opposite the High Priest felt as uncomfortable as ever, and waiting for him to speak was no less excruciating.

The stark reminder of his own mortality only served to emphasize his Superior's longevity. How did the High Priest achieve it? More importantly, if he'd discovered the key to long life, why was he so secretive about it? What right did he have to hoard such a prize for his own exclusive use?

His Eminence finally opened his mouth to speak. "You have been assigning men to every corner of the kingdom—men you do not like. Why have you yielded to favoritism?"

Goultzar said nothing in response, but anger began to well up within him. The High Priest should be happy that he'd been worshiping in the temple wholeheartedly for a change. That hadn't been possible until he removed the distractions.

His Superior apparently cared more about playing politics.

It didn't matter to Goultzar. Let the old man sit in his little room. Assignments were decided by the Archprimus, and he had no intention of backing away from what he had done.

The High Priest's eyes continued to bore into him. He had the feeling that His Eminence knew exactly what he was thinking, but it made no difference to him.

"There might be surprises in store for you," his Superior said dryly. He flicked a hand. "Leave me."

Goultzar left pondering the High Priest's comment about surprises. What might it mean?

He didn't have long to wait before finding out. As he exited the room, another priest was about to enter it. It was Zattu.

Normally he would have demanded to know why Zattu had abandoned his post. He didn't get a chance to ask.

"Archprimus," said Zattu, acknowledging him with a cool nod. "I have been recalled by His Eminence. It seems he has need of my services." With that he pushed through into the High Priest's room and closed the door.

The High Priest had blatantly undermined his Archprimus. And there was nothing Goultzar could do about it.

"YOU CALLED FOR ME, YOUR MAJESTY." Lord Boedwyk executed a clumsy bow, his bushy eyebrows bobbing up and down alarmingly.

King Krasmir waved him to a seat, trying not to wince as his guest swayed perilously close to a priceless vase on his way to the chair.

Settling into his seat with a deep sigh, the nobleman closed his eyes for a moment. Then, after opening his eyes again, his gaze traveled upward, his attention drawn to some feature of interest on the ceiling.

The king decided to open the conversation before the situation became even more awkward.

"I understand you have considerable knowledge of the Rogandan priesthood, My Lord."

Boedwyk nodded modestly. "It is true that I have made a thorough study of the priests of the dark gods and their various rituals," he acknowledged. "Indeed at one time I briefly considered a vocation as a priest myself."

The king's eyebrows rose in surprise.

"When I was a child I occasionally painted my face and clothed myself in priestly garb, precisely imitating their practices. Purely for my own amusement, you understand. I also memorized their various chants." He steepled his fingers thoughtfully. "I once led a group of stray cats in the Call to Fear. My feline apprentices were incapable of delivering the usual responses, but they nevertheless entered in with considerable enthusiasm. The caterwauling soon attracted a large and animated audience. Sadly, not all of the bystanders were equally able to appreciate the solemnity of the occasion. The incident prompted my parents to confiscate my robes and ban any further development of my budding talent for religious expression."

A mad laugh escaped the king's lips, in mockery of his best attempts to restrain it. He quickly smothered the outburst with a throaty cough.

Wasting no time before moving to safer ground, he observed, "I have heard whispers of tensions within the temple at Rog. Are you aware of the mechanics of leadership succession within the priesthood?"

"I can shed light on the historical precedents, Your Majesty. I must make my appeal to history since no High Priest has been inducted in living memory. The current incumbent is notoriously long-lived."

Similar reports had reached the king. He wondered if the High Priest's successor was becoming impatient.

"And the second in command is the Archprimus?"

"Yes, Your Majesty. Normally the High Priest serves until his death, at which point the Archprimus succeeds him."

"Who chooses the new Archprimus?"

"The outgoing Archprimus chooses his own successor. It is thought that such an approach is best suited to promoting harmony, at least for a while."

"What happens if conflict arises between the High Priest and the Archprimus?"

"A documented history of such conflict exists, of course. The outcome has invariably been the death of one, or occasionally both, of the men."

The king did not hide his surprise. "Are you suggesting the priests murder each other?"

Lord Boedwyk chortled appreciatively. "Your Majesty is unusually candid given the delicacy of such matters. One of the benefits of your station, I imagine." He looked suddenly mortified. "I meant no offense, of course!"

He quickly recovered himself. "The records speak of Nehrvina the Awful escorting the departed to Paradise. No mention is made of the circumstances of their passing."

"I have been wondering if anything is expected of the crown at such times," said the king.

"Nothing is expected at all, Your Majesty. Any attempt to involve yourself would be viewed as unwelcome interference."

"So I should simply sit back and let them battle it out?"

The nobleman nodded happily. "Your wisdom does you great credit, Your Majesty." He instantly looked horrified. "Please pardon my wayward tongue! I did not mean to be condescending!"

"Get over yourself, My Lord," growled the king. He softened his words with a genial smile. "It seems it is my turn to ask for pardon. Please remember that being candid is a benefit of my station."

Lord Boedwyk rewarded him with a laugh of delight.

The king returned a genuine smile. "I am grateful to you, My Lord. Please consider yourself released."

The nobleman departed with a bow and a cheery wave, leaving the king shaking his head and chuckling with amusement.

16

Kamash stood forlornly on the beach of his little island. It was hard to believe he must leave it again, and so soon after returning.

Gharpin had already climbed aboard the little boat, but he seemed content to allow Kamash whatever time he needed to say his goodbyes. Perhaps the Ahran was beginning to understand. Perhaps he, too, had learned to treasure a haven from the restless confusion of humankind.

Wondering if he might be turning his back on the island for the last time, Kamash released a quiet sigh as he pushed the little craft away from the sand and stepped in. Before long the boat was skipping over the water in a steady breeze.

Noticing the easy familiarity with which Gharpin steered the boat and managed the sail, the old man sat quietly and watched as the island slowly dwindled in size. His former home had long vanished from sight before Kamash finally found the resolve to direct his thoughts to the future. Catching the eye of his shipmate, he silently dipped his head in gratitude for his help. Then he directed his full attention to the boat.

. . .

IF THE ELEMENTS had united in saluting Kamash's return to the island, he could hardly be surprised if they took exception to his departure. In any event, the steady breeze that carried them from the island quickly deteriorated into a gale, and dark clouds gathered ominously on the horizon.

Gharpin did not seem perturbed in the least. Turning the boat westward, he handed the tiller to Kamash and reefed the sail. He then rummaged in the bottom of the boat until he found a storm jib, celebrating his discovery with a whoop of glee. Raising the jib, he took the tiller back from Kamash and settled into place once more with a grunt of satisfaction.

Kamash observed the process with considerable fascination. Having almost always sailed alone, he had been forced to rely entirely on his own skills. Sharing the boat with a competent seaman made for a refreshing change.

He soon discovered that Gharpin had an uncanny instinct for the weather. Using only the storm jib to propel the little craft through the heavy swell, the Ahran initiated a series of unlikely course corrections that saw them skirting around the worst of the storm front.

Simply watching Gharpin at work left Kamash feeling exhausted. Nevertheless he readily accepted the tiller when it became obvious his companion was too weary to continue.

Lying down in the bottom of the boat, the Ahran was soon soundly asleep.

THE STORM HAD BLOWN itself out, but only after blowing them far off course.

Their voyage would now be much longer than planned, but Kamash was not concerned. They had brought aboard an abundant supply of provisions, and one or other of the numerous islands dotted around these waters would provide them with fresh water if they needed it.

Turning the boat about, he headed once more in the direction of Rogand.

Calm seas and favorable winds had driven them forward for several hours when Gharpin called a sharp warning. Looking up, Kamash spotted a sail on the horizon. A ship was approaching from the southeast and moving steadily in their direction. They could never match its speed, but there might still be time for them to avoid it if they decided it was necessary.

A small island lay off the port bow, and after a few hurried words and much waving of hands, they swung about and set a course toward it. Their boat was a tiny speck on a vast ocean, and Kamash was hopeful that the island would shield them from view before the sailors on the ship became aware of them. If the ship was Rogandan or Varasan, their caution was unnecessary. The look on Gharpin's face suggested otherwise.

Sailing to the far side of the island, they reefed the sail and waited. Kamash watched tensely as the minutes passed.

Eventually the ship came into view again. The look on Gharpin's face left no doubt about its origins. After passing the island, it continued on the same course as previously. There was no sign that their little craft had been spotted.

Finally able to relax, Kamash hoisted the sail while Gharpin took the tiller. To the amazement of Kamash, his companion pointed the boat in the direction of the disappearing Ahran vessel instead of resuming their course toward Rogand.

"What are you doing?" he demanded.

Gharpin pointed toward the Ahran ship with a frown. "Where?" he growled.

The old man threw up his hands. "I have no idea where they're going, and I don't want to know!"

If Gharpin understood his meaning, he gave no indication of it. He held his course, a determined look on his face.

Kamash shook his head in exasperation. The language barrier prevented discussion, reasoned or otherwise. What could he do? Wrestling for control of the tiller was not an option he would even consider.

He sighed in resignation. It seemed they would be chasing the Ahran ship.

The ship's masts were already disappearing below the horizon when he looked up. "You do realize we can't keep pace with them."

With no response from Gharpin, he shrugged. What did it matter? The Ahrans might hold to their current course, but without visual contact there was no chance Gharpin could steer in exactly the same direction. In the vastness of the ocean, the smallest deviation would guarantee a wide divergence in the courses of the two vessels. Even if the final destination of the larger vessel was within reach, they would probably never discover it.

Gharpin must have been equally aware of these realities, yet he appeared undismayed. He sat at the tiller, staring grimly ahead, betraying no sign of tiredness.

Kamash decided to leave his companion to it. After sailing around searching for a couple of days they would be forced to give up anyway, and he could see no real harm in another detour. If they ran short of food they would just go hungry for a while.

With the conditions unusually good and his eyes drooping uncontrollably, there would never be a better time to take a nap. Stretching out in the bottom of the boat, he closed his eyes.

THE LITTLE BOAT glided through the water, Kamash at the tiller. When Gharpin had finally succumbed to exhaustion, he raised his eyebrows questioningly before relinquishing his seat. The Ahran had yielded control only after the old man had answered the unspoken question with a firm nod, accompanied by a sigh of resignation. When he awoke, he sat peering forward intently.

Open sea lay before them with no sign of ships. Islands were dotted about throughout these seas, but none of those nearby were large enough to support habitation. Kamash eyed his companion hopefully. Surely even Gharpin must be ready to admit defeat soon.

Then the tiniest hint of a mast appeared, far ahead. Kamash immediately swung the boat about, steering for the nearest island. To the old man's relief, they reached its shelter long before they could have been seen.

The vessel was unmistakably Ahran. Even Kamash felt certain it was the same vessel they had been following.

Gharpin moved to the tiller, waving at Kamash to move aside. The old man complied, rolling his eyes in mute protest. His companion ignored him.

As soon as the ship had disappeared entirely, Gharpin resumed their journey, continuing in the same direction as before. Kamash understood. The Ahran ship had probably stopped somewhere—almost certainly at an island—before heading back the way it had come. If they were fortunate, sailing back along its wake might lead them to the island it had visited.

They had not sailed for long before several islands came into view.

As they drew closer, Kamash spotted a thin plume of smoke rising lazily into the air from one of them. Surprised to find such a small island inhabited, he pointed to it at once. Gharpin immediately changed tack, steering instead for a closer island that was even smaller.

"Will they be able to see us?" asked Kamash, pointing to the island with the smoke.

Gharpin clearly understood the question. He responded with a shrug.

They soon reached the smaller island. Anchoring the boat in the sheltered waters behind a promontory, they quickly removed the sail.

Swimming to the rocks and clambering out of the water, they peered out toward the larger island. It was too far away to draw firm conclusions, but it seemed almost certain that the island was inhabited. Having chosen a not dissimilar setting for his self-imposed exile, Kamash understood why someone might choose to live in such isolation. But he also knew how unusual such behavior was. Who was living there, and why? And, more importantly, why had they received a visit from an Ahran ship?

Such questions were better answered by the Varasans or the

Rogandans. They could send a warship with armed sailors to explore the island. Kamash and Gharpin merely needed to ensure they could provide details of its location.

"We can leave after dark," Kamash suggested.

His companion shook his head. "Dark is good. Good for quiet visit."

Just the suggestion of spying was enough to flood Kamash with alarm again.

"You can't be serious!" he said.

"Serious?" Gharpin seemed to consider. He finally returned a determined nod. "Serious," he said, poking at his own chest.

He swept an arm across the vastness of the ocean before pointing at the island. "Why Ahrans? Why here?" He shook his head. "No good, no good."

Kamash readily understood these concerns, but he had no desire to go anywhere near the island, in the dark or not. He could well believe that Ahran captains would be expected to gather intelligence for the empire while traveling abroad, but he saw no reason to suppose they were trained as spies. Even if Gharpin had received such coaching, he himself was certainly not equipped to do it.

The sun set without any resolution to Kamash's concerns. Frustrated at his inability to sustain the simplest of conversations with Gharpin, he eyed his companion uneasily. The two men had been sharing a simple meal using supplies from their boat, and they were almost finished. What was Gharpin planning to do next? Did he expect Kamash to help him?

It occurred to him to wonder what his companion might do if he found himself among his countrymen once more. Would he grasp the opportunity to put the past behind him and make common cause with the Ahrans, in spite of everything that had happened?

He quickly saw he had no reason for doubt. Even in the failing light, a glance at the former captain showed his face rigid with determination.

Gharpin was a man on a mission. He would never rest until it was accomplished.

THE BOAT GLIDED SILENTLY FORWARD, Gharpin sitting keen-eyed at the tiller. In the moonlight, the sail would surely be visible from the island. Thankfully the moon had not yet risen.

The island was little more than a smudge against the brightly twinkling stars, but it stood out enough to show them where they needed to go. Landing on a beach was out of the question—they would need to find a suitable place to anchor nearby.

The island loomed larger, and Kamash's heart began to pound. As Gharpin steered them in close to the beach they saw fires flickering brightly among the trees. Figures were briefly outlined as they moved in front of them. It wasn't possible to guess anything about the identity of the people or why they were there.

Turning the boat about, Gharpin swung into a rocky bay not far from the beach. Low hills overlooked the sea, with a gully emptying into the little bay. For anyone willing to grope over rocks in the dark, the gully might provide a path onto the island.

The thought held no appeal for Kamash. Drawing close to his companion, he hissed, "This is a bad idea!"

If Gharpin understood the warning, he ignored it. "I go," he said softly. "Sun comes, you go." His hand flicked away from the island, out to sea.

He didn't pause for a reply. Slipping over the side, he struck out for the shore.

Kamash saw him reach the rocks. He pulled himself out of the water and stood dripping for a while. Then, slowly and carefully, he climbed toward the gully. A moment later he was lost in the darkness.

The old man sat alone in the boat, tense and unhappy. How long would his companion be gone? Gharpin would be careful, wouldn't he? Surely he would do nothing worse than sneak around for a while. When he discovered nothing sinister, he'd return. He should be back well before dawn.

The night had scarcely begun, though, and he didn't find the waiting easy. Anxious and jumpy, he flinched at the slightest sound.

Each time, concluding there was no reason for concern, he would peer into the darkness, hoping for his friend's return.

The hours wore by without any sign of Gharpin. Perhaps he had been forced to hide. It was also possible that he had been caught. What if he had injured himself climbing in the darkness? Kamash steadfastly pushed the more morbid possibilities from his mind.

At some point he realized that he was at risk as well. If Gharpin was spotted, it would be obvious that a boat had reached the island. Enemies might be searching for him at that very moment.

Was there another boat on the island? They might be in trouble if there was.

Clammy palms and a pounding heart told him he was becoming overwrought. Closing his eyes, he took in a deep breath and tried to calm himself.

KAMASH COULD DENY it no longer. The sky was showing clear signs of brightening.

What should he do? If he left now, Gharpin might arrive to find himself stranded. If he waited much longer, he might be seen from the island as he was leaving.

Eventually he decided to take Gharpin's words seriously. "Sun comes, you go." He would return as soon as it was dark. If Gharpin had been forced to hide for some reason, he would reappear under the cover of darkness.

Rowing clear of the rocks, he hoisted the sail and made for the nearby smaller island.

A sleepless night lay behind him, with the prospect of another to come. As soon as the boat was safely hidden, he threw out the anchor and lay down to rest.

The afternoon was wearing away by the time he woke. He helped himself to food and drink and waited restlessly for the sun to set again.

Gharpin might find his way back to the boat that night, but

Kamash was no longer hopeful about it. He couldn't continue to avoid the question that had been nagging at him. What should he do?

He could take the risk of doing a search of his own. Or he could resume the journey to Rog, and lead a rescue team back to the island. The sun set without him reaching a decision.

Sailing back to the island, he anchored the boat and sat wrestling with his thoughts.

A full hour passed before he decided. He could never live with himself if he made no attempt to discover the fate of the Ahran. Gharpin might be lying injured nearby. Sailing away might be condemning him to a slow and painful death.

With a sigh of resignation he lowered himself into the sea, swam to the rocks, and struggled ashore. Having committed himself, he took a deep breath and followed Gharpin into the gully.

17

Kamash reached the top of the gully without seeing Gharpin or anyone else. All activity seemed to be centered around the beach. Moving as noiselessly as he could, he crept forward in that direction.

He continued until he reached the edge of a large clearing. People were moving about, their shapes revealed in the dim light from a couple of large fires. He could also make out the outlines of a number of huts within the clearing.

None of the people seemed especially alert. That gave him hope. If Gharpin had been found, or even seen, surely the coastline would be swarming with people searching for his boat.

With no way to resolve the mystery of the Ahran's disappearance, he took the only option available to him. Positioning himself well out of the range of any firelight, he settled down to watch and wait.

A couple of hours had passed with nothing to show for it, when he felt a hand settle firmly on his shoulder. Leaping to his feet and spinning around in alarm, he barely managed to restrain himself from crying out.

Kamash found himself confronted with the familiar visage of

Gharpin. Still trying to calm his racing heart, he gaped in wide-eyed amazement. Finally he threw up his hands in exasperation.

Apparently surprised at the reaction he had provoked, the Ahran responded with a dispassionate shrug. Pointing across the clearing at two small buildings, he began speaking animatedly in a low voice.

Kamash could not understand a word of it. "Stop! I don't understand you," he said. He was forced to repeat it with increasing intensity before Gharpin's flow of words eventually came to an end.

His companion pointed into the clearing, then touched his ears.

"You heard them talking. And they speak your language."

Pointing once more at the buildings, Gharpin held up his arms, tightly connecting them immediately below his wrists.

"Bound at the wrists," murmured Kamash. "Prisoners!"

Gharpin held up three fingers.

"Three people," said Kamash.

The Ahran nodded. He held both hands wide, palms facing. Then he lifted them high, bringing them down slowly on either side of his head.

A couple of minutes went by before the old man made sense of the action. "A crown!" he said. "One of the three people is royal."

Gharpin cupped a hand on each side of his chest and looked at his companion expectantly.

Kamash frowned. "A woman?"

The Ahran grinned in triumph. Holding up one finger, he repeated first the crown movement and then the woman movement. He then held up two fingers, repeating the crown movement before cupping a hand between his legs.

The old man frowned. "A woman and a man, both of them royal?"

He stared at Gharpin in astonishment. "King Rupert and Princess Teylee? You mean they're here?"

Ignoring the question, Gharpin held up three fingers. Then he repeated the movements indicating a crown and a woman.

"A third captive? Also royal?" Kamash shook his head in confusion.

It didn't make sense. For one glorious moment he felt certain they'd found the abducted king and princess. But a third royal? That couldn't be right. He must have misunderstood what Gharpin was trying to communicate.

A rough voice called out words Kamash did not understand.

Gharpin froze. Grabbing Kamash's arm, he pulled him away from the clearing.

A second voice was shouting now. The two men ran through the trees, heading for the boat.

Throwing a glance over his shoulder, Kamash saw torches bobbing in their direction. Too many torches. He raced after Gharpin, desperate to keep up.

As the sounds of the sea grew louder, he tripped on a root. Falling headlong, his head hit the ground hard. He lay stunned, blinded by pain and unable to orient himself.

An arm reached down. He was dragged to his feet. Head throbbing, the old man took a stumbling step, then another. Gharpin urged him to greater efforts.

They were in the gully now. Angry shouts rang in his ears. Their pursuers were gaining on them.

Dragging him across the rocks, Gharpin propelled him into the water. He gasped a breath as he went under. Buoyed up by Gharpin, he splashed out feebly for the boat.

Then he was alone. Gharpin reached the boat in a few hurried strokes and hauled himself aboard. Freeing the anchor with a mighty tug, he hurriedly released the sail. An oar appeared in front of Kamash, and he clutched hold of it.

Loud splashes sounded behind them. Time was running out.

Kamash reached the boat. Abandoning his attempts to clamber aboard, he hung on grimly as the boat began to drift away from the rocks.

They were moving too slowly. With swimmers almost upon them, Gharpin reached again for the oar. Kamash felt a hand grab at him, trying to pull him away from the boat. Then abruptly the hand went slack as Gharpin landed a heavy blow on the man's head.

A breeze began to fill the sail, and they picked up speed. Gharpin sat at the tiller, leaving the old man to hang on as best he could. The effort and the pain were too much. As his hold on the boat began to slip, the Ahran appeared and hauled him aboard.

Kamash began to mumble. "Do...they have...a boat?"

Then everything went black.

His eyes opened on thin clouds skidding across a blue sky. The boat lurched suddenly, setting his head pounding. He closed his eyes, waiting for the aching to ease.

After a while he rolled onto one side. Propping himself up on one arm, he peered toward the stern. Gharpin sat calmly at the tiller. Seeing the old man awake, he gave him a wink.

The effort was too much for Kamash. Lying back again, he closed his eyes and drifted off to the slap of the boat plowing through the waves.

When he woke again the sky was ablaze with stars. The pounding in his head had subsided at last.

Sitting up cautiously, he looked around. The boat was racing through a moderate swell, driven by a stiff breeze. They appeared to be sailing almost due east.

Clearly Gharpin had not left the tiller. Moving to his side, Kamash found him barely able to function. Gently wresting the tiller from the Ahran's hands, he waved him forward. Gharpin was asleep almost before he collapsed into the bottom of the boat.

There was so much to ponder. They had been fortunate indeed to escape from the island. He wished he could speak with Gharpin. Had they been pursued?

He wondered again about the prisoners. Who were they?

The priority now was to pass on what they had discovered.

It would be too late of course. With outsiders discovering the island, the Ahrans would move the prisoners as soon as another ship arrived. By the time they returned with Varasan or Rogandan warships, there would probably be no one there.

He wondered if it might have been possible to rescue the prisoners, but he quickly discarded the idea. With so many guards about, any attempt to spirit away three prisoners would have been a recipe for disaster.

In the end they had done well to escape themselves.

He felt sure Gharpin had an important story to tell. Getting him safely to Rog would be enough of an achievement.

RUPERT AND TASHA watched warily as the latest Ahran ship appeared around the end of the island and anchored offshore. Longboats were soon making their way to the little beach.

Rupert tried not to imagine what the Ahrans might do next. Anticipating a fresh round of violations would not help anyone.

A group of guards were soon heading their way. To his surprise they had another captive in tow.

Tasha aimed a puzzled glance in his direction. He returned a shrug.

The Ahran leader approached, dragging the captive in front of Rupert. "I'm sure you weren't expecting a visit from your sister," he gloated.

Rupert stared in alarm at the captive. Her head was bowed, but even without a clear glimpse at her face he knew it was not Essanda. Opening his mouth to contradict the leader, he caught a momentary glimpse of the woman's eyes. His mouth snapped shut, his mocking smile melting away even before it appeared on his lips.

"Essanda! How do you come to be here?" he asked, loading as much dismay into his voice as he could muster.

Once more her head hung low, and she offered no reply.

The horror on Tasha's face almost undid him. With an effort he restrained the impulse to blurt out the truth.

The leader remained oblivious. "There's work to be done," he barked, waving his guards back toward the beach. All of them followed him except two. It wasn't hard to guess why they had been left behind.

"You're the last person I expected to see here," he told the newcomer, speaking loudly in Arvenian. "I have no words for my dismay when I saw you."

The sentiment was not entirely feigned. It must have been a terrible misfortune for the woman to find herself in these circumstances. And he was beginning to wonder if impersonating Essanda might have been a deliberate ploy to save her.

"Thank you!" she said, speaking quietly but with great intensity. Then, more loudly. "I never expected to see you either, Rupert. Not in these circumstances." She covered her face with her hands. "All I can think about is Steffan. He will be so distraught!"

Tasha was beginning to look confused, and Rupert drew both of them into an embrace.

"Thank you for not exposing my pretense!" the woman whispered again.

"You mean this is not your sister?" hissed Tasha.

"We need to talk," murmured Rupert. "Let's see if we can shake off these guards."

He led them swiftly toward the hut he was now sharing with Tasha. The guards trailed behind at a distance.

"We have a couple of minutes at best," said Rupert.

"They think they kidnapped Queen Essanda," the woman told them hurriedly. "They would have succeeded, too, if I hadn't taken her place."

Tasha stared at her in alarm. "They'll kill you at once if they find out the truth!"

The woman nodded. "I'd be dead already if you hadn't played along."

The guards were drawing closer.

Rupert managed one last question. "So who are you?"

"You can call me Essanda," she replied with a wink.

SHULKAHR, the Ahran responsible for the guards and the captives on the island, watched in irritation as the final boatload was ferried across from the supply ship. The vessel had arrived as expected. The surprise package among its cargo was another matter entirely.

It made no difference to him how many prisoners were delivered to the island. Not if he had warning. On this occasion he'd received none. He hated surprises.

Further, the Arvenian queen had been delivered in very poor condition—exactly what he might have expected of a clumsy fool like Kahrlin. Shulkahr cared nothing for her welfare, but powerful people, like Bolnyk, who had appointed him, or even the Grand Vizier himself, almost certainly had plans for her. He would be held accountable whenever it was his turn to hand over.

TWENTY-FOUR HOURS HAD PASSED before he was able to properly establish a new routine. At last he could relax.

"Intruders! Spying on us!"

Startled, he looked up to see one of his men pointing off into the trees.

"Get after them!" he shouted.

Leaping into action, he hastily rounded up a half dozen men. After passing around lighted torches, he sent them after the intruders. Then he found several others and instructed them to guard the prisoners with extra vigilance.

Restless and impatient, he waited for the searchers' return.

Eventually he spotted one of the pursuers returning. Several others straggled behind him.

The look on the men's faces was not promising.

"Well?" Shulkahr demanded.

"There were two men. It's impossible to know how long they'd been observing us."

"Where are they now?" he growled.

"We chased them. But they had too much of a head start. They got away. They had a small boat anchored nearby."

Other stragglers joined the conversation as they arrived.

"It wasn't a longboat, so they didn't come from a ship."

"They must have been fishermen."

"Yeah. A bit too inquisitive for their own good."

"They couldn't be Rogandan. Rogand is too far away."

"Nah. Varasans or Castelans for sure."

"That's enough!" Shulkahr shouted. "I'm tired of your wild guesses!"

He glared at them. "There's no way to find out how much they heard—not now you've let them escape!"

"Even if they overheard us talking, they wouldn't have understood a word. None of the people in this region understand Ahran."

"It isn't just how much they heard, you idiot!" he retorted. "It's how much they saw!"

He shook his head in annoyance. "How did they find the island? It's nowhere near any trading routes. It has to be one of the smallest pimples of rock in this part of the ocean."

"Perhaps they were blown off course in the recent storm," someone suggested.

"It makes no difference!" he snarled. "You all know what this means. We'll have to abandon the settlement. We have no choice now it's been compromised. You've got a lot of work ahead of you."

A howl of protest greeted his words.

"Silence, you fools!" he roared. "You've got no one to blame but yourselves!"

He paused until he had calmed down enough to think. "The next supply ship is due in another week. When it leaves we'll leave with it. All of us, including the three prisoners."

None of them said a word.

Gazing moodily out to sea, Shulkahr faced his real dilemma. Leaving the island wasn't the worst difficulty confronting him. Where would he take the prisoners? Without any way of consulting with Bolnyk, he'd be forced to make it up as he went along.

He faced his men grimly. This was their fault, and he wasn't going to let them off lightly.

"In the meantime you will remove every trace of our presence."

They instantly found their voices again. "That's impossible!"

"What's impossible is two intruders escaping from a crowd of armed guards! Somehow you let it happen."

He scowled at them. "I've been far too easy on you. As of now, someone will be positioned at the highest point of the island throughout daylight hours. We won't be caught by surprise again. And the coastline will be patrolled constantly, day and night. The entire length of it!"

Shulkahr ignored the groans. They'd let the intruders escape, but they wouldn't be the ones who wore the consequences.

When Bolnyk had first appointed him in Dessue's place, Shulkahr couldn't believe his luck. It was a high profile assignment, one that was certain to attract the attention of the chief minister. How had everything managed to unravel so spectacularly?

A huge amount of effort had gone into establishing and maintaining this prison hideaway. Now he had to tear it all down.

He refused to let himself dwell on what would happen when the Grand Vizier found out.

18

"Ship ahead!"

Perched high in the rigging of the Rogandan warship, the lookout was pointing west.

"How many masts?" bellowed the captain.

"Three, Cap'n!"

"Is it Ahran?"

The reply drifted faintly down. "Can't tell! We need to get closer."

Captain Pultek turned to the helmsman. Jerking his head toward the lookout, he ordered, "Follow his directions."

"Set more sail!" he bellowed, looking on with satisfaction as sailors hurried to scramble aloft.

Glancing behind, he saw the two accompanying vessels altering course as well. Keeping up would be their problem. He wouldn't be waiting for them.

Lord Kulferan himself had tasked Pultek with finding and following Ahran ships. The commander seemed to think the best hope of locating Princess Teylee and the Castelan king was to tail the Ahrans.

It would be easier if the Ahran ships weren't so fast. Most Rogandan vessels, including his own, were two masters. Almost every

Ahran ship he'd spotted in recent times had three masts. The empire seemed intent on sending its best ships to Rogand. That didn't bode well.

He'd asked Lord Kulferan directly if they were at war with the empire. The commander had replied that King Krasmir was not likely to declare war while any hope remained of recovering his daughter. When Pultek left the meeting, he had been authorized to use force only in self defense or if it meant the princess and her betrothed could be safely rescued.

He made his way to the wheel.

"Think we'll catch 'em?" asked the helmsman.

The captain frowned into the distance. "Not if they spot us."

He shouted up at the lookout. "If we're getting too close I want to know!"

"Aye, Cap'n!"

As the pursuit dragged on, the three ships in his squadron became strung out. The nearest one was still within reach, but it was slowly slipping behind. The mast was all that could be seen of the other.

Standing beside the helmsman, Pultek scowled back at the other vessels. "What are those idiots about?"

The helmsman grinned, exposing yellowing teeth with dark gaps between them. "Their problem is they don't 'ave you as cap'n."

A call from aloft dragged their attention back to the Ahran ship.

"They're turning!" The lookout was pointing to the northwest.

The helmsman swung the wheel, and the ship slowly came around.

Only a few minutes passed before the lookout called again. "We're gaining on 'em."

The captain reacted immediately. "Reef some sail!"

Sailors sprang into action.

"Make sure we keep our distance!" he called to the lookout.

The man waved an acknowledgment.

Tiny splotches began to appear on the horizon. Islands lay ahead.

"They're slowing down!" called the lookout. Moments later he shouted, "I can see the island they're heading for." Then, "I think they've seen us!"

Pultek yelled up to the sailors still aloft. "Prepare to reef the sails!"

He swung around to face the bosun. "Break out the weapons!" he ordered.

The bosun immediately sent men below.

The Ahran vessel had anchored off a small beach. They were still several minutes away from the island, but they were beginning to close on it. The captain saw three longboats in the water. One of them was already pulling in to the beach. Quickly loaded with passengers, it was ready to return before the other boats had even arrived.

A line of people stood ready to board the moment the other two boats drew in to the sand.

Pultek's gaze flicked back to the Ahran ship. Armed men lined its side. He snorted. His men could handle them.

His own ship began to slow as they drew closer. Archers stood expectantly on his deck, bows at the ready. "Hold your fire, men!" he called. "Wait for my orders."

The Ahran ship was already beginning to move, its anchors barely clear of the water. His helmsman spun the wheel, and they slowly drew alongside it.

As they were passing the stern of the other vessel, he caught a brief glimpse of the activity on its landward side. All three longboats had reached the ship and disgorged their passengers. People were scrambling up rope nets, desperate to reach the deck. The first boat was being frantically hauled aboard. The other two longboats were already drifting away from the ship, abandoned by the Ahran sailors in their haste.

Any opportunity to board the other vessel was fast disappearing. Although his ship was moving faster, he was slowing while they were gaining speed. If he could force the Ahrans toward the island while he still had forward momentum, it might be possible to board their ship.

"Cut them off!" he ordered the helmsman.

Slowly, painfully slowly, the ship began to turn.

The island lay on one side, with Pultek's vessel on the other. And the gap was closing. Nevertheless, the Ahrans were picking up speed. They might still slip through.

"Hoist more sail!" he shouted.

As his sailors responded, a stream of arrows flew from the other ship. Pultek saw at a glance that the Ahrans were targeting his men in the rigging.

"Return fire!" he yelled.

Chaos soon reigned on the decks of both vessels. Picked out by Ahran shafts, several Rogandan sailors aloft were sent crashing to the deck. His own archers struck the Ahran helmsman, causing momentary confusion as the other captain hurried to replace him.

The volley from their opponents proved only too effective. Hindered in their attempts to set more sail, the Rogandans had failed to pick up speed quickly enough. They watched helplessly as the Ahran vessel slipped neatly through the gap, its stern missing their bowsprit by a matter of yards.

People were still clinging to rope nets on the other side of the Ahran vessel. It occurred to him to wonder if Princess Teylee and King Rupert might be among them. With stray arrows flying everywhere, the risk of hitting them was too great.

"Hold your fire!" the captain bellowed.

His men managed to hoist the sails, but too late to make a difference.

Their reduced speed had allowed both of the other ships in his squadron to draw closer.

Calling for the signalman, he pointed toward the nearest of the two. "Signal them to join the pursuit," he ordered.

Then he pointed toward the other ship. "Signal them to search the island."

As the signalman set to work, the captain returned his attention to the chase.

The Ahran ship was proving to be the faster vessel. He could only glare after it in impotent fury as it slowly diminished in size.

A GUARD CAME RUNNING into the Ahran encampment, calling excitedly. Immediately the Ahran leader began shouting instructions. Guards raced around frantically, gathering items and dumping them on the beach.

Rupert saw at a glance that the so-called Essanda had been listening intently to the shouting. Once more he envied the agent's fluency in the Ahran language.

"A ship has been sighted," she said. "It's heading for the island. The guard thinks it's Ahran."

"Sounds like we'll be leaving soon," said Rupert.

She held up a hand for silence. "There's more! Another ship is trailing it. And it isn't Ahran."

Tasha's eyes had gone wide. "They're searching for us!"

Guards were hurrying in their direction. "Try to stay together!" hissed Rupert.

The guards were in no mood to be patient. "To the beach! Move!"

Shoved forward roughly, Rupert hardly noticed that he was being manhandled with unnecessary force. One question alone occupied his thoughts. Was it possible they would be rescued at last?

THE SUPPLY SHIP was arriving two days early, but a foreign vessel was not far behind it. It might barely be possible to evacuate in time. They would need to be ready to leave the moment the ship arrived.

At least they had some warning. Placing a guard at the highest point of the island was proving to be a canny move.

Even before his lookout finished shouting the news, Shulkahr realized he'd been thrown a lifeline. Until that moment, the island was being evacuated solely due to a major security lapse, one for which he was responsible. The appearance of a foreign vessel in hot pursuit of the supply ship changed everything. Evacuation had now become essential.

It would go a long way toward rehabilitating him in the eyes of Bolnyk and his master if he oversaw a successful extraction. Incredibly, he found himself thoroughly prepared for just that.

It was possible that the pursuit came as a direct result of the earlier incursion by two unidentified intruders, but no one would ever know for certain.

Whatever the reason for this latest exposure, the settlement was a secret no longer. Attempting to remove all evidence of their presence was now a waste of time. He grunted in satisfaction. It was one less thing to think about.

The prisoners arrived, hustled along by a group of guards. Nothing mattered to Shulkahr now except extracting the prisoners.

They stood with heads bowed, saying nothing. They seemed more than usually submissive, but he was not deceived. The subtle signs were there. They were dreaming of escape, of rescue.

Let them dream. "I'm not letting you out of my sight," he growled. Hope was a fickle mistress.

The supply ship glided around the island, anchors thrown overboard before it had properly slowed. The captain was in a hurry.

The first longboat was quickly in the water. Shulkahr noted with satisfaction that it was empty apart from rowers.

Moving forward onto the beach with the prisoners, he saw a brawl breaking out behind him. The idiots couldn't be left unsupervised for a minute. Leaving the prisoners with other guards, he hurried back.

"What are you fools arguing about?" he roared.

They stared at him sullenly. No one answered.

There was no time to get to the bottom of it. "Get onto the beach! Now! The next person I see fighting will stay here."

They moved off without a word.

Returning to the beach, he was annoyed to see the first longboat already full and ready to return to the ship. It didn't matter though. Two more longboats had been lowered, and they were already on their way.

Then the foreign ship appeared around the edge of the island. It had arrived more quickly than he could possibly have imagined.

Getting the prisoners to the ship had now become critical. As the first of the boats arrived, men pressed forward insistently, trying to force their way into it.

"Move aside," he shouted.

Either they didn't hear or they ignored him. Physically dragging two guards from the boat, he drew his sword. "The prisoners are getting into the boat. I'm getting in with them." He waved his sword. "Anyone who tries to board without my permission will get a taste of this."

As he clambered aboard, the other longboat arrived. The remaining guards raced for it, pushing and shoving in their eagerness to secure a place.

"Go!" he shouted. The rowers bent their backs, and the boat pulled away from the beach.

The foreign ship was nearing the island. He could see men with bows stretched out along its deck. Another vessel had appeared behind it too. The situation was becoming critical.

The Ahran ship lay immediately ahead. They were barely going to reach it in time.

Nets had been thrown over the side of the vessel, and men were clinging to them, waiting for those above them to climb onto the deck.

They reached the ship at last.

"Start climbing!" Shulkahr ordered the prisoners. When they didn't move, he drew a knife and held it to the throat of the princess. "Unless you want me to carve her pretty neck, you'll do as I say."

That got them moving. All of them grabbed the net, with him behind them. But the men above were not moving. When a succession of stray arrows whizzed overhead he realized why. The Ahran ship was under attack, and the decks were exposed. It was apparently safer on the net.

The ship was moving now. The two longboats drifted away, empty.

Shulkahr was becoming impatient. "Get moving!" he yelled to the people higher on the net. He was wasting his breath. Climbing upward as far as he could, he began haranguing the men above him, trying to stir them to action.

The ship was moving faster, and he saw that their pursuers had fallen behind. The flow of arrows appeared to have stopped as well. They were surely going to escape.

A second ship was swinging in behind them too, but it was going no faster than the first vessel.

Then he caught sight of a third ship, clearly heading for the island. They could search all they liked. They would find little of interest there.

He shook his head, astonished at how close it had been. They had barely made it out in time.

Glancing up he saw movement at last on the net above. It was time to get the prisoners onto the deck.

Looking down, he was baffled to find no sign of them. He swung his head around and then peered upward. They were nowhere to be found.

His heart skipped a beat. Where could they possibly have gone? He tried to remember the last time he had seen them. It was immediately before he climbed up to get people moving again.

He hadn't been gone for long. Yet in that short period of time they had somehow disappeared.

They could only have jumped into the sea. He peered back along the ship's wake, but he saw no sign of heads bobbing in the water. If they had been spotted from the pursuing ship, some attempt would have been made to pick them up. But the other ship had not turned aside or lowered a boat.

That meant they must have jumped while the other ship was still alongside. They would have been noticed otherwise.

He looked back at the island, disappearing in their wake. The prisoners must have been a lot closer to it when they jumped in, but they would still be hard pressed to swim to it, even with the tides on their side. If they were lucky enough to reach it, and if they got there before the foreign ship had left, they would soon be on their way back to their kingdoms.

He shook his head in denial.

He thought about the guards beside them on the ropes. If the prisoners leaped into the water from the net, they must have seen it.

He noticed for the first time that he was alone on the lower section of the net. All the guards had climbed above him. The last of them was about to disappear over the top onto the deck.

He shouted at the top of his voice, venting his frustration. He was wasting his breath. No one on deck would even hear him.

That was the moment when he realized all was lost. Of course the guards had seen the prisoners jumping from the ship. They couldn't possibly have failed to notice it. None of them would ever admit it though.

He understood why none of the guards had taken the risk of following them into the water. Why should they? They weren't ultimately responsible for the prisoners.

The blame would fall squarely on Shulkahr.

Returning without the captives did not bear thinking about. Taking a deep breath he leaped away from the net. He hit the water hard, disappearing briefly below the waves. When he surfaced, he looked up to find his ship already distant. If anyone had spotted him jumping, there was no indication of it.

Even before the first of the pursuing ships sailed past, his sword had begun to weigh him down. Treading water determinedly, he released the belt and let the weapon sink into the depths.

Left with only a knife in his belt, for a moment he wondered if he might live to regret being almost defenseless. He quickly dismissed the thought. It would be enough of a challenge to make it to the island without the extra burden. With it, his chances would be greatly diminished.

He squinted toward the island. It seemed so far away. But it was too late for regret.

Taking a deep breath, he started to swim.

19

Moody and unsettled, Bisri Ahuzza stood at the stern of the ship staring into the darkness. More than three hours had passed since the sun disappeared. Almost all of the sailors had gone below decks, away from the cold breeze that tirelessly brushed the hair from his face.

His ship lay at anchor not far from a secluded shoreline dimly visible in the moonlight. Rog was somewhere to the northwest, distant enough for Ahuzza to feel confident of their privacy.

He had no idea where the other Ahran ships were located. They had split up to avoid detection, and he was not sorry about it. The greater the distance between him and Rheibas, the better he liked it.

Even with Rheibas out of sight, the presence of Ronizah provided a constant reminder that the chief minister's eyes and ears were everywhere. The interpreter was beginning to weigh him down, like a millstone around his neck.

In appointing Ahuzza as envoy, had the emperor fully realized the potential for friction with the chief minister? Unforgiving and ruthless with his enemies, Rheibas was not a man any rational person wanted to cross.

A dull splash sounded below him. He stared down vacantly, half expecting to catch a glimpse of silver as a fish leaped from the water. With nothing visible in the darkness, he redirected his gaze to the shoreline.

Little as he desired company, he was beginning to wonder if he should go below decks when he was startled by a soft voice from below.

"Bisri Ahuzza?"

He stared down in astonishment. A dark figure dangled from a rope apparently attached to the stern of the ship.

"Who is it?" he demanded, speaking in a whisper.

"I was sent by King Krasmir. Is it safe to talk?"

Whoever it was spoke fluent Ahran.

"How do I know King Krasmir sent you?" For all he knew, it was one of Rheibas's men sent to trap him.

"The note you received after meeting with King Krasmir. I can tell you its contents."

His eyes went wide. He had read the note eagerly the moment he was alone. It made no sense. Perhaps it was coded. If so, he had no way to unlock it. At the first opportunity, he tore it into little pieces and tossed it into the sea. Then he had promptly forgotten about it.

"What did it say?" Ahuzza demanded breathlessly.

"Sightless fish dwell in deep waters," came the response.

So it was a pass phrase. The message had been intentionally cryptic.

"Why are you here?" he asked.

"You need to come with me, Bisri," the agent said insistently. "We believe your Grand Vizier wishes to prevent you from engaging directly with us. We think it likely that an attempt will be made on your life."

Disconcerting as the warning was, Ahuzza was not at all inclined to take it seriously. However unhappy Rheibas might be, surely he wasn't about to murder him. He had done nothing to warrant such an extreme reaction.

The agent spoke into the silence. "King Krasmir wanted to warn you, and to protect you in any way he can."

"How does he propose to protect me?" Ahuzza made no attempt to keep the skepticism from his voice.

"A Rogandan ship will return you to Kat Ahket whenever you are ready. In the meantime, King Krasmir wants to meet with you. His desire is to be frank and clear in what he communicates to the emperor."

So the Rogandan king expected him to simply slide down a rope and leave with this man? He stared at the dark figure, shivering in his wet garments. Did these people seriously think he would throw himself into their hands? What grounds did he have for trusting King Krasmir? And who was this agent anyway? How had he managed to elude the guards?

He had no doubt what his countrymen would conclude if they learned he had gone over to the Rogandans. They would certainly label him a traitor.

He couldn't possibly take the offer seriously. Nevertheless, it was alarming how tempting it felt.

He shook his head stubbornly. "Please thank the king for his offer. But I could never retain the trust and respect of my countrymen if I slipped away in secret and threw my lot in with a foreign ruler."

The agent didn't seem surprised. "Are you certain?"

"I am."

"Then I wish you all the best, Bisri," he murmured.

He left as silently as he had come.

Hurrying away from the stern Bisri Ahuzza hid himself in his cabin. He hoped desperately that the conversation had not been witnessed by anyone.

As he lay in his hammock trying to sleep, he pondered the agent's warning. Surely his life could not truly be in danger. The Rogandans were undoubtedly exaggerating, and why wouldn't they? They had an agenda of their own.

He sternly reminded himself that the emperor had given him an important task. He was determined to see it through.

BOLNYK BOWED as he entered the cabin on board the chief minister's ship the following day. "I have just received news, Your Eminence. A Rogandan agent has met with Bisri Ahuzza."

Rheibas raised his eyebrows. "Where and when?"

"The agent went to the bisri's ship late last night."

"What did they discuss?" asked Rheibas.

"Our agents were not able to overhear the conversation."

"Have you questioned Ronizah, Ahuzza's interpreter?"

"He was not involved, Your Eminence."

The chief minister scowled. "I warned Ahuzza. I told him to be careful."

Bolnyk found it hard to understand why someone as well informed as the bisri should need such a warning. If he was fool enough to ignore it, he deserved whatever he got.

"Unfortunate accidents can happen so easily at sea. Arrange one for the bisri."

Bolnyk bowed once more and departed.

As he emerged onto the deck he spotted the bosun. "I will need a longboat. Have it ready two hours before dawn. I will provide the crew."

The bosun hurried away to arrange it.

Bolnyk did not wait around for confirmation. He had work to do.

THE FOLLOWING night Bisri Ahuzza found himself standing at the stern once more. He didn't know for certain why he was there. Was some part of him hoping the agent would appear again and renew the offer to spirit him away?

"Bisri, what are you doing out here in this cold air?"

Taken completely by surprise, Ahuzza spun around to find Ronizah before him. After a quick bow, the interpreter stood staring at him quizzically.

"Why are you here if it's so cold, Ronizah?" asked Ahuzza testily.

"I have been asked to pass on a message. The chief minister

wishes to meet with you. He is planning to send a boat in the morning."

The bisri contented himself with a tight nod of acknowledgment.

After a deep bow, the interpreter departed, soon disappearing below decks.

Ahuzza was left in turmoil. A seemingly endless succession of questions flooded through his mind. What was the chief minister planning? Why had the message been delivered to Ronizah instead of to him directly? Could a sinister purpose lie behind the meeting? It was especially unnerving coming so soon after the agent's warning.

Restless and uneasy, he stood shivering, trying to convince himself it was due to the cold.

Eventually he made his way below decks. The irregular rocking of his hammock did nothing to soothe his jangled nerves. Desperate for the release of sleep, he closed his eyes. Yet the oblivion he craved refused to come. Long hours dragged by before he finally succumbed.

AHUZZA WOKE to a pounding on his cabin door. He groaned, opening his eyes reluctantly.

The muffled voice of his interpreter called, "Bisri! Are you awake?" How had he failed to notice the whining tone of the man's voice?

Stumbling out of his hammock, he called back, "What is it, Ronizah?"

"The chief minister's longboat has arrived. His senior agent is waiting for you."

His senior agent? Rhelbas had sent Bolnyk to collect him? The name banished every trace of sleepiness. He was fully alert.

Of all people, why did it have to be Bolnyk? Dismissive though he had been of Lord Torbury's allegations, Ahuzza was well aware of the man's reputation.

As he opened the door, he reminded himself sternly that the emperor himself had appointed him to his mission. He would not shrink from carrying it out. And what reason did he have to worry anyway? He'd done nothing to oppose Rheibas.

He would say as much to the chief minister's face if it proved necessary. Everyone knew the man had an uncanny knack for detecting falsehood. It would be obvious to him that Ahuzza was telling the truth.

Nevertheless, it seemed wise to take a couple of guards with him. It might seem little more than symbolic, but it would be making a statement. Passing a group of them as he moved toward the hatch, he selected two of their number and ordered them to accompany him. They immediately swung in behind him.

As he and his guards followed Ronizah onto the deck, he caught sight of Bolnyk at the side of the ship. Walking boldly to the agent, he glanced over the side. A longboat waited below. Rowers occupied all of the available seats apart from one at the stern.

He frowned at Bolnyk. "There isn't room for me and my guards."

"There is room for you in the prow, Bisri," Bolnyk replied coldly. "My orders referred to you alone. You will not require guards."

Ahuzza bristled. The agent showed none of the deference due a bisri, much less the handpicked envoy of the emperor. He glared disdainfully at the agent. "Either my guards travel with me, or I arrange my own transport to the chief minister's ship."

It must have been apparent to Bolnyk that Ahuzza had no intention of yielding. "There's space for them," he growled, waving the two guards irritably down to the boat. Ahuzza climbed down after them.

Ahuzza sat glowering in the prow as the longboat pulled away from his ship. His two guards crouched awkwardly in the middle of the boat, trying to keep out of the way of the rowers. Seated comfortably at the stern, Bolnyk ignored them all.

The rowers faced away from Ahuzza, but he felt certain he recognized one of the men immediately in front of him. The missing chunk of his left ear made him unmistakable. The bisri felt sure he had once seen the man in the company of Bolnyk.

Was it possible that these men were not sailors at all? Had Bolnyk chosen a crew from among his own henchmen? He began to wonder if he should have insisted on making his own way to Rheibas's ship.

He reminded himself once more of his status and his mission, but it didn't prevent a cold sweat from prickling his skin.

Long minutes passed, and the boat moved around a point into a narrow bay enclosed by rocky promontories on both sides. Waves splashed onto a lonely beach. The shoreline and the hills beyond it were deserted.

Bolnyk held up a hand, and the rowers ceased their labor. Getting up, he walked purposefully between the rowers, heading for the prow. Ahuzza watched his progress with wide eyes and pounding heart. As he reached the bisri, the agent thrust a hand into the bottom of the boat and retrieved an anchor.

"Bisri Ahuzza, the emperor finds you guilty of treason," he snapped.

At these words, the man with the missing ear spun around and pinned the bisri's arms to his side. Crying out for his guards, Ahuzza struggled to free himself. His guards could do nothing to help. Set on from every side, they were fighting for their lives.

In spite of the bisri's desperate thrashing, Bolnyk succeeded in looping the anchor rope three times around his neck. After knotting it tightly, the agent seemed to glimpse something over Ahuzza's shoulder. "Move!" he shouted to his men.

As the rowers bent to their task, both men threw him from the boat, sending the anchor in after him. As he went in he caught sight of his guards being thrown overboard as well.

Sucking in a huge breath as he hit the water, Ahuzza wrestled with the rope, frantic to remove it from his neck. But the weight of the anchor pulled it tight, dragging him relentlessly toward the bottom.

He carried a knife in his belt, and it was still in place. Retrieving it with trembling hands, he almost dropped it in his haste. Frantic, and struggling to grasp it firmly, he attacked the rope, sawing fiercely at it in a desperate attempt to free himself.

The knife was sharp. Severing the final strand, he felt the rope go slack. But he could hold his breath no longer. With the surface far above him, his despairing upward kick was nowhere near enough.

His lungs filled with water, panic sweeping away all coherent thought.

Consciousness returned grudgingly. He dimly heard a peculiar sequence of noises: labored gasp, haunting wail, gasp, wail, gasp—endlessly repeated. Confused and disoriented, he struggled to comprehend how the sounds coincided so exactly with his breathing.

He finally registered that the noises were coming from him.

A quiet voice spoke words he did not recognize.

Closing his eyes, he abandoned any attempt to make sense of the world around him.

He slept.

Ahuzza woke to a pounding head. He felt as if he had been beneath the waves, tumbling helplessly on the sand, his body pummeled by a relentless succession of breakers.

Fluid was pressed to his lips, and he drank submissively, grimacing at the taste. Then he closed his eyes again.

The pounding slowly eased, and he became aware he was lying on a comfortable bed.

"Where...am I?" He barely recognized his own voice.

"You are in the royal castle at Rog."

With an effort, Ahuzza propped himself up on one elbow and looked around. He decided he vaguely recognized the speaker.

The man saw it and nodded. "Yes, we have met already. On your ship."

Of course. He remembered water dripping from a dark figure. The agent.

"How?"

"We knew they would try to kill you. We arrived in a sloop as they were throwing you overboard. When they saw us they didn't wait around. We ignored them. Time was short—critically short. We barely reached you in time."

He paused. When Ahuzza said nothing, he continued.

"Fortunately for you, a healer had arrived just before we set out. A monk with rare skills. We brought him with us." The agent's lips twisted into a smile. "I thought you were done for. But he doesn't seem to know how to give up."

"And my guards?"

"They'd been brutally stabbed, but he got to them in time as well. You'll be able to see them later."

Ahuzza slumped with relief. "Can I meet this monk? To thank him?"

"Certainly. He isn't far away. But he speaks no Ahran."

The agent called out in a language Ahuzza didn't recognize.

A burly figure clad in the robes of a monk appeared in the doorway and approached the bed. A rare serenity encompassed the monk, and a gentleness that seemed incongruous for a man of his size.

The stranger gazed down at him, his eyes filled with compassion.

"Bisri Ahuzza," said the agent. "This is Brother Ander."

VOLUME 2—SEEDS OF HOPE

20

Bolnyk approached the emperor's throne, five steps behind the Grand Vizier. Not one to be easily daunted, he had told himself that the might of the emperor could never intimidate him. Now, admitted to this place for the first time, he was overawed in spite of himself. The menacing ranks of guards, the boastful grandeur of the chamber and its furnishings—everything about the imperial throne room reeked of power. The slightest whim of the emperor could end the life of any one of his subjects in a moment.

Rheibas did not seem at all intimidated, and Bolnyk took courage from that.

The emperor's greeting was blunt and to the point. "Where is Bisri Ahuzza?"

"I have grim news, Your Imperial Majesty. Even before I reached Rog the bisri had made independent contact with the Rogandans and their allies. After a recent conference with me, he set off to meet with them again at their invitation. I urged him to be careful, but he insisted on going alone. He has not been seen since. I regret to say there is every indication that he was murdered by the Rogandans."

The emperor glowered at him. "Why? How could such behavior benefit them?"

"Their motives are difficult to comprehend, Your Majesty. Why have they captured your daughter and refused to release her? They seem to think they can act with impunity where the empire is concerned. Perhaps the vastness of our physical separation convinces them they have nothing to fear by way of consequence."

"What do you propose?" demanded the emperor.

"The most effective response would be to return with an army."

The emperor scowled. "I have come to rely on your skills as a negotiator, Chief Minister. Those skills appear to have entirely deserted you!"

The Grand Vizier bent humbly. "I have been negotiating from a position of weakness, Your Majesty. I have become a tame lion. I can roar as fiercely as any wild animal, but without teeth I am little more than a carnival curiosity."

The emperor glared at him for a few moments. Finally he said, "Very well. You wish to catch the attention of the Rogandans. I will assign ten warships to the task, and as many soldiers as they will accommodate."

"So few, Your Majesty!"

"You will get no more!" the emperor snapped. "I am approving a show of force, not authorizing you to start a war. General Vholahr will command them. He will receive his orders directly from me, and he will not answer to you."

Rheibas bowed low.

The emperor's brows bristled. "My patience is wearing thin, Chief Minister. I have enough complications within my own empire—as you well know! Get my daughter back, and do it without embroiling me in a new catastrophe. You are dismissed!"

USHERED into the emperor's private audience chamber, General Vholahr bowed low.

"Come in, General." The emperor waved him irritably to a seat. "Rheibas has so far failed to retrieve my daughter from the Rogandans, and I fail to understand the reasons. I sent Bisri Ahuzza to monitor the situation on my behalf, and somehow he has disappeared. I am sending you to Rogand with a force of ten ships. You will carry on where he left off."

"Will the chief minister have authority over me and my men, Your Majesty?"

"He will not. I am sending you in a supporting role, and I certainly expect you to make contact with him when you arrive in the region. Nevertheless, you are to operate with complete independence. Under no circumstances are you to receive orders from anyone other than me."

The general dipped his head.

"Ensure that at least some of your soldiers speak Rogandan. If it is safe to do so, make contact with the Rogandan king. I want to be informed of whatever you learn."

"Under what circumstances am I authorized to use force?"

"I expect you to defend yourself vigorously if attacked. Beyond that, avoid even the appearance of aggression. I wish to retrieve my daughter without starting a war."

"So my men are largely intended as a show of force?"

"Precisely. The situation is volatile and confusing. I have chosen you because you combine military competence with unusual diplomatic subtlety. Do you understand what I require of you?"

"Yes, Your Majesty."

"Then you are dismissed."

General Vholahr bent low and departed.

Bolnyk scurried after the Grand Vizier, eager to be gone from the throne room. Only when it was behind him was he able to relax.

There had been moments when he felt almost afraid. The emperor seemed far from satisfied with his chief minister's handling of the Rogandan situation. Bolnyk had never before seen Rheibas bow to anyone, and it was alarming to witness the Grand

Vizier being called to account. After humbly pleading for provisions, his master had stooped submissively when the emperor threw him crumbs. It had been a stark reminder that, powerful as his master was, ultimate authority in the empire did not rest in his hands.

Curiously, Rheibas did not seem at all taken aback. In fact he seemed remarkably buoyant.

"How did you enjoy your first taste of the emperor's throne room, Bolnyk?"

"I was disappointed at his lack of support for your proposal, Your Eminence."

"For more troops?" Rheibas waved a hand indifferently. "Ten ships will be more than enough. I would have been satisfied with five."

The agent stared back at him in surprise.

Rheibas laughed. "I have access to more than enough men, Bolnyk. You of all people should know that. I lack one thing only. None of my men bear the imperial insignia on their uniforms." He grew serious. "The Rogandans have hunted down and killed our agents with impunity. They will think twice when they're facing the emperor's soldiers. If they kill just one of them, they'll have a war on their hands."

The strategy could not be simpler. Ever a master manipulator, Rheibas would have no difficulty steering the situation in whichever direction he chose.

"Leave me now," the chief minister said brusquely. "I have matters to attend to."

Bowing low, Bolnyk hurried away.

Disconcerting as the audience in the throne room had been, the impact quickly dissipated.

As time passed, he found the contrast between the emperor and his master more and more striking. Richly cloaked with every trapping of limitless power, His Imperial Majesty seemed hesitant to exercise it. Rheibas could not have been more different. To every outward appearance he was weak and insignificant. Yet he routinely surprised friends and enemies alike with his swift and decisive action.

Everything he did was carried out in the emperor's name. Credit for his successes was deflected to the emperor, with Rheibas deferring unfailingly to His Majesty in private as well as in public. Nevertheless, Bolnyk knew better than anyone how crafty his master was.

In practice, the chief minister had almost unrestricted access to the emperor's power. And he benefited more than anyone. The agent found it all very instructive.

Beyond all that, he could not ignore his own glow of satisfaction. Given his humble beginnings, he could never have dared to imagine being admitted to the emperor's presence. It said a great deal about the way Rheibas regarded him.

Having begun life as a nobody, he had found purpose, usefulness, and increasing authority under Rheibas. Over time he had been granted greater insight into his master's designs. Rheibas told him only what he needed to know, but Bolnyk felt sure that vastly more had been entrusted to him than to anyone else.

That thought brought to mind Rheibas's mysterious prisoner. After a bemusing introduction, Bolnyk had learned nothing further about who the man was or what Rheibas wanted from him. He had no idea what had become of him. Perhaps he was being held somewhere in Rogand.

The whole situation was beyond unusual. It was baffling, too. While normally very willing to include his senior agent in his plans, Rheibas had clearly decided to treat this case very differently. The implied lack of trust smarted. It also made the matter highly intriguing.

Bolnyk reminded himself to stay focused. He had more than enough to deal with. He couldn't afford to allow himself to become distracted.

Bolnyk approached the chief minister's reception room apprehensively, the afterglow from his visit to the emperor no more than a memory. A servant announced his presence, and he was ushered inside.

"The captain of one of our supply ships has just arrived in Kat Ahket, Your Eminence. He has brought alarming news."

Rheibas frowned at him. "Well?"

"Our royal prisoners have gone missing."

The frown instantly became a scowl. "How is that possible?! Where is this captain?"

"Waiting outside."

"Then bring him in!"

Hurrying to the door, Bolnyk waved the captain into the room.

The new arrival entered the room and bent low. He looked harried.

"How has this happened?" demanded the chief minister. "I want to know every detail! From the beginning. And do not dare to mislead me! I'll have your head if I discover you've gilded the truth even slightly."

The captain had gone pale. "Of course, Your Eminence." He blinked nervously, then began. "I was tasked with taking supplies to the island where the prisoners were being held. As we approached the island, our lookout spotted a foreign ship coming in behind us. Until that moment he had seen no sign of another ship."

"The fool is clearly blind!" spat Rheibas.

"We were surprised to find the guards ready to evacuate the island, with the prisoners. As soon as they saw us, they lined up on the beach, waiting to be collected."

"Why were they ready to leave?"

"I questioned the guards later, Your Eminence. A few days earlier a couple of fisherman were discovered on the island, watching the guards from the trees. They escaped in a small boat. The leader of the guards, Shulkahr, concluded that the island's location had been compromised. He decided they all needed to leave on the next supply vessel."

"Where is he? I want him here!"

"He is missing, Your Eminence."

The chief minister opened his mouth—most likely to yell. Apparently thinking better of it, he abruptly snapped his mouth shut again. "Go on," he finally managed.

"I launched three longboats as soon as it was possible, and we got everyone off the island. By then the foreign boat was almost on top of us. We retrieved the longboat crews, but had to abandon two of the longboats before we could haul them aboard. The people we rescued were hanging on to ropes on the side of the ship when we pulled the anchor. They couldn't climb onto the deck at first because of arrow fire. The foreigners tried to steer across our bow to cut off our escape. Some of our archers slowed them down, and we managed to slip past them. Once we were under way, we quickly outpaced them."

He paused, but the chief minister waved at him to continue.

"The foreign ship was not alone. Two others followed it in. One joined the chase, and the other headed to the island. As soon as I could, I sought out the leader of the guards. His name was Shulkahr. I discovered that Shulkahr never reached the deck. Nor did any of the three prisoners."

"Did you question the guards?"

"I did. I questioned them vigorously. All of them, including the guards who climbed the net last, denied any knowledge of what happened to the missing people."

"Where are these guards?" Rheibas's voice had gone quiet. Bolnyk recognized it as a dangerous sign.

"They dispersed as soon as we docked."

"Find them and bring them to me," Rheibas told Bolnyk curtly.

The agent bowed, saying nothing.

"What do you believe happened to the prisoners and to Shulkahr?" Rheibas asked the captain.

"If they were weakened by their captivity, they might have fallen into the water. Or perhaps they jumped, in an effort to escape. Shulkahr probably followed them in."

"On his own?"

"He might have felt responsible for them."

"Could they have swum to the island?"

"They would have had a considerable distance to swim. It would depend largely on the currents, but I think it unlikely."

The chief minister asked a few more questions before dismissing the captain. "Don't go anywhere. I might have other questions for you."

After bowing clumsily, the captain almost tripped over himself in his haste to leave the room.

Rheibas turned to his senior agent. "Shulkahr is known to me. Who appointed him to this position?" he asked.

Bolnyk's heart sank. "I did, Your Eminence."

His master's eyes narrowed. "I seem to recall another man—his name was Dessue—being placed in charge on the island. On the recommendation of Kahrlin, I believe. What became of him?"

Rheibas missed nothing. And his memory for detail was terrifying.

"I felt concerned that Dessue might be too soft. I replaced him with someone I expected to get the job done more effectively."

"So your action had nothing to do with your rivalry with Kahrlin?"

"Not at all, Your Eminence. I believed I was appointing the best man for the job. I apologize if I erred."

Rheibas said nothing for a long minute. Then he turned away from Bolnyk. "You are dismissed," he said coldly.

The senior agent left almost as hastily as the captain.

His master had chosen not to linger on the issue of Shulkahr's appointment, but as usual he had seen to the heart of it. Rheibas had guessed correctly. In spite of Bolnyk's bold denial, replacing Dessue had everything to do with Bolnyk's determination to undermine the man who recommended the appointment.

Kahrlin might be clever, but he was boastful and arrogant. More importantly, he lacked respect. He lusted after Bolnyk's position and status, and he made no secret of it. Bolnyk had witnessed first hand how the chief minister outmaneuvered his own challengers. Surely he could not be expected to behave any differently.

None of it would have mattered if it hadn't been for his own appointee's monumental blunders. Lax security had exposed the island to unfriendly eyes. That was bad enough. But Shulkahr's negligence in failing to effectively guard and restrain the prisoners during the evacuation was unforgivable.

Throwing himself into the water after them might have been the only sensible thing Shulkahr had done.

IT TOOK TWO WEEKS, but Bolnyk rounded up every one of the missing agents. He was relentless, sparing no energy in tracking them down.

By the time they were dragged before Rheibas, one at a time, they were justifiably terrified. After a lengthy interrogation, each of them was led away to be executed.

"Wringing the truth from them presented no challenges," observed Rheibas.

Bolnyk nodded stiffly. "Men are unusually pliable when they're frightened enough."

"It seems our captain told us the truth."

"It appears so, Your Eminence."

"On this occasion he has saved his life by doing so."

The senior agent dipped his head. "I will have him released."

Rheibas stared at him pointedly. "None of this should have been necessary, Bolnyk. Don't imagine I've failed to notice your contributions toward this debacle. Do not continue to test my patience."

The blood drained from the agent's face. To him the Grand Vizier's master plan remained a mystery. But clearly the stakes had never been higher. Why did it all have to unravel now?

The chief minister's brows drew together. He appeared to have forgotten his rebuke already. "Only one question matters now. Do our enemies realize that we no longer have the prisoners?"

With nothing to offer except guesses, Bolnyk decided to keep his mouth shut.

After musing for a few moments, Rheibas reached his conclusion. "We will act as though nothing has changed. If the prisoners are dead or still at large, the Rogandans will be none the wiser. A bluff will be as effective as the truth." He shrugged. "We will only be exposed if they have recovered the prisoners themselves. That could only have happened if they swam as far as the island. And if they did so before the foreign ship left."

Unsettled and tentative, Bolnyk felt adrift in uncharted waters. Knowing his master despised passivity, he decided to risk an observation. "The captain seems to think they drowned."

The chief minister treated the comment with disdain. "Guesswork holds no interest for me," he said coldly. "I will send a ship to the island and find out."

"Would you like me to arrange it, Your Eminence?" He hoped he didn't sound like he was pleading.

Rheibas directed an indifferent gaze toward him. "That will not be necessary. I understand that Kahrlin is ready for an assignment. His operation to abduct the Arvenian queen was masterful. I'm sure he would be interested to know what's become of her."

21

Will hurried after a servant on his way to King Krasmir's reception room. In response to his request for an urgent meeting, the king had agreed to receive him immediately.

The king was waiting for him when he arrived.

He bowed hastily. "I have just received a dispatch, Your Majesty. It has taken a while to reach us." He ran an unsteady hand across his brow. "I hardly know how to say this. Queen Essanda has been abducted by Ahran agents!"

The king appeared thunderstruck. "How is that possible?"

"She had traveled to Castel on a goodwill visit. King Steffan made sure she was well protected on the journey. She was abducted from a small garden adjoining her rooms in the palace."

King Krasmir's eyes narrowed in anger. "The Grand Vizier had already planned this when he met with us. I see no other way to interpret his remarks about the queen."

Will nodded. "I agree. And there is more. The Ahrans attempted to abduct King Delmar in his own capital. He escaped only thanks to the quick thinking of one of his agents."

This latest report came as no surprise to the king. "I recently received a dispatch with similar information. I have doubled the guards around my palace as a result. And I have given orders that I should be informed immediately if strangers are seen anywhere in the vicinity of the palace."

Will dipped his head in acknowledgment. "I am faced with a difficult decision. Should I remain here, or return to Arvenon? The dispatch offered no guidance."

"I will understand, whatever you decide," the king told him. He shook his head grimly. "The Grand Vizier has achieved one useful thing at least. By presenting our kingdoms with a common enemy he has succeeded in mightily reinforcing the alliance between us."

THE FOLLOWING day Will made his way back to the king's conference room. He arrived to find the king engaged in animated conversation with Lord Kulferan and Lady Tulinay.

"Welcome, Lord Torbury. I am aware that you requested a meeting with me, but unless your matters are urgent, I will meet with you later. We have news to share with you."

If the look on the king's face offered any indication, the king's news was mixed. Will decided to speak out immediately.

"I have good news for a change, Your Majesty. It is quickly conveyed, and very appropriate for this audience. But I am more than willing to leave the timing to you."

"Please proceed, Lord Torbury. We could all use some good news."

"I received a dispatch today that supersedes yesterday's news. Queen Essanda has not been abducted at all! The Ahrans made off with an agent impersonating her. As you might imagine, this information is extremely sensitive. The Ahrans are not aware they have the wrong person, and for her sake it is important that we maintain the deception. King Steffan apologizes for sending misleading information. He was himself subjected to the same false report, to ensure that his initial shock and outrage were real."

The king nodded in satisfaction. "That is a great relief, Lord Torbury. It is gratifying to know that the Ahrans don't have it all their own way. Is there a reason why this agent allowed herself to be abducted?"

"It was not part of the plan. I know no more than that."

"It might yet work in our favor." The king nodded to Lord Kulferan. "Please update Lord Torbury with our news."

Lord Kulferan was happy to oblige. "I followed your suggestion, Lord Torbury, and ordered our warships to tail Ahran vessels. A small squadron of three ships under a captain known as Pultek managed to do exactly that. They followed a ship to an island. The island was being hastily evacuated, presumably in response to their arrival. They were unable to prevent the ship from escaping—Ahran archers managed to slow them down enough to allow the ship to slip past them."

"Where was this island?" asked Will.

"West of Varacellan. It lies north of Savage Strait, not far from Baron Island. A cluster of tiny islands surrounds it, so it isn't close to any shipping lanes."

"Do they know why the Ahrans were on the island?"

"One of the ships landed a couple of boatloads of soldiers. They searched the island thoroughly. The Ahrans left in a hurry, so they took very little with them. It isn't possible to be certain of anything, but from their description it could well have been the place where the captives were being held."

"Was anyone still on the island?"

"No one. It was completely abandoned."

Lady Tulinay shook her head in disgust. "They could be anywhere now."

At that moment a knock sounded on the door.

"Enter," called the king.

An aide stepped into the room and bowed. "A man wishes to see you, Your Majesty. He is most insistent. I told him you were busy. I am aware you have met with him before, but I did not assume you would want to make a priority of meeting him again. Especially since he has an Ahran with him."

"Who is this man?" demanded the king.

"He says his name is Kamash."

"And who is the Ahran?" asked Will.

"Supposedly his name is Gharpin."

Will stared back at him in astonishment. The others were no less surprised.

"Show them in immediately!" ordered the king. "Then find my Ahran interpreter and bring him here."

"Bisri Ahuzza?" asked Will.

The king did not hesitate. "Have Bisri Ahuzza brought to us as well! Hurry!"

After a quick bow, the aide scampered from the room.

Will was struggling to contain his excitement. Could it be possible? Was this the missing captain who sailed with the princess? The one who the Grand Vizier claimed was lost at sea?

Kamash and the Ahran were shown into the room before anything further could be said.

The old man bent low, the foreigner copying him.

"Welcome, Kamash. I did not expect to see you again," the king said candidly.

"Thank you, Your Majesty. I no more expected it than you."

"I understand you have been asking to meet with me."

Kamash nodded. "We arrived in Rog a couple of days ago, Your Majesty. I have been trying to get an audience with you since that time."

The king glowered at this news. "I am sorry to hear of the delay."

Kamash shrugged, apparently satisfied at having achieved his goal. "May I introduce my companion, Gharpin? He is Ahran. Our communication has been very limited, but I believe he captained an Ahran ship. He is certainly a skilled sailor. He also seems to have a connection to Princess Neira."

Gharpin bowed. "Your Majesty," he said. He spoke the words in Rogandan, with a heavy accent.

"You speak Rogandan?" asked the king in surprise.

"Little Rogandan," replied Gharpin, his lips drawing back in a smile. He pointed at Kamash. "He teach."

The king nodded. "I bid you welcome, Gharpin."

He turned his attention to Kamash. "While we are waiting for an interpreter, perhaps you can tell us your news."

Agreeing without hesitation, Kamash proceeded to outline all that had happened since he returned to his island. He gradually unveiled his meeting with the shipwrecked Ahran, the painstaking process of teaching him Rogandan, their departure for Rog, the storm that blew them to the west, their visit to the island.

"I am impressed with your determination to follow and find the Ahran ship," Lord Kulferan told him.

"I was very reluctant," Kamash told him honestly. "We did so only at Gharpin's insistence. He was suspicious about their reason for being in the area."

"With good reason, it seems," concluded the king. "Do you know what he saw and heard on the island?"

The old man shook his head. "I have been waiting eagerly for an opportunity to find that out. Along with many other things, of course. Gharpin's history in particular."

They did not need to wait much longer before the king's interpreter arrived, Bisri Ahuzza with him.

A new round of introductions was carried out. When the bisri heard the name of the other Ahran, his eyes went wide.

Once the formalities were concluded, the king addressed Gharpin.

"All of us are eager to hear what you have to say, Gharpin. Please speak freely."

Once his words were translated, the Ahran began without hesitation.

"Thank you, Your Majesty. Determined as I was to survive, a part of me doubted that my story would ever be heard. It is therefore both surprising and satisfying to be able to speak to you now. Above all, I want the emperor to know the truth. I would be grateful beyond words if you can help me find a way to speak to him."

"If you are truly committed to speaking the truth, I will do whatever is in my power to help you," King Krasmir assured him.

Gharpin bowed. "I was privileged to captain the vessel that bore Her Imperial Highness Princess Neira to this region." He scowled. "I regret to say that Rheibas, the Grand Vizier of the Empire of Ahr, was also aboard my ship."

If he was aware of the consternation that greeted his words, Will saw no sign of it.

All of them listened intently as he spoke of the abandonment of the princess, the return trip to Kat Ahket, and the sabotage carried out by Rheibas and his men. He made it clear that daring to challenge the Grand Vizier had led to him paying a heavy price along with his entire crew.

After being washed ashore barely alive, against the odds, he spoke of his amazement when Kamash arrived. He could scarcely believe it when he realized that Kamash had access to a sturdy little boat. When they set out for Rog, he had never been so happy. Then the Ahran ship appeared.

The questions multiplied when he began to relate his experiences on the island.

"What was their reason for being there?" asked the king.

"I hid as close to them as I dared. They were speaking Ahran, and I listened to them for hours. Their purpose for being there was to guard three royals—two women and one man. One of the women hadn't been there for long. They never mentioned their names. I only heard them use disparaging nicknames I won't mention."

"Who did these guards report to?" asked Lady Tulinay.

"A man called Shulkahr had been placed in charge on the island. I don't know who he reported to. But they understood themselves to be working for the Grand Vizier."

"Was the emperor aware of their mission?"

"Not as far as I could tell, although they believed they were working for the benefit of the empire." He snorted. "With Rheibas directing their efforts?" He shook his head in disbelief.

"What were they planning to do with the prisoners?"

"They didn't seem to know anything about such plans."

The captain shrugged. "Then Kamash arrived. Not long after that they discovered us, and we ran for the boat. We barely escaped with our lives."

King Krasmir had been listening intently to the translation. When the captain finished, he nodded gratefully to him. Then he shook his head with wonder. "Once more we find ourselves greatly indebted to you, Kamash!" he said. "My only regret is that the solitude you long for has been denied once more."

Kamash bowed in response.

With a moment's pause at last, Bisri Ahuzza took the opportunity to ask Gharpin a rapid-fire series of questions. After a brief but heroic attempt at translation, the interpreter accepted defeat. All of them watched patiently as the two men engaged in a spirited interaction.

When they finally came to an end, Bisri Ahuzza spoke briefly to the interpreter.

"He wants me to tell you that he believes Captain Gharpin's account," the interpreter told them. "He especially asked me to apologize to you, Lord Torbury."

Hearing Lord Torbury's name, the bisri bowed formally to Will.

"He says it would have been much simpler for him, and for everyone, if he had believed you from the beginning."

Will bowed in his turn. "Please convey my compliments to the bisri. I can only imagine how difficult it must be to discover he has been so deceived."

Catching the attention of the interpreter, Gharpin spoke rapidly to him.

"The captain wishes to know how you are proposing to contact the emperor."

"We need to be sensible," warned Lady Tulinay. "We can't just put the captain and the bisri on one of our ships and send them to Kat

Ahket. If they were intercepted, no one would benefit except the Grand Vizier."

Lord Kulferan nodded soberly. "I agree. The voyage is long and perilous. And apart from that, the design of Rogandan and Ahran ships is noticeably different. A Rogandan ship would become increasingly conspicuous the closer it came to Ahr-chitani. I could not guarantee their safety."

Captain Gharpin leaped to his feet when their words were translated. "We cannot sit here and do nothing!"

An animated conversation followed. After watching it silently for many minutes, Will decided to intervene.

"May I speak?"

King Krasmir seized upon the request. "By all means, Lord Torbury! You have the floor."

Will began at once. "I would like to offer a suggestion."

Every eye was upon him.

"The Grand Vizier's position gives him access to considerable resources, and he has not been sparing with those resources. He has been freely moving ships and men wherever he chooses, almost without hindrance. However, from what Bisri Ahuzza has told us about the emperor's attitude, it seems evident that the Grand Vizier is furthering his own interests rather than the cause of the Empire of Ahr. It isn't clear what those interests are. Even his closest associates might not be aware of exactly what he is trying to achieve."

With no immediate comment, Will continued. "We are faced with a number of pressing challenges. We need to limit the Grand Vizier's freedom of movement, we need to make the emperor aware of the true situation, and we need to do it quickly. So far we have seen Ahran agents rather than the emperor's soldiers. That is likely to change. Sooner or later the Grand Vizier will find a way to escalate tensions."

A number of heads nodded.

"Here is what I believe we should do..."

22

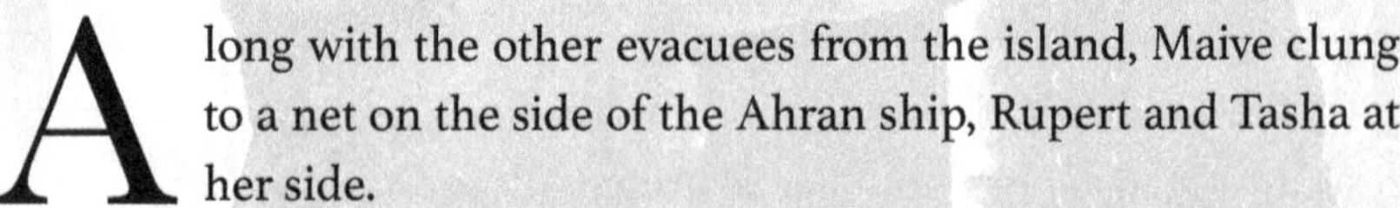

Along with the other evacuees from the island, Maive clung to a net on the side of the Ahran ship, Rupert and Tasha at her side.

Sudden hope sprang up within her as another vessel, most likely Rogandan, appeared unexpectedly, heading straight toward them.

The Ahrans hastily raised anchors, and the ship slowly began to pick up speed as it fled from the oncoming vessel. The Rogandans pulled level on the opposite side of the ship, apparently trying to cut off their escape.

No one was moving on the net above them. Given the stray arrows flying about, Maive well understood their hesitation. The leader of the guards was less sympathetic. Clearly annoyed, he climbed upward to prod them into action.

Maive turned to her companions. "This is our chance!" she hissed, jerking her head downward. "We have to go now!"

Rupert and Tasha peered uncertainly down at the water.

They apparently needed some encouragement. Launching herself away from the side of the ship, she hit the water hard. To her immense relief, she resurfaced to see Rupert and Tasha following her in. They submerged briefly, then their heads reappeared nearby.

Maive glanced up at the net, already some distance away. A couple of heads were turned in their direction.

So their escape had been noticed. Yet none of the guards had followed them into the water. She smiled grimly to herself. Sooner or later they would have reason to regret it.

Incredibly, the leader of the guards must still be distracted. Knowing that every moment was vital, Maive began swimming strongly toward the island. The others swam behind her. Her sole focus was to get as far away from the ship as possible before the leader realized they were missing.

The Rogandans would not have seen them when they jumped—the position of their ship prevented it. But a second vessel, presumably also Rogandan, had joined the chase. Seeing it heading right for them, they hastily swam to one side, waving and calling as it passed. All attention must have been fixed on the Ahran vessel ahead, because no one noticed them.

The leader of the guards must surely know they were missing by now. The ship was steadily receding into the distance, and Maive could see no sign of heads in the water behind them. But they could not afford to lessen their efforts.

She returned her attention to the island. Already she felt herself tiring, and it was so far away. Then to her amazement she spotted a new ship heading for the island.

The others had seen it too. "Could it be Rogandan?" asked Tasha.

Rupert was squinting toward it. "It doesn't look Ahran."

They watched as a longboat made its way to the beach and men spread out to search the island.

"Let's get closer," suggested Maive. "We'll stay out of sight if they're Ahrans."

Even the hint of a rescue was enough to drive them forward with renewed energy.

Many weary minutes dragged by before Rupert voiced her unspoken fear. "The island isn't getting any closer."

"I've been thinking the same thing," Tasha confessed.

Maive paused and began to tread water. "We must be in a current. I've swum in currents before. We need to swim to one side."

"But that won't get us to the beach," protested Tasha.

Maive shook her head. "No, it won't. But we don't have a choice. If we keep this up we'll wear ourselves out going nowhere."

The others nodded reluctantly. They began swimming along the shoreline instead of toward it, hoping to approach the island from the side.

At first Maive thought the strategy was working. The beach began to disappear from sight as they moved around the island. At the same time, though, she saw that the current was pulling them away from the land. In mockery of their best efforts, the island, and the ship anchored beside it, was steadily moving out of reach. Any hope of rescue was disappearing with it.

"I'm not sure how much longer I can keep this up." Tasha sounded weary and a little desperate.

Maive felt tired too, but she was determined not to give up. "Don't fight the current. Let it carry you for a couple of minutes. Just while we decide what to do."

She spun around in the water, eventually pointing in the opposite direction. "The current's taking us toward that little island. Maybe we can go ashore there." It was their best chance—maybe their only chance—of survival.

Rupert was squinting toward the island. "Won't the current just sweep us past it?"

"Not if we get out of it in time."

Tasha nodded. She seemed too weary to speak.

All talk ended as they refocused their energies on the new target.

Swimming with the current made a huge difference. The island drew closer surprisingly quickly. Reaching it wasn't straightforward though. Maive began heading out of the current sooner than the others. It was immediately apparent that she had made the right decision.

It was also clear that Tasha was in trouble.

"Rupert!" Maive pointed to Tasha, who was moving sluggishly at a time when she needed to put in extra energy.

Seeing what was happening, Rupert began calling encouragement to Tasha. "Swim to me!" he urged. When she didn't respond, he called, "I'm coming to you!"

Maive couldn't leave them to struggle alone. Striking out strongly toward Tasha, she reached her side not long after Rupert.

"Grab one of Rupert's ankles and one of mine, Tasha. We'll do some swimming for you."

Towing someone for more than a couple of minutes would have been challenging for Maive at any time. She was attempting it when almost spent, and Rupert was no better off. All three of them were flirting with disaster.

But Maive had underestimated Tasha's spirit. Rallying, the princess let go of their ankles. Propelling herself forward with new energy, she steered herself out of the current.

The island drew ever closer. Maive dared to believe they were going to make it. The last strokes felt almost out of reach, but she gritted her teeth and pushed on. Then her kicking feet brushed against a rock.

No sandy beach awaited them. Embracing the only available option, they dragged themselves out of the sea onto some rocks. Somehow they had survived. They were free.

For many minutes they lay exhausted, too weary to celebrate. Maive was the first to stir. Getting to her feet, she looked around, assessing their situation. Their new refuge appeared to be small and covered with trees.

Peering back in the direction they had come, she saw the other island. It seemed such a short distance away. She almost felt like she could reach out and touch it.

As she watched, a ship detached itself from the land. In the vastness of the ocean it seemed so close to them—heartbreakingly so. She stood helplessly as it sailed slowly away, heading in the direction the other ships had taken.

"I suppose they had no reason to stay."

It was Rupert who had spoken. Swiveling her head, she saw he had positioned himself beside her.

"No," she replied. "They waited longer than I expected."

"At least we're alive. We have you to thank for that. And for our freedom."

She shrugged. "Freedom isn't going to mean much if we're stranded here."

Tasha joined them. "I'm thirsty. Do you think there's fresh water on this island?"

"We might be lucky," Maive replied. "Let's do some exploring."

They set off together, heading for the trees.

To her relief, the island boasted at least one spring, and it didn't take long to find it. Scooping the crystal clear liquid into their cupped hands, they sipped it cautiously. Then, delighted at its freshness, they eagerly slaked their thirst.

"Food is going to be more of a challenge," said Rupert.

Maive nodded. "There might be seabird eggs among the rocks. But we'll need a lot more than that to keep us alive."

"There are plenty of fish in the sea of course," said Tasha. "I've caught fish before. But never with my bare hands." She glanced at them self-consciously.

Rupert shrugged. "I haven't either." He glanced around at the trees. "The guards left plenty of supplies on the island. We can't swim there, but could we build a raft? If we had some kind of sail, the current shouldn't be an issue."

"I'm not sure how we could build a raft without any tools. We don't even have a knife."

Tasha was staring out to sea. "What's that?" she asked, pointing into the water just offshore.

All of them stared in the direction she was indicating. At first Maive saw nothing, then she spotted something bobbing in the water. Was it a seal?

"It's a head!" said Rupert.

She narrowed her eyes, peering intently. "You're right!" she exclaimed in surprise.

"Is it one of the guards?" asked Tasha anxiously.

Rupert's face had gone hard. "If it is, he deserves to drown."

"We can't just leave him to die," Tasha protested.

"What do you want to do?" asked Maive.

Rupert released a heavy sigh. "I suppose we should at least try to rescue him."

He made to head back to the water, but Maive forestalled him.

"I'll do it. Agents are trained for situations like this."

Leaving the trees, she headed back across the rocks and eased herself into the water.

Rupert and Tasha stood watching from the water's edge.

"Tell me if I'm going in the wrong direction," she shouted. Then, calling upon her weary limbs to make a new effort, she headed out to sea.

Outward progress wasn't hard to achieve. But she knew once she was caught in the current, it would be extremely difficult to break free. She could never have achieved her purpose if the unknown swimmer hadn't been carried almost to her.

She realized as she reached him that it was the leader of the guards. He was nearly done for. Hope rose in his eyes when he realized someone was coming for him. The hope immediately died away when he saw who it was.

It would have been so easy to leave him to the ocean. After the way he had treated his captives, his end would have been fitting.

Ignoring her uncertainties, she approached him from behind. "Don't fight me," she said, only just remembering to limit herself to Arvenian. "I'm here to help."

He was too far gone to struggle. Grasping hold of him around his chest as she had been taught, she began kicking her legs vigorously, desperate to break free of the current once more. There would be no hope for either of them if they were swept past the island.

Just when she began to think all was lost, the rocks drew within reach at last. With the final residue of her failing strength, she propelled them to safety. Hands reached down and pulled them from the water.

While clutching the guard tightly to herself, she had noticed a dagger in his belt. The guard now lay prostrate on the ground, too weak to move. Retrieving it, she handed it to Rupert.

"Keep this safe," she told him, before whispering, "Remember that I'm supposed to speak only Arvenian."

Nodding, he secured the knife in his belt. Then he leaned toward Tasha, passing on the message to her as well.

Between them, Rupert and Tasha dragged the guard away from the rocks and into a clearing among the trees. She followed on wobbly legs.

Stretching him out on the ground, they sat on a fallen log nearby to watch him.

They could manage without her. With a sigh of relief, she permitted herself to collapse on the ground.

MAIVE WOKE to find stars twinkling above her. She sat up and looked around.

The guard she had rescued was lying nearby. He hadn't moved, and he appeared to still be asleep.

Rupert had managed to light a fire, presumably using the knife. He had positioned himself not far from the guard, and he was keeping a watchful eye on him. Tasha was resting on the opposite side of the fire.

Feeling surprisingly refreshed after such a short rest, Maive got up. As she moved closer to the fire to examine the guard, she caught him snapping his eyelids shut.

She laughed scornfully. "Everything has changed," she told him frankly. "The sooner you accept that the better." She spoke in Arvenian, confident he understood the language. "King Rupert now has your knife. He's a trained fighter, and he's in the best condition of any of us. I wouldn't suggest testing him."

Giving up the pretense, the guard opened his eyes. He didn't try to get up.

She crossed her arms and stared down at him. "We haven't been introduced. My name is Essanda. You may call me 'Your Majesty.'"

He studied her quietly for a few moments. "I am Shulkahr. Why did you save me?"

Her lip curled in an ironic grin. "During my brief time as your guest, you won me over with your charm and your generous spirit." Then she willed her face to relax. "Not all of us show the same contempt for human life and dignity as you Ahrans."

He glared back at her. "I am what I am. Not all of us have been born to a life of ease and privilege."

She shrugged. "I am no stranger to hardship."

"I know all about you. And I am well aware of your history. You were betrayed and attacked by your own countrymen. Men in the pay of the king of Rogand, whose armies invaded your kingdom."

When she did not respond, he added, "Ahrans do not seem to have a monopoly on contempt for human life and dignity." He shook his head in scorn. "How quickly you have forgotten. These same Rogandans are now your treasured allies."

"It is true that human nature is not determined by our place of birth," she acknowledged. "Our values and priorities are shaped first by our parents and our community. But our leaders have great influence—for good or for ill. The previous king of Rogand proved that, as you said. His successor has indeed become our ally—because he has chosen a different path." She eyed him calmly. "Perhaps the Empire of Ahr is not so fortunate in its leaders."

"The empire might seem unfortunate if you value weakness," he sneered.

"So I should have left you to drown?" she asked.

He went silent. "I owe you my life," he admitted reluctantly. "I do not forget my debts."

It was a concession of sorts. But she was no fool. She harbored no illusions about how much they could expect from him.

One last thing needed to be said. "Some believe that cruelty demonstrates strength, and mercy exposes weakness. But things aren't always as they appear. Cruelty is the first refuge of the insecure. True strength deals out mercy as freely as judgment."

She didn't wait around for him to disagree.

23

Shulkahr's rescue had shaken him almost as much as the ordeal that prompted it. He was alive, but at what cost? Not only had the roles been reversed, he now found himself indebted to a former captive. The humiliation was unbearable.

The island had been far away when he went into the water. Nevertheless, believing himself to be a strong swimmer, he expected that with perseverance he would reach the island. The Rogandan ship anchored off the beach would present a problem, but he decided to face that when the time came.

His confidence proved to be wildly misplaced and his best attempts futile. Swept helplessly away by the current, he had abandoned hope before the Arvenian queen appeared and towed him to shore. Without her he would have drowned. He owed his life to a captive, and a foreign queen at that. It was mortifying.

As if that wasn't enough, while lying exhausted beside the fire he had overheard another of his former captives, King Rupert, talking to the princess.

"You've been sitting there so long!" the king had said. "You should take a break."

"He might need my help," she replied simply.

"He doesn't deserve it," the king had growled.

"No, he doesn't. But if we treat him the way he treated us, how are we any better?"

He didn't respond, and after a moment she added, "What's troubling you, Rupert?"

"You mean apart from the fact that we're stranded on a tiny island with no food and no prospect of rescue?"

She laughed, a cheerful sound that seemed incongruous in light of their situation. "We've made it this far."

"And we've done it together," he replied. The angst was gone from his voice. He sounded almost content.

The king must have moved away, because their conversation did not continue.

Shulkahr was left restless and unsettled. Something about the princess's laugh evoked memories of his childhood, of carefree times before his mother's untimely death soured his life. A forgotten ache gnawed at him, seeking release. Unwilling to allow it to surface, he shoved it back down, determined to push it away.

As he lay wrestling with his thoughts, the unsavory truth about his current condition slowly penetrated his defenses. The princess had been watching at his side solely because she was concerned about him.

The situation was unendurable. Being beholden to one person was more than he could stomach. He refused to be further obligated to these people.

He could see only one way forward. For the moment he would work with them. Stranded on a tiny island as they were, any pooling of resources would benefit them all. After that he would consider any debt repaid.

Cooperating did not mean he would soften his attitude toward them. As soon as an opportunity arose, he would reverse the roles again. Next time it would be final.

THE HIGHER UP THE tree Shulkahr climbed, the more it began to sway. As it started to bend, he tied a vine to it and threw the other end to the ground. Rupert grabbed it and pulled tight. Shulkahr then began bouncing up and down vigorously. Before long the tree began to creak ominously.

"That's enough!" shouted Rupert. "It's about to break!"

His warning came too late. With an almighty crack, the trunk of the tree split. Shulkahr rode it to the ground, tumbling off as he landed.

Both Rupert and Essanda hurried over, staring down at him in alarm.

Shulkahr lay stunned for a moment. After carefully testing each of his limbs, he announced, "I don't seem to have broken anything."

"Your dedication is admirable," Rupert told him. "But there's no need to kill yourself."

The former guard slowly clambered to his feet. Although he would never have admitted it, he couldn't remember when he'd last enjoyed himself so much.

He'd allowed himself to go to seed on the island. Leading a group of guards had not played to his strengths. He much preferred hands-on pursuits—the higher the energy the better.

The arrival of the princess cut across his thoughts. She'd been gone for some time, foraging for anything safe to eat.

A few small eggs lay in her hands. "Food is served," she announced brightly.

Borrowing the knife from Rupert, Essanda took one of the eggs and poked a small hole in each end. Then she lifted the egg to her mouth and sucked out its contents. Poking holes in one egg at a time, she handed them around.

"I only found eleven," Tasha said ruefully.

"Don't worry," Essanda told her as she handed Tasha the last of the eggs. "I'm satisfied with two. All of you have been working harder than me anyway."

Rupert and Tasha protested, but Shulkahr remained silent. He saw no reason to complain as long as he wasn't the one missing out. Nevertheless, the irony of the situation was not lost on him. His former prisoners were freely sharing what little they had with him. In spite of his harshness toward them, they were treating him as an equal.

It was hard to believe they were all royal. They seemed so normal, quite unlike any royals he had ever heard of. He'd never met Her Imperial Highness Princess Neira, but from everything he knew of her, she differed from these three in almost every possible way. The idea that commoners could warm to their sovereigns had never occurred to him. Yet it wouldn't surprise him to hear that the subjects of these royals both loved and admired them.

He frowned, shaking his head. Maybe he was getting soft.

"Time to get back to work," Rupert said to Shulkahr.

He nodded absently, following the youthful king back to where they had been building the raft. After gathering a collection of tree trunks, they were binding them together as best they could with vines. Tasha and Essanda were weaving palm fronds together to make a crude sail.

The biggest challenge would be the mast. They had acquired a suitable tree trunk. None of them were quite sure how to secure it to the raft.

He glanced across at Essanda, hard at work on the sail. She might be slender, but she was tough. He remembered the confident ease with which she towed him to the island. She must have already been exhausted, but she found the strength to do it.

Nothing about her was what he would have expected from a queen, much less the mother of three children. Something about her didn't add up, although he couldn't identify it.

He frowned in bemusement, trying to make sense of it.

Rupert's voice cut across his thoughts. "I think I know how we might secure the mast."

He looked up to see the king lashing a long branch to one corner of the raft using vines. Then he secured the other end to the mast, most of the way to the top.

"That might work," agreed Shulkahr.

The two of them repeated the exercise until the mast was supported on four sides.

"It only has to stay upright long enough for us to reach the island," Rupert observed.

Shulkahr held up a makeshift tiller. "We can use this to steer the raft. It shouldn't be hard to attach it."

"How is the sail?" asked Rupert.

"As good as it's likely to get," Essanda replied. She didn't look overly confident, but after looking at it closely, Shulkahr doubted he could have done any better.

Rupert eyed the weather. "The conditions look good, but the sun will be setting soon. Should we chance it now, or leave it until the morning?"

"We leave in the morning," asserted Shulkahr. "And that's final!"

Rupert stared at him. "Thank you for your *opinion*, Shulkahr," he said pointedly. He turned to the others. "What do you think?"

"I'm hungry," said Tasha wistfully.

"I am too," agreed Essanda. "But it might be wise to wait until daylight. What do you think, Rupert?"

The king shrugged. "I'm of two minds. I'm looking forward to eating a proper meal, but I'm also weary. I suspect I'll be better prepared in the morning."

"Very well," said Tasha with a sigh. "If the rest of you can wait, I can too."

ALL FOUR OF them stood glumly at the water's edge, staring at the other island. The sun had barely risen, but they didn't need its light to tell them they should have set out the previous day.

The strong wind that sprang up in the night had whipped the waves into a frenzy. They didn't have far to go, but in these conditions it would be dangerous folly to attempt any kind of journey on their makeshift raft.

Shulkahr knew he was being irrational, but he felt annoyed. "It shouldn't have taken a whole day to build the raft," he spat. "It was just my luck to be stranded with royal incompetents."

The others glanced in his direction, but none of them chose to bite. That made him angrier.

He raised his hands heavenward. "Without me and my knife you'd be stranded here. I should have left you to starve!"

Rupert's face had gone hard. "No one forced you to jump in after us."

"If you'd had the sense to stay on the ship I wouldn't have needed to."

Stepping forward, the king planted himself in front of Shulkahr, glaring at him coldly. "Wherever this island is located, it's well within the territorial waters of Castel. You're in my kingdom now! You've given me more than enough reason to execute you. As king, it's my right and privilege. Don't push your luck."

Shulkahr snorted. The fool had just admitted he was soft.

He'd heard more than enough. A sneer on his lips, he brought up both arms and lunged forward suddenly with all his strength.

He wasn't nearly fast enough. Twisting lightly aside, the king thrust out a leg, using Shulkahr's momentum against him.

The Ahran crashed to the ground. Before he could blink, a foot landed heavily on his neck, pinning him helplessly.

The foot ground his face into the dirt. "Give me one reason why I shouldn't kill you."

With his life on the line, Shulkahr realized he'd seriously misjudged this man. He'd mistaken restraint for weakness. He wouldn't do it again.

It was his turn to exercise restraint. His opportunity would come if he was patient.

Forcing his body to relax, he quit struggling. "No reason," he sputtered, barely able to speak with his face in the dirt.

Abruptly the foot was gone. Rupert stood back and let him get up.

He clambered to his feet, his face burning red.

The queen mistook his blush for anger. She stared at him with narrowed eyes. "Next time, if he doesn't kill you, I will."

He stared back at her. She meant it, and he didn't doubt she would follow through on her threat.

His brows furrowed. Something about her wasn't right—he was sure of it.

"Do you doubt me?" she growled.

He hastily broke eye contact, shifting his gaze to the ground. She soon moved away, ignoring him completely.

The rest of the day passed miserably for all of them. Fresh water was plentiful, but they had nothing to eat. And the hours wore away with no sign of the weather improving.

All of them were avoiding Shulkahr now. Improbable as it might have seemed, he had established a fragile bond with his former captives. That bond had been shattered.

He told himself only a fool would care what a group of captives thought.

They lay down around a fire that night, but Shulkahr couldn't settle. He had the impression that none of the others were sleeping any better than he did.

As the hours dragged on, he tried to make sense of his inner churning. He knew the others saw him as behaving badly. What he couldn't understand was why that bothered him. He concluded that he was being weak. It had been folly to allow circumstances to influence his thinking and behavior. For a brief time he had treated them as if they mattered. His fellow agents would mock him unmercifully if they knew. And he deserved it. He didn't allow himself to think about what Bolnyk would have to say.

He managed to get some sleep in the end. It wasn't restful.

In the morning the wind had eased, but the waves remained choppy. Noon came and went with only a minor improvement in the conditions. All of them were becoming impatient.

The king chose a moment when they were all together. "Are you willing to risk it?"

The princess and the queen both nodded.

He turned to Shulkahr. "Are you coming?"

A sharp retort rose to his tongue, but he bit it back. He nodded. “I’ll take the risk.”

The four of them carried the raft to the water’s edge and put it in. The princess held it while the queen retrieved the sail. Shulkahr attached the rudder. Then they climbed aboard.

Raising the sail was a tense moment, but it held together as the wind caught it. The raft rocked alarmingly, and they hastily sat down to improve its stability. Shulkahr had taken the rudder, and he steered in the general direction of the other island.

The further they ventured into open water, the heavier the swell became. A bigger than usual wave rolled toward them, and Shulkahr swung the rudder desperately, trying to steer into it. He was only partly successful. Smashing into the raft side on, the wave twisted it violently, almost swamping them. One of the four supports holding up the mast broke free, but the others held. The mast was now leaning to one side, but the sail continued to catch the wind. Somehow the logs were holding together.

“I’m not sure how many more like that we can survive,” said the king grimly.

No one else spoke.

Shulkahr peered ahead intently, trying to anticipate the next threat. He didn’t have long to wait.

It came in the form of a series of three huge waves, rolling inexorably toward them. This time he managed to swing the raft around before they arrived. The flimsy craft rose, creaking and groaning as the first wave swept beneath them. Then the second reached them. Tilting ominously, the raft twisted enough to leave it exposed to the full force of the third wave.

A giant wall of water smashed into the fragile platform. The vines that bound it together were torn loose, allowing several logs to separate from the rest of the raft. Two of the remaining mast supports broke free, bringing the mast crashing down. The sail fell onto the princess, almost launching her into the water. The impact broke the sail apart. Pieces of it began drifting away with the tide.

Huddled with the other passengers on what remained of the raft,

Shulkahr stared longingly toward their goal. The island seemed so close. But it was beyond their reach.

Then the queen picked up a piece of the sail, and held it aloft. The king quickly followed her lead. The princess grabbed a third piece before it floated out of reach. All three of them knelt on the raft, using their bodies as masts.

Somehow the rudder had remained connected. Positioning himself beside it, Shulkahr fought the elements to steer them in the right direction. Slowly, sluggishly, the raft responded.

No further giant waves appeared to assault them. It was as if the ocean, having pummeled the little craft almost to oblivion, had lost interest in them.

Incredibly, the island drew closer. Shulkahr hardly dared to breathe. He had the sense to hold his course until they had passed the little beach. Then he turned toward the island.

The change of direction proved too much for the crippled vessel. Struck by a larger than usual wave as it came around, it broke apart.

Nevertheless, the raft had carried them most of the way. The vines binding it together had done their job for long enough. Pitched into the water, the fugitives struck out for the beach, swimming with the tide.

Shulkahr emerged as the laggard. By the time he pulled himself from the water, the others were already wandering among the pile of supplies abandoned beside the beach, searching for food.

The princess called out in excitement. "Over here! I've found some bread."

He arrived in time to hear the queen's response. "Well done, Tasha! I'm so hungry I don't care how stale it is." Both of them were biting hungrily into the food.

His eyes went wide. The conversation had been in Rogandan. Yet he had been reliably informed that the Arvenian queen spoke her own language, and nothing more.

It all came together in a rush. He'd known something wasn't right about her, but he hadn't been able to put the pieces together. Now the truth had been laid bare. Whoever she was, she wasn't Queen Essanda. She'd been masquerading the whole time.

The operation to abduct the Arvenian queen had been masterminded by Kahrlin. He'd captured an impostor. The arrogant fool thought he was so clever. He'd be in for a very big surprise.

The fake queen was staring at him. From the look on her face, she knew she'd been exposed.

"Was it my eyes?" she asked.

He looked at her blankly. "What about your eyes?"

She didn't enlighten him.

"If you're asking what gave you away, it started with your heroic rescue." His lip curled into a sneer. "You were far too strong and too clever for your own good. You should have left me to drown."

The other two had ceased their search and joined them.

"He knows." The impostor sounded tired.

The king frowned. "What are we going to do with him?"

The princess was staring out to sea. "I think we might have bigger things to worry about."

Shulkahr followed her gaze. A ship was gliding around the edge of the island. He saw at a glance that it was Ahran.

The mock queen grabbed the arm of the king. "Is there anywhere we can hide?"

Shulkahr snorted. "Save your energy. This island was chosen for a reason."

A boat was lowered from the ship and set out for the shore. All four of them stood watching as if mesmerized.

As it approached the beach, Shulkahr saw a face he recognized. The man poised in the prow of the boat was Kahrlin.

24

Commodore Pultek stood at the helm as the Princess Teylee plowed through another wave. He smiled in satisfaction at the creaking of the ship's timbers. It was good to be back at sea.

The ship that interrupted the Ahran evacuation of the island was now a memory. Frustrating as that engagement had been, his energy and initiative had gained him favorable attention from Lord Kulferan. As a reward, he had been promoted and given command of a newly commissioned ship, named for the missing princess.

The Princess Teylee was one of a kind. Sporting three masts, she was the fastest ship in the Rogandan navy. And Lord Kulferan had sent the Princess off laden with a full complement of fighting men. Pultek was itching to put the Ahrans to the test. He had no doubt that the outcome would be very different next time.

Commodore Pultek's squadron had also grown as a result of his promotion. Five ships now sailed under his command. It was true that the other four were older and less nimble than his flagship, but they would play their part.

A great deal of responsibility had been placed on his shoulders, and he was more than ready to embrace it. His squadron would no longer search for the princess. The hunt would continue, but that task had been assigned to other ships. He had been given a new strategy.

Sailing conditions were ideal—fine weather coupled with steady winds. Having sent his orders to the other captains in his squadron, Pultek set off in search of his quarry.

Steering north of Rog, he continued until he was well clear of the islands that dotted the ocean near the mainland. Then he turned west, heading toward Varas, and Castel beyond it. He had positioned two ships on either side of the Princess and instructed their captains to hold a steady course. Between them, the ships now covered a broad sweep of ocean. If any of them sighted an Ahran vessel, they would signal the nearest vessel, which would in turn notify the Princess. Pultek intended to waste no time before pursuing any ship unlucky enough to come in sight.

Nothing was predictable at sea. Conditions could change in a moment, and only the unexpected was inevitable. Nevertheless, on this occasion fate seemed determined to smile upon the commodore and his newly commissioned flagship.

Having cleared the islands and turned west, they sailed for only a few hours before the lookout called, "A signal, Cap'n!"

None of the men had adopted his new title, but Pultek didn't care.

The signalman relayed the message. "A ship sighted to the northwest, Cap'n."

"Is it Ahran?"

"No indication yet."

"West by northwest!" Pultek ordered the helmsman. "Steer a course to intercept them."

"Set full sail!" he bellowed.

Sailors immediately scrambled aloft.

Pultek grunted with satisfaction as the Princess responded. He had never experienced such speed and responsiveness.

"Sail ahead!"

The call from the lookout came much sooner than he expected.

"How many masts?"

"Three, Cap'n!"

He turned to the bosun. "Get the soldiers onto the deck! Make sure the archers are ready for action!"

By the time everyone was positioned, the sails could be clearly seen from the helm.

"Are they changing course?" he shouted to the lookout.

"No, Cap'n."

Pultek smirked at his helmsman. "They think we're Ahrans. They're not used to being chased by ships with three masts." He stared at his quarry. "Everything is about to change," he promised.

They were upon the other ship before the Ahrans realized anything was wrong. By the time sailors scurried into the rigging to set more sail, it was too late.

The commander of the soldiers had positioned himself beside Pultek.

"Tell me as soon as we're in arrow range," Pultek ordered.

The commander nodded, but no advice was necessary. The Ahrans hadn't waited to get into range to begin firing at the Princess. As soon as shafts were whizzing over the deck, Pultek gave the order.

"Target the men in the rigging!" he ordered.

A volley of arrows shot upward, and sailors crashed to the deck.

Pultek watched in grim satisfaction. "I learned that trick from you," he growled.

"Bring her alongside!" he ordered the helmsman.

"It's your job now," he told the soldier.

Hurrying down to the deck, the commander shouted orders to his men. As soon as the two ships were close enough, grappling hooks were thrown onto the other vessel. Ahran sailors retrieved axes and began hacking desperately at the ropes. But archers targeted them mercilessly, and more grappling hooks were thrown for every one they severed.

Soldiers were soon leaping across the gap onto the Ahran ship. As hand-to-hand fighting raged across the deck, men began assaulting the forecastle.

Taken by surprise and heavily outnumbered, the Ahran

defenders found that bravery was not enough. The Ahran captain had no choice but to surrender.

The commander reported back to Pultek. "The ship is yours, Commodore! My men have disarmed the survivors and have them under guard. No Ahrans remain below decks."

"Your casualties?"

"Relatively light, I am pleased to say."

"Well done, Commander. What is their cargo?"

"Supplies, mostly."

"Any clues as to their intentions?"

"Their captain tried to destroy his papers, but my men prevented him from completing the task. Unfortunately his orders are written in the Ahran language. I have no one who can translate them."

"They will be sent to Rog. Your men performed admirably today, Commander. Please convey my compliments to them."

The papers seized from the Ahran captain, along with the captured sailors and agents, were transferred by Pultek to the slowest of his ships, along with a strong contingent of guards. A skeleton crew took over the vessel and set a course for Rog.

As previously directed by Lord Kulferan, Pultek renamed the captured Ahran vessel the King Rupert. He transferred to it the remainder of the crew from the ship now on its way to Rog. Their numbers were bolstered with sailors from the other vessels in his squadron, along with soldiers drawn from all of his ships.

Communicating effectively while transferring personnel at sea proved challenging. However the seas remained calm, and his men performed admirably.

With the transfers almost complete, Pultek arranged for the most capable of his captains to join him. "Captain Bezai, I'm placing you in command of the King Rupert. I am sure you will work tirelessly to deliver on my expectations."

Captain Bezai made no effort to hide his delight, and he wasted no time in transferring to his new vessel.

As the afternoon wore on, Pultek had begun to wonder if urgent matters requiring his attention would never end. With the tasks finally behind him, he had every reason to be satisfied.

His flagship had performed magnificently. As he cast his eyes across the ships clustered around him, his gaze lingered on the newest addition to his squadron. The captain and the men he placed on the captured ship had more than fulfilled his expectations, and they well deserved a vessel better suited to their skills.

The three remaining crews were now dissatisfied and grumbling. Their complaints didn't bother Pultek at all. That day's efforts were only the beginning.

Signaling his orders to the squadron, he led the ships on a course westward, the new three-master close by on his starboard side. From now on the Princess Teylee and the King Rupert would be hunting together.

PULTEK LED his squadron as far as Baron Island without encountering another Ahran vessel. At that point he could have sailed south toward Maranelle after either rounding Baron Island or traversing Savage Strait. He chose instead to bring his ships about and head back toward the east.

Winds were light, and progress slow. In the afternoon of their second day, a lookout on the King Rupert signaled the Princess Teylee. Positioning the Princess near the other vessel, he invited Captain Bezai to join him. A boat was duly launched, and the captain came aboard.

"Welcome, Captain," Pultek told him, leading him to his cabin. "I am eager to hear your news."

The captain bowed. "Thank you, Commodore. About an hour ago we came upon a fishing boat. As soon as they were certain we were not Ahrans, they made obvious efforts to catch our attention. We sent a boat to investigate, and they told us they had chanced upon two Ahran ships anchored off an island beside their fishing grounds. They wanted us to send the Ahrans away."

Pultek's eyebrows rose. "I wonder what they're up to on the island."

"Could they be holding the princess there?"

"It doesn't seem likely. I'm guessing they would search for a location well away from prying eyes." Pultek paused for a moment, musing. "Did the fishermen say how many masts these ships had?"

"Three, Commodore. They were very definite about that."

Pultek grinned. "This might be just the opportunity we've been searching for. If it ends well, Captain, a couple of your disgruntled fellow captains might find themselves with a three-master of their own."

THE ROGANDAN ARMY commander called a quiet command, and eight longboats from the Princess Teylee and the King Rupert glided silently through the moderate swell, heading for two tall ships sitting at anchor off a small island. A bonfire twinkled on the beach, faintly illuminating a number of dark shapes clustered around it.

The army commander watched tensely from the forecastle of one of the smaller Rogandan ships in Pultek's squadron.

He noted with satisfaction that the moon had not yet risen. The conditions perfectly suited the soldiers crammed into the boats even now approaching their targets.

Abruptly the boats separated, four moving alongside each of the vessels. It was too dark to see the action, but the commander could imagine grappling hooks flying high into the air, dull thunks sounding as they gripped the side of the ship. He knew that men would already be shimmying up the ropes.

Sentries must have been posted, because loud shouts of warning were soon echoing across the water.

Lanterns threw light onto the deck of each ship. On the ship anchored furthest from the island, he saw armed Ahran sailors reaching the side of the ship just as the first attackers climbed onto the deck. Shouting ferociously, the two groups assaulted their enemies. The deck quickly degenerated into a confused mass of men struggling back and forth. He could see more defenders emerging from the hatch with every minute that passed, but in the chaos they seemed to be having difficulty reaching the ship's side quickly enough to stem the tide of Rogandans climbing aboard. He had the clear impression that most of the attackers had reached the deck and joined the fight.

The Ahran sailors showed they were not frightened of combat, and they fought with reckless bravery. He knew that Rheibas's agents would be battling beside them. By reputation the agents were self-reliant, and many of them boasted unusual fighting skills.

But he had confidence in the Rogandan soldiers facing the Ahrans. They were experienced fighters, handpicked for this assignment.

As the fighting intensified, he sensed that the discipline of the soldiers was beginning to have an impact. He didn't doubt the courage of the Ahran crew, but they were sailors, not soldiers.

As for the Ahran agents, they were almost certainly too few in number to decide the outcome. And in spite of their prowess, they were accustomed to relying on themselves. His men had been trained to fight as a company.

It quickly became evident that on the other ship the assault was not going so well. Only a few attackers made it onto the deck before the defenders reached the ship's side. Ahran sailors hacked through some of the ropes attached to grappling hooks. Men were sent plunging into the sea, and in one case, directly onto a longboat still disgorging soldiers. The longboat capsized, pitching its occupants into the water.

The Rogandans on the deck fought ferociously to protect a space for others to clamber up behind them. They achieved their goal at the cost of their lives.

The attackers had gained a precarious foothold. Greatly outnumbered and under constant pressure, they ran the risk of being overwhelmed at any moment.

The commander had not failed to notice that additional pressure was about to be applied from a different direction.

As soon as the alarm sounded, the men on shore had left their bonfire and hurried to their longboats. They rowed frantically toward the nearest ship where the Rogandans were hanging on by a thread.

The army commander had been holding in reserve four longboats from the other ships in the squadron, all of them loaded with soldiers. He now ordered them forward urgently.

The longboats from the island were racing toward the Rogandan boats still sending men aloft. Most likely the Ahrans did not carry grappling hooks as a matter of course in their longboats. With no way of climbing aloft themselves, they must have decided to disrupt the flow of attackers onto the deck. Eventually they might be able to use the attackers' ropes to climb to the deck themselves.

Two of the Rogandan reserve longboats arrived at the same time as the Ahrans. The resulting melee was so chaotic the commander could not determine who was winning.

The other two longboats held in reserve rowed to the other side of the Ahran ship. The commander lost sight of them once they rounded the stern, but he knew they would climb aboard and attack the defenders from behind. He could only wait impatiently for the first of them to appear.

At that moment he saw that his men had taken control of the first ship. A few Ahran defenders had been rounded up and disarmed. They now sat on the deck under heavy guard.

As he watched, men descended the ropes to one of the longboats below. Rowing hastily to the ship that was still in dispute, they too disappeared from sight as they rounded the stern.

His reserves appeared to have prevented the Ahrans from the island from reinforcing the defenders. It was impossible to know exactly what was happening, but a lot of men seemed to be in the water.

He saw at last Rogandans soldiers clambering onto the deck from the far side. By the time the defenders moved to respond, the new arrivals had established a foothold.

With the defenders surrounded and under pressure from both sides, the initiative began to tilt in favor of the attackers. Before another thirty minutes had passed, the second ship was also firmly under the control of the commander's soldiers. The Ahrans had all been killed or captured.

"Notify Commodore Pultek that the Ahran ships are his," the commander ordered.

PERHAPS IT SHOULD HAVE BEEN SIMPLER the second time, but taking command of two captured vessels in the dark complicated Pultek's task enormously. His first action was to spread the surviving Ahrans across two of his older ships. Both ships set off for Rog well before dawn, manned by skeleton crews supported by soldiers. Men wounded in the recent battle returned with them.

With three of his original ships now on their way to Rog, Pultek was well short of the required complement both of sailors and of soldiers. Three-masted ships carried more crew, and his command now included four of the vessels. It was becoming increasingly obvious that he could not continue his operation without correcting these shortfalls.

In the meantime, his men desperately needed to rest. After ensuring that every ship was well defended, he ordered his captains to lower anchors and wait for the dawn.

As soon as the sun rose, the whole squadron set sail for Rog.

Pultek had managed barely two hours of sleep. Bone-weary as he was, he was nevertheless ecstatic. He had been tasked with disrupting the Grand Vizier's activities by capturing or disabling his ships, and within days he had succeeded in doing precisely that. His squadron must surely have dealt a significant blow to the Ahran operation. He could only guess at the bemusement of the Grand Vizier when he learned that three of his vessels had simply vanished.

Best of all, the Rogandan navy had received an important boost. Having set out with a single three-master, Pultek was returning with four.

He couldn't wait to see the expression on Lord Kulferan's face.

25

As Kahrlin's longboat approached the beach, the impostor leaned toward the Castelan king. "Give me the knife," she urged.

The king handed it to her without hesitation, and she hid it beneath her clothing.

Shulkahr scowled at the woman. Her short-lived masquerade was coming to an end. Captives didn't carry knives. And the knife belonged to him anyway.

He would disarm her the moment Kahrlin's men landed.

She must have read his thoughts, because she murmured, "You owe me this much, at least."

A wave of irritation rose in him at the reminder of his debt. Nevertheless, he would not allow her to keep the knife. The situation had changed, and she was a fool if she couldn't see that.

The longboat slid onto the sand, and Kahrlin leaped out. The gloating look on the agent's face made Shulkahr sick to his stomach.

Abruptly changing his mind about the knife, he decided to let the situation play out. For the moment, the woman could keep it. Perhaps she might do him a favor and dispose of Kahrlin.

The self-satisfied fool was smirking at him. "You can relax now,

Shulkahr. A competent agent has finally arrived." He waved lazily toward the other three. "Seize them! Tie their hands and get them into the boat."

Stung by Kahrlin's contempt, Shulkahr opened his mouth to deliver his own barb. Then, on the brink of exposing the impostor, he realized that to do so at that moment would play into Kahrlin's hands. He needed to choose his timing. Kahrlin would be the one reporting on the mission when they returned. Why give him the information now? Knowing him, he'd find a way to rationalize his mistake and take credit for uncovering the truth.

No, the revelation about the Arvenian queen was better saved for a more appropriate audience. Satisfying himself reluctantly with a contemptuous glance at Kahrlin, he followed the captives into the boat.

When they reached the ship, Kahrlin herded the captives below decks, accompanied by four guards. "You can come, too," he told Shulkahr.

He led the way to a storeroom below the waterline. Entering it, he held a candle high. "This will be your new quarters," he told them. "I hope you find it to your liking."

He handed the candle to Shulkahr. "I can't spare anyone to guard them," he sniffed. "You can do it. It might give you a chance to redeem yourself."

Without waiting for an answer, he left the room and bolted the door. The sound of laughter faded as Kahrlin walked away with his guards.

Furious and humiliated, Shulkahr glared at the captives. "This is your fault!" he spat.

The king glared back at him. "It's true that you wouldn't be in this position if not for us. You'd be floating face down somewhere out at sea!"

Shulkahr suddenly noticed that all three of them were unbound. And the king once again had the knife. The princess had retrieved the blade from the other woman while he was distracted and used it to cut their bonds.

Slumping to the floor with an angry growl, Shulkahr grudgingly accepted that once more he was in the weaker position. For the moment.

"Why didn't you tell him?" The woman was peering at him suspiciously.

"That you're not Queen Essanda?" A mocking smile came to his face. "Don't imagine I was holding back for your sake. It's purely a matter of timing. In case you weren't aware, the man who originally brought you in is the same idiot who just collected us. He's known as Kahrlin. Taking him down in front of the right audience will be well worth the wait."

She regarded him seriously. "When will we be taken before the Grand Vizier?"

He frowned at her. Something about her tone wasn't right. Not only did she not sound terrified, there was a suppressed eagerness in her tone.

He peered at her suspiciously. "Why would you want to see him?"

"I want to know why he had us abducted." She sounded casual. A bit too casual.

It all came to him in a rush. He gaped at her open-mouthed. "That's why you wanted a knife! You think you're going to assassinate him!" He laughed mockingly. "Do you really imagine he'd let you get close enough to do that?"

A flush of anger passed across her face, but she quickly mastered herself.

"That *is* what you were planning, isn't it?" He looked at her in open amazement. "So you took the place of the queen, not to save her, but because you wanted to take down the chief minister?" He stared stupidly at her, shaking his head in unbelief. Finally a mad laugh burst out of him. "It's too much!"

The woman was watching him with narrowed eyes, but she didn't speak.

Finally he mastered himself. "I'm sorry to disappoint you, 'Your Majesty.' But I've seen enough of the way His Eminence works to know that none of you should ever expect to set eyes on him. Much less get anywhere near him. He's far too smart for that."

"Why?" The king's skepticism was obvious.

"Because if he ever met with you directly, it would be as good as admitting he knew you were abducted. He'd have to kill you. Don't misunderstand me! You'll be killed in a heartbeat if he decides you're no longer useful. But if he ever decides it would be more profitable to work with you, he might want to reinstate you."

"How could he possibly expect us to work with him?" scoffed the king. "No one would be that stupid after what he's done."

"How certain are you that he's responsible for anything that's happened to you?"

All three of them were staring at him as if he were a carnival curiosity. "How can you even ask such a question?" asked the princess.

"What proof do you have?"

"Bolnyk abducted us," retorted the king. "And he's the Grand Vizier's right hand man."

"What if Bolnyk was working on his own, without the chief minister's knowledge? From everything I heard, Bolnyk took you when an unexpected opportunity presented itself. No one planned it—certainly not the chief minister."

The king scoffed at him once more. "Your chief minister is Bolnyk's master, and he's done nothing to set the situation right. Any reasonable person would hold him equally responsible."

"As far as the chief minister is concerned, only one person's opinion counts. That person is the emperor. If the emperor accepts his version of events, nothing else matters."

None of them knew what to say.

"The chief minister is the smartest man alive. You might as well accept that now. It might give you a faint hope of extending your pitiful lives."

"He isn't smarter than Lord Torbury," the king said stubbornly.

"The Arvenian army commander? The one whose son went missing? He might be a clever strategist where armies are involved.

Matching wits with someone like the chief minister is a different matter entirely."

"I wouldn't bet against Lord Torbury."

Shulkahr's lip curled into a condescending sneer. "We will see."

"THE CHIEF MINISTER will see you now."

Kahrlin followed the servant into the chief minister's cabin. It was unpretentious and simply appointed. Rheibas had never been overly concerned with appearances.

"I hear you have retrieved the captives," Rheibas began.

The agent bowed modestly. "They had made their way back to the island, Your Eminence. Fortunately I was able to extract them without incident."

"You have done well. What of Shulkahr?"

"He was with them on the island."

Rheibas cocked an eyebrow.

"They seemed to be on friendly terms," offered Kahrlin.

"Where is he now?"

"I brought him back with the captives, Your Eminence."

"Dispose of him. I have no tolerance for failure."

Kahrlin bowed.

"Don't go anywhere, Kahrlin. I might have further need of you. You are dismissed."

The agent bent once more and left the cabin, struggling to conceal his elation.

On his way out, he noticed Bolnyk waiting outside the door.

The man was rapidly becoming irrelevant. Kahrlin wondered if he was aware of it. After a brief comment, he ignored his rival and made his way onto the deck.

"Fetch Shulkahr," he told one of his men imperiously.

The bosun was nearby. "Arrange for a longboat to be launched immediately," Kahrlin said. "I'll need an extra anchor." After a moment's reflection, he added, "Make that two. I'll provide the crew."

By the time Shulkahr arrived, his crew were climbing down to the longboat.

"Come with me," he told Shulkahr.

"Where are we going? I need to see Bolnyk. And the chief minister."

"You'll have to see them later. We have work to do for the chief minister."

Shulkahr glowered, but subsided. He followed Kahrlin down to the boat.

Kahrlin sat at the back of the boat, facing the rowers. He positioned Shulkahr in the bow.

As they rowed away from the chief minister's ship, Kahrlin stole an occasional glance toward the other man. He looked anxious and distracted. He had every reason to be.

The chief minister's ship disappeared from sight as the longboat rounded a head. Kahrlin glanced down into the water. It was too deep for the bottom to be visible.

He nodded to the two rowers closest to the bow. Turning swiftly, they each wound an anchor rope around the startled Shulkahr. Then they threw him overboard, tossing the anchors in after him.

It was done in a moment.

The doomed man managed to shout, "Wait! There's something you don't—"

Then he was gone.

Kahrlin nodded again, and the longboat came about, heading back to the ship.

Having enjoyed unprecedented access to the chief minister for so long, it was a major adjustment for Bolnyk to find himself waiting. It had become a consistent experience of late. He tried to remind himself that his master juggled many priorities and had every reason to be preoccupied.

He had positioned himself near Rheibas's cabin, ready to seize an opportunity as soon as one emerged.

The door opened and Kahrlin emerged. If the look on his face offered any indication, he was currently basking in the favor of his master.

"I imagine he will see you now," Kahrlin offered indifferently as he breezed past.

Bolnyk ignored him. His rival might think he was very clever, but he was not aware that some of his most trusted men were loyal to Bolnyk.

Consequently, Bolnyk already knew what had happened to Shulkahr. The fool had deserved his fate. He had not repaid Bolnyk's faith in him.

Nevertheless, it was galling that Rheibas had given the task to another person. Perhaps it was his way of showing consideration to the man who had appointed Shulkahr, but somehow Bolnyk doubted it.

Approaching the chief minister's door, he knocked, willing himself to remain calm. He couldn't afford the luxury of dwelling on Kahrlin. He was bearing news that would not please his master. More than ever he needed to steer a careful course.

"Enter," growled the voice of Rheibas.

Bowing low, he pushed his way into the cabin.

"Bolnyk," intoned his master indifferently. "What bad tidings are you bringing this time?"

Had Rheibas caught wind of what he was about to say?

"Our agents at Rog report that a Rogandan squadron just sailed into the harbor, Your Eminence. The squadron consisted of five ships. Three were of Ahran design, all of them with three masts."

"Impossible!" spat Rheibas.

"That is not all. Three other Rogandan vessels have docked in recent days bearing prisoners. Our agents are certain the prisoners were Ahran."

He had Rheibas's full attention now. "Is there more?"

Bolnyk nodded soberly. "Three ships bearing our agents appear to have gone missing. No reports have been received of their whereabouts, and there have been no sightings for many days."

The chief minister was scowling. "What is your conclusion from all this?"

"That the Rogandans are attacking and seizing our ships. Any survivors are taken prisoner. The ships are then repurposed for use in their own navy."

"Utterly detestable, if clever. Three ships, you say."

Bolnyk nodded.

"Who is responsible for the dispatch of our ships?"

"I am, Your Eminence."

The chief minister's voice became a growl. "Then how have you allowed this to happen?"

The question was monstrously unfair. Bolnyk offered no response.

Rheibas seemed uninterested in a reply. "I want to know which ships are missing. Exactly—get me details. And find out if more have gone missing since. While you're at it, confirm that the prisoners are Ahran. Don't keep me waiting!"

Bolnyk stooped low in acknowledgment.

"And circulate an order for all ships in the region to maintain high alert at all times. You are dismissed!"

THE CHIEF MINISTER'S next summons to Kahrlin was not long in coming. The agent entered the cabin and bowed low.

"I have a task for you, Kahrlin. An extremely sensitive one. I am relying on your utmost discretion. And I need you to carry it out quickly and effectively."

Kahrlin bowed once more. "I am at your disposal, Your Eminence."

"I need you to hire enough competent sailors to man three ships. Make sure all of your sailors know how to fight. The ships need teeth—fill them with mercenaries. A high proportion of your mercenaries need to be capable archers. Hire only Rogandans. Is that clear?"

"Perfectly, Your Eminence. Are there limits on the funding?"

"Money is no object."

"Should I hire captains for these ships?"

The chief minister shook his head firmly. "I will identify people of our own to carry out that role." He bared his teeth. "Our enemies think they are very clever. They will discover they are nowhere near clever enough."

The agent stood waiting to be dismissed.

"You have one week. I have high hopes for you, Kahrlin. Do not disappoint me! You are dismissed."

After bowing low, Kahrlin hurried away. A monumental task lay ahead of him, but he couldn't have been more jubilant.

As he entered Rheibas's cabin, Bolnyk's heart was pounding uncomfortably. Never had he felt more uncertain in the presence of his master.

A few days previously, Kahrlin had disappeared with the most capable of the agents. It was whispered that he was engaged in a highly sensitive and critically important mission on behalf of the chief minister. The situation was unusually galling, not least because most of the agents now assisting Kahrlin had originally been selected and trained by Bolnyk.

A lifetime must surely have passed since his master led Bolnyk into the emperor's throne room. Such honors were faded memories. People looked away now when he approached. He had not been summoned by Rheibas for days, and everyone knew it. Once more in the chief minister's cabin, he felt only apprehension.

His master seemed to notice him at last. "Ah. Bolnyk."

He stood awkwardly at attention, restless under the cold scrutiny of the chief minister.

For years he had drawn from a seemingly boundless reserve of confidence, never doubting his ability to achieve whatever his master demanded of him. In recent days that self-assurance had deserted him completely. He understood why—his master had lost faith in him. Nevertheless, the suddenness and completeness of the change remained as mystifying as it was alarming.

His entire adult life had been consumed in a tireless effort to further the interests of the man before him. That same man had become a stranger. Every night Bolnyk lay awake, desperate for the numbing oblivion of sleep. But its release was denied him. His mind, constantly churning with the injustice of his plight, refused to set him free.

A simmering anger had begun to bubble, close to the surface. Difficult as it was to ignore, he forced it down. He could not afford for Rheibas to sense it.

"You have served me faithfully for many years, Bolnyk."

His brows drew together. Whatever he might have been expecting, it wasn't that.

"You deserve a chance. A proper chance. An opportunity to demonstrate again the capabilities that made you so valuable to me."

The ice in his heart began to thaw. His master had his full attention.

"I have been planning an operation. A highly sensitive and very special operation. I assigned the legwork to Kahrlin, but he is not the right person to lead it. I need someone who is dependable beyond doubt. Someone whose loyalty goes beyond self-interest."

He stared at Bolnyk forthrightly. "Are you that man, Bolnyk?"

"I am, Your Eminence." He tried not to sound too desperate.

"Excellent." Rheibas was actually smiling. "Then here is what I need you to do..."

26

General Vholahr peered distastefully across the endless succession of rolling waves. He had participated in many amphibious operations, but this operation was different. Never before had he spent so many days stranded on a ship with nothing to do.

He was there to provide bargaining support to the chief minister, yet there had been no contact from him since arriving in the region.

The emperor had also charged Vholahr with making contact with the Rogandans, but the situation harbored enough uncertainty that he was unwilling to risk any kind of connection before the chief minister briefed him on the current state of negotiations.

Much as his men needed time on dry land, it was out of the question. Any landing would only risk inflaming tensions with the Rogandans. All they could do was circle endlessly outside of Rogandan territorial waters.

That left them at the mercy of wind and wave. Thankfully conditions had improved over the previous couple of days. Prior to that, storms had battered them relentlessly, tossing them about on mountainous seas. Sea sickness had incapacitated many of his soldiers, and at times he himself had barely been able to stand.

None of it would have mattered if he was making forward progress on the emperor's mission. He shook his head in frustration.

As if in mockery of his thoughts, he looked up to see the ship's captain hurrying toward him, a grave look on his face. "We have just received a signal, General! Two of our ships are under attack."

"What?! We will move to their support immediately." He pointed to the other ships in sight. "Signal them to join us!"

The captain hurried to the helm, shouting orders as he went.

As the ship slowly began to come about, the general called for his captains. "Get the men armed and on deck. It appears we will see action at last!"

Men began scurrying about, heading for their assigned stations. Everyone was in place long before they saw any sign of fighting. The men were becoming restless when five ships came into sight. Their design showed that the vessels were all Ahran.

As they drew closer he saw two ships on either side of a third ship, attacking it from both directions. Two other ships nearby were engaged in close fighting. It made no sense. Why would Ahrans be attacking Ahrans?

As they approached, the three attackers disengaged. Setting full sail, they were soon disappearing in the direction of Rog.

The captain approached. "Should we pursue them, General?"

The general shook his head. "We can't know where they might lead us. No, this attack needs to be investigated, and it needs to be done immediately. We can't afford to be caught unprepared a second time."

A couple of hours passed before men from every ship had gathered in response to his orders. In the absence of a large enough room, and with the weather moderate, they clustered on the forecastle.

"I want to know what happened," the general began. "In order."

An army captain, heavily bandaged from multiple wounds, responded first. "Two of our ships were in the same vicinity when three other ships appeared. They were clearly Ahran, so we did nothing to prevent them coming alongside. As soon as they were close enough, bowmen appeared and opened fire. We were not expecting an attack, and they caught us unprepared. As you know, we have few archers among our ranks. We could not prevent them from sweeping the decks with arrows before they boarded."

"How many men did you lose?"

"Fifty at least. They pulled us close with grappling hooks, then they boarded from both sides. Most of our men had sheltered below decks. Once hand-to-hand fighting started, they poured out of the hatch, and it turned into a real fight. We were outnumbered, but we gave a good account of ourselves. When they saw you approaching, they took their wounded and jumped back onto their own ships."

Another captain reported in. "We had a similar experience, although we were only facing one attacker. Their archers also took out a lot of our men. They lost plenty of men themselves when they boarded. If they hadn't withdrawn when they did, we might have been able to board them. When they saw you coming, they ran like rabbits. They only left their dead behind."

"Who were they?"

"It's hard to be certain, but they weren't speaking Ahran," the first captain said. "One of the crew recognized a few Rogandan words."

"Rogandan navy or pirates?"

The captain shrugged. "It's impossible to say. They showed discipline in removing their wounded, but they didn't fight like regular soldiers."

The second captain nodded. "I agree. The real mystery is how they came to be sailing Ahran ships. Those ships were definitely Ahran-built."

The general frowned. "There are too many unanswered questions for my liking. Nevertheless, you've acquitted yourselves well under difficult circumstances. Convey my appreciation to your men." He eyed them grimly. "As of now, all of our ships will stay in formation. And we clearly need archers. If we're lacking bows, find a way to manufacture some."

He dismissed them, and they returned to their ships.

"What do you make of all that?" the general asked his aide. "Who were the attackers, and what was their purpose? And how did they gain possession of three of our ships?"

"I can only guess, General," the aide replied. "I'm wondering if they knew they were attacking army transports. It's possible they thought we were merchants."

"They know nothing about Ahran ship design if they think we're merchants."

"But why would they attack army ships, General? Is it in retaliation for us having supposedly abducted their princess?"

The general snorted. "They could begin by explaining why they abducted our princess!" He shook his head. "If they want a war, they'll get one."

He glared out across the water. "It's past time we heard from the chief minister. His negotiations appear to have achieved nothing. I am planning to ask the emperor to assemble a serious force, and the chief minister will not find it easy to dissuade me."

AFTER ABANDONING THE ATTACK, Bolnyk led his little squadron back to the island where they had first taken on board the Rogandan fighters.

The mercenaries had been transported to the island as they were hired by Kahrlin. After a few days, when a sufficient number had assembled, three of the chief minister's newest ships arrived and disembarked their crews. The ships had been turned over to the mercenaries under the command of Bolnyk.

Two other trusted agents joined him—one to captain each of the vessels. Once they were all aboard, the ships set sail and departed. Surrounded by men of dubious character, Bolnyk had made it clear that none of them would receive payment unless all of them promptly carried out his every command.

The original Ahran crews had settled down on the island to wait for the return of their ships.

When the fighting was over, Bolnyk returned the mercenaries to the island and ferried them ashore. As the original crews boarded the ships once more, he gathered the mercenaries and addressed them.

"You have fulfilled the terms of your agreement," he told them. "You will shortly be collected and returned to Rogand. In the meantime, supplies have been laid out for you. Eat and drink your fill!"

"What about our pay?" a rough voice demanded.

"A worthy question!" he replied. "Your payment has been buried for safekeeping. You will find the full amount over there, beneath those spades." He pointed. "Dig it up at your leisure." He surveyed them with a humorless smile. "I am sure you will make every effort to share it fairly."

A group of mercenaries gathered threateningly around him and his men. "Don't think you're going anywhere! Not until we see our payment."

He folded his arms indifferently.

None of the mercenaries showed any interest in feasting. All eyes were on the digging. The first of the treasure was exposed within a few minutes. It was clearly a sizable hoard. Every one of the mercenaries abandoned Bolnyk, racing to claim their share.

A single longboat remained for Bolnyk's use. Climbing aboard with his men, he set off for one of the ships. As they climbed onto the deck, they saw that fighting had broken out between the mercenaries at the diggings.

Bolnyk had no interest in waiting around for the outcome. He gave the order, and the three ships weighed anchor and sailed away. He didn't even spare a backward glance at the island.

As soon as they were underway, he was joined by the agents who had captained the other two ships during the attack. Their faces were strained.

"What happened?" one of them asked, not trying to hide his consternation. "We were supposed to be taking ships back from Rogandans! Rogandans who'd captured them from our own people!"

The other was nodding vigorously. "We were attacking Ahran navy ships! I only realized it when we boarded them, and I found myself fighting men in imperial uniforms! I called off the attack immediately."

"You did the right thing," grunted Bolnyk, his brows furrowed.

Nothing about the operation had been as he expected. "I have no idea what went wrong. We were in the location where the ships were supposedly last seen."

Both men began speaking animatedly. "If anyone finds out we led an attack on the emperor's soldiers, we'll be dead men!"

"It was the chief minister's operation. We were just following his orders!"

"That's right! He'll protect us. Won't he?"

"Why did Kahrlin bury the mercenaries' pay? They're normally paid individually."

"I have no idea. Making them divide the spoils makes no sense. It's a recipe for conflict."

The flow of words continued uninterrupted as they glanced back toward the island.

Bolnyk didn't interrupt them. What could he say? He was no longer sure about anything.

Throughout the journey his mind churned uneasily, trying to make sense of all that had happened. His thoughts moved well beyond that operation. A seismic shift had taken place in his standing with Rheibas, and he was struggling to understand what had precipitated it.

Important questions had been raised by the operation he had just led on Rheibas's behalf. Had a careful plan somehow gone terribly wrong? Or, more alarmingly, was he merely an unwitting dupe in the most recent of the chief minister's devious schemes?

Having worked with Rheibas for a very long time, he was confident he could read him as well as anyone. He would know the truth when he stood before his master.

He would also know if he had any kind of a future.

"Enter," growled Rheibas.

Pushing into the cabin, Bolnyk bowed low, trying to calm his racing heart. So much hung on this interaction.

For a long moment, the chief minister stared at him, his features expressionless. "I have been briefed on your mission," he finally announced with an angry scowl.

Bolnyk kept his own face impassive. "We sailed to the location you described, Your Eminence," he said. "The ships we found there were not manned by Rogandans."

The chief minister's eyes flashed. "I warned you! I told you this mission was extremely sensitive! Yet you dared to attack the emperor's soldiers! Are you trying to destroy me?"

Bolnyk gazed calmly back at him. "The emperor's soldiers were attacked by a group of Rogandan mercenaries. The emperor has no need to know who was behind the attack."

Rheibas was incredulous. "You want me to lie to the emperor? Just to cover your mistake?"

A flush rose involuntarily to Bolnyk's face. It was indignation rather than embarrassment—he knew Rheibas well enough to recognize his posturing for what it was.

Deception was integral to the way the chief minister operated—Bolnyk had seen ample evidence of that throughout his life. Not much time had passed since he personally witnessed the chief minister lying brazenly to the emperor.

Rheibas hadn't finished. "I've protected you, Bolnyk—elevated you. I took you into the emperor's throne room! But even I have my limits. Don't expect me to constantly be available to rescue you from your own stupidity."

He waved a hand dismissively. "I'll decide what to do with you later. In the meantime don't leave this ship. You are dismissed!"

Bowing tightly, Bolnyk left the chief minister's cabin.

His worst fears had been confirmed. He was being cast aside like a worn out rag.

It wasn't difficult to guess who would be brought in to take his place. No doubt Kahrlin was already celebrating his predecessor's demise. He shrugged. Let his rival enjoy his moment in the sun—in time he would be discarded too.

His thoughts returned to the recent operation. Rheibas had said nothing of substance about it. Nevertheless, Bolnyk felt able to make a few intelligent guesses.

In spite of the chief minister's bluster, Bolnyk felt sure imperial soldiers had always been the target of the attack. Perhaps Rheibas was looking for an incident—a spark to ignite a war against the Rogandans.

Whatever his schemes, he would undoubtedly make sure his former senior agent was on hand to take the blame. He shook his head in disgust.

He wondered what had become of his mercenaries. Were they being returned to Rogand as promised? He didn't believe it for a minute.

Burying their payment was unprecedented. It must surely have been done for a reason. It wasn't hard to guess that the mercenaries would fight bitterly over the loot. Bolnyk had himself encouraged them to eat and drink their fill. It wasn't until after he left that he learned the supplies laid out for them consisted mainly of alcohol. Getting drunk wasn't going to help them stay calm.

At that moment, whoever had survived would be waiting anxiously on the island, wondering why they hadn't been collected. They would be facing starvation.

No doubt Rheibas would eventually send a team back—probably under Kahrlin—to finish off any survivors. Their bodies would be buried in the mass grave they had so helpfully dug for themselves. With no mercenaries left to claim their payment, it would be gathered together and returned to the chief minister.

Ingenious as the whole thing was, the sheer cynicism of it was breathtaking. The scale of the brutality was unusual, even for Rheibas.

Bolnyk had served Rheibas devotedly for years. Yet until his master turned on him, he never thought to question whether the man was worthy of such devotion. Recent events had answered the question emphatically.

Curiously, with all hope gone for any future of his own, he felt more calm and composed than he had for a very long time.

Abruptly it occurred to him to wonder again about the mysterious prisoner that Rheibas had shipped with him to Rogand. Who was he, and what did Rheibas want with him?

For that matter, where was he being hidden?

King Krasmir had aggressively hunted down many of the Ahran agents operating within his kingdom. Individuals continued to operate, but Krasmir had somehow succeeded in rooting out every Ahran base on Rogandan soil. How he had done it baffled Bolnyk, although it was no longer his concern.

It did mean that the prisoner was not likely to be located anywhere in Rogand. He might be confined on an island somewhere. It seemed unlikely though. Bolnyk had the impression that Rheibas wanted him close at hand. Why else would he have brought him aboard when he sailed from Kat Ahket?

The more he thought about it, the more likely it seemed that the man was locked away in the hold of that very ship.

With no longer anything to lose, Bolnyk headed for the hatch, hungry for answers.

27

Since displacing Bolnyk, Kahrlin had been spending a great deal of time with the chief minister. He could still scarcely believe how much of his day was spent sitting across from the second most powerful person in the empire. He had no doubt about one thing: power was intoxicating.

The ship that Rheibas used as a base was the scene of seemingly endless activity, with people and messages arriving and departing constantly. His private cabin was the central hub of it all.

The latest visitor was a servant. Handing a dispatch to the chief minister, the man bowed low and scurried away.

Rheibas watched his departing back thoughtfully before breaking open the seal and unrolling the parchment. As he read, his lips curled slowly into a satisfied smirk.

He glanced toward Kahrlin. "I understand that General Vholahr is anchored nearby with his squadron. He wishes to meet with me. Arrange a boat to take me to him."

Kahrlin got up and departed.

It wasn't difficult for the agent to guess what had prompted the general's communication. Nevertheless he didn't doubt that Rheibas would manage to appear suitably shocked when informed about the recent attack.

He knew that the chief minister had been avoiding contact with the general. It seemed that the time was finally right for them to meet. He didn't blame Rheibas for his aloofness. If he understood the situation correctly, the general was only there to provide support anyway.

He smiled to himself. The Rogandans must have thought they were so clever capturing three of the chief minister's ships. The unwitting fools had no idea they were furthering his purposes marvelously. They were clearly ill equipped to face an adversary like him.

No more than a couple of hours passed before Kahrlin delivered the chief minister to the general's ship. They boarded together, and Rheibas waved him forward, indicating he should remain to hear the conversation.

"Welcome to my ship, Chief Minister. You have proven difficult to track down."

"I can only apologize, General Vholahr! I have been much occupied of late. Three of my ships disappeared several days ago. I am at a loss to know what happened, but all the evidence points to the Rogandans. They apparently attacked and captured the ships and imprisoned the crews. For what purpose I cannot say."

"I can enlighten you as to their purpose," growled the general. "Two of the ships in my squadron recently suffered an unprovoked attack. That attack was carried out by Rogandans, and in three Ahran ships."

"You astonish me, General! My attempts to negotiate with the Rogandans and their allies have been frustrated at every turn. I have learned to expect nothing worthwhile from them. But as far as I know we are not at war. Such an attack is contemptible, even by their standards."

"I intend to ask the emperor to dispatch a credible force. Our current display is nothing more than a token."

"I urge you to show moderation, General! We must do everything in our power to avoid embroiling the empire in a war, especially one so far from home."

"May I remind you, Chief Minister, that I am not the one provoking a war!"

"I understand your frustration. I truly do! Perhaps there is a middle course."

"What do you suggest?"

"The emperor authorized ten ships. Perhaps he would be willing to release thirty more. A total of forty ships should be more than enough to show we cannot be trifled with. I doubt that too many others could be provisioned in any reasonable time frame anyway."

The general's eyebrows had gone up. "I was planning to request half that number. Nevertheless, in view of what has happened you have my support."

"Can I leave this matter in your hands, General? I have more than enough to occupy my attention already."

The general bowed stiffly. "Leave it to me. Now, please join me for refreshments, Chief Minister. I am eager to hear your assessment of the local situation."

A HOODED FIGURE stepped quietly up to the chief minister's empty cabin. His arrival was not met with a challenge of any kind.

Two guards normally stood at attention outside the door. That day they lay sprawled on the floor, sleeping soundly beside another guard.

The guards had not succumbed to weariness—they were incapacitated. Not long after Kahrlin had left with the chief minister, a fellow guard had brought them wine. An unexpected break from the constant demands of their master offered a perfect excuse for a small celebration, and all three settled down to enjoy themselves. None of them, including the guard who had brought the wineskins, were aware that the wine had been drugged.

After eyeing the motionless forms for a moment, the cloaked

figure stepped carefully over them, opened the door, and slipped inside the cabin.

Finding an unused parchment, the intruder brought it to the chief minister's desk. Dipping a quill into an exquisite ink pot, he scratched away patiently until words had almost filled the page. As soon as the ink was dry, he rolled up the document.

A candle stood at one side of the desk. Lighting it, he melted some wax and dribbled several large blobs across the edge of the rolled parchment. Finally, he wrote a single word on the outside of the document.

The visitor seemed to know where to find everything he needed. Retrieving a hidden key, he unlocked a drawer and removed the chief minister's official seal. After pressing the seal firmly onto the soft wax, he returned it to its hiding place. Then he tidied the desk, snuffed out the candle, and left the cabin.

Knowing that the guards would soon begin to stir, he stepped carefully over their prone figures and stole away as silently as he had come.

ONE OF THE many nameless servants of the chief minister scurried about his master's ship, looking for a particular agent. The man he sought was leaning over the rail staring at the horizon.

"This is for you," said the servant importantly, handing him a document bearing the seal of the chief minister.

"Why is it for me?" demanded the agent skeptically. "It isn't addressed to me."

The servant shrugged. "I was told to give it to Zhukha. That's you."

"Who told you that?"

"He didn't say who he was. But Kahrlin instructed him to give the document to you. It's sensitive. It's something His Eminence wants done urgently."

The agent eyed the servant loftily. "Kahrlin told me nothing about it. And he isn't here—he left with the chief minister a while ago. This isn't my responsibility. It can wait until they get back."

The servant shook his head obstinately. "I was told it has to be done now. His Eminence will not be happy if you ignore his orders."

"*Who* told you?" Zhukha repeated.

"I already said! I don't know!"

Rolling the document over in his hand, Zhukha fingered the seal absently. As he did, a barely legible word on one side caught his eye. Pulling it closer, he squinted at the writing. "It does have my name on it! But it's so badly smudged I can barely read it. You put your hand on the ink, you idiot!"

"I did not! It was like that already!" retorted the servant, hurrying away before the agent could say anything further.

Zhukha rolled his eyes. Then he turned his full attention to the parchment, ignoring the servant.

Breaking the seal, he unrolled the document and scrutinized its message carefully. The orders were simple enough. He was directed to two large crates in the hold and instructed to take them ashore. The destination was a deserted beach. It lay to the southeast, just beyond a headland with a large dead tree standing alone at the end of it. No one would be there to meet him. He should leave the boxes above the waterline. They would be collected later. He should destroy the document once the task was completed. When he returned to the ship he was to tell no one of the mission.

He hesitated for a moment when he saw that the document wasn't signed. It was, of course, sealed with the chief minister's seal. After a moment's thought, he realized he wouldn't know the chief minister's signature even if he saw it. He had no idea how His Eminence signed documents. Did he use one of his titles, or simply sign it with his name?

Zhukha shrugged. Most likely the chief minister didn't sign documents at all. The seal was signature enough.

Searching out the bosun, he requested a longboat and a crew, explaining that he had urgent business on behalf of the chief minister. Seeing uncertainty on the bosun's face, he allowed him a glimpse of the document and its seal. He was careful to conceal the contents.

The boat was duly prepared, and Zhukha led a group of sailors to the location of the crates in the hold. The crates were large and unusually heavy. It took four sailors to lug them onto the deck. Maneuvering them down into the longboat was a considerable achievement.

The beach referred to in the parchment proved to be considerably further away than Zhukha expected. Eventually the crates were manhandled ashore and left above the waterline as instructed. Several hours had passed by the time the boat returned to the ship.

HALF AN HOUR HAD PASSED since the crates came to a final halt and the last sounds ceased from the departing sailors. It was time to move. Reaching for a long metal tool, Bolnyk levered off the top of his crate and climbed out of it.

Moving to the other crate, he pried off its top as well.

"You can come out now. We're free, at least for the moment," said Bolnyk, speaking in Rogandan.

He handed over a bag. "I packed a few supplies. We need to leave. It's impossible to know how long we have before they'll begin chasing us."

The other man stretched uncomfortably. "I've been confined to small rooms for a very long time. I'm not too confident about my ability to walk long distances."

"Just do the best you can."

He nodded. "I suppose I should thank you for breaking me out. Except that he'll probably kill both of us if we're caught."

"I know how to shake off pursuers," growled Bolnyk. "Just stick to me." He studied his companion closely. "I still don't know who you are, or what the chief minister wants with you, but you can keep your little secrets, at least for the moment. You'd better be clear about one thing though. I'll kill you myself if you try to head off on your own."

The other man shrugged. "We may as well get going."

One final thing needed to be done before they left. Replacing the lids on the crates, Bolnyk used the metal tool to bash a large hole in each lid. After dragging the crates back into the water, both men piled rocks in through the holes until the crates were barely afloat. Bolnyk then towed them out into deeper water. Once the waves were lapping around his neck, he allowed the crates to fill with water and sink.

Returning to the shore, Bolnyk did his best to smooth away the drag marks. With the obvious traces of their location removed, they set off inland, moving as quickly as they were able.

THE LIGHT WAS FADING from the sky when Kahrlin finally returned to the ship with the chief minister. Rheibas did not immediately release Kahrlin. A number of pressing issues demanded attention, and the night was well advanced before either of them retired to their beds. Kahrlin was weary enough for sleep to claim him almost immediately.

He was awakened before dawn by a commotion. Instantly alert, he armed himself and threw on a nightgown. Pushing through the door, he headed for the chief minister's quarters. Two men had been stopped by the guards at the door. The men were extremely agitated, seemingly incapable of calming down.

Rheibas appeared and took in the scene. Ordering the entire group to follow him, he led them to the deck.

He faced the men. "Speak to me," he growled.

Both of the guards were trembling with fear. One of them began talking, but he wasn't even vaguely coherent.

Finally Rheibas lost his temper. "If one of you doesn't start talking sense, I'll have both of you tied to the mast and whipped senseless."

That got their attention. The second guard managed to calm down enough to make himself understood. "We were drugged, Your Eminence!"

The chief minister's eyes narrowed. "How were you drugged?"

The guard shifted nervously. "Someone brought us wine."

"So you were having a little celebration while you were on guard duty?"

Neither of the men spoke.

"And the man you were guarding?"

"W...when we came to, he was...gone."

Rheibas had gone deathly quiet, and Kahrlin saw that the blood had drained from his face.

"He is...GONE?!" The chief minister's voice might have been calm, but Kahrlin saw the rage in his eyes. "If he is not back by dawn, both of you will pay with your lives!"

He turned his back on the men. "Find Bolnyk and bring him here," he spat.

Although Rheibas had not specifically directed the order to him, Kahrlin set off at once in search of his predecessor. Whenever he saw agents he recognized, he pressed them into service.

He didn't return until they had searched the ship thoroughly.

"There is no sign of Bolnyk, Your Eminence."

The chief minister stood silently with his eyes half closed. He appeared to be struggling to master himself. Finally he spoke, addressing himself to Kahrlin. "Whatever happened here could not have been achieved without help. I want to know who was involved, and what they did. I don't care what it takes to extract the truth. I expect a full report in two hours."

Kahrlin hurried away. He knew what to do. The first fifteen minutes he spent among the crew—he told them enough to terrify anyone with something to hide. Then he sat down to wait.

The news raced through the ship like wildfire. When he deemed the time was ripe, he called people onto the deck in groups. Some of them were exhibiting obvious signs of anxiety. After extracting them, Kahrlin began applying pressure.

Within half an hour he knew about the drugged guards outside the chief minister's cabin as well as outside the prisoner's cell below decks. It took him another hour to find out about the parchment and the crates. He had to threaten to drag Zhukha in front of the chief minister before the agent was willing to reveal the contents of the parchment.

Before two hours had elapsed, Kahrlin had assembled everyone with even the vaguest role in what had taken place. Most, if not all of them, had been unwitting dupes, but he suspected that Rheibas wasn't likely to concern himself with fine distinctions.

As soon as he was able to piece together a full outline of what had happened, he reported to the chief minister. Rheibas regarded him with narrowed eyes as he spoke.

"Most of those involved did not understand the implications of their actions, Your Eminence," Kahrlin concluded. "Apart from Bolnyk, I've seen no clear evidence that anyone was intentionally disloyal."

"What actions have you taken?" demanded Rheibas.

"Since time was critical, I sent three boats filled with armed men to the place where the crates were delivered. They left as dawn was breaking. The men have been ordered to follow the fugitives."

The chief minister nodded tightly. "You have done well, Kahrlin."

He gazed darkly toward a group of men huddling restlessly off to one side of the deck. "Regardless of the final outcome, there will be consequences for what has happened today."

He turned to Kahrlin. "Take another boat and go after them. Do not…" He paused, frowning. "Do not fail me, Kahrlin," he finally growled.

Kahrlin set off the moment a boat was ready. He had sent Zhukha to direct the earlier party, but he knew roughly where to go, and he expected to find three longboats beached at the right location.

It took longer than he had hoped to find the beach. His boat soon joined the others drawn up on the sand. The crates were nowhere in sight.

Many footprints led away from the beach, and he followed them with his men. The tracks led up and over a series of low hills, then directly across a broad plain toward a stand of trees. A wide stream flowed beside the trees, and at that point the tracks became confused.

Wading along the stream, he eventually found a place where a large group had left the stream. Following the new tracks, they came to another stream. Another hour passed before any of his men found tracks again.

Leaving the stream, he set off again with his men. The tracks wound through the trees, eventually leading over another hill and down onto a new plain. A dense forest covered the plain.

Kahrlin came upon the earlier group of searchers just before he reached a broad river.

An agent he recognized saw him coming and moved to join him.

"We have men searching both sides of the river, but they haven't seen any sign of Bolnyk."

"How long have you been here?"

"A couple of hours." The agent shrugged. "It isn't surprising. Bolnyk is probably the best tracker we have."

"We don't *have* him!" spat Kahrlin. "He's working against us, not for us. We're *hunting* him! Enough talking—get back to your search."

After two more hours had passed with no sign of the fugitives' tracks, Kahrlin sent a couple of men ahead to scout. They returned within an hour.

"We crossed a series of streams," one of them told him. "Beyond that, the forest becomes almost impassable." He shook his head. "Bolnyk chose a perfect place to lose us. And he knows how to cover his tracks. There's no way we'll ever find him."

Kahrlin refused to accept it. As the sun was setting, he called the men together. "Build fires. We'll camp here overnight and carry on the search in the morning."

Reluctance showed on every face, but none of them argued.

The following day brought no better success. When the sun began to approach the western horizon, Kahrlin finally accepted that they were not going to find Bolnyk, or Rheibas's prisoner. The fugitives had gotten clean away.

Rheibas would be furious. Kahrlin remembered his final words. *"Do not...Do not fail me, Kahrlin."*

He had the impression that Rheibas had caught himself on the brink of saying something else. Had he been about to order Kahrlin not to return at all if he didn't come back with the fugitives?

He'd been the one who figured out what had happened, and he wasn't responsible for any of it. Rheibas surely wouldn't blame him. Would he?

Having taken Bolnyk's place at the chief minister's side with restless enthusiasm, Kahrlin had held nothing but contempt for his displaced rival. It now occurred to him to wonder if Bolnyk had actually been set free.

For the first time, he felt a tiny flash of envy for his predecessor.

28

One of King Krasmir's servants located Will as he sat in the gardens outside his rooms in the palace. He had been enjoying a relaxed conversation with Thomas and Brother Ander.

The servant addressed himself to Will. "King Krasmir wishes to meet with you urgently, My Lord." As if to emphasize the seriousness, he hurried away without waiting for a response.

Will exchanged an intrigued glance with the others. As he was getting up to go, the king himself appeared.

"Please pardon the intrusion, Lord Torbury," he said, sparing a nod for Thomas and Brother Ander. "I have received a request for an audience, and I would be glad if you would join me."

"I would be honored to do so, Your Majesty. Who is this man?"

"His name is Kahrlin. He claims to represent the Grand Vizier of Ahr."

Will's eyebrows went up in surprise. There must surely be a great deal to learn from someone with access to the Grand Vizier. A glance at Thomas suggested the possibilities were clear to him as well.

"Would you be willing to allow my companions to attend the interview, Your Majesty?"

After a moment's hesitation, the king shrugged. "I don't see why not. It can't hurt for Arvenon to be well represented."

The three men followed the king back into the palace.

It struck Will that the presence of Brother Ander had been especially fortuitous. Asking for his friends to be included was asking a lot, and he felt certain he had the monk to thank for the king's positive response.

There was no real reason for Brother Ander to be present at the coming interview of course. The person who needed to be there was Thomas. But the king had no awareness of the Stone of Knowing.

The king was, however, one of the few people aware of Brother Ander's role in the recovery of Bisri Ahuzza. The incident had only served to boost Brother Ander's already formidable reputation. Will had the feeling the king was eager to do anything he could to keep the monk close at hand, just in case his services might one day be required.

They settled themselves in one of the king's reception rooms, along with Lady Tulinay and Lord Kulferan. After a brief conversation about how to approach the interaction, the king issued instructions for Kahrlin to be admitted to the room.

Kahrlin entered the room, and offered a small bow. An aide to the king offered brief introductions, then left.

The agent didn't seem overawed by the situation, nor did he seem troubled by the frosty reception he encountered.

Will studied the stranger carefully before permitting himself a brief glance at Thomas. He was gratified to see his friend fully focused on the Ahran.

"You requested an audience on behalf of the Grand Vizier," the king observed coolly.

"Yes, Your Majesty. His Eminence wanted to make another attempt to reach an understanding with Rogand. He regrets your decision to take three of his ships by force. Using those vessels to carry out an unprovoked attack on two vessels of the Imperial Navy—on the high seas, and without a declaration of war—is a disappointing move that has prompted the emperor to strengthen his presence in the region."

Will exchanged bemused glances with the king and his nobles. Choosing to ignore their confusion, Kahrlin continued.

"We expect significant reinforcements any day. Once they arrive, the potential for escalation must surely increase. The Grand Vizier wishes to avoid any further deterioration in relations. He therefore proposes a summit conference with you as a matter of urgency."

He paused, surveying their faces. Then he added, "I understand you are still searching for three missing members of the royalty. He believes he might be in a position to provide information about them, should you be interested."

"We are open to any information you might care to offer," the king observed darkly.

"I regret that I am not privy to particulars. No one apart from the Grand Vizier is in a position to provide details."

The king was clearly unimpressed with this answer. He nevertheless responded diplomatically. "We will discuss the Grand Vizier's proposal. Should we wish to pursue a further meeting, we will need to know how to contact him. My aide will discuss practicalities with you as you leave."

With a cursory bow, Kahrlin left the room.

Animated conversation broke out the moment he was gone.

"What do you make of this purported attack on the emperor's ships?" asked the king, frowning.

Will didn't hesitate. "I suspect that when the Grand Vizier learned that we had taken three of his ships, he saw an opportunity. He used three of his own ships to launch an attack on the imperial navy, and blamed that attack on us."

The king looked dubious. "His own men attacked their countrymen?"

Will shook his head. "He would almost certainly have used mercenaries."

The notion made sense to Lady Tulinay. "A while ago I received persistent reports of people looking for mercenaries to hire," she said.

"It wasn't clear at the time who was doing the recruiting, or for what purpose. It seems we have our answer."

"The Grand Vizier is a devious man," offered Lord Kulferan, "if not quite as clever as he imagines."

"He is certainly devious," agreed Lady Tulinay. "There is some mystery surrounding these mercenaries. From all reports, they vanished entirely after signing up. I wonder what other purposes he is planning to use them for."

"He may not have plans for them at all," said Will. "He doesn't strike me as a man who likes loose ends. It wouldn't surprise me to discover he found a way to dispose of them after their raid on the emperor's navy."

Others were raising eyebrows, but Thomas inclined his head slightly, apparently confirming Will's guesses.

"I have a more immediate concern," said Lord Kulferan. "I was not aware that the emperor had naval ships close to our shores. If he is increasing that force, we need to urgently consider the possibility of an escalation into armed conflict, not least because the Grand Vizier seems intent on provoking a war for reasons known only to himself. Based on hints from both Princess Neira and Bisri Ahuzza, it seems unlikely that our navy is as strong as theirs. If they send enough ships, we may not be able to prevent them from landing a force."

"The key uncertainty is how many ships the emperor will send," offered Will. "We know he sent three ships with Bisri Ahuzza, but we have no way of knowing how many ships are currently in the region, nor how many more he will send in response to any request from the Grand Vizier."

Lady Tulinay responded quickly. "Our best intelligence suggests the emperor has no more desire for a war than we do. He will want to limit the size of any force he sends. It will also take time to fit out and send a fleet of any size."

Lord Kulferan shook his head impatiently. "All we can do is guess at the emperor's response, and we cannot base our preparations on guesswork. We must take measures to strengthen our army, and we must do it now! It will take time for the nobles to assemble and dispatch local levies."

"I sincerely hope you are right, My Lady," the king told Lady Tulinay. "Until we can be certain, it seems prudent to have too many troops on hand rather than too few."

He turned to his commander. "Do what you need to do, My Lord. You have my full support."

The meeting seemed almost at an end.

"Would either of you like to offer any thoughts?" the king asked Brother Ander and Thomas.

Both men shook their heads.

In spite of their response, Will didn't doubt that Thomas had a great deal to say, and he was impatient for the meeting to end.

As they were leaving the king's reception room, a man approached Will and handed him a dispatch. Will recognized the courier as Varasan. Without opening the document, Will returned with Thomas and Brother Ander to their rooms in the palace.

When the monk excused himself for a few minutes, Will seized his opportunity. "I'm eager to hear what you can tell me, Thomas. Let me read this message first, though, in case it needs urgent attention."

Opening the dispatch, he saw that it was a message from King Delmar. Since one of Delmar's agents had taken the place of Queen Essanda, it came as no surprise that the king was eager for any update on the search for her, King Rupert, and Princess Teylee.

Will threw it aside with a sigh as he settled into a chair. "It's from King Delmar. He wants to know if we've made any progress on finding the missing royals."

"I might be able to help with that," said Thomas.

Will surged to his feet, trying to contain his excitement. "So this Kahrlin knows their whereabouts?"

Thomas nodded. "They managed to jump into the sea as the Ahran ship was taking them from the island where they had been held. They returned to the same island."

Will grimaced, passing a hand across his face. "Do you mean that if we'd returned to the island ourselves, they would be free now?"

"So it seems," Thomas confirmed. "The Grand Vizier sent a ship back to find them. Kahrlin was in charge of the mission. After he had recaptured them, he deposited them on another island."

"Do you know where?"

"I have a general idea. The landmarks were clear in his mind."

"We have to alert King Krasmir immediately! We mustn't fail this time!"

Thomas looked alarmed. "The king will want to know how we discovered the location."

Will waved a hand dismissively. "I'll simply tell him I've just received the information from a confidential source. He saw that courier hand me a dispatch. He'll assume the Varasans have uncovered the location and passed it on."

"Will he know that the man is Varasan?"

"You can be sure the king knows everything that goes on in his palace!" Will found a parchment and a quill. "Describe the location as well as you can."

Writing swiftly, Will documented everything Thomas was able to tell him. "I need to get this to the king urgently. Is there anything else important you learned from the Ahran?"

"I learned a lot," Thomas assured him. "But nothing that can't wait until you've notified the king. The sooner he sends someone to the island, the better."

Will hurried away. After seeking an urgent meeting with King Krasmir, he passed on the news, handing over the information about the island's location.

The king did not hesitate. A fire had come to his eyes, and he hastened away to organize a force to be sent to the island.

With nothing useful to contribute to the operation, Will returned to find Thomas in conversation with the monk.

Brother Ander got to his feet as soon as Will walked in the door. "Would you like me to leave, Will?" he asked.

"Not at all! Please stay. You're as deeply invested as any of us."

The monk nodded and sat down again.

Something was bothering Thomas. The look on his face said he was feeling extremely uncomfortable.

"I hope you don't mind, Will, but I decided it was time Brother Ander knew about the Stone of Knowing."

After an initial wave of alarm had passed over him, Will shrugged. "Have you told him about the scroll?"

Thomas shook his head.

"Then it's time we did. I suspect we can trust him." Will gazed at Brother Ander with a wry smile.

Beginning at once, Will launched into a brief description of the scroll and what it had revealed about the three stones. Finally he retrieved the Stone of Authority and handed it to Brother Ander.

The monk shook his head in amazement. "A number of mysteries are starting to become clear." His face became serious. "You have given me a great deal to think about. One thing is clear to me: it is a great privilege, as well as a responsibility, to be the stewards of such resources. God must have placed these stones in our hands for a reason."

Will locked eyes with him. "I hardly need to say that we must keep the existence of all three stones a closely guarded secret. I am trusting you to honor that."

"Most certainly," Brother Ander replied, nodding slowly as if to emphasize his words. "Please be assured that I will never reveal the existence of any of these stones, or that you are their guardians."

With a grunt of satisfaction, Will turned back to Thomas. "What else did you learn from the Ahran?"

"He appears to be the Grand Vizier's senior agent right now. Bolnyk has been displaced, and he's gone missing, along with a mysterious prisoner that the Grand Vizier was holding."

Will's eyebrows had gone up. "Gone missing?"

"Yes. He found a way to leave the Grand Vizier's ship undetected. He went ashore."

"You mean he's wandering around somewhere in Rogand?"

"That's what Kahrlin believes. He led a large group of men on a man hunt. They never found Bolnyk."

Will was almost licking his lips. "I'd give a lot to get hold of that man! I have a score to settle with him."

"Bolnyk was involved in the attack on the imperial navy too," continued Thomas. "He led the operation."

"Is that why the Grand Vizier displaced him?" asked Brother Ander.

Thomas shook his head. "The attack was ordered by the Grand Vizier. Kahrlin hired the mercenaries and delivered them to a location where Bolnyk collected them for the raid."

Will's brows were furrowed. "Casting him aside is undoubtedly another example of the Grand Vizier's devious mind at work. Given that Bolnyk has been the key player in everything from the abductions to the recent naval attack, the Grand Vizier might have decided to shift the blame onto him. He could simply claim that his senior agent acted without his authority or knowledge, undermining his best attempts to negotiate."

"There's even a grain of truth in it," said Thomas. "The Grand Vizier might have taken full advantage of the capture of King Rupert and Princess Teylee, but we know that Bolnyk acted on his own initiative when he first took them."

"And it was Bolnyk who oversaw the drowning of Bisri Ahuzza," added Brother Ander.

"What you're saying is we have no hard evidence of the Grand Vizier's direct involvement," growled Will. "He's been very clever. It can't hurt to get access to Bolnyk though. Can you identify where he went ashore?"

"Only roughly. It was southeast of Rog, but I can't be too specific."

Will nodded. "It's a start. I'll speak to the king and Lord Kulferan. I'm sure they'll be willing to send patrols into the area."

KAHRLIN REPORTED to the chief minister's cabin as soon as he returned to his ship.

"Well?" demanded Rheibas.

"They seem willing to meet with you, Your Eminence."

"Who was present at this meeting?"

"King Krasmir, a noblewoman called Lady Tulinay, the head of his security, which I presume means his spy network, and Lord Kulferan, his army commander. No other Rogandans. There were three Arvenians present: Lord Torbury, the army commander, a Thomas Stablehand, and a monk, Brother Ander."

The chief minister cocked an eyebrow. "Did these last two contribute anything?"

"Nothing at all."

"The Arvenians have sunk low indeed if such men are representing them," snorted Rheibas.

He paused thoughtfully. To Kahrlin's eye, he had a gloating look on his face.

"Move the royal captives to a different island immediately," he ordered. "And don't allow them to get settled. I won't risk them being discovered a second time."

He stared coolly at Kahrlin. "If they've agreed to meet, I have preparation to do. You have your orders. You are dismissed!"

THE AHRAN GUARD could not decide whether to be gratified at being chosen or irritated at being left on the island by Kahrlin. The three royal captives had already been transferred to the ship and secured in the hold, and the final group of guards were waiting for Kahrlin in a longboat. Once they left, he would be alone on the island.

"You have enough supplies?" asked Kahrlin.

He nodded. "Yes. Buried out of sight."

"Are you confident you can remain hidden if anyone lands on this island?"

"Yes. There's a cave near the beach. I have hidden the entrance. No one will ever find it."

Kahrlin seemed satisfied. "Watch for ships throughout the

daylight hours. I want to know if anyone even passes by. Do you understand?"

He nodded again.

"Good. I'll expect a full briefing when you're collected in a few days."

The guard watched as Kahrlin climbed into the boat, returned to his ship, and sailed away.

The vessel slowly dwindled to nothing.

Settling down with a sigh and peering out across an empty sea, he commenced his lonely vigil.

UNDER FULL SAIL in a three-masted ship on a special mission for Lord Kulferan, Captain Bezai led a small squadron of two-masted Rogandan vessels in a search for the island where the captive Castelan king, Rogandan princess, and Arvenian queen were supposedly being held. With Commodore Pultek otherwise occupied, he had been granted the honor of leading this mission.

It had been impressed on him that speed was critical, and after Rogandan rescuers had previously missed out so narrowly on reaching the captives in time, he was not willing to wait for slower ships in his squadron.

Although his vessel soon outpaced the others, it didn't concern him. His ship had a full complement of soldiers, many of them capable archers.

The directions had been less than specific. He knew the general vicinity, and he knew he needed to find a small island, positioned between two larger islands each with tall rocky peaks. With islands aplenty in the region, he had no alternative but to carry out a careful search. He was accordingly planning to order the other ships in his squadron to spread out once all of them arrived in the right area.

A protracted search proved unnecessary. His ship located the island surprisingly quickly. With no sign of Ahran vessels anywhere nearby, he put ashore several longboats filled with soldiers. They spread out over the island, searching thoroughly. In the end they found clear indications of recent habitation, including a number of buildings that had been hastily abandoned. They also dug up buried supplies. But they found no sign of people. Returning to the ship, their leader declared the island deserted.

Bezai had been instructed to return immediately if he found the island abandoned. He waited only until the rest of his squadron reached him, then he set sail once more for Rog.

29

Bisri Ahuzza stared moodily ahead as the island of Ahrchitani slowly came into view. The beating heart of the empire lay before him, dazzling in its glory. For the bisri, drawing close to it had always stirred pride, along with a deep sense of belonging. For the first time it felt strangely alien.

He wondered why he had never noticed the brooding menace of the mountain that overlooked the capital of Kat Ahket. Nothing remained of its towering peak except a jagged crater. The vista whispered of the frailty of humankind. If the mountain ever erupted again, no city dweller would be safe, from the emperor to the most wretched. The power of nature was a great leveler.

He allowed his eyes to be drawn lower, across the bustling harbor of Kat Ahket to the glittering palace that lay beyond it. He could only guess at what awaited him there.

Gharpin stood at his side. The former captain seemed unusually taciturn, and Ahuzza wondered what might be on his mind. Perhaps his thoughts were with his crew, every one of them lost at sea thanks to the sabotage instigated by the chief minister. So many men who would never return to their families.

Ahuzza's two guards were standing nearby. They at least had survived. He had brought them because they had also witnessed the chief minister's treachery, and it was possible that the emperor might wish to question them.

A familiar voice broke across his thoughts. "What are you anticipating most, Bisri? The surprise and delight of the emperor at your unexpected return, or the consternation of the chief minister's people at your impossible escape from a watery grave?"

The question drew a grim smile from Ahuzza as he turned his attention to the speaker. "I'm more interested in their reaction when they discover that I've sailed to Kat Ahket with the infamous Shallam—one of King Krasmir's most capable agents."

"Hardly infamous. My goal is to be invisible, although I'm willing to settle for inconspicuous. In any event, I certainly won't be at your side when you meet the emperor."

Shallam's dry humor was one of many things Ahuzza appreciated about him. After risking his life climbing aboard Ahuzza's ship to warn him, the agent had played a key role in rescuing him from drowning. It was hardly surprising that the bisri was predisposed to like him. But Shallam had proven to be unexpectedly good company on the voyage to Kat Ahket, and Ahuzza had come to consider him a friend.

There was one question he had never put to Shallam. "I know your parents are responsible for your fluency in both Rogandan and Ahran. But how did you end up working for King Krasmir?"

Shallam smiled. "You want the truth? I found myself with a choice between working for King Krasmir or for Rheibas, your chief minister. What I knew about Rheibas made it an easy choice."

"It took me far too long to see the truth about Rheibas!"

"You shouldn't berate yourself. He's exceptionally good at hiding his true nature."

"He didn't manage to hide it from you!"

"That's because I think like a spy. Spies find ways to ferret out other people's secrets. You're a diplomat. You're more interested in finding ways of working with other people."

There might have been truth in what Shallam was saying, but Ahuzza wasn't prepared to let himself off that easily. He would be approaching things very differently in future.

"Have you decided how to approach the palace?" Shallam asked. "Are you aiming for bold or subtle?"

"Subtle is much more my style. I also think I'll have a better chance of reaching there alive if no one recognizes me."

Shallam nodded approvingly. "I think you're wise. While you're there, I'll do my best to mingle with the crowd. With any luck I might learn something useful."

"What about me?" asked Gharpin. "We never decided whether I should go to the palace with you immediately or wait until you've made contact with the emperor."

"Now that we're almost there, I'm inclined to think you and my two guards should wait," Ahuzza replied. "All of us have important testimony that implicates the chief minister. It might be wise to avoid any possibility that we could be eliminated at one stroke. If my meeting with the emperor proceeds without incident, I will ask his permission to call for you all. I have no doubt that the emperor will be eager to hear what you have to say."

"That seems prudent," agreed Shallam.

Gharpin nodded his agreement.

As they drew closer to the harbor, Commodore Pultek approached. "Lord Torbury seems to have been right about sailing here in one of our newly acquired Ahran ships rather than my Rogandan-designed three-master. I admit I wasn't enthusiastic about exchanging vessels with Captain Bezai for this mission, but now I'm glad I did. We don't appear to have attracted any attention at all. I'll be taking no risks, though. I'll anchor in the bay rather than pulling in to one of the docks. I'll make a boat available for shore visits. Hopefully that will allow us to avoid attention, at least for a while."

Ahuzza and Shallam disappeared below to prepare for the trip. Ahuzza returned to the deck clad in an unremarkable cloak with a hood to hide his face. Shallam was similarly attired.

A boat was lowered, and after climbing down to it, they were rowed to the shore. Before returning to the ship, the sailors agreed to watch for a prearranged signal, and to send a boat whenever they received it.

The men knew that the quickest way to the palace would be to hire a carriage. However, to avoid drawing attention to themselves they set off walking instead. With the morning not yet spent, they felt they could afford the time.

"How are you planning to arrange an audience with the emperor?" asked Shallam as their destination drew closer.

"I made some preparations before we left the ship," Ahuzza replied. "I'll need your help though."

"Whatever you need," Shallam assured him.

Ahuzza retrieved a parchment from his robe. "This document states that the imperial envoy, Bisri Ahuzza, urgently requests a private audience with the emperor. You'll need to give it to a particular servant. I can tell you his name and how to locate him."

"What about a reply?" asked Shallam.

"You'll need to wait for it. It could take hours, depending on how busy the servant is. The timing of the interview will depend on the emperor's schedule. I imagine that His Majesty has been told I was lost at sea though, so I expect my message will get his attention. I'll be surprised if I need to wait long for an audience."

After sending Shallam away with detailed instructions, Ahuzza settled down to wait.

The afternoon dragged away with no sign of his friend returning, and Ahuzza began to wonder if something had gone wrong. Becoming ever more restless, he decided he would go to the palace to investigate if the sun set before Shallam appeared.

Ahuzza was still hesitating well after the sun sank below the horizon. Unsettled as he was, he knew that leaving the agreed location meant that Shallam would not be able to find him. He briefly contemplated hiring someone to search on his behalf, but the risks were too great to ignore.

In the end he acknowledged that the only sensible course was to continue waiting.

Several hours of darkness had gone by before Shallam eventually returned.

"What happened?" demanded the bisri, trying unsuccessfully to master his agitation.

"It didn't take long to find the servant," Shallam replied, "but he didn't seem in any hurry. He questioned me closely about who I was, and especially why you didn't deliver the message yourself if you were present in the city."

"What did you tell him?"

"What we agreed. That I was your servant, and that you were keeping out of sight due to the sensitive nature of your business. But he'd never seen me before, and I think I roused his suspicions. He asked me a lot of questions."

"What did you do?"

"I answered them. I didn't see I had any choice."

"Do you think he realized you weren't who you were claiming to be?"

Shallam grinned. "I doubt it. I like to think I'm good at what I do. When he eventually decided to give up the questioning, he left without telling me what he was going to do or how long it would take. He only returned two hours ago."

"Two hours ago! Why did it take you so long to get here?"

"It quickly became obvious that I was being followed, so I decided to provide them with some exercise. Once I was confident I'd shaken them, I returned here. I don't think it would be wise to remain here though. It would be safer to return to the ship. I can tell you the outcome while we're signaling the boat."

Ahuzza made to head for the road.

"Not that way!" Shallam called softly. "Follow me! I suspect I know the back alleys of this city as well as you know the major roads."

Even with Shallam wanting to be followed, Ahuzza barely managed to keep up with him. It wasn't difficult to see how the agent had succeeded in losing his pursuers. Shallam wended his way rapidly through streets and alleys, keeping out of sight and avoiding anyone loitering suspiciously in the dark.

Arriving breathless at the designated location on the shore, Ahuzza saw that Shallam had somehow acquired a burning torch. After he had waved the agreed signal, they settled down to wait.

By then, Ahuzza was almost bursting with impatience. “Do I have an audience with the emperor?” he demanded.

“You do,” confirmed the agent. “Although it’s with the imperial crown prince rather than the emperor.”

“Why?” He could make no sense of it. Why wouldn’t the emperor want to speak with him?

Shallam could only shrug. “He didn’t say. You have an audience the day after tomorrow at noon.”

“The day after tomorrow? My note said it was urgent!”

Shallam gave the bisri a wry smile before looking away. “I have a feeling it’s going to be a long two days,” he muttered.

ARRIVING at the palace at the appointed time, Bisri Ahuzza was ushered into the emperor’s reception room. His request for a private audience had been honored, although it was indeed Crown Prince Ahreitas who greeted him rather than the emperor.

“Bisri Ahuzza! Welcome! I am most gratified to see that reports of your death were exaggerated.”

“Thank you, Your Imperial Highness,” the bisri replied, bowing low. “I am grateful to be received by you. I trust that His Imperial Majesty is not unwell.”

“Ah, so you are not aware,” the crown prince replied. “Rheibas requested reinforcements. His negotiations with the Rogandans have apparently stalled. My father decided to do more than simply dispatch the requested soldiers—he sailed with them. He is determined to find out what is going so badly wrong. He appointed me regent in his absence.”

The news filled Ahuzza with alarm. “I fear for His Majesty’s safety!” he exclaimed.

The crown prince frowned. "You believe the Rogandans will try to harm him? I have no doubt he will be well protected by his men."

"No, Your Highness. My concern lies solely with the intentions of the chief minister."

"Be careful what you say, Bisri," growled the crown prince. "It is no small matter to slander the chief minister of the empire!"

"This is not slander, Your Highness!" retorted Ahuzza. "After appointing me as his envoy, the emperor sent me to make independent contact with the Rogandans. In doing so I was able to uncover what the chief minister has been doing there. To prevent me from reporting back to the emperor, he ordered my execution, on the pretext that the emperor had found me guilty of treason! My rescuers barely reached me in time. I was fortunate to survive."

"You were present when the chief minister ordered your execution?"

"I did not personally witness him giving the order," Ahuzza admitted. "The accusation against me was delivered by Bolnyk, the chief minister's senior agent. His men restrained me while he knotted an anchor rope around my neck and threw me overboard with the anchor. The chief minister might not have been directly involved, but Bolnyk only ever carries out the wishes of his master."

The crown prince frowned. "I've never understood what possessed Rheibas to drag Bolnyk from the gutter."

He considered Ahuzza gravely. "These are weighty charges, Bisri, and they must be properly investigated. I also wish to hear whatever you have learned in Rogand. All in good time. I have many responsibilities to attend to. While a formal inquiry is being set up, I will arrange accommodation for you. I will also ensure that you are properly guarded—purely for your own safety of course. You seem to have been making powerful enemies."

"But I must warn the emperor, Your Highness!"

The crown prince eyed him condescendingly. "My father's safety is not your concern, Ahuzza," he said haughtily. "His men are well able to ensure his security."

Calling for the imperial guards, he nodded toward Ahuzza.

"Escort the bisri to a secure apartment. Make sure that he is well provided for, but ensure that he remains safely under your protection until I notify you."

With that, the crown prince appeared to lose interest in the bisri entirely. Accompanied by his aides, he left the room without a backward glance.

Dismayed and downcast, Ahuzza allowed himself to be led away by the imperial guards. He wondered if he should have mentioned Gharpin, but he found it hard to imagine that the captain's testimony would have swayed the crown prince.

After a long delay, he was taken to a small palace apartment overlooking the city and ushered inside. The guards left with a promise of refreshments, locking the door behind them.

A brief inspection revealed that the apartment was comfortable, well appointed, and entirely self contained. It also confirmed that the door to the apartment provided the only access to the room. The outer wall featured a single large window, its shutters thrown wide to reveal an impressive outlook across the city. Unfortunately the window was perched several stories above the ground, offering no opportunity for escape.

Ahuzza groaned in frustration. It was now apparent that he had sailed past the emperor without realizing it. If only they could have met at sea. The emperor had personally appointed Ahuzza—he surely would not have ignored the warnings of his own envoy.

As regent, Crown Prince Ahreitas should have taken the threat to his father more seriously. A new and deeply disturbing possibility now occurred to him. Why had the crown prince sidelined Ahuzza and dismissed his concerns? Was it possible he was in league with Rheibas? Or was he simply willing to benefit by turning a blind eye to Rheibas's treachery? It wouldn't be the first time an heir to the throne had become weary of waiting his turn.

In any event, there could be no doubt that the emperor was sailing into deadly peril. Worse, the men charged with protecting him would be looking in the wrong direction. Alert to any threat from the

Rogandans, they would see no reason to guard their master against his own people.

The more Ahuzza's mind churned through the possible scenarios, the more alarmed he became. But there was nothing he could do. He was a prisoner in all but name.

30

The first full day of Ahuzza's confinement dragged by with nothing more remarkable than a brief social call from a winged visitor. Flying into the room through the open window, a bird fluttered about for a few moments before flying out again.

The freedom of the bird provoked considerable envy from the bisri. Had he been fortunate enough to possess wings, he would have fled the room in an instant.

He thought about Shallam and Gharpin, and Pultek and the ship, hoping they hadn't encountered trouble while waiting to hear from him. If they had decided to wait, it was likely they wouldn't be going anywhere for a very long time.

If only he had a way of getting a message to them. There was nothing preventing them from setting out to warn the emperor. Gharpin's testimony needed to be heard no less than his own. But who could he trust with a message? He knew plenty of people in Kat Ahket, including a number who were worthy of his trust. None of them had any idea he was in the city though, and he had no way of reaching them even if they did.

He had slept poorly the previous night. It had nothing to do with the bed—his mind simply refused to quit. With the crown prince unwilling to take his concerns seriously, it wasn't clear to him who else might be in a position to safeguard the interests of the emperor. The sovereign's personal bodyguards were sworn to defend him with their lives, but how could they be effective without a proper awareness of the threats they were facing?

The more he thought about the emperor sailing off in support of Rheibas, the more it alarmed him. The chief minister's agenda was a mystery, but two things were clear—his behavior was neither open nor transparent, and he was acting in his own interests, not in the interests of the emperor.

How far might Rheibas be willing to go? Was the life of the emperor at risk? In the absence of clear answers, Ahuzza could only guess. He was left with nothing to do but agonize helplessly.

Consequently, he waited until he was drooping with weariness before retiring for a second time. Closing the shutters, he lay down and waited for exhaustion to claim him. It was not until the early hours of the morning that he succumbed at last.

The release of sleep came at a price. Caught up in the distorted reality of a dream, Ahuzza found himself afloat in the sea, not far from the ship that bore the emperor. Standing on deck, the emperor seemed unaware that the vessel was sailing directly toward a massive whirlpool. No one on board showed any awareness of the peril, the helmsman maintaining his course steadfastly until the ship was almost in the grip of the maelstrom.

Below them in the water, Ahuzza began swimming frantically in the direction of the ship, shouting at the top of his lungs in a desperate attempt to deliver a warning. His efforts proved futile. Along with the ship, he was swept into the whirlpool, spinning helplessly as he sank lower and lower into the vortex.

A giant crab suddenly surfaced beside the circling ship, tapping a claw rhythmically against the hull. Before he could make any sense of the bizarre experience, Ahuzza woke with a start. Someone was tapping on the shutters of his window.

Rising blearily from his bed, he stumbled to the window and

opened the shutters a crack. The tapping ceased abruptly, and he dimly glimpsed a dark figure hanging from a rope outside his window. He drew back in alarm. A hood covered the head of the intruder, but a voice he recognized said softly, "Is it safe to come in?"

After staring wide-eyed for a moment, he grasped the rope and swung the interloper into the room. "What are you doing here, Shallam?" he breathed incredulously as the agent released the rope and removed his hood.

"I came to find out what your situation was," the agent replied quietly, a smile on his face. "It occurred to me you might not want to remain stuck in here."

"You certainly got that right!" Ahuzza assured him. "How do you propose to get me out though? There are guards stationed permanently outside the door."

"Are you any good with ropes?" asked Shallam calmly.

Seeing the astonishment on Ahuzza's face, he added, "It's only five floors to the ground. I'm confident you can manage the descent."

After hesitating for a long moment, Ahuzza nodded reluctantly. "I'll try. Being stranded here indefinitely is not something I'm willing to consider. Not for any reason."

"I'll show you how to do it," Shallam assured him. "I'll make sure you've got it right before I let you attempt a descent."

First he instructed Ahuzza to put on a sturdy cloak. "You'll need that to avoid rope burn," he said. Then he handed him a thick pair of gloves and told him to put them on.

Pulling in plenty of slack, Shallam ran the rope between his legs, pulling it around his left leg and up over his right shoulder. Running it across the back of his neck, he brought it under his left arm, stretching out his arm to grasp it firmly below his waist. Then he reached up with his right hand and grasped the rope at head height.

"You'll use your left hand to control the speed of your descent," he said. "When you relax your grip on the rope, it will slide through your hand and you'll slide downward. Place your feet on the wall of the building and allow your body to lean outward. Then push away from the wall with your feet and slide down a short distance before letting your feet come back onto the wall again. It works best if you use a hopping motion. You simply repeat that until you reach the ground. When you want to descend, your left hand should be away from your body. To stop, draw your left hand across your body and grasp the rope tightly."

Shallam stepped out of the rope and helped Ahuzza wrap it around his own body in the correct way. Then he repeated his instructions.

"Do you understand?" he asked.

Ahuzza nodded. He pointed to a second rope hanging outside the window. "What's that for?"

"That rope is for me," Shallam told him, reaching for it. "I'll be descending beside you. If you need help, I'll be right there."

Once he was satisfied that they were both ready, Shallam stepped onto the window sill. "Don't look down!" he warned Ahuzza. "Focus on the wall in front of you." Then with a little hop, he lowered himself a short distance.

As Ahuzza took his place on the window sill, he broke out in a cold sweat. With his hands suddenly clammy, he was grateful for the gloves. He stood trembling for a couple of long minutes, hanging out over the void.

"You can do it!" whispered Shallam.

With a little hop, Ahuzza lowered himself a tiny distance. To his amazement, it worked. Repeating the movement, he landed beside Shallam.

"The rope is starting to burn my shoulder," he whispered, grimacing.

"The best way to end that is to reach the bottom," the agent told him, hopping downward a little further.

Ignoring the discomfort, Ahuzza followed him down. The descent was going surprisingly well until they reached a shuttered window on the floor below.

"We need a bigger hop this time," Shallam whispered, nodding his head toward the window below. "If we land on the shutters, it might wake whoever's in that room."

He demonstrated by lowering himself the entire length of the window in one smooth motion.

Ahuzza's attempt at the same maneuver yielded a very different outcome. Managing to descend just half the distance, he landed on the shutters with the whole weight of his body. The noise sounded deafening in the stillness. Remarkably, the shutters remained closed. Ahuzza hung there helplessly, barely able to control his shaking.

"Once more!" Shallam urged.

Closing his eyes, Ahuzza forced himself to do another hop. This time he cleared the shutters.

"Well done!" whispered Shallam. "Let's not wait around to see if that room was occupied." So saying, he hopped downward once more, resting while he waited for the bisri.

The rest of the descent felt to Ahuzza like a waking nightmare. Somehow both of them reached the ground in safety. Incredibly, no one appeared to have been roused in the process. Leaving the ropes, Shallam led them to the shelter of some trees nearby.

"Wait here," he said. "There's a simple way to get onto the roof where I tied the ropes. I'll climb up and untie them."

After he had reached the ground, Ahuzza's limbs had begun shaking uncontrollably. He sat down in an attempt to master his trembling, watching distractedly as the agent disappeared once more on his way back up to the top of the building.

After a few minutes, he untied the ropes and they fell to the ground. Climbing back down from the roof, Shallam retrieved the ropes. Coiling them swiftly, he put one over each shoulder.

By then Ahuzza felt able to move. Setting off after Shallam, he wound his way back through the darkened streets of the city. They reached the shore without incident. Signaling the ship, they settled down to wait for a boat to arrive.

Less than two hours passed from the time Shallam arrived at Ahuzza's window to the moment Commodore Pultek and Gharpin welcomed them aboard.

"When can we leave?" the bisri asked, waiting impatiently for Shallam to translate the question for Pultek.

"The tide should turn in about an hour," Pultek replied. "I expect we can be well clear of the bay before dawn." His brows furrowed. "Not a moment too soon, either. We were beginning to attract attention. Just before sunset I spotted a couple of port officials pointing in our direction. I don't think we could have avoided a visit if we were still here at sunrise."

Pultek excused himself to oversee preparations for their departure. As soon as they were underway, Ahuzza, Shallam, and Gharpin joined the commodore in his cabin.

Pressure had slowly been building inside the bisri since his escape from the palace, and now the dam burst at last. Everything poured out—his conversation with the crown prince, the decision to confine him under guard, his frustration about being denied an opportunity to warn the emperor.

Apart from Shallam's translation for the benefit of Pultek, all of them listened in silence, and when he came to an end, they politely gave him time to recover himself.

Needing to deflect attention elsewhere, Ahuzza asked Shallam, "How did you find me?"

"It took a while. It cost me some coin too. But eventually I was able to discover exactly where you were being held. Getting you out proved a lot easier than I feared. You did well with the rope." Seeing the look on Ahuzza's face, he chuckled. "I'll be happy to help you perfect your technique any time you like."

The bisri shuddered. "I won't be sorry if I never touch another rope again."

The agent jerked his head back in the direction of Kat Ahket. "It won't be too long before the guards discover you're missing. They'll be wondering how you managed to disappear without trace. I imagine the crown prince won't be too pleased."

"He certainly won't," said Ahuzza emphatically. After hesitating for a moment, he revealed his fears about the crown prince and his possible motives.

"We need to warn the emperor as a matter of urgency," he concluded. "How quickly can you get us back to Rogand?" he asked the commodore.

“This ship is fast, and while you were gone Captain Gharpin familiarized me with a few aspects of its design I was unfamiliar with,” Pultek told him. “I also took the opportunity to drill my men. Bad weather aside, we’ll be there sooner than you could possibly imagine.”

Dawn found them plowing swiftly through a moderate swell, favorable winds filling their sails. Ahr-chitani had already dwindled to a tiny dot behind them.

The breeze whipped the hair from Bisri Ahuzza’s face as he stood leaning against the rail, gazing at a horizon that revealed nothing apart from the endless wave crests rolling toward them.

A single question dominated his thoughts—would they reach the emperor in time?

31

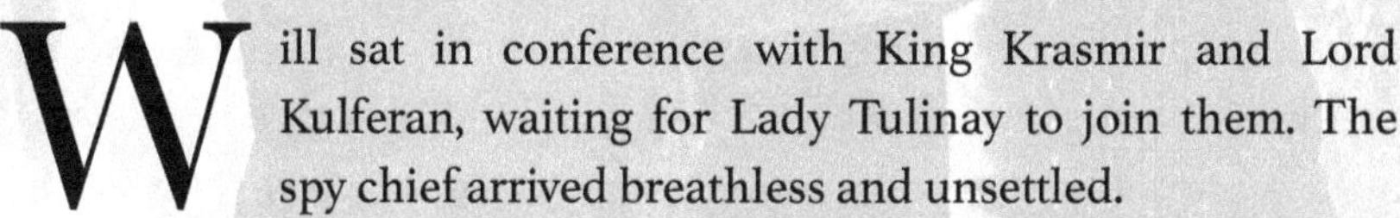

Will sat in conference with King Krasmir and Lord Kulferan, waiting for Lady Tulinay to join them. The spy chief arrived breathless and unsettled.

"I have news—a lot of news! Most importantly, an Ahran fleet has been sighted!"

Lord Kulferan frowned. "How many ships?"

"The report came from a merchant, so it's difficult to be certain. He counted fifteen, but he was sure there were more."

"Where did he see them?" asked Will.

"About two days out from Rogand. They were heading in this direction. They didn't appear to be in a hurry."

"We could use some bad weather right now," Will muttered, shaking his head.

His own attempts at using the Stone of Authority to influence the weather had been far from encouraging. Not for the first time, he wished that Amyra had traveled with him to Rogand. If it came to an invasion, they would be forced to rely on more conventional methods to overcome the Ahrans.

A grim look had come over the king's face. "So the threatened reinforcements are almost here." He turned to his commander. "How advanced are your preparations?"

Lord Kulferan was already on his feet, anxious to leave. "The first levies have arrived, Your Majesty. I have men searching out landing points that might be suitable for a large force." He shook his head. "There are far too many possible locations for the Ahrans to use. Before we can be confident of our defenses, there is a great deal that needs to be done."

"Go!" the king told him. "I won't be far behind you. I intend to notify the nobles within the hour."

The commander hurried away.

King Krasmir had turned to face Will. "Will Arvenon stand with us, Lord Torbury?"

The king's voice was calm, but with the moment of truth upon him at last, the tension in his face betrayed his uncertainty. Will wasn't surprised. Not many years had passed since Rogand invaded the neighboring kingdoms, inflicting great suffering and distress, and neither the king nor anyone else could magically undo the damage.

"Arvenon will stand with you, Your Majesty. Letting go of the past is difficult for many, but King Steffan understands what is at stake here."

The king was clearly relieved. "Please express my gratitude to your sovereign, My Lord."

Will bowed.

"You suggested there is other news," the king told Lady Tulinay.

"Yes!" the spy chief confirmed. "A patrol has brought in two men from the region where Bolnyk and his companion went missing."

Will's heart began to race at the prospect of confronting the man who had murdered his son.

"Do you think you would recognize Bolnyk if you saw him again?" Lady Tulinay asked Will.

He did not hesitate. "Most certainly!"

The king was eager to be gone. "Please find out if he has any useful information. We need any help we can get."

. . .

THE DUNGEONS under the royal castle at Rog were largely vacant under King Krasmir. Nevertheless, guards stood alert as Will followed Lady Tulinay into an occupied section. She came to a halt before an iron door that offered a square viewing hole at eye level. Peering in, Will saw that the prisoner was Bolnyk.

Will glanced at Lady Tulinay. "It's him."

"You're certain?"

He nodded.

"Then I'll have him restrained. I didn't want to do it before we were confident of his identity."

She waved forward a group of guards. "We need to talk to the prisoner. Secure him!"

Unlocking the door, four guards went inside. Three of them stood watchfully by as the fourth attached leg irons to the prisoner's ankles. He did not resist.

The guards left the cell and stood aside to allow Will to enter. Lady Tulinay followed him in.

The appearance of the Ahran agent suggested he had been through hard times since last Will had seen him. His eyes seemed sunken, and his clothes were torn and ragged.

Bolnyk gazed at them indifferently for a moment, then a frown came to his face. "I know you," he said, eyeing Will.

Will stared back at him coldly. "I'm the man whose son you murdered."

The prisoner's eyes narrowed. "I was following orders."

"And you think that absolves you? You were the one who killed my son! Your Grand Vizier didn't do it!"

"It wasn't personal," Bolnyk returned indifferently.

An icy calm had settled over Will. Approaching the agent, he leaned forward aggressively until he was inches from Bolnyk's face. "Maybe I'll kill you now," he purred. "And just so there's no misunderstanding, it will certainly be personal."

Lady Tulinay apparently decided the time had come to intervene.

Dragging Will back, she positioned herself between him and the prisoner. "Give me one reason why we shouldn't execute you."

"You want to bring down the chief minister. I'm the only one who can do that."

Will scoffed at the claim. "You're the only one who's going to be brought down! You've been very busy on your Grand Vizier's behalf, and he's going to blame you for all of it. He'll say you acted independently. It will be your word against his. It isn't hard to guess who the emperor's going to believe."

"Unless I provide proof," Bolnyk returned quietly.

Will glared at him. "What proof?"

The prisoner refused to say another word.

Glowering at him in frustration, Will berated himself for not bringing Thomas.

Lady Tulinay jostled Will from the room. As soon as they were out of earshot she rounded furiously on him. "What game do you think you were playing? You don't get to decide about his execution! If he is executed, it won't be purely to satisfy your need for revenge!"

Will glared back at her. "It's personal for me, and I won't pretend otherwise."

"Then in future you won't be going anywhere near him."

His fury abated as they walked away. As soon as he had mastered himself, she asked, "Do you think he has proof?"

Will snorted. "I doubt it. Notice he didn't actually say that he has! It's probably no more than a ploy. He's lived by deceit and manipulation—he wants to keep us hanging so we'll let him live for a while longer."

She didn't seem convinced. "If there's any truth to his claim, we can't afford to ignore it. There's far too much at stake. I'll explore it with him later." She glowered at Will. "Sometime when you're not around."

Thomas sat with Brother Ander. Will had joined them as they

were discussing the arrival of the emperor's ships. The news had spread rapidly through the palace, and the tension in the air was almost palpable.

"What do you think about the ships, Will?" Thomas asked anxiously.

Will waved a hand dismissively. "Bolnyk is being held in the dungeons right now! That's of much more interest to me."

Will's mind was clearly buzzing, and they eyed him uneasily as he paced restlessly back and forth.

"I need you to get a look at him, Thomas! I want to know if he has proof of the Grand Vizier's involvement, or if he's just lying."

Thomas nodded. "Of course. I'll go if you can arrange it."

The appearance of Bolnyk had clearly reawakened the trauma of Ethen's captivity. It was obvious that Will was not himself.

Will's intensity brought back uncomfortable memories for Thomas. No one but the Grand Vizier would benefit if he remained in this state. "You can't let Bolnyk get to you, Will! All of us are relying on you. We need you more than ever right now."

Will offered nothing more than a grunt in response.

"You're going to have to forgive him, Will," Brother Ander said calmly.

"Forgive him?! Never! He doesn't deserve it!"

The monk was not deterred. "No, he doesn't," he agreed. "I don't deserve forgiveness either. Not after some of the things I've done. But if God is willing to extend mercy to me, how can I do less to others?"

He paused, gazing at Will in concern. "Your anger will consume you if you don't let it go."

Will grunted again, although he seemed less agitated than before.

"You're right. Both of you," he conceded. "It isn't going to be easy, but I'll do my best to be calm and measured where Bolnyk is concerned." A wry smile came to his lips. "It isn't actually an option. Until I can manage to do that, Lady Tulinay isn't going to let me anywhere near him."

With the threat of war uppermost in every mind, it was clear to Will that access to Bolnyk would soon be viewed as a low priority. He wasted no time in meeting with Lady Tulinay.

"Have you learned anything useful from Bolnyk?" asked Will.

The spy chief scowled. "He has a few things to say—when it suits him. But he's short on details."

"Would you allow me to meet with him one more time?"

Her lips twisted in an ironic grin. "So you can carve him up into little pieces?"

"No. You can expect a different approach from me. I won't pretend my feelings have changed, and you'll never convince me he doesn't richly deserve anything I might do to him. But I'm no fool. None of us can afford the luxury of personal vendettas. Especially now. I'm willing to let King Krasmir decide whether and when Bolnyk's life should come to an end."

She eyed him suspiciously. "How do I know you're telling the truth?"

He sighed. "Because I make a habit of telling the truth. Ask anyone. You'll soon discover that I'm a man of my word."

"And where are these people who can vouch for you?"

"Arvenon, Castel, Varas," he said mildly. "Aen-irac, too, if you're looking for somewhere closer to home."

She scowled at him. "Your answers are about as useful as Bolnyk's."

Cocking an eyebrow, he gazed at her knowingly. "I'm not trying to be glib. I've heard reports of the spy network you oversee, Lady Tulinay. Even the Varasans and Castelans envy its reach! I know your agents have compiled a detailed profile on me. There's no point in denying it! The most cursory examination of that information will quickly confirm what I'm saying."

She rolled her eyes. "The report you refer to certainly exists, and you can be assured that I have studied it carefully. I might add that it also warns you're a smooth talker."

He executed a little bow.

"Why should I make it a priority for you to meet with Bolnyk again?" she demanded.

"I want to ask him some questions in the presence of my friend and countryman, Thomas Stablehand. The reason for including Thomas is that he is unusually adept at discerning falsehood and deceit. Bolnyk claims to have evidence that implicates the Grand Vizier. We need to know if there's anything worth pursuing, and we need to know now. We might not have a lot of time."

The spy chief was studying him closely through narrowed eyes. "Very well," she said finally. "Don't come armed. You'll be sitting across a table from Bolnyk. It will be a wide table. I will decide when the interview is over, but you can certainly expect it to end the moment personal feelings make an appearance."

"And what about the other man? Can we meet with him too?"

"No," she said flatly. "I'm letting you meet with Bolnyk because there's an outside chance he might prove useful. But we have a foreign army on our doorstep! I'm not setting up interviews for you with every prisoner that catches your fancy. There's no point anyway—he refuses to answer questions."

He wouldn't need to answer questions if Thomas was present in the room. But Will couldn't say that. In the face of her stubborn resistance, there was no point in pursuing it further.

He bowed. "You have my thanks, My Lady. I promise there will be no surprises from my end when we meet with Bolnyk."

WILL LED Thomas into a room dominated by a very large table. On one side of the table sat Lady Tulinay with an aide at her side. Across from her sat Bolnyk, his wrists chained and secured to the table.

"Lord Torbury," said the spy chief with a welcoming nod. "You have already met Bolnyk." She ignored Thomas, probably in a considerate attempt to preserve his anonymity.

Having been waved to seats located on the same side of the table as Lady Tulinay, Will and Thomas made themselves comfortable. Both of them immediately turned their full attention to Bolnyk.

Will addressed the agent. "Are you aware of the Grand Vizier's purpose in coming here?"

Bolnyk gazed back at him dispassionately. "Your question would be better directed to the man who escaped with me from the chief minister's ship."

"Who is he, and why was he being held captive? And how is he aware of the Grand Vizier's intentions?"

"If I knew the answers to any of those questions, I wouldn't need to direct you to him."

"You spoke of evidence of the Grand Vizier's duplicity. What is the nature of this evidence?"

"The evidence is for the eyes of the emperor alone."

"If you expect us to put you in front of the emperor you'll need to do better than that."

Bolnyk's mouth clamped shut.

Glancing at Thomas, Will saw his friend blink twice. By prior agreement, blinking twice meant that Bolnyk did indeed have evidence.

Will headed in a different direction. "What do you know of reinforcements from the emperor?"

Bolnyk offered no response. His body language made it clear they would get nothing further from him.

Aiming a grateful nod at Lady Tulinay, Will got to his feet and headed for the door, closely followed by Thomas.

The spy chief followed them outside.

"Well?" she asked.

"I am satisfied that he has evidence," Will told her. "That means his life is worth preserving, and it also means we need to find a way to get him in front of the emperor."

She eyed him curiously. "Why the sudden change in your attitude?"

Will shrugged. "When he first arrived I found it very hard to be objective. I'm sure that won't surprise you given our history."

"And what convinced you about the evidence? He didn't say a word about it."

"That's what convinced me. If he was lying to save his life, I would have expected him to have plenty to say."

She didn't seem satisfied. "Why say nothing, though? How does that benefit him?"

Thomas finally decided to help. "Perhaps he's conflicted. He's angry with the Grand Vizier, but even so, it can't be easy to turn against someone he's served for so long. Some part of him might still be hoping the Grand Vizier will decide it was a mistake to have cast him aside."

The spy chief was looking at Thomas as if she was noticing him for the first time. Thomas didn't seem to be enjoying the attention.

"Do you believe you can convince Bolnyk to work with us?" Will asked her.

She shrugged. "If your friend here is right, Bolnyk might never fully cooperate until it's obvious his master has abandoned him completely."

Will nodded. After thanking her once more for setting up the interview, he left with Thomas.

The moment they returned to their rooms, Will turned eagerly to Thomas.

"What did you discover?"

"I was shocked when I saw Bolnyk. He's a different man from the one I saw previously. The Grand Vizier's betrayal is something he never thought possible, and it's scarred him deeply. Some part of him is still hoping that things will return to normal, even though deep down he knows that isn't going to happen."

"If he's conflicted, he hasn't completely changed sides. We can't lose sight of who he is. He might be wounded, but he's still dangerous."

Thomas nodded. "He's capable of doing a lot of damage if given the chance."

"What about the former prisoner he escaped with?"

"Bolnyk was telling the truth. He doesn't know who the prisoner is, and he has no idea what the Grand Vizier wants with the man. The time they spent together after landing in Rogand left him none the wiser."

"Why did they escape together?"

"Bolnyk was entirely responsible for that. He wanted a simple and effective way to hit back at the Grand Vizier."

"And what about Bolnyk's evidence?"

"The evidence exists. It's a document."

"What's in it?"

"I can't be certain." Seeing Will's surprise, he added, "Bolnyk has handled a lot of documents over the years he's served the Grand Vizier, all of them written in Ahran. You're aware that I can't read. Even if I could, I don't understand Ahran. That means I can't make a lot of sense of Bolnyk's memories of the contents. I was able to identify which document is relevant, but it doesn't help."

Will threw up his hands in frustration.

"And there's another complication. Bolnyk thinks there might be a problem if he uses this document against the Grand Vizier. The problem is somehow connected with Princess Neira, but I can't tell you any more than that."

Will buried his head in his hands.

Thomas wasn't finished. "There's something else going on as well. It involves the priests of the dark gods, although I can't tell if the main contact is the Archprimus—the second in charge—or the High Priest himself."

"Why can't you tell?"

"The Ahrans have a title that means nothing to me, and that's how Bolnyk thinks about him. There have been meetings with priests, but they've always been hooded and unrecognizable."

"What's the purpose of the connection?"

"Bolnyk doesn't know. He believes there's some kind of power struggle going on within the priesthood, but he doesn't know what the priests want from the Grand Vizier."

"What's in it for the Grand Vizier?"

"Bolnyk has absolutely no idea."

32

Roused from sleep long before she was ready, Princess Teylee opened her eyes to find herself staring into the unyielding face of an Ahran guard.

"Get up!" he growled. "You're being moved!"

Throwing a small lump of hard bread at her feet, he turned on his heel and strode away.

A glance to one side showed her that her fellow captives had been woken as well.

Pulling herself to her feet, Tasha stretched uncomfortably. Her back was aching, but that was hardly surprising after another night sleeping on the ground.

"The early days of our captivity feel like a distant memory," she told Rupert wistfully.

He nodded. "Remember Dessue, the first guard in charge of us? He was impossibly benevolent, although I probably didn't see it that way at the time."

"It's been a continual downward slide since then," she agreed.

"They've come down especially hard on us since our escape," the pretend queen observed. "It seems they've been told to keep us alive and to keep their hands off us. Beyond that, they clearly have unlimited discretion to do as they see fit."

Tasha shrugged. "It wouldn't matter so much if they didn't keep changing our location."

Leaving them in one location for any length of time was apparently considered a security risk. The problem was that the guards had no interest in constantly building new shelters for the prisoners. If the prisoners wanted shelter, they had to build it themselves.

"Are we going to sleep under the stars again at the new location?" she asked, screwing up her nose.

"I imagine it will depend on the weather," Rupert replied.

Their companion gazed up at the sky. "We should be able to do it a while longer. At least until the rainy season starts."

"More delightful hours spent with the hard earth at my back," said Tasha with a sigh.

Rupert stared at the guards, busy preparing for another departure. "I wonder how much longer this will go on. They can't keep holding us forever."

Neither of the women responded. It was a topic they preferred not to dwell on.

He gazed at the Varasan agent. "What will you do if we never get to see the Grand Vizier?"

She shrugged. "One way or another I'll find him. And when I do I'll kill him."

"Why do you hate him so much?" he asked.

She gazed off into the distance without speaking. When she finally replied, her mouth was tight. "I had an Ahran father and a Varasan mother. We were living on the island of Ahr-shesan. There was a revolt there, and he came to put it down. My parents were good people. They'd done nothing wrong, and he well knew it. He had them executed anyway, along with five hundred others. He wanted to make a statement." After a pause, she added tersely, "I don't like to talk about it."

Her voice trailed off, and she continued staring at nothing.

Reaching out, Tasha placed a tentative hand on her shoulder. She couldn't find words. Maybe it was another subject better left alone.

Soon they were bustled into a boat and rowed to a ship. The guards didn't let up on them until they were locked in the hold without food or water or light.

The day was rapidly turning into one of those times when Tasha wondered if she could bear it for another minute. Closing her eyes, she released a shuddering sigh.

In response Rupert groped his way over and threw an arm around her shoulder, drawing her close. She gazed up at him in the darkness, appreciating afresh his warmth, his solidity, and his determination to win through in spite of everything. She had lived through the worst of times with him at her side. Always he had treated her with respect and consideration.

"We'll make it through this, and we'll do it together," he said determinedly.

"Together," she echoed, returning a tender smile she knew he couldn't see.

KAHRLIN FOUND himself summoned to Rheibas's cabin.

His master looked up from his desk when Kahrlin arrived. "Send a message to our contact among the priests. Tell him that the moment has arrived."

The agent bowed an acknowledgment.

Rheibas got to his feet and stretched himself to his full height. "The time has come to meet with Krasmir and his ragtag band. Are you prepared?"

"I am, Your Eminence."

"Are there any hindrances?"

"None that I am aware of."

"Then summon them to the meeting! "

The chief minister's lip peeled back to reveal his teeth. "It's time the Rogandans did some dancing, and to our tune."

WILL SAT in his usual seat conferring with King Krasmir, Lady Tulinay, and Lord Kulferan. The group had developed into an informal council of war, meeting early each morning before the main business of the day began.

The irony of his current role was not lost on Will, given his reputation as the architect of the Rogandan defeat in Agon's war. He guessed that his inclusion gave tangible expression to the alliance King Steffan had promised in the event of an attack. He also hoped that the king appreciated his strategic insights. Above all, he felt humbled by the trust the king placed in him.

What Krasmir's other nobles thought of his involvement was another matter entirely. He didn't know and had no desire to find out. That said, it wasn't hard to guess. The locals referred to Will as the Lash of the Devil—King Krasmir himself had told him as much.

His musing was interrupted by a servant who hurried in with a dispatch for the spy chief. She quickly scanned it.

"It's finally come. The Grand Vizier proposes that we follow through on the summit discussed with his senior agent Kahrlin. He points to the risks associated with any continuation of the 'current misunderstandings.' He urges us to meet with him as a matter of great urgency."

"Where does the snake propose to meet?" growled the king.

"On board his ship," she replied.

Lord Kulferan gave a mocking laugh. "We cannot possibly agree to that! It would pose an unacceptable risk. The man's history of treachery is far too well established."

The king was scowling. "We'd be doing his emperor a favor if we engaged in some treachery of our own and rid the world of him entirely."

Will nodded gravely. "Satisfying as that would be, Your Majesty, it might better serve the cause of international harmony if we let the emperor dispose of him—after we get the captives back. In the meantime, our own plans are in motion. They need time to come to full fruition."

The king sputtered, but he accepted the change in tone.

The others shot Will a grateful look.

Will had every sympathy for the king. He understood better than anyone the impact of a beloved child's abduction. Whenever the king's simmering anger threatened to bubble over, Will recognized the signs and worked deftly to steer the king in a more helpful direction.

There could be no doubt that King Krasmir understood perfectly well what Will was doing. Thus far at least he had tolerated it with good grace.

"We could provide a ship of our own," Lord Kulferan suggested.

"Or we could suggest a suitable location ashore," Lady Tulinay offered.

Will wasn't convinced. "Allowing them to land on Rogandan soil might be sending the wrong message."

The king grunted his agreement. "It took far too much effort to root out their previous footholds—I'm not letting them back in. Besides, I can't imagine them agreeing. For all they know we could have an army waiting over the hill."

"I believe a Varasan diplomatic vessel recently docked in Rog Harbor," observed Will. "As far as we're aware, the Ahrans still believe they abducted Queen Essanda rather than a Varasan impostor. From their perspective, that leaves Varas as the one kingdom in the region with no active grievance against them. In view of that, perhaps we could prevail upon the Varasans to offer their ship as a neutral location."

"A suggestion worth considering. Lady Tulinay, please explore it with the Varasans on my behalf."

As the meeting broke up, Will leaned toward the king. "I would like to propose that Brother Ander be present on board, Your Majesty."

The king frowned back at him. "You want him to attend the conference?" he asked in disbelief.

"Not at all. My request is prompted by his unusual healing gift. I see it as a precautionary measure to have him available."

"It's hard to believe that it might be necessary. But I will concede that the Grand Vizier is unpredictable. I suppose it is acceptable, provided he stays out of the way."

Will contented himself with a grateful nod.

The king was eyeing him shrewdly. "If I know you at all, Lord Torbury, your next request will be for Thomas Stablehand to be allowed to keep Brother Ander company."

"An excellent suggestion, Your Majesty! I'm glad you thought of it."

The king rolled his eyes, but he didn't seem to have strong objections to the notion.

So much about the Grand Vizier was unknown, and the pressing need for insight into his plans and motives made it crucial that Thomas was present with the Stone of Knowing. Not for the first time, Will had traded on the king's respect for Brother Ander to achieve the result they needed.

THE IMPERIAL ADMIRAL sought out the emperor. "We have reached Rogandan waters, Your Majesty. I am keeping our ships well away from land, as you instructed."

The emperor nodded gravely. "Search out the chief minister, and General Vholahr. I want their reports as a matter of urgency. Make the request in your name, not in mine."

"At once, Your Majesty."

The admiral withdrew with a bow and began rapidly issuing orders. Four ships soon separated from the fleet and set off in search of the other Ahrans.

Two full days passed before the admiral again appeared before the emperor. "I have received two dispatches, Your Majesty."

Taking the dispatches, the emperor opened and carefully scanned the first of them. He turned to the admiral. "General Vholahr acknowledges your arrival. There has been no further change in his situation. He will hold his squadron at its current location until he receives new orders."

The second dispatch appeared to be more consequential. "The chief minister is about to join a summit meeting with the Rogandans, and he urgently requests your presence," the emperor told the admiral. "I will join him at the indicated location. Bring three additional ships for close support. The rest can follow at a distance."

After hastily signaling the rest of the fleet, the admiral set a course for the location of the meeting.

BISRI AHUZZA WAS RESTING below decks when he received an invitation to join Commodore Pultek at the helm. Shallam was included in the invitation.

"My lookout has spotted a number of ships ahead. All of them have three masts. It is possible we have reached the emperor's fleet."

Barely able to contain his excitement, Ahuzza asked, "Can we contact them?"

"Of course," Pultek replied. "They might regard us as hostile when they find out who we are, though."

"I will speak to them," Ahuzza assured him.

The ships ahead were traveling slowly, and before long Pultek was able to reach them. A boat was lowered, and Ahuzza was rowed to the nearest ship. A net was lowered for him, and he climbed aboard.

Several soldiers surrounded him as soon as he stepped onto the deck.

"I am Bisri Ahuzza, envoy to the emperor," Ahuzza told them confidently. "I need to speak with your captain."

The soldiers appeared suspicious, but they nevertheless led him to the captain who was standing at the helm. Ahuzza thought he vaguely recognized the captain, but he couldn't be certain.

"I need to speak with you privately—on a matter of considerable urgency, Captain," the bisri told him.

After considering him for a moment, the captain nodded. “I know who you are, Bisri. Follow me.” Setting off toward his cabin, he waved Ahuzza to his side.

As soon as they were alone, Ahuzza said, “I need to reach the emperor on a pressing matter. His Highness the Crown Prince informed me that the emperor had joined the fleet in sailing to Rogand. Can you please direct me to His Majesty urgently?”

It proved significant that the captain knew Ahuzza to be genuine. He said without hesitation, “Several ships have gone on ahead. The emperor is with the admiral on the flagship.” He then described the location.

“Thank you, Captain! Please excuse me. I must do everything in my power to reach the emperor before his meeting.”

None of the soldiers hindered Ahuzza as he climbed down to the boat. After being returned to the ship, he climbed aboard and gave the location to Commodore Pultek.

Soon the ship was plowing through the waves under full sail, racing for the emperor’s destination.

Thus far everything had gone as well as it possibly could. The most important question remained. Would they reach the emperor in time?

33

The ship bearing the Grand Vizier of the Empire of Ahr and his senior agent sailed north before turning east. Avoiding the harbor at Rog, it sailed into a quiet bay nestled among the cliffs of a rugged coastline. Rheibas had agreed to the rendezvous location and also to the proposal that the Varasans host the conference. The conference vessel was sitting at anchor in the bay. No other ships were nearby, apart from a small Rogandan vessel anchored within signaling range.

After a boat was lowered, Rheibas and Kahrlin climbed down to it. By prior arrangement, once they were delivered to the conference vessel, the boat would return to their ship, and the ship would withdraw.

A rope net had been lowered for them, and Kahrlin climbed aboard the Varasan ship ahead of Rheibas. The four guards who followed offered no more than token security, but Kahrlin knew his master was not expecting to need protection.

They were offered a muted greeting once they reached the deck, then without further comment the Grand Vizier was ushered to a seat at a large table positioned in the middle of the main deck.

Kahrlin stared at the arrangement curiously. An ornate wooden table seemed out of place positioned in the middle of an open deck. He could only imagine the difficulty of maneuvering such a heavy item of furniture onto the ship. Nevertheless, with the vessel lying at anchor in the shelter of a quiet bay, the deck felt surprisingly steady, its gentle rocking barely noticeable.

The other delegates had already arrived. The man at the head of the table rose to his feet. "I am Lord Talmon. As the envoy of the Kingdom of Varas, I am your host today." He nodded toward each of the other seated participants. "Seated around the table are King Krasmir of Rogand, Lord Torbury of Arvenon, Lord Giddel of Castel, and the Grand Vizier of the Empire of Ahr. I believe the Grand Vizier proposed this summit. I will therefore offer him the opportunity to speak first."

As the Varasan's words were translated into Rogandan, Kahrlin scanned the audience. Most of the people present on the deck were not known to him. He was not surprised to see Lady Tulinay and Lord Kulferan hovering near their king. More interesting was the presence of Thomas Stablehand and Brother Ander, both of them at pains to stay in the background.

Rheibas did not immediately respond to Lord Talmon's invitation. He had been slowly surveying every person on the deck, by no means limiting himself to those seated at the table, and he clearly intended to complete his observations before saying anything. When he had finished, he glanced briefly at his senior agent, his eyebrows raised questioningly. Kahrlin responded with a tight nod.

Satisfied with the outcome, Rheibas directed his attention at last to the representatives of the local kingdoms. "I have informed you that the emperor has seen fit to increase the size of his force in this region. His action is in direct response to the unprovoked aggression directed at ships belonging to the imperial navy."

He paused, studying the faces opposite him. He received nothing in return except a stony silence.

Kahrlin was not surprised. The Rogandans and their allies had nothing to do with the attack on the Ahran navy ships, and none of them were stupid. They would undoubtedly have guessed that the attack had been staged by the Grand Vizier in retaliation for the Rogandans capturing three of his ships.

Kahrlin could only marvel once more at the masterful simplicity of Rheibas's counterstroke. If the chief minister's enemies had not fully appreciated his shrewdness before, perhaps they were beginning to grasp it now.

"Very little time remains to us to reach an understanding," Rheibas continued. "For my part, my sole desire is to see the honor of the empire upheld. Beyond that, I am willing to put the past behind me."

"What is it you want?" asked King Krasmir bluntly, his voice a growl.

"Let us begin instead with what you want," Rheibas replied boldly. "Am I right in supposing that the missing royals weigh most heavily on your minds?" He didn't wait for an answer. "Unfortunate as their absconding might be, I believe it is within my power to arrange their safe return."

King Krasmir's eyes narrowed. "And what would you be expecting in exchange?"

It was a key question, and Kahrlin didn't know the answer to it.

"My expectations are modest and reasonable. To begin with, the Princess Neira must be released from her current imprisonment. Once that is done, I wish to negotiate a trade agreement that places the empire on an equal footing with the kingdoms in this region. Beyond that, there are a few...minor matters I wish to explore with the Arvenian delegation."

Every face around the table wore a frown once his words were translated. It was clear to Kahrlin that they were not willing to trust a word he said.

King Krasmir was the first to respond. "If you wish to be taken seriously, release the hostages."

Rheibas sighed loudly. "I will try to be patient with your posturing. At best, any claim that I am holding hostages demonstrates a profound ignorance of me and of my intentions. At worst, it reveals an unjustified animosity that does not flatter you."

Even as he was speaking, a lookout called out a warning. "Four ships approaching! All bearing three masts!"

The Rogandan king was on his feet in an instant. "So you propose to attack us during a peace conference?" he bellowed. "Or are you hoping to take us hostage as well?"

"Please!" Rheibas replied calmly. "You misunderstand entirely. I no more expected ships to arrive than you did. It is most likely the vanguard of the reinforcements I warned you about."

The ships could now be seen from the deck, and Kahrlin soon saw that Rheibas was right. They were clearly of Ahran design. He worked hard at suppressing a smirk. The timing of their arrival could not have been more perfect.

Rheibas's words were translated, but if the others heard it, they gave no indication. The Rogandans had clustered together, flanked by Lord Torbury and the Varasan and Castelan envoys. Prompted by King Krasmir, the captain of the Varasan vessel began issuing orders frantically, and signals were sent to the smaller ship stationed nearby. That ship in turn seemed to be relaying the signals to other ships not visible from the deck.

Within minutes, other sails began to appear from the direction of Rog. A standoff between the Ahran and Rogandan navies appeared imminent.

In the midst of the confusion, Thomas Stablehand approached Lord Torbury and whispered in his ear. Torbury responded by speaking quietly but forcefully to his huddled allies. They slowly seemed to calm down. Glancing around, Kahrlin saw that Thomas had made himself inconspicuous once more.

Rheibas watched it all with an inscrutable smile.

A boat was launched from one of the newly arrived Ahran vessels. All eyes were upon it, and Kahrlin saw at once that the conference would not proceed until it reached them.

Throughout the excitement, Rheibas had been sitting calmly, an indulgent look on his face. He looked for all the world like a tolerant uncle, unruffled as he watched an unruly group of nephews and nieces run amok. He showed no apparent interest in the Ahran boat as it drew ever closer.

The boat disappeared from sight as it pulled in alongside the Varasan ship, but Kahrlin watched with great interest as a rope net was lowered over the side to allow its occupants to climb aboard. Two sailors appeared and were greeted by the Varasan envoy, Lord Talmon. After a brief conversation with the sailors, Lord Talmon called over King Krasmir, Lord Torbury, and Lord Giddel. The group huddled for a few minutes, then the sailors disappeared back down the rope. Their boat was soon being rowed away.

Not many minutes passed before another boat arrived alongside. Kahrlin watched with interest to see who would be joining them. He guessed it would be an Ahran admiral.

The first person to appear was an Ahran imperial guard. He was followed by the emperor himself.

Kahrlin looked on with mouth agape. Shooting a glance at Rheibas, he saw that his master had gone pale. He otherwise gave nothing away.

Lord Talmon greeted the emperor with great deference, as did the representatives of the other kingdoms.

The Grand Vizier had pushed himself to his feet the moment the emperor appeared. He now stooped low. "It is both unexpected and gratifying that you have chosen to join us, Your Imperial Majesty. Your august presence is a balm to our spirits, and access to your ineffable wisdom is more than we could have hoped for."

The emperor offered his chief minister no more than a curt nod before he took the offered seat.

"Thank you for coming so swiftly in response to our invitation, Your Imperial Majesty," said King Krasmir.

Another swift glance at Rheibas showed his eyes narrowed. The Rogandan king seemed to have taken him by surprise.

The emperor did not look happy. "Invitation or not, I needed little inducement to come, in spite of the hazards of the journey. It is beyond time I saw for myself what is going on here. Where is my daughter, King Krasmir, and why has she not been returned to her people?"

"It will give me great pleasure to reunite you with your daughter, Your Majesty," the Rogandan king replied. "For her own safety we were unwilling to entrust her to your Grand Vizier, given that he had previously left her to die on a remote island. I would only ask in return that you prevail upon him to release the people he has abducted and held captive. I am referring to my daughter, Princess Teylee, as well as King Rupert of Castel and Queen Essanda of Arvenon."

Rheibas bristled. "These are monstrous falsehoods, Your Majesty! I have already explained the true situation to you regarding your daughter. Her Highness was abducted from my ship by Rogandan pirates, almost certainly acting on behalf of their king." He aimed a poisonous glare in Krasmir's direction. "As for these so-called abductions, it is beneath me to involve myself in such atrocities. My understanding is that the princess and the king absconded, presumably for the purpose of eloping. I can hardly be held responsible for that. Nor is it my fault if the Arvenian queen later chose to visit her brother in their romantic hideaway."

The Rogandan king turned to the emperor, fury on his face. "This despicable attempt by Your Majesty's servant to explain away his provocative outrages does no credit to him, nor to the empire whose interests he claims to represent."

"Do you have proof of your assertions, King Krasmir?" the emperor asked calmly.

"We do," the king replied. He nodded to an aide, who disappeared below decks.

While he was gone, Krasmir continued. "I must also mention the son of Lord Torbury, who was abducted by Bolnyk, the Grand Vizier's senior agent. The boy was murdered at the hands of Bolnyk. Lord Torbury endured the horror of witnessing it personally."

As his words were being translated, the aide returned with a man in chains. Kahrlin recognized the new arrival at once. It was Bolnyk.

Rheibas seized the initiative. "I see that the Rogandans have

Bolnyk in their custody, and I can only express my delight that he has been apprehended. He deserves great censure for his behavior. In recent times it became evident to me that he was operating on his own initiative, carrying out actions I could never condone. The moment I discovered this, I removed him from any position of responsibility. Until recently he was being held on my ship, but he managed to escape while I was absent. He escaped using a letter he wrote in my name and stamped with my seal. He has done all of us a service by turning himself in to the Rogandans."

The emperor frowned at Bolnyk. "What do you have to say for yourself?" he demanded.

Bolnyk had been watching Rheibas closely. He appeared hesitant when he first arrived, but the chief minister's words seemed to have decided him. "For many years I have been acting as the chief minister's senior agent, Your Majesty. He placed me in that position in large measure because of my willingness to carry out his orders without question, however unprincipled those orders might be. I have done things in his service that would generally be regarded as contemptible. Murder is not the worst of them."

In spite of his admission, Bolnyk did not appear repentant. "It is true that I was responsible for the abduction of Lord Torbury's son," he continued. "I also later took advantage of an opportunity to abduct Princess Teylee and King Rupert. None of those abductions were carried out on the chief minister's orders. Far from disowning them though, he immediately proceeded to take full advantage of them. I murdered Lord Torbury's son on the explicit orders of the chief minister. As for the abduction of Queen Essanda, that was planned and carried out by the chief minister's new favorite, Kahrlin." He pointed an accusing finger at Kahrlin. "The operation was ordered by the chief minister. The chief minister also masterminded the attack by Rogandan mercenaries on three imperial navy ships. Kahrlin hired the mercenaries, and I led the attack, in the mistaken belief that we were attacking ships seized by the Rogandans. I called the attack off as soon as I realized the true situation."

The emperor was scowling at Bolnyk with barely controlled rage.

"And were you also responsible for abandoning my daughter on a deserted island?" he demanded.

"I was involved, Your Majesty, but I was following the orders of the chief minister. He invented the pirate story for the benefit of the Rogandans, and for the benefit of Your Majesty. He gave a different explanation to Princess Neira. Her Imperial Highness was told that she had been abandoned by Captain Gharpin without the knowledge of the chief minister. The chief minister is skilled at twisting the facts to suit his purposes."

Rheibas waved a hand contemptuously. "We are listening to the ravings of a dangerous and desperate man. By his own assessment he is unprincipled and contemptible. He admits to being a murderer and an abductor. Nothing he says can be believed."

He turned to Krasmir. "You appear to have embraced the fantasies peddled by this renegade. Has he offered you a single shred of proof?"

Almost as if the question was a signal, a Rogandan servant approached Bolnyk and pressed a parchment into his hand. Bolnyk's eyes went wide when he examined it.

"How did you come by this?" he demanded.

The servant offered no response, but his eyes flicked momentarily to Thomas Stablehand. Other eyes followed his glance, to the obvious discomfort of the Arvenian.

Bolnyk held the document out to the emperor, who hesitated for a moment before taking it.

He frowned when he read it. "This is stamped with your seal," he growled, staring at Rheibas.

"What is it?" Rheibas asked innocently.

The emperor scowled at him. "It is a letter from you to my daughter. It proves that you have lied to me!"

34

Kahrlin watched wide-eyed as the emperor waved the parchment in Rheibas's face. "This letter you wrote to the princess acknowledges that she was indeed abandoned on a deserted island, and it confirms Bolnyk's claim that you gave different explanations to different people. It also concedes that you lied to the Rogandans about the supposed pirate incident."

Rheibas glared at Bolnyk with narrowed eyes. He had gone pale with anger, but he didn't speak.

The emperor turned to Bolnyk. "The letter orders you to destroy it. Why did you choose to disobey those orders?"

Bolnyk shook his head. "I cannot explain my own behavior, Your Majesty. I initially intended to destroy it as soon as the princess had read it. When the time came, I hesitated. Something told me it might prove significant. So I hid it instead."

The emperor waved the document at Rheibas. "I demand an explanation!"

"The explanation is very simple, Your Majesty. This document that I supposedly authored is nothing more than a fabrication."

"It is stamped with your seal!"

Rheibas was not perturbed. "Bolnyk had access to my seal. He clearly wrote the letter in an attempt to implicate me. As I have already told you, he recently used the same trick to escape from my ship! After writing a letter in my name and sealing it with my seal, he hid himself in a crate. The letter ordered one of my men to transfer that crate to the shore. Witnesses on my ship can confirm these facts!"

He raised his hands heavenward in frustration. "Bolnyk claims I ordered him to destroy the document before you. By his own account he disobeyed a direct order to further his own interests. I have found such behavior to be consistent with his attitude. The man was once useful to me, and to the empire. In recent times he became dangerous and unreliable to the point where I was forced to stand him down." Rheibas shook his head regretfully.

"The truth about this document is more straightforward," he continued. "I have never seen it, but the details Your Majesty has revealed suggest it was written solely for the purpose of discrediting me."

The emperor had thrown up his hands in irritation. "What am I expected to believe?" he demanded.

As they had been speaking, another ship of Ahran design had appeared. After drawing alongside one of the imperial navy ships, presumably for the sake of communication, Kahrlin saw the new arrival separate itself and launch a boat. The boat was at that moment pulling in alongside the Varasan vessel hosting the summit.

Others noticed it too, one of them approaching the emperor and whispering in his ear. All conversation ceased while the gathering waited for the arrival of whoever was climbing the rope net.

Ahuzza clambered onto the deck of the ship, his two guards and Captain Gharpin close behind him.

The first face Ahuzza recognized was that of the emperor. He at once bowed deeply. "Your Majesty!"

"You are welcome, Bisri Ahuzza!" the emperor exclaimed gladly. "I am gratified to see you alive and well."

Almost immediately the bisri noticed the chief minister sitting across from His Majesty. The sight of Rheibas openly engaged in conference with the emperor, free and unrestrained, filled the bisri with unease.

Rheibas had clearly been taken by surprise at Ahuzza's appearance, for all that he tried to mask it. As soon as he spotted Gharpin though, his face burned red. Distracted by the new arrivals, no one appeared to have noticed apart from Ahuzza.

Belatedly the bisri noticed Bolnyk—in chains, which brought Ahuzza at least some satisfaction. The agent was standing wide-eyed, staring at him as if he were seeing a ghost. Ahuzza snorted. His would-be murderer had good reason to be shocked.

"I see the man who tried to murder me and my guards has been apprehended," he said tightly, staring at Bolnyk.

Rheibas wasted no time responding. "We now have further confirmation of Bolnyk's treason from the lips of Bisri Ahuzza, a reliable witness. It seems the perfidy of my former associate runs deeper than I had imagined," he said grimly. "I sincerely regret having raised him from the gutter. He has not repaid the confidence I placed in him."

"He acted on your orders!" cried Ahuzza.

"Do you have evidence of that, Bisri, or did you simply assume it?" demanded Rheibas reasonably. "I know the answer, of course. No evidence exists, because I gave no such order."

The same reasoning had been used by the crown prince, and hearing it from the chief minister only heightened Ahuzza's frustration. He himself would never again be taken in by Rheibas's lies. Disappearing into the depths with an anchor tied around his neck had seen to that. But the emperor was the one who needed to be convinced.

Rheibas faced his sovereign. "Have I ever failed you before, Your Majesty? It is true that I have been unable to resolve the Rogandan crisis, but I hope the reasons are becoming clear. I have been undermined at every turn, and by a man who owed his position of power and privilege solely to me." He shook his head sadly.

Ahuzza was not impressed by the chief minister's attempts at deception, but he eyed his sovereign anxiously, not at all certain what he might be thinking.

The emperor did not immediately respond to Rheibas's assertions. "Who is this accompanying you, Bisri?" he asked with a frown, nodding toward the Ahran captain.

Gharpin bowed low. "I am Captain Gharpin, Your Majesty. I captained the ship that carried Her Highness Princess Neira from Kat Ahket."

The emperor's eyes went wide. "I have been told that you were lost at sea!"

"That is very close to the truth, Your Majesty. My ship went down in a storm after being sabotaged. When we took to the boats, we found that the timbers had been staved in. It was a miracle that I survived. Sadly, my crew were not so fortunate. I was washed ashore on a remote island and rescued there."

"Your ship was sabotaged, Captain? Who was responsible for such an outrage?" demanded the emperor.

Gharpin pointed to Rheibas. "The chief minister. His men inflicted the damage immediately before they transferred to another ship with their master."

"Ridiculous!" scoffed Rheibas. "What possible motive could I have for such a heinous act?"

Gharpin's face twisted with anger. "That question, at least, is easy to answer," he growled. "You wished to make certain that none of my crew lived to tell the emperor that you had abandoned his daughter and her personal guard to die on a remote island."

Heartened that Gharpin had at last found the ear of the emperor, Ahuzza aimed a glance at the chief minister.

In no way abashed, the chief minister waded immediately into the attack.

"By your own admission you oversaw the loss of one of the finest ships in the emperor's fleet, Gharpin. And you assure us that the ship went down with the loss of all hands. Such a disaster is unimaginable! We can only ask how it is that you survived, when every other life was lost? In my naivety, I believed that a captain put the safety of his crew ahead of his own." He glared at Gharpin. "The results of your negligence have been catastrophic, and yet you have the temerity to blame me for sabotage?"

Facing the emperor once more, Rheibas sighed deeply. "Although the honor of Your Majesty has suffered greatly due to a series of misdeeds, the perpetrators now stand before you." His finger flicked first to Bolnyk then to Gharpin. "Each of them is bent on shifting the blame, and it seems I have become their favored target. I am beginning to wonder if they are part of a conspiracy."

Ahuzza listened to his words with growing agitation. The emperor had been presented with Gharpin's testimony as well as his own, and undoubtedly King Krasmir and his allies had already made statements of their own, yet there was no clear sign that any of it had stuck. Was it possible that, in spite of all the evil he had instigated, Rheibas might yet slither away?

Glancing around, he saw that others shared his frustration. King Krasmir and his allies knew the truth, whatever lies Rheibas might spout. But they risked a war with the empire if they took matters into their own hands. The emperor needed an opportunity to reach his own conclusion.

"I am aware that Your Majesty has received wildly different accounts from different people," Rheibas continued, "accounts that are impossible to reconcile. Even though a great deal of slander has been directed at me, I am prepared to disregard it, knowing that such opinions were formed in ignorance of the true situation. To demonstrate that I bear no animosity, I would like to offer a gesture of goodwill. I believe that much of the misunderstanding with the Rogandans and their allies lies around the prolonged absence of the Rogandan princess, the Castelan king, and the Arvenian queen. I well understand the discomfort associated with their disappearance. I confess to similar discomfort in connection with our own Princess Neira. Having stumbled upon the location of their hideaway, I am in a unique position to restore the missing royals, and I propose to do so immediately. It need hardly be said that they could have returned home of their own accord at any time, but I will speak no more of that. I should forewarn you that they were not pleased about being extracted from their retreat against their will. I ask you to overlook that. I saw it as a necessary price for them to pay to bring this quarrel to an end."

It was a masterful performance. Even though Ahuzza understood the true character of the chief minister, it was hard to remain untouched by the force of his words, and the apparent sincerity with which they were expressed.

"What exactly are you proposing?" asked the emperor.

"If you will allow me, I will return to my ship to make arrangements for the three royals to be delivered here. King Krasmir has promised to return Princess Neira to the care of Your Majesty. If he delivers on his promise, all of us can return to this ship tomorrow afternoon for the handover. With those steps completed, it is my hope we can begin negotiations around less contentious matters, such as a mutual trade agreement."

"You are wasting your time protesting your innocence," Lord Torbury said coldly. "Nevertheless, you are right in suggesting that the return of the three missing royals is of primary concern to the allied kingdoms, just as the return of his daughter is, I am sure, the primary concern of the emperor. By all means let us settle those issues before addressing the matter of your duplicity."

Rheibas contented himself with an indulgent smile.

"You mentioned matters you wanted to explore with the Arvenian delegation," Torbury added. "What is the nature of those matters?"

"Perhaps you could join me as I return to my ship," suggested Rheibas. "That will give us an opportunity to discuss them freely."

"Why not discuss them here?" demanded Torbury.

"Are you afraid of me, Lord Torbury?" asked Rheibas mildly.

Torbury's reply was caustic. "You mistake me entirely. I do not fear you. But I will never be fool enough to trust you. You delude yourself if you think you can induce me to voluntarily place myself in your power."

"I think you underestimate us both, Lord Torbury. Nevertheless, I am willing to defer our discussions until tomorrow."

The emperor had not offered any clear indication of his position, and all eyes turned to him.

"The return of my daughter and the three other royals is a necessary precondition for any further discussion," he stated flatly. "I am willing to reconvene when that has taken place." Turning to Rheibas, he glared at him with narrowed eyes. "I must warn you that I am far from satisfied with the account you have given. I will make a final judgment tomorrow."

Lord Talmon bowed. "I pronounce this conference closed for today," he declared formally. "Thank you all for your participation."

It took time for boats to be summoned for the emperor and for Rheibas. While they were waiting, King Krasmir approached Bisri Ahuzza and Gharpin.

"You are welcome to remain with us if you wish," he said.

Both of them bowed when his words were translated. However Ahuzza shook his head. "Your offer is gracious, Your Majesty, but the emperor has invited us to join him on his ship. The captain and I are hoping for further opportunity to interact with him, and he has yet to hear the testimony of my guards."

"Of course," the king replied. "We are grateful to you all. The timing of your arrival was uncanny! I trust you did not encounter difficulties when you arrived in Kat Ahket. The emperor must have already left."

"I was detained by the crown prince," Ahuzza told him frankly. "Fortunately Shallam was able to extract me from the palace."

Krasmir lowered his voice. "Are you suggesting that the crown prince is implicated in the Grand Vizier's schemes?" he asked with a frown.

The bisri shrugged. "It is difficult to say. He said he was confining me for my own protection, and it's possible he was sincere." He paused. "A more immediate issue is occupying my mind. I set out to warn the emperor. He now has most of the facts at his disposal, but he has also been subjected to the full force of Rheibas's lies. Thankfully, he seems to have reservations about what Rheibas has told him. We will do what we can to help him see the truth."

"I wish you both good success," King Krasmir told them.

No further interaction took place between the various parties. Rheibas was rowed away, soon followed by the emperor. Ahuzza, Gharpin, and the bisri's two guards traveled with the emperor in his boat. Only after they had boarded his ship did Ahuzza allow himself to relax.

THE MOMENT the guests were being returned to their ships, Will took Thomas aside. He was barely able to contain his eagerness.

"You finally got your chance to see him, Thomas!" he hissed. "What did you learn?"

Thomas grimaced. "Almost nothing useful."

Will stared at him incredulously. "How is that possible?"

"I'll explain later," Thomas murmured uncomfortably, flicking his eyes back over Will's shoulder.

Will turned to see King Krasmir approaching.

The king looked grim. "The emperor has now been presented with the best evidence available, but he still hasn't made it clear where he stands."

"His position isn't entirely clear," agreed Will dryly. He shook his head. "Seeing the Grand Vizier in action was certainly enlightening. The man is devious beyond belief! Without doubt he's the most accomplished liar I have encountered. I shudder to think how many people he has trampled on to reach his current exalted position. I don't doubt he's proven useful to the emperor, but I wonder how well the emperor—who appears to be a reasonable person—understands him."

A snort sounded from Bolnyk who was standing nearby. "I served him for years, and even I don't understand him. I do know what he's capable of though. He's more than devious enough to conceal his true character from the emperor."

All of them fell to musing silently.

Will was the first to speak. "Whatever we have learned about him, we haven't answered the question that troubles me most: what is his agenda in all this maneuvering?"

Bolnyk had one final piece of advice. "That question should be directed to the person I brought from his ship. I've told you that already."

With that, the former agent turned away, making it plain that he had nothing further to say.

Will turned to Lady Tulinay. "I need to interview your other prisoner, as a matter of urgency. Please do not refuse me! He might hold the key to all of this."

"Very well," she replied. "I will write a letter for you to give the guards in the dungeon. If you leave now though, you might miss the start of tomorrow's conference. You might also miss the return of the hostages."

"I don't care," he assured her. "To me this seems more important."

"If you're returning to Rog," King Krasmir told him, "Lord Kulferan can accompany you and bring back Princess Neira. Commodore Pultek can take you as far as Rog. Captain Bezai is currently at Rog—he can bring you back. I will send a couple of other ships as well for security."

"Thank you, Your Majesty."

It wasn't difficult for Will to guess why the king wanted to send Pultek back to Rog. The commodore was currently commanding a ship seized from the Ahrans, and it made no sense to flaunt that fact in front of them.

"May I offer a suggestion?" Will asked, his face grim.

"By all means, Lord Torbury."

"It might be wise if everyone involved in this conference spends the night in another location. Somewhere very well guarded."

35

Will and Lord Kulferan were soon plowing through the waves on their way to Rog. Thomas and Brother Ander sailed with them.

As soon as an opportunity presented itself, Will called Thomas and Brother Ander to his side.

"Why weren't you able to learn anything useful, Thomas?"

Thomas winced. "The Grand Vizier is unlike anyone I have encountered. My worst nightmare cannot compare with a few minutes probing his thoughts and memories. I've never attempted anything so difficult or so taxing."

"But you must surely have discovered something!"

"Astonishingly little, I'm sorry to say. To begin with, the only language he understands is Ahran. He was thinking hard and drawing a lot on memories while responding to the accusations against him, but I didn't understand any of it. The same was true for his memories of spoken interactions. Images weren't hidden from me, but that's what made it so traumatic. His thoughts were filled with horrific images from his past—torture, brutal executions, and worse—most of them perpetrated directly or indirectly by him. He kept working them over and over in his mind, to the point where I couldn't bear to look. His mind truly is a cesspit."

"Did you get any idea at all of what he's up to?"

"Two things did emerge through the confusion. The first involves a prisoner. I suspect it's the man we're going to meet—as soon as I see him I'll know. The prisoner is at the very forefront of the Grand Vizier's mind, but I couldn't make any sense of why. The other thing was more of an impression than anything. He's planning something big—something to do with the conference. But I don't know exactly what."

Having set high hopes on Thomas's insights through the stone, Will couldn't help but be bitterly disappointed. Nevertheless, he held his peace. Although he held a stone himself that might seem almost limitless in its potential, his personal experience had featured frustrating limitations as often as great power.

In any event, a visit to the prisoner might well provide the answers they were seeking.

"What about the emperor?"

"He's a very different kind of person. He has his flaws, but for the most part he's straightforward and honorable."

That at least was something to celebrate.

Darkness fell before they reached Rog, and the night was well advanced by the time they docked. They parted from Lord Kulferan after agreeing to return to the ship at dawn.

Late as the hour was, Will was not willing to delay the meeting with the prisoner even for a moment. Accordingly Thomas and Brother Ander trailed after him to the dungeons. Lady Tulinay's letter provided them the access she had promised, and a guard led them to the cell where the prisoner was being held.

"Can we go inside to talk with him?" asked Will.

The guard shrugged. "If you want to. He's shown no hint of violent tendencies."

Retrieving a large key, he unlocked the iron door and pushed it open before handing Will a burning torch. Then without a backward glance he returned to the meager comforts of his guard station.

Will pushed his way into the cell to find a bleary-eyed man of late middle-age stretched out upon a low bed. Thomas and the monk followed him in.

A brief glance at Thomas yielded a barely perceptible nod. So this was indeed the man on the mind of the Grand Vizier.

The man didn't get up from his bed. "Welcome," he said. "I don't often receive visitors, particularly at this time of night." He glanced at Thomas, eyed Brother Ander curiously, then turned his full attention to Will. The sword at Will's side briefly caught his eye, but he seemed fixated on his visitor's face. Will guessed his scarred visage was the reason.

"What brings you here at such an hour?" To Will the prisoner's cheerful tone seemed forced.

"I am Lord Torbury, and my companions are Thomas Stablehand and Brother Ander. We have some questions for you. The first is simple. Who are you?"

The prisoner couldn't seem to decide whether to be intrigued or terrified. When he finally spoke, he seemed surprisingly bold.

"I haven't heard of any of you. I am Rogandan by birth. I have lived most of my life in or around Rog, although a few years ago I made the mistake of traveling to Kat Ahket. I was eventually unfortunate enough to capture the attention of the Grand Vizier. He brought me here as a prisoner on his ship. A fellow prisoner decided to escape and brought me with him."

He waved a hand around his cell tragically. "As you can see, I have merely exchanged one jail for another. I am not entirely complaining, though. I prefer King Krasmir's dungeon over the finest cabin the Grand Vizier's ship has to offer." He paused. "I must say the food is only marginally better though."

"You have plenty to say," Will told him.

"I rarely have the pleasure of company," the prisoner replied. "The Grand Vizier refused to let anyone speak with me, and although I spent a lot of time with Bolnyk after we escaped, he was no conversationalist. When I first arrived I decided to hold my tongue, and since then none of King Krasmir's people have shown any interest in me. I've been starved of human contact." He gazed at Will thoughtfully. "You might look fierce, but I get a feeling none of you are especially vicious. So I decided to take a chance."

"You still haven't told us who you are," Will reminded him.

"No, I seem to be easily distracted. After being silent for so long, it's intoxicating to have an opportunity to speak." He sighed. "I'm still straying from the point, aren't I? Who am I? I've been many things, a mystic among them, but the truth is I'm a nobody. I do have the dubious distinction of being a nobody who briefly advised the late King Agon on the topic of living forever, if you can believe that. Unfortunately for me it happened to be a topic close to his heart."

Getting to his feet, he gave a little bow. "My name is Chalno."

CHALNO LOOKED at the blank faces of his visitors and smiled.

"I see you have never heard of me. The tiny part of me that desires fame and recognition is tempted to be dismayed by that, but anonymity is a much more useful achievement, at least in my case."

"What does the Grand Vizier want with you?" asked Lord Scarface. He was clearly the one in charge. The other two hadn't uttered a word.

"Ah the Grand Vizier. I haven't been missing him in the slightest. He was my host for far too long." He sighed noisily. "I left Rogand just before the death of King Agon, may Malzakh gnaw his bones! I had good reason to get as far away from him as I could. My wanderings eventually led me to the empire, and in time I became acquainted with the sleaziest corners of Kat Ahket. I might have done a little too much boasting about some topics better left alone. Sadly for me, I caught the attention of the ravenous monster known as Rheibas—the Grand Vizier."

"What topics was he so interested in?"

Chalno shook his head, wagging a finger reprovingly. "Now, now,

My Lord. That is not a safe question to ask. Not safe for me, that is. You will learn nothing from me on that topic. Not unless you happen to possess the fabled Stone of Knowing, of course."

Laughing heartily at his own witticism, he failed at first to notice their faces. When he did, it filled him with dread.

"Surely not you as well!" The blood drained from his face. "That *is* what you're here about, *isn't* it?" he asked incredulously.

They gave no reply, but they didn't need to.

He shook his head in stubborn denial. "You won't get another word out of me. Even if you torture me! I already know how to endure torture, thanks to the Grand Vizier."

"You misunderstand us," asserted the nobleman. "We only want to know what the Grand Vizier is planning."

They were wasting their time. Climbing onto his bed, he curled into a protective ball, waiting for the blows to begin.

Nothing happened. Nothing at all. After a few minutes he dared to take a peek. The room was dark and empty. A moment later the guard appeared and locked his door.

He was alone once more.

THE MOMENT they were clear of the dungeon, Will turned to Thomas.

"Well?" he asked.

"Chalno has given us plenty to think about," Thomas replied. "He was overflowing with information."

Will sighed with relief.

"I'll try to give you the important pieces, although I'm still working to sort it all out in my mind."

"There's no hurry. We have until dawn," Will assured him.

Thomas returned a wry smile. "I guessed that none of us would be getting any sleep tonight."

He shrugged in resignation. "I might as well make a start. Apparently it all began when King Agon discovered a scroll among the effects of Lord Drettroth after his death. The scroll apparently outlined a ritual to buy unending life from the dark gods. The beneficiary had to be willing to pay, of course."

"What was the price?" asked Brother Ander curiously.

"Blood. For someone like Agon, rivers of it! Agon couldn't make sense of Drettroth's document, so he turned to a mystic for help. That mystic was Chalno. He tried to be clever with the king, and it nearly cost him his life. In the end he managed to convince Agon that he had unraveled the mysteries of the scroll, and even that he had performed the ritual and acquired unending life himself, although at a much more modest cost given his lowly estate. It was mostly bluff, although to this day he isn't sure whether the ritual had any effect or not. Agon left after Chalno explained to him what he needed to do to achieve the same result."

Will smiled grimly. "Agon didn't achieve unending life. I can personally vouch for that."

"Chalno wasn't willing to wait around for Agon to try it out. He realized he would never be safe in Rogand while Agon was alive, so he booked passage on a merchant ship. He eventually made his way to Kat Ahket. He arrived with no money and no understanding of the language. He eked out an existence telling stories in taverns to anyone who would listen—mostly merchants who understood a little Rogandan. Not surprisingly, his most impressive tale involved his consultations with the Rogandan king regarding unending life. As he told us, word of his stories eventually reached the Grand Vizier. That's where our problems began.

"Chalno later discovered that Rheibas, the Grand Vizier, had assembled an extensive collection of ancient documents from other lands. Collecting them and studying them used to be his favorite hobby—back in the days when he still had time for a hobby. He liked to read of ancient kings—how they became powerful and what brought them down. But he especially enjoyed imaginative tales. Rheibas knew about the scroll that talks about the stones. He'd somehow gotten hold of a copy and had it translated. He later told Chalno he didn't believe a word of it, but it fascinated him, and he never stopped imagining what his life would be like if he possessed the stones."

"It's no wonder Chalno caught his attention, with all his talk about King Agon and unending life," said Will.

"Exactly. Rheibas wanted Chalno's opinion on the scroll, so he gave him a Rogandan translation to read. By then Chalno had realized that Rheibas was at least as dangerous as Agon. He needed to give Rheibas something. He didn't want to talk about Drettroth's ritual, because he guessed Rheibas would want it enacted immediately. That might soon lead to him concluding that Chalno was a fraud. Rogand seemed a very long way away, so he talked instead about the great age of the High Priest at the Temple of the Dark Gods at Rog. He wondered aloud if the High Priest had the Stone of Vitality, or had perhaps discovered some other way of extending his life."

Will groaned. "So he got the Grand Vizier's hopes up."

Thomas nodded.

"How did they communicate?" asked Brother Ander. "Does he speak Ahran?"

Thomas grimaced. "At first Rheibas brought in an interpreter. After using his services, he confined him until the next time he was needed. Eventually he instructed him to teach Chalno the Ahran language. It took a long time, but Chalno eventually became reasonably fluent. By then he and the interpreter had become friends. Rheibas ordered the interpreter's execution, making sure it was done in front of Chalno. The result was predictable—Chalno became terrified of Rheibas."

The monk shook his head in dismay.

"After that Rheibas was able to speak with him in private. Their conversations were just the beginning. Rheibas sent agents to Rogand, and eventually to the other kingdoms as well. He began to hear tales about a commander able to inspire incredible devotion from his men—a commander who had never been defeated. He even heard about Lord Drettroth invading Arvenon so he could pursue a youth who had something he wanted.

"He questioned Chalno closely about these things. Chalno had the impression that he gradually came to the conclusion that the stones described by the scroll were not only real, but available to be seized by someone with sufficient determination and resources. After that he didn't meet with Chalno as often. But he kept him close, and refused to let anyone speak with him. He also threatened Chalno with dire consequences if he dared to speak to anyone."

"So the Grand Vizier is after the stones!" exclaimed Will.

Thomas nodded sadly. "It seems to be the reason behind everything he's done—his schemes, his infiltration, his abductions, his threats about war."

"He's been trying to flush out the stones," said Will. "And he's done an admirable job. He manufactured a threat significant enough to bring us into the open to counter it. He's probably guessed that I have the Stone of Authority, even if he's drawn that conclusion for the wrong reasons. And he won't find it hard to guess who has the Stone of Vitality once he hears of a monk who performs miraculous healings and even resurrections. Assuming he doesn't still think the High Priest has it. With that in mind, I'll tell Lord Kulferan I've heard vague whispers of a threat to the High Priest, and ask him to send a warning to the temple before we leave."

"I think I can guess why Rheibas filled his mind with horrific memories during the conference," said Thomas morosely. "He wanted to distract and confuse anyone with the Stone of Knowing who might be trying to read him. It also explains why Chalno was so much on his mind. He knew that everything he was doing would be exposed if someone with the Stone of Knowing got to Chalno."

Will frowned. "Why did he keep Chalno alive?"

"Chalno constantly asked himself the same question. He's quite skilled at sounding mysterious, and he worked hard to foster the idea that he had a unique ability to make sense of ancient scrolls. He also concluded that Rheibas wanted to be able to talk to someone about the stones. Apart from Chalno no one was safe."

"We can't tell the emperor any of this," said Will. "He wouldn't believe it anyway."

"No," agreed Thomas. "The emperor is a reasonable man. Probably a bit too reasonable to take any of this seriously, even if we were willing to expose the existence of the stones."

Will wasn't too dismayed. "At least we're no longer groping about in the dark," he said. "We understand what we're up against, the three of us in particular. We know that the Grand Vizier isn't going to stop until he gets the stones, and we know we can't let that happen, because the consequences are too terrible to contemplate."

"What can we do?" asked Thomas miserably.

Will shrugged. "We have until tomorrow afternoon. I'll think of something."

36

Thomas watched gloomily as Captain Bezai's ship drew closer to the Varasan vessel hosting the conference.

A tight knot had begun to twist his stomach. Heartening as it was to have the Grand Vizier's plans exposed at last, it had left him with nothing but apprehension about the future. Once more the Stone of Knowing threatened not only his peaceful existence but his life. He longed for Elena's calming presence, and he would have given a lot for the enthusiastic embrace of his children.

At least this time he faced the uncertainties of the future with Will and Brother Ander at his side.

Thomas had no idea what Will was thinking. The commander had been pensive and distracted throughout the return journey, leaning on the rail staring out to sea for much of the time. Brother Ander seemed his usual placid self, which meant he had very little to say.

"Why are there no servants to groom me appropriately?" demanded a petulant voice from across the deck. "I can't possibly be presented to my father with my hair like this!"

Princess Neira had been roused well before dawn to allow the ship to get underway when the sun rose. She had been moody and disagreeable ever since. Thomas knew her reaction to be little more than nerves—she had, after all, been separated from her father for months, enduring some truly harrowing circumstances during that time. It didn't make the strident edge to her voice any less grating.

Uman, her long-suffering personal guard, hovered at her side as ever, his face inscrutable. Being unable to speak, he offered no comment on her behavior.

Having reached the Varasan vessel, the sails were reefed and anchors released. A boat was lowered, and all of them climbed down to it. Before long they were scrambling up a rope net toward the deck of the Varasan ship.

The princess was first over the rail, closely followed by Uman. Thomas heard a squeal of joy, followed by the sound of the princess bursting into tears. He reached the deck in time to see her lose herself in her father's embrace.

Following the others to the side of King Krasmir, he was able to hear a translation of the emperor's interaction with the princess.

"My daughter! You are safe at last!"

"I have missed you so much, Father!" she managed. Having said it, she immediately dissolved into tears again.

The emperor gave her a few moments to recover herself, then he gently held her at arm's length, looking into her eyes. "I have been told you were left to die on a remote island, Neira. Is that true?"

For a long moment she hesitated. Bringing the stone into contact with his skin, Thomas witnessed the battle raging within her. Notwithstanding her lofty heritage, the princess felt small and insecure, of little value either to her father or to the empire. She harbored no doubts about what Rheibas wanted her to say. Absolving the Grand Vizier would place him in her debt, increasing her esteem in his eyes. The lure of such an outcome dazzled and enticed her.

At the same time, she despised him. The lower status of his birth predisposed her to look down on him, but she had also discovered from bitter personal experience that he was deceitful and dishonorable.

As she lingered, undecided, Uman gave her a sharp nudge. The reproachful expression on his face spoke as plainly as words.

His intervention seemed to decide her. A pout came to her lips. "It is true, Father. I survived only by a miracle. Rheibas is unusually skilled at deflecting blame, but he was the one responsible."

The emperor kissed her lightly on the forehead. "Good girl. Rheibas has been very useful to me for many years, and I would not cast him aside without good reason. Nevertheless, having been presented with all the evidence, I no longer have any doubt about the truth. But I wanted to hear it plainly from your own lips."

He turned to King Krasmir. "Thank you for keeping my daughter safe, Your Majesty. I am in your debt." It was the first time the emperor had addressed the king with such an honorific.

"It was both an honor and a pleasure, Your Majesty," returned the king, managing to keep any trace of irony from his tone.

"For now I will withdraw with my daughter," said the emperor. "Do not imagine I have forgotten the provocations of Rheibas though. I will deal decisively with him as soon as you have your daughter and her friends back."

With that he left, taking Princess Neira and her guard with him.

The moment they had gone, King Krasmir called Will, Thomas, and Brother Ander aside. A desolate look covered his face. "There's no good way to communicate this," he said. "Before the emperor arrived, we were visited by Kahrlin, the Grand Vizier's man. He said his master demands that I deliver the three of you to his ship for "negotiations", using force if necessary. He says one hostage will be released for each of you. He made it clear that if I refuse we will never see the hostages again. He also said that the Grand Vizier will kill them without hesitation if I try to involve the emperor."

The king regarded them with a haunted look in his eyes. "It need hardly be said that I refused his demands outright. Kahrlin said I would be offered one final chance. He would return in three hours for my decision. If his boat is empty when it reaches the Grand Vizier's ship, all three hostages will be executed immediately."

"I will go," said Brother Ander without hesitation. "I will appeal to him to release Princess Teylee in my place."

Thomas stared at the monk wide-eyed.

"It seems we have little choice," said Will grimly. "I will go too."

"This is madness!" protested the king. "What guarantee is there that he will release any of the hostages? What prevents him from simply adding you to his collection?"

When none of them replied, the king continued. "He has abandoned subtlety entirely, which surely means he is becoming desperate. He must be aware that the emperor is no longer deceived by his posturing. There is no telling what he is capable of."

Will nodded. "If he suspects the emperor is turning against him, he knows he's running out of options. He won't go quietly—he'll come up with a new strategy, and it might be one that doesn't require the hostages. We need to get them back while we still can."

His heart pounding, Thomas was struggling to breathe. Memories flooded into his mind. In Drettroth's fortress he'd been given an impossible choice between handing the stone to a madman or dying a horrible death. He'd chosen the costly path, and incredibly, he'd survived, but only because first Simon and then Brother Vangellis had willingly sacrificed their lives. Was it finally his turn to make the ultimate sacrifice?

By agreeing to go, his friends had backed him into a corner. Resisting the temptation to feel resentful, he acknowledged he could never live with himself if he shrank back out of fear and allowed them to go alone. As much as he questioned the Grand Vizier's sincerity about releasing the hostages, there was no way to be certain. He could not ignore a genuine opportunity just to save his own skin.

With a sigh of resignation, he made his choice. He and his friends would die together.

Knowing that the power of speech would abandon him if he didn't respond soon, he somehow ground out the words. "I will go."

The king covered his face with his hands. After a few moments he took a deep breath, then exhaled slowly. "I offered myself in place of my daughter," he told them frankly. "Kahrlin laughed at me." He threw up his hands in exasperation. "I don't understand what the Grand Vizier is hoping to achieve! Please pardon my bluntness, but I cannot see why he wants any of you. His current hostages give him vastly more leverage. And surely I am more valuable to him than my daughter!"

"He undoubtedly has his reasons," Will replied. "I imagine we'll find out soon enough what they are."

"I will call for the emperor to join me," cried the king. "Together we can easily overcome him!"

Will shook his head firmly. "You can't give him an excuse to follow through on his threat. As long as there's the faintest chance of the hostages being released, you must avoid even the appearance of provocation." His face became grim. "If you don't get the hostages back by sundown, destroy him without hesitation! Do not allow him any opportunity to escape!"

King Krasmir stared at them with haunted eyes. "So you are willingly going to your deaths?"

Will remained undaunted. "If there is a way to win free, we will find it. But if it costs our lives to end this, then so be it."

The king's face set hard. "I swear to you that I will not rest until every one of you has been released, or the Grand Vizier is dead!"

THOMAS STOOD TENSELY beside Will and Brother Ander as Kahrlin's longboat drew closer. Leaning toward Will in agitation, he exclaimed quietly, "Agreeing to go to Rheibas is one thing, but surely we can't take the stones with us! It's much too risky!"

Will shook his head. "Rheibas wants the stones, and we want the hostages. If we go without the stones, we'll have nothing to bargain with, and he'll have no further reason to keep the hostages alive. Besides, the stones might give us an edge, and we're going to need all the help we can get if we want to bring him down."

"But there are so many things that could go wrong!"

Will remained unmoved. "Don't forget that Rheibas has read the scroll. He knows that the stones will be useless to him if he takes them by force. He needs us to give them to him."

"We can't give him the stones for any reason!" protested Thomas.

Will gazed back at him calmly. "Of course not. If it comes to the worst, we'll throw them into the sea." He looked at them both. "Agreed?" he asked quietly.

Thomas and Brother Ander nodded their agreement.

THOMAS SAT in the prow of the longboat watching absently as the rowers bent to their task. Will and Brother Ander sat before him. Kahrlin sat at the stern steering the boat, a satisfied smirk lingering on his face.

Once his decision lay behind him, a surprising sense of calm had settled over Thomas. He didn't want to die. He wanted to grow old with Elena in the serenity of Newhaven, to dandle grandchildren on his knee. Nevertheless he was determined to play whatever role he could in setting the hostages free.

And the situation surely wasn't entirely hopeless. This time he was not alone, and Will must have some kind of a plan. In any event, he knew Will wouldn't stand passively by if the Grand Vizier proved faithless. Thomas was no soldier, but he would do anything he could to support his friend.

As they rounded a point, Thomas glanced behind to find that the Varasan ship had disappeared from view. Beyond the next point he spotted a three-masted ship lying at anchor. It quickly became clear they were nearing their destination.

A rope net had been lowered for them, and Kahrlin waved them toward it. Will ascended first, followed by Brother Ander and Thomas. Emerging onto the deck they found the Grand Vizier awaiting them, his face unreadable. The stone was touching

Thomas's skin, and after his previous experience he found himself reluctant to look at the Grand Vizier. He needn't have worried. This time no barrage of horror awaited him. Rheibas was no longer bothering to mask his thoughts.

The language barrier did not prevent Thomas from seeing his purpose clearly. Before he could whisper a warning to Will, a group of guards emerged from the hatch. Behind them trailed King Rupert, Princess Teylee, and a woman Thomas did not recognize, their hands bound before them. Their faces were defiant, but they did not appear to be in good condition. Then another figure appeared, similarly bound, wearing the garb of a priest of the dark gods. His hood had been thrown back. The many scars and the blue paint that covered his face did not entirely obscure the deep wrinkles that spoke of great age. Even without having previously met him, Thomas knew he was looking at the High Priest.

Rheibas shouted an order, and all except ten of the guards followed Kahrlin below decks. Three guards stood protectively around the Grand Vizier, another four positioned themselves behind the three captives and the priest, while the other three took up positions behind the new arrivals.

The stone revealed Kahrlin's frustration at being excluded from what was about to happen. He might have seen it differently if he realized that Rheibas intended to ensure total secrecy by killing every witness.

The interpreter standing beside Rheibas had no more idea of his fate than the guards, and he proceeded to relay the Grand Vizier's words in Arvenian. None of the guards understood what was being said—none of them spoke Arvenian, and Rheibas spoke to the interpreter too quietly for them to hear.

"I imagine that you have spoken to my former prisoner," Rheibas began, addressing the three newcomers. After a pause, he added, "I can see from your faces that you have. I believe I can therefore assume you understand my purpose in coming to this region."

When none of them denied it, he continued. "Unless I am greatly mistaken, I have assembled a most unusual group of people. One of you has exercised great authority over a number of years, to extraordinary effect." He nodded at Will.

"One of you has built a remarkable reputation, and not just as a healer." He dipped his head in the direction of Brother Ander. "I understand a mob savagely beat you and left you for dead. You got up and walked away." He shook his head in wonder.

"Your companion," and here he paused and surveyed Thomas curiously, "appears to be unexceptional in every way. Yet he hides a rare gift of exceptional insight. At our recent meeting with the emperor, it unexpectedly emerged that you were the one who found Bolnyk's hidden document." He bared his teeth in the semblance of a smile. "We have a servant's indiscreet glance to thank for identifying you. I must say that finding the document was a truly marvelous achievement on your part!"

He turned toward the High Priest. "I freely acknowledge that the presence of the priest may be little more than a distraction, although I would never dismiss the possibility that anyone with such unusual longevity is hiding secrets of their own. But I honor agreements when I make them, and that is the primary reason he is here. I won't go into details of this agreement, but it's fair to say it will reshape Rogand in significant ways. None of that need concern us now, though."

Rheibas was clearly enjoying himself. "Did you realize I set a test for you? You will remember Kahrlin's first meeting with King Krasmir, because all three of you were present. When Kahrlin briefed me later, imagine my surprise when he reported that the audience included a monk and a commoner. He couldn't account for it, and I didn't enlighten him with my guesses. He attended that meeting knowing the exact location of the island where our friends had been placed." He waved toward the three hostages. "Remarkably, Rogandan ships soon appeared at that very location. I had already moved the three royals, of course, but I left someone behind on the island to watch for visitors. I was not disappointed. The incident offered great encouragement to me. It showed me I was steering the correct course."

He frowned. "I must confess that one thing remains a mystery to me. Every indication suggests that each of you is aware of the others' gifts. Why hasn't one of you found a way to appropriate them all for yourselves? I can only imagine what you might have achieved, for example, Lord Torbury. You might have begun with the throne of Arvenon, and I don't doubt it would have proven little more than a stepping stone. I find such hesitancy unfathomable. I would never have shown the same indecisiveness."

He shook his head. "No matter. It is time we made a beginning. I think you know what I want. A voluntary gift from each of you will save the lives of the captives. Who is going to be first?"

It came as no surprise to hear him speak of a voluntary gift. Having read the scroll, Rheibas understood that the stones would be useless if taken by force. But he was a fool if he expected them to simply give him what he wanted.

None of them moved.

Rheibas issued a sharp command. Drawing his sword, the guard behind the High Priest ran his prisoner through.

The priest crumpled. He did not cry out, but his face revealed his agony. The stone revealed to Thomas an abrupt and tormented end to the celebrated longevity of the priest.

Anger warred with compassion on the face of Brother Ander. Before the guards could react, he hurried across the deck to the fallen priest and knelt beside him. Placing a hand on his wound, he mouthed a fervent prayer.

As Thomas watched, life stirred in the old man. The grimace cleared abruptly from the priest's face, and he opened his eyes. Standing up, Brother Ander reached down a hand and helped him to his feet.

Rheibas applauded enthusiastically. "Splendid! Truly splendid! A remarkable performance!"

Then he scowled. "Do not think to test my patience. I will not tolerate any further miraculous recoveries." He waved a hand to the guard previously assigned to Brother Ander, and the man escorted the monk at sword point back to his original place. Two other guards converged on them, and the monk's arms and legs were securely trussed.

Another sharp command to the guard standing behind Princess Teylee resulted in the appearance of a knife at her throat. "If I hear nothing from any of you in two minutes, the princess will die."

37

Everything had been happening far too quickly for Thomas. Able to foresee Rheibas's intentions as he issued each command, the knowledge came too late for him to warn Will or to think of a way to prevent what was about to happen. Once more Rheibas had succeeded in distracting him, as he had during the meeting with the emperor. This time, instead of using images of horror, the Grand Vizier had flooded his own mind with images of everything he had instigated. The revelations had been as overwhelming as they were revealing, screening his next steps until he was actually carrying them out.

Thomas wasn't going to let Rheibas have it all his own way though. There was one thing he could do.

Lifting up his voice, Thomas spoke loudly enough for all to hear.

"The Grand Vizier has credited me with a rare gift of exceptional insight. For once he is telling the truth! However, I need no unusual perception to assure you he has no intention of ever releasing his hostages, or of letting us live—not even if we were able to give him what he wants. So much for honoring his agreements! No one witnessing this little drama—and that includes the interpreter as well as every guard present on the deck—will live to see another dawn. He plans to have every one of us killed! That is the reason he sent Kahrlin below with most of the guards. He still needs them once he is finished here."

The interpreter had gone pale. When Rheibas demanded a translation of Thomas's words, the interpreter did more than just comply —he shouted it for the benefit of the guards.

Rheibas decided in a moment that no further translation would be needed. At his barked command, one of the guards ran his sword through the interpreter. Then, with the help of a second guard, the killer threw the interpreter's body overboard.

It was too late. The damage had been done. Many of the guards were becoming noticeably restless.

Rheibas commanded one of them to fetch Kahrlin. When the guard boldly refused, Rheibas immediately ordered the others to kill him. Most hesitated, but the two who had disposed of the interpreter obeyed, and another body was soon disappearing over the side into the water.

One of the two loyalists ran to the hatch and opened it, calling for Kahrlin. The agent soon appeared, a host of guards at his back, with sailors following them onto the deck. In a fury, Rheibas commanded him to kill the nine remaining guards. The two men fool enough to carry out his orders were not to be spared.

All nine were soon fighting for their lives. A few of them had the sense to band together, and others fought back to back. Many of the guards from below deck milled around uselessly, unable to reach the fighting.

Thomas had won the prisoners a brief reprieve. Will had come aboard armed, and no one had attempted to remove his weapons. He now cut the ropes binding Brother Ander. Handing him a knife, he said, "Free the hostages!"

Both Brother Ander and Will weaved their way through the fighting, reaching the three at the same moment as three of Kahrlin's men. Will held off the guards while Brother Ander cut the bonds of King Rupert, Princess Teylee, and the Varasan agent masquerading as Queen Essanda.

Hastily retrieving discarded weapons, the king and the agent hurried to the support of Will.

Thomas cowered alone on the other side of the ship. Fighting now raged across the deck. Having been sentenced to death, the besieged guards fought with the desperation of men with nothing to lose. Nevertheless, there could be no doubt about the final outcome.

As the last of the guards finally went down, Rheibas bellowed a command. Moments later, Thomas felt a knife at his throat.

Rheibas spoke again, this time to Will and his companions. No one remained to translate his words, but his meaning was clear enough. He was warning that Thomas's life would end unless they laid down their weapons.

At that moment a splintering crash sounded, and the ship shuddered violently. Thomas was thrown to the deck, along with the guard holding the knife. In the sudden movement the blade nicked his throat, and he felt warm blood seeping down his neck. Frantically exploring the wound with one hand, he concluded the cut wasn't deep. His body went slack with relief.

The clasp around his neck had twisted, removing the stone from contact with his skin. He didn't care. Too much was going on around him to make sense of its revelations anyway.

The ship shook again, then slowly began moving through the water. The anchors had broken free, or else their cables had broken.

A shower of water sprayed the deck as a huge whale—almost the same length as the ship—breached beside them before disappearing into the depths. The whale was not long gone before gigantic tentacles appeared over the rail. Thomas watched with mouth agape as a tentacle swept the deck, barely missing him. Giant suckers fastened onto two guards as it passed. They disappeared with it over the side, screaming in terror.

The remaining guards had lost all interest in the prisoners. Thomas spotted Rheibas crouching warily beside the main mast, scowling helplessly as chaos engulfed his ship.

Peering about in search of his companions, Thomas glanced up as mighty tentacles wrapped around the mizzen mast. Unable to withstand the force, the mast gave way with a resounding crack. He scurried frantically out of its way as it came crashing down onto the main deck, bringing spars, sails, and lines with it. Anyone unfortunate enough to be caught in its path was crushed. The tentacles that brought it down now ranged freely about the ship, adding to the madness.

Will and Brother Ander were crouching beside the rail on the other side of the deck, the High Priest and the freed hostages beside them. Thomas set out for them, dodging flailing tentacles and falling timbers. He was halfway there when a figure rose up before him. It was Kahrlin. Recognizing Thomas, he drew his knife and stepped menacingly toward him. Before Thomas could react, a broken spar still attached to the rigging swung down and knocked the agent senseless. Trembling uncontrollably, Thomas stepped over him and resumed his journey.

Somehow he reached his friends unharmed.

Relief showed on Will's face. "You found us, Thomas! I couldn't see you!" Then he saw the blood. "Are you hurt?" he asked in alarm.

"It's nothing. Just a scratch," Thomas replied. He leaned closer to Will, pointing a finger toward the huge squid. "Did you do this?"

Wild-eyed and disheveled, Will surveyed the scene. "I summoned the creature," he confirmed quietly. "I have no control over it though! We're in as much danger as anyone else!"

As if to emphasize his assessment, Princess Teylee screamed in terror. Glancing in her direction, Thomas saw a huge eye peering over the rail. The entire head rose into view, alien and dreadful. Then the creature abruptly sank out of sight beneath the vessel, its tentacles gliding away behind it.

"I've heard tales of giant squid attacking ships," breathed King Rupert in awe. "I never believed for a minute any of it was true."

A strange calm settled over the crippled ship. Dazed men wandered aimlessly, picking their way among fallen spars, shredded sails, and the tangles of unidentifiable debris that lay strewn across the deck.

Thomas, Brother Ander, and Will stood warily beside the former captives. King Rupert and the counterfeit queen stood at the ready with drawn swords, but no one paid them any attention.

Almost no one. Humbled by forces beyond his control, Rheibas had not forgotten them. He glared toward them with calculating eyes from his refuge beside the main mast. Even now he had not abandoned his schemes to relieve them of the stones.

But the nightmare was far from over. The tentacles returned, rising lazily from the deep on the opposite side of the ship and bringing a sudden end to the respite.

A damaging hail of spars and tangled lines rained from above as giant limbs claimed the foremast and tore it down. Missing the deck, it crashed sideways through the hull not far from Thomas, leaving a gaping hole behind it.

This time the creature seemed more intent on tearing the ship apart than on hunting down the terrified fugitives cowering on its deck. Planks flew through the air as great tentacles clawed at the breach.

The ship had been drifting out to sea, and for the first time Thomas noticed it was beginning to list. Their side of the deck was slowly sinking.

"Can't you do something about this creature?" pleaded Thomas.

"I'm working on it!" Will replied tensely.

After falling into the sea, one of the ship's boats now floated peacefully on the seaward side of the vessel. Before anyone could seek refuge in it, the huge whale reappeared, surfacing behind the ship. Launching itself backward from the water, it landed squarely on the little boat. Water sprayed in every direction, and splintered pieces of wood soon littered the surface.

The whale hit the side of the ship with a jarring thud, knocking Thomas from his feet. He looked up to see the tentacles finally disappearing from view.

Moments later he saw the reason for the giant cephalopod's retreat. Fighting for its life, it had wrapped itself around the snout of the whale. They all stared in fascinated consternation as the two giants of the deep joined battle. Tentacles flailed wildly while the great tail of the leviathan slapped the water. Then the whale sank beneath the waves, dragging its intended meal with it. Soon nothing remained except a trail of bubbles.

The tiny humans perched precariously on the tilting deck had little to celebrate. By now all of them were acutely aware that the vessel was sinking. They eyed the water uncertainly, fearful of what else might be lurking in its depths.

Continuing to settle lower, the ship abruptly lurched of its own accord, leaning at an alarming angle. Men began sliding across the deck toward the rails, a few falling into the water. Thomas soon spotted figures dragging themselves onto chunks of floating debris.

Then with a creaking and groaning of timbers, the ship keeled over. Tossed carelessly into the ocean, Thomas surfaced to see the ship towering above him. Desperately swimming away from it, he tried to ignore the objects large and small splashing down around him. Wooden yards and booms, tangled lines, pieces of sail—anything not secured to the ship—plummeted into the water. There was no way to escape the deadly rain. Somehow emerging unscathed, he began scanning the surface anxiously, hoping his companions had also escaped injury.

Even before he spotted them all, a huge piece of sailcloth came down, suspended between broken spars. Rupert and Tasha were directly in its path, and it settled over them like a shroud. Thomas waited impatiently for them to swim out from underneath it, but he saw only signs of their struggles. Gradually it occurred to him that they must have become ensnared.

Brother Ander apparently reached the same conclusion, because he dived below the cloth, Will's knife poised in his hand. Fully expecting Will to join the monk, Thomas glanced about for his friend. When he finally located him, he saw the Varasan agent helping him onto a large piece of wood. Will seemed dazed, his head covered with blood. One of the falling objects must have picked him out.

Only the aged High Priest seemed aware of the drama below the sailcloth. Floating nearby on a support of his own, he stared at Thomas as if waiting for him to do something.

Shamed into action, Thomas took a deep breath and dived. Coming up beneath the cloth, he saw both the king and the princess entangled in lines. The monk had just succeeded in cutting the princess free. Seeing Thomas, he waved him to her aid, and moved to help the king.

Frantic for air, the princess seemed confused. Thomas grabbed her and led her beyond the enveloping sailcloth and upward. She broke the surface gasping desperately. Impatient to return to the others, he saw to his relief that her struggles had attracted the attention of the Varasan. As the agent moved to the aid of the princess, Thomas took a deep breath and dived back down.

Neither Brother Ander nor the king could have survived this long without air, yet he saw the monk still working frantically to free the king. Then Thomas discovered how they had continued so long. Stretching up, the king tilted back his head to claim a small pocket of air above him. The trapped air was now exhausted though, and no other pockets were in sight. Swimming toward the king, Thomas managed to free one limb from entanglement at the same moment the monk severed the final line. As Thomas led the king to freedom, Brother Ander set out after them, his attempts noticeably feeble.

The king surfaced, gasping weakly. The Varasan woman was ready. Grasping hold of him, she pulled him to safety.

Not pausing for a minute, Thomas filled his lungs and dived back under the water. The monk had not cleared the sailcloth, and his arms were flailing ineffectually. He clearly had no resources left.

There was not a moment to lose. Ducking back under the sail, Thomas grabbed him and pushed him clear. With the last of his strength he thrust him toward the surface. Dimly he saw an ancient arm reach down to grasp the robe of the monk and pull him with surprising strength toward safety.

Attempting to swim out from under the sail, Thomas felt resistance. Looking down he saw that his own leg had become entangled. Reaching down, he fumbled endlessly with the twisted lines. Finally succeeding in freeing his leg, he knew it had taken too long. The surface wasn't far away, but he no longer had the strength to reach it.

Thomas had passed beyond the limit of his own endurance. He struggled weakly as water filled his lungs, but he struggled in vain.

His fading thought was not one of regret, but of gratitude for a life rich beyond his imagining.

A FACE APPEARED, one he should have recognized. Words sounded, but he could not grasp their meaning.

Then, accompanied by much coughing and spluttering, everything came rushing back.

Thomas found himself lying on a flat piece of wood, large enough to accommodate his whole body. Brother Ander, astride his own piece of wood, was bending over him. The monk looked barely able to function himself.

Brother Ander turned to address the Varasan woman. "Thank you for retrieving him. I couldn't have done it."

Then the monk's eyes moved away, and a smile lit his face. There was nothing wry about it. It was a heart-felt smile, without reservation, reaching to his eyes. Following his gaze, Thomas was astonished to see the ghost of a smile on the High Priest's face, softening the deep lines of his ancient visage. With an effort he turned away, sensing it was not his place to intrude upon the moment.

Other voices reached him, and he turned his head to see the newly freed king propped up on an elbow, talking to the princess. Both of them rested on floating debris. Facing the other direction, he found Will floating beside him, stretched out on his own little raft. Blood had stained his hair a deeper shade of red. His eyes were closed, but his chest rose and fell rhythmically.

Will's eyes fluttered open. Seeing Thomas, his lips parted in a feeble smile. "Welcome back," he managed.

The monk paddled over to them and leaned in to examine Will's head. "My apologies for taking so long to notice this, Will," he said.

Laying a hand on the wound, he prayed simply, then leaned back. "How does that feel?"

"My head has stopped pounding," reported Will. He explored the wound with his hand. "It doesn't hurt at all. Thank you, Brother Ander!"

The monk smiled wearily and moved away.

As time passed, Thomas gradually became more aware of his surroundings. The ship lay crippled in the water, but much of it was still visible. Other survivors clung to floating objects of their own.

Not far away Thomas spotted Kahrlin kneeling atop a substantial piece of the hull. Reaching down, the agent dragged a dripping Grand Vizier from the water. Rheibas appeared to be bleeding freely from a gash on his leg, but he was alive. His wound was staining the water red, and Kahrlin knelt beside his master, apparently trying to staunch the flow of blood.

Thomas shook his head in bemusement. How was it possible that the person responsible for all the trauma, all the grief, had managed to survive?

Twisting the clasp of the stone, he peered at Rheibas once more. No distractions blocked his explorations this time; such tactics were beyond the chief minister in his current state. Hidden ambitions welled up at last—a mental image of Rheibas sitting in state upon an imposing throne in the heart of what Thomas didn't doubt was Kat Ahket. Whatever his eventual plans for Rogand, it seemed that after acquiring the stones Rheibas intended to begin with the Empire of Ahr. In light of this information, his plan to dispose of Princess Neira took on a new significance.

Returning the stone to its usual position, Thomas reached over and nudged Will, pointing out Rheibas and his lackey.

He soon discovered that other eyes were on the two Ahrans. A voice nearby rang out in a language Thomas didn't understand. Twisting around to identify the speaker, he saw it was the Varasan agent. From the tone of her voice, she had been taunting the two men.

Kahrlin was staring back at her in shock. Unconcealed hatred showed on Rheibas's face.

A fin appeared in the water near the beleaguered men, drawing their attention away. The Ahrans watched wide-eyed as it circled their tiny wooden island ominously. Then the island rocked violently, pitching both men into the water.

A head emerged, jaws yawning wide to reveal rows of razor-sharp teeth. Snatching Rheibas, it sank out of sight. Kahrlin's cry of dismay was cut short as he too disappeared, carried off by a second predator.

Thomas stared aghast at the empty platform, now rocking gently in the swell.

He faced Will. "Was that you?" he whispered.

Haunted eyes stared back at him. "I had nothing to do with it." Will's brows drew together. "Somehow, though..." he began.

"It seems fitting," Thomas finished for him.

The Varasan agent had witnessed the demise of the Grand Vizier with evident satisfaction.

"What did you say to Rheibas earlier, when you were calling out?" Will asked her.

"I told him he'd promoted the wrong bootlicker. I said that Bolnyk abducted two royals, and Kahrlin didn't even manage one. I was speaking in Ahran, which would have made it clear I wasn't Queen Essanda."

Will grunted in approval. "They weren't as clever as they thought, and it's satisfying to know they discovered the truth before the end."

The agent stared into the water where Rheibas had disappeared. "It wouldn't shock me if that shark gets indigestion," she growled. Seeing Thomas looking at her quizzically, she told him, "I've dreamed of bringing the Grand Vizier down since I was a child. Now he's gone, and not by my hand. The shark cheated me, although I suppose I should be grateful."

"Why did you want to bring him down?" asked Thomas.

She briefly described Rheibas's role in the unjust execution of her parents. "Suddenly my parents were gone," she added bitterly. "There was no dignity in their deaths. They'd been sentenced for sedition, so their bodies were thrown into a mass grave. There was no ceremony to remember them, and no opportunity for a confused and horrified child to grieve their loss."

Thomas stared at her, appalled.

"I found myself an orphan, left to fend for myself on the streets. Fortunately a widow found me and took me in. She was a good woman who set about raising me and loving me. She told me the day would come when I needed to forget him and focus my energies elsewhere."

The Varasan smiled wryly. "It seems she was right. About needing to focus elsewhere, at least. Whatever the future might bring, the time has finally come for me to find a new expression for my energy."

Brother Ander had been listening. "Invest your energy in pursuits that bring life and hope," he said with a weary smile. "Make sure your legacy counts for something when your time comes."

"I will ponder your words," she promised.

As they fell silent, Thomas peered numbly around him, weighed down and overwhelmed by what he had heard and witnessed.

The Grand Vizier had inflicted damage exceeding anything Thomas could comprehend. Countless lives had been destroyed at his whim. And once he learned of the stones, entire kingdoms had been thrown into turmoil. All to satisfy his rapacious appetite for power.

Now he was gone, snatched away in a moment. After having such a significant role in the affairs of the world, his departure from it had been undignified and without ceremony. Very few would miss him.

So much upheaval. So much destruction. And what had been the point of it all?

Everything went quiet, apart from the slap-slap of the water on the floating debris. Clinging stubbornly to his makeshift raft, Thomas continued to drift. Other predators were undoubtedly prowling below, but the knowledge didn't move him. He had stared death in the face and survived. For that moment at least, he remained undaunted.

As they continued to float, something nudged him from below, reawakening his alarm. Then a gray body surfaced beside him, and the unforgettable smile of a dolphin greeted his startled gaze. The creature chittered once, then submerged its head again.

It took another gentle nudge before he finally grasped what was required of him. Remaining perched on his little raft, he grabbed hold of the dorsal fin and allowed the dolphin to propel him through the water. Glancing back a couple of minutes later he saw his companions strung out behind him, similarly conveyed. A large pod of the creatures surrounded the little group, sporting about them before leaping joyfully above the waves. Their exuberance washed over him, buoying up his spirits and chasing away his memories of the darkness.

After a few moments his mount disappeared and another took its place. When he glanced behind once more, he saw that the remains of the ship were already far away.

A profound sense of serenity began to settle over him. Having refused to yield to the paralyzing embrace of fear, he had set foot on a path that promised only a terrible death. By a miracle he had avoided the looming disaster, only to be snatched away to an abrupt ending he never anticipated.

Having passed through the gates of death, he had been restored, beyond expectation and beyond hope. And now, in the most improbable of conclusions, he was returning home, borne along joyfully by the sublimest of earth's creatures.

In later years he remembered this journey as one of the purest joys of his entire life.

Leaning sideways to lay his head on the body of the dolphin, he allowed the last of the tension to drain from his body.

He was at peace.

38

Spotting the castaways, a fishing boat diverted from its course to pick them up. As the boat approached, their dolphin escorts glided silently away and headed out to sea, presumably in search of fish.

Will climbed aboard with the others, warmly expressing his appreciation to the fisherman and his son for rescuing them. The fisherman was well aware of the presence of the Rogandan and Ahran fleets, and confirmed that they were still in the area. He readily agreed to take them all to King Krasmir.

Will positioned himself in the bow, away from the others.

Thomas soon joined him there. "Thank you," he said quietly.

"For what?" asked Will.

"For that magnificent experience!" Thomas replied.

Will responded with a wink.

The others were distracted, none of them able to stop talking about the dolphins. Will understood perfectly. After the horrors they had endured, the timely arrival of the gentle creatures had done more to lift their spirits than he could have believed possible.

"I was astonished at how effectively you enlisted the aid of the dolphins," Thomas told him.

"They are intelligent creatures," Will replied. "It was much easier than I expected to convey what I needed them to do."

"You seemed to have a connection with them when we first sailed to Rog," Thomas observed.

"Yes. I needed to work on it though. If I seemed distracted when we sailed back from Rog, it was because I was concentrating on strengthening my links with sea creatures, particularly larger ones. I had no clear idea what I might do with those links, but couldn't see any other way to make use of the Stone of Authority."

"The opportunity arose, and you made good use of it."

Will nodded. "When the Grand Vizier had us at his mercy, I summoned the largest creatures of the deep available. I was as surprised as anyone by the giant squid—I believe they are rarely seen in shallow waters. All I intended was to create a distraction, but it quickly spiraled out of control. I could easily have been responsible for our deaths!"

"You have no reason to reproach yourself. We survived."

"That had a lot to do with you and Brother Ander," Will told him. "You used the Stone of Knowing to good effect when you warned the interpreter, and Brother Ander once more achieved the impossible with the help of the Stone of Vitality."

A wry smile came to Thomas's face. "It's ironic that the stones played such a big part in the Grand Vizier's downfall. He got to see them at work first hand, but he'll never get his hands on them. The shark made certain of that."

"Yes, the shark did us a favor. It arrived without encouragement from me, as you already know. I could summon a shark, but I'm not sure I have the mastery to direct it to do exactly what it did. I'm sure the Stone of Authority would be capable of it in the hands of the right person. But in the end the Grand Vizier was brought down without our involvement, and I'm perfectly content with that."

Will wondered if Thomas had discovered anything new about Rheibas's intentions. "Did you learn anything more about what he was hoping to achieve if he managed to get his hands on the stones?"

Thomas nodded. "He had an unguarded moment just before the

shark took him. He had his sights set on the emperor's crown. The stones would have helped deliver it. Eventually he would have needed to dispose of the princess anyway, and he saw a way to use her to create a crisis that might bring the stones into the open. We're fortunate indeed that he didn't succeed."

Their conversation was cut short when the Varasan ship used for the conference came into view. Before long they had pulled alongside. Will was the last out of the fishing boat, and he didn't leave before sincerely thanking the fishermen once again.

They found King Krasmir still aboard. The king was stunned speechless when they appeared one after another over the rail. When he caught sight of his daughter, though, his joy could not be contained. No one witnessing their reunion could have remained unmoved by it. For Will it was especially poignant, knowing better than anyone what the king must be experiencing.

As soon as King Krasmir was able to detach himself, he sent a message to the emperor, inviting him to join them for a full debriefing. While they were waiting, he went to each of the other new arrivals, welcoming them and congratulating them on their safe return. Not surprisingly, he remained longest with King Rupert, but no one was neglected. He greeted the High Priest with appropriate deference, and earnestly expressed his gratification at his rescue.

When he came to Will, he did not hide his relief at his safe return. "Allowing you to leave this morning was beyond uncomfortable, and I'm immensely relieved to welcome you back! I can't begin to imagine what I would have told your king."

"Your daughter's life was at stake, Your Majesty, and there seemed at least a faint chance I could do something to secure her release. After what I went through with my son, I could never have lived with myself if I didn't try."

"I am forever in your debt, Lord Torbury." He dipped his head in salute. Then he glanced at Will's clothing, still wet from the time he spent in the water. "How did all of you manage to escape his clutches?"

"That is a surprising story, Your Majesty."

Before he could relate it, the arrival of the emperor was announced.

After welcoming his honored guest, King Krasmir introduced the released hostages.

"Your Imperial Majesty, it gives me great pleasure to introduce you to King Rupert of Castel. And this is my daughter, Princess Teylee, to whom he is betrothed. Their companion in captivity was not Queen Essanda of Arvenon as her captors believed. This woman impersonated the queen in order to protect her. As a result, she endured on the queen's behalf a brutal abduction at the hands of Kahrlin, the Grand Vizier's senior agent. I have not introduced her by name out of respect for her request that her anonymity be preserved."

The emperor's demeanor showed how he felt about his most senior official having placed him in such a position. "I can see at a glance that none of you have been well treated," he acknowledged. "I can only apologize most sincerely for what you have endured at the hands of my chief minister. He denied any involvement, suggesting the betrothed couple had eloped, then absconded. He claimed the queen later visited her brother of her own accord. In view of his abhorrent behavior and his deception, it need hardly be said that Rheibas is no longer my chief minister."

He addressed the princess. "I profoundly regret the ordeal you have suffered."

Princess Teylee bowed. "Thank you, Your Majesty. All of us understand that the Grand Vizier was acting only on his own behalf." She looked at her father. "Knowing that he invented a report about us eloping might help explain why the guards tried to force us together. At first they gave each of us a hut, but later they demolished one of them. When the weather was bad enough, we were forced to shelter together."

King Krasmir didn't speak, but his face had gone dark with anger.

King Rupert faced Krasmir calmly. "You can rest assured that the Grand Vizier's efforts were in vain, Your Majesty." He grinned at the princess. "That isn't because our ordeal did anything to diminish my affection for your daughter."

She returned a grin of her own.

"Perhaps the Grand Vizier was hoping to reinforce his version of the truth," suggested Lady Tulinay with a frown.

"More likely he was looking for ways to further increase his leverage," scowled Krasmir.

King Rupert nodded. "That occurred to us as well. Any child we produced would be heir to the Castelan throne, as well as being Your Majesty's grandchild."

The emperor appeared more uncomfortable than ever. "Where is Rheibas now?" he asked.

"He is dead, Your Majesty," Will replied bluntly.

Both the emperor and King Krasmir regarded him in astonishment.

"How did that happen?" asked the king.

"As you told us, Your Majesty, the Grand Vizier sent Kahrlin to say that the hostages would only be released if the Arvenians visited him on his ship for what he called 'negotiations.' He was referring to Brother Ander, Thomas Stablehand, and me. We agreed to go in the hope that he would honor his promise and release them. When we arrived he claimed we had something he wanted. He didn't say what it was. He said unless we gave it to him, he would kill the hostages immediately."

Lady Tulinay was shaking her head. "It sounds like he was making a demand none of you could satisfy, thereby giving himself an excuse to kill the hostages."

"No doubt he intended to kill you as well," added King Krasmir. "Not least because the three of you witnessed Bolnyk's murder of Lord Torbury's son."

"It quickly became obvious to us that he intended to kill us all," agreed Will.

"How did you escape?" asked the king.

"Before he said anything to us, Rheibas sent Kahrlin and most of his men below deck, leaving behind an interpreter and a few armed men. He clearly didn't want witnesses. After killing us, he was going to have the interpreter and the others killed as well. Thomas announced that to the interpreter, who then told everyone else. Rheibas immediately had the interpreter killed and recalled Kahrlin and the others. When they arrived, he told them to kill the men on deck. A battle broke out. It didn't last long, but it bought us some time."

The emperor was clearly appalled. "How was Rheibas killed?"

"At this point nature intervened in a remarkable way," Will continued. "Incredible as it sounds, the ship was attacked by a giant squid. The squid in turn was attacked by a huge whale, but not before it had damaged the ship so badly it sank. While we were in the water, we saw a shark take Rheibas. Another shark took Kahrlin almost immediately. We stayed together and were eventually picked up by a fishing boat."

Will made no mention of the dolphins. The story was incredible enough already.

He turned to the emperor. "We don't know what became of the other survivors, but I'm sure that most of them are still in the area. It isn't far away. They will confirm my account."

The emperor immediately spoke to one of his aides. The man left the ship at once. After excusing himself, the emperor then spent a considerable time consulting quietly with other aides. He continued until a boat pulled alongside the ship and the missing aide returned. After a whispered conversation, the emperor once more addressed his hosts.

"The survivors are being rescued," the emperor explained. "An investigation is underway into their behavior. While they have not conducted themselves in a manner worthy of their emperor, I recognize they were following orders. They will be given a proper opportunity to explain themselves before I decide their fate."

He shook his head in astonishment. "I confess your tale is so bizarre it defies belief, Lord Torbury. Nevertheless, the other survivors have confirmed your account. It seems that justice has been served on Rheibas for his misdeeds, the sentence having been carried out by nature itself. I have never heard of such a thing!"

"What of Bolnyk, Your Majesty?" asked King Krasmir. "His crimes were committed against the empire as well as against Rogand and Arvenon. I am willing to hand him over to you for judgment if you are willing to take him."

"Gladly, Your Majesty," the emperor replied. "You have my promise he will be held to account."

Before the emperor left, he approached King Krasmir with one final suggestion. Will was one of the few within earshot. Neither of them seemed to object to his presence.

"I am told that your oldest son is of marriageable age, King Krasmir. It has not escaped my attention that any alliance between the empire and Rogand might be strengthened by a union between your son and my daughter."

The king's mouth opened, then he snapped it shut.

His dilemma was painfully obvious to Will. "As someone with no vested interest, might I offer a thought on the subject, Your Majesties?" he asked.

"Of course," said the king at once.

The emperor nodded as soon as the request was translated.

"It strikes me that events have conspired in such a way that Princess Neira's experience of Rogand has been profoundly disagreeable. After being rescued from certain death on a remote Rogandan island, she was fortunate to survive her initial attempt to reach Rog by sea. When she did arrive, it was necessary to confine her for her own protection. Rheibas found a way to contact her anyway. The letter he entrusted to Bolnyk exposed his attempts to manipulate her."

His eyebrows drew together. "I'm not sure if Your Majesty is aware of the full impact of Rheibas's scheming. In addition to the abductions and murder carried out by his agents, he has been actively stoking fears of an Ahran invasion, drawing upon an ever increasing naval presence to reinforce his threats. From the beginning he targeted the surrounding kingdoms as well as Rogand, both with his threats and his abductions. That is the reason King Steffan sent me to Rog. As a result Her Highness spent months in the capital in a climate of fear and uncertainty toward Ahrans in general, with no clarity about her own future, all the while cut off from the familiar comfort and security of her father's authority.

"I have no doubt she would not hesitate to do anything required of her for the sake of her father and the empire. However, if she marries the crown prince she will face a lifetime in Rogand, with her best years spent in service to the kingdom as its queen. In light of all she has endured, I fear that the prospect might seem disheartening. It might even seem to her like a heavy sentence."

He dipped his head respectfully. "I know I speak on behalf of my own king when I say that the arrival of Your Majesty has transformed our situation. A catastrophe has been averted, and you have lifted us from despondency to hope. It is not necessary for you to yield up your brightest jewel to secure the gratitude and friendship of the kingdoms of the region. You have achieved that already."

He bent low. "I have spoken very freely. Please pardon me if my words appear in any way presumptuous."

The emperor addressed himself to King Krasmir. "Do these sentiments echo your own thoughts, Your Majesty?"

The king nodded gravely. "Lord Torbury's analysis of the situation is perceptive, and I can only concur. In particular, I agree that all of us are in the debt of Your Imperial Majesty. Having come here with a willingness to search out the truth, you at once saw to the heart of it, in spite of a determined attempt by Rheibas to deceive you. No greater token of your goodwill is necessary."

The emperor nodded. Turning to Will, he regarded him thoughtfully. "You have given me much to consider, Lord Torbury. I compliment you on your diplomatic skills. It is not difficult to see why your sovereign appointed you as his representative."

He turned to the king. "In view of what both of you have said, it might be wisest to allow Neira to return to Kat Ahket."

With that, he bade them farewell and departed. He left with a promise to leave behind an official with authority to commence negotiations on trade agreements and a mutual assistance treaty.

As soon as he was gone, King Krasmir turned to Will. "It seems there is to be no end to my indebtedness toward you, Lord Torbury!" he exclaimed. "I could see no way to refuse the emperor's request without causing him grave offense, and no way to accept it without forever alienating my son—not to mention my wife—no doubt along with the rest of the kingdom! You have neatly extricated me from a very delicate situation."

"It is the least I could do, Your Majesty. There is one other matter I wished to raise with you. A former prisoner of Rheibas is currently being held in your dungeons. Having met with him and questioned him closely, I do not believe he has done anything worthy of punishment. Could you please ask one of your people to examine his case?"

"I will follow it up," the king promised.

Then he frowned. "Do you have any idea what Rheibas wanted with the High Priest?"

Will shrugged. "He said he was honoring an agreement. He didn't offer details, but he said it would result in significant change for Rogand. Do you have enemies among the priesthood, Your Majesty?"

"My agents believe that the Archprimus, the second in charge, thinks I am not sufficiently in thrall to the dark gods."

"In that case, if I had to guess, I'd say that the Archprimus agreed to deliver the High Priest to Rheibas, although for what purpose I cannot say with any certainty. In return, Rheibas promised the Archprimus he'd get rid of you and your family. Presumably the Archprimus would further benefit by stepping into the role of High Priest. That might have allowed him some measure of influence over who replaced you."

The king reacted with fury. "I have been careful never to interfere with the priests, but I will not tolerate insurrection!" he snapped.

"It may not be necessary for you to do anything, Your Majesty. I suspect the High Priest will be more than eager to deal with the matter."

Glancing toward the priest, Will found him talking with Brother Ander. "I haven't mentioned it, but after we arrived on Rheibas's ship, he decided to show he was serious by ordering the High Priest killed. One of his men ran him through. Before anyone could stop him, Brother Ander hurried over and restored him. The High Priest later returned the favor by pulling Brother Ander from the water when he was about to drown. We might be witnessing the beginning of an unlikely friendship."

The king looked at the two men in amazement. "This has been a day of surprises!" he exclaimed.

BISRI AHUZZA STOOD at the rail of the emperor's ship, watching the water foam about the bow as the vessel plowed through the swell. Rogand lay behind them; they were returning at last to Kat Ahket, the imperial fleet clustered around them.

Looking up, he saw the emperor approaching. He bowed low.

"I have a request for you, Bisri. You seem to have reached an understanding with the Rogandans and their allies. It's apparent to me that they trust you. I wish to appoint you as my ambassador to the region."

Ahuzza bowed again. "You do me great honor, Your Majesty."

"I imagine you will need to learn both Rogandan and Arvenian," the emperor observed.

The bisri tried not to sound too eager. "I will apply myself diligently to the task," he promised.

The emperor gazed off into the horizon. "It seems I will be much distracted in the near future. Spending time with my daughter is long overdue."

Ahuzza looked at him quizzically.

"I proposed a marriage alliance with the Rogandan crown prince," the emperor told him with a sigh. "Lord Torbury said some pretty words to deflect me from my purpose, but it was nevertheless apparent that the notion terrified King Krasmir. I can only conclude that Neira has not left a favorable impression."

"I am sure Her Highness will both appreciate and benefit from your attention, Your Majesty."

"I see you share their opinion," observed the emperor gloomily. "The situation is clearly worse than I realized."

Horrified, Ahuzza opened his mouth to protest.

The emperor waved him to silence. "Don't bother to deny it, Ahuzza. You will be of little use to me as an ambassador if you're too frightened to tell me the truth." He frowned. "One thing puzzles me. Why did you travel to Kat Ahket to see me, when I had already received a message from Krasmir requesting a meeting?"

"It was Lord Torbury's suggestion to employ a backup plan, Your Majesty. Captain Gharpin and I sailed together to meet with you. But in case something went wrong, King Krasmir sent a message with a merchant as well. It seems the message reached you first."

"I would not have expected a merchant to reach me," the emperor told him. "These have been challenging times for merchants. Ahrans have not been welcome in Rogand, and few Rogandans have dared to travel to Kat Ahket."

"The Rogandans located a merchant who was unusually capable and persistent."

The emperor snorted. "Such qualities are hardly surprising in a smuggler. I had this so-called merchant thrown into jail as soon as he had delivered the message."

A look of horror played across Ahuzza's face before he could prevent it.

"Don't trouble yourself, Ahuzza. I arranged for him to be released with a stern warning after a couple of days in the lockup." He shook his head stoically. "I doubt it will make any difference."

Ahuzza looked at the emperor tentatively. "If I may raise a different matter, Your Majesty, I believe I will owe the crown prince an explanation when I return."

The emperor's eyebrows went up inquiringly.

"When I arrived in Kat Ahket he graciously agreed to receive me. I warned him about the chief minister and expressed my concerns about a possible threat to you. He told me I was raising serious allegations that needed investigation. He then placed me in protective custody. He explained it was for my own safety."

"And he later changed his mind and released you?"

"No. I escaped."

The emperor burst into laughter. "There is more to you than meets the eye, Bisri! I am delighted!"

He studied Ahuzza shrewdly. "And you have been wondering if my son might have been in league with Rheibas?"

Ahuzza felt color rising to his face. "The thought did occur to me, Your Majesty."

The emperor chuckled. "You needn't trouble yourself. My son hated Rheibas more than most—he despised the man. Much as I appreciate your concerns on my behalf, the young whelp does nothing without my knowledge. He never sneezes without me finding out about it!" A wry grin came to his face. "As for you escaping from under his nose, set your mind at rest. I will deal with the matter."

He slapped Ahuzza heartily on the back. "There's something refreshingly transparent about you, Bisri. I hope you never lose that quality!"

39

Rupert stood in a palace garden, holding Tasha's hands lightly in his own and gazing wistfully into her eyes.

"This has felt like the longest week of my life," he said with a sigh. "Harrowing as our captivity was, at least I was able to spend every day with you. Now I have to make an appointment to see you. And even then we're never truly alone." He threw a sideways glance at the chaperone hovering nearby. "I've been missing you, Tasha!"

"I've been missing you, too." She took a step closer, and his heart began to pound. "I want to spend the rest of my life with you, Rupert," she breathed.

He gazed at her in helpless longing. If it were possible, he'd marry her tomorrow and never leave her side again.

Both of them knew it wasn't that simple.

"I need to leave for Castel tomorrow," he told her, reluctantly bringing the moment to an end.

"Does it have to be so soon?"

The crestfallen look on her face tugged at his heart, but he couldn't escape his responsibilities.

"I've been away from my kingdom far too long. My subjects must have wondered if I'd ever return. And they believed that my sister—the last of our line—had been taken from them as well." He shook his head. "I can't delay this any longer. But I will return the moment our wedding has been arranged. After that we can be together always."

"We'd better talk to my parents," she said.

Leading him inside, she took him to a room in the royal apartments where they found both of her parents sitting restlessly.

Queen Deka jumped up when they appeared. Seeing the look on Tasha's face, she cried, "Whatever is wrong?"

"Rupert is leaving tomorrow," Tasha told them. "He won't be back until the wedding."

"There, there," the queen said, wrapping a comforting arm around her daughter.

Before long she began sniffling herself. Drawing back, she gazed at Tasha mournfully. "I thought I'd lost you!" she said. "Then at last you were restored to me. But now you'll marry and go away, and I'll never see you again!"

"Don't be silly, Mother," Tasha replied. "We'll visit Rog whenever we can."

"And you'll always be welcome at Castel Citadel," Rupert added. "You can stay for as long as you like."

Their efforts were in vain. After a brief attempt to rally, the queen abandoned herself completely to despondency. Dissolving into tears, she buried her face in Tasha's shoulder.

The king raised his hands helplessly. "We completely understand, Rupert. You must do your duty to your kingdom. I'm sure I don't need to tell you that you will always be welcome here."

After saying his farewells, Rupert excused himself. Tasha accompanied him out of the royal apartments.

"Will I see you tomorrow before I go?" he asked.

"Of course," she assured him. "And I will wait impatiently for your return."

A RED-TINTED SUNRISE SAW WILL, Thomas, and Brother Ander gathered at a small dock in Rog Harbor. The little group had come to farewell Kamash and his friend Gharpin. King Rupert had departed for Castel by ship the previous day, accompanied by much pomp and ceremony, and Will knew that an official send off would also have been arranged for Kamash if the old man hadn't firmly rejected any such notion. He also knew that King Krasmir had found time to express his thanks and say his goodbyes in private.

"So you're finally going back to your island again, Kamash!" said Thomas. "But not alone this time."

"I am joining him for one month only," said Gharpin. "I am helping him get a start."

Brother Ander grinned at the former captain. "Your Rogandan has improved a lot!"

The Ahran shrugged, jerking his head in the direction of Kamash. "I like him better when I do not understand him."

His remark drew a chuckle from Kamash. "Rude as Gharpin might be, it will be good to have some company while I get established again."

"What will happen when the month is up?" asked Will.

"The emperor sends a ship. To bring me to Kat Ahket," Gharpin replied. "Then he gives me a new ship. I am Captain Gharpin again!"

"Congratulations!" they all cried in unison.

"Even after he leaves we won't entirely lose touch," Kamash told them. "He's promised to look in on me whenever he's in the region."

"That's excellent news! We wish you well—both of you. All of us owe you a lot!" Will told them.

The others echoed his sentiments.

After a final round of farewells, the two men climbed into the boat and guided it toward the channel. Will and his friends stood and watched until they had sailed out of sight.

Thomas stared after them. "Partings never seem to get any easier," he said, a catch in his voice.

"No, they do not," agreed Will.

Turning their backs on the dock, the three Arvenians headed back toward the city.

Delmar stood at an open window, gazing absently out across the city of Varacellan to the sea beyond.

A knock sounded, and a servant appeared. “You have a visitor, Your Majesty,” he announced, before silently departing.

Delmar looked up to find Maive standing hesitantly at the door. Their eyes met, and Delmar’s heart skipped a beat. The day had finally come.

“Maran said you wanted to speak with me, Your Majesty,” she said. Her cheeks colored faintly as she faced him.

“I can’t tell you how relieved I am to find you safe and well! Our parting was awkward, and I’m very sorry for that. I’ve often wished I could have our time over again.”

She didn’t respond, so he continued. “You saved my life, and I never thanked you properly. Worse, I left you feeling awkward and uncomfortable.”

“You have no need to apologize, Your Majesty. I said things I regret too.”

He tried to read her eyes. Was it possible she had also dreamed of a different outcome?

“The significance of your service cannot be overstated, Maive. I understand that both King Rupert and Princess Teylee are alive only because of you. Castel and Arvenon, as well as Varas, are deeply in your debt. None of us will forget it.” He paused. “Are you planning to continue as an agent now that the threat is behind us?”

She shook her head decisively. “I’m hoping for a more peaceful life in the future.”

He smiled. “Does that mean you can tell me your real name now?”

After a moment’s hesitation, a dimpled smile transformed her face. Had he imagined she wasn’t a beauty?

"My name really is Maive," she told him.

He beamed at her.

A question had been plaguing him. "You've needed to impersonate a queen, Maive. Did it sour you on everything royal?"

"I have never confused pretense with reality," she replied carefully.

She hadn't answered his question, but the faint blush on her cheeks told a tale of its own.

"I hope you will pardon my directness, but I would like to get to know you, Maive. You as a person, not as an agent. Would you be willing to let me do that?"

She looked uncertain, and he took a deep breath. "Something happened when we were together," he told her plainly. "I can't pretend to understand it, but I felt like I came alive." He looked her in the eye. "You told me it meant nothing to you. Were you speaking the truth?"

She looked away, remaining silent for a long moment without responding. Then she shook her head, unable to meet his eyes.

His heart soared. "Whatever was awoken back then might not survive the experience of us getting to know each other properly. But I would like to give it a chance."

The tension had slowly been easing from her face. "I would like that too, Your Majesty."

Taking a step toward her, he reached out and took her hand. "Please walk with me. We have some attractive gardens in the palace grounds, and I would like to show them to you."

She nodded shyly but seemed content to walk hand in hand beside him.

"If we are going to get to know each other properly, you'd better begin by calling me Delmar," he told her with a smile.

THOMAS HAD BECOME restless to return to his family, and he knew that Will was no less eager to be gone. Eventually Will managed to conclude his business with King Krasmir, and they prepared to leave.

To their delight, Brother Ander had decided to join them for at least part of the journey. He was planning to return to Arvenon after spending some time in Aen-irac. Since Thomas and Will planned to make their journey on horseback, it made sense for him to travel with them for a while.

"Is the king planning to give you an official farewell?" Thomas asked Will.

"He would if I'd let him. Lord Kulferan and Lady Tulinay seem to have tolerated me well enough, but the other nobles must be smarting at the special attention I've received from the king. I have no interest in adding fuel to that particular fire."

Nevertheless, as they were about to depart, King Krasmir himself rode up, escorted by a detachment of royal guards. Dismounting, the king approached them.

"We are grateful to you for the gift of the horses, Your Majesty," said Will.

The king waved it away. "It is the least I can do. I owe you more than I can possibly repay, Lord Torbury." He regarded Will frankly. "A king chooses his friends carefully, and I hope you know that I have come to regard you as a friend. It need hardly be said that you are welcome here at any time."

Will bowed low in response. "I am humbled by your words, Your Majesty. For my part, I hold you in high esteem. Rogand is fortunate indeed to be led by you, and I value your friendship greatly."

The king turned to Thomas. "I confess you are a mystery to me, Thomas Stablehand. I cannot shake the feeling that things would have turned out very differently if you had not been here, but I cannot explain why. In any event, you will also find a welcome in Rogand should you ever decide to return."

Thomas thanked him sincerely.

Lastly King Krasmir addressed the monk. "I wish I could convince you to make your home in Rogand permanently, Brother Ander. Nevertheless, you have assured me that you intend to return at some point, and I will hold you to that. Everyone who knows you will look forward eagerly to that day."

"I thank you for your kindness, Your Majesty," the monk replied. "God willing, I will visit often in the years to come."

Greatly heartened by the king's words, they left the palace. After riding through Rog, they guided their horses onto the main trade route heading south.

There was no shortage of things to talk about.

At one point Will asked Brother Ander, "Have you been to see the High Priest?"

"Yes," he replied. "Several times."

"Inside the temple?" Will asked in surprise. "The place sounds horrific from everything I've heard."

The monk shook his head. "I went inside briefly on my first visit. I found it so oppressive I had to leave. The High Priest was gracious enough to meet with me in the temple grounds."

Will's eyes grew wide with surprise. "That's totally unheard of!" he exclaimed. "He never leaves the temple! Everyone knows that."

Brother Ander shrugged. "We met with him on Rheibas's ship."

"Those were exceptional circumstances," Will returned. Abruptly changing the subject, he asked, "Do you know how he got to be so old? We know he doesn't have the Stone of Vitality."

Thomas grinned. "I suppose he could have invoked the ritual in Drettroth's scroll—the one that relied upon a bargain with the dark gods."

"I believe the explanation is much more simple," the monk replied calmly. "He told me that many of his forbears were long-lived. Apparently it runs in the family."

"Not an especially attractive explanation," said Will disappointedly.

Brother Ander smiled. "My mentor, Brother Elias, used to say that a simple explanation rarely draws a crowd, but it most often turns out to be the truth."

"Did you find out how he came to be on Rheibas's ship?" asked Thomas.

"He didn't say a lot about it, but I believe it was a power play on the part of his second-in-command, the Archprimus."

"Presumably he's had the man removed."

"There was no need. The High Priest told me a struggle broke out among the priests during his abduction. The Archprimus succeeded in taking him, but he was badly wounded in the process. It seems he didn't make it through the night."

"Thereby ending the power struggle," observed Will. "I'm sure the High Priest has rooted out the other conspirators by now."

"I believe so."

"What did the two of you talk about?" asked Thomas curiously.

"Many things," the monk replied, "but mostly theology."

"Do you think you'll see him again?"

"I hope so. He invited me to visit him again next time I'm in Rog."

WHEN THEY REACHED the borders of Aen-irac, both Thomas and Will were sorely tempted to divert with Brother Ander to visit old friends. But a long journey lay ahead of them and their families drew them onward. They parted after the monk promised to pass on their greetings.

As soon as he found a suitable moment, Thomas asked Will, "What will you do with the Stone of Authority?"

"Return it to Amyra," Will replied without hesitation.

"Will the two of you share it?"

"Perhaps, under exceptional circumstances. Only if it involves animals though. To be honest, I'll be glad to see the last of it." A grimace came to his face. "However hard I try I can't get the memory of that giant squid out of my head."

Pressing on to Arnost, they arrived to an enthusiastic welcome from their families. Swarming around Thomas and Will eagerly, their children left no room for Amyra or Elena to even reach their husbands. However, as soon as both men retrieved gifts from their saddlebags, the children ran off in great excitement to enjoy their new prizes.

For a while Thomas lost sight of all else in the joy of his reunion with Elena.

A short time later a dazzling burst of sunlight drew Elena's attention heavenward. "Someone's pleased to have Will back again," she said with a smile.

Up to that point the day had been overcast, with dark clouds blotting out the sun. Sunlight was now streaming through a large opening in the clouds above them, shafts of light picking out the two couples.

"I see you've handed it over already, Will," Thomas exclaimed.

"I completely forgot to bring a gift for Amyra," he returned, "so I had to give her something."

She punched him in mock anger.

"What about you, Elena?" Amyra asked.

Elena patted her bodice with a grin. "Thomas was just as eager for a handover. But he's assured me he didn't only bring gifts for the children."

Chatting happily, the four of them wandered into the palace.

KING STEFFAN WAS NO LESS delighted to see Will and Thomas return safely. He was greatly relieved to hear that all of the hostages had been released, not least because it meant that Queen Essanda could come into the open at last. Hiding herself away might have been essential to preserve the fiction that she had been abducted, but it had also become increasingly difficult for the king to bear. He wasted no time in sending a message to Newhaven.

As soon as an opportunity presented itself, the king sat down with Amyra and Elena to hear an account of the dramatic conclusion to the saga in Rogand. All of them listened with amazement as Will and Thomas laid out the unlikely outcome of the Grand Vizier's scheming.

Amyra shook her head in wonder. "Perhaps we'll finally be able to enjoy an extended season of peace." She eyed Will and Thomas shrewdly. "I have a feeling that both of you understated your own role in what happened. I'll look forward to quizzing Brother Ander next time he visits."

The king nodded. "I'm eager to see him and hear his account myself. Brother Ander has become more remarkable than ever—if such a thing were possible."

He addressed himself to Will and Thomas. "What are you planning to do now?"

"Return home with our families, Your Majesty," Will replied.

"I could use your input on a few matters while you're here, Will," the king observed. "But I know what my wife would say. I can almost hear her telling me that after everything you've been through, the only pressing need for both of you is to spend time with your families."

He gazed at the two women. "I'm sure Amyra and Elena must have been starting to wonder if you would ever return!"

They said nothing to contradict him.

He sighed. "I managed without you while you were in Rogand, Will, and there's no reason I can't continue to do so."

After a single night in Arnost, the two families set out for home, accompanied by a group of soldiers. Both Will and Thomas tried to decline the protection, but the king wouldn't yield.

When the time came to part ways, Thomas insisted that the soldiers continue on with Will. "You know how strongly Anneka and Rellan feel about Newhaven's privacy. And we don't need the protection. Not here."

"I scarcely know how to thank you, Thomas," Will told him. "I dragged you into danger once again, and it could so easily have been the end of us this time."

"You've never done it for your own sake," Thomas replied. "And we needed to be there—all three of us. It could have ended very badly without the help of the stones."

They parted with a confused mixture of regret and eagerness to reach their homes.

. . .

THE SUN WAS SINKING low in the sky when Thomas and Elena and the children finally reached Newhaven. Voices rose up to greet them, and they responded with cheery greetings of their own. Reaching their hut, the children raced inside, eager to rediscover everything they had left behind.

Stepping inside, Thomas took Elena in his arms. "We're home at last!"

He kissed her deeply, ignoring the noisy reaction of the children. "As soon as the children are asleep we'll find a quiet corner," he promised. "There's so much I still haven't heard about your time in Arnost."

She smiled up at him, a sigh of contentment passing her lips.

"I've never wanted fame or palaces, Elena," he whispered. "This is where I belong—right here with you."

40

30 years after the death of the Grand Vizier

With the Arvenian delegation drawing closer to Rog, a guard rode up to Lord Torbury's carriage, bringing an end to Thomas's conversation with his friend.

"A messenger has arrived from King Rimek, My Lord," the guard announced, addressing himself to Will. "The king is planning to greet the delegation in person. We expect to reach Rog by mid-afternoon."

"Thank you, Captain," Will replied.

The guard bowed and rode away.

"King Rimek." Will shook his head. "I'm still not used to it."

"It isn't surprising," Thomas replied. "You and King Krasmir were good friends over many years."

"I'm finding it harder to accept change these days," Will acknowledged. "I'm getting too old to be bothered with it. Still, young Rimek deserves his opportunity. He's waited long enough."

"He's certainly needed to be patient. And he isn't exactly young—he's in his early fifties!"

Will grunted. "Fifty sounds young to me."

Thomas laughed. "In that case I suppose you must think of King Aiden as a mere child. He isn't forty yet."

"He's a good boy," Will conceded. "His father would have been proud of him."

The mention of Aiden's father prompted Thomas to glance at the carriage behind them. Elena and Amyra were chatting enthusiastically with Essanda, the Dowager Queen of Arvenon since the passing of King Steffan two years previously at the age of 71. Elena might be a commoner, but preserving such boundaries held no more interest for Essanda than it had for her late husband.

"I suppose I'd better make myself presentable," said Will abruptly.

Thomas grinned. Will's appearance was always presentable, and his mind remained sharp as a dagger.

"I want you to take a good look at the Lestanorian ambassador, Thomas. He's certain to put in an appearance. I want to know if Lestanor is behind the recent trouble with the plains nomads." He looked at Thomas sharply. "You did bring it, didn't you!"

"Of course," Thomas assured him, patting his chest. As always, the Stone of Knowing rested securely on its clasp beneath his tunic. "I'll see what I can learn."

He glanced up at the sky. "Those dark clouds look threatening. We're incredibly fortunate to have avoided rain completely these last few days. I hope the weather doesn't intrude on the ceremony in a couple of days' time."

Will waved a hand dismissively. "Being fortunate has nothing to do with it. Rain won't interrupt the coronation any more than it did our journey."

Thomas's eyes went wide. "Do you mean to say you badgered poor Amyra into using the Stone of Authority—just to keep yourself dry?" He shook his head. "You're an old tyrant."

"Me? A tyrant? Ha!" he snorted. "Don't waste your sympathy on Amyra—she's more than capable of looking after herself!"

Thomas just grinned at him.

"Besides, it was never about me," Will insisted. "The queen is traveling with us. She's too old to be caught in the rain."

"She's younger than any of us," Thomas reminded him.

"Everyone's younger than us these days," grumbled Will.

The arrival of King Rimek brought an end to their conversation. Climbing down from the carriage, all of them bent at the waist.

After greeting the dowager queen and her companions, Rimek turned to Will and Thomas.

"Lord Torbury, Thomas Stablehand, you are both very welcome."

"Our sincere condolences on the loss of your father, Your Majesty," said Will. "He was a worthy king and a good man."

"He held you in high regard, Lord Torbury. He especially looked forward to your visits."

"It was an honor to know him."

"I trust that Arvenon understands that I value our alliance no less than my father. These are uncertain times."

"Lestanor?" asked Will.

The king nodded. "The new king has been flexing his muscles."

"The nomad tribes have been restive of late," Will told him. "We have wondered if Lestanor is behind it."

"Rogand also shares a border with the plains in the southwest," Rimek observed, "and we have noted similar stirrings. Whatever ambitions Lestanor's king might harbor, I am confident he will show restraint while we stand firmly together." Rimek smiled. "I am hopeful we will not need to draw upon your tactical genius anytime soon."

"My son Ethen might be of more use, Your Majesty. He shows considerable promise."

"I will gladly meet with him as often as King Aiden is willing to release him," the king replied. "In the meantime, I hope you will join me later. I find myself confronted with a number of strategic challenges, and I would value your wisdom."

"It would be an honor."

After a smile and a quick nod, King Rimek remounted and returned to the city.

As they rolled into Rog and headed for the palace, Thomas mused on Will's effortless transition from blustery old rogue to smooth-talking diplomat. The strange thing was that both identities reflected who he was. Thomas knew better than anyone how much the world needed men like Will, and he could only appreciate him in all his guises.

Dark clouds brooded heavily as the morning of the coronation dawned, but, just as Will had promised, the sky cleared well before the event got under way. The palace boasted extensive grounds, and the ceremony would be taking full advantage of them. In addition to nobles, officials, and envoys, King Rimek intended to admit a large contingent of commoners to the palace grounds to observe the coronation. Accordingly he made arrangements for a broad area to be cordoned off to accommodate the common people. Thomas had heard that refreshments would be freely provided to all after the formalities were over.

The coronation would also be the official commissioning of the new family crest, featuring a bear on a field of green. Even in the absence of visible opposition to his rule, Rimek understood that he needed to build a popular base of his own. Krasmir had often been likened to a bear, both before and after his coronation, and Rimek intended to use the symbol both to honor his father and to leverage Krasmir's popularity with commoners and nobles alike.

Thomas and Elena were led to preferred seating along with other members of the Arvenian delegation, and Thomas was delighted to discover Brother Ander among the group. He couldn't suppress a grin when he noted that the monk had been positioned as far away as possible from the large contingent of priests of the dark gods.

Brother Ander might have established a remarkable bond with the former High Priest, but his friend was long gone. The priest's prolonged tenure had finally concluded just two years after the Grand Vizier's demise, ending once and for all any suggestion that the dark gods had granted him immortality. Thomas had no doubt that the current incumbent wanted nothing to do with a foreign monk.

Other members of foreign delegations were positioned nearby, and Thomas was delighted to catch sight of an older man he recognized as Bisri Ahuzza. He decided to greet the Ahran as soon as he had an opportunity. A sullen faced man sat apart from the others. Bringing the stone into contact with his skin, Thomas confirmed he was looking at the Lestanorian ambassador. In a matter of moments he had mentally compiled a substantial list of observations to pass on to Will.

The ceremony got underway, commanding Thomas's full attention. In spite of his proficiency in Rogandan, Thomas understood very little of it, presumably because it relied upon archaic words no longer in common use. When it finished, loud cheering arose.

The king and his wife together raised high a staff featuring the new royal emblem, prompting a new round of applause. The flag rippled in the breeze, revealing a bear standing upright with arms outstretched.

Then a movement behind the king brought the cheering to an abrupt end.

Extensive woodlands fringed the grounds in which the ceremony was being held. To Thomas's amazement, two bears emerged from the trees, trotting purposefully toward the official party. Everyone backed away except the king, who stood boldly in their path. Guards belatedly hurried forward with drawn swords, but he waved them back. One of the bears was little more than a baby, and it held something between its teeth. The other bear was large and intimidating.

Bypassing the king, the baby bear shuffled toward the observers in the front row. Sitting on the very end of the row was Queen Deka, clad in mourning attire following the recent death of her husband, King Krasmir. After lifting its head high for all to see, the little bear opened its mouth and deposited a large white flower at the feet of the astonished dowager queen. Then it turned and ambled back to the forest.

Approaching the king, the large bear raised itself high on two legs and released a loud roar. Then it bent low, as if in homage, before spinning around and shambling off after its offspring.

For a moment complete silence reigned. Then a mighty shout arose as the people paid noisy homage to their king, enthusiastically affirming the honor bestowed by the bear. The commoners were delirious with excitement, and even the nobles were visibly impressed.

The king began to circulate among the people. As he passed nearby, Thomas overheard him say to one of the nobles, "I was as surprised as you!" Reaching the barrier separating the nobles from the common folk, the king horrified his guards by stepping over it to mingle with his people. He was soon swallowed up by a cheering mob.

With many old friends close at hand, Thomas still found time for a warm and informative interaction with Bisri Ahuzza. He was gratified to hear that the connection with the empire remained as robust as ever.

The festivities continued unabated as the day wore away. The sun was setting before the grounds were finally cleared of revelers.

That night Thomas and Elena sat with Will and Amyra in a palace apartment.

"The visit from the bears was very impressive," Thomas told Will. "Was Amyra in on your little surprise?"

Amyra opened her mouth to speak, but Will got in first. "I thought Rimek deserved a bit of a boost—just to get him started," he said. "It will be up to him from here."

"I was most definitely *not* expecting anything like that," Amyra assured Thomas. "He claimed he needed the stone in case the horses were unsettled." She cocked an eyebrow in Will's direction. "I should have known he'd pull some kind of stunt!"

"I knew exactly what to do with the bears, because Amyra's been trying to train me for years," said Will with a cheeky smile. "With little success, I'm sorry to say."

All of them burst into laughter except Amyra, although she didn't seem too displeased.

Queen Essanda and Brother Ander appeared, and loud voices and laughter quickly filled the room.

Before long King Delmar and Queen Maive joined them, prompting an enthusiastic greeting.

"Did you bring your children?" asked Amyra hopefully. "It's much too long since I saw them last."

"No," replied Maive with a smile. "They're not little anymore. The two of them are well able to fend for themselves."

"And we needed to leave someone in charge during our absence," added Delmar.

The energy level increased even more with the arrival of King Rupert and Queen Tasha.

"How are the twins and their sisters?" asked Essanda eagerly.

"All grown up," Rupert assured her. "I expect we'll be calling you over for a wedding or two before long."

"You hardly look a day older!" Elena told Tasha. "What's your secret?"

"I credit my husband," she replied with a grin. "He manages to keep a smile on my face no matter what happens. I must say you look remarkable yourself, Elena!"

"To me she's as beautiful as the day I first saw her face," said Thomas. He gazed fondly into Elena's eyes, dismissing with a grin the hoots from the other men.

"It's so good to see you all!" cried Essanda. "There was barely an opportunity to greet one another at the ceremony. When did you arrive in Rog?"

"Not until last night," Rupert replied. He indicated Delmar and Maive. "The four of us sailed together, and unfortunately we were delayed by adverse winds."

"I hope you weren't visited by a giant squid," quipped Amyra.

"That's no way to refer to Her Imperial Highness Princess Neira," chided Will, setting them off into gales of horrified laughter.

Animated conversation continued well into the night. As they reminisced, they discovered that their shared history had been transformed into memories of narrow escapes and ultimate triumph. Real as the horror had been, it had been left to wither in the past, blotted out by the vitality that flowed from their deliverance.

THE DAYS FOLLOWING the coronation proved to be a busy time for Brother Ander. His assistance with physical ailments was in heavy demand among both rulers and common folk, and he responded to them all without distinction. Wherever possible, he drew in local healers, intent on supporting rather than supplanting them.

Having developed significant friendships with every royal in the region, including the new king of Rogand and his wife, he also found himself taken aside for consultations on a wide range of topics. Giving freely of his time and wisdom, he received gratitude and friendship in return.

Intending to remain behind in Rogand for a season, he bade each of the visitors farewell as they departed, promising to come to them as soon as he could.

Thomas made a point of taking him aside as he was about to leave.

"All of us are getting older, Brother Ander. Apart from you, that is," he added with a grin. "Would you please be willing to conduct our funerals when the time comes? We'll try to send a message when the end seems to be getting close. I'm speaking on behalf of Will and Amyra, as well as Elena and myself."

"Of course," Brother Ander replied without hesitation. "I will pray that such necessities are long delayed!"

After embracing him one last time, Thomas joined the others. Their carriage rolled away, slowly dwindling in size. A distant waving of many arms provided the monk with a final glimpse of his friends before they were lost to sight.

EPILOGUE

Brother Ander stood silently before the open grave, his mind rich with memories. Fifteen years had passed since the coronation of King Rimek, fifteen years filled with unnumbered joys and griefs.

As so often seemed to be the case, he had sensed that the time was near. He had arrived at Newhaven in time to see Thomas Stablehand end his life at peace, surrounded by his children and grandchildren. Thomas had attained a great age, and he left the world grateful for a final blessing from his oldest friend—the man who had taken up the mantle laid down by another treasured friend, the long-departed Brother Vangellis.

A final expression of respect remained for Brother Ander to perform. Standing before the grave he began the committal, surrounded by grieving children, grandchildren, and many others from the Newhaven community.

Brother Ander aside, Thomas was the last of his generation. Both Anneka and Rellan were gone, leaving the Newhaven community to thrive under the leadership of their children. Four years previously, Thomas and Elena had traveled to the Torbury holdings to comfort Amyra as Brother Ander buried Will. They laid him to rest near his lifelong friend Rufe Sarjant and Rufe's wife Peggy. Amyra had passed away the following year, joining Will and her mother Dahra in the little graveyard.

Elena had hung on for two more years, eventually departing at the age of 78. Thomas had never recovered from her loss.

Now he was being laid to rest beside her, near the graves of her father Rubin, their friend Haldek, and his own parents, Axel and Marya.

Thomas and Elena left behind their three children, Tamara, Andy, and Delia. The monk had watched them grow from their infancy, conducted their marriages, and celebrated as between them they bore ten children of their own.

Dragging his thoughts back to the present, he addressed the gathered mourners.

"Thomas Stablehand was a simple man—a man of integrity and honor. No hidden agendas lay behind his ready smile. Simple as he was, he made a monumental contribution, not just to the lives of those he knew and loved, but to Arvenon and the kingdoms surrounding it. He was known and respected by kings, queens, and nobles, as well as countless commoners like himself. More than once he faced almost certain death without flinching, solely for the sake of others. He never spoke of the full darkness and horror of those times. I was present on one of those occasions, and I saw first hand his bravery and his willingness to sacrifice himself. A great evil was averted that day, in no small part because of his involvement. Perhaps he was never appropriately honored for his deeds, but he was content with that.

"None of that is why you are here today. You are here to honor the memory of the ordinary man you knew and respected—a man who loved his wife, cared for and provided for his children, and worked tirelessly in support of this community. Many of you learned to ride and to handle horses under the patient guidance of Thomas Stablehand. Thankfully, he has passed on his gift with the animals to his daughter Delia." He smiled in the direction of Thomas and Elena's youngest.

He gazed around him. "None of us live forever, however worthy our lives and contributions might have been. Thankfully though, we can enter eternity without fear or dread. One has gone before us, one willing to forgive our wrongs and discharge our debts if we will trust him to do so. It is into his loving arms and his gracious care that I commit Thomas Stablehand today."

Flowers were scattered lovingly over Thomas's remains as his body was slowly lowered into the ground. The grave was then sealed with fresh earth.

When the burial was over, the monk led the mourners away, encouraging them to celebrate Thomas's life as they reminisced together.

Brother Ander remained with them for several days. As he was preparing to go, Tamara took him aside.

"My father asked me to remind you of something he requested you to do. Apparently he spoke to you about it after my mother's funeral."

The monk smiled. "Yes, I remember the conversation. I will do as he asked." After thanking her, he said his farewells and left.

At the time, Thomas had drawn him aside. "Could you please do me a favor?" he had asked. "When I'm gone, go to the place where you used to sit with Brother Gerome to chat and watch the sunset. You'll find a package there, buried beneath a large rock. Please take it with you when you leave Newhaven."

Searching out the location, Brother Ander found the rock and dug up the package. He took it with him when he departed.

Two full days passed before he opened the package. He found in it a letter written by Will, and two pieces of tightly wrapped cloth. Unfolding the pieces of cloth, he discovered the Stone of Knowing hidden inside one, along with its clasp and chain. The Stone of Authority lay within the other.

Unrolling Will's letter, he sat down to read it.

Brother Ander,

I am writing this on behalf of Thomas, Elena, Amyra, and myself.

We have long agonized over what to do with the stones after our passing. We have seen the enormous good that can flow from their use. We have also seen the chaos that follows when a truly evil person gets as much as a sniff of them. I myself experienced the terrible consequences of Agon acquiring the Stone of Authority. Both Dret-troth and Rheibas came uncomfortably close in their pursuit of the stones.

A number of options presented themselves.

We could each pass our stone to one of our children, leaving it to them to deal with the burden. The scroll indicated that others before us had followed this path, although the outcomes it reported were far from encouraging. And how would we choose between our children?

We could hide them where no one could find them. None of us were able to convince ourselves that this option would prove effective in the long term.

We could try to destroy them, perhaps by crushing them into tiny grains. Who could guess what might happen if we scattered the grains? If the powers of a stone reside in many of its grains, the effect might be to greatly expand their reach, and more unpredictably than ever.

After pondering and discussing these matters over many years, we together agreed on the simple plan of bequeathing the stones to you.

All three of the stones now rest in your hands. Had it been Rheibas, he wouldn't have wasted a minute before setting out to rule the known world. Perhaps you might decide to embark upon a great endeavor of your own. Perhaps you will simply use them for good, like the original Goodman Tomas in the scroll. Perhaps you will hide or even destroy them.

You must decide. We have no desire to encumber you with requests, recommendations, or even suggestions. We trust you to do with them as you see fit.

In taking this course, we recognize we are placing a great burden on you. We can think of no one better able to shoulder such a burden.

This letter comes with our grateful thanks and sincerest regards,

Will Prentis,

also for Amyra, Thomas, and Elena.

Brother Ander sat without moving for a very long time, pondering what he should do.

The stones had been entrusted to him. Nevertheless, even before he finished reading Will's letter he knew he would not keep them for his own use.

It wasn't a question of doubting himself and his motivations; there were practical considerations he could not ignore. Trouble had found him from the moment he used the Stone of Vitality without constraint. Any person bold enough to use all three stones would draw conflict as surely as honey attracted bears.

That would not have deterred Rheibas. Someone like him would wield the power of the stones without hesitation or moderation, ruthlessly destroying any who dared oppose him. But Brother Ander was not Rheibas. Nor was he unique. He felt sure that responsibility for all three stones would quickly become a heavy burden for most reasonable people.

The situation also forced him to confront a decision he had been deferring. How much longer could he continue to use the Stone of Vitality? With the monk's own generation little more than a memory, his longevity was already becoming proverbial. How could he possibly explain it as the years continued to stretch on?

Some kind of decision would be needed before long, although he saw no immediate urgency. He could be certain only of two things: he would not keep the stones himself, and he would not burden one person with all three of them. Beyond that he could not be sure of anything.

Eventually he placed the Stone of Knowing around his neck, making sure it wasn't touching his skin. Then he carefully secured the Stone of Authority within his robe.

Finally he put the stones from his mind and resumed his wanderings.

Obedient to a timeless ritual, the sun reached down once more to kiss the horizon. Another day was drawing to a close.

Settling himself on a grassy hillside, Brother Ander gazed into the heavens, eager to savor the extravagant display already claiming the sky.

Wondrous as it was, it left him restless. That day, like every day before it, had known when its span was over. Yet here he was, five years after receiving the stones, still without a conclusion.

He could sidestep the issue no longer—the time had come. He would resolve it in the morning, before he did anything else.

Stretching himself out on the grass, he abandoned himself to sleep.

He woke well before dawn, confronted immediately with the troublesome question. What should he do with the stones?

Throughout his life he had seen evil in many of its guises, and he well knew the propensity for wrongdoing that had dogged humankind from the beginning. Allowing the stones to pass into unknown hands seemed risky at best, and grossly irresponsible at worst.

Hiding them seemed attractive if it could be done effectively. After all, the talismans had emerged in his lifetime after lying hidden for countless years—perhaps centuries. He had passed through many lonely regions in his tireless wanderings. One of them would surely do as a new hiding place.

And yet he could find no peace with such a conclusion. The more he pondered it, the more he realized that basing a decision entirely on fear required him to elevate evil more highly than it deserved.

Familiar words from his Holy Book came to mind.

> "As for man, his days are like grass.
> As a flower of the field, so he flourishes.
> For the wind passes over it, and it is gone.
> Its place remembers it no more.
> But the Lord's loving kindness is from everlasting to
> everlasting with those who fear him."

No human endured for long—he well knew it, having conducted more funerals than he could count. Evil sometimes far outlasted the one who initiated it, but his own experience confirmed that the grace and mercy of the Almighty outlasted everything.

Why should he be afraid?

He saw at last what should have been clear from the beginning—he needed to dispose of the stones in a manner consistent with their original purpose.

No human artisan had crafted the stones. They were neither his, nor anyone else's, to hide or destroy.

Nor were they to be shunned. Malign intent had played no part in their origins. Fashioned by one who was unfailingly good, they had always been intended to be used.

It occurred to him to wonder if Will and Thomas and the others would have seen it the way he did. He had no way to be certain, but they knew him well, and Will's letter made it clear they trusted him to do as he saw fit.

Choosing to embrace hope, he decided at last. He would pass them on to three different individuals.

All that remained was to choose the recipients. In recent times the stones had rested in the hands of Thomas and Elena, Amyra and Will, Kamash, and himself. All of them were ordinary people, and none were prepared for what awaited them. Yet each had risen to the challenge. There was no reason to think others would do any less.

He felt confident he would recognize the right people when he came upon them. They would be no more perfect than the previous stewards, but the responsibility for final outcomes rested in the hands of the one who had fashioned and sent the stones.

A time would come for him to yield up the Stone of Vitality. Like Kamash before him, he would do so without regret. Having already exceeded a normal lifespan, he had no desire to live on endlessly. He would miss the familiar surge of joy as the sick unfailingly responded to his prayer, but he was content. Another could take up where he left off.

A great weight had been lifted from his mind. With a nod of satisfaction, Brother Ander shouldered his meager possessions and rose to his feet.

A pre-dawn glimmer had begun to lighten the sky. The sun was ready to burst forth, resurrected, like a butterfly released from its cocoon.

Turning toward the east, he set off with his face to the rising sun.

The End

The saga of *The Stone Cycle* ends with this final installment

---

Ready for more?

Don't miss the first novel in Allan N. Packer's second epic fantasy series!

The Hard Edge of Magic (The Ruptured Kingdom Book 1)

NOTE FROM THE AUTHOR

Thank you for reading *The Stone of Vitality Complete Set*. Huge thanks for staying on the journey to the very end of the series!

Don't forget to leave a review. Reviews make a huge difference to me as well as benefiting other readers.

I also very much appreciate feedback from my readers. I'd love to hear what you thought of the series—please feel free to send me an email.

What's next? Having thoroughly enjoyed my years in Arvenon and the surrounding kingdoms, I decided it was time to move on. The result is my second epic fantasy series, The Ruptured Kingdom! Check out the first novel in the series now: The Hard Edge of Magic, described below.

To be kept up to date on new releases, sign up to my mailing list at www.allanpacker.com. New subscribers will receive an exclusive bonus ebook, The Rending: A Prequel to The Cost of Knowing. The novelette is a complete story four chapters (13,000 words) in length that provides additional context to Anneka's story. The novelette, also separately available in audiobook and print format, is also described below.

Hungry and desperate, Kylen knows what it's like to be an outcast. Plucked from the streets by a tight-lipped stranger, he begins to dream of a better life. But his rescuer turns out to be a renegade mage. In an instant Kylen finds himself transformed from a person of no account to a dangerous fugitive.

But much more than his life might be at stake. Dark forces are stirring, and an ancient evil is poised, ready to be unleashed on an unsuspecting kingdom. Comfortable and arrogant, the kingdom's mages are bent on destroying the one person capable of saving them.

On the run with his mentor, Kylen tries to ignore the voices whispering about his destiny. Of what use is a fabled destiny when you're struggling to survive?

If you enjoy epic fantasy with gripping action and relatable characters in a compelling coming of age saga, then try the novels of The Ruptured Kingdom *now!*

Endings may be beginnings in disguise

Anneka is comfortable and confident, a noblewoman of consequence living a life of privilege. Until the day her world is torn apart.

After losing everything she most cares about, she must abandon her home and her way of life in an attempt to secure the future of those who depend on her.

No one, least of all Anneka, could anticipate a deeper significance to her struggle. Yet her journey will one day influence the fate of kingdoms.

ACKNOWLEDGMENTS

With the series now at an end, it's time to offer series-wide acknowledgments.

First, my wife Merilyn has graciously persisted as my alpha reader through multiple revisions of every novel, with changes having often been instigated by her feedback. The stories are invariably better for her input.

Heartfelt thanks to the beta readers who've stuck it out throughout the series: Merilyn, Andrew Menzies, Deborah, Ray, and Cherilyn White. In spite of his busy schedule, Stephen only missed once. Roly Edwardes joined the team for the final novel. I'm grateful to all of them for their feedback. It always makes a difference.

As the series progressed I have come to increasingly appreciate my developmental editor, Mary Novak. Her keen insights and helpful critiques have always proven invaluable.

Karri Klawiter has been wonderfully creative with the covers and always a pleasure to work with throughout the series.

Brian Plush managed some final additions to his excellent map in time for this novel, and I'm grateful for his skilful contribution.

Deborah's time has become ever busier with her growing family and her own writing, and I'm thankful for her meticulous proofreads throughout the series.

When I published the first novel, I had no thought of audiobooks. Since Greg John agreed to narrate them, I have been fortunate to connect with an appreciative and growing audience. I am very grateful to my ever-reliable beta listener, Arpenny Hart, who has consistently offered valuable and encouraging feedback. I thoroughly agree with her assessment that Greg has narrated the stories "with great clarity, energy and emotion."

I published *The Stone of Knowing* in early 2019, but almost three decades have slipped away since I first started writing it. Through it all, I've been a grateful recipient of the grace and mercy of God. Seasons come and go, but his steadfast love never changes.

ABOUT THE AUTHOR

Allan Packer writes epic fantasy, and the novels and novelettes of *The Stone Cycle* are his first published fiction.

Allan grew up surrounded by books and became an avid reader during his childhood. In his university years fantasy displaced science fiction as his favorite genre, thanks primarily to J. R. R. Tolkien. He later shared this love with his four children by reading *The Lord of the Rings* to them aloud—a three-month marathon he completed twice during their formative years.

Born in Australia, Allan has lived and worked on three continents, and spent one quarter of his working years abroad. Having worked as an IT professional throughout his career, he was first published as a technical author.

Today he lives with his wife in Adelaide, South Australia, near their children and a small but growing band of grandchildren.

Allan is currently working on his second epic fantasy series.

PART III

LIST OF CHARACTERS AND RESEARCH NOTES

THE STONE OF VITALITY

LIST OF CHARACTERS

- *Agon* - previous king of Rogand
- *Ahreitas* - imperial crown prince of Ahr
- *Ahuzza* - Ahran bisri (nobleman), special envoy of the emperor of Ahr
- *Aiden* - crown prince of Arvenon, son of Steffan and Essanda
- *Ander* - a monk; former Arvenian soldier who traveled with Will and later commanded soldiers at the Battle of Torbury Scarp
- *Andy* - son of Thomas and Elena
- *Ashloh* - princess of Rogand, daughter of King Krasmir and Queen Deka; younger twin of Crown Prince Rimek
- *Attalnar* - early king of Arvenon
- *Amyra* - wife of Will Prentis; holder of the Stone of Authority; formerly Ahnya, daughter of Sheylha
- *Anneka* - former noblewoman who leads a community hidden away in the forest near Erestor
- *Beldisel* - Erestorian nobleman with holdings adjacent to those of Lord Torbury
- *Bolnyk* - Ahran agent

- *Boedwyk* - Rogandan nobleman
- *Breysen* - retainer to Lord Torbury (Will Prentis); former sailor, soldier, and mercenary
- *Burnett* - scribe to King Attalnar of Arvenon, from Earlsford
- *Burtelen* - high-ranking Arvenian nobleman from Erestor who is a close confidante of King Steffan; played a crucial role in bringing an army from Erestor to the battle at Torbury Scarp
- *Charlotte* - princess of Arvenon, daughter of Steffan and Essanda
- *Dahra* - mother of Amyra; formerly Sheylha, the Seer
- *Deka* - wife of Krasmir and queen of Rogand
- *Delia* - daughter of Thomas and Elena
- *Delmar* - king of Varas, a neighboring kingdom to Arvenon, and ally of King Steffan of Arvenon
- *Drettroth* - high-ranking Rogandan nobleman who commanded the Rogandan army during the invasion of Arvenon; known as Vilkami during his childhood
- *Duke of Erestor* - King Steffan's uncle, and the regent during the king's absence during the Rogandan invasion; the senior member of the nobility in Erestor
- *Eisgold* - Castelan nobleman formerly commanding the Castelan army; exiled after the Battle of Torbury Scarp for ignoring orders at a crucial moment in the battle
- *Elena* - wife of Thomas Stablehand
- *Essanda* - Queen of Arvenon, formerly a princess of Castel
- *Ethen* - son of Will and Amyra
- *Gharpin* - captain of an Ahran ship
- *Goultzar* - Archprimus, second in command to the High Priest of the Dark Gods of Rogand
- *Haldek* - former Rogandan soldier who unwittingly helped Will on more than one significant occasion; living in a tiny forest community with Elena, Rubin, and Thomas
- *Hourahn* - emperor of Ahr

- *Istel* - king of Castel, a neighboring kingdom to Arvenon, father of Rupert and Essanda, and father-in-law and ally of King Steffan of Arvenon
- *Jaxin* - retainer to the Duke of Erestor and later Lord Burtelen and their key representative at the docks in Maranelle
- *Jonas* - senior army leader and close confidante of Will Prentis; fought at the Battle of Torbury Scarp
- *Hender* - bowman living in Anneka and Rellan's forest community
- *Kaifet* - Ahran agent tasked with meeting the Rogandan High Priest
- *Karevis* - Varasan nobleman and commander of the Varasan army; played a key role at the Battle of Torbury Scarp
- *Kamash* - Rogandan who chose to exile himself to a remote island
- *Krasmir* - king of Rogand, formerly a wealthy and powerful Rogandan baron
- *Kulferan* - Rogandan nobleman and army commander
- *Kyla* - princess of Rogand, daughter of King Krasmir and Queen Deka
- *Leonid* - prince of Arvenon, son of Steffan and Essanda
- *Millie* - daughter of Will and Amyra
- *Neira* - imperial princess of the Empire of Ahr
- *Ranauld* - Arvenian count and a senior leader in the army at Torbury Scarp; a close confidante of King Steffan and a friend of Will Prentis
- *Rellan* - Arvenian soldier from Erestor who led a cavalry force to the battlefield at Torbury Scarp with his twin brother Kuper; connected with Anneka's forest community
- *Rheibas* - Grand Vizier of the Empire of Ahr
- *Rimek* - crown prince of Rogand, son of King Krasmir and Queen Deka

- *Rubin* - father of Elena
- *Rufe Sarjant* - respected and physically imposing Arvenian soldier; a close friend of Will Prentis and a key leader in the army
- *Rupert* - king of Castel, brother to Essanda, son of King Istel
- *Steffan the Second* - king of Arvenon
- *Tamara* - daughter of Thomas and Elena
- *Teylee* - Rogandan princess, daughter of King Krasmir and Queen Deka
- *Thomas Stablehand* - possessor of the Stone of Knowing
- *Torbury* - title granted to Will Prentis by King Steffan; Will Prentis was elevated to the Arvenian peerage as Lord Torbury in honor of his efforts in defeating the Rogandans
- *Uman* - guard and servant to Princess Neira
- *Vangellis* - Arvenian monk who became a key mentor to Thomas; role model to Brother Ander; killed at Lord Drettroth's stronghold
- *Will Prentis* - commander of the Arvenian army, greatly respected by his soldiers as well as King Steffan due to his remarkable qualities; fluent in Rogandan and widely traveled

THE HOPE OF VITALITY

LIST OF CHARACTERS

- *Agon* - previous king of Rogand
- *Ahreitas* - imperial crown prince of Ahr
- *Ahuzza* - Ahran bisri (nobleman), special envoy of the emperor of Ahr
- *Aiden* - crown prince of Arvenon, son of Steffan and Essanda
- *Akohlsa* - Ahran agent working with Kahrlin
- *Ander* - a monk; former Arvenian soldier who traveled with Will and later commanded soldiers at the Battle of Torbury Scarp
- *Andy* - son of Thomas and Elena
- *Ashloh* - princess of Rogand, daughter of King Krasmir and Queen Deka; younger twin of Crown Prince Rimek
- *Atmek* - Rogandan priest reporting to Goultzar, the Archprimus
- *Amyra* - wife of Will Prentis; holder of the Stone of Authority; formerly Ahnya, daughter of Sheylha
- *Anneka* - former noblewoman who leads a community hidden away in the forest near Erestor
- *Bolnyk* - senior Ahran agent

- *Bezai* - Rogandan naval captain
- *Boedwyk* - eccentric Rogandan nobleman
- *Charlotte* - princess of Arvenon, daughter of Steffan and Essanda
- *Dahra* - mother of Amyra; formerly Sheylha, the Seer
- *Dannhur* - Rogandan soldier assigned as a guard to Brother Ander
- *Deka* - queen of Rogand; wife of Krasmir and mother of Crown Prince Rimek, Princess Ashloh, Princess Kyla, and Princess Teylee
- *Delia* - daughter of Thomas and Elena
- *Delmar* - king of Varas, a neighboring kingdom to Arvenon, and ally of King Steffan of Arvenon
- *Dessue* - Ahran guard leader
- *Drettroth* - high-ranking Rogandan nobleman who commanded the Rogandan army during the invasion of Arvenon; known as Vilkami during his childhood
- *Eisgold* - Castelan nobleman formerly commanding the Castelan army; exiled after the Battle of Torbury Scarp for ignoring orders at a crucial moment in the battle
- *Elena* - wife of Thomas Stablehand
- *Essanda* - Queen of Arvenon, formerly a princess of Castel
- *Ethen* - son of Will and Amyra
- *Galvas* - Varasan agent
- *Gharpin* - captain of an Ahran ship
- *Ghonik* - Rogandan soldier assigned as a guard to Brother Ander
- *Giddel* - Castelan envoy, based in Rogand
- *Goultzur* - Archprimus, second in command to the High Priest of the Dark Gods of Rogand
- *Haldek* - former Rogandan soldier who unwittingly helped Will on more than one significant occasion; living in a tiny forest community with Elena, Rubin, and Thomas
- *Hennis* - Arvenian army captain serving under Rufe Sarjant

- *Hourahn* - emperor of Ahr
- *Kahrlin* - senior Ahran agent in Castel
- *Karevis* - Varasan nobleman and commander of the Varasan army; played a key role at the Battle of Torbury Scarp
- *Kamash* - Rogandan who chose to exile himself to a remote island
- *Krasmir* - king of Rogand, formerly a wealthy and powerful Rogandan baron
- *Kulferan* - Rogandan nobleman and army commander
- *Kyla* - princess of Rogand, daughter of King Krasmir and Queen Deka
- *Kyleth* - Rogandan soldier assigned as a guard to Brother Ander
- *Leonid* - prince of Arvenon, son of Steffan and Essanda
- *Maive* - Varasan agent
- *Maran* - senior agent answering to King Delmar of Varas
- *Millie* - daughter of Will and Amyra
- *Neira* - imperial princess of the Empire of Ahr
- *Pultek* - Rogandan naval captain
- *Ranauld* - Arvenian count and a senior leader in the army at Torbury Scarp; a close confidante of King Steffan and a friend of Will Prentis
- *Rellan* - Arvenian soldier from Erestor who led a cavalry force to the battlefield at Torbury Scarp with his twin brother Kuper; married to Anneka; lives at the Newhaven forest community
- *Rheibas* - Grand Vizier of the Empire of Ahr
- *Rimek* - crown prince of Rogand, son of King Krasmir and Queen Deka
- *Roethen* - rich Rogandan merchant living in Rog
- *Rubin* - father of Elena
- *Rufe Sarjant* - respected and physically imposing Arvenian soldier; a close friend of Will Prentis and a key leader in the army

- *Rupert* - king of Castel, brother to Essanda, son of King Istel
- *Shallam* - Rogandan agent, fluent in Ahran
- *Shulkahr* - Ahran leader
- *Steffan the Second* - king of Arvenon
- *Talmon* - Varasan envoy, based in Rogand
- *Tamara* - daughter of Thomas and Elena
- *Teylee* - Rogandan princess, daughter of King Krasmir and Queen Deka, also known as Tasha
- *Thomas Stablehand* - possessor of the Stone of Knowing
- *Thorsel* - Castelan nobleman
- *Torbury* - title granted to Will Prentis by King Steffan; Will Prentis was elevated to the Arvenian peerage as Lord Torbury in honor of his efforts in defeating the Rogandans
- *Tulinay* - Rogandan noblewoman; head of King Krasmir's spy network
- *Uman* - guard and servant to Princess Neira
- *Vangellis* - Arvenian monk who became a key mentor to Thomas; role model to Brother Ander; killed at Lord Drettroth's stronghold
- *Vholahr* - senior Ahran general
- *Will Prentis* - commander of the Arvenian army, greatly respected by his soldiers as well as King Steffan due to his remarkable qualities; fluent in Rogandan and widely traveled
- *Yetvar* - leader of Rogandan shepherds
- *Zattu* - senior Rogandan priest
- *Zhukha* - Ahran agent

RESEARCH NOTES

THE HOPE OF VITALITY

Spoiler Alert!

The reader is advised to avoid this section before finishing *The Hope of Vitality*.

Rappelling with a single rope

In helping Bisri Ahuzza to escape from his room five floors above the ground, Shallam used a technique similar to the Dülfersitz. The technique is demonstrated live here:

- https://www.youtube.com/watch?v=j23eZhTOv3s
- https://www.youtube.com/watch?v=CLQoIltdYdo

From Wikipedia: https://en.wikipedia.org/wiki/Dülfersitz

The Dülfersitz (named after its inventor, mountaineer Hans Dülfer), also known as body rappel is a classical, or non-mechanical abseiling technique, used in rock climbing and mountaineering. It is not used frequently any more, since the introduction of belay devices. In the Dülfersitz, the rope is wound around the body, and the speed of descent is controlled using the friction of the rope against the body.

The advantages of the Dülfersitz are that one can descend without a climbing harness or belay device, and because the rope is not kinked or subjected to concentrated forces, it does not experience as much wear. The major disadvantage of this method is that intense heat is generated by the friction on the shoulder, neck and thigh, which can be painful, and can damage clothing.

Giant Sea Creatures

Giant squid and sperm whales are described below, as are sailing ships similar to those depicted in *The Stone of Vitality* and *The Hope of Vitality*. In each case, the source is Wikipedia. A few general observations follow.

• It's easy to lose sight of how small three-masted medieval sailing ships were, especially by modern standards. The carracks used by Christopher Columbus, Vasco de Gama, and Magellan typically measured around 20m in length, less than half as long as many modern superyachts.

• At 16m to 20m from end to end, sperm whales are almost the same length as the carracks used by these explorers.

• Giant squid are smaller, measuring 10m to 13m from the tip of their tentacles to their posterior fins, but not by a lot.

Giant Squid

From Wikipedia: https://en.wikipedia.org/wiki/Giant_squid

The giant squid (Architeuthis dux) is a species of deep-ocean dwelling squid in the family Architeuthidae. It can grow to a tremendous size, offering an example of abyssal gigantism: recent estimates put the maximum size at around 12–13 m (39–43 ft) for females and 10 m (33 ft) for males, from the posterior fins to the tip of the two long tentacles (longer than the colossal squid at an estimated 9–10 m (30–33 ft), but substantially lighter, due to the tentacles making up most of the length). The mantle of the giant squid is about 2 m (6 ft 7 in) long (more for females, less for males), and the length of the squid excluding its tentacles (but including head and arms) rarely exceeds 5 m (16 ft).

The known predators of adult giant squid include sperm whales, pilot whales, southern sleeper sharks, and in some regions killer whales.

The elusive nature of the giant squid and its foreign appearance, often perceived as terrifying, have firmly established its place in the human imagination. Representations of the giant squid have been known from early legends of the kraken through books such as *Moby-Dick* and *Twenty Thousand Leagues Under the Sea* on to novels such as Ian Fleming's *Dr. No*, Peter Benchley's *Beast* (adapted as a film called *The Beast*), and Michael Crichton's *Sphere* (adapted as a film), and modern animated television programs.

In particular, the image of a giant squid locked in battle with a sperm whale is a common one, although the squid is the whale's prey and not an equal combatant.

Sperm Whale

From Wikipedia: https://en.wikipedia.org/wiki/Sperm_whale

The sperm whale or cachalot (Physeter macrocephalus) is the largest of the toothed whales and the largest toothed predator.

Mature males average 16 metres (52 ft) in length but some may reach 20.7 metres (68 ft), with the head representing up to one-third of the animal's length.

Sperm whales usually dive between 300 to 800 metres (980 to 2,620 ft), and sometimes 1 to 2 kilometres (3,300 to 6,600 ft), in search of food. Such dives can last more than an hour. They feed on several species, notably the giant squid, but also the colossal squid, octopuses, and fish such as demersal rays and sharks, but their diet is mainly medium-sized squid.

Medieval Sailing Ships

From Wikipedia: https://en.wikipedia.org/wiki/Carrack

A carrack is a three- or four-masted ocean-going sailing ship that was developed in the 14th to 15th centuries in Europe, most notably in Portugal. Evolved from the single-masted cog, the carrack was first used for European trade from the Mediterranean to the Baltic and quickly found use with the newly found wealth of the trade between

Europe and Africa and then the trans-Atlantic trade with the Americas. In their most advanced forms, they were used by the Portuguese for trade between Europe and Asia starting in the late 15th century, before eventually being superseded in the 17th century by the galleon, introduced in the 16th century.

Famous carracks:

Santa María, in which Christopher Columbus made his first voyage to America in 1492.

- Tons burthen est. 108 tons BM
- Estimated hull length 19 m (62 ft)
- Estimated keel length 12.6 m (41 ft)
- Beam est. 5.5 m (18 ft)
- Draught est. 3.2 m (10 ft)
- Propulsion sail
- Complement 40

São Gabriel, flagship of Vasco da Gama, in the 1497 Portuguese expedition from Europe to India by circumnavigating Africa.

- Tons burthen ~ 100 tons
- Length 25.7 m (84 ft 4 in)
- Beam 8.5 m (27 ft 11 in)
- Draft 2.3 m (7 ft 7 in)
- Propulsion sail
- Complement ~60

Victoria, the first ship in history to circumnavigate the globe (1519 to 1522), and the only survivor of Magellan's expedition for Spain.

- Tonnage 85
- Length 18 to 21 metres (59 to 69 ft)
- Complement 55

www.ingramcontent.com/pod-product-compliance
Lightning Source LLC
Chambersburg PA
CBHW020533310726
48979CB00014B/2317/J

* 9 7 8 1 9 2 3 2 1 8 1 1 6 *